S0-BNU-643

Ex-Libris

Thelma
Snyder

ERRINGTON BEHELD A WILD, DISTORTED FIGURE RUNNING TOWARD HIM, WITH ITS
HEAD DOWNWARD, AND BEARING ALOFT A SMOKING PINE TORCH.—Page 22.

—*Thelma.*

THELMA.

A NORWEGIAN PRINCESS.

By MARIE CORELLI,

Author of "A Romance of Two Worlds," "Wormwood," etc.

A. L. BURT COMPANY, PUBLISHERS,
52-58 DUANE STREET, NEW YORK

THELMA.

THELMA.

BOOK I.

THE LAND OF THE MIDNIGHT SUN.

CHAPTER I.

"Dream by dream shot through her eyes, and each
Outshone the last that lighted."

SWINBURNE.

MIDNIGHT,—without darkness, without stars! Midnight,
—and the unwearied sun stood, yet visible in the heavens,
like a victorious king throned on a dais of royal purple
bordered with gold. The sky above him,—his canopy,—
gleamed with a cold yet lustrious blue, while across it
slowly flitted a few wandering clouds of palest amber, deepening, as they sailed along, to a tawny orange. A broad
stream of light falling, as it were, from the centre of the
magnificent orb, shot lengthwise across the Altenfjord,
turning its waters to a mass of quivering and shifting color
that alternated from bronze to copper,—from copper to silver and azure. The surrounding hills glowed with a warm,
deep violet tint, flecked here and there with touches of
bright red, as though fairies were lighting tiny bonfires on
their summits. Away in the distance a huge mass of rock
stood out to view, its rugged lines transfigured into ethe-
real loveliness by a misty veil of tender rose pink,—a hue
curiously suggestive of some other and smaller sun that
might have just set. Absolute silence prevailed. Not even
the cry of a sea-mew or kittiwake broke the almost deathlike stillness,—no breath of wind stirred a ripple on the
glassy water. The whole scene might well have been the
fantastic dream of some imaginative painter, whose ambition soared beyond the limits of human skill. Yet it was

only one of those million wonderful effects of sky and sea which are common in Norway, especially on the Altenfjord, where, though beyond the Arctic circle, the climate in summer is that of another Italy, and the landscape a living poem fairer than the visions of Endymion.

There was one solitary watcher of the splendid spectacle. This was a man of refined features and aristocratic appearance, who, reclining on a large rug of skins which he had thrown down on the shore for that purpose, was gazing at the pageant of the midnight sun and all its stately surroundings, with an earnest and rapt expression in his clear hazel eyes.

"Glorious! beyond all expectation, glorious!" he murmured half aloud, as he consulted his watch and saw that the hands marked exactly twelve on the dial. "I believe I'm having the best of it, after all. Even if those fellows get the *Eulalie* into good position they will see nothing finer than this."

As he spoke he raised his field-glass and swept the horizon in search of a vessel, his own pleasure yacht,—which had taken three of his friends, at their special desire, to the opposite island of Seiland,—Seiland, rising in weird majesty three thousand feet above the sea, and boasting as its chief glory the great peak of Jedkè, the most northern glacier in all the wild Norwegian land. There was no sign of a returning sail, and he resumed his study of the sumptuous sky, the colors of which were now deepening and burning with increasing lustre, while an array of clouds of the deepest purple hue swept gorgeously together beneath the sun as though to form his footstool.

"One might imagine that the trump of the Resurrection had sounded, and that all this aerial pomp,—this strange silence,—was just the pause, the supreme moment before the angels descended," he mused, with a half-smile at his own fancy, for though something of a poet at heart, he was much more of a cynic. He was too deeply imbued with modern fashionable atheism to think seriously about angels or Resurrection trumps, but there was a certain love of mysticism and romance in his nature, which not even his Oxford experiences and the chilly dullness of English materialism had been able to eradicate. And there was something impressive in the sight of the majestic orb holding such imperial revel at midnight,—something almost unearthly in the light and life of the heavens, as compared with the reverential and seemingly worshipping silence of the earth,—that, for a few moments, awed him into a sense of the spiritual and unseen. Mythical passages from the poets he loved came into his memory, and stray fragments of old songs and ballads he had known in his childhood returned to him with haunting persistence. It was, for him, one of those sudden halts in life which we all experience,—an instant,—when time and the world seem to stand still, as though to permit us easy breathing; a brief space,—in which we are allowed to stop and wonder awhile at the strange unaccountable force within us, that enables us to stand with such calm, smiling audacity, on our small pin's point of the present, between the wide dark gaps of past and future; a small hush,—in which the gigantic engines of the universe appear to revolve no more, and the immortal Soul of man itself is subjected and over-ruled by supreme and eternal Thought. Drifting away on those delicate imperceptible lines that lie between reality and dreamland, the watcher of the midnight sun gave himself up to the half painful, half delicious sense of being drawn in, absorbed, and lost in infinite imaginings, when the intense stillness around him was broken by the sound of a voice singing, a full, rich contralto, that rang through the air with the clearness of a golden bell. The sweet liquid notes were those of an old Norwegian mountain melody, one of those wildly pathetic *folk-songs* that seem to hold all the sorrow, wonder, wistfulness, and indescribable yearning of a heart too full for other speech than music. He started to his feet and looked around him for the singer. There was no one visible. The amber streaks in the sky were leaping into crimson flame; the Fjord glowed like the burning lake of Dante's vision; one solitary sea-gull winged its graceful, noiseless flight far above, its white pinions shimmering like jewels as it crossed the radiance of the heavens. Other sign of animal life there was none. Still the hidden voice rippled on in a stream of melody, and the listener stood amazed and enchanted at the roundness and distinctness of every note that fell from the lips of the unseen vocalist.

"A woman's voice," he thought; "but where is the woman?"

Puzzled, he looked to the right and left, then out to the shining Fjord, half expecting to see some fisher-maiden rowing along, and singing as she rowed, but there was no sign of any living creature. While he waited, the voice suddenly ceased, and the song was replaced by the sharp grating of a keel on the beach. Turning in the direction of this sound, he perceived a boat being pushed out by invisible hands towards the water's edge from a rocky cave, that jutted upon the Fjord, and, full of curiosity, he stepped towards the arched entrance, when,—all suddenly and unexpectedly,—a girl sprang out from the dark interior, and standing erect in her boat, faced the intruder. A girl of about nineteen she seemed, taller than most women,—with a magnificent uncovered mass of hair, the color of the midnight sunshine, tumbled over her shoulders, and flashing against her flushed cheeks and dazzlingly fair skin. Her deep blue eyes had an astonished and certainly indignant expression in them, while he, utterly unprepared for such a vision of loveliness at such a time and in such a place, was for a moment taken aback and at a loss for words. Recovering his habitual self-possession quickly, however, he raised his hat, and, pointing to the boat, which was more than half way out of the cavern, said simply—

"May I assist you?"

She was silent, eyeing him with a keen glance which had something in it of disfavor and suspicion.

"I suppose she doesn't understand English," he thought, "and I can't speak a word of Norwegian. I must talk by signs."

And forthwith he went through a labored pantomime of gesture, sufficiently ludicrous in itself, yet at the same time expressive of his meaning. The girl broke into a laugh—a laugh of sweet amusement which brought a thousand new sparkles of light into her lovely eyes.

"That is very well done," she observed graciously, speaking English with something of a foreign accent. "Even the Lapps would understand you, and they are very stupid, poor things!"

Half vexed by her laughter, and feeling that he was somehow an object of ridicule to this tall, bright-haired maiden, he ceased his pantomimic gestures abruptly and stood looking at her with a slight flush of embarrassment on his features.

"I know your language," she resumed quietly, after a brief pause, in which she had apparently considered the stranger's appearance and general bearing. "It was rude of me not to have answered you at once. You can help me if you will. The keel has caught among the pebbles, but we can easily move it between us." And, jumping lightly out of her boat, she grasped its edge firmly with her strong white hands, exclaiming gaily, as she did so, " Push ! "

Thus adjured, he lost no time in complying with her request, and, using his great strength and muscular force to good purpose, the light little craft was soon well in the water, swaying to and fro as though with impatience to be gone. The girl sprang to her seat, discarding his eagerly proffered assistance, and, taking both oars, laid them in their respective rowlocks, and seemed about to start, when she paused and asked abruptly—

" Are you a sailor ? "

He smiled. " Not I ! Do I remind you of one ? "

" You are strong, and you manage a boat as though you were accustomed to the work. Also you look as if you had been at sea."

" Rightly guessed ! " he replied, still smiling ; " I certainly *have* been at sea ; I have been coasting all about your lovely land. My yacht went across to Seiland this afternoon."

She regarded him more intently, and observed, with the critical eye of a woman, the refined taste displayed in his dress, from the very cut of his loose travelling coat, to the luxurious rug of fine fox-shins, that lay so carelessly cast on the shore at a little distance from him. Then she gave a gesture of hauteur and half-contempt.

" You have a yacht? Oh ! then you are a gentleman. You do nothing for your living ? "

" Nothing, indeed ! " and he shrugged his shoulders with a mingled air of weariness and self-pity, " except one thing —I live ! "

" Is that hard work ? " she inquired wonderingly.

" Very."

They were silent then, and the girl's face grew serious as she rested on her oars, and still surveyed him with a straight, candid gaze, that, though earnest and penetrating, had nothing of boldness in it. It was the look of one in whose past there were no secrets—the look of a child who is satisfied with the present and takes no thought for the future. Few women look so after they have entered their teens. Social artifice, affectation, and the insatiate vanity that modern life encourages in the feminine nature—all these things soon do away with the pellucid clearness and steadfastness of the eye—the beautiful, true, untamed expression, which, though so rare, is, when seen infinitely more be-witching than all the bright arrows of coquetry and spark-ling invitation that flash from the glances of well-bred so-ciety dames, who have taken care to educate their eyes if not their hearts. This girl was evidently not trained prop-erly; had she been so, she would have dropped a curtain over those wide, bright windows of her soul; she would have remembered that she was alone with a strange man at midnight—at midnight, though the sun shone; she would have simpered and feigned embarrassment, even if she could not feel it. As it happened, she did nothing of the kind, only her expression softened and became more wistful and earnest, and when she spoke again her voice was mel-low with a suave gentleness, that had something in it of compassion.

"If you do not love life itself," she said, "you love the beautiful things of life, do you not? See yonder! There is what we call the meeting of night and morning. One is glad to be alive at such a moment. Look quickly! The light soon fades."

She pointed towards the east. Her companion gazed in that direction, and uttered an exclamation,—almost a shout, —of wonder and admiration. Within the space of the past few minutes the aspect of the heavens had completely changed. The burning scarlet and violet hues had all melted into a transparent yet brilliant shade of pale mauve, —as delicate as the inner tint of a lilac blossom,—and across this stretched two wing-shaped gossamer clouds of watery green, fringed with soft primrose. Between these cloud-wings, as opaline in lustre as those of a dragon-fly, the face of the sun shone like a shield of polished gold, while his rays, piercing spear-like through the varied tints of emerald, brought an unearthly radiance over the land-scape—a lustre as though the moon were, in some strange way, battling with the sun for mastery over the visible un-iverse, though, looking southward, she could dimly be per-ceived, the ghost of herself—a poor, fainting, pallid god-dess,—a perishing Diana.

Bringing his glance down from the skies, the young man turned it to the face of the maiden near him, and was startled at her marvellous beauty—beauty now heightened by the effect of the changeful colors that played around her. The very boat in which she sat glittered with a bronze-like, metallic brightness as it heaved gently to and fro on the silvery green water; the midnight sunshine bathed the falling glory of her long hair, till each thick tress, each clustering curl, appeared to emit an amber spark of light. The strange, weird effect of the sky seemed to have stolen into her eyes, making them shine with witch-like brilliancy,—the varied radiance flashing about her brought into strong relief the pureness of her profile, draw-ing as with a fine pencil the outlines of her noble forehead, sweet mouth, and rounded chin. It touched the scarlet of her bodice, and brightened the quaint old silver clasps she wore at her waist and throat, till she seemed no longer an earthly being, but more like some fair wondering sprite from the legendary Norse kingdom of *Alfheim*, the "abode of the Luminous Genii."

She was gazing upwards,—heavenwards,—and her ex-pression was one of rapt and almost devotional intensity. Thus she remained for some moments, motionless as the picture of an expectant angel painted by Raffaele or Cor-reggio; then reluctantly and with a deep sigh she turned her eyes towards earth again. In so doing she met the fixed and too visibly admiring gaze of her companion. She started, and a wave of vivid color flushed her cheeks. Quickly recovering her serenity, however, she saluted him slightly, and, moving her oars in unison, was on the point of departure.

Stirred by an impulse he could not resist, he laid one hand detainingly on the rim of her boat.

"Are you going now?" he asked.

She raised her eyebrows in some little surprise and smiled.

"Going?" she repeated. "Why, yes. I shall be late in getting home as it is."

"Stop a moment," he said eagerly, feeling that he could not let this beautiful creature leave him as utterly as a midsummer night's dream without some clue as to her origin and destination. "Will you not tell me your name?"

She drew herself erect with a look of indignation.

"Sir, I do not know you. The maidens of Norway do not give their names to strangers."

"Pardon me," he replied, somewhat abashed. "I mean no offense. We have watched the midnight sun together, and—and—I thought——"

He paused, feeling very foolish, and unable to conclude his sentence.

She looked at him demurely from under her long, curling lashes.

"You will often find a peasant girl on the shores of the Altenfjord watching the midnight sun at the same time as yourself," she said, and there was a suspicion of laughter in her voice. "It is not unusual. It is not even necessary that you should remember so little a thing."

"Necessary or not, I shall never forget it," he said with sudden impetuosity. "You are no peasant! Come; if I give you my name will you still deny me yours?"

Her delicate brows drew together in a frown of haughty and decided refusal. "No names please my ears save those that are familiar," she said, with intense coldness. "We shall not meet again. Farewell!"

And without further word or look, she leaned gracefully to the oars, and pulling with a long, steady, resolute stroke, the little boat darted away as lightly and swiftly as a skimming swallow out on the shimmering water. He stood gazing after it till it became a distant speck sparkling like a diamond in the light of sky and wave, and when he could no more watch it with unassisted eyes, he took up his field glass and followed its course attentively. He saw it cutting along as straightly as an arrow, then suddenly it dipped round to the westward, apparently making straight for some shelving rocks, that projected far into the Fjord. It reached them; it grew less and less—it disappeared. At the same time the lustre of the heavens gave way to a pale pearl-like uniform grey tint, that stretched far and wide, folding up as in a mantle all the regal luxury of the Sun-king's palace. The subtle odor and delicate chill of the coming dawn stole freshly across the water. A light haze rose and obscured the opposite islands. Something of the tender melancholy of autumn, though it was late June, toned down the aspect of the before brilliant landscape. A lark rose swiftly from its nest in an adjacent meadow, and soaring higher and higher, poured from its tiny throat a cascade of delicious melody. The midnight sun no longer shone at midnight; his face smiled with a sobered serenity through the faint early mists of approaching morning.

CHAPTER II.

"Viens donc—je te chanterai des chansons que les esprits des cimetières m'ont apprises!"

MATURIN.

"Baffled!" he exclaimed, with a slight vexed laugh, as the boat vanished from his sight. "By a woman, too! Who would have thought it?"

Who would have thought it, indeed! Sir Philip Bruce-Errington, Baronet, the wealthy and desirable *parti* for whom many match-making mothers had stood knee-deep in the chilly though sparkling waters of society, ardently plying rod and line with patient persistence, vainly hoping to secure him as a husband for one of their highly proper and passionless daughters,—he, the admired, long-sought-after " eligible," was suddenly rebuffed, flouted—by whom? A stray princess, or a peasant. He vaguely wondered, as he lit a cigar and strolled up and down on the shore, meditating, with a puzzled, almost annoyed expression on his handsome features. He was not accustomed to slights of any kind, however trifling; his position being commanding and enviable enough to attract flattery and friendship from most people. He was the only son of a baronet as renowned for eccentricity as for wealth. He had been the spoilt darling of his mother; and now, both his parents being dead, he was alone in the world, heir to his father's revenues, and entire master of his own actions. And as part of the penalty he had to pay for being rich and good-looking to boot, he was so much run after by women that he found it hard to understand the haughty indifference with which he had just been treated by one of the most fair, if not the fairest of her sex. He was piqued, and his *amour propre* was wounded.

"I'm sure my question was harmless enough," he mused, half crossly. " She might have answered it."

He glanced out impatiently over the Fjord. There was no sign of his returning yacht as yet.

"What a time those fellows are!" he said to himself. " If the pilot were not on board, I should begin to think they had run the *Eulalie* aground."

He finished his cigar and threw the end of it into the water; then he stood moodily watching the ripples as they rolled softly up and caressed the shining brown shore at his feet, thinking all the while of that strange girl, so wonder-fully lovely in face and form, so graceful and proud of bear-ing, with her great blue eyes and masses of dusky gold hair.

His meeting with her was a sort of adventure in its way —the first of the kind he had had for some time. He was subject to fits of weariness or caprice, and it was in one of these that he had suddenly left London in the height of the season, and had started for Norway on a yachting cruise with three chosen companions, one of whom, George Lori-mer, once an Oxford fellow-student, was now his " chum " —the Pythias to his Damon, the *fidus Achates* of his closest confidence. Through the unexpected wakening up of energy in the latter young gentleman, who was usually of a most sleepy and indolent disposition, he happened to be quite alone on this particular occasion, though, as a general rule, he was accompanied in his rambles by one if not all three of his friends. Utter solitude was with him a rare occurrence, and his present experience of it had chanced in this wise. Lorimer the languid, Lorimer the lazy, Lorimer who had remained blandly unmoved and drowsy through all the magnificent panorama of the Norwegian coast, includ-ing the Sogne Fjord and the toppling peaks of the Justedäl glaciers; Lorimer who had slept peacefully in a hammock on deck, even while the yacht was passing under the loom-ing splendors of Melsnipa; Lorimer, now that he had arrived at the Alten Fjord, then at its loveliest in the full glory of the continuous sunshine, developed a new turn of mind, and began to show sudden and abnormal interest in the scenery. In this humor he expressed his desire to " take a sight " of the midnight sun from the island of Seiland, and also declared his resolve to try the nearly im-possible ascent of the great Jedkè glacier.

Errington laughed at the idea. " Don't tell me," he said, " that you are going in for climbing. And do you suppose I believe that you are interested—*you* of all people—in the heavenly bodies?"

" Why not ? " asked Lorimer, with a candid smile. " I'm not in the least interested in earthly bodies, except my own. The sun's a jolly fellow. I sympathize with him in his present condition. He's in his cups—that's what's the matter—and he can't be persuaded to go to bed. I know his feelings perfectly ; and I want to survey his gloriously inebriated face from another point of view. Don't laugh, Phil ; I'm in earnest! And I really have quite a curiosity to try my skill in amateur mountaineering. Jedkè's the very place for a first effort. It offers difficulties, and "— this with a slight yawn—" I like to surmount difficulties ; it's rather amusing."

His mind was so evidently set upon the excursion, that Sir Philip made no attempt to dissuade him from it, but excused himself from accompanying the party on the plea that he wanted to finish a sketch he had recently begun. So that when the *Eulalie* got up her steam, weighed anchor, and swept gracefully away towards the coast of the adjacent islands, her owner was left, at his desire, to the seclusion of a quiet nook on the shore of the Altenfjord, where he succeeded in making a bold and vivid picture of the scene before him. The colors of the sky had, however, defied his palette, and after one or two futile attempts to transfer to his canvas a few of the gorgeous tints that illumed the landscape, he gave up the task in despair, and resigned himself to the *dolce far niente* of absolute enjoyment. From his half pleasing, half melancholy reverie the voice of the unknown maiden had startled him, and now,—now she had left him to resume it if he chose,—left him, in chill displeasure, with a cold yet brilliant flash of something like scorn in her wonderful eyes.

Since her departure the scenery, in some unaccountable way, seemed less attractive to him, the songs of the birds, who were all awake, fell on inattentive ears ; he was haunted by her face and voice, and he was, moreover, a little out of humor with himself for having been such a blunderer as to give her offense, and thus leave an unfavorable impression on her mind.

" I suppose I *was* rude," he considered after a while. " She seemed to think so, at any rate. By Jove ! what a crushing look she gave me ! A peasant ? Not she ! If she had said she was an empress I shouldn't have been much surprised. But a mere common peasant, with that regal figure and those white hands ! I don't believe it. Perhaps our pilot, Valdemar, knows who she is ; I must ask him."

All at once he bethought himself of the cave whence she had emerged. It was close at hand—a natural grotto, arched and apparently lofty. He resolved to explore it. Glancing at his watch he saw it was not yet one o'clock in the morning, yet the voice of the cuckoo called shrilly from the neighboring hills, and a circling group of swallows flitted around him, their lovely wings glistening like jewels in the warm light of the ever-wakeful sun. Going to the entrance of the cave, he looked in. It was formed of rough rock, hewn out by the silent work of the water, and its floor was strewn thick with loose pebbles and polished stones. Entering it, he was able to walk upright for some few paces, then suddenly it seemed to shrink in size and to become darker. The light from the opening gradually narrowed into a slender stream too small for him to see clearly where he was going, thereupon he struck a fusee. At first he could observe no sign of human habitation, not even a rope, or chain, or hook, to intimate that it was a customary shelter for a boat. The fusee went out quickly, and he lit another. Looking more carefully and closely about him, he perceived on a projecting shelf of rock, a small antique lamp, Etruscan in shape, made of iron and wrought with curious letters. There was oil in it, and a half-burnt wick; it had evidently been recently used. He availed himself at once of this useful adjunct to his explorations, and lighting it, was able by the clear and steady flame it emitted, to see everything very distinctly. Right before him was an uneven flight of steps leading down to a closed door.

He paused and listened attentively. There was no sound but the slow lapping of the water near the entrance; within, the thickness of the cavern walls shut out the gay carolling of the birds, and all the cheerful noises of awakening nature. Silence, chillness, and partial obscurity are depressing influences, and the warm blood flowing through his veins, ran a trifle more slowly and coldly as he felt the sort of uncomfortable eerie sensation which is experienced by the jolliest and most careless traveller, when he first goes down to the catacombs in Rome. A sort of damp, earthy shudder creeps through the system, and a dreary feeling of general hopelessness benumbs the faculties; a morbid state of body and mind which is only to be remedied by a speedy return to the warm sunlight, and a draught of generous wine.

Sir Philip, however, held the antique lamp aloft, and descended the clumsy steps cautiously, counting twenty steps in all, at the bottom of which he found himself face to face

with the closed door. It was made of hard wood, so hard
as to be almost like iron. It was black with age, and covered with quaint carvings and inscriptions ; but in the middle, standing out in bold relief among the numberless
Runic figures and devices, was written in large well-cut letters the word—

THELMA.

" By Jove ! " he exclaimed, " I have it ! The girl's name,
of course ! This is some private retreat of hers, I suppose,
—a kind of boudoir like my Lady Winsleigh's, only with
rather a difference."

And he laughed aloud, thinking of the dainty gold-satin
hangings of a certain room in a certain great mansion in
Park Lane, where an aristocratic and handsome lady-leader
of fashion had as nearly made love to him as it was possible for her to do without losing her social dignity.

His laugh was echoed back with a weird and hollow
sound, as though a hidden demon of the cave were mocking
him, a demon whose merriment was intense but also horrible. He heard the unpleasant jeering repetition with a kind
of careless admiration.

" That echo would make a fortune in *Faust*, if it could be
persuaded to back up Mephistopheles with that truly fiendish ' *Ha ha!* ' " he said, resuming his examination of the
name on the door. Then an odd fancy seized him, and he
called loudly—

" Thelma ! "

" Thelma ! " shouted the echo.

" Is that her name ? "

" Her name ! " replied the echo.

" I thought so ! " And Philip laughed again, while the
echo laughed wildly in answer. " Just the sort of name to
suit a Norwegian nymph or goddess. *Thelma* is quaint
and appropriate, and as far as I can remember there's no
rhyme to it in the English language. *Thelma !* " And he
lingered on the pronunciation of the strange word with a
curious sensation of pleasure. " There is something mysteriously suggestive about the sound of it ; like a chord of
music played softly in the distance. Now, can I get through
this door, I wonder ? "

He pushed it gently. It yielded very slightly, and he
tried again and yet again. Finally, he put down the lamp
and set his shoulder against the wooden barrier with all his

force. A dull creaking sound rewarded his efforts, and inch by inch the huge door opened into what at first appeared immeasurable darkness. Holding up the light he looked in, and uttered a smothered exclamation. A sudden gust of wind rushed from the sea through the passage and extinguished the lamp, leaving him in profound gloom. Nothing daunted he sought his fusee case; there was just one left in it. This he hastily struck, and shielding the glow carefully with one hand, relit his lamp, and stepped boldly into the mysterious grotto.

The murmur of the wind and waves, like spirit-voices in unison, followed him as he entered. He found himself in a spacious winding corridor, that had evidently been hollowed out in the rocks and fashioned by human hands. Its construction was after the ancient Gothic method; but the wonder of the place consisted in the walls, which were entirely covered with shells,—shells of every shape and hue,—some delicate as rose-leaves, some rough and prickly, others polished as ivory, some gleaming with a thousand irridescent colors, others pure white as the foam on high billows. Many of them were turned artistically in such a position as to show their inner sides glistening with soft tints like the shades of fine silk or satin,—others glittered with the opaline sheen of mother-o'-pearl. All were arranged in exquisite patterns, evidently copied from fixed mathematical designs,—there were stars, crescents, roses, sunflowers, hearts, crossed daggers, ships and implements of war, all faithfully depicted with extraordinary neatness and care, as though each particular emblem had served some special purpose.

Sir Philip walked along very slowly, delighted with his discovery, and,—pausing to examine each panel as he passed,—amused himself with speculations as to the meaning of this beautiful cavern, so fancifully yet skillfully decorated.

"Some old place of worship, I suppose," he thought. "There must be many such hidden in differents parts of Norway. It has nothing to do with the Christian faith, for among all these devices I don't perceive a single cross."

He was right. There were on crosses; but there were many designs of the sun—the sun rising, the sun setting, the sun in full glory, with all his rays embroidered round him in tiny shells, some of them no bigger than a pin's head.

What a waste of time and labor," he mused. " Who would undertake such a thing nowadays? Fancy the patience and delicacy of finger required to fit all these shells in their places! and they are embedded in strong mortar too, as if the work were meant to be indestructible."

Full of pleased interest, he pursued his way, winding in and out through different arches, all more or less richly ornamented, till he came to a tall, round column, which seemingly supported the whole gallery, for all the arches converged towards it. It was garlanded from top to bottom with their roses and their leaves, all worked in pink and lilac shells, interspersed with small pieces of shining amber and polished malachite. The flicker of the lamp he carried, made it glisten like a mass of jewel-work, and, absorbed in his close examination of this unique specimen of ancient art, Sir Philip did not at once perceive that another light beside his own glimmered from out the furthest archway a little beyond him,—an opening that led into some recess he had not as yet explored. A peculiar lustre sparkling on one side of the shell-work however, at last attracted his attention, and, glancing up quickly, he saw, to his surprise, the reflection of a strange radiance, rosily tinted and brilliant.

Turning in its direction, he paused, irresolute. Could there be some one living in that furthest chamber to which the long passage he had followed evidently led? some one who would perhaps resent his intrusion as an impertinence? some eccentric artist or hermit who had made the cave his home? Or was it perhaps a refuge for smugglers? He listened anxiously. There was no sound. He waited a minute or two, then boldly advanced, determined to solve the mystery.

This last archway was lower than any of those he had passed through, and he was forced to take off his hat and stoop as he went under it. When he raised his head he remained uncovered, for he saw at a glance that the place was sacred. He was in the presence, not of Life, but Death. The chamber in which he stood was square in form, and more richly ornamented with shell-designs than any other portion of the grotto he had seen, and facing the east was an altar hewn out of the solid rock and studded thickly with amber, malachite and mother-o'-pearl. It was covered with the incomprehensible emblems of a bygone creed

2

worked in most exquisite shell-patterns, but on it,—as though in solemn protest against the past,—stood a crucifix of ebony and carved ivory, before which burned steadily a red lamp.

The meaning of the mysterious light was thus explained, but what chiefly interested Errington was the central object of the place,—a coffin,—of rather a plain granite sarcophagus which was placed on the floor lying from north to south. Upon it,—in strange contrast to the sombre coldness of the stone,—reposed a large wreath of poppies freshly gathered. The vivid scarlet of the flowers, the gleam of the shining shells on the walls, the mournful figure of the ivory Christ stretched on the cross among all those pagan emblems,— the intense silence broken only by the slow drip, drip of water trickling somewhere behind the cavern,—and more than these outward things,—his own impressive conviction that he was with the imperial Dead—imperial because past the sway of empire—all made a powerful impression on his mind. Overcoming by degrees his first sensations of awe, he approached the sarcophagus and examined it. It was solidly closed and mortared all round, so that it might have been one compact coffin-shaped block of stone so far as its outward appearance testified. Stooping more closely, however, to look at the brilliant poppy-wreath, he started back with a slight exclamation. Cut deeply in the hard granite he read for the second time that odd name—

THELMA.

It belonged to some one dead, then—not to the lovely living woman who had so lately confronted him in the burning glow of the midnight sun? He felt dismayed at his unthinking precipitation,—he had, in his fancy, actually associated *her*, so full of radiant health and beauty, with what was probably a mouldering corpse in that hermetically sealed tenement of stone! This idea was unpleasant, and jarred upon his feelings. Surely she, that golden-haired nymph of the Fjord, had nothing to do with death! He had evidently found his way into some ancient tomb. "Thelma" might be the name or title of some long-departed queen or princess of Norway, yet, if so, how came the crucifix there,—the red lamp, the flowers?

He lingered, looking curiously about him, as if he fancied the shell-embroidered walls might whisper some answer to his thoughts. The silence offered no suggestions. The plaintive figure of the tortured Christ suspended on the cross maintained an immovable watch over all things, and there was a subtle, faint odor floating about as of crushed spices or herbs. While he still stood there absorbed in perplexed conjectures, he became oppressed by want of air. The red hue of the poppy-wreath mingled with the softer glow of the lamp on the altar,—the moist glitter of the shells and polished pebbles, seemed to dazzle and confuse his eyes. He felt dizzy and faint—and hastily made his way out of that close death-chamber into the passage, where he leaned for a few minutes against the great central column to recover himself. A brisk breath of wind from the Fjord came careering through the gallery, and blew coldly upon his forehead. Refreshed by it, he rapidly overcame the sensation of giddiness, and began to retrace his steps through the winding arches, thinking with some satisfaction as he went, what a romantic incident he would have to relate to Lorimer and his other friends, when a sudden glare of light illumined the passage, and he was brought to an abrupt standstill by the sound of a wild " Halloo ! " The light vanished ; it reappeared. It vanished again, and again appeared, flinging a strong flare upon the shell-worked walls as it approached. Again the fierce " Halloo ! " resounded through the hollow cavities of the subterranean temple, and he remained motionless, waiting for an explanation of this unlooked-for turn to the events of the morning.

He had plenty of physical courage, and the idea of any addition to his adventure rather pleased him than otherwise. Still, with all his bravery, he recoiled a little when he first caught sight of the extraordinary being that emerged from the darkness—a wild, distorted figure that ran towards him with its head downwards, bearing aloft in one skinny hand a smoking pine-torch, from which the sparks flew like so many fireflies. This uncanny personage, wearing the semblance of man, came within two paces of Errington before perceiving him ; then, stopping short in his headlong career, the creature flourished his torch and uttered a defiant yell.

Philip surveyed him coolly and without alarm, though so weird an object might well have aroused a pardonable distrust, and even timidity. He saw a misshapen dwarf, not quite four feet high, with large, ungainly limbs out of all proportion to his head, which was small and compact. His features were of almost feminine fineness, and from under his shaggy brows gleamed a restless pair of large, full, wild blue eyes. His thick, rough flaxen hair was long and curly, and hung in disordered profusion over his deformed shoulders. His dress was of reindeer skin, very fancifully cut, and ornamented with beads of different colors,—and twisted about him as though in an effort to be artistic, was a long strip of bright scarlet woollen material, which showed up the extreme pallor and ill-health of the meagre countenance, and the brilliancy of the eyes that now sparkled with rage as they met those of Errington. He, from his superior height, glanced down with pity on the unfortunate creature, whom he at once took to be the actual owner of the cave he had explored. Uncertain what to do, whether to speak or remain silent, he moved slightly as though to pass on ; but the shock-headed dwarf leaped lightly in his way, and, planting himself firmly before him, shrieked some unintelligible threat, of which Errington could only make out the last words, " Nifleheim " and " Nastrond."

" I believe he is commending me to the old Norwegian *inferno*," thought the young baronet with a smile, amused at the little man's evident excitement. " Very polite of him, I'm sure ! But, after all, I had no business here. I'd better apologize." And forthwith he began to speak in the simplest English words he could choose, taking care to pronounce them very slowly and distinctly.

" I cannot understand you, my good sir ; but I see you are angry. I came here by accident. I am going away now at once."

His explanation had a strange effect. The dwarf drew nearer, twirled himself rapidly round three times as though waltzing ; then, holding his torch a little to one side, turned up his thin, pale countenance, and, fixing his gaze on Sir Philip, studied every feature of his face with absorbing interest. Then he burst into a violent fit of laughter.

" At last—at last ? " he cried in fluent English. " Going now? Going, you say? Never ! never ! You will never go away any more. No, not without something stolen ! The dead have summoned you here ! Their white bony fingers have dragged you across the deep ! Did you not hear their voices, cold and hollow as the winter wind, calling, calling you, and saying,' Come, come, proud robber, from over the far seas ; come and gather the beautiful rose of the northern forest'? Yes, Yes ! You have obeyed the dead—the dead who feign sleep, but are ever wakeful;—you have come as a thief in the golden midnight, and the thing you seek is the life of Sigurd! Yes—yes! it is true. The spirit cannot lie. You must kill, you must steal! See how the blood drips, drop by drop, from the heart of Sigurd! And the jewel you steal—ah, what a jewel!—you shall not find such another in Norway!"

His excited voice sank by degrees to a plaintive and forlorn whisper, and dropping his torch with a gesture of despair on the ground, he looked at it burning, with an air of mournful and utter desolation. Profoundly touched, as he immediately understood the condition of his companion's wandering wits, Errington spoke to him soothingly.

"You mistake me," he said in gentle accents; "I would not steal anything from you, nor have I come to kill you. See," and he held out his hand, "I wouldn't harm you for the world. I didn't know this cave belonged to you. Forgive me for having entered it. I am going to rejoin my friends. Good-bye!"

The strange, half-crazy creature touched his outstretched hand timidly, and with a sort of appeal.

"Good-bye, good-bye!" he muttered. "That is what they all say,—even the dead,—good-bye; but they never go—never, never! You cannot be different to the rest. And you do not wish to hurt poor Sigurd?"

"Certainly not, if *you* are Sigurd," said Philip, half laughing; "I should be very sorry to hurt you."

"You are *sure?*" he persisted, with a sort of obstinate eagerness. "You have eyes which tell truths; but there other things which are truer than eyes—things in the air, in the grass, in the waves, and they talk very strangely of you. I know you, of course! I knew you ages ago—long before I saw you dead on the field of battle, and the black-haired Valkyrie galloped with you to Valhalla! Yes; I knew you long before that, and you knew me; for I was your King, and you were my vassal, wild and rebellious—not the proud, rich Englishman you are to-day."

Errington started. How could this Sigurd, as he called himself, be aware of either his wealth or nationality?

The dwarf observed his movement of surprise with a cunning smile.

"Sigurd is wise,—Sigurd is brave! Who shall deceive him? He knows you well; he will always know you. The

old gods teach Sigurd all his wisdom—the gods of the sea
and the wind—the sleepy gods that lie in the hearts of the
flowers—the small spirits that sit in shells and sing all day
and all night." He paused, and his eyes filled with a wistful look of attention. He drew closer.

"Come," he said earnestly, "come, you must listen to
my music; perhaps you can tell me what it means."

He picked up his smouldering torch and held it aloft
again; then, beckoning Errington to follow him, he led the
way to a small grotto, cut deeply into the wall of the
cavern. Here there were no shell patterns. Little green
ferns grew thickly out of the stone crevices, and a minute
runlet of water trickled slowly down from above, freshen-
ing the delicate frondage as it fell. With quick, agile fingers
he removed a loose stone from this aperture, and as he did
so, a low shuddering wail resounded through the arches—a
melancholy moan that rose and sank, and rose again in
weird, sorrowful minor echoes.

" Hear her," murmured Sigurd plaintively. " She is always complaining; it is a pity she cannot rest! She is a
spirit, you know. I have often asked her what troubles
her, but she will not tell me; she only weeps ! "

His companion looked at him compassionately. The
sound that so affected his disordered imagination was nothing but the wind blowing through the narrow hole formed
by the removal of the stone; but it was useless to explain
this simple fact to one in his condition.

" Tell me," and Sir Philip spoke very gently, " is this
your home ? "

The dwarf surveyed him almost scornfully. " *My* home ! "
he echoed. " My home is everywhere—on the mountains,
in the forests, on the black rocks and barren shores ! My
soul lives between the sun and the sea; my heart is with
Thelma ! "

Thelma ! Here was perhaps a clue to the mystery.

" Who is Thelma ? " asked Errington somewhat hurriedly.

Sigurd broke into violent and derisive laughter. " Do
you think I will tell *you* ? " he cried loudly. " *You*,—one
of that strong, cruel race who must conquer all they see;
who covet everything fair under heaven, and will buy it,
even at the cost of blood and tears ! Do you think I will
unlock the door of my treasure to *you* ? No, ɴᴏ; besides."

and his voice sank lower, " what should you do with Thelma?
She is dead!"

And, as if possessed by a sudden access of frenzy, he
brandished his pine-torch wildly above his head till it showered a rain of bright sparks above him, and exclaimed furiously—

" Away, away, and trouble me not! The days are not
yet fulfilled,—the time is not yet ripe. Why seek to hasten
my end? Away, away, I tell you! Leave me in peace!
I will die when Thelma bids me; but not till then!"

And he rushed down the long gallery and disappeared in
the furthest chamber, where he gave vent to a sort of long,
sobbing cry, which rang dolefully through the cavern and
then subsided into utter silence.

Feeling as if he were in a chaotic dream, Errington pursued his interrupted course through the winding passages
with a bewildered and wondering mind. What strange
place had he inadvertently lighted on? and who were the
still stranger beings in connection with it? First the beautiful girl herself; next the mysterious coffin, hidden in its
fanciful shell temple; and now this deformed madman, with
the pale face and fine eyes; whose utterances, though incoherent, savored somewhat of poesy and prophecy. And
what spell was attached to that name of Thelma? The
more he thought of his morning's adventure, the more puzzled he became. As a rule, he believed more in the commonplace than in the romantic—most people do. But
truth to tell, romance is far more common than the commonplace. There are few who have not, at one time or
other of their lives, had some strange or tragic episode
woven into the tissue of their every-day existence; and it
would be difficult to find one person even among humdrum
individuals, who, from birth to death, has experienced nothing out of the common.

Errington generally dismissed all tales of adventure as
mere exaggerations of heated fancy; and, had he read in
some book, of a respectable nineteenth-century yachtsman
having such an interview with a madman in a sea-cavern,
he would have laughed at the affair as an utter improb-
ability, though he could not have explained why he considered it improbable. But now it had occurred to himself, he was both surprised and amused at the whole circumstance; moreover, he was sufficiently interested and
curious to be desirous of sifting the matter to its foundation.

It was, however, somewhat of a relief to him when he again reached the outer cavern. He replaced the lamp on the shelf where he had found it, and stepped once more into the brilliant light of the very early dawn, which then had all the splendor of full morning. There was a deliciously-balmy wind, the blue sky was musical with a chorus of larks, and every breath of air that waved aside the long grass sent forth a thousand odors from hidden beds of wild thyme and bog-myrtle.

He perceived the *Eulalie* at anchor in her old place on the Fjord; she had returned while he was absent on his explorations. Gathering together his rug and painting materials, he blew a whistle sharply three times; he was answered from the yacht, and presently a boat, manned by a couple of sailors, came skimming over the water towards him. It soon reached the shore, and, entering it, he was speedily rowed away from the scene of his morning's experience back to his floating palace, where, as yet, none of his friends were stirring.

"How about Jedkè?" he inquired of one of his men. "Did they climb it?"

A slow grin overspread the sailor's brown face.

"Lord bless you, no, sir! Mr. Lorimer, he just looked at it and sat down in the shade ; the other gentleman played pitch-and-toss with pebbles. They was main hungry too, and ate a mighty sight of 'am and pickles. Then they came on board and all turned in at once."

Errington laughed. He was amused at the utter failure of Lorimer's recent sudden energy, but not surprised. His thoughts were, however, busied with something else, and he next asked—

"Where's our pilot?"

"Valdemar Svensen, sir? He went down to his bunk as soon as we anchored, for a snooze, he said."

"All right. If he comes on deck before I do, just tell him not to go ashore for anything till I see him. I want to speak to him after breakfast."

"Ay, ay, sir."

Whereupon Sir Philip descended to his private cabin. He drew the blind at the port-hole to shut out the dazzling sunlight, for it was nearly three o'clock in the morning, and quickly undressing, he flung himself into his berth with a slight, not altogether unpleasant, feeling of exhaustion. To the last, as his eyes closed drowsily, he seemed to hear the slow drip, drip of the water behind the rocky cavern, and the desolate cry of the incomprehensible Sigurd, while through these sounds that mingled with the gurgle of little waves lapping against the sides of the *Eulalie*, the name of " Thelma " murmured itself in his ears till slumber drowned his senses in oblivion.

CHAPTER III.

"Hast any mortal name,
Fit appellation for this dazzling frame,
Or friends or kinsfolk on the citied earth?"

KEATS.

" THIS is positively absurd," murmured Lorimer, in mildly injured tones, seven hours later, as he sat on the edge of his berth, surveying Errington, who, fully dressed and in the highest spirits, had burst in to upbraid him for his laziness while he was yet but scantily attired. " I tell you, my good fellow, there are some things which the utmost stretch of friendship will *not* stand. Here am I in shirt and trousers with only one sock on, and you dare to say you have had an adventure! Why, if you had cut a piece out of the sun, you ought to wait till a man is shaved before mentioning it."

" Don't be snappish, old boy!" laughed Errington gaily. " Put on that other sock and listen. I don't want to tell those other fellows just yet, they might go making inquiries about her——"

" Oh, there is a ' her ' in the case, is there?" said Lorimer, opening his eyes rather widely. " Well, Phil! I thought you had had enough, and something too much, of women."

" This is not a woman!" declared Philip with heat and eagerness, " at least not the sort of woman *I* have ever known! This is a forest-empress, sea-goddess, or sun-angel! I don't know *what* she is, upon my life!"

Lorimer regarded him with an air of reproachful offense. " Don't go on—please don't!" he implored. " I can't stand it—I really can't! Incipient verse-mania is too much for me. Forest-empress, sea-goddess, sun-angel—by Jove! what next? You are evidently in a very bad way. If I remember rightly, you had a flask of that old green Chartreuse with you. Ah! that accounts for it! Nice stuff, but a little too strong."

Errington laughed, and, unabashed by his friend's rail-
lery, proceeded to relate with much vivacity and graphic
fervor the occurrences of the morning. Lorimer listened
patiently with a forbearing smile on his open, ruddy countenance. When he had heard everything he looked up and
inquired calmly—

"This is not a yarn, is it?"

"A yarn!" exclaimed Philip. "Do you think I would
invent such a thing?"

"Can't say," returned Lorimer imperturbably. "You
are quite capable of it. It's a very creditable crammer,
due to Chartreuse. Might have been designed by Victor
Hugo; it's in his style. Scene, Norway—midnight. Mysterious maiden steals out of a cave and glides away in a
boat over the water; man, the hero, goes into cave, finds a
stone coffin, says—'Qu'est-ce que c'est? Dieu! C'est la
mort!' Spectacle affreux! Staggers back perspiring;
meets mad dwarf with torch; mad dwarf talks a good deal
—mad people always do,—then yells and runs away. Man
comes out of cave and—and—goes home to astonish his
friends; one of them won't be astonished,—that's me!"

"I don't care," said Errington. "It's a true story for
all that. Only, I say, don't talk of it before the others;
let's keep our own counsel——"

"No poachers allowed on the Sun-Angel Manor!" interrupted Lorimer gravely. Philip went on without heeding
him.

"I'll question Valdemar Svensen after breakfast. He
knows everybody about here. Come and have a smoke on
deck when I give you the sign, and we'll cross-examine
him."

Lorimer still looked incredulous. "What's the good of
it?" he inquired languidly. "Even if it's all true you had
much better leave this goddess, or whatever you call her,
alone, especially if she has any mad connections. What do
you want with her?"

"Nothing!" declared Errington, though his color heightened. "Nothing, I assure you! It's just a matter of curiosity with me. I should like to know who she is—that's
all! The affair won't go any further."

"How do you know?" and Lorimer began to brush his
stiff curly hair with a sort of vicious vigor. "How can you
tell? I'm not a spiritualist, nor any sort of a humbug at
all, I hope, but I sometimes indulge in presentiments. Be-

fore we started on this cruise, I was haunted by that dismal old ballad of Sir Patrick Spens—

> 'The King's daughter of Norroway
> 'Tis thou maun bring her hame!'

And here you have found her, or so it appears. What's to come of it, I wonder?"

"Nothing's to come of it; nothing *will* come of it!" laughed Philip. "As I told you, she said she was a peasant. There's the breakfast-bell! Make haste, old boy, I'm as hungry as a hunter!"

And he left his friend to finish dressing, and entered the saloon, where he greeted his two other companions, Alec, or, as he was oftener called, Sandy Macfarlane, and Pierre Duprèz; the former an Oxford student,—the latter a young fellow whose acquaintance he had made in Paris, and with whom he had kept up a constant and friendly intercourse. A greater contrast than these two presented could scarcely be imagined. Macfarlane was tall and ungainly, with large loose joints that seemed to protrude angularly out of him in every direction,—Duprèz was short, slight and wiry, with a dapper and by no means ungraceful figure. The one had formal *gauche* manners, a never-to-be-eradicated Glasgow accent, and a slow, infinitely tedious method of expressing himself,—the other was full of restless movement and pantomimic gesture, and being proud of his English, plunged into that language recklessly, making it curiously light and flippant, though picturesque, as he went. Macfarlane was destined to become a shining light of the established Church of Scotland, and therefore took life very seriously,—Duprèz was the spoilt only child of an eminent French banker, and had very little to do but enjoy himself, and that he did most thoroughly, without any calculation or care for the future. On all points of taste and opinion they differed widely; but there was no doubt about their both being good-hearted fellows, without any affectation of abnormal vice or virtue.

"So you did not climb Jedkè after all!" remarked Errington laughingly, as they seated themselves at the breakfast table.

"My friend, what would you!" cried Duprèz. "I have not said that I will climb it; no! I never say that I will do anything, because I'm not sure of myself. How can I be? It is that *cher enfant*, Lorimer, that said such brave words!

See : . . . we arrive ; we behold the shore—all black, great, vast ! . . . rocks like needles, and, higher than all, this most fierce Jedkè—bah ! what a name !—straight as the spire of a cathedral. One must be a fly to crawl up it, and we, we are not flies—*ma foi !* no ! Lorimer, he laugh, he yawn—so ! He say, ' not for me to-day ; I very much thank you ! ' And then, we watch the sun. Ah ! that was grand, glorious, beautiful ! " And Duprèz kissed the tips of his fingers in ecstacy.

" What did *you* think about it, Sandy ? " asked Sir Philip.

" I didna think much," responded Macfarlane, shortly. " It's no sae grand a sight as a sunset in Skye. And it's an uncanny business to see the sun losin' a' his poonctooal- ity, and remainin' stock still, as it were, when it's his plain duty to set below the horizon. Mysel', I think it's been fair over-rated. It's unnatural an' oot o' the common, say what ye like."

" Of course it is," agreed Lorimer, who just then saun- tered in from his cabin. " Nature *is* most unnatural. I always thought so. Tea for me, Phil, please ; coffee wakes me up too suddenly. I say, what's the programme to-day ? "

" Fishing in the Alten," answered Errington promptly.

" That suits me perfectly," said Lorimer, as he leisurely sipped his tea. " I'm an excellent fisher. I hold the line and generally forget to bait it. Then,—while it trails harm- lessly in the water, I doze ; thus both the fish and I are happy."

" And this evening," went on Errington, " we must return the minister's call. He's been to the yacht twice. We're bound to go out of common politeness."

" Spare us, good Lord ! " groaned Lorimer.

" What a delightfully fat man is that good religious ! " cried Duprèz. " A living proof of the healthiness of Nor- way ! "

" He's not a native," put in Macfarlane ; " he's frae' Yorkshire. He's only been a matter of three months here, filling the place o' the settled meenister who's awa' for a change of air."

" He's a precious specimen of a humbug, anyhow," sighed Lorimer drearily. " However, I'll be civil to him as long as he doesn't ask me to hear him preach. At that suggestion I'll fight him. He's soft enough to bruise easily."

" Ye're just too lazy to fight onybody," declared **Macfar- lane.**

Lorimer smiled sweetly. " Thanks, awfully ! I dare say you're right. I've never found it worth while as yet to exert myself in any particular direction. No one has asked me to exert myself; no one wants me to exert myself; therefore, why should I ? "

" Don't ye want to get on in the world ? " asked Macfarlane, almost brusquely.

" Dear me, no ! What an exhausting idea ! Get on in the world—what for ? I have five hundred a year, and when my mother goes over to the majority (long distant be that day, for I'm very fond of the dear old lady), I shall have five thousand—more than enough to satisfy any sane man who doesn't want to speculate on the Stock Exchange. *Your* case, my good Mac, is different. You will be a celebrated Scotch divine. You will preach to a crowd of pious numskulls about predestination, and so forth. You will be stump-orator for the securing of seats in paradise. Now, now, keep calm !—don't mind me. It's only a figure of speech ! And the numskulls will call you a ' rare powerfu' rousin' preacher '—isn't that the way they go on ? and when you die—for die you must, most unfortunately—they will give you a three-cornered block of granite (if they can make up their minds to part with the necessary bawbees) with your name prettily engraved thereon. That's all very nice; it suits some people. It wouldn't suit me."

" What *would* suit you ? " queried Errington. " You find everything more or less of a bore."

" Ah, my good little boy ! " broke in Duprèz. " Paris is the place for you. You should live in Paris. Of that you would never fatigue yourself."

" Too much absinthe, secret murder and suicidal mania," returned Lorimer, meditatively. " That was a neat idea about the coffins though. I never hoped to dine off a coffin."

" Ah ! you mean the Taverne de l'Enfer ? " exclaimed Duprèz. " Yes ; the divine waitresses wore winding sheets, and the wine was served in imitation skulls. Excellent ! I remember ; the tables were shaped like coffins."

" Gude Lord Almighty ! " piously murmured Macfarlane. " What a fearsome sicht ! "

As he pronounced these words with an unusually marked accent, Duprèz looked inquiring.

" What does our Macfarlane say ? "

" He says it must have been a ' fearsome sicht,' " repeated Lorimer, with even a stronger accent than Sanby's own, "which, *mon cher* Pierre, means all the horrors in your language; *affreux, epouvantable, navrant*—anything you like, that is sufficiently terrible."

" *Mais, point du tout!* " cried Duprèz energetically. "It was charming! It made us laugh at death—so much better than to cry! And there was a delicious child in a winding-sheet; brown curls, laughing eyes and little mouth; ha, ha! but she was well worth kissing!"

" I'd rather follow ma own funeral, than kiss a lass in a winding-sheet," said Sandy, in solemn and horrified tones. " It's just awfu' to think on."

" But, see, my friend," persisted Duprèz, "you would not be permitted to follow your own funeral, not possible,— *voila!* Your *are* permitted to kiss the pretty one in the winding-sheet. It *is* possible. Behold the difference!"

" Never mind the Taverne de l'Enfer just now," said Errington, who had finished his breakfast hurriedly. " It's time for you fellows to get your fishing toggery on. I'm off to speak to the pilot."

And away he went, followed more slowly by Lorimer, who, though he pretended indifference, was rather curious to know more, if possible, concerning his friend's adventure of the morning. They found the pilot, Valdemar Svensen, leaning at his ease against the idle wheel, with his face turned towards the eastern sky. He was a stalwart specimen of Norse manhood, tall and strongly built, with thoughtful, dignified features, and keen, clear hazel eyes. His chestnut hair, plentifully sprinkled with gray, clustered thickly over a broad brow, that was deeply furrowed with many a line of anxious and speculative thought, and the forcible brown hand that rested lightly on the spokes of the wheel, told its own tale of hard and honest labor. Neither wife nor child, nor living relative had Valdemar; the one passion of his heart was the sea. Sir Philip Errington had engaged him at Christiansund, hearing of him there as a man to whom the intricacies of the Fjords, and the dangers of rock-bound coasts, were more familiar than a straight road on dry lake, and since then the management of the *Eulalie* had been entirely entrusted to him. Though an eminently practical sailor, he was half a mystic, and believed in the wildest legends of his land with more implicit faith than many so-called Christians believe in their sacred doctrines. He doffed his red cap respectfully now as Er-

rington and Lorimer approached, smilingly wishing them
" a fair day." Sir Philip offered him a cigar, and, coming
to the point at once, asked abruptly—

" I say, Svensen, are there any pretty girls in Bosekop ? "

The pilot drew the newly lit cigar from his mouth, and
passed his rough hand across his forehead in a sort of grave
perplexity.

" It is a matter in which I am foolish," he said at last,
" for my ways have always gone far from the ways of
women. Girls there are plenty, I suppose, but——" he
mused with pondering patience for awhile. Then a broad
smile broke like sunshine over his embrowned countenance, as he continued, " Now, gentlemen, I do remember
well ; it is said that at Bosekop yonder, are to be found
some of the homeliest wenches in all Norway."

Errington's face fell at this reply. Lorimer turned away
to hide the mischievous smile that came on his lips at his
friend's discomfiture.

" I *know* it was that Chartreuse," he thought to himself. " That and the midnight sun-effects. Nothing
else ! "

" What ! " went on Philip. " No good-looking girls at all
about here, eh ? "

Svensen shook his head, still smilingly.

" Not at Bosekop, sir, that I ever heard of."

" I say ! " broke in Lorimer, " are there any old tombs
or sea-caves, or places of that sort close by, worth explor-
ing ? "

Valdemar Svensen answered this question readily, almost
eagerly.

" No, sir ! There are no antiquities of any sort ; and as
for caves, there are plenty, but only the natural formations
of the sea, and none of these are curious or beautiful on this
side of the Fjord."

Lorimer poked his friend secretly in the ribs.

" You've been dreaming, old fellow ! " he whispered slyly.
" I knew it was a crammer ! "

Errington shook him off good-humoredly.

" Can you tell me," he said, addressing Valdemar again in
distinct accents, " whether there is any place, person, or
thing near here called *Thelma ?* "

The pilot started ; a look of astonishment and fear came
into his eyes ; his hand went instinctively to his red cap, as
though in deference to the name.

"The Fröken Thelma!" he exclaimed, in low tones. "Is it possible that you have seen her?"

"Ah, George, what do you say now?" cried Errington delightedly. "Yes, yes, Valdemar; the Fröken Thelma, as you call her. Who is she? . . . What is she?—and how can there be no pretty girls in Bosekop if such a beautiful creature as she lives there?"

Valdemar looked troubled and vexed.

"Truly, I thought not of the maiden," he said gravely. "'Tis not for me to speak of the daughter of Olaf," here his voice sank a little, and his face grew more and more sombre. "Pardon me, sir, but how did you meet her?"

"By accident," replied Errington promptly, not caring to relate his morning's adventure for the pilot's benefit. "Is she some great personage here?"

Svensen sighed, and smiled somewhat dubiously.

"Great? Oh, no; not what you would call great. Her father, Olaf Güldmar, is a *bonde*,—that is, a farmer in his own right. He has a goodly house, and a few fair acres well planted and tilled,—also he pays his men freely,—but those that work for him are all he sees,—neither he nor his daughter ever visit the town. They dwell apart, and have nothing in common with their neighbors."

"And where do they live?" asked Lorimer, becoming as interested as he had formerly been incredulous.

The pilot leaned lightly over the rail of the deck and pointed towards the west.

"You see that great rock shaped like a giant's helmet, and behind it a high green knoll, clustered thick with birch and pine?"

They nodded assent.

"At the side of the knoll is the *bonde's* house, a good eight-mile walk from the outskirts of Bosekop. Should you ever seek to rest there, gentlemen," and Svensen spoke with quiet resolution, "I doubt whether you will receive a pleasant welcome."

And he looked at them both with an inquisitive air, as though seeking to discover their intentions.

"Is that so?" drawled Lorimer lazily, giving his friend an expressive nudge. "Ah! *We* shant trouble them! Thanks for your information, Valdemar! We don't intend to hunt up the—what d'ye call him?—the *bonde*, if he's at all surly. Hospitality that gives you greeting and a dinner for nothing,—that's what suits *me*."

o marry you, for nothing but a sun-empress will suit
w."

Don't be a fool, George," said Errington, half vexedly,
he hot color mounted to his face in spite of himself. " It
ll idle curiosity, nothing else. After what Svensen told
I'm quite as anxious to see this gruff old *bonde* as his
ughter."

Lorimer held up a reproachful finger. " Now, Phil,
on't stoop to duplicity—not with me, at any rate. Why
disguise your feelings? Why, as the tragedians say, endeavor to crush the noblest and best emotions that ever
warm the *boo-zum* of man? Chivalrous sentiment and admiration for beauty,—chivalrous desire to pursue it and catch
it and call it your own,—I understand it all, my dear boy!
But my prophetic soul tells me you will have to strangle the
excellent Olaf Güldmar—heavens! what a name!—before
it will be allowed to make love to his fair *chee-ild.* Then
't forget the madman with the torch,—he may turn up
the most unexpected fashion and give you no end of
uble. But, by Jove, it *is* a romantic affair, positively
ite stagey! Something will come of it, serious or comic.
I wonder which?"

Errington laughed, but said nothing in reply, as their
two companions ascended from the cabin at that moment,
in full attire for the fishing expedition, followed by the
teward bearing a large basket of provisions for luncheon,—
nd all private conversation came to an end. Hastening
he rest of their preparations, within twenty minutes they
vere skimming across the Fjord in a long boat manned by
our sailors, who rowed with a will and sent the light
raft scudding through the water with the swiftness of an
arrow. Landing, they climbed the dewy hills spangled
thick with forget-me-nots and late violets, till they reached
a shady and secluded part of the river, where, surrounded
by the songs of hundreds of sweet-throated birds, they commenced their sport, which kept them well employed till a
late hour in the afternoon.

34

" Our people are not without
with a touch of wistful and appea
your journey, gentlemen, you have
as you know. But Olaf Güldmar is
he has the pride and fierceness of olde
and customs are different; and few like
feared."

" You know him then?" inquired Erri

" I know him," returned Valdemar quie
daughter is fair as the sun and the sea. Bu
place to speak of them——." He broke off,
slightly embarrassed pause, asked, " Will the *h*
to sail to-day ? "

" No Valdemar," answered Errington indifferentl
till to-morrow, when we'll visit the Kaa Fjord if the w
keeps fair."

" Very good, sir," and the pilot, tacitly avoiding
further converse with his employer respecting the mys
rious Thelma and her equally mysterious father, turned
examine the wheel and compass as though something ther
needed his earnest attention. Errington and Lorime
strolled up and down the polished white deck arm-in-arm,
talking in low tones.

" You didn't ask him about the coffin and the dwarf,"
said Lorimer.

" No; because I believe he knows nothing of either, and
it would be news to him which I'm not bound to give. If
I can manage to see the girl again the mystery of the cave
may explain itself."

" Well, what are you going to do? "

Errington looked meditative. " Nothing at present
We'll go fishing with the others. But, I tell you what, i
you're up to it, we'll leave Duprèz and Macfarlane at t
minister's house this evening and tell them to wait for
there,—once they all begin to chatter they never know h
time goes. Meanwhile you and I will take the boat
row over in search of this farmer's abode. I believe th
a short cut to it by water; at any rate I know the w
went."

" ' I know the way she went home with her
posy ! ' " quoted Lorimer, with a laugh. " You
Phil, ' a very palpable hit ' ! Who would have tho
Clara Winsleigh needn't poison her husband a

CHAPTER IV.

"Thou art violently carried away from grace ; there is a devil haunts thee in the likeness of a fat old man,—a tun of man is thy companion."   SHAKESPEARE.

THE Reverend Charles Dyceworthy sat alone in the small dining-room of his house at Bosekop, finishing a late tea, and disposing of round after round of hot buttered toast with that suave alacrity he always displayed in the consumption of succulent eatables. He was a largely made man, very much on the wrong side of fifty, with accumulations of unwholesome fat on every available portion of his body. His round face was cleanly shaven and shiny, as though its flabby surface were frequently polished with some sort of luminous grease instead of the customary soap. His mouth was absurdly small and pursy for so broad a countenance,—his nose seemed endeavoring to retreat behind his puffy cheeks as though painfully aware of its own insignificance,—and he had little, sharp, ferret-like eyes of a dull mahogany brown, which were utterly destitute of even the faintest attempt at any actual expression. They were more like glass beads than eyes, and glittered under their scanty fringe of pale-colored lashes witk a sort of shallow cunning which might mean malice or good-humor,—no one looking at them could precisely determine which. His hair was of an indefinite shade, neither light nor dark, somewhat of the tinge of a dusty potato before it is washed clean. It was neatly brushed and parted in the middle with mathematical precision, while from the back of his head it was brought forward in two projections, one on each side, like budding wings behind his ears. It was impossible for the most fastidious critic to find fault with the Reverend Mr. Dyceworthy's hands. He had beautiful hands, white, soft, plump and well-shaped,—his delicate filbert nails were trimmed with punctilious care, and shone with a pink lustre that was positively charming. He was evidently an amiable man, for he smiled to himself over his tea,—he had a trick of smiling,—ill-natured people said he did it on purpose, in order to widen his mouth and make it more in proportion to the size of his face. Such remarks, however, emanated only from the spiteful and envious who could not succeed in winning the social popularity that everywhere attended Mr. Dyceworthy's movements. For he was undoubtedly popular,—no one could deny that. In the small Yorkshire town where he usually had his abode, he came little short of being adored by the women of his own particular sect, who crowded to listen to his fervent discourses, and came away from them on the verge of hysteria, so profoundly moved were their sensitive souls by his damnatory doctrines. The men were more reluctant in their admiration, yet even they were always ready to admit " that he was an excellent fellow, with his heart in the right place."

He had a convenient way of getting ill at the proper seasons, and of requiring immediate change of air, whereupon his grateful flock were ready and willing to subscribe the money necessary for their beloved preacher to take repose and relaxation in any part of the world he chose. This year, however, they had not been asked to furnish the usual funds for travelling expenses, for the resident minister of Bosekop, a frail, gentle old man, had been seriously prostrated during the past winter with an affection of the lungs, which necessitated his going to a different climate for change and rest. Knowing Dyceworthy as a zealous member of the Lutheran persuasion, and, moreover, as one who had in his youth lived for some years in Christiania, —thereby gaining a knowledge of the Norwegian tongue, —he invited him to take his place for his enforced time of absence, offering him his house, his servants, his pony-carriage and an agreeable pecuniary *douceur* in exchange for his services,—proposals which the Reverend Charles eagerly accepted. Though Norway was not exactly new to him, the region of the Alten Fjord was, and he at once felt, though he knew not why, that the air there would be the very thing to benefit his delicate constitution. Besides, it looked well for at least *one* occasion, to go away for the summer without asking him congregation to pay for his trip. It was generous on his part, almost noble.

The ladies of his flock wept at his departure and made him socks, comforters, slippers, and other consoling gear of the like description to recall their sweet memories to his saintly mind during his absence from their society. But, truth to tell, Mr. Dyceworthy gave little thought to these fond and regretful fair ones ; he was much too comfortable at Bosekop to look back with any emotional yearning to the ugly, precise little provincial town he had left behind him. The minister's quaint, pretty house suited him perfectly; the minister's servants were most punctual in their services; the minister's phaeton conveniently held his cumbrous person, and the minister's pony was a quiet beast, that trotted good-temperedly wherever it was guided, and shied at nothing. Yes, he was thoroughly comfortable,—as comfortable as a truly pious fat man deserves to be, and all the work he had to do was to preach twice on Sundays, to a quiet, primitive, decently ordered congregation, who listened to his words respectfully though without displaying any emotional rapture. Their stolidity, however, did not affect him,—he preached to please himself,—loving above all things to hear the sound of his own voice, and never so happy as when thundering fierce denunciations against the Church of Rome. His thoughts seemed tending in that direction now, as he poured himself out his third cup of tea and smilingly shook his head over it, while he stirred the cream and sugar in,—for he took from his waistcoat pocket a small glittering object and laid it before him on the table, still shaking his head and smiling with a patient, yet reproachful air of superior wisdom. It was a crucifix of mother-o'-pearl and silver, the symbol of the Christian faith. But it seemed to carry no sacred suggestions to the soul of Mr. Dyceworthy. On the contrary, he looked at it with an expression of meek ridicule,—ridicule that bordered on contempt.

"A Roman," he murmured placidly to himself, between two large bites of toast. "The girl is a Roman, and thereby hopelessly damned."

And he smiled again,—more sweetly than before, as though the idea of hopeless damnation suggested some peculiarly agreeable reflections. Unfolding his fine cologne-scented cambric handkerchief, he carefully wiped his fat white fingers free from the greasy marks of the toast, and, taking up the objectionable cross gingerly, as though it were red-hot, he examined it closely on all sides. There were some words engraved on the back of it, and after some trouble Mr. Dyceworthy spelt them out. They were "*Passio Christi, conforta me. Thelma.*"

He shook his head with a sort of resigned cheerfulness.

"Hopelessly damned," he murmured again gently, "unless——"

What alternative suggested itself to his mind was not precisely apparent, for his thoughts suddenly turned in a more frivolous direction. Rising from the now exhausted tea-table, he drew out a small pocket-mirror and surveyed himself therein with a mild ·approval. With the extreme end of his handkerchief he tenderly removed two sacrilegious crumbs that presumed to linger in the corners of his piously pursed mouth. In the same way he detached a morsel of congealed butter that clung pertinaciously to the end of his bashfully retreating nose. This done, he again looked at himself with increased satisfaction, and, putting by his pocket-mirror, rang the bell. It was answered at once by a tall, strongly built woman, with a colorless, stolid countenance,—that might have been carved out of wood for any expression it had in it.

" Ulrika," said Mr. Dyceworthy blandly, " you can clear the table."

Ulrika, without answering, began to pack the tea-things together in a methodical way, without clattering so much as a plate or spoon, and, piling them compactly on a tray, was about to leave the room, when Mr. Dyceworthy called to her, " Ulrika ! "

" Sir ? "

" Did you ever see a thing like this before ? " and he held up the crucifix to her gaze.

The woman shuddered, and her dull eyes lit up with a sudden terror.

" It is the witch's charm ! " she muttered thickly, while her pale face grew yet paler. " Burn it, sir !—burn it, and the power will leave her."

Mr. Dyceworthy laughed indulgently. " My good woman, you mistake," he said suavely. " Your zeal for the true gospel leads you into error. There are thousands of misguided persons who worship such a thing as this. It is often all of our dear Lord they know. Sad, very sad ! But still, though they, alas ! are not of the elect, and are plainly doomed to perdition,—they are not precisely what are termed witches, Ulrika."

" *She* is," replied the woman with a sort of ferocity ; " and, if I had my way, I would tell her so to her face, and see what would happen to her then ! "

" Tut, tut ! " remarked Mr. Dyceworthy amiably. " The days of witchcraft are past. You show some little ignorance, Ulrika. You are not acquainted with the great advancement of recent learning."

" Maybe, maybe," and Ulrika turned to go ; but she muttered sullenly as she went, " There be them that know and could tell, and them that will have her yet."

She shut the door behind her with a sharp clang, and, left to himself, Mr. Dyceworthy again smiled—such a benignant, fatherly smile! He then walked to the window and looked out. It was past seven o'clock, an hour that elsewhere would have been considered evening, but in Bosekop at that season it still seemed afternoon.

The sun was shining brilliantly, and in the minister's front garden the roses were all wide awake. A soft moisture glittered on every tiny leaf and blade of grass. The penetrating and delicious odor of sweet violets scented each puff of wind, and now and then the call of the cuckoo pierced the air with a subdued, far-off shrillness.

From his position Mr. Dyceworthy could catch a glimpse through the trees of the principal thoroughfare of Bosekop—a small, primitive street enough, of little low houses, which, though unpretending from without, were roomy and comfortable within. The distant, cool sparkle of the waters of the Fjord, the refreshing breeze, the perfume of the flowers, and the satisfied impression left on his mind by recent tea and toast—all these things combined had a soothing effect on Mr. Dyceworthy, and with a sigh of absolute comfort he settled his large person in a deep easy chair and composed himself for pious meditation.

He meditated long,—with fast-closed eyes and open mouth, while the earnestness of his inward thoughts was clearly demonstrated now and then by an irrepressible,—almost triumphant,—cornet-blast from that trifling elevation of his countenance called by courtesy a nose, when his blissful reverie was suddenly broken in upon by the sound of several footsteps crunching slowly along the garden path, and, starting up from his chair, he perceived four individuals clad in white flannel costumes and wearing light straw hats trimmed with fluttering blue ribbons, who were leisurely sauntering up to his door, and stopping occasionally to admire the flowers on their way. Mr. Dyceworthy's face reddened visibly with excitement.

" The gentlemen from the yacht," he murmured to himself, hastily settling his collar and cravat, and pushing up his cherubic wings of hair more prominently behind his ears. " I never thought they would come. Dear me ! Sir Philip Errington himself, too ! I must have refreshments instantly."

And he hurried from the room, calling his orders to Ulrika as he went, and before the visitors had time to ring, he had thrown open the door to them himself, and stood smiling urbanely on the threshold, welcoming them with enthusiasm,—and assuring Sir Philip especially how much honored he felt, by his thus visiting, familiarly and unannounced, his humble dwelling. Errington waved his many compliments good-humoredly aside, and allowed himself and his friends to be marshalled into the best parlor, the drawing-room of the house, a pretty little apartment whose window looked out upon a tangled yet graceful wilderness of flowers.

" Nice, cosy place this," remarked Lorimer, as he seated himself negligently on the arm of the sofa. " You must be pretty comfortable here ? "

Their perspiring and affable host rubbed his soft white hands together gently.

" I thank Heaven it suits my simple needs," he answered meekly. " Luxuries do not become a poor servant of God."

" Ah, then your are different to many others who profess to serve the same Master," said Duprèz with a *sourire fin* that had the devil's own mockery in it. " *Monsieur le bon Dieu* is very impartial ! Some serve Him by constant over-feeding, others by constant over-starving ; it is all one to Him apparently ! How do you know which among His servants He likes best, the fat or the lean ? "

Sandy Macfarlane, though slightly a bigot for his own form of doctrine, broke into a low chuckle of irrepressible laughter at Duprèz's levity, but Mr. Dyceworthy's flabby face betokened the utmost horror.

" Sir," he said gravely, " there are subjects concerning which it is not seemly to speak without due reverence. He knoweth His own elect. He hath chosen them out from the beginning He summoned forth from the million, the glorious apostle of reform, Martin Luther——"

" *Le bon gaillard !* " laughed Duprèz. " Tempted by a pretty nun ! What man could resist ! Myself, I would try to upset all the creeds of this world if I saw a pretty nun worth my trouble. Yes, truly ! A pity though, that

the poor Luther died of over-eating; his exit from life was
so undignified ! "

" Shut up, Duprèz," said Errington severely. " You displease Mr. Dyceworthy by your fooling."

" Oh, pray do not mention it, Sir Philip," murmured the
reverend gentleman with a mild patience. " We must ac-
custom ourselves to hear with forbearance the opinions o
all men, howsoever contradictory, otherwise our vocation
of no avail. Yet is it sorely grievous to me to consid.
that there should be any person or persons existent wh
lack the necessary faith requisite for the performance of
God's promises."

" Ye must understand, Mr. Dyceworthy," said Macfarlane in his slow, deliberate manner, " that ye have before ye
a young Frenchman who doesna believe in onything except
himsel'—and even as to whether he himsel' is a mon or a
myth, he has his doots—vera grave doots."

Duprèz nodded delightedly. " That is so ! " he exclaimed.
" Our dear Sandy puts it so charmingly ! To be a myth
seems original,—to be a mere man, quite ordinary. I believe it is possible to find some good scientific professor
who would prove me to be a myth—the moving shadow of
a dream—imagine !—how perfectly poetical ! "

" You talk too much to be a dream, my boy," laughed
Errington, and turning to Mr. Dyceworthy, he added, " I'm
afraid you must think us a shocking set. We are really
none of us very religious, I fear, though," and he tried to
look serious; " if it had not been for Mr. Lorimer, we
should have come to church last Sunday. Mr. Lorimer
was, unfortunately, rather indisposed."

" Ya-as ! " drawled that gentleman, turning from the little window where he had been gathering a rose for his button-hole. " I was knocked up; had fits, and all that sort of
thing; took these three fellows all their time on Sunday to
hold me down ! "

" Dear me ! " and Mr. Dyceworthy was about to make
further inquiries concerning Mr. Lorimer's present state of
health, when the door opened, and Ulrika entered, bearing
a large tray laden with wine and other refreshments. As
she set it down, she gave a keen, covert glance round the
room, as though rapidly taking note of the appearance and
faces of all the young men, then, with a sort of stiff curt-
sey, she departed as noiselessly as she had come,—not,

however, without leaving a disagreeable impression on Errington's mind.

"Rather a stern Phyllis, that waiting-maid of yours," he remarked, watching his host, who was carefully drawing the cork from one of the bottles of wine.

Mr. Dyceworthy smiled. "Oh, no, no! not stern at all," he answered sweetly. "On the contrary, most affable and kind-hearted. Her only fault is that she is a little zealous, —over-zealous for the purity of the faith; and she has suffered much; but she is an excellent woman, really excellent! Sir Philip, will you try this Lacrima Christi?"

"Lacrima Christi!" exclaimed Duprèz. "You do not surely get that in Norway?"

"It seems strange, certainly," replied Mr. Dyceworthy, "but it is a fact that the Italian or Papist wines are often used here. The minister whose place I humbly endeavor to fill has his cellar stocked with them. The matter is easy of comprehension when once explained. The benighted inhabitants of Italy, a land lost in the darkness of error, still persist in their fasts, notwithstanding the evident folly of their ways—and the Norwegian sailors provide them with large quantities of fish for their idolatrous customs, bringing back their wines in exchange."

"A very good idea," said Lorimer, sipping the Lacrima with evident approval—"Phil, I doubt if your brands on board the *Eulalie* are better than this."

"Hardly so good," replied Errington with some surprise, as he tasted the wine and noted its delicious flavor. "The minister must be a fine *connoisseur*. Are there many other families about here, Mr. Dyceworthy, who know how to choose their wines so well?"

Mr. Dyceworthy smiled with a dubious air.

"There is one other household that in the matter of choice liquids is almost profanely particular," he said. "But they are people who are ejected with good reason from respectable society, and,—it behooves me not to speak of their names."

"Oh, indeed!" said Errington, while a sudden and inexplicable thrill of indignation fired his blood and sent it in a wave of color up to his forehead—"May I ask——"

But he was interrupted by Lorimer, who, nudging him slyly on one side, muttered, "Keep cool, old fellow! *You* can't tell whether he's talking about the Güldmar folk!

Be quiet—you don't want every one to know your little game."

Thus adjured, Philip swallowed a large gulp of wine, to keep down his feelings, and strove to appear interested in the habits and caprices of bees, a subject into which Mr. Dyceworthy had just inveigled Duprèz and Macfarlane.

"Come and see my bees," said the Reverend Charles almost pathetically. "They are emblems of ever-working and patient industry,—storing up honey for others to partake thereof."

"They wudna store it up at a', perhaps, if they knew that," observed Sandy significantly.

Mr. Dyceworthy positively shone all over with beneficence.

"They *would* store it up, sir; yes, they would, even if they knew! It is God's will that they should store it up; it is God's will that they should show an example of unselfishness, that they should flit from flower to flower sucking therefrom the sweetness to impart into strange palates unlike their own. It is a beautiful lesson; it teaches us who are the ministers of the Lord to likewise suck the sweetness from the flowers of the living gospel, and impart it gladly to the unbelievers who shall find it sweeter than the sweetest honey!"

And he shook his head piously several times, while the pores of his fat visage exuded holy oil. Duprèz sniggered secretly. Macfarlane looked preternaturally solemn.

"Come," repeated the reverend gentleman, with an inviting smile. "Come and see my bees,—also my strawberries! I shall be delighted to send a basket of the fruit to the yacht, if Sir Philip will permit me?"

Errington expressed his thanks with due courtesy, and hastened to seize the opportunity that presented itself for breaking away from the party.

"If you will excuse us for twenty minutes or so, Mr. Dyceworthy," he said, "Lorimer and I want to consult a fellow here in Bosekop about some new fishing tackle. We shan't be gone long. Mac, you and Duprèz wait for us here. Don't commit too many depredations on Mr. Dyceworthy's strawberries."

The reason for their departure was so simply and naturally given, that it was accepted without any opposing remarks. Duprèz was delighted to have the chance of amusing himself by harassing the Reverend Charles with

open professions of utter atheism, and Macfarlane, who
loved an argument more than he loved whiskey, looked forward to a sharp discussion presently concerning the superiority of John Knox, morally and physically, over Martin
Luther. So that when the others went their way, their departure excited no suspicion in the minds of their friends,
and most unsuspecting of all was the placid Mr. Dyceworthy, who, had he imagined for an instant the direction
which they were going, would certainly not have dis-
coursed on the pleasures of bee-keeping with the calmness
and placid conviction, that always distinguished him when
holding forth on any subject that was attractive to his
mind. Leading the way through his dewy, rosegrown garden, and conversing amicably as he went, he escorted Macfarlane and Duprèz to what he called with a gentle humor
his "Bee-Metropolis," while Errington and Lorimer returned to the shore of the Fjord, where they had left their
boat moored to a small, clumsily constructed pier,—and
entering it, they set themselves to the oars and pulled
away together with the long, steady, sweeping stroke rendered famous by the exploits of the Oxford and Cambridge
men. After some twenty minutes' rowing, Lorimer looked
up and spoke as he drew his blade swiftly through the
bright green water.

"I feel as though I were aiding and abetting you in
some crime, Phil. You know, my first impression of this
business remains the same. You had much better leave it
alone."

"Why?" asked Errington coolly.

"Well, 'pon my life I don't know why. Except that,
from long experience, I have proved that it's always dangerous and troublesome to run after a woman. Leave her
to run after you—she'll do it fast enough."

"Wait till you see her. Besides, I'm not running after
any woman," averred Philip with some heat.

"Oh, I beg your pardon—I forgot. She's not a woman;
she's a Sun-angel. You are rowing, not running, after a
Sun-angel. Is that correct? I say, don't drive through
the water like that; you'll pull the boat round."

Errington slackened his speed and laughed. "It's only
curiosity," he said, lifting his hat, and pushing back the
clustering dark-brown curls from his brow. "I bet you
that sleek Dyceworthy fellow meant the old *bonde* and
his daughter, when he spoke of persons who were 'ejected'

from the social circles of Bosekop. Fancy Bosekop society presuming to be particular—what an absurd idea!"

"My good fellow, don't pretend to be so deplorably ignorant! Surely you know that a trumpery village or a twopenny town is much more choice and exclusive in its 'sets' than a great city? I wouldn't live in a small place for the world. Every inhabitant would know the cut of my clothes by heart, and the number of buttons on my waistcoat. The grocer would copy the pattern of my trousers,—the butcher would carry a cane like mine It would be simply insufferable. To change the subject, may I ask you if you know which way you are going, for it seems to me we're bound straight for a smash on that uncomfortable-looking rock, where there is certainly no landing-place."

Errington stopped pulling, and, standing up in the boat, began to examine the surroundings with keen interest. They were close to the great crag "shaped like a giant's helmet," as Valdemar Svenson had said. It rose sheer out of the water, and its sides were almost perpendicular. Some beautiful star-shaped sea anemones clung to it in a varicolored cluster on one projection, and the running ripple of the small waves broke on its jagged corners with a musical splash, and sparkle of white foam. Below them, in the emerald mirror of the Fjord, it was so clear that they could see the fine white sand lying at the bottom, sprinkled thick with shells and lithe moving creatures of all shapes, while every now and then, there streamed past them, brilliantly tinted specimens of the Medusæ, with their long feelers or tendrils, looking like torn skins of crimson and azure floss silk.

The place was very silent; only the sea-gulls circled round and round the summit of the great rock, some of them occasionally swooping down on the unwary fishes, their keen eyes perceived in the waters beneath, then up again they soared, swaying their graceful wings and uttering at intervals that peculiar wild cry that in solitary haunts sounds so intensely mournful. Errington gazed about him in doubt for some minutes, then suddenly his face brightened. He sat down again in the boat and resumed his oar.

"Row quietly, George," he said in a subdued tone. "Quietly—round to the left."

The oars dipped noiselessly, and the boat shot forward,— then swerved sharply round in the direction indicated,—

and there before them lay a small sandy creek, white and
shining as though sprinkled with powdered silver. From
this, a small but strongly-built wooden pier ran out into the
sea. It was carved all over with fantastic figures, and in it,
at equal distances, were fastened iron rings, such as are
used for the safe mooring of boats. One boat was there already, and Errington recognized it with delight. It was
that in which he had seen the mysterious maiden disappear.
High and dry on the sand, out of reach of the tides, was a
neat sailing-vessel; its name was painted round the stern
— *The Valkyrie.*

As the two friends ran their boat on shore, and fastened
it to the furthest ring of the convenient pier, they caught
the distant sound of the plaintiff " coo-cooing " of turtle
doves.

" You've done it this time, old boy," said Lorimer, speaking in a whisper, though he knew not why. " This is the
old *bonde's* own private landing-place evidently, and here's a
footpath leading somewhere. Shall we follow it ? "

Philip emphatically assented, and, treading softly, like
the trespassers they felt themselves to be, they climbed the
ascending narrow way that guided them up from the sea-
shore, round through a close thicket of pines, where their
footsteps fell noiselessly on a thick carpet of velvety green
moss, dotted prettily here and there with the red gleam of
ripening wild strawberries. Everything was intensely still,
and as yet there seemed no sign of human habitation. Suddenly a low whirring sound broke upon their ears, and Errington, who was a little in advance of his companion,
paused abruptly with a smothered exclamation, and drew
back on tip-toe, catching Lorimer by the arm.

" By Jove ! " he whispered excitedly, " we've come right
up to the very windows of the house. Look ! "

Lorimer obeyed, and for once, the light jest died upon his
lips. Surprise and admiration held him absolutely silent.

CHAPTER V.

"Elle filait et souriait—et je crois qu'elle enveloppa mon cœur
avec son fil."—HEINE.

BEFORE them, close enough for their outstretched hands
to have touched it, was what appeared to be a framed picture, exquisitely painted,—a picture perfect in outline,

matchless in color, faultless in detail,—but which was in reality nothing but a large latticed window thrown wide open to admit the air. They could now see distinctly through the shadows cast by the stately pines, a long, low, rambling house, built roughly, but strongly, of wooden rafters, all overgrown with green and blossoming creepers; but they scarcely glanced at the actual building, so strongly was their attention riveted on the one window before them. It was surrounded by an unusually broad framework, curiously and elaborately carved, and black as polished ebony. Flowers grew all about it,—sweet peas, mignonette, and large purple pansies—while red and white climbing roses rioted in untrained profusion over its wide sill. Above it was a quaintly built dovecote, where some of the strutting fan-tailed inhabitants were perched, swelling out their snowy breasts, and discoursing of their domestic trials in notes of dulcet melancholy; while lower down, three or four ring-doves nestled on the roof in a patch of sunlight, spreading up their pinions like miniature sails, to catch the warmth and lustre.

Within the deep, shadowy embrasure, like a jewel placed on dark velvet, was seated a girl spinning,—no other than the mysterious maiden of the shell cavern. She was attired in a plain, straight gown, of some soft white woolen stuff, cut squarely at her throat; her round, graceful arms were partially bare, and as the wheel turned swiftly, and her slender hands busied themselves with the flax, she smiled, as though some pleasing thought had touched her mind. Her smile had the effect of sudden sunshine in the dark room where she sat and span,—it was radiant and mirthful as the smile of a happy child. Yet her dark blue eyes remained pensive and earnest, and the smile soon faded, leaving her fair face absorbed and almost dreamy. The whirr-whirring of the wheel grew less and less rapid,—it slackened,—it stopped altogether,—and, as though startled by some unexpected sound, the girl paused and listened, pushing away the clustering masses of her rich hair from her brow. Then rising slowly from her seat, she advanced to the window, put aside the roses with one hand, and looked out,—thus forming another picture as beautiful, if not more beautiful, than the first.

Lorimer drew his breath hard. " I say, old fellow," he whispered; but Errington pressed his arm with vice-like firmness, as a warning to him to be silent, while they both stepped further back into the dusky gloom of the pine boughs.

The girl, meanwhile, stood motionless, in a half-expectant attitude, and, seeing her there, some of the doves on the roof flew down and strutted on the ground before her, coo-cooing proudly, as though desirous of attracting her attention. One of them boldly perched on the window-sill; she glanced at the bird musingly, and softly stroked its opaline wings and shining head without terrifying it. It seemed delighted to be noticed, and almost lay down under her hand in order to be more conveniently caressed. Still gently smoothing its feathers, she leaned further out among the clambering wealth of blossoms, and called in a low, penetrating tone, " Father! father! is that you? "

There was no answer; and, after waited a minute or two, she moved and resumed her former seat, the stray doves flew back to their customary promenade on the roof, and the drowsy whirr-whirr of the spinning-wheel murmured again its monotonous hum upon the air.

" Come on, Phil," whispered Lorimer, determined not to be checked this time; " I feel perfectly wretched! It's mean of us to be skulking about here, as if we were a couple of low thieves waiting to trap some of those birds for a pigeon-pie. Come away,—you've seen her; that's enough."

Errington did not move. Holding back a branch of pine, he watched the movements of the girl at her wheel with absorbed fascination.

Suddenly her sweet lips parted, and she sang a weird, wild melody, that seemed, like a running torrent, to have fallen from the crests of the mountains, bringing with it echoes from the furthest summits, mingled with soft wailings of a mournful wind.

He voice was pure as the ring of fine crystal—deep, liquid, and tender, with a restrained passion in it that stirred Errington's heart and filled it with a strange unrest and feverish yearning,—emotions which were new to him, and which, while he realized their existence, moved him to a sort of ashamed impatience. He would have willingly left his post of observation now, if only for the sake of shaking off his unwonted sensations; and he took a step or two backwards for that purpose, when Lorimer, in his turn, laid a detaining hand on his shoulder.

" For Heaven's sake, let us hear the song through! " he

said in subdued tones. "What a voice! A positive golden flute!"

His rapt face betokened his enjoyment, and Errington, nothing loth, still lingered, his eyes fixed on the white-robed slim figure framed in the dark old rose-wreathed window—the figure that swayed softly with the motion of the wheel and the rhythm of the song,—while flickering sunbeams sparkled now and then on the maiden's dusky gold hair, or touched up a warmer tint on her tenderly flushed cheeks, and fair neck, more snowy than the gown she wore. Music poured from her lips as from the throat of a nightingale. The words she sang were Norwegian, and her listeners understood nothing of them; but the melody,—the pathetic appealing melody,—soul-moving as all true melody must be, touched the very core of their hearts, and entangled them in a web of delicious reveries.

"Talk of Ary Scheffer's Gretchen!" murmured Lorimer with a sigh. "What a miserable, pasty, milk-and-watery young person she is beside that magnificent, unconscious beauty! I give in, Phil! I admit your taste. I'm willing to swear that she's a Sun-Angel if you like. Her voice has convinced me of that."

At that instant the song ceased. Errington turned and regarded him steadfastly.

"Are *you* hit, George?" he said softly, with a forced smile.

Lorimer's face flushed, but he met his friend's eyes frankly.

"I am no poacher, old fellow," he answered in the same quiet accents; "I think you know that. If that girl's mind is as lovely as her face, I say, go in and win!"

Sir Philip smiled. His brow cleared and an expression of relief settled there. The look of gladness was unconscious; but Lorimer saw it at once and noted it.

"Nonsense!" he said in a mirthful undertone. "How can I go in and win, as you say? What am I to do? I can't go up to that window and speak to her,—she might take me for a thief."

"You look like a thief," replied Lorimer, surveying his friend's athletic figure, clad in its loose but well-cut yachting suit of white flannel, ornamented with silver anchor buttons, and taking a comprehensive glance from the easy pose of the fine head and handsome face, down to the trim foot with the high and well-arched instep. "very much like a thief? I wonder I haven't noticed it before. Any London policeman would arrest you on the mere fact of your suspicious appearance."

Errington laughed. "Well, my boy, whatever my looks may testify, I am at this moment an undoubted trespasser on private property,—and so are you for that matter. What shall we do?"

"Find the front door and ring the bell," suggested George promptly. "Say we are benighted travellers and have lost our way. The *bonde* can but flay us. The operation, I believe, is painful, but it cannot last long."

"George, you are incorrigible! Suppose we go back and try the other side of this pine-wood? That might lead us to the front of the house."

"I don't see why we shouldn't walk coolly past that window," said Lorimer. "If any observation is made by the fair 'Marguerite' yonder, we can boldly say we have come to see the *bonde*."

Unconsciously they had both raised their voices a little during the latter part of their hasty dialogue, and at the instant when Lorimer uttered the last words, a heavy hand was laid on each of their shoulders,—a hand that turned them round forcibly away from the window they had been gazing at, and a deep, resonant voice addressed them.

"The *bonde*? Truly, young men, you need seek no further,—I am Olaf Güldmar!"

Had he said, "I am an Emperor!" he could not have spoken with more pride.

Errington and his friend were for a moment speechless,— partly from displeasure at the summary manner in which they had been seized and twisted round like young uprooted saplings, and partly from surprise and involuntary admiration for the personage who had treated them with such scant courtesy. They saw before them a man somewhat above the middle height, who might have served an aspiring sculptor as a perfect model for a chieftain of old Gaul, or a dauntless Viking. His frame was firmly and powerfully built, and seemed to be exceptionally strong and muscular; yet an air of almost courtly grace pervaded his movements, making each attitude he assumed more or less picturesque. He was broad-shouldered and deep-chested; his face was full and healthily colored, while his head was truly magnificent. Well-poised and shapely, it indicated power, will, and wisdom ; and was furthermore adorned by a rough, thick mass of snow-white hair that shone in the sunlight like spun silver. His beard was short and curly, trimmed after the fashion of the warriors of old Rome ; and, from under his fierce, fuzzy, grey eyebrows, a pair of senti- nel eyes, that were keen, clear, and bold as an eagle's, looked out with a watchful steadiness—steadiness that like the sharp edge of a diamond, seemed warranted to cut through the brittle glass of a lie. Judging by his outward appearance, his age might have been guessed at as between fifty-eight and sixty, but he was, in truth, seventy-two, and more strong, active, and daring than many another man whose years are not counted past the thirties. He was curiously attired, after something of the fashion of the Highlander, and something yet more of the ancient Greek, in a tunic, vest, and loose jacket all made of reindeer skin, thickly embroidered with curious designs worked in coarse thread and colored beads ; while thrown carelessly over his shoul- ders and knotted at his waist, was a broad scarf of white woollen stuff, or *wadmel*, very soft-looking and warm. In his belt he carried a formidable hunting-knife, and as he faced the two intruders on his ground, he rested one hand lightly yet suggestively on a weighty staff of pine, which was notched all over with quaint letters and figures, and terminated in a curved handle at the top. He waited for the young man to speak, and finding they remained sil- ent, he glanced at them half angrily and again repeated his words—

"I am the *bonde*,—Olaf Güldmar. Speak your business and take your departure ; my time is brief!"

Lorimer looked up with his usual nonchalance,—a faint smile playing about his lips. He saw at once that the old farmer was not a man to be trifled with, and he raised his cap with a ready grace as he spoke.

"Fact is," he said frankly, " we've no business here at all—not the least in the world. We are perfectly aware of it! We are tresspassers, and we know it. Pray don't be hard on us, Mr.—Mr. Güldmar!"

The *bonde* glanced him over with a quick lightening of the eyes, and the suspicion of a smile in the depths of his curly beard. He turned to Errington.

"Is this true? You came here on purpose, knowing the ground was private property ? "

Errington, in his turn, lifted his cap from his clustering

brown curls with that serene and stately court manner which was to him second nature.

"We did," he confessed, quietly following Lorimer's cue, and seeing also that it was best to be straightforward. "We heard you spoken of in Bosekop, and we came to see if you would permit us the honor of your acquaintance."

The old man struck his pine-staff violently into the ground, and his face flushed wrathfully.

"Bosekop!" he exclaimed. "Talk to me of a wasp's nest! Bosekop! You shall hear of me there enough to satisfy your appetite for news. Bosekop! In the days when my race ruled the land, such people as they that dwell there would have been put to sharpen my sword on the grindstone, or to wait, hungry and humble, for the refuse of the food left from my table!"

He spoke with extraordinary heat and passion,—it was evidently necessary to soothe him. Lorimer took a covert glance backward over his shoulder towards the lattice window, and saw that the white figure at the spinning-wheel had disappeared.

"My dear Mr. Güldmar," he then said with polite fervor, "I assure you I think the Bosekop folk by no means deserve to sharpen your sword on the grindstone, or to enjoy the remains of your dinner! Myself, I despise them! My friend here, Sir Philip Errington, despises them—don't you, Phil?"

Errington nodded demurely.

"What my friend said just now is perfectly true," continued Lorimer. "We desire the honor of your acquaintance,—it will charm and delight us above all things!"

And his face beamed with a candid, winning, boyish smile, which was very captivating in its own way, and which certainly had its effect on the old *bonde*, for his tone softened, though he said gravely—

"My acquaintance, young men, is never sought by any. Those who are wise, keep away from me. I love not strangers, it is best you should know it. I freely pardon your trespass; take your leave, and go in peace."

The two friends exchanged disconsolate looks. There really seemed nothing for it, but to obey this unpleasing command. Errington made one more venture.

"May I hope, Mr. Güldmar," he said with persuasive courtesy, "that you will break through your apparent rule of seclusion for once and visit me on board my yacht? You have no doubt seen her—the *Eulalie*—she lies at anchor in the Fjord."

The *bonde* looked him straight in the eyes. "I have seen her. A fair toy vessel to amuse an idle young man's leisure! You are he that in that fool's hole of a Bosekop, is known as the 'rich Englishman,'—an idle trifler with time,—an aimless wanderer from those dull shores where they eat gold till they die of surfeit! I have heard of you, —a mushroom knight, a fungus of nobility,—an ephemeral growth on a grand decaying old tree, whose roots lie buried in the annals of a far forgotten past."

The rich, deep voice of the old man quivered as he spoke, and a shadow of melancholy flitted across his brow. Errington listened with unruffled patience. He heard himself, his pleasures, his wealth, thus made light of, without the least offense. He met the steady gaze of the *bonde* quietly, and slightly bent his head as though in deference to his remarks.

"You are quite right," he said simply. "We modern men are but pigmies compared with the giants of old time. Royal blood itself is tainted nowadays. But, for myself, I attach no importance to the mere appurtenances of life,— the baggage that accompanies one on that brief journey. Life itself is quite enough for me."

"And for me too," averred Lorimer, delighted that his friend had taken the old farmer's scornful observations so good-naturedly. "But, do you know, Mr. Güldmar, you are making life unpleasant for us just now, by turning us out? The conversation is becoming interesting! Why not prolong it? We have no friends in Bosekop, and we are to anchor here for some days. Surely you will allow us to come and see you again?"

Olaf Güldmar was silent. He advanced a step nearer, and studied them both with such earnest and searching scrutiny, that as they remembered the real attraction that had drawn them thither, the conscious blood mounted to their faces, flushing Errington's forehead to the very roots of his curly brown hair. Still the old man gazed as though he sought to read their very souls. He muttered something to himself in Norwegian, and, finally, to their utter astonishment, he drew his hunting-knife from its sheath, and with a rapid, wild gesture, threw it on the ground and placed his foot upon it.

"Be it so!" he said briefly. "I cover the blade! You

are men ; like men you speak truth. As such, I receive
you ! Had you told me a lie concerning your coming here,
—had you made pretense of having lost your way, or other
such shifty evasion, your path would never have again
crossed mine. As it is,—welcome ! "

And he held out his hand with a sort of royal dignity,
still resting one foot on the fallen weapon. The young
men, struck by his action and gratified by his change of
manner and the genial expression that now softened his
rugged features, were quick to respond to his friendly
greeting, and the *bonde*, picking up and re-sheathing his
hunting-knife as if he had done nothing at all out of the
common, motioned them towards the very window on which
their eyes had been so long and so ardently fixed.

"Come ! " he said. " You must drain a cup of wine with
me before you leave. Your unguided footsteps led you by
the wrong path,—I saw your boat moored to my pier, and
wondered who had been venturesome enough to trample
through my woodland. I might have guessed that only a
couple of idle boys like yourselves, knowing no better,
would have pushed their way to a spot that all worthy
dwellers in Bosekop, and all true followers of the Lutheran
devilry, avoid as though the plague were settled in it."

And the old man laughed, a splendid, mellow laugh, with
the ring of true jollity in it,—a laugh that was infectious,
for Errington and Lorimer joined in it heartily without
precisely knowing why. Lorimer, however, thought it
seemly to protest against the appellation " idle boys."

" What do you take us for, sir ? " he said with lazy good-
nature. " I carry upon my shoulders the sorrowful burden
of twenty-six years,—Philip, there, is painfully conscious
of being thirty,—may we not therefore dispute the word
' boys ' as being derogatory to our dignity ? You called us
' men ' a while ago,—remember that ! "

Olaf Güldmar laughed again. His suspicious gravity
had entirely disappeared, leaving his face a beaming mirror
of beneficence and good-humor.

" So you *are* men," he said cheerily, " men in the bud,
like leaves on a tree. But you seem boys to a tough old
stump of humanity such as I am. That is my way,—my
child Thelma, though they tell me she is a woman grown,
is always a babe to me. 'Tis one of the many privileges of
the old, to see the world about them always young and full
of children."

And he led the way past the wide-open lattice, where they could dimly perceive the spinning-wheel standing alone, as though thinking deeply of the fair hands that had lately left it idle, and so round to the actual front of the house, which was exceedingly picturesque, and literally overgrown with roses from ground to roof. The entrance door stood open ;—it was surrounded by a wide, deep porch richly carved and grotesquely ornamented, having two comfortable seats within it, one on each side. Through this they went, involuntarily brushing down as they passed, a shower of pink and white rose-leaves, and stepped into a wide passage, where upon walls of dark, polished pine, hung a large collection of curiously shaped weapons, all of primitive manufacture, such as stone darts and rough axes, together with bows and arrows and two-handled swords, huge as the fabled weapon of William Wallace.

Opening a door to the right the *bonde* stood courteously aside and bade them enter, and they found themselves in the very apartment where they had seen the maiden spinning.

"Sit down, sit down!" said their host hospitably. "We will have wine directly, and Thelma shall come hither. Thelma! Thelma! Where is the child? She wanders hither and thither like a mountain sprite. Wait here, my lads, I shall return directly."

And he strode away, leaving Errington and Lorimer delighted at the success of their plans, yet somewhat abashed too. There was a peace and gentle simplicity about the little room in which they were, that touched the chivalrous sentiment in their natures and kept them silent. On one side of it, half a dozen broad shelves supported a goodly row of well-bound volumes, among which the time-honored golden names of Shakespeare and Scott glittered invitingly, together with such works as Chapman's Homer, Byron's "Childe Harold," the Poems of John Keats, Gibbon's Rome, and Plutarch; while mingled with these were the devotional works in French of Alphonse de Liguori, the "Imitation," also in French,—and a number of books with titles in Norwegian,—altogether an heterogenous collection of literature, yet not without interest as displaying taste and culture on the part of those to whom it belonged. Errington, himself learned in books, was surprised to see so many standard works in the library of one who professed to be nothing but a Norwegian farmer, and his respect for

the sturdy old *bonde* increased. There were no pictures in
the room,—the wide lattice window on one hand, looking
out on the roses and pine-wood, and the other smaller one,
close to the entrance door, from which the Fjord was distinctly visible, were sufficient pictures in themselves, to
need no others. The furniture was roughly made of pine,
and seemed to have been carved by hand,—some of the
chairs were very quaint and pretty and would have sold in
a bric-a-brac shop for more than a sovereign apiece. On
the wide mantle-shelf was a quantity of curious old china
that seemed to have been picked up from all parts of the
world,—most of it was undoubtedly valuable. In one dark
corner stood an ancient harp ; then there was the spinning-
wheel,—itself a curiosity fit for a museum,—testifying
dumbly of the mistress of all these surroundings, and on
the floor there was something else,—something that both
the young men were strongly inclined to take posession of.
It was only a bunch of tiny meadow daisies, fastened together with a bit of blue silk. It had fallen,—they guessed
by whom it had been worn,—but neither made any remark,
and both, by some strange instinct, avoided looking at it,
as though the innocent little blossoms carried within them
some terrible temptation. They were conscious of a certain embarrassment, and making an effort to break through
it, Lorimer remarked softly—

"By Jove, Phil, if this old Güldmar really knew what
you are up to, I believe he would bundle you out of this
place like a tramp ! Didn't you feel a sneak when he said
we had told the truth like men ? "

Philip smiled dreamily. He was seated in one of the
quaintly carved chairs, half absorbed in what was evidently
a pleasing reverie.

"No; not exactly," he replied. "Because we *did* tell
him the truth ; we did want to know him, and he's worth
knowing too ! He is a magnificent-looking fellow ; don't you
think so ? "

"Rather ! " assented Lorimer, with emphasis. "I wish
there were any hope of my becoming such a fine old buffer
in my *decadence,*—it would be worth living for if only to
look at myself in the glass now and then. He rather startled me when he threw down that knife, though. I suppose
it is some old Norwegian custom ? "

"I suppose so," Errington answered, and then was silent,
for at that moment the door opened and the old farmer re-

turned, followed by a girl bearing a tray glittering with flasks of Italian wine, and long graceful glasses shaped like round goblets, set on particularly slender stems. The sight of the girl disappointed the eager visitors, for though she was undeniably pretty, she was not Thelma. She was short and plump, with rebellious nut-brown locks, that rippled about her face and from under her close white cap with persistent untidiness. Her heeks were as round and red as love-apples, and she had dancing blue eyes that appeared for ever engaged in good-natured efforts to outsparkle each other. She wore a spotless apron, lavishly trimmed with coquettish little starched frills,—her hands were, unfortunately, rather large and coarse,—but her smile, as she set down the tray and curtsied respectfully to the young men, was charming, disclosing as it did, tiny teeth as even and white as a double row of small pearls.

"That is well, Britta," said Güldmar, speaking in English, and assisting her to place the glasses. "Now, quick! . . . run after thy mistress to the shore,—her boat cannot yet have left the creek,—bid her return and come to me, —tell her there are friends here who will be glad of her presence."

Britta hurried away at once, but Errington's heart sank. Thelma had gone!—gone, most probably, for one of those erratic journeys across the Fjord to the cave where he had first seen her. She would not come back, he felt certain; not even at her father's request would that beautiful, proud maiden consent to alter her plans. What an unlucky destiny was his! Absorbed in disappointed reflections, he scarcely heard the enthusiastic praises Lorimer was diplomatically bestowing on the *bonde's* wine. He hardly felt its mellow flavor on his own palate, though it was in truth delicious, and fit for the table of a monarch. Güldmar noticed the young baronet's abstraction, and addressed him with genial kindness.

"Are you thinking, Sir Philip, of my rough speeches to you yonder? No offense was meant, no offense! . . ." the old fellow paused, and laughed over his wine-glass. 'Yet I may as well be honest about it! Offense *was* meant; but when I found that none was taken, my humor changed."

A slight, half-weary smile played on Errington's lips. "I assure you, sir," he said, "I agreed with you then and agree with you now in every word you uttered. You took my measure very correctly, and allow me to add that no one can be more conscious of my own insignificance that I am myself. The days we live in are insignificant; the chronicle of our paltry doings will be skipped by future readers of the country's history. Among a society of particularly useless men, I feel myself to be one of the most useless. If you could show me any way to make my life valuable——"

He paused abruptly, and his heart beat with inexplicable rapidity. A light step and the rustle of a dress was heard coming through the porch; another perfumed shower of rose-leaves fell softly on the garden path; the door of the room opened, and a tall, fair, white-robed figure shone forth from the dark background of the outer passage; a figure that hesitated on the threshold, and then advanced noiselessly and with a reluctant shyness. The old *bonde* turned round in his chair with a smile.

"Ah, here she is!" he said fondly. "Where hast thou been, my Thelma?"

CHAPTER VI.

"And Sigurd the Bishop said,
 'The old gods are not dead,
 For the great Thor still reigns,
 And among the Jarls and Thanes
 The old witchcraft is spread.'"
                LONGFELLOW'S *Saga of King Olaf.*

THE girl stood silent, and a faint blush crimsoned her cheeks. The young men had risen at her entrance, and in one fleeting glance she recognized Errington, though she gave no sign to that effect.

"See, my darling," continued her father, "here are English visitors to Norway. This is Sir Philip Errington, who travels through our wild waters in the great steam yacht now at anchor in the Fjord; and this is his friend, Mr.— Mr.—Lorimer,—have I caught your name rightly, my lad?" he continued, turning to George Lorimer with a kindly smile.

"You have, sir," answered that gentleman promptly, and then he was mute, feeling curiously abashed in the presence of this royal-looking young lady, who, encircled by her father's arm, raised her deep, dazzling blue eyes, and serenely bent her stately head to him as his name was mentioned.

The old farmer went on, " Welcome them, Thelma mine!
—friends are scarce in these days, and we must not be ungrateful for good company. What! what! I know honest
lads when I see them! Smile on them, my Thelma!—and
then we will warm their hearts with another cup of wine."

As he spoke, the maiden advanced with a graceful, even
noble air, and extending both her hands to each of the visitors in turn, she said—

" I am your servant, friends; in entering this house you
do possess it. Peace and heart's greeting!"

The words were a literal translation of a salutation perfectly common in many parts of Norway—a mere ordinary
expression of politeness; but, uttered in the tender, penetrating tones, of the most musical voice they had ever
heard, and accompanied by the warm, frank, double hand-
clasp of those soft, small, daintily shaped hands, the effect
on the minds of the generally self-possessed, fashionably
bred young men of the world, was to confuse and bewilder
them to the last degree. What could they answer to this
poetical, quaint formula of welcome? The usual lati-
tudes, such as " Delighted, I'm sure;" or, " Most happy—
am charmed to meet you?" No; these remarks, deemed
intelligent by the lady rulers of London drawing-rooms,
would, they felt, never do here. As well put a gentleman
in modern evening dress *en face* with a half-nude scornfully beautiful statue of Apollo, as tro out threadbare, in-
sincere commonplaces in the hearing of this clear-eyed child
of nature, whose pure, perfect face seemed to silently repel
the very passing shadow of a falsehood.

Philip's brain whirled round and about in search of some
suitable reply, but could find none; and Lorimer felt himself blushing like a schoolboy, as he stammered out something incoherent and eminently foolish, though he had sense
enough left to appreciate the pressure of those lovely hands
as long as it lasted.

Thelma, however, appeared not to notice their deep embarrassment—she had not yet done with them. Taking
the largest goblet on the table, she filled it to the brim with
wine, and touched it with her lips,—then with a smile in
which a thousand radiating sunbeams seemed to quiver and
sparkle, she lifted it towards Errington. The grace of her
attitude and action wakened him out of his state of dreamy
bewilderment—in his soul he devoutly blessed these ancient
family customs, and arose to the occasion like a man.

Clasping with a tender reverence the hands that upheld the goblet, he bent his handsome head and drank a deep draught, while his dark curls almost touched her fair ones, —and then an insane jealousy possessed him for a moment, as he watched her go through the same ceremony with Lorimer.

She next carried the now more than half-emptied cup to the *bonde*, and said as she held it, laughing softly—

"Drink it all, father !—if you leave a drop, you know these gentlemen will quarrel with us, or you with them."

"That is true !" said Olaf Güldmar with great gravity ; "but it will not be my fault, child, nor the fault of wasted wine."

And he drained the glass to its dregs and set it upside down on the table with a deep sigh of satisfaction and refreshment. The ceremony concluded, it was evident the ice of reserve was considered broken, for Thelma seated herself like a young queen, and motioned her visitors to do the same with a gesture of gracious condescension.

"How did you find your way here ? " she asked with sweet, yet direct abruptness, giving Sir Philip a q ick glance, in which there was a sparkle of mirth, though her long lashes veiled it almost instantly.

Her entire lack of stiffness and reserve set the young men at their ease, and they fell into conversation freely, though Errington allowed Lorimer to tell the story of their trespass in his own fashion without interference. He instinctively felt that the young lady who listened with so demure a smile to that plausible narrative, knew well enough the real motive that had brought them thither. though she apparently had her own reasons for k eping silence on the point, as whatever she may have thoug t, she said nothing.

Lorimer skillfully avoided betraying the fact that they had watched her through the window, and had listened to her singing. And Thelma heard all the explanations patiently till Bosekop was mentioned, and then her fair face grew cold and stern.

"From whom did you hear of us there ? " she inquired. "We do not mix with the people,—why should they speak of us ? "

"The truth is," interposed Errington, resting his eyes with a sense of deep delight on the beautiful rounded figure and lovely features that were turned towards him; "I heard of you first through my pilot—one Valdemar Svensen."

" Ha, ha ! " cried old Güldmar with some excitement, " there is a fellow who cannot hold his tongue ! What have I said to thee, child ? A bachelor is no better than a gossiping old woman. He that is always alone must talk, if it be only to woods and waves. It is the married men who know best how excellent it is to keep silence ! "

They all laughed, though Thelma's eyes had a way of looking pensive even when she smiled.

" You would not blame poor Svensen because he is alone, father ? " she said. " Is he not to be pitied ? Surely it is a cruel fate to have none to love in all the wide world. Nothing can be more cruel ! "

Güldmar surveyed her humorously. " Hear her ! " he said. " She talks as if she knew all about such things ; and if ever a child was ignorant of sorrow, surely it is my Thelma ! Every flower and bird in the place loves her. Yes ; I have thought sometimes the very sea loves her. It must ; she is so much upon it. And as for her old father " —he laughed a little, though a suspicious moisture softened his keen eyes—" why, he doesn't love her at all. Ask her ! She knows it."

Thelma rose quickly and kissed him. How deliciously those sweet lips pouted, thought Errington, and what an unreasonable and extraordinary grudge he seemed to bear towards the venerable *bonde* for accepting that kiss with so little apparent emotion !

" Hush, father ! " she said. " These friends can see too plainly how much you spoil me. Tell me,"—and she turned with a sudden pretty imperiousness to Lorimer, who started at her voice as a racehorse starts at its rider's touch,— " what person in Bosekop spoke of us ? "

Lorimer was rather at a loss, inasmuch as no one in the small town had actually spoken of them, and Mr. Dyceworthy's remarks concerning those who were " ejected with good reason from respectable society," might not, after all, have applied to the Güldmar family. Indeed, it now seemed an absurd and improbable supposition. Therefore he replied cautiously—

" The Reverend Mr. Dyceworthy, I think, has some knowledge of you. Is he not a friend of yours ? "

These simple words had a most unexpected effect. Olaf Güldmar sprang up from his seat flaming with wrath. It

was in vain that his daughter laid a restraining hand upon
his arm. The name of the Lutheran divine had sufficed to
put him in a towering passion, and he turned furiously
upon the astonished Errington.

" Had I known you came from the devil, sir, you should
have returned to him speedily, with hot words to hasten
your departure ! I would have split that glass to atoms before I would have drained it after you ! The friends of a
false heart are no friends for me,—the followers of a pretended sanctity find no welcome under my roof ! Why not
have told me at once that you came as spies, hounded on by
the liar Dyceworthy ? Why not have confessed it openly ?
. . . . and not have played the thief's trick on an old
fool, who, for once, misled by your manly and upright bearing, consented to lay aside the rightful suspicions he at first
entertained of your purpose ? Shame on you, young men !
shame ! "

The words coursed impetuously from his lips; his face
burned with indignation. He had broken away from his
daughter's hold, while she, pale and very still, stood leaning
one hand upon the table. His white hair was tossed back
from his brow ; his eyes flashed ; his attitude though venge-
ful and threatening, was at the same time so bold and commanding that Lorimer caught himself lazily admiring the
contour of his figure, and wondering how he would look in
marble as an infuriated Viking.

One excellent thing in the dispositions of both Errington
and Lorimer was that they never lost temper. Either they
were too lazy or too well-bred. Undoubtedly they both
considered it " bad form." This indifference stood them in
good stead now. They showed no sign whatever of offense,
though the old farmer's outbreak of wrath was so sudden
and unlooked for, that they remained for a moment silent
out of sheer surprise. Then rising with unruffled serenity,
they took up their caps preparatory to departure. Errington's gentle, refined voice broke the silence.

" You are in error, Mr. Güldmar," he said in chilly but
perfectly polite tones. " I regret you should be so hasty in
your judgment of us. If you accepted us as ' men ' when
you first met us, I cannot imagine why you should now
take us for spies. The two terms are by no means synony-
mous. I know nothing of Mr. Dyceworthy beyond that he
called upon me, and that I, as in duty bound, returned his
call. I am ignorant of his character and disposition. I

may add that I have no desire to be enlightened respecting them. I do not often take a dislike to anybody, but it so happens that I have done so in the case of Mr. Dyceworthy. I know Lorimer doesn't care for him, and I don't think my other two friends are particularly attached to him. I have nothing more to say, except that I fear we have outstayed our welcome. Permit us now to wish you good evening. And you,"—he hesitated, and turned with a low bow to Thelma, who had listened to his words with a gradually dawning brightness on her face—" you will, I trust, exonerate us from any intentional offense towards your father or yourself? Our visit has proved unlucky, but—"

Thelma interrupted him by laying her fair little hand on his arm with a wistful, detaining gesture, which, though seemingly familiar, was yet perfectly sweet and natural. The light touch thrilled his blood, and sent it coursing through his veins at more than customary speed.

" Ah, then, you also will be foolish !" she said, with a naïve protecting air of superior dignity. "Do you not see my father is sorry? Have we all kissed the cup for nothing, or was the wine wasted? Not a drop was spilt; how then, if we are friends should we part in coldness? Father, it is you to be ashamed,—not these gentleman, who are strangers to the Altenfjord, and know nothing of Mr. Dyceworthy, or an other person dwelling here. And when their vessel sails away again over the wide seas to their own shores, how will you have them think of you? As one whose heart was all kindness, and who helped to make their days pass pleasantly? or as one who, in unreasonable anger, forgot the duties of sworn hospitality?"

The *bonde* listened to her full, sweet, reproachful voice as a tough old lion might listen to the voice of its tamer, uncertain whether to yield or spring. He wiped his heated brow and stared around him shamefacedly. Finally, as though swallowing his pride with a gulp, he drew a long breath, took a couple of determined strides forward, and held out his hands, one to Errington and the other to Lorimer, by whom they were warmly grasped.

" There, my lads," he said rapidly. "I'm sorry I spoke ! Forgive and forget ! That is the worst of me—my blood is up in a minute, and old though I am, I'm not old enough yet to be patient. And when I hear the name of that sneak Dyceworthy—by the gates of Valhalla, I feel as if my own house would not hold me ! No, no; don't go yet ! Nearly ten? Well, no matter, the night is like the day here. you see—it doesn't matter when one goes to bed. Come and sit in the porch awhile; I shall get cool out there. Ah, Thelma, child! I see thee laughing at thy old father's temper! Never mind, never mind; is it not for thy sake after all?"

And, holding Errington by the arm, he led the way into the fine old porch, Lorimer following with rather a flushed face, for he, as he passed out of the room, had managed to pick up and secrete the neglected little bunch of daisies, before noticed as having fallen on the floor. He put them quickly in his breast pocket with a curious sense of satisfaction, though he had no intention of keeping them, and leaned idly against the clambering roses, watching Thelma, as she drew a low stool to her father's feet and sat there. A balmy wind blew in from the Fjord, and rustled mysteriously among the pines; the sky was flecked here and there with fleecy clouds, and a number of birds were singing in full chorus. Old Güldmar heaved a sigh of relief, as though his recent outburst of passion had done him good.

"I will tell you, Sir Philip," he said, ruffling his daughter's curls as he spoke,—" I will tell you why I detest the villian Dyceworthy. It is but fair you should know it. Now, Thelma!—why that push to my knee? You fear I may offend our friends again? Nay, I will take good care. And so, first of all, I ask you, what is your religion? Though I know you cannot be Lutherans."

Errington was somewhat taken aback by the question. He smiled.

"My dear sir," he replied at last; " to be frank with you, I really do not think I have any religion. If I had, I suppose I should call myself a Christian, though, judging from the behavior of Christians in general, I cannot be one of them after all,—for I belong to no sect, I go to no church, and I have never read a tract in my life. I have a profound reverence and admiration for the character and doctrine of Christ, and I believe if I had had the privilege of knowing and conversing with Him, I should not have deserted Him in extremity as his timorous disciples did. I believe in an all-wise Creator; so you see I am not an atheist. My mother was an Austrian and a Catholic, and I have a notion that, as a small child, I was brought up in that creed; but I'm afraid I don't know much about it now."

The *bonde* nodded gravely. " Thelma, here," he said, " is a Catholic, as her mother was—" he stopped abruptly, and a deep shadow of pain darkened his features. Thelma looked up,—her large blue eyes filled with sudden tears, and she pressed her father's hand between her own, as though in sympathy with some undeclared grief; then she looked at Errington with a sort of wistful appeal. Philip's heart leaped as he met that soft beseeching glance, which seemed to entreat his patience with the old man for her sake,—he felt himself drawn into a bond of union with her thoughts, and in his innermost soul he swore as knightly a vow of chivalry and reverence for the fair maiden, who thus took him into her silent confidence, as though he were some gallant Crusader of old time, pledged to defend his lady's honor unto death. Olaf Güldmar, after a long and apparently sorrowful pause, resumed his conversation.

"Yes," he said, "Thelma is a Catholic, though here she has scarcely any opportunity for performing the duties of her religion. It is a pretty and a graceful creed,—well fitted for women. As for me, I am made of sterner stuff, and the maxims of that gentle creature, Christ, find no echo in my soul. But you, young sir," he added, turning suddenly on Lorimer, who was engaged in meditatively smoothing out on his palm one of the fallen rose-petals— "you have not spoken. What faith do you profess? It is no curiosity that prompts me to ask,—I only seek not to offend."

Lorimer laughed languidly. "Upon my life, Mr. Güldmar, you really ask too much of me. I haven't any faith at all; not a shred! It's been all knocked out of me. I tried to hold on to a last remaining bit of Christian rope in the universal ship-wreck, but that was torn out of my hands by a scientific professor, who ought to know what he is about, and—and—now I drift along anyhow!"

Güldmar smiled dubiously; but Thelma looked at the speaker with astonished, regretful eyes.

"I am sorry," she said simply. "You must be often unhappy."

Lorimer was not disconcerted, though her evident pity caused an unwonted flush on his face.

"Oh no," he said in answer to her, "I am not a miserable sort of fellow by any means. For instance, I'm not afraid of death,—lots of very religious people are horribly afraid of it, though they all the time declare it's the only path to heaven. They're not consistent at all. You see I believe

5

in nothing,—I came from nothing,—I am nothing,—I shall be nothing. That being plain, I am all right."

Güldmar laughed. " You are an odd lad," he said good-humoredly. " You are in the morning of life; there are always mists in the morning as there are in the evening. In the light of your full manhood you will see these things differently. Your creed of Nothing provides no moral law, —no hold on the conscience, no restraint on the passions,— don't you see that ? "

Lorimer smiled with a very winning and boyish candor. " You are exceedingly good, sir, to credit me with a conscience ! I don't think I have one,—I'm sure I have no passions. I have always been too lazy to encourage them, and as for moral law,—I adhere to morality with the greatest strictness, because if a fellow is immoral, he ceases to be a gentleman. Now, as there are very few gentlemen nowadays, I fancy I'd like to be one as long as I can."

Errington here interposed. " You mustn't take him seriously. Mr. Güldmar," he said; " he's never serious himself, I'll give you his character in a few words. He belongs to no religious party, it's true,—but he's a first-rate fellow,—the best fellow I know ! "

Lorimer glanced at him quietly with a gratified expression on his face. But he said nothing, for Thelma was regarding him with a most bewitching smile.

" Ah ! " she said, shaking a reproachful finger at him, " you do love all nonsense, that I can see ! You would make every person laugh, if you could,—is it not so ? "

" Well, yes," admitted George, " I think I would ! But it's a herculean task sometimes. If you had ever been to London, Miss Güldmar, you would understand how difficult it is to make people even smile,—and when they do, the smile is not a very natural one."

" Why ? " she exclaimed. " Are they all so miserable ? "

" They pretend to be, if they're not," said Lorimer ; " it is the fashion there to find fault with everything and everybody."

"That is so," said Güldmar thoughtfully. " I visited London once and thought I was in hell. Nothing but rows of hard, hideously built houses, long streets, and dirty alleys, and the people had weary faces all, as though Nature had refused to bless them. A pitiful city,—doubly pitiful to the eyes of a man like myself, whose life has been passed among fjords and mountains such as these. Well, now, as neither of you are Lutherans,—in fact, as neither of you seem to know what you are," and he laughed, " I can be frank, and speak out as to my own belief. I am proud to say I have never deserted the faith of my fathers, the faith that makes a man's soul strong and fearless, and defiant of evil,—the faith that is supposed to be crushed out among us, but that is still alive and rooted in the hearts of many who can trace back their lineage to the ancient Vikings as I can,—yes!—rooted firm and fast,—and however much some of the more timorous feign to conceal it, in the tacit acceptance of another creed, there are those who can never shake it off, and who never desire to forsake it. I am one of these few. Shame must fall on the man who willfully deserts the faith of his warrior-ancestry! Sacred to me for ever be the names of Odin and Thor!"

He raised his hand aloft with a proud gesture, and his eyes flashed. Errington was interested, but not surprised : the old *bonde's* declaration of his creed seemed eminently fitted to his character. Lorimer's face brightened,—here was a novelty—a man, who in all the conflicting storms of modern opinion, sturdily clung to the traditions of his forefathers.

" By Jove!" he exclaimed eagerly, " I think the worship of Odin would suit me perfectly! It's a rousing, fighting sort of religion,—I'm positive it would make a man of me. Will you initiate me into the mysteries, Mr. Güldmar? There's a fellow in London who writes poetry on Indian subjects, and who, it is said, thinks Buddhism might satisfy his pious yearnings,—but I think Odin would be a personage to command more respect than Buddha,—at any rate, I should like to try him. Will you give me a chance?"

Olaf Güldmar smiled gravely, and rising from his seat, pointed to the western sky.

" See yonder threads of filmy white," he said, " that stretch across the wide expanse of blue! They are the lingering, fading marks of light clouds,—and even while we watch them, they shall pass and be no more. Such is the emblem of your life, young man—you that would, for an idle jest or pastime, presume to search into the mysteries of Odin! For you they are not,—your spirit is not of the stern mould that waits for death as gladly as the bridegroom waits for the bride! The Christian heaven is an abode for girls and babes.—Valhalla is the place for men! I tell you, my creed is as divine in its origin as any that ever existed on the earth! The Rainbow Bridge is a fairer pathway from death to life than the doleful Cross,—and better far the dark summoning eyes of a beauteous Valkyrie, than the grinning skull and cross-bones, the Christian emblem of mortality. Thelma thinks,—and her mother before her thought also,—that different as my way of belief is to the accepted new creeds of to-day, it will be all right with me in the next world—that I shall have as good a place in heaven as any Christian. It may be so,—I care not! But see you,—the key-note of all the civilization of to-day is discontent, while I,—thanks to the gods of my fathers, am happy, and desire nothing that I have not."

He paused and seemed absorbed. The young men watched his fine inspired features with lively interest. Thelma's head was turned away from them so that her face was hidden. By-and-by he resumed in quieter tones—

"Now, my lads, you know what we are—both of us accursèd in the opinion of the Lutheran community. My child belongs to the so-called idolatrous Church of Rome. I am one of the very last of the ' heathen barbarians,' "—and the old fellow smiled sarcastically, " though, truth to tell, for a barbarian, I am not such a fool as some folks would have you think. If the snuffling Dyceworthy and I competed at a spelling examination, I'm pretty sure 'tis I would have the prize! But, as I said,—you know us,—and if our ways are likely to offend you, then let us part good friends before the swords are fairly drawn."

"No sword will be drawn on my side, I assure you, sir," said Errington, advancing and laying one hand on the *bonde's* shoulder. " I hope you will believe me when I say I shall esteem it an honor and a privilege to know more of you."

"And though you won't accept me as a servant of Odin," added Lorimer, " you really cannot prevent me from trying to make myself agreeable to you. I warn you, Mr. Güldmar, I shall visit you pretty frequently! Such men as you are not often met with."

Olaf Güldmar looked surprised. " You really mean it?" he said. " Nothing that I have told you affects you? You still seek our friendship?"

They both earnestly assured him that they did, and as

they spoke Thelma rose from her low seat and faced them with a bright smile.

"Do you know," she said, "that you are the first people who, on visiting us once, have ever cared to come again? Ah, you look surprised, but it is so, is it not, father?"

Güldmar nodded a grave assent.

"Yes," she continued demurely, counting on her little white fingers, "we are three things—first, we are accursèd; secondly, we have the evil eye; thirdly, we are not respectable!"

And she broke into a peal of laughter, ringing and sweet as a chime of bells. The young men joined her in it; and, still with an amused expression on her lovely face, leaning her head back against a cluster of pale roses, she went on—

"My father dislikes Mr. Dyceworthy so much, because he wants to—to—oh, what is it they do to savages, father? Yes, I know,—to convert us,—to make us Lutherans. And when he finds it all no use, he is angry; and, though he is so religious, if he hears any one telling some untruth about us in Bosekop, he will add another thing equally untrue, and so it grows and grows, and—why! what is the matter with you?" she exclaimed in surprise as Errington scowled and clenched his fist in a peculiarly threatening manner.

"I should like to knock him down!" he said briefly under his breath.

Old Güldmar laughed and looked at the young baronet approvingly.

"Who knows, who knows!" he said cheerfully. "You may do it some day! It will be a good deed! I will do it myself if he troubles me much more. And now let us make some arrangement with you. When will you come and see us again?"

"You must visit me first," said Sir Philip quickly. "If you and your daughter will honor me with your company to-morrow, I shall be proud and pleased. Consider the yacht at your service."

Thelma, resting among the roses, looked across at him with serious, questioning eyes—eyes that seemed to be asking his intentions towards both her and her father.

Güldmar accepted the invitation at once, and, the hour for their visit next day being fixed and agreed upon, the young men began to take their leave. As Errington

clasped Thelma's hand in farewell, he made a bold venture.
He touched a rose that hung just above her head almost
dropping on her hair.

"May I have it?" he asked in a low tone.

Their eyes met. The girl flushed deeply, and then grew
pale. She broke off the flower and gave it to him,—then
turned to Lorimer to say good-bye. They left her then,
standing under the porch, shading her brow with one hand
from the glittering sunlight, as she watched them descending the winding path to the shore, accompanied by her
father, who hospitably insisted on seeing them into their
boat. They looked back once or twice, always to see the
slender, tall white figure standing there like an angel resting in a bower of roses, with the sunshine flashing on a
golden crown of hair. At the last in the pathway Philip
raised his hat and waved it, but whether she condescended
to wave her hand in answer he could not see.

Left alone, she sighed, and went slowly into the house to
resume her spinning. Hearing the whirr of the wheel, the
servant Britta entered.

"You are not going in the boat, Fröken?" she asked in
a tone of mingled deference and affection.

Thelma looked up, smiled faintly, and shook her head in
the negative.

"It is late, Britta, and I am tired."

And the deep blue eyes had an intense dreamy light
within them as they wandered from the wheel to the wide-
open window, and rested on the majestic darkness of the
overshadowing, solemn pines.

CHAPTER VII.

"In mezzo del mio core c' è una spina;
    Non c' è barbier che la possa levare,—
    Solo il mio amore colla sua manina"
                                    Rime Popolari.

ERRINGTON and Lorimer pulled away across the Fjord in
a silence that lasted for many minutes. Old Güldmar stood
on the edge of his little pier to watch them out of sight.
So, till their boat turned the sharp corner of the protecting
rock, that hid the landing-place from view, they saw his
picturesque figure and gleaming silvery hair outlined
clearly against the background of the sky—a sky now

tenderly flushed with pink like the inside of a delicate shell.
When they could no longer perceive him they still rowed on
speaking no word,—the measured, musical plash of the oars
through the smooth, dark olive-green water alone breaking
the stillness around them. There was a curious sort of
hushed breathlessness in the air ; fantastic, dream-like lights
and shadows played on the little wrinkling waves; sudden
flushes of crimson came and went in the western horizon,
and over the high summits of the surrounding mountains
mysterious shapes, formed of purple and grey mist, rose up
and crept softly downwards, winding in and out deep
valleys and dark ravines, like wandering spirits sent on
some secret and sorrowful errand. After a while Errington
said almost vexedly—

"Are you struck dumb, George? Haven't you a word
to say to a fellow ? "

"Just what I was about to ask *you*," replied Lorimer
carelessly ; "and I was also going to remark that we
hadn't seen your mad friend up at the Güldmar residence."

"No. Yet I can't help thinking he has something to do
with them, all the same," returned Errington meditatively.
"I tell you, he swore at me by some old Norwegian infernal
place or other. I dare say he's an Odin worshipper, too.
But never mind him. What do you think of *her* ? "

Lorimer turned lazily round in the boat, so that he faced
his companion.

"Well, old fellow, if you ask me frankly, I think she is
the most beautiful woman I ever saw, or, for that matter,
ever heard of. And I am an impartial critic—perfectly impartial."

And, resting on his oar, he dipped the blade musingly in
and out of the water, watching the bright drops fall with
an oil-like smoothness as they trickled from the polished
wood and glittered in the late sunshine like vari-colored
jewels. Then he glanced curiously at Philip, who sat
silent, but whose face was very grave and earnest,—even
noble, with that shade of profound thought upon it. He
looked like one who had suddenly accepted a high trust, in
which there was not only pride, but tenderness. Lorimer
shook himself together, as he himself would have expressed
it, and touched his friend's arm half-playfully.

"You've met the king's daughter of Norroway after all,
Phil ; " and his light accents had a touch of sadness in
them ; " and you'll have to bring her home, as the old song

says. I believe the 'eligible' is caught at last. The 'woman' of the piece has turned up, and your chum must play second fiddle—eh, old boy?"

Errington flushed hotly, but caught Lorimer's hand and pressed it with tremendous fervor.

"By Jove, I'll wring it off your wrist if you talk in that fashion, George!" he said, with a laugh. "You'll always be the same to me, and you know it. I tell you," and he pulled his moustache doubtfully, "I don't know quite what's the matter with me. That girl fascinates me! I feel a fool in her presence. Is that a sign of being in love I wonder?"

"Certainly not!" returned George promptly; "for *I* feel a fool in her presence, and I'm not in love."

"How do you know that?" And Errington glanced at him keenly and inquiringly.

"How do I know? Come, I like that! Have I studied myself all these years for nothing? Look here,"—and he carefully drew out the little withering bunch of daisies he had purloined—"these are for you. I knew you wanted them, though you hadn't the impudence to pick them up, and I had.. I thought you might like to put them under your pillow, and all that sort of thing, because if one is resolved to become love-lunatic, one may as well do the thing properly out and out,—I hate all half-measures. Now, if the remotest thrill of sentiment were in me, you can understand, I hope, that wild horses would not have torn this adorable posy from my possession! I should have kept it, and you would never have known of it," and he laughed softly. "Take it, old fellow! You're rich now, with the rose she gave you besides. What is all your wealth compared with the sacred preciousness of such blossoms! There, don't look so awfully estatic, or I shall be called upon to ridicule you in the interests of common sense. So you're in love with the girl at once, and have done with it. Don't beat about the bush!"

"I'm not sure about it," said Philip, taking the daisies gratefully, however, and pressing them in his pocket-book. "I don't believe in love at first sight!"

"I do," returned Lorimer decidedly. "Love is electricity. Two telegrams are enough to settle the business, —one from the eyes of the man, the other from those of the woman. You and Miss Güldmar must have exchanged a dozen such messages at least."

"And you?" inquired Errington persistently. "You had the same chance as myself."

George shrugged his shoulders. "My dear boy, there are no wires of communication between the Sun-angel and myself; nothing but a blank, innocent landscape, over which perhaps some day, the mild lustre of friendship may beam. The girl is beautiful—extraordinarily so; but I'm not a 'man o' wax,' as Juliet's gabbling old nurse says—not in the least impressionable."

And forthwith he resumed his oar, saying briskly as he did so—

"Phil, do you know those other fellows must be swearing at us pretty forcibly for leaving them so long with Dyceworthy. We've been away two hours!"

"Not possible!" cried Errington, amazed, and wielding his oar vigorously. "They'll think me horribly rude. By Jove, they must be bored to death!"

And, stimulated by the thought of the penance their friends were enduring, they sent the boat spinning swiftly through the water, and rowed as though they were trying for a race, when they were suddenly pulled up by a loud "Halloo!" and the sight of another boat coming slowly out from Bosekop, wherein two individuals were standing up, gesticulating violently.

"There they are!" exclaimed Lorimer. "I say, Phil, they've hired a special tub, and are coming out to us."

So it proved. Duprèz and Macfarlane had grown tired of waiting for their truant companions, and had taken the first clumsy wherry that presented itself, rowed by an even clumsier Norwegian boatman, whom they had been compelled to engage also, as he would not let his ugly punt out of his sight, for fear some harm might chance to befall it. Thus attended, they were on their way back to the yacht. With a few long, elegant strokes, Errington and Lorimer soon brought their boat alongside, and their friends gladly jumped into it, delighted to be free of the company of the wooden-faced mariner they had so reluctantly hired, and who now, on receiving his fee, paddled awkwardly away in his ill-constructed craft, without either a word of thanks or salutation. Errington began to apologize at once for his long absence, giving as a reason for it, the necessity he found himself under of making a call on some persons of importance in the neighborhood, whom he had, till now, forgotten.

"My good Phil-eep!" cried Duprèz, in his cheery sing-song accent, "why apologize? We have amused ourselves! Our dear Sandy has a vein of humor that is astonishing! We have not wasted our time. No! We have made Mr. Dyceworthy our slave; we have conquered him; we have abased him! He is what we please,—he is for all gods or for no god,—just as we pull the string! In plain words, *mon cher*, that amiable religious is drunk!"

"Drunk!" cried Errington and Lorimer together. "Jove! you don't mean it?"

Macfarlane looked up with a twinkle of satirical humor in his deep-set grey eyes.

"Ye see," he said seriously, "the Lacrima, or Papist wine as he calls it, was strong—we got him to take a good dose o't—a vera fair dose indeed. Then, doun he sat, an' fell to convairsing vera pheelosophically o' mony things,—it wad hae done ye gude to hear him,—he was fair lost in the mazes o' his metapheesics, for twa flies took a bit saunter through the pleasant dewy lanes o' his forehead, an' he never raised a finger to send them awa' aboot their beeziness. Then I thoct I wad try him wi' the whusky—I had ma pocket flask wi' me—an' O mon! he was sairly glad and gratefu' for the first snack o't! He said it was deevilish fine stuff, an' so he took ane drappikie, an' anither drappikie, and yet anither drappikie,"—Sandy's accent got more and more pronounced as he went on—"an' after a bit, his heed dropt doun, an' he took a wee snoozle of a minute or twa, —then he woke up in a' his strength an' just grappit the flask in his twa hands an' took the hale o't off at a grand, rousin' gulp! Ma certes! after it ye shuld ha' seen him laughin' like a feekless fule, an' rubbin' an' rubbin' his heed, till his hair was like the straw kicked roond by a mad coo!"

Lorimer lay back in the stern of the boat and laughed uproariously at this extraordinary picture, as did the others.

"But that is not all," said Duprèz, with delighted mischief sparkling in his wicked little dark eyes; "the dear religious opened his heart to us. He spoke thickly, but we could understand him. He was very impressive! He is quite of my opinion. He says all religion is nonsense, fable, imposture,—Man is the only god, Woman his creature and subject. Again,—man and woman conjoined, make up divinity, necessity, law. He was quite clear on that point.

Why did he preach what he did not believe, we asked? He almost wept! He replied that the children of this world liked fairy-stories and he was paid to tell them. It was his bread and butter,—would we wish him to have no bread and butter? We assured him so cruel a thought had no place in our hearts! Then he is amorous—yes! the good fat man is amorous! He would have become a priest, but on close examination of the confessionals he saw there was no possibility of seeing, much less kissing a lady penitent through the grating. So he gave up that idea! In his form of faith he *can* kiss, he says,—he *does* kiss!—always a holy kiss, of course! He is so ingenuous,—so delightfully frank, it is quite charming!"

They laughed again. Sir Philip looked somewhat disgusted.

"What an old brute he must be!" he said. "Somebody ought to kick him—a holy kick, of course, and therefore more intense and forcible than other kicks."

"You begin, Phil," laughed Lorimer, "and we'll all follow suit. He'll be like that Indian in 'Vathek' who rolled himself into a ball; no one could resist kicking as long as the ball bounded before them,—we, similarly, shall not be able to resist, if Dyceworthy's fat person is once left at our mercy."

"That was a grand bit he told us, Errington," resumed Macfarlane. "Ye should ha' heard him talk aboot his love-affair! . . . . the saft jelly of a man that he is, to be making up to ony woman."

At that moment they ran alongside of the *Eulalie* and threw up their oars.

"Stop a bit," said Errington. "Tell us the rest on board."

The ladder was lowered; they mounted it, and their boat was hauled up to its place.

"Go on!" said Lorimer, throwing himself lazily into a deck arm-chair and lighting a cigar, while the others leaned against the yacht rails and followed his example. "Go on, Sandy—this is fun! Dyceworthy's amours must be amusing. I suppose he's after that ugly wooden block of a woman we saw at his house who is so zealous for the 'true gospel'?"

"Not a bit of it," replied Sandy, with immense gravity. "The auld Silenus has better taste. He says there's a young lass running after him, fit to break her heart aboot

him,—puir thing, she must have vera little choice o' men !
He hasna quite made up his mind, though he admeets she's
as fine a lass as ony man need require. He's sorely
afraid she has set herself to catch him, as he says she's an
eye like a warlock for a really strong good-looking fellow
like himself," and Macfarlane chuckled audibly. " Maybe
he'll take pity on her, maybe he wont; the misguided
lassie will be sairly teazed by him from a' he tauld us in his
cups. He gave us her name,—the oddest in a' the warld for
sure,—I canna just remember it."

" I can," said Duprèz glibly. " It struck me as quaint
and pretty—Thelma Güldmar."

Errington started so violently, and flushed so deeply,
that Lorimer was afraid of some rash outbreak of wrath on
his part. But he restrained himself by a strong effort. He
merely took his cigar from his mouth and puffed a light
cloud of smoke into the air before replying, then he said
coldly—

" I should say Mr. Dyceworthy, besides being a drunk-
ard, is a most consummate liar. It so happens that the
Güldmars are the very people I have just visited,—highly
superior in every way to anybody we have yet met in Norway. In fact, Mr. and Miss Güldmar will come on board
to-morrow. I have invited them to dine with us; you will
then be able to judge for yourselves whether the young lady
is at all of the description Mr. Dyceworthy gives of her."

Duprèz and Macfarlane exchanged astonished looks.

" Are ye quite sure," the latter ventured to remark cautiously, " that ye're prudent in what ye have done? Remember ye have asked no pairson at a' to dine with ye as
yet,—it's a vera sudden an' exceptional freak o' hospitality."

Errington smoked on peacefully and made no answer.
Duprèz hummed a verse of a French *chansonnette* under his
breath and smiled. Lorimer glanced at him with a lazy
amusement.

" Unburden yourself, Pierre, for heaven's sake ! " he said.
" Your mind is as uncomfortable as a loaded camel. Let it
lie down, while you take off its packages, one by one, and
reveal their contents. In short, what's up ? "

Duprèz made a rapid, expressive gesture with his hands.

" *Mon cher*, I fear to displease Phil-eep ! He has invited
these people; they are coming,—*bien !* there is no more to
say."

" I disagree with ye," interposed Macfarlane. " I think

Errington should hear what *we* ha' heard; it's fair an' just to a mon that he should understand what sort o' folk are gaun to pairtake wi' him at his table. Ye see, Errington, ye should ha' thought a wee, before inviting pairsons o' unsettled an' dootful chairacter——"

"Who says they are?" demanded Errington half-angrily. "The drunken Dyceworthy?"

"He was no sae drunk at the time he tauld us," persisted Macfarlane in his most obstinate, most dictatorial manner. "Ye see, it's just this way——"

"Ah, *pardon!*" interrupted Duprèz briskly. "Our dear Sandy is an excellent talker, but he is a little slow. Thus it is, *mon cher* Errington. This gentleman named Güldmar had a most lovely wife—a mysterious lady, with an evident secret. The beautiful one was never seen in the church or in any town or village; she was met sometimes on hills, by rivers, in valleys, carrying her child in her arms. The people grew afraid of her; but, now, see what happens! Suddenly, she appears no more; some one ventures to ask this Monsieur Güldmar, 'What has become of Madame?' His answer is brief. 'She is dead!' Satisfactory so far, yet not quite; for, Madame being dead, then what has become of the corpse of Madame? It was never seen,—no coffin was ever ordered,—and apparently it was never buried! *Bien!* What follows? The good people of Bosekop draw the only conclusion possible—Monsieur Güldmar, who is said to have a terrific temper, killed Madame and made away with her body. *Voila!*"

And Duprèz waved his hand with an air of entire satisfaction.

Errington's brow grew sombre. "This is the story, is it?" he asked at last.

"It is enough, is it not?" laughed Duprèz. "But, after all, what matter? It will be novel to dine with a mur——"

"Stop!" said Philip fiercely, with so much authority that the sparkling Pierre was startled. "Call no man by such a name till you know he deserves it. If Güldmar was suspected, as you say, why didn't somebody arrest him on the charge?"

"Because, ye see," replied Macfarlane, "there was not sufficient proof to warrant such a proceeding. Moreover, the actual meenister of the parish declared it was a' richt, an' said this Güldmar was a mon o' vera queer notions, an'

maybe, had buried his wife wi' certain ceremonies peculiar
to himself——What's wrong wi' ye now ? "

For a light had flashed on Errington's mind, and with the
quick comprehension it gave him, his countenance cleared.
He laughed.

" That's very likely," he said ; " Mr. Güldmar is a character. He follows the faith of Odin, and not even Dyceworthy can convert him to Christianity."

Macfarlane stared with a sort of stupefied solemnity.

" Mon ! " he exclaimed, " ye never mean to say there's an
actual puir human creature that in this blessed, enlightened
nineteenth century of ours, is so far misguidit as to worship
the fearfu' gods o' the Scandinavian meethology ? "

" Ah ! " yawned Lorimer, " you may wonder away, Sandy,
but it's true enough ! Old Güldmar is an Odinite. In this
blessed, enlightened nineteenth century of ours, when
Christians amuse themselves by despising and condemning
each other, and thus upsetting all the precepts of the Master they profess to follow, there is actually a man who sticks
to the traditions of his ancestors. Odd, isn't it ? In this
delightful, intellectual age, when more than half of us are
discontented with life and yet don't want to die, there is a
fine old gentleman, living beyond the Arctic circle, who is
perfectly satisfied with his existence—not only that, he
thinks death the greatest glory that can befall him. Comfortable state of things altogether ! I'm half inclined to
be an Odinite too."

Sandy still remained lost in astonishment. " Then ye
don't believe that he made awa' wi' his wife ? " he inquired
slowly.

" Not in the least ! " returned Lorimer decidedly ;
" neither will you, to-morrow, when you see him. He's a
great deal better up in literature than you are, my boy, I'd
swear, judging from the books he has. And when he mentioned his wife, as he did once, you could see in his face he
had never done *her* any harm. Besides, his daughter—"

" Ah ! but I forgot," interposed Duprèz again. " The
daughter, Thelma, was the child the mysteriously vanished
lady carried in her arms, wandering with it all about the
woods and hills. After her disappearance, another thing
extraordinary happens. The child also disappears, and
Monsieur Güldmar lives alone, avoided carefully by every
respectable person. Suddenly the child returns, grown to
be nearly a woman—and they say, lovely to an almost im-

possible extreme. She lives with her father. She, like her strange mother, never enters a church, town, or village— nowhere, in fact, where persons are in any numbers. Three years ago, it appears, she vanished again, but came back at the end of ten months, lovelier than ever. Since then she has remained quiet—composed—but always apart,—she may disappear at any moment. Droll, is it not, Errington? and the reputation she has is natural!"

"Pray state it," said Philip, with freezing coldness. "The reputation of a woman is nothing nowadays. Fair game—go on!"

But his face was pale, and his eyes blazed dangerously. Almost unconsciously his hand toyed with the rose Thelma had given him, that still ornamented his button-hole.

"Mon Dieu!" cried Duprèz in amazement. "But look not at me like that! It seems to displease you, to put you *en fureur*, what I say! It is not my story,—it is not I,— I know not Mademoiselle Güldmar. But as her beauty is considered superhuman, they say it is the devil who is her *parfumeur*, her *coiffeur*, and who sees after her complex-ion; in brief, she is thought to be a witch in full practice, dangerous to life and limb."

Errington laughed loudly, he was so much relieved.

"Is that all?" he said with light contempt. "By Jove! what a pack of fools there must be about here,—ugly fools too, if they think beauty is a sign of witchcraft. I wonder Dyceworthy isn't scared out of his skin if he positively thinks the so-called witch is setting her cap at him."

"Ah, but he means to convairt her," said Macfarlane se-riously. "To draw the evil oot o' her, as it were. He said he wad do't by fair means or foul."

Something in these latter words struck Lorimer, for, rais-ing himself in his seat, he asked, "Surely Mr. Dyceworthy, with all his stupidity, doesn't carry it so far as to believe in witchcraft?"

"Oh, indeed he does," exclaimed Duprèz; "he believes in it *à la lettre!* He has Bible authority for his belief. He is very firm—firmest when drunk!" And he laughed gaily.

Errington muttered something not very flattering to Mr. Dyceworthy's intelligence, which escaped the hearing of his friends; then he said—

"Come along, all of you, down into the saloon. We want something to eat. Let the Güldmars alone; I'm not

a bit sorry I've asked them to come to-morrow. I believe
you'll all like them immensely."

They all descended the stair-way leading to the lower
part of the yacht, and Macfarlane asked as he followed his
host—

"Is the lass vera bonnie did ye say?"

"Bonnie's not the word for it this time," said Lorimer,
coolly answering instead of Errington. "Miss Güldmar is
a magnificent woman. You never saw such a one, Sandy,
my boy; she'll make you sing small with one look; she'll
wither you up into a kippered herring! And as for you,
Duprèz," and he regarded the little Frenchman critically,
"let me see,—you *may* possibly reach up to her shoulder,
—certainly not beyond it."

"*Pas possible!*" cried Duprèz. "Mademoiselle is a
giantess."

"She needn't be a giantess to overtop you, *mon ami,*"
laughed Lorimer with a lazy shrug. "By Jove, I *am*
sleepy, Errington, old boy; are we never going to bed?
It's no good waiting till it's dark here, you know."

"Have something first," said Sir Philip, seating himself
at the saloon table, where his steward had laid out a tasty
cold collation. "We've had a good deal of climbing about
and rowing; it's taken it out of us a little."

Thus hospitably adjured, they took their places, and
managed to dispose of an excellent supper. The meal concluded, Duprèz helped himself to a tiny liqueur glass of
Chartreuse, as a wind-up to the exertions of the day, a mild
luxury in which the others joined him, with the exception
of Macfarlane, who was wont to declare that a "mon without his whusky was nae mon at a'," and who, therefore,
persisted in burning up his interior mechanism with alcohol
in spite of the doctrines of hygiene, and was now absorbed
in the work of mixing his lemon, sugar, hot water, and
poison—his usual preparation for a night's rest.

Lorimer, usually conversational, watched him in abstracted silence. Rallied on this morose humor, he rose,
shook himself like a retriever, yawned, and sauntered to
the piano that occupied a dim corner of the saloon, and
began to play with that delicate, subtle touch, which,
though it does not always mark the brilliant pianist, distinguishes the true lover of music, to whose ears a rough
thump on the instrument, or a false note would be most exquisite agony. Lorimer had no pretense to musical talent;

when asked, he confessed he could " strum a little," and he hardly seemed to see the evident wonder and admiration he awakened in the minds of many to whom such " strumming " as his was infinitely more delightful than more practiced, finished playing. Just now he seemed undecided, —he commenced a dainty little prelude of Chopin's, then broke suddenly off, and wandered into another strain, wild, pleading, pitiful, and passionate,—a melody so weird and dreamy that even the stolid Macfarlane paused in his toddy-sipping, and Duprèz looked round in some wonderment.

" *Comme c'est beau, ça !* " he murmured.

Errington said nothing ; he recognized the tune as that which Thelma had sung at her spinning-wheel, and his bold bright eyes grew pensive and soft, as the picture of the fair face and form rose up again before his mind. Absorbed in a reverie, he almost started when Lorimer ceased playing, and said lightly—

" By-bye, boys ! I'm off to bed ! Phil, don't wake me so abominably early as you did this morning. If you do, friendship can hold out no longer—we must part ! "

" All right ! " laughed Errington good-humoredly, watching his friend as he sauntered out of the saloon ; then seeing Duprèz and Macfarlane rise from the table, he added courteously, " Don't hurry away on Lorimer's account, you two. I'm not in the least sleepy,—I'll sit up with you to any hour."

" It is droll to go to bed in broad daylight," said Duprèz. " But it must be done. *Cher Philippe,* your eyes are heavy. ' To bed, to bed,' as the excellent Madame Macbeth says. Ah ! *quelle femme !* What an exciting wife she was for a man ? Come, let us follow our dear Lorimer,— his music was delicious. Good night or good morning ? . . . I know not which it is in this strange land where the sun shines always ! It is confusing ! "

They shook hands and separated. Errington, however, unable to compose his mind to rest, went into his cabin merely to come out of it again and betake himself to the deck, where he decided to walk up and down till he felt sleepy. He wished to be alone with his own thoughts for awhile—to try and resolve the meaning of this strange new emotion that possessed him,—a feeling that was half pleasing, half painful, and that certainly moved him to a sort of shame. A man, if he be strong and healthy, is always more or less ashamed when Love, with a single effort, proves him

to be weaker than a blade of grass swaying in the wind.
What! all his dignity, all his resoluteness, all his authority
swept down by the light touch of a mere willow wand? for
the very sake of his own manhood and self-respect, he cannot help but be ashamed! It is as though a little nude,
laughing child mocked at a lion's strength, and made him a
helpless prisoner with a fragile daisy chain. So the god
Eros begins his battles, which end in perpetual victory,—
first fear and shame,—then desire and passion,—then conquest and possession. And afterwards? ah! . . . afterwards the pagan deity is powerless,—a higher God, a
grander force, a nobler creed must carry Love to its
supreme and best fulfillment.

CHAPTER VIII.

"Le vent qui vient à travers la montagne
M'a rendu fou!"

VICTOR HUGO.

IT was half an hour past midnight. Sir Philip was left
in absolute solitude to enjoy his meditative stroll on deck,
for the full radiance of light that streamed over the sea and
land was too clear and brilliant to necessitate the attendance of any of the sailors for the purpose of guarding the
Eulalie. She was safely anchored and distinctly visible to
all boats or fishing craft crossing the Fjord, so that unless
a sudden gale should blow, which did not seem probable in
the present state of the weather, there was nothing for the
men to do that need deprive them of their lawful repose.
Errington paced up and down slowly, his yachting shoes
making no noise, even as they left no scratch on the spotless white deck, that shone in the night sunshine like polished silver. The Fjord was very calm,—on one side it
gleamed like a pool of golden oil in which the outline of
the *Eulalie* was precisely traced, her delicate masts and
spars and drooping flag being drawn in black lines on the
yellow water as though with a finely pointed pencil. There
was a curious light in the western sky ; a thick bank of
clouds, dusky brown in color, were swept together and
piled one above the other in mountainous ridges, that rose
up perpendicularly from the very edge of the sea-line, while
over their dark summits a glimpse of the sun, like a giant's
eye, looked forth, darting dazzling descending rays through

the sullen smoke-like masses, tinging them with metallic green and copper hues as brilliant and shifting as the bristling points of lifted spears. Away to the south, a solitary wreath of purple vapor floated slowly as though lost from some great mountain height; and through its faint, half disguising veil the pale moon peered sorrowfully, like a dying prisoner lamenting joy long past, but unforgotten.

A solemn silence reigned; and Errington, watching sea and sky, grew more and more absorbed and serious. The scornful words of the proud old Olaf Güldmar rankled in his mind and stung him. "An idle trifler with time—an aimless wanderer!" Bitter, but, after all, true! He looked back on his life with a feeling kin to contempt. What had he done that was at all worth doing? He had seen to the proper management of his estates,—well! any one with a grain of self-respect and love of independence would do the same. He had travelled and amused himself,—he had studied languages and literature,—he had made many friends; but after all said and done, the *bonde's* cutting observations had described him correctly enough. The do-nothing, care-nothing tendency, common to the very wealthy in this age, had crept upon him unconsciously; the easy, cool, indifferent nonchalance common to men of his class and breeding was habitual with him, and he had never thought it worth while to exert his dormant abilities. Why then, should he now begin to think it was time to reform all this,—to rouse himself to an effort,—to gain for himself some honor, some distinction, some renown that should mark him out as different to other men? why was he suddenly seized with an insatiate desire to be something more than a mere "mushroom knight, a fungus of nobility"— why? if not to make himself worthy of—ah! There he had struck a suggestive key-note! Worthy of what? of whom? There was no one in all the world, excepting perhaps Lorimer, who cared what became of Sir Philip Errington, Baronet, in the future, so long as he would, for the present, entertain and feast his numerous acquaintances and give them all the advantages, social and political, his wealth could so easily obtain. Then why, in the name of well-bred indolence, should he muse with such persistent gloom, on his general unworthiness at this particular moment? Was it because this Norwegian maiden's grand blue eyes had met his with such beautiful trust and candor?

He had known many women, queens of society, titled

beauties, brilliant actresses, sirens of the world with all their witcheries in full play, and he had never lost his self-possession or his heart ; with the loveliest of them he had always felt himself master of the situation, knowing that in their opinion he was always " a catch," " an eligible," and, therefore, well worth winning. Now, for the first time, he became aware of his utter insignificance,—this tall, fair goddess knew none of the social slang—and her fair, pure face, the mirror of a fair, pure soul, showed that the " eligibility " of a man from a pecuniary point of view was a consideration that would never present itself to her mind. What she would look at would be the man himself,—not his pocket. And, studied from such an exceptional height,—a height seldom climbed by modern marrying women,—Philip felt himself unworthy. It was a good sign ; there are great hopes of any man who is honestly dissatisfied with himself. Folding his arms, he leaned idly on the deck-rails, and looked gravely and mus-ingly down into the motionless water where the varied hues of the sky were clearly mirrored,—when a slight creaking, cracking sound was heard, as of some obstacle grazing against or bumping the side of the yacht. He looked, and saw, to his surprise, a small rowing boat close under the gunwale, so close indeed that the slow motion of the tide heaved it every now and then into a jerky collision with the lower framework of the *Eulalie*—a circumstance which explained the sound which had attracted his attention. The boat was not unoccupied—there was some one in it lying straight across the seats, with face turned upwards to the sky—and, walking noiselessly to a better post of observa-tion, Errington's heart beat with some excitement as he recognized the long, fair, unkempt locks, and eccentric attire of the strange personage who had confronted him in the cave—the crazy little man who had called himself " Sigurd." There he was, beyond a doubt, lying flat on his back with his eyes closed. Asleep or dead ? He might have been the latter,—his thin face was so pale and drawn,—his lips were so set and colorless. Errington, astonished to see him there, called softly—

" Sigurd ! Sigurd ! " There was no answer ; Sigurd's form seemed inanimate—his eyes remained fast shut.

" Is he in a trance ? " thought Sir Philip wonderingly ; " or has he fainted from some physical exhaustion ? "

He called again, but again received no reply. He now

observed in the stern of the boat a large bunch of pansies, dark as velvet, and evidently freshly gathered,—proving that Sigurd had been wandering in the deep valleys and on the sloping sides of the hills, where these flowers may be frequently found in Norway during the summer. He began to feel rather uncomfortable, as he watched that straight stiff figure in the boat, and was just about to swing down the companion-ladder for the purpose of closer inspection, when a glorious burst of light streamed radiantly over the Fjord, —the sun conquered the masses of dark cloud that had striven to conceal his beauty, and now,—like a warrior clad in golden armor, surmounted and trod down his enemies, shining forth in all his splendor. With that rush of brilliant effulgence, the apparently lifeless Sigurd stirred, —he opened his eyes, and as they were turned upwards, he naturally, from his close vicinity to the side of the *Eulalie*, met Errington's gaze fixed inquiringly and somewhat anxiously upon him. He sprang up with such sudden and fierce haste that his frail boat rocked dangerously and Philip involuntarily cried out—

"Take care!"

Sigurd stood upright in his swaying skiff and laughed scornfully.

"Take care!" he echoed derisively. "It is you who should take care! You,—poor miserable moth on the edge of a mad storm! It is you to fear—not I! See how the light rains over the broad sky. All for me! Yes, all the light, all the glory for me; all the darkness, all the shame for you!"

Errington listened to these ravings with an air of patience and pitying gentleness, then he said with perfect coolness—

"You are quite right, Sigurd! You are always right, I am sure. Come up here and see me; I won't hurt you! Come along!"

The friendly tone and gentle manner appeared to soothe the unhappy dwarf, for he stared doubtfully, then smiled,— and finally, as though acting under a spell, he took up an oar and propelled himself skillfully enough to the gangway, where Errington let down the ladder and with his own hand assisted his visitor to mount, not forgetting to fasten the boat safely to the steps as he did so. Once on deck, Sigurd gazed about him perplexedly. He had brought his bunch of pansies with him, and he fingered their soft leaves thoughtfully. Suddenly his eyes flashed.

" You are alone here ? " he asked abruptly.

Fearing to scare his strange guest by the mention of his companions, Errington answered simply—

" Yes, quite alone just now, Sigurd."

Sigurd took a step closer towards him. " Are you not afraid ? " he said in an awe-struck, solemn voice.

Sir Philip smiled. " I never was afraid of anything in my life ! " he answered.

The dwarf eyed him keenly. " You are not afraid," he went on, " that I shall kill you ? "

" Not in the least," returned Errington calmly. " You would not do anything so foolish, my friend."

Sigurd laughed. " Ha ha ! You call me ' friend.' You think that word a safeguard ! I tell you, no ! There are no friends now ; the world is a great field of battle,—each man fights the other. There is no peace,—none anywhere ! The wind fights with the forests ; you can hear them slashing and slaying all night long—when it *is* night—the long, long night ! The sun fights with the sky, the light with the dark, and life with death. It is all a bitter quarrel ; none are satisfied, none shall know friendship any more ; it is too late ! We cannot be friends ! "

" Well, have it your own way," said Philip good-naturedly, wishing that Lorimer were awake to interview this strange specimen of human wit gone astray ; " we'll fight if you like. Anything to please you ! "

" We *are* fighting," said Sigurd with intense passion in his voice. " You may not know it ; but I know it ! I have felt the thrust of your sword ; it has crossed mine. Stay ! " and his eyes grew vague and dreamy. " Why was I sent to seek you out—let me think—let me think ! "

And he seated himself forlornly on one of the deck chairs and seemed painfully endeavoring to put his scattered ideas in order. Errington studied him with a gentle forbearance ; inwardly he was very curious to know whether this Sigurd had any connection with the Güld- mars, but he refrained from asking too many questions. He simply said in a cheery tone—

" Yes, Sigurd,—why did you come to see me ? I'm glad you did ; it's very kind of you, but I don't think you even know my name."

To his surprise, Sigurd looked up with a more settled and resolved expression of face, and answered almost as connectedly as any sane man could have done.

" I know your name very well," he said in a low composed manner. " You are Sir Philip Errington, a rich English nobleman. Fate led you to *her* grave—a grave that no strange feet have ever passed, save yours—and so I know you are the man for whom her spirit has waited,— she has brought you hither. How foolish to think she sleeps under the stone, when she is always awake and busy, —always at work opposing me! Yes, though I pray her to lie still, she will not!"

His voice grew wild again, and Philip asked quietly—

" Of whom are you speaking, Sigurd?"

His steady tone seemed to have some compelling influence on the confused mind of the half-witted creature, who answered readily and at once—

" Of whom should I speak but Thelma? Thelma, the beautiful rose of the northern forest—Thelma——"

He broke off abruptly with a long shuddering sigh, and rocking himself drearily to and fro, gazed wistfully out to the sea. Errington hazarded a guess as to the purpose of that coffin hidden in the shell cavern.

" Do you mean Thelma living? . . . or Thelma dead?"

" Both," answered Sigurd promptly. " They are one and the same,—you cannot part them. Mother and child, —rose and rosebud! One walks the earth with the step of a queen, the other floats in the air like a silvery cloud; but I see them join and embrace and melt into each other's arms till they unite in one form, fairer than the beauty of angels! And you—you know this as well as I do—you have seen Thelma, you have kissed the cup of friendship with her; but remember!—not with me—not with me!"

He started from his seat, and, running close up to Errington, laid one meagre hand on his chest.

" How strong you are, how broad and brave," he exclaimed with a sort of childish admiration. " And can you not be generous too?"

Errington looked down upon him compassionately. He had learned enough from his incoherent talk to clear up what had seemed a mystery. The scandalous reports concerning Olaf Güldmar were incorrect,—he had evidently laid the remains of his wife in the shell-cavern, for some reason connected with his religious belief, and Thelma's visits to the sacred spot were now easy of comprehension. No doubt it was she who placed fresh flowers there every day, and kept the little lamp burning before the crucifix as a sign of the faith her departed mother had professed, and which she herself followed. But who was Sigurd, and what was he to the Güldmars? Thinking this, he replied to the dwarf's question by a counter-inquiry.

"How shall I be generous, Sigurd? Tell me! What can I do to please you?"

Sigurd's wild blue eyes sparkled with pleasure.

"Do!" he cried. "You can go away, swiftly, swiftly over the seas, and the Altenfjord need know you no more! Spread your white sails!" and he pointed excitedly up to the tall tapering masts of the *Eulalie.* "You are king here. Command and you are obeyed! Go from us, go! What is there here to delay you? Our mountains are dark and gloomy,—the fields are wild and desolate,—there are rocks, glaciers and shrieking torrents that hiss like serpents gliding into the sea! Oh, there must be fairer lands than this one,—lands where oceans and sky are like twin jewels set in one ring,—where there are sweet flowers and fruits and bright eyes to smile on you all day—yes! for you are as a god in your strength and beauty—no woman will be cruel to *you!* Ah! say you will go away!" and Sigurd's face was transfigured into a sort of pained beauty as he made his appeal. "That is what I came to seek you for, —to ask you to set sail quickly and go, for why should you wish to destroy me? I have done you no harm as yet. Go!—and Odin himself shall follow your path with blessings!"

He paused, almost breathless with his own earnest pleading. Errington was silent. He considered the request a mere proof of the poor creature's disorder. The very idea that Sigurd seemed to entertain of his doing him any harm, showed a reasonless terror and foreboding that was simply to be set down as caused by his unfortunate mental condition. To such an appeal there could be no satisfactory reply. To sail away from the Altenfjord and its now most fascinating attractions, because a madman asked him to do so, was a proposion impossible of acceptance, so Sir Philip said nothing. Sigurd, however, watching his face intently, saw, or thought he saw, a look of resolution in the Englishman's clear, deep grey eyes,—and with the startling quickness common to many whose brains, like musical instruments, are jarred, yet not quite unstrung, he grasped the meaning of that expression instantly.

"Ah! cruel and traitorous!" he exclaimed fiercely.

"You will not go; you are resolved to tear my heart out for your sport! I have pleaded with you as one pleads with a king and all in vain—all in vain! You will not go? Listen, see what you will do," and he held up the bunch of purple pansies, while his voice sank to an almost feeble faintness. "Look!" and he fingered the flowers, "look! . . . they are dark and soft as a purple sky,—cool and dewy and fresh;—they are the thoughts of Thelma; such thoughts! So wise and earnest, so pure and full of tender shadows!—no hand has grasped them rudely, no rough touch has spoiled their smoothness! They open full-faced to the sky, they never droop or languish; they have no secrets, save the marvel of their beauty. Now you have come, you will have no pity,—one by one you will gather and play with her thoughts as though they were these blossoms, —your burning hand will mar their color,—they will wither and furl up and die, all of them,—and you,—what will you care? Nothing! no man ever cares for a flower that is withered,—not even though his own hand slew it."

The intense melancholy that vibrated through Sigurd's voice touched his listener profoundly. Dimly he guessed that the stricken soul before him had formed the erroneous idea that he, Errington, had come to do some great wrong to Thelma or her belongings, and he pitied the poor creature for his foolish self-torture.

"Listen to me, Sigurd," he said, with a certain imperativeness; "I cannot promise you to go away, but I can promise that I will do no harm to you or to—to—Thelma. Will that content you?"

Sigurd smiled vacantly and shook his head. He looked at the pansies wistfully and laid them down very gently on one of the deck benches.

"I must go," he said in a faint voice :—"She is calling me."

"Who is calling you?" demanded Errington astonished.

"She is," persisted Sigurd, walking steadily to the gang-way. "I can hear her! There are the roses to water, and the doves to feed, and many other things." He looked steadily at Sir Philip, who, seeing he was bent on departure, assisted him to descend the companion ladder into his little boat. "You are sure you will not sail away?"

Errington balanced himself lightly on the ladder and smiled.

" I am sure, Sigurd! I have no wish to sail away. Are you all right there?"

He spoke cheerily, feeling in his own mind that it was scarcely safe for a madman to be quite alone in a cockle-shell of a boat on a deep Fjord, the shores of which were indented with dangerous rocks as sharp as the bristling teeth of fabled sea-monsters, but Sigurd answered him almost contemptuously.

" All right!" he echoed. " That is what the English say always. All right! As if it were ever wrong with me, and the sea! We know each other,—we do each other no harm. *You* may die on the sea, but *I* shall not! No, there is another way to Valhalla!"

" Oh, I dare say there are no end of ways," said Errington good-temperedly, still poising himself on the ladder, and holding on to the side of his yacht, as he watched his late visitor take the oars and move off. " Good-bye, Sigurd! Take care of yourself! Hope I shall see you again soon."

But Sigurd replied not. Bending to the oars, he rowed swiftly and strongly, and Sir Philip, pulling up the ladder and closing the gangway, saw the little skiff flying over the water like a bird in the direction of the Güldmar's landing-place. He wondered again and again what relationship, if any, this half-crazed being bore to the *bonde* and his daughter. That he knew all about them was pretty evident; but how? Catching sight of the pansies left on the deck bench, Errington took them, and, descending to the saloon, set them on the table in a tumbler of water.

" Thelma's thoughts, the poor little fellow called them," he mused, with a smile. " A pretty fancy of his, and linked with the crazy imaginings of Ophelia too. 'There's pansies, that's for thoughts,' *she* said, but Sigurd's idea is different; he believes they are Thelma's own thoughts in flower. 'No rough touch has spoiled their smoothness,' he declared; he's right there, I'm sure. And shall I ruffle the sweet leaves; shall I crush the tender petals? or shall I simply transform them, from pansies into roses,—from the dream of love,—into love itself?"

His eyes softened as he glanced at the drooping rose he wore, which Thelma herself had given him, and as he went to his sleeping cabin, he carefully detached it from his button-hole, and taking down a book,—one which he greatly prized, because it had belonged to his mother,—he prepared to press the flower within its leaves. It was the " Imitation of Christ," bound quaintly and fastened with silver clasps, and as he was about to lay his fragrant trophy on the first page that opened naturally of itself, he glanced at the words that there presented themselves to his eyes.

"Nothing is sweeter than love, nothing stronger, nothing higher, nothing wider, nothing more pleasant, nothing fuller or better in heaven or in earth!" And with a smile, and a warmer flush of color than usual on his handsome face, he touched the rose lightly yet tenderly with his lips and shut it reverently within its sacred resting-place.

CHAPTER IX.

"Our manners are infinitely corrupted, and wonderfully incline to the worse; of our customs there are many barbarous and monstrous."
MONTAIGNE.

THE next day was very warm and bright, and that pious Lutheran divine, the Reverend Charles Dyceworthy, was seriously encumbered by his own surplus flesh material, as he wearily rowed himself across the Fjord towards Olaf Güldmar's private pier. As the perspiration bedewed his brow, he felt that Heaven had dealt with him somewhat too liberally in the way of fat—he was provided too amply with it ever to excel as an oarsman. The sun was burning hot, the water was smooth as oil, and very weighty—it seemed to resist every stroke of his clumsily wielded blades. Altogether it was hard, uncongenial work,—and, being rendered somewhat flabby and nerveless by his previous evening's carouse with Macfarlane's whisky, Mr. Dyceworthy was in a plaintive and injured frame of mind. He was bound on a mission—a holy and edifying errand, which would have elevated any minister of his particular sect. He had found a crucifix with the name of Thelma engraved thereon,—he was now about to return it to the evident rightful owner, and in returning it, he purposed denouncing it as an emblem of the " Scarlet Woman, that sitteth on the Seven Hills," and threatening all those who dared to hold it sacred, as doomed to eternal torture, " where the worm dieth not." He had thought over all he meant to say ; he had planned several eloquent and rounded sentences, some of which he murmured placidly to himself as he propelled his slow boat along.

" Yea!" he observed in a mild sotto-voce—" ye shall be

cut off root and branch! Ye shall be scorched even as
stubble,—and utterly destroyed." Here he paused and
mopped his streaming forehead with his clean perfumed
handkerchief. "Yea!" he resumed peacefully, "the wor-
shippers of idolatrous images are accursèd; they shall
have ashes for food and gall for drink! Let them turn and
repent themselves, lest the wrath of God consume them as
straw whirled on the wind. Repent! . . . or ye shall
be cast into everlasting fire. Beauty shall avail not, learning shall avail not, meekness shall avail not; for the
fire of hell is a searching, endless, destroying——"
here Mr. Dyceworthy, by plunging one oar with too
much determination into the watery depths, caught a
crab, as the saying is, and fell violently backward
in a somewhat undignified posture. Recovering himself slowly, he looked about him in a bewildered way,
and for the first time noticed the vacant, solitary appearance of the Fjord. Some object was missing; he realized
what it was immediately—the English yacht *Eulalie* was
gone from her point of anchorage.

"Dear me!" said Mr. Dyceworthy, half aloud, "what a
very sudden departure! I wonder, now, if those young
men have gone for good, or whether they are coming back
again? Pleasant fellows, very pleasant! flippant, perhaps,
but pleasant."

And he smiled benevolently. He had no remembrance
of what had occurred, after he had emptied young Macfarlane's flask of Glenlivet; he had no idea that he had been
almost carried from his garden into his parlor, and there
flung on the sofa and left to sleep off the effects of his
strong tipple; least of all did he dream that he had betrayed any of his intentions towards Thelma Güldmar, or
given his religious opinions with such free and undisguised
candor. Blissfully ignorant on these points, he resumed
his refractory oars, and after nearly an hour of laborious effort, succeeded at last in reaching his destination. Arrived at the little pier, he fastened up his boat, and with
the lofty air of a thoroughly moral man, he walked deliberately up to the door of the *bonde's* house. Contrary to
custom, it was closed, and the place seemed strangely silent and deserted. The afternoon heat was so great that
the song-birds were hushed, and in hiding under the cool
green leaves,—the clambering roses round the porch hung
down their bright heads for sheer faintness,—and the only

sounds to be heard were the subdued coo-cooing of the doves on the roof, and the soft trickling rush of a little mountain stream that flowed through the grounds. Somewhat surprised, though not abashed, at the evident " not-at-home " look of the farm-house, Mr. Dyceworthy rapped loudly at the rough oaken door with his knuckles, there being no such modern convenience as a bell or a knocker. He waited sometime before he was answered, repeating his summons violently at frequent intervals, and swearing irreligiously under his breath as he did so. But at last the door was flung sharply open, and the tangle-haired, rosy-cheeked Britta confronted him with an aspect which was by no means encouraging or polite. Her round blue eyes sparkled saucily, and she placed her bare, plump, red arms, wet with recent soapsuds, akimbo on her sturdy little hips, with an air that was decidedly impertinent.

" Well, what do you want ? " she demanded with rude abruptness.

Mr. Dyceworthy regarded her in speechless dignity. Vouchsafing no reply, he attempted to pass her and enter the house. But Britta settled her arms more defiantly than ever, and her voice had a sharper ring as she said—

" It's no use your coming in ! There's no one here but me. The master has gone out for the day."

" Young woman," returned Mr. Dyceworthy with polite severity, " I regret to see that your manners stand in sore need of improvement. Your master's absence is of no importance to me. It is with the Fröken Thelma I desire to speak."

Britta laughed and tossed her rough brown curls back from her forehead. Mischievous dimples came and went at the corners of her mouth—indications of suppressed fun.

" The Fröken is out too," she said demurely. " It's time she had a little amusement ; and the gentlemen treat her as if she were a queen ! "

Mr. Dyceworthy started, and his red visage became a trifle paler.

" Gentlemen ? What gentlemen ? " he demanded with some impatience.

Britta's inward delight evidently increased.

" The gentlemen from the yacht, of course," she said. " What other *gentlemen* are there ? " This with a contemptous up-and-down sort of look at the Lutheran minister's portly form. " Sir Philip Errington was here with his friend yesterday evening and stayed a long time,—and to-day a fine boat with four oars came to fetch the master and Fröken Thelma, and they are all gone for a sail to the Kaa Fjord or some other place near here—I cannot remember the name. And I am *so* glad!" went on Britta, clasping her plump hands in ecstasy. "They are the grandest, handsomest *Herren* I hav ever s·en,—and one can tell they think wonders of the Fröken—nothing is too good for her!"

Mr. Dyceworthv's face was the picture of dismay. This was a new turn to the course of events, and one, more-over, that he had never once contemplated. Britta watched him amusedly.

"Will you leave any message for them when they re-turn?" she asked.

"No," said the minister dubiously. "Yet, stay; yes! I will! Tell the Fröken that I have found something which belongs to her, and that when she wishes to have it, I will myself bring it."

Britta looked cross. "If it is hers you have no business to keep it," she said brusquely. "Why not leave it,—what-ever it is,—with me?"

Mr. Dyceworthy regarded her with a bland and lofty air.

"I trust no concerns of mine or hers to the keeping of a paid domestic," he said. "A domestic, moreover, who de-serts the ways of her own people,—who hath dealings with the dwellers in darkness,—who even bringeth herself to for-get much of her own native tongue, and who devoteth her-self to——"

What he would have said was uncertain, as at that mo-ment he was nearly thrown down by a something that slipped agilely between his legs, pinching each fat calf as it passed—a something that looked like a ball, but proved to be a human creature—no other than the crazy Sigurd, who, after accomplishing his uncouth gambol successfully, stood up, shaking back his streaming fair locks and laughing wildly.

"Ha, ha!" he exclaimed. "That was good; that was clever! If I had upset you now, you would have said your prayers backward! What are you here for? This is no place for you! They are all gone out of it. *She* has gone—all the world is empty! There is nothing any-where but air, air, air!—no birds, no flowers, no trees, no sunshine! All gone with her on the sparkling, singing water!" and he swung his arms round violently, and snapped his fingers in the minister's face. " What an ugly man your are!" he exclaimed with refreshing candor. " I think you are uglier than I am! You are straight,—but you are like a load of peat—heavy and barren and fit to burn. Now, I—I am the crooked bough of a tree, but I have bright leaves where a bird hides and sings all day! You—you have no song, no foliage; only ugly and barren and fit to burn!" He laughed heartily, and, catching sight of Britta, where she stood in the doorway entirely unconcerned at his eccentric behavior, he went up to her and took hold of the corner of her apron. " Take me in, Britta dear—pretty Britta!" he said coaxingly. " Sigurd is hungry! Britta, sweet little Britta,—come and talk to me and sing! Good-bye, fat man!" he added suddenly, turning round once more on Dyceworthy. " You will never overtake the big ship that has gone away with Thelma over the water. Thelma will come back,—yes! . . . . but one day she will go never to come back." He dropped his voice to a mysterious whisper. " Last night I saw a little spirit come out of a rose,—he carried a tiny golden hammer and nail, and a ball of cord like a rolled-up sunbeam. He flew away so quickly I could not follow him; but I know where he went! He fastened the nail in the heart of Thelma, deeply, so that the little drops of blood flowed,—but she felt no pain; and then he tied the golden cord to the nail and left her, carrying the other end of the string with him—to whom? Some other heart must be pierced! Whose heart?" Sigurd looked infinitely cunning as well as melancholy, and sighed deeply.

The Reverend Mr. Dyceworthy was impatient and disgusted.

" It is a pity," he said with an air of solemn patience, " that this hapless creature, accursèd of God and man, is not placed in some proper abode suitable to the treatment of his affliction. You, Britta, as the favored servant of a —a—well, let us say, of a peculiar mistress, should persuade her to send this—this—person away, lest his vagaries become harmful."

Britta glanced very kindly at Sigurd, who still held her apron with the air of a trustful child.

" He's no more harmful than you are," she said promptly, in answer to the minister's remark. " He's a good fellow

and if he talks strangely he can make himself useful,—
which is more than can be said of certain people. He can
saw and chop the wood, make hay, feed the cattle, pull a
strong oar, and sweep and keep the garden,—can't you,
Sigurd?" She laid her hand on Sigurd's shoulder, and he
nodded his head emphatically, as she enumerated his different talents. "And as for climbing,—he can guide you
anywhere over the hills, or up the streams to the big waterfalls—no one better. And if you mean by peculiar,—that
my mistress is different to other people, why, I know she
is, and am glad of it,—at any rate, she's a great deal too
kind-hearted to shut this poor boy up in a house for mad-
men! He'd die if he couldn't have the fresh air." She
paused, out of breath with her rapid utterance, and Mr.
Dyceworthy held up his hands in dignified astonishment.

"You talk too glibly, young woman," he said. "It is
necessary that I should instruct you without loss of time, as
to how you should be sparing of your words in the presence of your superiors and betters——"

Bang! The door was closed with a decision that sent a
sharp echo through the silent, heated air, and Mr. Dyceworthy was left to contemplate it at his leisure. Full of
wrath, he was about to knock peremptorily and insist that
it should be re-opened; but on second thoughts he decided
that it was beneath his dignity to argue with a servant,
much less with a declared lunatic like Sigurd,—so he made
the best of his way back to his boat, thinking gloomily of
the hard labor awaiting him in the long pull back to
Bosekop.

Other thoughts, too, tortured and harrassed his brain,
and as he again took the oars and plied them wearily
through the water, he was in an exceedingly unchristian
humor. Though a specious hypocrite, he was no fool. He
knew the ways of men and women, and he thoroughly realized the present position of affairs. He was quite aware
of Thelma Güldmar's exceptional beauty,—and he felt
pretty certain that no man could look upon her without
admiration. But up to this time, she had been, as it were,
secluded from all eyes,—a few haymakers and fishermen
were the only persons of the male sex who had ever been
within the precincts of Olaf Güldmar's dwelling, with the
exception of himself, Dyceworthy,—who, being armed with
a letter of introduction from the actual minister of Bosekop, whose place, he, for the present, filled, had intruded his

company frequently and persistently on the *bonde* and his daughter, though he knew himself to be entirely unwelcome. He had gathered together as much as he could, all the scraps of information concerning them; how Olaf Güldmar was credited with having made away with his wife by foul means; how nobody even knew where his wife had come from; how Thelma had been mysteriously educated, and had learned strange things concerning foreign lands, which no one else in the place understood anything about; how she was reputed to be a witch, and was believed to have cast her spells on the unhappy Sigurd, to the destruction of his reason,—and how nobody could tell where Sigurd himself had come from.

All this Mr. Dyceworthy had heard with much interest, and as the sensual part of his nature was always more or less predominant, he had resolved in his own mind that here was a field of action suitable to his abilities. To tame and break the evil spirit in the reputed witch; to convert her to the holy and edifying Lutheran faith; to save her soul for the Lord, and take her beautiful body for himself; these were Mr. Dyceworthy's laudable ambitions. There was no rival to oppose him, and he had plenty of time to mature his plans. So he had thought. He had not bargained for the appearance of Sir Philip Bruce-Errington on the scene, —a man, young, handsome, and well-bred, with vast wealth to back up his pretensions, should he make any.

"How did he find her out?" thought the Reverend Charles, as he dolefully pulled his craft along. "And that brutal pagan Güldmar, too, who pretends he cannot endure strangers!"

And as he meditated, a flush of righteous indignation crimsoned his flabby features.

"Let her take care," he half muttered, with a smile that was not pleasant; "let her take care! There are more ways than one to bring down her pride! Sir Philip Errington must be too rich and popular in his own country to think of wishing to marry a girl who is only a farmer's daughter after all. He may trifle with her; yes! . . . and he will help me by so doing. The more mud on her name, the better for me; the more disgrace, the more need of rescue, and the more grateful she will have to be. Just a word to Ulrika,—and the scandal will spread. Patience, patience!"

And somewhat cheered by his own reflections, though

still wearing an air of offended dignity, he rowed on, glancing up every now and then to see if the *Eulalie* had returned, but her place was still empty.

Meanwhile, as he thought and planned, other thoughts and plans were being discussed at a meeting which was held in a little ruined stone hut, situated behind some trees on a dreary hill just outside Bosekop. It was a miserable place, barren of foliage,—the ground was dry and yellow, and the hut itself looked as if it had been struck by lightning. The friends, whose taste had led them to select this dilapidated dwelling as a place of conference, were two in number, both women,—one of them no other than the minister's servant, the drear-faced Ulrika. She was crouched on the earth-floor in an attitude of utter abasement, at the feet of her companion,—an aged dame of tall and imposing appearance, who, standing erect, looked down upon her with an air of mingled contempt and malevolence. The hut was rather dark, for the roof was not sufficiently destroyed to have the advantage of being open to the sky. The sunlight fell through holes of different shapes and sizes,—one specially bright patch of radiance illumining the stately form, and strongly marked, though withered features of the elder woman, whose eyes, deeply sunken in her head, glittered with a hawk-like and evil lustre, as they rested on the prostrate figure before her. When she spoke, her accents were harsh and commanding.

" How long ? " she said, " how long must I wait ? How long must I watch the work of Satan in the land ? The fields are barren and will not bring forth; the curse of bitter poverty is upon us all : and only he, the pagan Güldmar, prospers and gathers in harvest, while all around him starve ! Do I not know the devil's work when I see it,—I, the chosen servant of the Lord ? " And she struck a tall staff she held violently into the ground to emphasize her words. " Am I not left deserted in my age ? The child Britta,—sole daughter of my sole daughter,—is she not stolen, and kept from me ? Has not her heart been utterly turned away from mine ? All through that vile witch,—accurséd of God and man ! She it is who casts the blight on our land ; she it is who makes the hands and hearts of our men heavy and careless, so that even luck has left the fishing ; and yet you hesitate,—you delay, you will not fulfill your promise ! I tell you, there are those in Bosekop who, at my bidding, would cast her naked into the Fjord, and leave her there, to sink or swim according to her nature!"

"I know," murmured Ulrika humbly, raising herself slightly from her kneeling posture; "I know it well! . . . . but, good Lovisa, be patient! I work for the best! Mr. Dyceworth will do more for us than we can do for ourselves; he is wise and cautious——"

Lovisa interrupted her with a fierce gesture. "Fool!" she cried. "What need of caution? A witch is a witch, burn her, drown her! There is no other remedy! But two days since, the child of my neighbor Engla passed her on the Fjord; and now the boy has sickened of some strange disease, and 'tis said he will die. Again, the drove of cattle owned by Hildmar Bjorn were herded home when she passed by. Now they are seized by the murrain plague! Tell your good saint Dyceworthy these things; if he can find no cure, *I* can,—and *will!*"

Ulrika shuddered slightly as she rose from the ground and stood erect, drawing her shawl closely about her.

"You hate her so much, Lovisa?" she asked, almost timidly.

Lovisa's face darkened, and her yellow, claw-like hand closed round her strong staff in a cruel and threatening manner.

"Hate her!" she muttered, 'I have hated her ever since she was born! I hated her mother before her! A nest of devils, every one of them; and the curse will always be upon us while they dwell here."

She paused and looked at Ulrika steadily.

"Remember!" she said, with an evil leer on her lips, "I hold a secret of yours that is worth the keeping! I give you two weeks more; within that time you must act! Destroy the witch,—bring back to me my grandchild Britta, or else—it will be *my* turn!"

And she laughed silently. Ulrika's face grew paler, and the hand that grasped the folds of her shawl trembled violently. She made an effort, however, to appear composed, as she answered—

"I have sworn to obey you, Lovisa,—and I will. But tell me one thing—how do you know that Thelma Güldmar is indeed a witch?"

"How do I know?" almost yelled Lovisa. "Have I lived all these years for nothing? Look at her! Am *I* like her? Are *you* like her? Are any of the honest

women of the neighborhood like her? Meet her on the
hills with knives and pins,—prick her, and see if the blood
will flow! I swear it will not—not one drop! Her skin is
too white; there is no blood in those veins—only fire!
Look at the pink in her cheeks,—the transparency of her
flesh,—the glittering light in her eyes, the gold of her hair,
it is all devil's work, it is not human, it is not natural! I
have watched her,—I used to watch her mother, and curse
her every time I saw her—ay! curse her till I was breathless with cursing——"

She stopped abruptly. Ulrika gazed at her with as much
wonder as her plain, heavy face was capable of expressing.
Lovisa saw the look and smiled darkly.

"One would think *you* had never known what love is!"
she said, with a sort of grim satire in her tone. "Yet even
your dull soul was on fire once! But I—when I was young,
I had beauty such as you never had, and I loved—Olaf
Güldmar."

Ulrika uttered an exclamation of astonishment. "You!
and yet you hate him now?"

Lovisa raised her hand with an imperious gesture.

"I have grown hate like a flower in my breast," she said,
with a sort of stern impressiveness. "I have fostered it
year after year, and now,—it has grown too strong for me!
When Olaf Güldmar was young he told me I was fair;
once he kissed my cheek at parting! For those words,—
for that kiss,—I loved him then—for the same things I hate
him now! When I knew he had married, I cursed him;
on the day of my own marriage with a man I despised, I
cursed him! I have followed him and all his surroundings
with more curses than there are hours in the day! I have
had some little revenge—yes!"—and she laughed grimly
—"but I want more! For Britta has been caught by his
daughter's evil spell. Britta is mine, and I must have her
back. Understand me well!—do what you have to do without delay! Surely it is an easy thing to ruin a woman!"

Ulrika stood as though absorbed in meditation, and said
nothing for some moments. At last she murmured as
though to herself—

"Mr. Dyceworthy could do much—if——"

"Ask him, then," said Lovisa imperatively. "Tell him
the village is in fear of her. Tell him that if he will do
nothing *we* will. And if all fails, come to me again; and
remember! . . . I shall not only act,—I shall *speak!*"

And emphasizing the last word as a sort of threat, she turned and strode out of the hut.

Ulrika followed more slowly, taking a different direction to that in which her late companion was seen rapidly disappearing. On returning to the minister's dwelling, she found that Mr. Dyceworthy had not yet come back from his boating excursion. She gave no explanation of her absence to her two fellow-servants, but went straight up to her own room —a bare attic in the roof—where she deliberately took off her dress and bared her shoulders and breast. Then she knelt down on the rough boards, and clasping her hands, began to writhe and wrestle as though she were seized with a sudden convulsion. She groaned and tortured the tears from her eyes; she pinched her own flesh till it was black and blue, and scratched it with her nails till it bled,—and she prayed inaudibly, but with evident desperation. Sometimes her gestures were frantic, sometimes appealing; but she made no noise that was loud enough to attract attention from any of the dwellers in the house. Her stolid features were contorted with anguish,—and had she been an erring nun of the creed she held in such bitter abhorrence, who, for some untold crime, endured a self-imposed penance, she could not have punished her own flesh much more severely.

She remained some quarter of an hour or twenty minutes thus; then rising from her knees, she wiped the tears from her eyes and re-clothed herself,—and with her usual calm, immovable aspect—though smarting from the injuries she had inflicted on herself—she descended to the kitchen, there to prepare Mr. Dyceworthy's tea with all the punctilious care and nicety befitting the meal of so good a man and so perfect a saint.

CHAPTER X.

"She believed that by dealing nobly with all, all would show themselves noble; so that whatsoever she did became her."

HAFIZ.

As the afternoon lengthened, and the sun lowered his glittering shield towards that part of the horizon where he rested a brief while without setting, the *Eulalie*,—her white sails spread to the cool, refreshing breeze,—swept gracefully and swiftly back to her old place on the Fjord, and her anchor dropped with musical clank and splash, just as Mr. Dyceworthy entered his house, fatigued, perspiring, and ill-tempered at the non-success of his day. All on board the yacht were at dinner—a dinner of the most tasteful and elegant description, such as Sir Philip Errington well knew how to order and superintend, and Thelma, leaning against the violet velvet cushions that were piled behind her for her greater ease, looked,—as she indeed was,—the veritable queen of the feast. Macfarlane and Duprèz had been rendered astonished and bashful by her excessive beauty. From the moment she came on board with her father, clad in her simple white gown, with a deep crimson hood drawn over her fair hair, and tied under her rounded chin, she had taken them all captive—they were her abject slaves in heart, though they put on very creditable airs of manly independence and nonchalance. Each man in his different way strove to amuse or interest her, except, strange to say, Errington himself, who, though deeply courteous to her, kept somewhat in the background and appeared more anxious to render himself agreeable to old Olaf Güldmar, than to win the good graces of his lovely daughter. The girl was delighted with everything on board the yacht,—she admired its elegance and luxury with child-like enthusiasm; she gloried in the speed with which its glittering prow cleaved the waters; she clapped her hands at the hiss of the white foam as it split into a creaming pathway for the rushing vessel; and she was so unaffected and graceful in all her actions and attitudes, that the slow blood of the cautious Macfarlane began to warm up by degrees to a most unwonted heat of admiration. When she had first arrived, Errington, in receiving her, had seriously apologized for not having some lady to meet her, but she seemed not to understand his meaning. Her naïve smile and frankly uplifted eyes put all his suddenly conceived notions of social stiffness to flight.

"Why should a lady come?" she asked sweetly. "It is not necessary? . . . ."

"Of course it isn't!" said Lorimer promptly and delightedly. "I am sure we shall be able to amuse you, Miss Güldmar."

"Oh,—for that!" she replied, with a little shrug that had something French about it, "I amuse myself always! I am amused now,—you must not trouble yourselves!"

As she was introduced to Duprèz and Macfarlane, she

gave them each a quaint, sweeping curtsy, which had the effect of making them feel the most ungainly lumbersome fellows on the face of the earth. Macfarlane grew secretly enraged at the length of his legs,—while Pierre Duprèz, though his bow was entirely Parisian, decided in his own mind that it was jerky, and not good style. She was perfectly unembarrassed with all the young men; she laughed at their jokes, and turned her glorious eyes full on them with the unabashed sweetness of innocence; she listened to the accounts they gave her of their fishing and climbing excursions with the most eager interest,—and in her turn, she told them of fresh nooks and streams and waterfalls, of which they had never even heard the names. Not only were they enchanted with her, but they were thoroughly delighted with her father, Olaf Güldmar. The sturdy old pagan was in the best of humors,—and seemed determined to be pleased with everything,—he told good stories,—and laughed that rollicking, jovial laugh of his with such unforced heartiness that it was impossible to be dull in his company,—and not one of Errington's companions gave a thought to the reports concerning him and his daughter, which had been so gratuitously related by Mr. Dyceworthy.

They had had a glorious day's sail, piloted by Valdemar Svensen, whose astonishment at seeing the Güldmars on board the *Eulalie* was depicted in his face, but who prudently forebore from making any remarks thereon. The *bonde* hailed him good-humoredly as an old acquaintance, —much in the tone of a master addressing a servant,—and Thelma smiled kindly at him,—but the boundary line between superior and inferior was in this case very strongly marked, and neither side showed any intention of overstepping it. In the course of the day, Duprèz had accidentally lapsed into French, whereupon to his suprise Thelma had answered him in the same tongue,—though with a different and much softer pronunciation. Her " *bien zoli!* " had the mellifluous sweetness of the Provençal dialect, and on his eagerly questioning her, he learned that she had received her education in a large convent at Arles, where she had learned French from the nuns. Her father overheard her talking of her school-days, and he added—

" Yes, I sent my girl away for her education, though I know the teaching is good in Christiania. Yet it did not seem good enough for her. Besides, your modern ' higher education ' is not the thing for a woman,—it is too heavy and commonplace. Thelma knows nothing about mathematics or algebra. She can sing and read and write,—and, what is more, she can spin and sew; but even these things were not the first consideration with me. I wanted her disposition trained, and her bodily health attended to. I said to those good women at Arles—' Look here,—here's a child for you! I don't care how much or how little she knows about accomplishments. I want her to be sound and sweet from head to heel—a clean mind in a wholesome body. Teach her self-respect, and make her prefer death to a lie. Show her the curse of a shrewish temper, and the blessing of cheerfulness. That will satisfy me!' I dare say, now I come to think of it, those nuns thought me an odd customer; but, at any rate, they seemed to understand me. Thelma was very happy with them, and considering all things"—the old man's eyes twinkled fondly—" she hasn't turned out so badly!"

They laughed,—and Thelma blushed as Errington's dreamy eyes rested on her with a look, which, though he was unconscious of it, spoke passionate admiration. The day passed too quickly with them all,—and now, as they sat at dinner in the richly ornamented saloon, there was not one among them who could contemplate without reluctance the approaching break-up of so pleasant a party. Dessert was served, and as Thelma toyed with the fruit on her plate and sipped her glass of champagne, her face grew serious and absorbed,—even sad,—and she scarcely seemed to hear the merry chatter of tongues around her, till Errington's voice asking a question of her father roused her into swift attention.

" Do you know any one of the name of Sigurd ?" he was saying, " a poor fellow whose wits are in heaven let us hope,—for they certainly are not on earth."

Olaf Güldmar's fine face softened with pity, and he replied—

" Sigurd ? Have you met him then ? Ah, poor boy, his is a sad fate! He has wit enough, but it works wrongly; the brain is there, but 'tis twisted. Yes, we know Sigurd well enough—his home is with us in default of a better. Ay, ay! we snatched him from death—perhaps unwisely,— yet he has a good heart, and finds pleasure in his life."

" He is a kind of poet in his own way," went on Errington, watching Thelma as she listened intently to their conversation. " Do you know he actually visited me on board here last night and begged me to go away from the Alten-fjord altogether? He seemed afraid of me, as if he thought I meant to do him some harm."

"How strange!" murmured Thelma. "Sigurd never speaks to visitors,—he is too shy. I cannot understand his motive!"

"Ah, my dear!" sighed her father. "Has he any motive at all? . . . and does he ever understand himself? His fancies change with every shifting breeze! I will tell you," he continued, addressing himself to Errington, "how he came to be, as it were, a bit of our home. Just before Thelma was born, I was walking with my wife one day on the shore, when we both caught sight of something bumping against our little pier, like a large box or basket. I managed to get hold of it with a boat-hook and drag it in; it was a sort of creel such as is used to pack fish in, and in it was the naked body of a half-drowned child. It was an ugly little creature—a newly born infant deformity—and on its chest there was a horrible scar in the shape of a cross, as though it had been gashed deeply with a pen-knife. I thought it was dead, and was for throwing it back into the Fjord, but my wife,—a tender-hearted angel—took the poor wretched little wet body in her arms, and found that it breathed. She warmed it, dried it, and wrapped it in her shawl,—and after awhile the tiny monster opened its eyes and stared at her. Well! . . . somehow, neither of us could forget the look it gave us,—such a solemn, warning, pitiful, appealing sort of expression! There was no resisting it,—so we took the foundling and did the best we could for him. We gave him the name of Sigurd,—and when Thelma was born, the two babies used to play together all day, and we never noticed anything wrong with the boy, except his natural deformity, till he was about ten or twelve years old. Then we saw to our sorrow that the gods had chosen to play havoc with his wits. However, we humored him tenderly, and he was always manageable. Poor Sigurd! He adored my wife; I have known him listen for hours to catch the sound of her footstep; he would actually deck the threshold with flowers in the morning that she might tread on them as she passed by." The old *bonde* sighed and rubbed his hand across his eyes with a gesture half of pain, half of impatience—" And now he is Thelma's slave,—a regular servant to her. She can manage him best of us all,—he is as docile as a lamb, and will do anything she tells him."

" I am not surprised at that," said the gallant Duprèz; "there is reason in such obedience ! "

Thelma looked at him inquiringly, ignoring the implied compliment.

" You think so ? " she said simply " I am glad ! I al-ways hope that he will one day be well in mind,—and every little sign of reason in him is pleasant to me."

Duprèz was silent. It was evidently no use making even an attempt at flattering this strange girl; surely she must be dense not to understand compliments that most other women compel from the lips of men as their right ? He was confused—his Paris breeding was no use to him—in fact he had been at a loss all day, and his conversation had, even to himself, seemed particularly shallow and frothy. This Mademoiselle Güldmar, as he called her, was by no means stupid—she was not a mere moving statue of lovely flesh and perfect color whose outward beauty was her only recommendation,—she was, on the contrary, of a most su-perior intelligence,—she had read much and thought more, —and the dignified elegance of her manner, and bearing would have done honor to a queen. After all, thought Du-prèz musingly, the social creeds of Paris *might* be wrong— it was just possible ! There might be women who were womanly,—there might be beautiful girls who were neither vain nor frivolous,—there might even be creatures of the feminine sex, besides whom a trained Parisian coquette would seem nothing more than a painted fiend of the neuter gender. These were new and startling considerations to the feather-light mind of the Frenchman,—and unconsciously his fancy began to busy itself with the old romantic histor-ies of the ancient French chivalry, when faith, and love, and loyalty, kept white the lilies of France, and the stately cour-tesy and unflinching pride of the *ancien régime* made its name honored throughout the world. An odd direction in-deed for Pierre Duprèz's reflection to wander in—he, who never reflected on either past or future, but was content to fritter away the present as pleasantly as might be—and the only reason to which his unusually serious reverie could be attributed was the presence of Thelma. She certainly had a strange influence on them all, though she herself was not aware of it,—and not only Errington, but each one of his companions had been deeply considering during the day,

that notwithstanding the unheroic tendency of modern living, life itself might be turned to good and even noble account, if only an effort were made in the right direction.

Such was the compelling effect of Thelma's stainless mind
reflected in her pure face, on the different dispositions of all
the young men ; and she, perfectly unconscious of it, smiled
at them, and conversed gaily,—little knowing as she talked,
in her own sweet and unaffected way, that the most profound resolutions were being formed, and the most noble
and unselfish deeds, were being planned in the souls of her
listeners,—all forsooth ! because one fair, innocent woman
had, in the clear, grave glances of her wondrous sea-blue
eyes, suddenly made them aware of their own utter unworthiness. Macfarlane, meditatively watching the girl
from under his pale eyelashes, thought of Mr. Dyceworthy's
matrimonial pretensions, with a humorous smile hovering on
his thin lips.

"Ma certes ! the fellow has an unco' gude opeenion o'
himsel'," he mused. "He might as well offer his hand in
marriage to the Queen while he's aboot it,—he wad hae just
as muckle chance o' acceptance."

Meanwhile, Errington, having learned all he wished to
know concerning Sigurd, was skillfully drawing out old
Olaf Güldmar, and getting him to give his ideas on things
in general, a task in which Lorimer joined.

"So you don't think we're making any progress nowadays ?" inquired the latter with an appearance of interest,
and a lazy amusement in his blue eyes as he put the question.

"Progress !" exclaimed Güldmar. "Not a bit of it ! It
is all a going backward ; it may not seem apparent, but it
is so. England, for instance, is losing the great place she
once held in the world's history,—and these things always
happen to all nations when money becomes more precious
to the souls of the people than honesty and honor. I take
the universal wide-spread greed of gain to be one of the
worst signs of the times,—the forewarning of some great
upheaval and disaster, the effects of which no human mind
can calculate. I am told that America is destined to be the
dominating power of the future,—but I doubt it ! Its politics are too corrupt,—its people live too fast, and burn their
candle at both ends, which is unnatural and most unwholesome ; moreover, it is almost destitute of Art in its highest
forms,—and is not its confessed watchward ' the almighty

Dollar ?' And such a country as that expects to arrogate to itself the absolute sway of the world? I tell you, *no*— ten thousand times *no!* It is destitute of nearly every-thing that has made nations great and all-powerful in his-toric annals,—and my belief is that what has been, will be again,—and that what has never been, will never be."

"You mean by that, I suppose, that there is no possi-bility of doing anything new,—no way of branching out in some better and untried direction?" asked Errington.

Olaf Güldmar shook his head emphatically. "You can't do it," he said decisively. "Everything in every way has been begun and completed and then forgotten over and over, in this world,—to be begun and completed and for-gotten again, and so on to the end of the chapter. No one nation is better than another in this respect,—there is,—there can be nothing new. Norway, for example, has had its day; whether it will ever have another I know not,—at any rate, I shall not live to see it. And yet, what a past! ——" He broke off and his eyes grew meditative.

Lorimer looked at him. "You would have been a Viking, Mr. Güldmar, had you lived in the old days," he said with a smile.

"I should, indeed!" returned the old man, with an un-consciously haughty gesture of his head; "and no better fate could have befallen me! To sail the seas in hot pursuit of one's enemies, or in search of further conquest,—to feel the very wind and sun beating up the blood in one's veins, —to live the life of a *man*—a true man! . . in all the pride and worth of strength, and invincible vigor!—how much better than the puling, feeble, sickly existence, led by the majority of men to-day! I dwell apart from them as much as I can,—I steep my mind and body in the joys of Nature, and the free fresh air,—but often I feel that the old days of the heroes must have been best,—when Gorm the Bold and the fierce Siegfried seized Paris, and stabled their horses in the chapel where Charlemagne lay buried!"

Pierre Duprèz looked up with a faint smile. "Ah, *par-don!* But that was surely a very long time ago!"

"True!" said Güldmar quietly. "And no doubt you will not believe the story at this distance of years. But the day is coming when people will look back on the little chronicle of your Empire,—your commune,—your republic, all your little affairs, and will say, ' Surely these things are myths ; they occurred,—if they occurred at all,—a very long time ago ! ' "

" Monsieur is a philosopher ! " said Duprèz, with a good-humored gesture ; " I would not presume to contradict him."

" You see, my lad," went on Güldmar more gently, " there is much in our ancient Norwegian history that is forgotten or ignored by students of to-day. The travellers that come hither come to see the glories of our glaciers and fjords,—but they think little or nothing of the vanished tribe of heroes who once possessed the land. If you know your Greek history, you must have heard of Pythias, who lived three hundred and fifty-six years before Christ, and who was taken captive by a band of Norseman and carried away to see ' the place where the sun slept in winter.' Most probably he came to this very spot, the Altenfjord,— at any rate the ancient Greeks had good words to say for the ' Outside Northwinders,' as they called us Norwegians, for they reported us to be ' persons living in peace with their gods and themselves.' Again, one of the oldest tribes in the world came among us in times past,—the Phœnicians,— there are traces among us still of their customs and manners. Yes ! we have a great deal to look back upon with pride as well as sorrow,—and much as I hear of the wonders of the New World, the marvels and the go-ahead speed of American manners and civilization,—I would rather be a Norseman than a Yankee." And he laughed.

" There's more dignity in the name, at any rate," said Lorimer. " But I say, Mr. Güldmar, you are ' up ' in history much better than I am. The annals of my country were grounded into my tender soul early in life, but I have a very hazy recollection of them. I know Henry VIII. got rid of his wives expeditiously and conveniently,—and I dis-tinctly remember that Queen Elizabeth wore the first pair of silk stockings, and danced a kind of jig in them with the Earl of Leicester ; these things interested me at the time,— and they now seen firmly impressed on my memory to the exclusion of everything else that might possibly be more important."

Old Güldmar smiled, but Thelma laughed outright and her eyes danced mirthfully.

" Ah, I do know you now ! " she said, nodding her fair head at him wisely. " You are not anything that is to be believed ! So I shall well understand you,—that is, you are a very great scholar,—but that it pleases you to pretend you are a dunce!"

Lorimer's face brightened into a very gentle and winning softness as he looked at her.

"I assure you, Miss Güldmar, I am not pretending in the least. I'm no scholar. Errington is, if you like! If it hadn't been for him, I should never have learned anything at Oxford at all. He used to leap over a difficulty while I was looking at it. Phil, don't interrupt me,—you know you did! I tell you he's up to everything: Greek, Latin, and all the rest of it,—and, what's more, he writes well,—I believe,—though he'll never forgive me for mentioning it,—that he has even published some poems."

"Be quiet, George!" exclaimed Errington, with a vexed laugh. "You are boring Miss Güldmar to death!"

"What is *boring*?" asked Thelma gently, and then turning her eyes full on the young Baronet, she added, "I like to hear that you will pass your days sometimes without shooting the birds and killing the fish; it can hurt nobody for you to write." And she smiled that dreamy pensive smile of hers that was so infinitely bewitching. "You must show me all your sweet poems!"

Errington colored hotly. "They are all nonsense, Miss Güldmar," he said quickly. "There's nothing 'sweet' about them, I tell you frankly! All rubbish, every line of them!"

"Then you should not write them," said Thelma quietly. "It is only a pity and a disappointment."

"I wish every one were of your opinion," laughed Lorimer, "it would spare us a lot of indifferent verse."

"Ah! you have the chief Skald of all the world in your land!" cried Güldmar, bringing his fist down with a jovial thump on the table. "He can teach you all that you need to know."

"*Skald*?" queried Lorimer dubiously. "Oh, you mean bard. I suppose you allude to Shakespeare?"

"I do," said the old *bonde* enthusiastically, "he is the only glory of your country I envy! I would give anything to prove him a Norwegian. By Valhalla! had he but been one of the Bards of Odin, the world might have followed the grand old creed still! If anything could ever persuade me to be a Christian, it would be the fact that Shakespeare was one. If England's name is rendered imperishable, it will be through the fame of Shakespeare alone,—just as we have a kind of tenderness for degraded modern Greece, because of Homer. Ay, ay! countries and nations are worthless enough ; it is only the great names of heroes that endure, to teach the lesson that is never learned sufficiently,—namely, that man and man alone is fitted to grasp the prize of immortality."

" Ye believe in immortality ? " inquired Macfarlane seriously.

Güldmar's keen eyes lighted on him with fiery impetuousness.

" Believe in it? I possess it! How can it be taken from me? As well make a bird without wings, a tree without sap, an ocean without depths, as expect to find a man without an immortal soul! What a question to ask? Do *you* not possess heaven's gift? and why should not I ? "

" No offense," said Macfarlane, secretly astonished at the old *bonde's* fervor,—for had not he, though himself intending to become a devout minister of the Word,—had not he now and then felt a creeping doubt as to whether, after all, there was any truth in the doctrine of another life than this one. " I only thocht ye might have perhaps questioned the probabeelity o't, in your own mind ? "

" I never question Divine authority," replied Olaf Güldmar, " I pity those that do ! "

" And this Divine authority ? " said Durprèz suddenly with a delicate sarcastic smile, " how and where do you perceive it ? "

" In the very Law that compels me to exist, young sir," said Güldmar,—" in the mysteries of the universe about me,—the glory of the heavens,—the wonders of the sea! You have perhaps lived in cities all your life, and your mind is cramped a bit. No wonder, . . . you can hardly see the stars above the roofs of a wilderness of houses. Cities are men's work,—the gods have never had a finger in the building of them. Dwelling in them, I suppose you cannot help forgetting Divine authority altogether ; but here,—here among the mountains, you would soon remember it ! You should live here,—it would make a man of you ! "

" And you do not consider me a man ? " inquired Duprèz with imperturbable good-humor.

Güldmar laughed. " Well, not quite ! " he admitted candidly, " there's not enough muscle about you. I confess I like to see strong fellows—fellows fit to rule the planet on

which they are placed. That's my whim!—but you're a
neat little chap enough, and I dare say you can hold your
own!"

And his eyes twinkled good-temperedly as he filled himself another glass of his host's fine Burgundy, and drank it
off, while Durprèz, with a half-plaintive, half-comical shrug
of resignation to Güldmar's verdict on his personal appearance, asked Thelma if she would favor them with a song.
She rose from her seat instantly, without any affected
hesitation, and went to the piano. She had a delicate touch,
and accompanied herself with great taste,—but her voice,
full, penetrating, rich and true,—was one of the purest and
most sympathetic ever possessed by woman, and its freshness was unspoilt by any of the varied "systems" of torture invented by singing-masters for the ingenious destruction of the delicate vocal organ. She sang a Norwegian
love-song in the original tongue, which might be roughly
translated as follows :—

> " Lovest thou me for my beauty's sake?
>   Love me not then !
>   Love the victorious, glittering Sun,
>   The fadeless, deathless, marvellous One!
>
> "Lovest thou me for my youth's sake ?
>   Love me not then !
>   Love the triumphant, unperishing Spring,
>   Who every year new charms doth bring !
>
> " Lovest thou me for treasure's sake ?
>   Oh, love me not then !
>   Love the deep, the wonderful Sea,
>   Its jewels are worthier love than me !
>
> "Lovest thou me for Love's own sake ?
>   Ah sweet, then love me !
>   More than the Sun and the Spring and the Sea,
>   Is the faithful heart I will yield to thee ! "

A silence greeted the close of her song. Though the
young men were ignorant of the meaning of the words still
old Güldmar translated them for their benefit, they could
feel the intensity of the passion vibrating through her ringing tones,—and Errington sighed involuntarily. She heard
the sigh, and turned round on the music-stool laughing.

" Are you so tired, or sad, or what is it ? " she asked
merrily. " It is too melancholy a tune ? And I was foolish to sing it,—because you cannot understand the meaning

of it. It is all about love,—and of course love is always sorrowful."

" Always ? " asked Lorimer, with a half-smile.

" I do not know," she said frankly, with a pretty deprecatory gesture of her hands,—" but all books say so! It must be a great pain, and also a great happiness. Let me think what I can sing to you now,—but perhaps you will yourself sing ? "

" Not one of us have a voice, Miss Güldmar," said Errington. " I used to think I had, but Lorimer discouraged my efforts."

" Men shouldn't sing," observed Lorimer ; " if they only knew how awfully ridiculous they look, standing up in dress-coats and white ties, pouring forth inane love-ditties that nobody wants to hear, they wouldn't do it. Only a a woman looks pretty while singing."

" Ah, that is very nice ! " said Thelma, with a demure smile. " Then I am agreeable to you when I sing ? "

Agreeable ? This was far too tame a word—they all rose from the table and came towards her, with many assurances of their delight and admiration ; but she put all their compliments aside with a little gesture that was both incredulous and peremptory.

" You must not say so many things in praise of me," she said, with a swift upward glance at Errington, where he leaned on the piano regarding her. " It is nothing to be able to sing. It is only like the birds, but we cannot understand the words they say, just as you cannot understand Norwegian. Listen,—here is a little ballad you will all know," and she played a soft prelude, while her voice, subdued to a plaintive murmur, rippled out in the dainty verses of Sainte-Beuve—

> " Sur ma lyre, l'autre fois
> Dans un bois,
> Ma main préludait à peine ;
> Une colombe descend
> En passant,
> Blanche sur le luth d'ébène.

> " Mais au lieu d'accords touchants,
> De doux chants,
> La colombe gemissante
> Me demande par pitié
> Sa moitié
> Sa moitié loin d'elle absente ! "

She sang this seriously and sweetly till she came to the last three lines, when, catching Errington's earnest gaze, her voice quivered and her cheeks flushed. She rose from the piano as soon as she had finished, and said to the *bonde*, who had been watching her with proud and gratified looks—

"It is growing late, father. We must say good-bye to our friends and return home."

"Not yet!" eagerly implored Sir Philip. "Come up on deck,—we will have coffee there, and afterwards you shall leave us when you will."

Güldmar acquiesced in this arrangement, before his daughter had time to raise any objection, and they all went on deck, where a comfortable lounging chair was placed for Thelma, facing the most gorgeous portion of the glowing sky, which on this evening was like a moving mass of molten gold, split asunder here and there by angry ragged-looking rifts of crimson. The young men grouped themselves together at the prow of the vessel in order to smoke their cigars without annoyance to Thelma. Old Güldmar did not smoke, but he talked,—and Errington after seeing them all fairly absorbed in an argument on the best methods of spearing salmon, moved quietly away to where the girl was sitting, her great pensive eyes fixed on the burning splendors of the heavens.

"Are you warm enough there?" he asked, and there was an unconscious tenderness in his voice as he asked the question, "or shall I fetch you a wrap?"

She smiled. "I have my hood," she said. "It is the warmest thing I ever wear, except, of course, in winter."

Philip looked at the hood as she drew it more closely over her head, and thought that surely no more becoming article of apparel ever was designed for woman's wear. He had never seen anything like it either in color or texture, —it was of a peculiarly warm, rich crimson, like the heart of a red damask rose, and it suited the bright hair and tender, thoughtful eyes of its owner to perfection.

"Tell me," he said, drawing a little nearer and speaking in a lower tone, "have you forgiven me for my rudeness the first time I saw you?"

She looked a little troubled.

"Perhaps also I was rude," she said gently. "I did not know you. I thought—"

"You were quite right," he eagerly interrupted her. "It

was very impertinent of me to ask you for your name. I should have found it out for myself, as I *have* done."

And he smiled at her as he said the last words with marked emphasis. She raised her eyes wistfully.

"And you are glad?" she asked softly and with a sort of wonder in her accents.

"Glad to know your name? glad to know *you!* Of course! Can you ask such a question?"

"But why?" persisted Thelma. "It is not as if you were lonely,—you have friends already. We are nothing to you. Soon you will go away, and you will think of the Altenfjord as a dream,—and our names will be forgotten. That is natural!"

What a foolish rush of passion filled his heart as she spoke in those mellow, almost plaintive accents,—what wild words leaped to his lips and what an effort it cost him to keep them back. The heat and impetuosity of Romeo,—whom up to the present he had been inclined to consider a particularly stupid youth,—was now quite comprehensible to his mind, and he, the cool, self-possessed Englishman, was ready at that moment to outrival Juliet's lover, in his utmost excesses of amorous folly. In spite of his self-restraint, his voice quivered a little as he answered her—

"I shall never forget the Altenfjord or you, Miss Güldmar. Don't you know there are some things that cannot be forgotten? such as a sudden glimpse of fine scenery,—a beautiful song, or a pathetic poem?" She bent her head in assent. "And here there is so much to remember—the light of the midnight sun,—the glorious mountains, the loveliness of the whole land!"

"Is it better than other countries you have seen?" asked the girl with some interest.

"Much better!" returned Sir Philip fervently. "In fact, there is no place like it in my opinion." He paused at the sound of her pretty laughter.

"You are—what is it?—ecstatic!" she said mirthfully. "Tell me, have you been to the south of France and the Pyrenees?"

"Of course I have," he replied. "I have been all over the Continent,—travelled about it till I'm tired of it. Do you like the south of France better than Norway?"

"No,—not so very much better," she said dubiously. "And yet a little. It is so warm and bright there, and the people are gay. Here they are stern and sullen. My

father loves to sail the seas, and when I first went to school
at Arles, he took me a long and beautiful voyage. We went
from Christiansund to Holland, and saw all those pretty
Dutch cities with their canals and quaint bridges. Then
we went through the English Channel to Brest,—then by
the Bay of Biscay to Bayonne. Bayonne seemed to me
very lovely, but we left it soon, and travelled a long way by
land, seeing all sorts of wonderful things, till we came to
Arles. And though it is such a long route, and not one for
many persons to take, I have travelled to Arles and back
twice that way, so all there is familiar to me,—and in some
things I do think it better than Norway."

"What induced your father to send you so far away from
him?" asked Philip rather curiously.

The girl's eyes softened tenderly. "Ah, that is easy to
understand!" she said. "My mother came from Arles."

"She was French, then?" he exclaimed with some surprise.

"No," she answered gravely. "She was Norwegian, because her father and mother both were of this land. She
was what they call 'born sadly.' You must not ask me
any more about her, please!"

Errington apologized at once with some embarrassment,
and a deeper color than usual on his face. She looked up at
him quite frankly.

"It is possible I will tell you her history some day," she
said, "when we shall know each other better. I do like to
talk to you very much! I suppose there are many Englishmen like you?"

Philip laughed. "I don't think I am at all exceptional!
why do you ask?"

She shrugged her shoulders. "I have seen some of
them," she said slowly, "and they are stupid. They shoot,
shoot,—fish, fish, all day, and eat a great deal. . . ."

"My dear Miss Güldmar, I also do all these things!"
declared Errington amusedly. "These are only our surface
faults. Englishmen are the best fellows to be found anywhere. You mustn't judge them by their athletic sports,
or their vulgar appetites. You must appeal to their hearts
when you want to know them."

"Or to their pockets, and you will know them still better!" said Thelma almost mischievously, as she raised herself in her chair to take a cup of coffee from the tray that
was then being handed to her by the respectful steward.

' Ah, how good this is ! It reminds me of our coffee luncheon at Arles ! "

Errington watched her with a half-smile, but said no more, as the others now came up to claim their share of her company.

" I say ! " said Lorimer, lazily throwing himself full length on the deck and looking up at her, " come and see us spear a salmon to-morrow, Miss Güldmar. Your father is going to show us how to do it in the proper Norse style."

" That is for men," said Thelma loftily. " Women must know nothing about such things."

" By Jove ! " and Lorimer looked profoundly astonished. " Why, Miss Güldmar, women are going in for everything nowadays ! Hunting, shooting, bull-fighting, duelling, horse-whipping, lecturing,—heaven knows what ! They stop at nothing—salmon-spearing is a mere trifle in the list of modern feminine accomplishments."

Thelma smiled down upon him benignly. " You will always be the same," she said with a sort of indulgent air. " It is your delight to say things upside down ? But you shall not make me believe that women do all these dreadful things. Because, how is it possible ? The men would not allow them ! "

Errington laughed, and Lorimer appeared stupefied with surprise.

" The men—would—not—allow them ? " he repeated slowly. " Oh, Miss Güldmar, little do you realize the state of things at the present day ! The glamor of Viking memories clings about you still ! Don't you know the power of man has passed away, and that ladies do exactly as they like ? It is easier to control the thunderbolt than to prevent a woman having her own way."

" All that is nonsense ! " said Thelma decidedly. " Where there is a man to rule, he *must* rule, that is certain."

" Is that positively your opinion ? " and Lorimer looked more astonished than ever.

" It is everybody's opinion, of course ! " averred Thelma. " How foolish it would be if women did not obey men ! The world would be all confusion ! Ah, you see you cannot make me think your funny thoughts; it is no use ! " And she laughed and rose from her chair, adding with a gentle persuasive air, " Father dear, is it not time to say good-bye?"

" Truly I think it is!" returned Güldmar, giving himself a shake like an old lion, as he broke off a rather tedious conversation he had been having with MacFarlane. " We shall have Sigurd coming to look for us, and poor Britta will think we have left her too long alone. Thank you, my lad!" this to Sir Philip, who instantly gave orders for the boat to be lowered. " You have given us a day of thorough, wholesome enjoyment. I hope I shall be able to return it in some way. You must let me see as much of you as possible."

They shook hands cordially, and Errington proposed to escort them back as far as their own pier, but this offer Güldmar refused.

" Nonsense!" he exclaimed cheerily. " With four oarsmen to row us along, why should we take you away from your friends? I won't hear of such a thing! And now, regarding the great fall of Njedegorze; Mr. Macfarlane here says you have not visited it yet. Well the best guide you can have there is Sigurd. We'll make up a party and go when it is agreeable to you; it is a grand sight,—well worth seeing. To-morrow we shall meet again for the salmon-spearing,—I warrant I shall be able to make the time pass quickly for you! How long do you think of staying here?"

" As long as possible!" answered Errington absently, his eyes wandering to Thelma, who was just then shaking hands with his friends and bidding them farewell.

Güldmar laughed and clapped him on the shoulder. " That means till you are tired of the place," he said good-humoredly. " Well you shall not be dull if I can prevent it! Good-bye, and thanks for your hospitality."

" Ah, yes!" added Thelma gently, coming up at that moment and laying her soft hand in his. " I have been so happy all day, and it is all your kindness! I am very grateful!"

" It is I who have cause to be grateful," said Errington hurriedly, clasping her hand warmly, " for your company and that of your father. I trust we shall have many more pleasant days together."

" I hope so too!" she answered simply, and then, the boat being ready, they departed. Errington and Lorimer leaned on the deck-rails, waving their hats and watching them disappear over the gleaming water, till the very last glimpse of Thelma's crimson hood had vanished, and then they turned to rejoin their companions, who were strolling up and down smoking.

"*Belle comme un ange!*" said Duprèz briefly. "In short, I doubt if the angels are so good-looking!"

"The auld pagan's a fine scholar," added Macfarlane meditatively. "He corrected me in a bit o' Latin."

"Did he, indeed?" And Lorimer laughed indolently. "I suppose you think better of him now, Sandy?"

Sandy made no reply, and as Errington persisted in turning the conversation away from the merits or demerits of their recent guests, they soon entered on other topics. But that night, before retiring to rest, Lorimer laid a hand on his friend's shoulder, and said quietly, with a keen look—

"Well, old man, have you made up your mind? Have I seen the future Lady Bruce-Errington?"

Sir Philip smiled,—then, after a brief pause, answered steadily—

"Yes, George, you have! That is,—if I can win her!"

Lorimer laughed a little and sighed. "There's no doubt about that, Phil." And eyeing Errington's fine figure and noble features musingly, he repeated again thoughtfully—"No doubt about that, my boy!" Then after a pause he said, somewhat abruptly, "Time to turn in—good night!"

"Good night, old fellow!" And Errington wrung his hand warmly, and left him to repose.

But Lorimer had rather a bad night,—he tossed and tumbled a good deal, and had dreams,—unusual visitors with him,—and once or twice he muttered in his sleep,—"No doubt about it—not the least in the world—and if there were——"

But the conclusion of this sentence was inaudible.

CHAPTER XI.

"Tu vas faire un beau rêve,
  Et t'enivrer d'un plaisir dangereux.
Sur ton chemin l'étoile qui se lève
  Longtemps encore éblouira tes yeux!"

DE MUSSET.

A FORTNIGHT passed. The first excursion in the *Eulalie* had been followed by others of a similar kind, and Errington's acquaintance with the Güldmars was fast ripening

into a pleasant intimacy. It had grown customary for the
young men to spend that part of the day which, in spite of
persistent sunshine, they still called evening, in the comfortable, quaint parlor of the old farmhouse,—looking at the
view through the rose-wreathed windows,—listening to the
fantastic legends of Norway as told by Olaf Güldmar,—or
watching Thelma's picturesque figure, as she sat pensively
apart in her shadowed corner spinning. They had fratern-
ized with Sigurd too—that is, as far as he would permit
them—for the unhappy dwarf was uncertain of temper, and
if at one hour he were docile and yielding as a child, the
next he would be found excited and furious at some imaginary slight that he fancied had been inflicted upon him.
Sometimes, if good-humored, he would talk almost ration-
ally,—only allowing his fancy to play with poetical ideas
concerning the sea, the flowers, or the sunlight,—but he was
far more often sullen and silent. He would draw a low
chair to Thelma's side, and sit there with half-closed eyes
and compressed lips, and none could tell whether he
listened to the conversation around him, or was utterly indifferent to it. He had taken a notable fancy to Lorimer,
but he avoided Errington in the most marked and persistent
manner. The latter did his best to overcome this unreasonable dislike, but his efforts were useless,—and deciding in
his own mind that it was best to humor Sigurd's vagaries,
he soon let him alone, and devoted his attention more
entirely to Thelma.

   One evening, after supper at the farmhouse, Lorimer, who
for some time had been watching Philip and Thelma conversing together in low tones near the open window, rose
from his seat quietly, without disturbing the hilarity of the
bonde, who was in the middle of a rollicking sea-story, told
for Macfarlane's entertainment,—and slipped out into the
garden, where he strolled along rather absently till he found
himself in the little close thicket of pines,—the very same
spot where he and Philip had stood on the first day of their
visit thither. He threw himself down on the soft emerald
moss and lit a cigar, sighing rather drearily as he did so.

   " Upon my life," he mused, with a half-smile, " I am very
nearly being a hero,—a regular stage-martyr,—the noble
creature of the piece ! By Jove, I wish I were a soldier !
I'm certain I could stand the enemy's fire better than this !
Self-denial ? Well, no wonder the preachers make such a
fuss about it. It's a tough, uncomfortable duty. But am

I self-denying? Not a bit of it! Look here, George Lori-mer"—here he tapped himself very vigorously on his broad chest—"don't you imagine yourself to be either virtuous or magnanimous! If you were anything of a man at all you would never let your feelings get the better of you,— you would be sublimely indifferent, stoically calm,—and, as it is,—you know what a sneaking, hang-dog state of envy you were in just now when you came out of that room! Aren't you ashamed of yourself,—rascal?"

The inner self he thus addressed was most probably abashed by this adjuration, for his countenance cleared a little, as though he had received an apology from his own conscience. He puffed lazily at his cigar, and felt some-what soothed. Light steps below him attracted his atten-tion, and, looking down from the little knoll on which he lay, he saw Thelma and Philip pass. They were walking slowly along a little winding path that led to the orchard, which was situated at some little distance from the house. The girl's head was bent, and Philip was talking to her with evident eagerness. Lorimer looked after them earnestly, and his honest eyes were full of trouble.

"God bless them both!" he murmured half aloud. "There's no harm in saying that, anyhow! Dear old Phil! I wonder whether——"

What he would have said was uncertain, for at that mo-ment he was considerably startled by the sight of a meagre, pale face peering through the parted pine boughs,—a face in which two wild eyes shone with a blue-green glitter, like that of newly sharpened steel.

"Hullo, Sigurd!" said Lorimer good-naturedly, as he recognized his visitor. "What are you up to? Going to climb a tree?"

Sigurd pushed aside the branches cautiously and ap-proached. He sat down by Lorimer, and, taking his hand, kissed it deferentially.

"I followed you. I saw you go away to grieve alone. I came to grieve also!" he said with a patient gentleness.

Lorimer laughed languidly. "By Jove, Sigurd, you're too clever for your age! Think I came away to grieve, eh? Not so, my boy—came away to smoke! There's a come-down for you! I never grieve—don't know how to do it. What *is* grief?"

"To love!" answered Sigurd promptly. "To see a beautiful elf with golden wings come fluttering, fluttering gently down from the sky,—you open your arms to catch her—so! . . . and just as you think you have her, she leans only a little bit on one side, and falls, not into your heart—no!—into the heart of some one else! That is grief, because, when she has gone, no more elves come down from the sky,—for you, at any rate,—good things may come for others,—but for *you* the heavens are empty!"

Lorimer was silent, looking at the speaker curiously.

"How do you get all this nonsense into your head, eh?" he inquired kindly.

"I do not know," replied Sigurd with a sigh. "It comes! But, tell me,"—and he smiled wistfully—"it is true, dear friend—good friend—it is all true, is it not? For you the heavens are empty? You know it!"

Lorimer flushed hotly, and then grew strangely pale. After a pause, he said in his usual indolent way—

"Look here, Sigurd; you're romantic! I'm not. I know nothing about elves or empty heavens. I'm all right! Don't you bother yourself about me."

The dwarf studied his face attentively, and a smile of almost fiendish cunning suddenly illumined his thin features. He laid his weak-looking white hand on the young man's arm and said in a lower tone—

"I will tell you what to do. Kill him!"

The last two words were uttered with such intensity of meaning that Lorimer positively recoiled from the accents, and the terrible look which accompanied them.

"I say, Sigurd, this won't do," he remonstrated gravely. "You mustn't talk about killing, you know! It's not good for you. People don't kill each other nowadays so easily as you seem to think. It can't be done, Sigurd! Nobody wants to do it."

"It *can* be done!" reiterated the dwarf imperatively. "It *must* be done, and either you or I will do it! He shall not rob us,—he shall not steal the treasure of the golden midnight. He shall not gather the rose of all roses——"

"Stop!" said Lorimer suddenly. "Who are you talking about?"

"Who!" cried Sigurd excitedly. "Surely you know. Of him—that tall, proud, grey-eyed Englishman,—your foe, your rival; the rich, cruel Errington. . . ."

Lorimer's hand fell heavily on his shoulder, and his voice was very stern.

"What nonsense, Sigurd! You don't know what you

are talking about to-day. Errington my foe! Good heavens! Why, he's my best friend! Do you hear?"

Sigurd stared up at him in vacant surprise, but nodded feebly.

"Well, mind you remember it! The spirits tell lies, my boy, if they say that he is my enemy. I would give my life to save his!"

He spoke quietly, and rose from his seat on the moss as he finished his words, and his face had an expression that was both noble and resolute.

Sigurd still gazed upon him. "And you,—you do not love Thelma?" he murmured.

Lorimer started, but controlled himself instantly. His frank English eyes met the feverishly brilliant ones fixed so appealingly upon him.

"Certainly not!" he said calmly, with a serene smile. "What makes you think of such a thing? Quite wrong, Sigurd,—the spirits have made a mistake again! Come along,—let us join the others."

But Sigurd would not accompany him. He sprang away like a frightened animal, in haste, and abruptly plunging into the depths of a wood that bordered on Olaf Güldmar's grounds, was soon lost to sight. Lorimer looked after him in a little perplexity.

"I wonder if he ever gets dangerous?" he thought. "A fellow with such queer notions might do some serious harm without meaning it. I'll keep an eye on him!"

And once or twice during that same evening, he felt inclined to speak to Errington on the subject, but no suitable opportunity presented itself—and after a while, with his habitual indolence, he partly forgot the circumstance.

On the following Sunday afternoon Thelma sat alone under the wide blossom-covered porch, reading. Her father and Sigurd,—accompanied by Errington and his friends,—had all gone for a mountain ramble, promising to return for supper, a substantial meal which Britta was already busy preparing. The afternoon was very warm,—one of those long, lazy stretches of heat and brilliancy in which Nature seems to have lain down to rest like a child tired of play, sleeping in the sunshine with drooping flowers in her hands. The very ripple of the stream seemed hushed, and Thelma, though her eyes were bent seriously on the book she held, sighed once or twice heavily as though she were tired. There was a change in the girl,—an undefinable something

seemed to have passed over her and toned down the redun-
dant brightness of her beauty. She was paler,—and there
were darker shadows than usual under the splendor of her
eyes. Her very attitude, as she leaned her head against
the dark, fantastic carving of the porch, had a touch of list-
lessness and indifference in it; her sweetly arched lips
drooped with a plaintive little line at the corners, and her
whole air was indicative of fatigue, mingled with sadness.
She looked up now and then from the printed page, and her
gaze wandered over the stretch of the scented, flower-filled
garden, to the little silvery glimmer of the Fjord from
whence arose, like delicate black streaks against the sky,
the slender masts of the *Eulalie*,—and then she would resume her reading with a slight movement of impatience.

The volume she held was Victor Hugo's " Orientales,"
and though her sensitive imagination delighted in poetry as
much as in sunshine, she found it for once hard to rivet her
attention as closely as she wished to do, on the exquisite
wealth of language, and glow of color, that distinguishes the
writings of the Shakespears of France. Within the house
Britta was singing cheerily at her work, and the sound of
her song alone disturbed the silence. Two or three pale-
blue butterflies danced drowsily in and out a cluster of
honeysuckle that trailed downwards, nearly touching
Thelma's shoulder, and a diminutive black kitten, with a
pink ribbon round its neck, sat gravely on the garden path,
washing its face with its tiny velvety paws, in that deliberate and precise fashion, common to the spoiled and petted
members of its class. Everything was still and peaceful as
became a Sunday afternoon,—so that when the sound of a
heavy advancing footstep disturbed the intense calm, the
girl was almost nervously startled, and rose from her seat
with so much precipitation, that the butterflies, who had
possibly been considering whether her hair might not be
some new sort of sunflower, took fright and flew far upwards, and the demure kitten scared out of its absurd self-
consciousness, scrambled hastily up the nearest little tree.
The intruder on the quietude of Güldmar's domain was the
Rev. Mr. Dyceworthy,—and as Thelma, standing erect in
the porch, beheld him coming, her face grew stern and resolute, and her eyes flashed disdainfully.

Ignoring the repellant, almost defiant dignity of the girl's
attitude, Mr. Dyceworthy advanced, rather out of breath

and somewhat heated,—and smiling benevolently, nodded his head by way of greeting, without removing his hat.

"Ah, Fröken Thelma!" he observed condescendingly. "And how are you to-day? You look remarkably well—remarkably so, indeed!" And he eyed her with mild approval.

"I am well, I thank you," she returned quietly. "My father is not in, Mr. Dyceworthy."

The Reverend Charles wiped his hot face, and his smile grew wider.

"What matter?" he inquired blandly. "We shall, no doubt, entertain ourselves excellently without him! It is with you alone, Fröken, that I am desirous to hold converse."

And, without waiting for her permission, he entered the porch, and settled himself comfortably on the bench opposite to her, heaving a sigh of relief as he did so. Thelma remained standing—and the Lutheran minister's covetous eye glanced greedily over the sweeping curves of her queenly figure, the dazzling whiteness of her slim arched throat, and the glitter of her rich hair. She was silent—and there was something in her manner as she confronted him that made it difficult for Mr. Dyceworthy to speak. He hummed and hawed several times, and settled his stiff collar once or twice as though it hurt him; finally he said with an evident effort—

"I have found a—a—trinket of yours—a trifling toy—which, perhaps, you would be glad to have again." And he drew carefully out of his waistcoat pocket, a small parcel wrapped up in tissue paper, which he undid with his fat fingers, thus displaying the little crucifix he had kept so long in his possession. "Concerning this," he went on, holding it up before her, "I am grievously troubled,—and would fain say a few necessary words——"

She interrupted him, reaching out her hand for the cross as she spoke.

"That was my mother's crucifix," she said in solemn, infinitely tender accents, with a mist as of unshed tears in her sweet blue eyes. "It was round her neck when she died. I knew I had lost it, and was very unhappy about it. I do thank you with all my heart for bringing it back to me!"

And the hauteur of her face relaxed, and her smile—that sudden sweet smile of hers,—shone forth like a gleam of sunshine athwart a cloud.

Mr. Dyceworthy's breath came and went with curious rapidity. His visage grew pale, and a clammy dew broke out upon his forehead. He took the hand she held out,—a fair, soft hand with a pink palm like an upcurled shell,—and laid the little cross within it, and still retaining his hold of her, he stammeringly observed—

"Then we are friends, Fröken Thelma! . . . . good friends, I hope?"

She withdrew her fingers quickly from his hot, moist clasp, and her bright smile vanished.

"I do not see that at all!" she replied frigidly. "Friendship is very rare. To be friends, one must have similar tastes and sympathies,—many things which we have not,—and which we shall never have. I am slow to call any person my friend."

Mr. Dyceworthy's small pursy mouth drew itself into a tight thin line.

"Except," he said, with a suave sneer, "except when 'any person' happens to be a rich Englishman with a handsome face and easy manners! . . . then you are not slow to make friends, Fröken,—on the contrary, you are remarkably quick!"

The cold haughty stare with which the girl favored him might have frozen a less conceited man to a pillar of ice.

"What do you mean?" she asks abruptly, and with an air of surprise.

The minister's little ferret-like eyes, drooped under their puffy lids, and he fidgeted on the seat with uncomfortable embarrassment. He answered her in the mildest of mild voices.

"You are unlike yourself, my dear Fröken!" he said, with a soothing gesture of one of his well-trimmed white hands. "You are generally frank and open, but to-day I find you just a little,—well!—what shall I say—secretive? Yes, we will call it secretive! Oh, fie!" and Mr. Dyceworthy laughed a gentle little laugh; "you must not pretend ignorance of what I mean! All the neighborhood is talking of you and the gentleman you are so often seen with. Notably concerning Sir Philip Errington,—the vile tongue of rumor is busy,—for, according to his first plans when his yacht arrived here, he was bound for the North Cape,—and should have gone there days ago. Truly, I think,—and there are others who think also in the same spirit of interest for you,—that the sooner this young man leaves our peaceful Fjord the better,—and the less he has to do with the maidens of the district, the safer we shall be from the risk of scandal." And he heaved a pious sigh.

Thelma turned her eyes upon him in wonderment.

"I do not understand you," she said coldly. "Why do you speak of *others*? No others are interested in what I do? Why should they be? Why should *you* be? There is no need!"

Mr. Dyceworthy grew slightly excited. He felt like a runner nearing the winning-post.

"Oh, you wrong yourself, my dear Fröken," he murmured softly, with a sickly attempt at tenderness in his tone. "You really wrong yourself! It is impossible,—for me at least, not to be interested in you,—even for our dear Lord's sake. It troubles me to the inmost depths of my soul to behold in you one of the foolish virgins whose light hath been extinguished for lack of the saving oil,—to see you wandering as a lost sheep in the paths of darkness and error, without a hand to rescue your steps from the near and dreadful precipice! Ay, truly! . . . my spirit yearneth for you as a mother for an own babe—fain would I save you from the devices of the evil one,—fain would I——" here the minister drew out his handkerchief and pressed it lightly to his eyes,—then, as if with an effort overcoming his emotion, he added, with the gravity of a butcher presenting an extortionate bill, "but first,—before my own humble desires for your salvation—first, ere I go further in converse, it behoveth me to enter on the Lord's business!"

Thelma bent her head slightly, with an air as though she said: "Indeed; pray do not be long about it!" And, leaning back against the porch, she waited somewhat impatiently.

"The image I have just restored to you," went on Mr. Dyceworthy in his most pompous and ponderous manner, "you say belonged to your unhappy——"

"She was not unhappy," interposed the girl, calmly.

"Ay, ay!" and the minister nodded with a superior air of wisdom. "So you imagine, so you think,—you must have been too young to judge of these things. She died——"

"I saw her die," again she interrupted, with a musing tenderness in her voice. "She smiled and kissed me,—then she laid her thin white hand on this crucifix, and, closing her eyes, she went to sleep. They told me it was death; since then I have known that death is beautiful!"

Mr. Dyceworthy coughed,—a little cough of quiet incredulity. He was not fond of sentiment in any form, and the girl's dreamily pensive manner annoyed him. Death "beautiful?" Faugh! it was the one thing of all others that he dreaded; it was an unpleasant necessity, concerning which he thought as little as possible. Though he preached frequently on the peace of the grave and the joys of heaven, —he was far from believing in either,—he was nervously terrified of illness, and fled like a frightened hare from the very rumor of any infectious disorder, and he had never been known to attend a death-bed. And now, in answer to Thelma, he nodded piously and rubbed his hands, and said—

"Yes, yes; no doubt, no doubt! All very proper on your part, I am sure! But concerning this same image of which I came to speak,—it is most imperative that you should be brought to recognize it as a purely carnal object, unfitting a maiden's eyes to rest upon. The true followers of the Gospel are those who strive to forget the sufferings of our dear Lord as much as possible,—or to think of them only in spirit. The minds of sinners, alas! are easily influenced,— and it is both unseemly and dangerous to gaze freely upon the carven semblance of the Lord's limbs! Yea, truly, it hath oft been considered as damnatory to the soul,—more especially in the cases of women immured as nuns, who encourage themselves in an undue familiarity with our Lord, by gazing long and earnestly upon his body nailed to the accursèd tree."

Here Mr. Dyceworthy paused for breath. Thelma was silent, but a faint smile gleamed on her face.

"Wherefore," he went on, "I do adjure you, as you desire grace and redemption, to utterly cast from you the vile trinket, I have,—Heaven knows how reluctantly! . . . returned to your keeping,—to trample upon it, and renounce it as a device of Satan . . . " He stopped, surprised and indignant, as she raised the much-abused emblem to her lips and kissed it reverently.

"It is the sign of peace and salvation," she said steadily; "to me, at least. You waste your words, Mr. Dyceworthy; I am a Catholic."

"Oh, say not so!" exclaimed the minister, now thoroughly roused to a pitch of unctuous enthusiasm. "Say

not so. Poor child! who knowest not the meaning of the
word used. Catholic signifies universal. God forbid a universal Papacy! You are not a Catholic—no! You are a
Roman—by which name we understand all that is most
loathsome and unpleasing unto God! But I will wrestle
for your soul,—yea, night and day will I bend my spiritual
sinews to the task,—I will obtain the victory,—I will exor-
cise the fiend! Alas, alas! you are on the brink of hell—
think of it!" and Mr. Dyceworthy stretched out his hand
with his favorite pulpit gesture. "Think of the roasting
and burning,—the scorching and withering of souls! Imagine, if you can, the hopeless, bitter, eternal damnation,"
and here he smacked his lips as though he were tasting
something excellent,—"from which there is no escape!
. . . for which there shall be no remedy!"

"It is a gloomy picture," said Thelma, with a quiet
sparkle in her eye. "I am sorry,—for *you*. But I am
happier,—my faith teaches of purgatory—there is always a
little hope!"

"There is none! there is none!" exclaimed the minister,
rising in excitement from his seat, and swaying ponderously
to and fro as he gesticulated with hands and head. "You
are doomed,—doomed! There is no middle course between
hell and heaven. It must be one thing or the other; God
deals not in half-measures! Pause, oh pause, ere you decide to fall! Even at the latest hour the Lord desires to
save your soul,—the Lord yearns for your redemption, and
maketh me to yearn also. Fröken Thelma!" and Mr. Dyceworthy's voice deepened in solemnity, "there is a way which
the Lord hath whispered in mine ears,—a way that pointeth
to the white robe and the crown of glory,—a way by which
you shall possess the inner peace of the heart with bliss on
earth as the forerunner of bliss in heaven!"

She looked at him steadfastly. "And that way is—
what?" she inquired.

Mr. Dyceworthy hesitated, and wished with all his heart
that this girl was not so thoroughly self-possessed. Any
sign of timidity in her would have given him an increase of
hardihood. But her eyes were coldly brilliant, and glanced
him over without the smallest embarrassment. He took
refuge in his never-failing remedy, his benevolent smile—a
smile that covered a multitude of hypocrisies.

"You ask a plain question, Fröken," he said sweetly,
"and I should be loth not to give you a plain answer. That

9

way—that glorious way of salvation for you is—·through *me !*"

And his countenance shone with smug self-satisfaction as he spoke, and he repeated softly, " Yes, yes ; that way is through me!"

She moved with a slight gesture of impatience. " It is a pity to talk any more," she said rather wearily. " It is all no use! Why do you wish to change me in my religion? I do not wish to change *you*. I do not see why we should speak of such things at all."

" Of course!" replied Mr. Dyceworthy blandly. " Of course you do not see. And why ? Because you are blind." Here he drew a little nearer to her, and looked covetously at the curve of her full, firm waist.

" Oh, why !" he resumed in a sort of rapture—·" why should we say it is a pity to talk any more? Why should we say it is all no use ? It *is* of use,—it is noble, it is edifying to converse of the Lord's good pleasure ! And what is His good pleasure at this moment ? To unite two souls in His service ! Yea, He hath turned my desire towards you, Fröken Thelma,—even as Jacob's desire was towards Rachel! Let me see this hand."· He made a furtive grab at the white taper fingers that played listlessly with the jessamine leaves on the porch, but the girl dexterously withdrew them from his clutch and moved a little further back, her face flushing proudly. " Oh, will it not come to me ? Cruel hand!" and he rolled his little eyes with an absurdly sentimental air of reproach. " It is shy—it will not clasp the hand of its protector! Do not be afraid, Fröken! . . . I, Charles Dyceworthy, am not the man to trifle with your young affections! Let them rest where they have flown! I accept them! Yea! . . . in spite of wrath and error and moral destitution,—my spirit inclineth towards you,—in the language of carnal men, I love you! More than this, I am willing to take you as my lawful wife——"

He broke off abruptly, somewhat startled at the bitter scorn of the flashing eyes that, like two quivering stars, were blazing upon him. Her voice, clear as a bell ringing in frosty air, cut through the silence like a sweep of a sword-blade.

" How dare you !" she said, with a wrathful thrill in her low, intense tones. " How dare you come here to insult me !"

Insult her! He,—the Reverend Charles Dyceworthy,—considered guilty of insult in offering honorable marriage to a mere farmer's daughter! He could not believe his own ears,—and in his astonishment he looked up at her. Looking, he recoiled and shrank into himself, like a convicted knave before some queenly accuser. The whole form of the girl seemed to dilate with indignation. From her proud mouth, arched like a bow, sprang barbed arrows of scorn that flew straightly and struck home.

"Always I have guessed what you wanted," she went on in that deep, vibrating tone which had such a rich quiver of anger within it; "but I never thought you would——" She paused, and a little disdainful laugh broke from her lips. "You would make *me* your wife—*me?* You think *me* likely to accept such an offer?" And she drew herself up with a superb gesture, and regarded him fixedly.

"Oh, pride, pride!" murmured the unabashed Dyceworthy, recovering from the momentary abasement into which he had been thrown by her look and manner. "How it overcometh our natures and mastereth our spirits! My dear, my dearest Fröken,—I fear you do not understand me! Yet it is natural that you should not; you were not prepared for the offer of my—my affections,"—and he beamed all over with benevolence,—" and I can appreciate a maidenly and becoming coyness, even though it assume the form of a repellant and unreasonable anger. But take courage, my—my dear girl!—our Lord forbid that I should wantonly play with the delicate emotions of your heart! Poor little heart! does it flutter?" and Mr. Dyceworthy leered sweetly. "I will give it time to recover itself! Yes, yes! a little time! and then you will put that pretty hand in mine"—here he drew nearer to her, "and with one kiss we will seal the compact!"

And he attempted to steal his arm round her waist, but the girl sprang back indignantly, and pulling down a thick branch of the clambering prickly roses from the porch, held it in front of her by way of protection. Mr. Dyceworthy laughed indulgently.

"Very pretty—very pretty indeed!" he mildly observed, eyeing her as she stood at bay barricaded by the roses. "Quite a picture! There, there! do not be frightened,—such shyness is very natural! We will embrace in the Lord another day! In the meantime one little word—*the* word—will suffice me,—yea, even one little smile,—to show

me that you understand my words,—that you love me "—
here he clasped his plump hands together in flabby ecstasy
—" even as you are loved ! "

His absurd attitude,—the weak, knock-kneed manner in
which his clumsy legs seemed, from the force of sheer sentiment, to bend under his weighty body, and the inanely
amatory expression of his puffy countenance, would have
excited most women to laughter,—and Thelma was perfectly conscious of his utterly ridiculous appearance, but
she was too thoroughly indignant to take the matter in a
hurmorous light.

"Love you!" she exclaimed, with a movement of irrepressible loathing. "You must be mad! I would rather
die than marry you!"

Mr. Dyceworthy's face grew livid and his little eyes
sparkled vindictively,—but he restrained his inward rage,
and merely smiled, rubbing his hands softly one against
the other.

"Let us be calm!" he said soothingly. "Whatever we
do, let us be calm! Let us not provoke one another to
wrath! Above all things, let us, in a spirit of charity and
patience, reason out this matter without undue excitement. My ears have most painfully heard your last words,
which, taken literally, might mean that you reject my honorable offer. The question is, *do* they mean this? I cannot,—I will not believe that you would foolishly stand in
the way of your own salvation,"—and he shook his head
with doleful gentleness. "Moreover, Fröken Thelma,
though it sorely distresses me to speak of it,—it is my
duty, as a minister of the Lord, to remiud you that an
honest marriage,—a marriage of virtue and respectability
such as I propose, is the only way to restore your reputation,—which, alas! is sorely damaged, and——"

Mr. Dyceworthy stopped abruptly, a little alarmed, as
she suddenly cast aside the barrier of roses and advanced
toward him, her blue eyes blazing.

"My reputation!" she said haughtily. "Who speaks of
it ? "

"Oh dear, dear me!" moaned the minister pathetically.
"Sad! . . . very sad to see so ungovernable a temper, so
wild and untrained a disposition! Alas, alas! how frail we
are without the Lord's support,—without the strong staff
of the Lord's mercy to lean upon! Not I, my poor child,
not I, but the whole village speaks of you; to you the

ignorant people attribute all the sundry evils that of late have fallen sorely upon them,—bad harvests, ill-luck with the fishing, poverty, sickness,"—here Mr. Dyceworthy pressed the tips of his fingers delicately together, and looked at her with a benevolent compassion,—" and they call it witchcraft,—yes! strange, very strange! But so it is,—ignorant as they are, such ignorance is not easily en-lightened,—and though I," he sighed, " have done my poor best to disabuse their minds of the suspicions against you, I find it is a matter in which I, though a humble mouth-piece of the Gospel, am powerless—quite powerless!"

She relaxed her defiant attitude, and moved away from him; the shadow of a smile was on her lips.

" It is not my fault if the people are foolish," she said coldly ; " I have never done harm to any one that I know of." And turning abruptly, she seemed about to enter the house, but the minister dexterously placed himself in her way, and barred her passage.

" Stay, oh, stay!" he exclaimed with unctuous fervor. " Pause, unfortunate girl, ere you reject the strong shield and buckler that the Lord has in His great mercy, offered you, in my person! For I must warn you,—Fröken Thelma, I must warn you seriously of the danger you run! I will not pain you by referring to the grave charges brought against your father, who is, alas! in spite of my spiritual wrestling with the Lord for his sake, still no bet-ter than a heathen savage ; no! I will say nothing of this. But what,—what shall I say,"—here he lowered his voice to a tone of mysterious and weighty reproach,—" what shall I say of your most unseemly and indiscreet companionship with these worldly young men who are visiting the Fjord for their idle pastime? Ah dear, dear! This is indeed a heavy scandal and a sore burden to my soul,—for up to this time I have, in spite of many faults in your disposition, considered you were at least of a most maidenly and de-corous deportment,—but now—now! to think that you should, of your own free will and choice, consent to be the plaything of this idle stroller from the wicked haunts of fashion,—the hour's toy of this Sir Philip Errington! Fröken Thelma, I would never have believed it of you!" And he drew himself up with ponderous and sorrowful dig-nity.

A burning blush had covered Thelma's face at the men-tion of Errington's name, but it soon faded, leaving her very pale. She changed her position so that she confronted Mr. Dyceworthy,—her clear blue eyes regarded him steadfastly.

" Is this what is said of me ? " she asked calmly.

" It is,—it is, most unfortunately ! " returned the minister, shaking his bullet-like head a great many times; then, with a sort of elephantine cheerfulness, he added, " but what matter ? There is time to remedy these things. I am willing to set myself as a strong barrier against the evil noises of rumor ! Am I selfish or ungenerous ? The Lord forbid it ! No matter how *I* am compromised, no matter how *I* am misjudged,—I am still willing to take you as my lawful wife Fröken Thelma,—but," and here he shook his forefinger at her with a pretended playfulness, " I will permit no more converse with Sir Philip Errington ; no, no ! I cannot allow it ! . . . I cannot, indeed ! "

She still looked straight at him,—her bosom rose and fell rapidly with her passionate breath, and there was such an eloquent breath of scorn in her face that he winced under it as though struck by a sharp scourge.

" You are not worth my anger ! " she said slowly, this time without a tremor in her rich voice. " One must have something to be angry with, and you—you are nothing ! Neither man nor beast,—for men are brave, and beasts tell no lies ! Your wife ! I ! " and she laughed aloud,—then with a gesture of command, " Go ! " she exclaimed, " and never let me see your face again ! "

The clear scornful laughter,—the air of absolute authority with which she spoke,—would have stung the most self-opinionated of men, even though his conscience were enveloped in a moral leather casing of hypocrisy and arrogance. And, notwithstanding his invariable air of mildness, Mr. Dyceworthy had a temper. That temper rose to a white heat just now,—every drop of blood receded from his countenance,—and his soft hands clenched themselves in a particularly ugly and threatening manner. Yet he managed to preserve his suave composure.

" Alas, alas ! " he murmured. " How sorely my soul is afflicted to see you thus, Fröken ! I am amazed—I am distressed ! Such language from your lips ! oh fie, fie ! And has it come to this ! And must I resign the hope I had of saving your poor soul ? and must I withdraw my spiritual protection from you ? " This he asked with a suggestive sneer of his prim mouth,—and then continued, " I must—

alas, I must! My conscience will not permit me to do more than pray for you! And as is my duty, I shall, in a spirit of forbearance and charity, speak warningly to Sir Philip concerning——"

But Thelma did not permit him to finish his sentence. She sprang forward like a young leopardess, and with a magnificent outward sweep of her arm motioned him down the garden path.

" Out of my sight,—*coward !* " she cried, and then stood waiting for him to obey her, her whole frame vibrating with indignation like a harp struck too roughly. She looked so terribly beautiful, and there was such a suggestive power in that extended bare white arm of hers, that the minister, though quaking from head to heel with disappointment and resentment, judged it prudent to leave her.

" Certainly, I will take my departure, Fröken! " he said meekly, while his teeth glimmered wolfishly through his pale lips, in a snarl more than a smile. "It is best you should be alone to recover yourself—from this—this undue excitement! I shall not repeat my—my—offer ; but I am sure your good sense will—in time—show you how very unjust and hasty you have been in this matter—and—and you will be sorry! Yes, indeed! I am quite sure you will be sorry! I wish you good day, Fröken Thelma! "

She made him no reply, and he turned from the house and left her, strolling down the flower-bordered path as though he were in the best of all possible moods with himself and the universe. But, in truth, he muttered a heavy oath under his breath—an oath that was by no means in keeping with his godly and peaceful disposition. Once, as he walked, he looked back,—and saw the woman he coveted now more than ever, standing erect in the porch, tall, fair and loyal in her attitude, looking like some proud empress who had just dismissed an unworthy vassal. A farmer's daughter! and she had refused Mr. Dyceworthy with disdain! He had much ado to prevent himself shaking his fist at her!

" The lofty shall be laid low, and the stiff-necked shall be humbled," he thought, as with a vicious switch of his stick he struck off a fragrant head of purple clover. " Conceited fool of a girl! Hopes to be ' my lady ' does she? She had better take care! "

Here he stopped abruptly in his walk as if a thought had struck him,—a malignant joy sparkled in his eyes, and he flourished his stick triumphantly in the air. " I'll have her yet!" he exclaimed half-aloud. "I'll set Lovisa on her!" And his countenance cleared; he quickened his pace like a man having some pressing business to fulfill, and was soon in his boat, rowing towards Bosekop with unaccustomed speed and energy.

Meanwhile Thelma stood motionless where he had left her,—she watched the retreating form of her portly suitor till he had altogether disappeared,—then she pressed one hand on her bosom, sighed, and laughed a little. Glancing at the crucifix so lately restored to her, she touched it with her lips and fastened it to a small silver chain she wore, and then a shadow swept over her fair face that made it strangely sad and weary. Her lips quivered pathetically ; she shaded her eyes with her curved fingers as though the sunlight hurt her,—then with faltering steps she turned away from the warm stretch of garden, brilliant with blossom, and entered the house. There was a sense of outrage and insult upon her, and though in her soul she treated Mr. Dyceworthy's observations with the contempt they deserved, his coarse allusion to Sir Philip Errington had wounded her more than she cared to admit to herself. Once in the quiet sitting-room, she threw herself on her knees by her father's arm-chair, and laying her proud little golden head down on her folded arms, she broke into a passion of silent tears.

Who shall unravel the mystery of a woman's weeping? Who shall declare whether it is a pain or a relief to the overcharged heart? The dignity of a crowned queen is capable of utterly dissolving and disappearing in a shower of tears, when Love's burning finger touches the pulse and marks its slow or rapid beatings. And Thelma wept as many of her sex weep, without knowing why, save that all suddenly she felt herself most lonely and forlorn like Sainte Beuve's—

"Colombe gemissante,
Qui demande par pitié
Sa moitié,
Sa moitié loin d'elle absente!"

CHAPTER XII.

"A wicked will,
A woman's will ; a cankered grandame's will!"
                                        King John.

"By Jove!"

And Lorimer, after uttering this unmeaning exclamation, was silent out of sheer dismay. He stood hesitating and looking in at the door of the Güldmar's sitting-room, and the alarming spectacle he saw was the queenly Thelma down on the floor in an attitude of grief,—Thelma giving way to little smothered sobs of distress,—Thelma actually crying! He drew a long breath and stared, utterly bewildered. It was a sight for which he was unprepared,—he was not accustomed to women's tears. What should he do? Should he cough gently to attract her attention, or should he retire on tip-toe and leave her to indulge her grief as long as she would, without making any attempt to console her? The latter course seemed almost brutal, yet he was nearly deciding upon it, when a slight creak of the door against which he leaned, caused her to look up suddenly. Seeing him, she rose quickly from her desponding position and faced him, her cheeks somewhat deeply flushed and her eyes glittering feverishly.

" Mr. Lorimer!" she exclaimed, forcing a faint smile to her quivering lips. "You here? Why, where are the others?"

"They are coming on after me," replied Lorimer, advancing into the room, and diplomatically ignoring the girl's efforts to hide the tears that still threatened to have their way. "But I was sent in advance to tell you not to be frightened. There has been a slight accident——"

She grew very pale. "Is it my father?" she asked tremblingly. "Sir Philip——"

"No, no!" answered Lorimer reassuringly. "It is nothing serious, really, upon my honor! Your father's all right,—so is Phil,—our lively friend Pierre is the victim. The fact is, we've had some trouble with Sigurd. I can't think what has come to the boy! He was as amiable as possible when we started, but after we had climbed about half-way up the mountain, he took it into his head to throw stones about rather recklessly. It was only fun, he said. Your father tried to make him leave off, but he was obstinate. At last, in a particularly bright access of playfulness, he got hold of a large flint, and nearly put Phil's eye out with it,—Phil dodged it, and it flew straight at Duprèz, splitting open his cheek in rather an unbecoming fashion——Don't look so horrified, Miss Güldmar,—it is really nothing!"

"Oh, but indeed it is something!" she said, with true womanly anxiety in her voice. "Poor fellow! I am so sorry! Is he much hurt? Does he suffer?"

"Pierre? Oh, no, not a bit of it! He's as jolly as possible! We bandaged him up in a very artistic fashion; he looks quite interesting, I assure you. His beauty's spoilt for a time, that's all. Phil thought you might be alarmed when you saw us bringing home the wounded,—that is why I came on to tell you all about it."

"But what can be the matter with Sigurd?" asked the girl, raising her hand furtively to dash off a few tear-drops that still hung on her long lashes. "And where is he?"

"Ah, that I can't tell you!" answered Lorimer. "He is perfectly incomprehensible to-day. As soon as he saw the blood flowing from Duprèz's cheek, he uttered a howl as if some one had shot him, and away he rushed into the woods as fast as he could go. We called him, and shouted his name till we were hoarse,—all no use! He wouldn't come back. I suppose he'll find his way home by himself?"

"Oh, yes," said Thelma gravely. "But when he comes I will scold him very much! It is not like him to be so wild and cruel. He will understand me when I tell him how wrong he has been."

"Oh, don't break his heart, poor little chap!" said Lorimer easily. "Your father has given him a terrible scolding already. He hasn't got his wits about him you know, —he can't help being queer sometimes. But what have *you* been doing with yourself during our absence?" And he regarded her with friendly scrutiny. "You were crying when I came in. Now, weren't you?"

She met his gaze quite frankly. "Yes!" she replied, with a plaintive thrill in her voice. "I could not help it! My heart ached and the tears came. Somehow I felt that everything was wrong,—and that it was all my fault——"

"Your fault!" murmured Lorimer, astonished. "My dear Miss Güldmar, what do you mean? What *is* your fault?"

"Everything!" she answered sadly, with a deep sigh. "I am very foolish; and I am sure I often do wrong without meaning it. Mr. Dyceworthy has been here and ——" she stopped abruptly, and a wave of color flushed her face.

Lorimer laughed lightly. "Dyceworthy!" he exclaimed. "The mystery is explained! You have been bored by 'the good religious,' as Pierre calls him. You know what *boring* means now, Miss Güldmar, don't you?" She smiled slightly, and nodded. "The first time you visited the *Eulalie*, you didn't understand the word, I remember,— ah!" and he shook his head—"if you were in London society, you'd find that expression very convenient,—it would come to your lips pretty frequently, I can tell you!"

"I shall never see London," she said, with a sort of re- signed air. "You will all go away very soon, and I—I shall be lonely——"

She bit her lips in quick vexation, as her blue eyes filled again with tears in spite of herself.

Lorimer turned away and pulled a chair to the open window.

"Come and sit down here," he said invitingly. "We shall be able to see the others coming down the hill. Noth- ing like fresh air for blowing away the blues." Then, as she obeyed him, he added, "What has Dyceworthy been saying to you?"

"He told me I was wicked," she murmured; "and that all the people here think very badly of me. But that was not the worst"—and a little shudder passed over her— "there was something else—something that made me very angry—so angry!"—and here she raised her eyes with a gravely penitent air—"Mr. Lorimer, I do not think I have ever had so bad and fierce a temper before!"

"Good gracious!" exclaimed Lorimer, with a broad smile. "You alarm me, Miss Güldmar! I had no idea you were a 'bad, fierce' person,—I shall get afraid of you —I shall, really!"

"Ah, you laugh!" and she spoke half-reproachfully. "You will not be serious for one little moment!"

"Yes I will! Now look at me," and he assumed a solemn expression, and drew himself up with an air of dignity. "I am all attention! Consider me your father-confessor, Miss Güldmar, and explain the reason of this 'bad, fierce' temper of yours."

She peeped at him shyly from under her silken lashes.

"It is more dreadful than you think," she answered in a low tone. "Mr. Dyceworthy asked me to marry him."

Lorimer's keen eyes flashed with indignation. This was beyond a jest,—and he clenched his fist as he exclaimed—

"Impudent donkey! What a jolly good thrashing he

deserves! . . . and I shouldn't be surprised if he got it one of these days! And so, Miss Güldmar,"—and he studied her face with some solicitude—" you were very angry with him?"

" Oh yes!" she replied, " but when I told him he was a coward, and that he must go away, he said some very cruel things——" she stopped, and blushed deeply; then, as if seized by some sudden impulse, she laid her small hand on Lorimer's and said in the tone of an appealing child, " you are very good and kind to me, and you are clever,—you know so much more than I do! You must help me,—you will tell me, will you not? . . . if it is wrong of me to like you all,—it is as if we had known each other a long time and I have been very happy with you and your friends. But you must teach me to behave like the girls you have seen in London,—for I could not bear that Sir Philip should think me wicked!"

" Wicked!" and Lorimer drew a long breath. " Good heavens! If you knew what Phil's ideas about you are, Miss Güldmar——"

" I do not wish to know," interrupted Thelma steadily. " You must quite understand me,—I am not clever to hide my thoughts, and—and—, *you* are glad when you talk sometimes to Sir Philip, are you not?" He nodded, gravely studying every light and shadow on the fair, up-turned, innocent face.

" Yes!" she continued with some eagerness, " I see you are! Well, it is the same with me,—I do love to hear him speak! You know how his voice is like music, and how his kind ways warm the heart,—it is pleasant to be in his company—I am sure you also find it so! But for me,—it seems it is wrong,—it is not wise for me to show when I am happy. I do not care what other people say,—but I would not have *him* think ill of me for all the world!"

Lorimer took her hand and held it in his with a most tender loyalty and respect. Her naïve, simple words had, all unconsciously to herself, laid bare the secret of her soul to his eyes,—and though his heart beat with a strange sickening sense of unrest that flavored of despair, a gentle reverence filled him, such as a man might feel if some little snow-white shrine, sacred to purity and peace, should be suddenly unveiled before him.

" My dear Miss Güldmar," he said earnestly, " I assure you, you have no cause to be uneasy! You must not believe a word Dyceworthy says—every one with a grain of common sense can see what a liar and hypocrite he is! And as for you, you never do anything wrong,—don't imagine such nonsense! I wish there were more women like you!"

"Ah, that is very kind of you!" half laughed the girl, still allowing her hand to rest in his. "But I do not think everybody would have such a good opinion." They both started, and their hands fell asunder as a shadow darkened the room, and Sir Philip stood before them.

"Excuse me!" he said stiffly, lifting his hat with cere-monious politeness. "I ought to have knocked at the door —I——"

"Why?" asked Thelma, raising her eyebrows in sur-prise.

"Yes—why indeed?" echoed Lorimer, with a frank look at his friend.

"I am afraid,"—and for once the generally good-humored Errington looked positively petulant—"I am afraid I in-terrupted a pleasant conversation!" And he gave a little forced laugh of feigned amusement, but evident vexation.

"And if it was pleasant, shall you not make it still more so?" asked Thelma, with timid and bewitching sweetness, though her heart beat very fast,—she was anxious. Why was Sir Philip so cold and distant? He looked at her, and his pent-up passion leaped to his eyes and filled them with a glowing and fiery tenderness,—her head drooped suddenly, and she turned quickly, to avoid that searching, longing gaze. Lorimer glanced from one to the other with a slight feeling of amusement.

"Well Phil," he inquired lazily, "how did you get here so soon? You must have glided into the garden like a ghost, for I never heard you coming."

"So I imagine!" retorted Errington, with an effort to be sarcastic, in which he utterly failed as he met his friend's eyes,—then after a slight and somewhat embarrassed pause he added more mildly! "Duprèz cannot get on very fast, —his wound still bleeds, and he feels rather faint now and then. I don't think we bandaged him up properly, and I came on to see if Britta could prepare something for him."

"But you will not need to ask Britta," said Thelma quietly, with a pretty air of authority, " for I shall myself do all for Mr. Duprèz. I understand well how to cure his wound, and I do think he will like me as well as Britta."

And, hearing footsteps approaching, she looked out at the window. "Here they come!" she exclaimed. "Ah, poor Monsieur Pierre! he does look very pale! I will go and meet them."

And she hurried from the room, leaving the two young men together. Errington threw himself into Olaf Güldmar's great arm-chair, with a slight sigh.

"Well?" said Lorimer inquiringly.

"Well!" he returned somewhat gruffly.

Lorimer laughed, and crossing the room, approached him and clapped a hand on his shoulder.

"Look here, old man!" he said earnestly, "don't be a fool! I know that 'love maketh men mad,' but I never supposed the lunacy would lead you to the undesirable point of distrusting your friend,—your true friend, Phil,— by all the Gods of the past and present!"

And he laughed again,—a little huskily this time, for there was a sudden unaccountable and unwished-for lump in his throat, and a moisture in his eyes which he had not bargained for. Philip looked up,—and silently held out his hand, which Lorimer as silently clasped. There was a moment's hesitation, and then the young baronet spoke out manfully.

"I'm ashamed of myself, George! I really am! But I tell you, when I came in and saw you two standing there, —you've no idea what a picture you made! . . . by Jove! . . . I was furious!" And he smiled. "I suppose I was jealous!"

"I suppose you were!" returned Lorimer amusedly. "Novel sensation, isn't it? A sort of hot, prickly, 'have-at-thee-villain' sort of thing; must be frightfully exhausting! But why you should indulge this emotion at *my* expense is what I cannot, for the life of me, understand!"

"Well," murmured Errington, rather abashed, "you see, her hands were in yours———"

"As they will be again, and yet again, I trust!" said Lorimer with cheery fervor. "Surely you'll allow me to shake hands with your wife?"

"I say, George, be quiet!" exclaimed Philip warningly, as at that moment Thelma passed the window with Pierre Duprèz leaning on her arm, and her father and Macfarlane following.

She entered the room with the stately step of a young queen,—her tall, beautiful figure forming a strong contrast to that of the narrow-shouldered little Frenchman, upon whom she smiled down with an air of almost maternal protection.

"You will sit here, Monsieur Duprèz," she said, leading him to the *bonde's* arm-chair which Errington instantly vacated, "and father will bring you a good glass of wine. And the pain will be nothing when I have attended to that cruel wound. But I am so sorry,—so very sorry, to see you suffer!"

Pierre did indeed present rather a dismal spectacle. There was a severe cut on his forehead as well as his cheek; his face was pale and streaked with blood, while the hastily-improvised bandages which were tied under his chin, by no means improved his personal appearance. His head ached with the pain, and his eyes smarted with the strong sunlight to which he had been exposed all the day, but his natural gaiety was undiminished, and he laughed as he answered—

"*Chère Mademoiselle*, you are too good to me! It is a piece of good fortune that Sigurd threw that stone—yes! since it brings me your pity! But do not trouble; a little cold water and a fresh handkerchief is all I need."

But Thelma was already practicing her own simple surgery for his benefit. With deft, soft fingers she laid bare the throbbing wound,—washed and dressed it carefully and skillfully,—and used with all such exceeding gentleness, that Duprèz closed his eyes in a sort of rapture during the operation, and wished it could last longer. Then taking the glass of wine her father brought in obedience to her order, she said in a tone of mild authority—

"Now, you will drink this Monsieur Pierre, and you will rest quite still till it is time to go back to the yacht; and to-morrow you will not feel any pain, I am sure. And I do think it will not be an ugly scar for long."

"If it is," answered Pierre, "I shall say I received it in a duel! Then I shall be great—glorious! and all the pretty ladies will love me!"

She laughed,—but looked grave a moment afterwards.

"You must never say what is not true," she said. "It is wrong to deceive any one,—even in a small matter."

Duprèz gazed up at her wonderingly, feeling very much like a chidden child.

"Never say what is not true!" he thought. "*Mon Dieu!* what would become of my life?"

It was a new suggestion, and he reflected upon it with astonishment. It opened such a wide vista of impossibilities to his mind.

Meanwhile old Güldmar was engaged in pouring out wine for the other young men, talking all the time.

"I tell thee, Thelma mine," he said seriously, "something must be very wrong with our Sigurd. The poor lad has always been gentle and tractable, but to-day he was like some wild animal for mischief and hardihood. I grieve to see it! I fear the time may come when he may no longer be a safe servant for thee, child!"

"Oh, father!"—and the girl's voice was full of tender anxiety—"surely not! He is too fond of us to do us any harm—he is so docile and affectionate!"

"Maybe, maybe!" and the old farmer shook his head doubtfully. "But when the wits are away the brain is like a ship without ballast—there is no safe sailing possible. He would not mean any harm, perhaps,—and yet in his wild moods he might do it, and be sorry for it directly afterwards. 'Tis little use to cry when the mischief is done, —and I confess I do not like his present humor."

"By-the-by," observed Lorimer, "that reminds me! Sigurd has taken an uncommonly strong aversion to Phil. It's curious but it's a fact. Perhaps it is that which upsets his nerves?"

"I have noticed it myself," said Errington, "and I'm sorry for it, for I've done him no harm that I can remember. He certainly asked me to go away from the Alten-fjord, and I refused,—I'd no idea he had any serious meaning in his request. But it's evident he can't endure my company."

"Ah, then!" said Thelma simply and sorrowfully, "he must be very ill,—because it is natural for every one to like you."

She spoke in perfect good faith and innocence of heart; but Errington's eyes flashed and he smiled—one of those rare, tender smiles of his which brightened his whole visage.

"You are very kind to say so, Miss Güldmar!"

"It is not kindness; it is the truth!" she replied frankly.

At that moment a very rosy face and two sparkling eyes peered in at the door.

"Yes, Britta!" Thelma smiled; "we are quite ready!"

Whereupon the face disappeared, and Olaf Güldmar led the way into the kitchen, which was at the same time the dining-room, and where a substantial supper was spread on the polished pine table.

The farmer's great arm-chair was brought in for Duprèz, who, though he declared he was being spoilt by too much attention, seemed to enjoy it immensely,—and they were all, including Britta, soon clustered round the hospitable board whereon antique silver and quaint glasses of foreign make sparkled bravely, their effect enhanced by the snowy whiteness of the homespun table-linen.

A few minutes set them all talking gaily. Macfarlane vied with the ever-gallant Duprèz in making a few compliments to Britta, who was pretty and engaging enough to merit attention, and who, after all, was something more than a mere servant, possessing, as she did, a great deal of her young mistress's affection and confidence, and being always treated by Güldmar himself as one of the family. There was no reserve or coldness in the party, and the hum of their merry voices echoed up to the cross-rafters of the stout wooden ceiling and through the open door and window, from whence a patch of the gorgeous afternoon sky could be seen, glimmering redly, like a distant lake of fire. They were in the full enjoyment of their repast, and the old farmer's rollicking " Ha, ha, ha ! " in response to a joke of Lorimer's, had just echoed jovially through the room, when a strong, harsh voice called aloud—" Olaf Güld-mar ! "

There was a sudden silence. Each one looked at the other in surprise. Again the voice called—" Olaf Güld-mar ! "

" Well ! " roared the *bonde* testily, turning sharply round in his chair, " who calls me ? "

" I do ! " and the tall, emaciated figure of a woman advanced and stood on the threshold, without actually entering the room. She dropped the black shawl that enveloped her, and, in so doing, disordered her hair, which fell in white, straggling locks about her withered features, and her dark eyes gleamed maliciously as she fixed them on the assembled party. Britta, on perceiving her, uttered a faint shriek, and without considering the propriety of her action, buried her nut-brown curls and sparkling eyes in Duprèz's coat-sleeve, which, to do the Frenchman justice, was exceedingly prompt to receive and shelter its fair burden. The *bonde* rose from his chair, and his face grew stern.

" What do you here, Lovisa Elsland ? Have you walked

thus far from Talvig to pay a visit that must needs be unwelcome?"

"Unwelcome I know I am," replied Lovisa, disdainfully noting the terror of Britta and the astonished glances of Errington and his friends—"unwelcome at all times,—but most unwelcome at the hour of feasting and folly,—for who can endure to receive a message from the Lord when the mouth is full of savory morsels, and the brain reels with the wicked wine? Yet I have come in spite of your iniquities, Olaf Güldmar,—strong in the strength of the Lord, I dare to set foot upon your accursèd threshold, and once more make my just demand. Give me back the child of my dead daughter! . . . restore to me the erring creature who should be the prop of my defenceless age, had not your pagan spells alienated her from me,—release her,—and bid her return with me to my desolate hearth and home. This done,—I will stay the tempest that threatens your habitation—I will hold back the dark cloud of destruction—I will avert the wrath of the Lord,—yes! for the sake of the past —for the sake of the past!"

These last words she muttered in a low tone, more to herself than to Güldmar; and, having spoken, she averted her eyes from the company, drew her shawl closely about her, and waited for an answer.

"By all the gods of my fathers!" shouted the *bonde* in a towering passion. "This passes my utmost endurance! Have I not told thee again and again, thou silly soul! . . . that thy grandchild is no slave? She is free—free to return to thee an' she will; free also to stay with us, where she has found a happier home than thy miserable hut at Talvig. Britta!" and he thumped his fist on the table. "Look up, child! Speak for thyself! Thou hast a spirit of thine own. Here is thy one earthly relation. Wilt go with her? Neither thy mistress nor I will stand in the way of thy pleasure."

Thus adjured Britta looked up so suddenly that Duprèz, —who had rather enjoyed the feel of her little nestling head hidden upon his arm,—was quite startled, and he was still more so at the utter defiance that flashed into the small maiden's round, rosy face.

"Go with *you!*" she cried shrilly, addressing the old woman, who remained standing in the same attitude, with an air of perfect composure. "Do you think I have forgotten how you treated my mother, or how you used to beat me and starve me? You wicked old woman! How dare you come here? I'm ashamed of you! You frightened my mother to death—you know you did! . . . and now you want to do the same to me! But you won't —I can tell you! I'm old enough to do as I like, and I'd rather die than live with you!"

Then, overcome by excitement and temper, she burst out crying, heedless of Pierre Duprèz's smiling nods of approval, and the admiring remarks he was making under his breath, such as—" *Brava, ma petite! C'est bien fait! c'est joliment bien dit! Mais je crois bien!*"

Lovisa seemed unmoved; she raised her head and looked at Güldmar.

" Is this your answer?" she demanded.

" By the sword of Odin!" cried the *bonde*, " the woman must be mad! *My* answer? The girl has spoken for herself,—and plainly enough too! Art thou deaf, Lovisa Elsland? or are thy wits astray?"

" My hearing is very good," replied Lovisa calmly, " and my mind, Olaf Güldmar, is as clear as yours. And, thanks to your teaching in mine early days,"—she paused and looked keenly at him, but he appeared to see no meaning in her allusion,—" I know the English tongue, of which we hear far too much,—too often! There is nothing Britta has said that I do not understand. But I know well it is not the girl herself that speaks—it is a demon in her,— and that demon shall be cast forth before I die! Yea, with the help of the Lord I shall——" She stopped abruptly and fixed her eyes, glowing with fierce wrath, on Thelma. The girl met her evil glance with a gentle surprise. Lovisa smiled malignantly.

" You know me, I think!" said Lovisa. " You have seen me before?"

" Often," answered Thelma mildly. " I have always been sorry for you."

" Sorry for me!" almost yelled the old woman. " Why —why are you sorry for me?"

" Do not answer her, child!" interrupted Güldmar angrily. " She is mad as the winds of a wild winter, and will but vex thee."

But Thelma laid her hand soothingly on her father's, and smiled peacefully as she turned her fair face again towards Lovisa.

" Why?" she said. " Because you seem so very lonely

and sad—and that must make you cross with every one
who is happy! And it is a pity, I think, that you do not
let Britta alone—you only quarrel with each other when
you meet. And would you not like her to think kindly of
you when you are dead?"

Lovisa seemed choking with anger,—her face worked
into such hideous grimaces, that all present, save Thelma,
were dismayed at her repulsive aspect.

"When I am dead!" she muttered hoarsely. "So you
count upon that already, do you? Ah! . . . but do
you know which of us shall die first!" Then raising her
voice with an effort she exclaimed—

"Stand forth, Thelma Güldmar! Let me see you closely
—face to face!"

Errington said something in a low tone, and the *bonde*
would have again interfered, but Thelma shook her head,
smiled and rose from her seat at table.

"Anything to soothe her, poor soul!" she whispered, as
she left Errington's side and advanced towards Lovisa till
she was within reach of the old woman's hand. She looked
like some grand white angel, who had stepped down from a
cathedral altar, as she stood erect and stately with a
gravely pitying expression in her lovely eyes, confronting
the sable-draped, withered, leering hag, who fixed upon her
a steady look of the most cruel and pitiless hatred.

"Daughter of Satan!" said Lovisa then, in intense
piercing tones that somehow carried with them a sense of
awe and horror. "Creature, in whose veins the fire of hell
burns without ceasing,—my *curse* upon you! My curse
upon the beauty of your body—may it grow loathsome in
the sight of all men! May those who embrace you, embrace
misfortune and ruin!—may love betray you and forsake you!
May your heart be broken even as mine has been!—may
your bridal bed be left deserted!—may your children wither
and pine from their hour of birth! Sorrow track you to
the grave!—may your death be lingering and horrible!
God be my witness and fulfill my words!"

And, raising her arms with wild gesture, she turned and
left the house. The spell of stupefied silence was broken
with her disappearance. Old Güldmar prepared to rush
after her and force her to retract her evil speech,—Errington was furious, and Britta cried bitterly. The lazy Lorimer was excited and annoyed.

"Fetch her back," he said, "and I'll dance upon her!"

But Thelma stood where the old woman had left her—she smiled faintly, but she was very pale. Errington approached her,—she turned to him and stretched out her hands with a little appealing gesture.

"My friend," she said softly, "do you think I deserve so many curses? Is there something about me that is evil?"

What Errington would have answered is doubtful,—his heart beat wildly—he longed to draw those little hands in his own, and cover them with passionate kisses,—but he was intercepted by old Güldmar, who caught his daughter in his arms and hugged her closely, his silvery beard mingling with the gold of her rippling hair.

"Never fear a wicked tongue, my bird!" said the old man fondly. "There is naught of harm that would touch thee either on earth or in heaven,—and a foul-mouthed curse must roll off thy soul like water from a dove's wing! Cheer thee, my darling—cheer thee! What! Thine own creed teaches thee that the gentle Mother of Christ, with her little white angels round her, watches over all innocent maids,—and thinkest thou she will let an old woman's malice and envy blight thy young days? No, no! *Thou* accursed?" And the *bonde* laughed loudly to hide the tears that moistened his keen eyes. "Thou art the sweetest blessing of my heart, even as thy mother was before thee! Come, come! Raise thy pretty head—here are these merry lads growing long-faced,—and Britta is weeping enough salt water to fill a bucket! One of thy smiles will set us all right again,—ay, there now!"—as she looked up and, meeting Philip's eloquent eyes, blushed, and withdrew herself gently from her father's arms,—"Let us finish our supper and think no more of yonder villainous old hag—she is crazy, I believe, and knows not what she says half her time. Now, Britta, cease thy grunting and sighing—'twill spoil thy face and will not mend the hole in thy grandmother's brain!"

"Wicked, spiteful, ugly old thing!" sobbed Britta; "I'll never, never, never forgive her!" Then, running to Thelma, she caught her hand and kissed it affectionately. "Oh, my dear, my dear! To think she should have cursed you, what dreadful, dreadful wickedness! Oh!" and Britta looked volumes of wrath. "I could have beaten her black and blue!"

Her vicious eagerness was almost comic—every one

laughed, including Thelma, though she pressed the hand of her little servant very warmly.

"Oh fie!" said Lorimer seriously. "Little girls mustn't whip their grandmothers; it's specially forbidden in the Prayer-book, isn't it, Phil?"

"I'm sure I don't know!" replied Errington merrily. "I believe there is something to the effect that a man may not marry his grandmother—perhaps that is what you mean?"

"Ah, no doubt!" murmured Lorimer languidly, as, with the others, he resumed his seat at the supper-table. "I knew there was a special mandate respecting one's particularly venerable relations, with a view to self-guidance in case they should prove troublesome, like Britta's good grandmamma. What a frightfully picturesque mouthing old lady she is!"

"She is *la petroleuse* of Norway!" exclaimed Duprèz. "She would make an admirable dancer in the Carmagnole!"

Macfarlane, who had preserved a discreet silence throughout the whole scene, here looked up.

"She's just a screech-owl o' mistaken piety," he said. "She minds me o' a glowerin' auld warlock of an aunt o' mine in Glasgie, wha sits in her chair a' day wi' ae finger on the Bible. She says she's gaun straight to heaven by special invitation o' the Lord, leavin' a' her blood relations howlin' vainly after her from their roastin' fires down below. Ma certes! she'll give ye a good rousin' curse if ye like! She's cursed me ever since I can remember her, —cursed me in and out from sunrise to sunset,—but I'm no the worse for't as yet,—an' it's dootful whether she's any the better."

"And yet Lovisa Elsland used to be as merry and lissom a lass as ever stepped," said Güldmar musingly. "I remember her well when both she and I were young. I was always on the sea at that time,—never happy unless the waves tossed me and my vessel from one shore to another. I suppose the restless spirit of my father was in me. I was never contented unless I saw some new coast every six months or so. Well! . . . . . Lovisa was always foremost among the girls of the village who watched me leave the Fjord,—and however long or short a time I might be absent, she was certain to be on the shore when my ship came sailing home again. Many a joke I have cracked with her and her companions—and she was a bonnie enough creature to look at then, I tell you,—though now she is like a battered figure-head on a wreck. Her marriage spoiled her temper,—her husband was as dark and sour a man as could be met with in all Norway, and when he and his fishing-boat sank in a squall off the Lofoden Islands, I doubt if she shed many tears for his loss. Her only daughter's husband went down in the same storm,—and he but three months wedded,—and the girl,—Britta's mother, —pined and pined, and even when her child was born took no sort of comfort in it. She died four years after Britta's birth—her death was hastened, so I have heard, through old Lovisa's harsh treatment,—anyhow the little lass she left behind her had no very easy time of it all alone with her grandmother,—eh Britta?"

Britta looked up and shook her head emphatically.

"Then," went on Güldmar, "when my girl came back the last time from France, Britta chanced to see her, and, strangely enough,"—here he winked shrewdly—"took a fancy to her face,—odd, wasn't it? However, nothing would suit her but that she must be Thelma's handmaiden, and here she is. Now you know her history,—she would be happy enough if her grandmother would let her alone; but the silly old woman thinks the girl is under a spell, and that Thelma is the witch that works it;"—and the old farmer laughed. "There's a grain of truth in the notion too, but not in the way she has of looking at it."

"All women are witches!" said Duprèz. "Britta is a little witch herself!"

Britta's rosy cheeks grew rosier at this, and she tossed her chestnut curls with an air of saucy defiance that delighted the Frenchman. He forgot his wounded cheek and his disfiguring bandages in the contemplation of the little plump figure, cased in its close-fitting scarlet bodice, and the tempting rosy lips that were in such close proximity to his touch.

"If it were not for those red hands!" he thought. "*Dieu!* what a charming child she would be! One would instantly kill the grandmother and kiss the granddaughter!"

And he watched her with admiration as she busied herself about the supper-table, attending to every one with diligence and care, but reserving her special services for Thelma, whom she waited on with a mingled tenderness and reverence, that were both touching and pretty to see.

The conversation now became general, and nothing further occurred to disturb the harmony and hilarity of the party—only Errington seemed somewhat abstracted, and answered many questions that were put to him at haphazard, without knowing, or possibly caring, whether his replies were intelligible or incoherent. His thoughts were dreamlike and brilliant with fairy sunshine. He understood at last what poets meant by their melodious musings, woven into golden threads of song—he seemed to have grasped some hitherto unguessed secret of his being—a secret that filled him with as much strange pain as pleasure. He felt as though he were endowed with a thousand senses,—each one keenly alive and sensitive to the smallest touch,—and there was a pulsation in his blood that was new and beyond his control,—a something that beat wildly in his heart at the sound of Thelma's voice, or the passing flutter of her white garments near him. Of what use to disguise it from himself any longer? He loved her! The terrible, beautiful tempest of love had broken over his life at last; there was no escape from its thunderous passion and dazzling lightning glory.

He drew a sharp quick breath—the hum of the gay voices around him was more meaningless to his ears than the sound of the sea breaking on the beach below. He glanced at the girl—the fair and innocent creature who had, in his imagination, risen to a throne of imperial height, from whence she could bestow on him death or salvation. How calm she seemed! She was listening with courteous patience to a long story of Macfarlane's whose Scotch accent rendered it difficult for her to understand. She was pale, Philip thought, and her eyes were heavy; but she smiled now and then,—such a smile! Even so sweetly might the " kiss-worthy " lips of the Greek Aphrodite part, could that eloquent and matchless marble for once breathe into life. He looked at her with a sort of fear. Her hands held his fate. What if she could not love him? What if he must lose her utterly? This idea overpowered him; his brain whirled, and he suddenly pushed away his untasted glass of wine, and rose abruptly from the table, heedless of the surprise his action excited.

" Hullo, Phil, where are you off to?" cried Lorimer. " Wait for me!"

" Tired of our company, my lad?" said Güldmar kindly, " You've had a long day of it,—and what with the climbing and the strong air, no doubt you'll be glad to turn in."

"Upon my life, sir," answered Errington, with some confusion, "I don't know why I got up just now! I was thinking,—I'm rather a dreamy sort of fellow sometimes, and——"

"He was asleep, and doesn't want to own it!" interrupted Lorimer sententiously. "You will excuse him; he means well! He looks rather seedy. I think, Mr. Güldmar, we'll be off to the yacht. By the way, you're coming with us to-morrow, aren't you?"

"Oh yes," said Thelma. "We will sail with you round by Soröe,—it is weird and dark and grand; but I think it is beautiful. And there are many stories of the elves and berg-folk, who are said to dwell there among the deep ravines. Have you heard about the berg-folk?" she continued, addressing herself to Errington, unaware of the effort he was making to appear cool and composed in her presence. "No? Then I must tell you to-morrow."

They all walked out of the house into the porch, and while her father was interchanging farewells with the others, she looked at Sir Philip's grave face with some solicitude.

"I am afraid you are very tired, my friend?" she asked softly, "or your head aches,—and you suffer?"

He caught her hands swiftly and raised them to his lips.

"Would you care much,—would you care at all, if I suffered?" he murmured in a low tone.

Then before she could speak or move, he let go her hands again, and turned with his usual easy courtesy to Güldmar. "Then we may expect you without fail to-morrow, sir! Good night!"

"Good night, my lad!"

And with many hearty salutations the young men took their departure, raising their hats to Thelma as they turned down the winding path to the shore. She remained standing near her father,—and, when the sound of their footsteps had died away, she drew closer still and laid her head against his breast.

"Cold, my bird?" queried the old man. "Why, thou art shivering, child!—and yet the sunshine is as warm as wine. What ails thee?"

"Nothing, father!" And she raised her eyes, glowing and brilliant as stars. "Tell me,—do you think often of my mother now!"

"Often!" And Güldmar's fine resolute face grew sad

and tender. " She is never absent from my mind! I see her
night and day, ay! I can feel her soft arms clinging round
my neck,—why dost thou ask so strange a question, little
one? Is it possible to forget what has been once loved?"

Thelma was silent for many minutes. Then she kissed
her father and said " good night." He held her by the hand
and looked at her with a sort of vague anxiety.

" Art thou well, my child?" he asked. " This little hand
burns like fire,—and thine eyes are too bright, surely, for
sleep to visit them? Art sure that nothing ails thee?"

"Sure, quite sure," answered the girl with a strange,
dreamy smile. " I am quite well,—and happy!"

And she turned to enter the house.

" Stay!" called the father. " Promise me thou wilt think
no more of Lovisa!"

"I had nearly forgotten her," she responded. " Poor
thing! She cursed me because she is so miserable, I suppose—all alone and unloved; it must be hard! Curses
sometimes turn to blessings, father! Good night!"

And she ascended the one flight of wooden stairs in the
house to her own bedroom—a little three-cornered place as
clean and white as the interior of a shell. Never once
glancing at the small mirror that seemed to invite her
charms to reflect themselves therein, she went to the quaint
latticed window and knelt down by it, folding her arms on
the sill while she looked far out to the Fjord. She could
see the English flag fluttering from the masts of the *Eulalie;* she could almost hear the steady plash of the oars
wielded by Errington and his friends as they rowed themselves back to the yacht. Bright tears filled her eyes, and
brimmed over, falling warmly on her folded hands.

" Would I care if you suffered?" she whispered. "Oh,
my love! . . . my love!"

Then, as if afraid lest the very winds should have heard
her half-breathed exclamation, she shut her window in
haste, and a hot blush crimsoned her cheeks.

Undressing quickly, she slipped into her little white bed
and, closing her eyes, fancied she slept, though her sleep
was but a waking dream of love in which all bright hopes
reached their utmost fulfillment, and yet were in some
strange way crossed with shadows which she had no power
to disperse. And later on, when old Güldmar slumbered
soundly, and the golden mid-night sunshine lit up every
nook and gable of the farmhouse with its lustrous glory,—

making Thelma's closed lattice sparkle like a carven jewel,
—a desolate figure lay prone on the grass beneath her window, with meagre pale face, and wide-open wild blue eyes
upturned to the fiery brillancy of the heavens. Sigurd
had come home;—Sigurd was repentant, sorrowful,
ashamed,—and broken-hearted.

CHAPTER XIII.

"O Love! O Love! O Gateway of Delight!
  Thou porch of peace, thou pageant of the prime
Of all God's creatures! I am here to climb
  Thine upward steps, and daily and by night
To gaze beyond them and to search aright
  The far-off splendor of thy track sublime."
           ERIC MACKAY'S *Love-letters of a Violinist.*

ON the following morning the heat was intense,—no
breath of wind stirred a ripple on the Fjord, and there was
a heaviness in the atmosphere which made the very brightness of the sky oppressive. Such hot weather was unusual
for that part of Norway, and according to Valdemar Svensen, betokened some change. On board the *Eulalie* everything was ready for the trip to Soröe,—steam was getting
up prior to departure,—and a group of red-capped sailors
stood prepared to weigh the anchor as soon as the signal
was given. Breakfast was over,—Macfarlane was in the
saloon writing his journal, which he kept with great exactitude, and Duprèz, who, on account of his wound, was
considered something of an invalid, was seated in a lounge
chair on deck, delightedly turning over a bundle of inflam-
matory French political journals received that morning.
Errington and Lorimer were pacing the deck arm in arm,
keeping a sharp look-out for the first glimpse of the returning boat which had been sent off to fetch Thelma and
her father. Errington looked vexed and excited,—Lorimer
bland and convincing.

"I can't help it, Phil!" he said. "It's no use fretting
and fuming at me. It was like Dyceworthy's impudence,
of course,—but there's no doubt he proposed to her,—and
it's equally certain that she rejected him. I thought I'd
tell you you had a rival,—not in me, as you seemed to
think yesterday,—but in our holy fat friend."

"Rival! pshaw!" returned Errington, with an angry
laugh. "He is not worth kicking!"

"Possibly not! Still I have a presentiment that he's the sort of fellow that won't take 'no' for an answer. He'll dodge that poor girl and make her life miserable if he can, unless——"

"Unless what?" asked Philip quickly.

Lorimer stopped in his walk, and, leaning against the deck-railings, looked his friend straight in the eyes.

"Unless you settle the matter," he said with a slight effort. "You love her,—tell her so!"

Errington laid one hand earnestly on his shoulder.

"Ah, George, you don't understand!" he said in a low tone, while his face was grave and full of trouble. "I used to think I was fairly brave, but I find I am a positive coward. I dare not tell her! She—Thelma—is not like other women. You may think me a fool,—I dare say you do,—but I swear to you I am afraid to speak, because—because, old boy,—if she were to refuse me,—if I knew there was no hope—well, I don't want to be sentimental,—but my life would be utterly empty and worthless,—so useless, that I doubt if I should care to live it out to the bitter end!"

Lorimer heard him in silence—a silence maintained partly out of sympathy, and partly that he might keep his own feelings well under control.

"But why persist in looking at the gloomy side of the picture?" he said at last. "Suppose she loves you?"

"Suppose an angel flew down from Heaven!" replied Philip, with rather a sad smile. "My dear fellow, who am I that I should flatter myself so far? If she were one of endse ordinary women to whom marriage is the be-all and tho-all of existence, it would be different—but she is not. Her thoughts are like those of a child or a poet,—why should I trouble them by the selfishness of my passion? for all passion *is* selfish, even at its best. Why should I venture to break the calm friendship she may have for me, by telling her of a love which might prove unwelcome!"

Lorimer looked at him with gentle amusement depicted in his face.

"Phil, you are less conceited than I thought you were," he said, with a light laugh, "or else you are blind—blind as a bat, old man! Take my advice,—don't lose any more time about it. Make the 'king's daughter of Norroway' happy, ... " and a brief sigh escaped him. "You are the man to do it. I am surprised at your density; Sigurd, the lunatic, has more perception. He sees which way the wind blows,—and that's why he's so desperately unhappy. He thinks—and thinks rightly too —that he will lose his ' beautiful rose of the northern forest,' as he calls her,—and that you are to be the robber. Hence his dislike to you. Dear me!" and Lorimer lit a cigarette and puffed at it complacently. " It seems to me that my wits are becoming sharper as I grow older, and that yours, my dear boy,—pardon me! . . . are getting somewhat blunted, otherwise you would certainly have perceived——" he broke off abruptly.

" Well, go on!" exclaimed Philip eagerly, with flashing eyes. " Perceived what?"

Lorimer laughed. " That the boat containing your Sunempress is coming along very rapidly, old fellow, and that you'd better make haste to receive her!"

This was the fact, and Duprèz had risen from his chair and was waving his French newspaper energetically to the approaching visitors. Errington hastened to the gangway with a brighter flush than usual on his handsome face, and his heart beating with a new sense of exhilaration and excitement. If Lorimer's hints had any foundation of truth —if Thelma loved him ever so little—how wild a dream it seemed! . . . why not risk his fate? He resolved to speak to her that very day if opportunity favored him,— and, having thus decided, felt quite masterful and heroic about it.

This feeling of proud and tender elation increased when Thelma stepped on deck that morning and laid her hands in his. For, as he greeted her and her father, he saw at a glance that she was slightly changed. Some restless dream must have haunted her—or his hurried words beneath the porch, when he parted from her the previous evening, had startled her and troubled her mind. Her blue eyes were no longer raised to his in absolute candor,—her voice was timid, and she had lost something of her usual buoyant and graceful self-possession. But she looked lovelier than ever with that air of shy hesitation and appealing sweetness. Love had thrown his network of light about her soul and body till, like Keats's " Madeleine,"

> " She seemed a splendid angel newly drest
> Save wings, for heaven!"

As soon as the Güldmars were on board, the anchor was

weighed with many a cheery and musical cry from the
sailors; the wheel revolved rapidly under Valdemar Svensen's firm hand,—and with a grand outward sweeping
curtsy to the majestic Fjord she left behind her, the *Eulalie*
steamed away, cutting a glittering line of white foam
through the smooth water as she went, and threading her
way swiftly among the clustering picturesque islands,—
while the inhabitants of every little farm and hamlet on
the shores, stopped for a while in their occupations to stare
at the superb vessel, and to dreamily envy the wealth of
the English *Herren* who could afford to pass the summer
months in such luxury and idleness. Thelma seated herself at once by Duprèz, and seemed glad to divert attention from herself to him.

"You are better, Monsieur Duprèz, are you not?" she
asked gently. "We saw Sigurd this morning; he came
home last night. He is very, very sorry to have hurt
you!"

"He need not apologize," said Duprèz cheerfully. "I
am delighted he gave me this scar, otherwise I am confi-
dent he would have put out the eye of Phil-eep. And that
would have been a misfortune! For what would the ladies
in London say if *le beau* Errington returned to them with
one eye! *Mon Dieu!* they would all be *en desespoir!*"

Thelma looked up. Philip was standing at some little
distance with Olaf Güldmar and Lorimer, talking and
laughing gaily. His cap was slightly pushed off his forehead, and the sun shone on his thick dark-chestnut curls;
his features, warmly colored by the wind and sea, were lit
up with mirth, and his even white teeth sparkled in an irresistible smile of fascinating good-humor. He was the
beau-ideal of the best type of Englishman, in the full tide
of youth, health and good spirits.

"I suppose he is a great favorite with all those beautiful
ladies?" she asked very quietly.

Something of gentle resignation in her tone struck the
Frenchman's sense of chivalry; had she been like any ordinary woman, bent on conquest, he would have taken a
mischievous delight in inventing a long list of fair ones
supposed to be deeply en amored of Errington's good looks,
—but this girl's innocent inquiring face inspired him with
quite a different sentiment.

"*Mais certainement!*" he said frankly and emphatically.
"Phil-eep is a favorite everywhere! Yet not more so with

women than with men. I love him extremely—he is a charming boy! Then you see, *chère Mademoiselle*, he is rich,—very rich,—and there are so many pretty girls who are very poor,—naturally they are enchanted with our Errington—*voyez-vous?*"

"I do not understand," she said, with a puzzled brow. "It is not possible that they should like him better because he is rich. He would be the same man without money as with it—it makes no difference!"

"Perhaps not to you," returned Duprèz, with a smile; "but to many it would make an immense difference! *Chère Mademoiselle*, it is a grand thing to have plenty of money, —believe me!"

Thelma shrugged her shoulders. "Perhaps," she answered indifferently. "But one cannot spend much on one's self, after all. The nuns at Arles used to tell me that poverty was a virtue, and that to be very rich was to be very miserable. They were poor,—all those good women, —and they were always cheerful."

"The nuns! *ah, mon Dieu!*" cried Duprèz. "The darlings know not the taste of joy—they speak of what they cannot understand! How should they know what it is to be happy or unhappy, when they bar their great convent doors against the very name of love!"

She looked at him, and her color rose.

"You always talk of *love*," she said, half reproachfully, "as if it were so common a thing! You know it is sacred —why will you speak as if it were all a jest?"

A strange emotion of admiring tenderness stirred Pierre's heart—he was very impulsive and impressionable.

"Forgive me!" he murmured penitently. Then he added suddenly, "You should have lived ages ago, *ma belle*, —the world of to-day will not suit you! You will be made very sorrowful in it, I assure you,—it is not a place for good women!"

She laughed. "You are morose," she said. "That is not like you! No one is good,—we all live to try and make ourselves better."

"What highly moral converse is going on here?" inquired Lorimer, strolling leisurely up to them. "Are you giving Duprèz a lecture, Miss Güldmar? He needs it.—so do I. Please give me a scolding!"

And he folded his hands with an air of demure appeal.

A sunny smile danced in the girl's blue eyes. "Always

you will be foolish!" she said. "One can never know you because I am sure you never show your real self to anybody. No,—I will not scold you, but I should like to find you out!"

"To find me out!" echoed Lorimer. "Why, what do you mean?"

She nodded her bright head with much sagacity.

"Ah, I do observe you often! There is something you hide; it is like when my father has tears in his eyes; he pretends to laugh, but the tears are there all the time. Now I see in you——" she paused, and her questioning eyes rested on his, seriously.

"This is interesting!" said Lorimer, lazily drawing a camp-stool opposite to her, and seating himself thereon. "I had no idea I was a human riddle. Can you read me, Miss Güldmar?"

"Yes," she answered slowly and meditatively. "Just a little. But I will not say anything; no—except this— that you are not altogether what you seem."

"Here, Phil!" called Lorimer, as he saw Errington approaching, arm in arm with Olaf Güldmar, "come and admire this young lady's power of perception. She declares I am not such a fool as I look!"

"Now," said Thelma, shaking her forefinger at him, "you know very well that I did not put it in that way. But is it not true, Sir Philip——" and she looked up for a moment, though her eyes drooped again swiftly under his ardent gaze, "is it not true that many people do hide their feelings, and pretend to be quite different to what they are?"

"I should say it was a very common fault," replied Errington. "It is a means of self-defense against the impertinent curiosity of outsiders. But Lorimer is free from it, —he has nothing to hide. At any rate, he has no secrets from me,—I'm sure of that!" And he clapped his hand heartily on his friend's shoulder.

Lorimer flushed slightly, but made no remark, and at that moment Macfarlane emerged from the saloon, where the writing of his journal had till now detained him. In the general handshaking and salutations which followed, the conversation took a different turn, for which Lorimer was devoutly thankful. His face was a tell-tale one,—and he was rather afraid of Philip's keen eyes. "I hope to Heaven he'll speak to her to-day," he thought, vexedly. "I hate being in suspense! My mind will be easier when I once know that he has gained his point,—and that there's not the ghost of a chance for any other fellow!"

Meanwhile the yacht skimmed along by the barren and rocky coast of Seiland; the sun was dazzling; yet there was a mist in the air as though the heavens were full of unshed tears. A bank of nearly motionless clouds hung behind the dark, sharp peaks of the Altenguard mountains, which now lay to the southward, as the vessel pursued her course. There was no wind; the flag on the mast flapped idly now and then with the motion of the yacht; and Thelma found herself too warm with her pretty crimson hood,—she therefore unfastened it and let the sunshine play on the uncovered gold of her hair. They had a superb view of the jagged glacier of Jedkè,—black in some parts, and in others white with unmelted snow,—and seeming, as it rose straight up against the sky, to be the majestic monument of some giant Viking. Presently, at her earnest request, Errington brought his portfolio of Norwegian sketches for Thelma to look at; most of them were excellently well done, and elicited much admiration from the *bonde*.

"It is what I have wondered at all my life," said he, "that skill of the brush dipped in color. Pictures surprise me as much as poems. Ah, men are marvellous creatures, when they are once brought to understand that they *are* men,—not beasts! One will take a few words and harmonize them into a song or a verse that clings to the world for ever; another will mix a few paints and dab a brush in them, and give you a picture that generation after generation shall flock to see. It is what is called genius, —and genius is a sort of miracle. Yet I think it is fostered by climate a good deal,—the further north, the less inspiration. Warmth, color, and the lightness of heart that a generally bright sky brings, enlarges the brain and makes it capable of creative power."

"My dear sir," said Lorimer, "England does not possess these climatic advantages, and yet Shakespeare was an Englishman."

"He must have travelled," returned Güldmar positively. "No one will make me believe that the man never visited Italy. His Italian scenes prove it,—they are full of the place and the people. The whole of his works, full of such wonderful learning, and containing so many types of different nations, show,—to *my* mind, at least,—that countries

11

were his books of study. Why I, who am only a farmer and proprietor of a bit of Norwegian land,—I have learned many a thing from simply taking a glance at a new shore each year. That's the way I used to amuse myself when I was young,—now I am old, the sea tempts me less, and I am fonder of my arm-chair; yet I've seen a good deal in my time—enough to provide me with memories for my declining days. And it's a droll thing, too," he added, with a laugh, "the further south you go, the more immoral and merry are the people; the further north, the more virtuous and miserable. There's a wrong balance somewhere,—but where, 'tis not easy to find out."

"Weel," said Macfarlane, "I can give ye a direct contradeection to your theory. Scotland lies to the north, and ye'll not find a grander harvest o' sinfu' souls anywhere between this an' the day o' judgment. I'm a Scotchman, an' I'm just proud o' my country—I'd back its men against a' the human race,—but I wadna say much for the stabeelity o' its women. I wad just tak to my heels and run if I saw a real, thumpin', red-cheeked, big-boned Scotch lassie makin' up to me. There's nae bashfulness in they sort, and nae safety."

"I will go to Scotland!" said Duprèz enthusiastically. "I feel that those—what do you call them, *lassies?*—will charm me!"

"Scotland I never saw," said Güldmar. "From all I have heard, it seems to me 'twould be too much like Norway. After one's eyes have rested long on these dark mountains and glaciers, one likes now and then to see a fertile sunshiny stretch of country such as France, or the plains of Lombardy. Of course there may be exceptions, but I tell you climatic influences have a great deal to do with the state of mind and morals. Now, take the example of that miserable old Lovisa Elsland. She is the victim of religious mania—and religious mania, together with superstition of the most foolish kind, is common in Norway. It happens often during the long winters; the people have not sufficient to occupy their minds; no clergyman—not even Dyceworthy—can satisfy the height of their fanaticism. They preach and pray and shriek and groan in their huts; some swear that they have the spirit of prophecy,—others that they are possessed of devils,—others imagine witchcraft, like Lovisa—and altogether there is such a howling on the name of Christ, that I am glad to be out of it,—for 'tis a sight to awaken the laughter and contempt of a pagan such as I am!"

Thelma listened with a slight shadow of pain on her features.

"Father is not a pagan," she declared, turning to Lorimer. "How can one be pagan if one believes that there is good in everything,—and that nothing happens except for the best?"

"It sounds to me more Christian than pagan," averred Lorimer, with a smile. "But it's no use appealing to *me* on such matters, Miss Güldmar. I am an advocate of the Law of Nothing. I remember a worthy philosopher who, —when he was in his cups,—earnestly assured me it was all right—' everything was nothing, and nothing was everything.' 'You are sure that is so?' I would say to him. ' My dear young friend—*hic*—I am positive! I have—*hic* —worked out the problem with—*hic*—care!' And he would shake me by the hand warmly, with a mild and moist smile, and would retire to bed walking sideways in the most amiable manner. I'm certain his ideas were correct as well as luminous."

They laughed, and then looking up saw that they were passing a portion of the coast of Seiland which was more than usually picturesque. Facing them was a great cavernous cleft in the rocks, tinted with a curious violet hue intermingled with bronze,—and in the strong sunlight these colors flashed with the brillancy of jewels, reflecting themselves in the pale slate-colored sea. By Errington's orders the yacht slackened speed, and glided along with an almost noiseless motion,—and they were silent, listening to the dash and drip of water that fell invisibly from the toppling crags that frowned above, while the breathless heat and stillness of the air added to the weird solemnity of the scene. They all rose from their chairs and leaned on the deck-rails, looking, but uttering no word.

"In one of these islands," said Thelma at last, very softly —"it was either Seiland or Soröe—they once found the tomb of a great chief. There was an inscription outside that warned all men to respect it, but they laughed at the warning and opened the tomb. And they saw, seated in a stone chair, a skeleton with a gold crown on its head and a great carved seal in its hand, and at its feet there was a stone casket. The casket was broken open, and it was full of gold and jewels. Well, they took all the gold and jewels, and buried the skeleton—and now,—do you know what happens? At midnight a number of strange persons are seen searching on the shore and among the rocks for the lost treasure, and it is said they often utter cries of anger and despair. And those who robbed the tomb all died suddenly."

"Served them right!" said Lorimer. "And now they are dead, I suppose the wronged ghosts don't appear any more?"

"Oh yes, they do," said Güldmar very seriously. "If any sailor passes at midnight, and sees them or hears their cries, he is doomed."

"But *does* he see or hear them?" asked Errington, with a smile.

"Well, I don't know," returned Güldmar, with a grave shake of his head. "I'm not superstitious myself, but I should be sorry to say anything against the berg-folk. You see they *may* exist, and it's no use offending them."

"And what do ye mean by the berg-folk?" inquired Macfarlane.

"They are supposed to be the souls of persons who died impenitent," said Thelma, "and they are doomed to wander on the hills till the day of judgment. It is a sort of purgatory."

Duprèz shook his fingers emphatically in the air.

"Ah, bah!" he said; "what droll things remain still in the world! Yes, in spite of liberty, equality, fraternity! You do not believe in foolish legends, Mademoiselle? For example,—do you think you will suffer purgatory?"

"Indeed yes!" she replied. "No one can be good enough to go straight to heaven. There must be some little stop on the way in which to be sorry for all the bad things one has done."

"'Tis the same idea as ours," said Güldmar. "We have two places of punishment in the Norse faith; one, *Nifle-heim*, which is a temporary thing like the Catholic purgatory; the other *Nastrond*, which is the counterpart of the Christian hell. Know you not the description of *Nifle-heim* in the *Edda*?—'tis terrible enough to satisfy all tastes. '*Hela*, or Death rules over the Nine Worlds of Nifleheim. Her hall is called Grief. Famine is her table, and her only servant is Delay. Her gate is a precipice, her porch Faintness, her bed Leanness,—Cursing and Howling are her tent. Her glance is dreadful and terrifying,—and her lips are blue with the venom of Hatred.' These words," he added, " sound finer in Norwegian, but I have given the meaning fairly."

" Ma certes ! " said Macfarlane chuckling. " I'll tell my aunt in Glasgie aboot it. This Nifleheim wad suit her pairfectly,—she wad send a' her relations there wi' tourist tickets, not available for the return journey ! "

" It seems to me," observed Errington, " that the Nine Worlds of Nifleheim have a resemblance to the different circles of Dante's Purgatory."

" Exactly so," said Lorimer. " All religions seem to me to be more or less the same,—the question *I* can never settle is,—which is the right one ? "

" Would you follow it if you knew ? " asked Thelma, with a slight smile. Lorimer laughed.

" Well, upon my life, I don't know ! " he answered frankly, " I never was a praying sort of fellow,—I don't seem to grasp the idea of it somehow. But there's one thing I'm certain of,—I can't endure a bird without song, —a flower without scent, or a *woman* without religion—she seems to me no woman at all."

" But *are* there any such women ? " inquired the girl surprised.

" Yes, there are undoubtedly ! Free-thinking, stumporator, have-your-rights sort of creatures. *You* don't know anything about them, Miss Güldmar—be thankful ! Now, Phil, how long is this vessel of yours going to linger here? "

Thus reminded, Errington called to the pilot, and in a few minutes the *Eulalie* resumed her usual speed, and bore swiftly on towards Soröe. This island, dreary and dark in the distance, grew somewhat more inviting in aspect on a nearer approach. Now and then a shaft of sunlight fell on some glittering point of felspar or green patch of verdure, —and Valdemar Svensen stated that he knew of a sandy creek where, if the party chose, they could land and see a small cave of exquisite beauty, literally hung all over with stalactites.

" I never heard of this cave," said Güldmar, fixing a keen eye on the pilot. " Art thou a traveller's guide to all such places in Norway ? "

Somewhat to Errington's surprise, Svensen changed color and appeared confused ; moreover, he removed his red cap altogether when he answered the *bonde*, to whom he spoke deferentially in rapid Norwegian. The old man laughed as he listened, and seemed satisfied; then, turning away, he linked his arm through Philip's, and said,

"You must pardon him, my lad, that he spoke in your presence a tongue unfamiliar to you. No offense was meant. He is of my creed, but fears to make it known, lest he should lose all employment—which is likely enough, seeing that so many of the people are fanatics. Moreover, he is bound to me by an oath,—which in olden days would have made him my serf,—but which leaves him free enough just now,—with one exception."

"And that exception?" asked Errington with some interest.

"Is, that should I ever demand a certain service at his hands, he dare not refuse it. Odd, isn't it? or so it seems to you," and Güldmar pressed the young man's arm lightly and kindly; "but our Norse oaths, are taken with great solemnity, and are as binding as the obligation of death itself. However, I have not commanded Valdemar's obedience yet, nor do I think I am likely to do so for some time. He is a fine, faithful fellow,—though too much given to dreams."

A gay chorus of laughter here broke from the little group seated on deck, of which Thelma was the centre,—and Güldmar stopped in his walk, with an attentive smile on his open, ruddy countenance.

"'Tis good for the heart to hear the merriment of young folks," he said. "Think you not my girl's laugh is like the ripple of a lark's song? just so clear and joyous?"

"Her voice is music itself!" declared Philip quickly and warmly. "There is nothing she says, or does, or looks,—that is not absolutely beautiful!"

Then, suddenly aware of his precipitation, he stopped abruptly. His face flushed as Güldmar regarded him fixedly, with a musing and doubtful air. But whatever the old man thought, he said nothing. He merely held the young baronet's arm a little closer, and together they joined the others,—though it was noticeable that during the rest of the day the *bonde* was rather abstracted and serious,—and that every now and then his eyes rested on his daughter's face with an expression of tender yearning and melancholy.

It was about two hours after luncheon that the *Eulalie* approached the creek spoken of by the pilot, and they were all fascinated by the loveliness as well as by the fierce grandeur of the scene. The rocks on that portion of Soröe appeared to have split violently asunder to admit some great in-rushing passage of the sea, and were piled up in toppling terraces to the height of more than two thousand feet above the level of the water. Beneath these wild and craggy fortresses of nature a shining stretch of beach had formed itself, on which the fine white sand, mixed with crushed felspar, sparkled like powdered silver. On the left-hand side of this beach could be distinctly seen the round opening of the cavern to which Valdemar Svensen directed their attention. They decided to visit it—the yacht was brought to a standstill, and the long-boat lowered. They took no sailors with them, Errington and his companions rowing four oars, while Thelma and her father occupied the stern. A landing was easily effected, and they walked toward the cavern, treading on thousands of beautiful little shells which strewed the sand beneath their feet. There was a deep stillness everywhere—the island was so desolate that it seemed as though the very sea-birds refused to make their homes in the black clefts of such steep and barren rocks.

At the entrance of the little cave Güldmar looked back to the sea.

"There's a storm coming!" he announced. "Those clouds we saw this morning have sailed thither almost as quickly as ourselves!"

The sky had indeed grown darker, and little wrinkling waves disturbed the surface of the water. But the sun as yet retained his sovereignty, and there was no wind. By the pilot's advice, Errington and his friends had provided themselves each with a pine torch, in order to light up the cavern as soon as they found themselves within it. The smoky crimson flare illuminated what seemed at a first glance to be a miniature fairy palace studded thickly with clusters of diamonds. Long pointed stalactites hung from the roof at almost mathematically even distances from one another,—the walls glistened with varying shades of pink and green and violet,—and in the very midst of the cave was a still pool of water in which all the fantastic forms and hues of the place mirrored themselves in miniature. In one corner the stalactites had clustered into the shape of a large chair overhung by a canopy, and Duprèz perceiving it, exclaimed—

" *Voilà!* A queen's throne! Come, Mademoiselle Güld mar, you must sit in it!"

"But I am not a queen," laughed Thelma. "A throne is for a king, also—will not Sir Philip sit there?"

"There's a compliment for you, Phil!" cried Lorimer, waving his torch enthusiastically. "Let us awaken the echoes with the shout of ' Long live the King!'"

But Errington approached Thelma, and taking her hand in his, said gently—

"Come! let me see you throned in state, Queen Thelma! To please me,—come!"

She looked up—the flame of the bright torch he carried illumined his face, on which love had written what she could not fail to read,—but she trembled as with cold, and there was a kind of appealing wonder in her troubled eyes. He drew closer, and pressed her hand more tightly; again he whispered, "Come, Queen Thelma!" As in a dream, she allowed him to lead her to the stalactite chair, and when she was seated therein, she endeavored to control the rapid beating of her heart, and to smile unconcernedly on the little group that surrounded her with shouts of mingled mirth and admiration.

"Ye just look fine!" said Macfarlane with undisguised delight. "Ye'd mak' a grand picture, wouldn't she, Errington?"

Philip gazed at her, but said nothing—his heart was too full. Sitting there among the glittering, intertwisted, and suspended rocks,—with the blaze from the torches flashing on her winsome face and luxuriant hair,—with that half-troubled, half-happy look in her eyes, and an uncertain shadowy smile quivering on her sweet lips, the girl looked almost dangerously lovely,—Helen of Troy could scarce have fired more passionate emotion among the old-world heroes than she unconsciously excited at that moment in the minds of all who beheld her. Duprèz for once understood what it was to reverence a woman's beauty, and decided that the flippant language of compliment was out of place—he therefore said nothing, and Lorimer, too, was silent, battling bravely against wild desires that were now, in his opinion, nothing but disloyalty to his friend. Old Güldmar's hearty voice aroused and startled them all.

"Now Thelma, child! If thou art a queen, give orders to these lads to be moving! 'Tis a damp place to hold a court in, and thy throne must needs be a cold one. Let us out to the blessed sunshine again—maybe we can climb one of yon wild rocks and get a view worth seeing."

" All right, sir ! " said Lorimer, chivalrously resolving that now Errington should have a chance. " Come on, Mac ! *Allons, marchons,*—Pierre ! Mr. Güldmar exacts our obedience ! Phil, you take care of the queen ! "

And skillfully pushing on Duprèz and Macfarlane before him, he followed Güldmar, who preceded them all,—thus leaving his friend in a momentary comparative solitude with Thelma. The girl was a little startled as she saw them thus taking their departure, and sprang up from her stalactite throne in haste. Sir Philip had laid aside his torch in order to assist her with both hands to descend the sloping rocks ; but her embarrassment at being left almost alone with him made her nervous and uncertain of foot,— she was hurried and agitated and anxious to overtake the others, and in trying to walk quickly she slipped and nearly fell. In one second she was caught in his arms and clasped passionately to his heart.

" Thelma ! Thelma ! " he whispered, " I love you, my darling—I love you ! "

She trembled in his strong embrace, and strove to release herself, but he pressed her more closely to him, scarcely knowing that he did so, but feeling that he held the world, life, time, happiness, and salvation in this one fair creature. His brain was in a wild whirl—the glitter of the stalactite cave turned to a gyrating wheel of jewel-work, there was nothing any more—no universe, no existence—nothing but love, love, love, beating strong hammer-strokes through every fibre of his frame. He glanced up, and saw that the slowly retreating forms of his friends had nearly reached the outer opening of the cavern. Once there, they would look back and——

" Quick, Thelma ! " and his warm breath touched her cheek. " My darling ! my love ! if you are not angry,— kiss me ! I shall understand."

She hesitated. To Philip that instant of hesitation seemed a cycle of slow revolving years. Timidly she lifted her head. She was very pale, and her breath came and went quickly. He gazed at her in speechless suspense,— and saw as in a vision the pure radiance of her face and star-like eyes shining more and more closely upon him. Then came a touch,—soft and sweet as a roseleaf pressed against his lips,—and for one mad moment he remembered nothing,—he was caught up like Homer's Paris in a cloud of gold, and knew not which was earth or heaven.

"You love me, Thelma?" he murmured in a sort of wondering rapture. " I cannot believe it, sweet! Tell me —you love me?"

She looked up. A new, unspeakable glory flushed her face, and her eyes glowed with the mute eloquence of awakening passion.

"Love you?" she said in a voice so low and sweet that it might have been the whisper of a passing fairy. "Ah, yes! more than my life!"

CHAPTER XIV.

"Sweet hands, sweet hair, sweet cheeks, sweet eyes, sweet mouth; Each singly wooed and won !"

DANTE ROSSETTI.

"HILLO, ho!" shouted Güldmar vociferously, peering back into the shadows of the cavern from whence the figures of his daughter and Errington were seen presently emerging. "Why, what kept you so long, my lad? We thought you were close behind us. Where's your torch?"

"It went out," replied Philip promptly, as he assisted Thelma with grave and ceremonious politeness to cross over some rough stones at the entrance, "and we had some trouble to find our way."

"Ye might hae called to us i' the way o' friendship," observed Macfarlane somewhat suspiciously, "and we wad hae lighted ye through."

"Oh, it was no matter!" said Thelma, with a charming smile. "Sir Philip seemed well to know the way, and it was not so very dark!"

Lorimer glanced at her and read plainly all that was written in her happy face. His heart sank a little; but, noticing that the old *bonde* was studying his daughter with a slight air of vexation and surprise, he loyally determined to divert the general attention from her bright blushes and too brilliantly sparkling eyes.

"Well! . . . here you both are, at any rate," he said lightly, "and I should strongly advise that we attempt no more exploration of the island of Soröe to-day. Look at the sky; and just now there was a clap of thunder."

"Thunder?" exclaimed Errington. " I never heard it!"

" I dare say not!" said Lorimer, with a quiet smile.
" Still *we* heard it pretty distinctly, and I think we'd better
make for the yacht."

" All right!" and Sir Philip sprang gaily into the long-
boat to arrange the cushions in the stern for Thelma. Never
had he looked handsomer or more high-spirited, and his
elation was noticed by all his companions.

" Something joyous has happened to our Phil-eep," said
Duprèz in a half-whisper. " He is in the air!"

" And something in the ither way has happened vera sud-
lenly to Mr. Güldmar," returned Macfarlane. " Th' auld
nan is in the dumps."

The *bonde's* face in truth looked sad and somewhat stern.
He scarcely spoke at all as he took his place in the boat
beside his daughter,—once he raised her little hand, looked
at t, and kissed it fondly.

They were all soon on their way back to the *Eulalie*,
over a sea that had grown rough and white-crested during
their visit to the stalactite cave. Clouds had gathered
thickly over the sky, and though a few shafts of sunlight
still forced a passage through them, the threatening darkness spread with steady persistency, especially to the
northern side of the horizon, where Storm hovered in the
shape of a black wing edged with coppery crimson. As
they reached the yacht a silver glare of lightning sprang
forth from beneath this sable pinion, and a few large
drops of rain began to fall. Errington hurried Thelma on
deck and down into the saloon. His friends, with Güldmar,
followed,—and the vessel was soon plunging through waves
of no small height on her way back to the Altenfjord. A
loud peal of thunder like a salvo of artillery accompanied
their departure from Soröe, and Thelma shivered a little as
she heard it.

" You are nervous, Mademoiselle Güldmar?" asked Duprèz, noticing her tremor.

" Oh no," she answered brightly. " Nervous? That is
to be afraid,—I am not afraid of a storm, but I do not like
it. It is a cruel, fierce thing; and I should have wished
to-day to be all sunshine—all gladness!" She paused, and
her eyes grew soft and humid.

" Then you have been happy to-day?" said Lorimer in a
low and very gentle voice.

She smiled up at him from the depths of the velvet
lounge in which Errington had placed her.

" Happy ? I do not think I have ever been so happy before ! " She paused, and a bright blush crimsoned her
cheeks ; then, seeing the piano open, she said suddenly,
" Shall I sing to you ? or perhaps you are all tired, and
would rather rest ? "

" Music *is* rest," said Lorimer rather dreamily, watching
her as she rose from her seat,—a tall, supple, lithe figure,
—and moved towards the instrument. " And *your* voice,
Miss Güldmar, would soothe the most weary soul that ever
dwelt in clay."

She glanced round at him, surprised at his sad tone.

" Ah, you are very, very tired, Mr. Lorimer, I am sure !
I will sing you a Norse cradle-song to make you go to
sleep. You will not understand the words though—will
that matter ? "

" Not in the least ! " answered Lorimer, with a smile.
" The London girls sing in German, Italian, Spanish, and
English. Nobody knows what they are saying : they
scarcely know themselves—but it's all right, and quite
fashionable."

Thelma laughed gaily. " How funny ! " she exclaimed.
" It is to amuse people, I suppose ! Well,—now listen."
And, playing a soft prelude, her rich contralto rippled forth
in a tender, passionate, melancholy melody,—so sweet and
heart-penetrating that the practical Macfarlane sat as one
in a dream,—Duprèz forgot to finish making the cigarette
he was daintily manipulating between his fingers, and
Lorimer had much ado to keep tears from his eyes. From
one song she glided to another and yet another ; her soul
seemed possessed by the very spirit of music. Meanwhile
Errington, in obedience to an imperative sign from old
Güldmar, left the saloon with him,—once outside the door,
the *bonde* said in a somewhat agitated voice—

" I desire to speak to you, Sir Philip, alone and undisturbed, if such a thing be possible."

" By all means ! " answered Philip. " Come to my ' den '
on deck. We shall be quite solitary there."

He led the way, and Olaf Güldmar followed him in
silence.

It was raining fiercely, and the waves, green towers of
strength, broke every now and then over the sides of the
yacht with a hissing shower of salt white spray. The
thunder rolled along the sky in angry reverberating echoes,
—frequent flashes of lightning leaped out like swords

drawn from dark scabbards,—yet towards the south the sky was clearing, and arrowy beams of pale gold fell from the hidden sun, with a soothing and soft lustre on the breast of the troubled water.

Güldmar looked about him, and heaved a deep sigh of refreshment. His eyes rested lovingly on the tumbling billows,—he bared his white head to the wind and rain.

"This is the life, the blood, the heart of a man!" he said, while a sort of fierce delight shone in his keen eyes. "To battle with the tempest,—to laugh at the wrath of waters,—to set one's face against the wild wind,—to sport with the elements as though they were children or serfs,—this is the joy of manhood! A joy," he added slowly, "that few so-called men of to-day can ever feel."

Errington smiled gravely. "Perhaps you are right, sir," he said; "but perhaps, at the same time, you forget that life has grown very bitter to all of us during the last hundred years or so. Maybe the world is getting old and used up, maybe the fault is in ourselves,—but it is certain that none of us nowadays are particularly happy, except at rare intervals when——"

At that moment, in a lull of the storm, Thelma's voice pealed upwards from the saloon. She was singing a French song, and the refrain rang out clearly—

"Ah! le doux son d'un baiser tendre!"

Errington paused abruptly in his speech, and turning towards a little closed and covered place on deck which was half cabin, half smoking-room, and which he kept as his own private sanctum, he unlocked it, saying—

"Will you come in here, sir? It's not very spacious, but I think it's just the place for a chat,—especially a private one."

Güldmar entered, but did not sit down,—Errington shut the door against the rain and beating spray and also remained standing. After a pause, during which the *bonde* seemed struggling with some inward emotion, he said resolutely—

"Sir Philip, you are a young man, and I am an old one. I would not willingly offend you—for I like you—yes!" And the old man looked up frankly: "I like you enough to respect you—which is more than I can say to many men I have known! But I have a weight on my heart that must be lifted. You and my child have been much together for many days,—and I was an old fool not to have foreseen the influence your companionship might have upon her. I may be mistaken in the idea that has taken hold of me—some wild words let fall by the poor boy Sigurd this morning, when he entreated my pardon for his misconduct of yesterday, have perhaps misled my judgment,—but—by the gods! I cannot put it into suitable words! I——"

"You think I love your daughter?" said Sir Philip quietly. "You are not mistaken, Sir! I love her with my whole heart and soul! I want you to give her to me as my wife."

A change passed over the old farmer's face. He grew deathly pale, and put out one hand feebly as though to seek some support. Errington caught it in his own and pressed it hard.

"Surely you are not surprised, Sir?" he added with eagerness. "How can I help loving her! She is the best and loveliest girl I have ever seen! Believe me,—I would make her happy!"

"And have you thought, young man," returned Güldmar slowly, "that you would make me desolate?—or, thinking it, have you cared?"

There was an infinite pathos in his voice, and Errington was touched and silent. He found no answer to this reproach. Güldmar sat down, leaning his head on his hand.

"Let me think a little," he said. "My mind is confused a bit. I was not prepared for——"

He paused and seemed lost in sorrowful meditation. By-and-by he looked up, and meeting Errington's anxious gaze, he broke into a short laugh.

"Don't mind me, my lad!" he said sturdily. "'Tis a blow, you see! I had not thought so far as this. I'll tell you the plain truth, and you must forgive me for wronging you. I know what young blood is, all the world over. A fair face fires it—and impulse makes it gallop beyond control. 'Twas so with me when I was your age,—though no woman, I hope, was ever the worse for my harmless love-making. But Thelma is different from most women,—she has a strange nature,—moreover, she has a heart and a memory,—if she once learns the meaning of love, she will never unlearn the lesson. Now, I thought, that like most young men of your type, you might, without meaning any actual evil, trifle with her—play with her feelings——"

"I understand, Sir," said Philip coolly, without displaying any offense. "To put it plainly, in spite of your liking for me, you thought me a snob."

This time the old man laughed heartily and unforcedly.

"Dear, dear!" he exclaimed. "You are what is termed in your own land, a peppery customer! Never mind—I like it. Why, my lad, the men of to-day think it fair sport to trifle with a pretty woman now and then——"

"Pardon!" interrupted Philip curtly. "I must defend my sex. We *may* occasionally trifle with those women who show us that they wish to be trifled with—but never with those who, like your daughter, win every man's respect and reverence."

Güldmar rose and grasped his hand fervently.

"By all the gods, I believe you are a true gentleman!" he said. "I ask your pardon if I have offended you by so much as a thought. But now"—and his face grew very serious—"we must talk this matter over. I will not speak of the suddenness of your love for my child, because I know, from my own past experience, that love is a rapid impulse—a flame ignited in a moment. Yes, I know that well!" He paused, and his voice trembled a little, but he soon steadied it and went on—"I think, however, my lad, that you have been a little hasty,—for instance, have you thought what your English friends and relatives will say to your marrying a farmer's daughter who,—though she has the blood of kings in her veins,—is, nevertheless, as this present world would judge, beneath you in social standing? I say, have you thought of this?"

Philip smiled proudly. "Certainly, sir, I have *not* thought of any such trifle as the opinion of society,—if that is what you mean. I have no relatives to please or displease—no friends in the truest sense of the world except Lorimer. I have a long list of acquaintances undoubtedly, —infinite bores, most of them,—and whether they approve or disapprove of my actions is to me a matter of profound indifference."

"See you!" said the *bonde* firmly and earnestly. "It would be an ill day for me if I gave my little one to a husband who might—mind! I only say *might*,—in the course of years, regret having married her."

"Regret!" cried Philip excitedly, then quieting down, he said gently. "My good friend, I do not think you understand me. You talk as if Thelma were beneath *me*. Good God! It is *I* who am infinitely beneath *her*! I am utterly unworthy of her in every way, I assure you—and I tell you so frankly. I have led a useless life, and a more or less selfish one. I have principally sought to amuse and interest myself all through it. I've had my vices to, and have them still. Beside Thelma's innocent white soul, mine looks villainous! But I can honestly say I never knew what love was till I saw her,—and now—well! I would give my life away gladly to save her from even a small sorrow."

"I believe you—I thoroughly believe you!" said Güldmar. "I see you love the child. The gods forbid that I should stand in the way of her happiness! I am getting old, and 'twas often a sore point with me to know what would become of my darling when I was gone,—for she is fair to look upon, and there are many human wolves ready to devour such lambs. Still, my lad, you must learn all. Do you know what is said of me in Bosekop?"

Errington smiled and nodded in the affirmative.

"You do?" exclaimed the old man, somewhat surprised. "You know they say I killed my wife—my wife! the creature before whom my soul knelt in worship night and day—whose bright head was the sunlight of life! Let me tell you of her, Sir Philip—'tis a simple story. She was the child of my dearest friend, and many years younger than myself. This friend of mine, Erik Erlandsen, was the captain of a stout Norwegian barque, running constantly between these wild waters and the coast of France. He fell in love with, and married a blue-eyed beauty from the Sogne Fjord, he carried her secretly away from her parents, who would not consent to the marriage. She was a timid creature, in spite of her queenly ways, and, for fear of her parents, she would never land again on the shores of Norway. She grew to love France,—and Erik often left her there in some safe shelter when he was was bound on some extra long and stormy passage. She took to the Catholic creed, too, in France, and learned to speak the French tongue, so Erik said, as though it were her own. At the time of the expected birth of her child, her husband had taken her far inland to Arles, and there business compelled him to leave her for some days. When he returned she was dead!—laid out for burial, with flowers and tapers round her. He fell prone on her body insensible,—and not for many hours did the people of the place dare to tell him that he was the father of a living child—a girl, with the great blue eyes and white skin of her mother. He would scarce look at it

—but at last, when roused a bit, he carried the little thing in his arms to the great Convent at Arles, and, giving the nuns money, he bade them take it and bring it up as they would, only giving it the name of Thelma. Then poor Erlandsen came home—he sought me out :—he said, ' Olaf, I feel that I am going on my last voyage. Promise you will see to my child—guard her, if you can, from an evil fate! For me there is no future!' I promised, and strove to cheer him—but he spoke truly—his ship went down in a storm on the Bay of Biscay, and all on board were lost. Then it was that I commenced my journeyings to and fro, to see the little maiden that was growing up in the Convent at Arles. I watched her for sixteen years—and when she reached her seventeenth birthday, I married her and brought her to Norway."

" And she was Thelma's mother ? " said Errington with interest.

" She was Thelma's mother," returned the *bonde*, " and she was more beautiful than even Thelma is now. Her education had been almost entirely French, but, as a child, she had learnt that I generally spoke English, and as there happened to be an English nun in the Convent, she studied that language and mastered it for the love of me—yes ! " he repeated with musing tenderness, " all for the love of me, —for she loved me, Sir Philip—ay ! as passionately as I loved her, and that is saying a great deal ! We lived a solitary happy life,—but we did not mix with our neighbors —our creeds were different,—our ways apart from theirs. We had some time of perfect happiness together. Three years passed before our child was born, and then "—the *bonde* paused awhile, and again continued,—" then my wife's health grew frail and uncertain. She liked to be in the fresh air, and was fond of wandering about the hills with her little one in her arms. One day—shall I ever forget it ! when Thelma was about two and a half years old, I missed them both, and went out to search for them, fearing my wife had lost her way, and knowing that our child could not toddle far without fatigue. I found them "—the *bonde* shuddered—" but how ? My wife had slipped and fallen through a chasm in the rocks,—high enough, indeed, to have killed her,—she was alive, but injured for life. She lay there white and motionless—little Thelma meanwhile sat smilingly on the edge of the rock, assuring me that her mother had gone to sleep ' *down there.*' Well ! " and Güld-

mar brushed the back of his hand across his eyes, " to make
a long story short, I carried my darling home in my arms
a wreck—she lingered for ten years of patient suffering, ten
long years! She could only move about on crutches,—the
beauty of her figure was gone—but the beauty of her face
grew more perfect every day! Never again was she seen
on the hills,—and so to the silly folks of Bosekop she
seemed to have disappeared. Indeed, I kept her very existence a secret,—I could not endure that others should
hear of the destruction of all that marvellous grace and
queenly loveliness! She lived long enough to see her
daughter blossom into girlhood,—then,—she died. I could
not bear to have her laid in the damp, wormy earth—you
know in our creed earth-burial is not practiced,—so I laid
her tenderly away in a king's tomb of antiquity,—a tomb
known only to myself and one who assisted me to lay her
in her last resting-place. There she sleeps right royally,
—and now is your mind relieved, my lad? For the reports
of the Bosekop folk must certainly have awakened some
suspicions in your mind?"

"Your story has interested me deeply, sir," said Errington; " but I assure you I never had any suspicions of you
at all. I always disregard gossip—it is generally scandalous, and seldom true. Besides, I took your face on trust,
as you took mine."

" Then," declared Güldmar, with a smile, " I have nothing more to say,—except "—and he stretched out both
hands—" may the great gods prosper your wooing! You
offer a fairer fate to Thelma than I had dreamed of for her
—but I know not what the child herself may say——"

Philip interrupted him. His eyes flashed, and he smiled.

" She loves me!" he said simply. Güldmar looked at
him, laughed a little, and sighed.

" She loves thee?" he said, relapsing into the *thee* and
thou he was wont to use with his daughter. " Thou hast
lost no time, my lad? When didst thou find that out?"

" To-day!" returned Philip, with that same triumphant
smile playing about his lips. " She told me so—yet even
now I cannot believe it!"

" Ah, well, thou mayest believe it truly," said Güldmar,
"for Thelma says nothing that she does not mean! The
child has never stooped to even the smallest falsehood."

Errington seemed lost in a happy dream. Suddenly he
roused himself and took Güldmar by the arm.

" Come," he said, " let us go to her ! She will wonder why we are so long absent. See ! the storm has cleared— the sun is shining. It is understood? You will give her to me ? "

" Foolish lad ! " said Güldmar gently. " What have I to do with it ? She has given herself to thee ! Love has over- whelmed both of your hearts, and before the strong sweep of such an ocean what can an old man's life avail? Nothing —less than nothing ! Besides, I *should* be happy—if I have regrets,—if I feel the tooth of sorrow biting at my heart— 'tis naught but selfishness. 'Tis my own dread of parting with her "—his voice trembled, and his fine face quivered with suppressed emotion.

Errington pressed his arm. " Our house shall be yours, sir ! " he said eagerly. " Why not leave this place and come with us ? "

Güldmar shook his head. " Leave Norway ! " he said— " leave the land of my fathers—turn my back on these mountains and fjords and glaziers? Never ! No, no, my lad, you're kind-hearted and generous as becomes you, and I thank you from my heart. But 'twould be impossible ! I should be like a caged eagle, breaking my wings against the bars of English conventionalities. Besides, young birds must make their nest without interference from the old ones."

He stepped out on deck as Errington opened the little cabin door, and his features kindled with enthusiasm as he looked on the the stretch of dark mountain scenery around him, illumined by the brilliant beams of the sun that shone out now in full splendor, as though in glorious defiance of the retreating storm, which had gradually rolled away in clouds that were tumbling one over the other at the ex- treme edge of the northern horizon, like vanquished armies taking to hasty flight.

" Could I stand the orderly tameness of your green En- gland, think you, after this ? " he exclaimed, with a compre- hensive gesture of his hand. " No, no ! When death comes —and 'twill not be long coming—let it find me with my face turned to the mountains, and nothing but their kingly crests between me and the blessed sky ! Come, my lad ! " and he relapsed into his ordinary tone. " If thou art like me when I was thy age, every minute passed away from thy love seems an eternity ! Let us go to her—we had best wait till the decks are dry before we assemble up here again."

They descended at once into the saloon, where they found Thelma being initiated into the mysteries of chess by Duprèz, while Macfarlane and Lorimer looked idly on. She glanced up from the board as her father and Errington entered, and smiled at them both with a slightly heightened color.

"This is such a wonderful game, father!" she said. "And I am so stupid, I cannot understand it! So Monsieur Pierre is trying to make me remember the moves."

"Nothing is easier!" declared Duprèz. "I was showing you how the bishop goes, so—cross-ways," and he illustrated his lesson. "He is a dignitary of the Church, you perceive *Bien!* it follows that he cannot go in a straight line, —if you observe them well, you will see that all the religious gentlemen play at cross purposes. You are very quick, Mademoiselle Güldmar,—you have perfectly comprehended the move of the castle, and the pretty plunge of the knight. Now, as I told you, the queen can do anything—all the pieces shiver in their shoes before her!"

"Why?" she asked, feeling a little embarrassed, as Sir Philip came and sat beside her, looking at her with an undoubtedly composed air of absolute proprietorship.

"Why? *Enfin*, the reason is simple!" answered Pierre. "The queen is a woman,—everything must give way to her wish!"

"And the king?" she inquired.

"Ah! *Le pauver Roi!* He can do very little—almost nothing! He can only move one step at a time, and that with much labor and hesitation—he is the wooden image of Louis XVI.!"

"Then," said the girl quickly, "the object of the game is to protect a king who is not worth protecting!"

Duprèz laughed. "Exactly! And thus, in this charming game, you have the history of many nations! Mademoiselle Güldmar has put the matter excellently! Chess is for those who intend to form republics. All the worry and calculation—all the moves of pawns, bishops, knights, castles, and queens,—all to shelter the throne which is not worth protecting! Excellent! Mademoiselle, you are not in favor of monarchies!"

"I do not know," said Thelma; "I have never thought of such things. But kings should be great men,—wise and powerful, better and braver than all their subjects, should they not?"

" Undoubtedly ! " remarked Lorimer ; " but, it's a curious thing, they seldom are. Now, our queen, God bless her—"

" Hear, hear ! " interrupted Errington, laughing good-humoredly. " I won't have have a word said against the dear old lady, Lorimer ! Granted that she hates London, and sees no fun in being stared at by vulgar crowds, I think she's quite right,—and I sympathize heartily with her liking for a cup of tea in peace and quiet with some old Scotch body who doesn't care whether she's a queen or a washerwoman."

" I think," said Macfarlane slowly, " that royalty has its duties, ye see, an' though I canna say I object to Her Majesty's homely way o' behavin', still there are a few matters that wad be the better for her pairsonal attention."

" Oh bother ! " said Errington gaily. " Look at that victim of the nation, the Prince of Wales ! The poor fellow hasn't a moment's peace of his life,—what with laying foundation stones, opening museums, inspecting this and visiting that, he is like a costermonger's donkey, that must gee-up or gee-wo as his master, the people bid. If he smiles at a woman, it is instantly reported that he's in love with her,—if he frankly says he considers her pretty, there's no end to the scandal. Poor royal wretch ! I pity him from my heart ! The unwashed, beer-drinking, gin-swilling classes, who clamor for shortened hours of labor, and want work to be expressly invented for their benefit, don't suffer a bit more than Albert Edward, who is supposed to be rolling idly in the very lap of luxury, and who can hardly call his soul his own. Why, the man can't eat a mutton-chop without there being a paragraph in the papers headed, ' Diet of the Prince of Wales.' His life is made an infinite bore to him, I'm positive ! "

Güldmar looked thoughtful. " I know little about kings or princes," he said, " but it seems to me, from what I *do* know, that they have but small power. They are mere puppets. In olden times they possessed supremacy, but now—"

" I will tell you," interrupted Duprèz excitedly, " who it is that rules the people in these times,—it is the *Pen*— *Madame la Plume.* A little black, sharp, scratching devil she is,—empress of all nations ! No crown but a point,— no royal robe save ink ! It is certain that as long as *Madame la Plume* gambols freely over her realms of paper, so long must kings and autocrats shake in their shoes and be uncertain of their thrones. *Mon Dieu!* if I had but the gift of writing, I would conquer the world!"

"There are an immense number of people writing just now, Pierre," remarked Lorimer, with a smile, "yet they don't do much in the conquering line."

"Because they are afraid!" said Duprèz. "Because they have not the courage of their opinions! Because they dare not tell the truth!"

"Upon my life, I believe you are right!" said Errington. "If there were a man bold enough to declare truths and denounce lies, I should imagine it quite possible that he might conquer the world,—or, at any rate, make it afraid of him."

"But is the world so full of lies?" asked Thelma timidly.

Lorimer looked at her gravely. "I fear so, Miss Güldmar! I think it has a tolerable harvest of them every year,—a harvest, too, that never fails! But I say, Phil! Look at the sun shining! Let us go up on deck,—we shall soon be getting back to the Altenfjord."

They all rose, threw on their caps, and left the saloon with the exception of Errington, who lingered behind, watching his opportunity, and as Thelma followed her father he called her back softly—

"Thelma!"

She hesitated, and then turned towards him,—her father saw her movement, smiled at her, and nodded kindly, as he passed through the saloon doors and disappeared. With a beating heart, she sprang quickly to her lover's side, and as he caught her in his arms, she whispered—

"You have told him?"

"Your father? Yes, my darling!" murmured Philip, as he kissed her sweet, upturned lips. "Be quite happy—he knows everything. Come, Thelma! tell me again you love me—I have not heard you say it properly yet!"

She smiled dreamily as she leaned against his breast and looked up into his eyes.

"I cannot say it properly!" she said. "There is no language for my heart! If I could tell you all I feel, you would think it foolish, I am sure, because it is all so wild and strange,"—she stopped, and her face grew pale,— "oh!" she murmured with a slight tremor; "it is terrible!"

"What is terrible, my sweet one?" asked Errington,

drawing her more closely, and folding her more tightly in his arms.

She sighed deeply. " To have no more life of my own ! " she answered, while her low voice quivered with intense feeling. " It has all gone—to you ! And yours has come to me !—is it not strange and almost sad ? How your heart beats, poor boy !—I can hear it throb, throb—so fast !— here, where I am resting my head." She looked up, and her little white hand caressed his cheek. " Philip," she said very softly, " what are you thinking about ? Your eyes shine so brightly—do you know you have beautiful eyes ? "

" Have I ? " he murmured abstractedly, looking down on that exquisite, innocent, glowing face, and trembling with the force of the restrained passion that kindled through him. " I don't know about that !—yours seem to me like two stars fallen from heaven ! Oh, Thelma, my darling !— God make me worthy of you."

He spoke with intense fervor,—kissing her with a tenderness, in which there was something of reverence as well as fear. The whole soul of the man was startled and roused to inexpressible devotion, by the absolute simplicity and purity of her nature—the direct frankness with which she had said her life was his—his !—and in what way was *he* fitted to be the guardian and possessor of this white lily from the garden of God ? She was so utterly different to all women as he had known them—as different as a bird of paradise to a common house-sparrow. Meanwhile, as these thoughts flitted through his brain, she moved gently from his embrace and smiled proudly, yet sweetly.

" Worthy of me ? " she said softly and wonderingly. " It is I that will pray to be made worthy of *you !* You must not put it wrongly, Philip ! "

He made no answer, but looked at her as she stood before him, majestic as a young empress in her straight, unadorned white gown.

" Thelma ! " he said suddenly, " do you know how lovely you are ? "

" Yes ! " she answered simply ; " I know it, because I am like my mother. But it is not anything to be beautiful,— unless one is loved,—and then it is different ! I feel much more beautiful now, since you think me pleasant to look at ! "

Philip laughed and caught her hand. " What a child

you are!" he said. "Now let me see this little finger."
And he loosened from his watch-chain a half-hoop ring of
brilliants. "This belonged to *my* mother, Thelma," he
continued gently, " and since her death I have always carried it about with me. I resolved never to part with it, except to——" He paused and slipped it on the third finger
of her left hand, where it sparkled bravely.

She gazed at it in surprise. "You part with it now?"
she asked, with wonder in her accents. "I do not understand!"

He kissed her. "No? I will explain again, Thelma!—
and you shall not laugh at me as you did the very first
time I saw you! I resolved never to part with this ring, I
say, except to—my promised wife. *Now* do you understand?"

She blushed deeply, and her eyes dropped before his
ardent gaze.

"I do thank you very much, Philip,"—she faltered
timidly,—she was about to say something further when
suddenly Lorimer entered the saloon. He glanced from
Errington to Thelma, and from Thelma back again to Errington,—and smiled. So have certain brave soldiers been
known to smile in face of a death-shot. He advanced with
his usual languid step and nonchalant air, and removing
his cap, bowed gravely and courteously.

"Let me be the first to offer my congratulations to the
future Lady Errington! Phil, old man! . . . I wish you
joy!"

CHAPTER XV.

"Why, sir, in the universal game of double-dealing, shall not the
cleverest tricksters play each other false by haphazard, and so betray their closest secrets, to their own and their friends' infinite
amazement?"—CONGREVE.

WHEN Olaf Güldmar and his daughter left the yacht that
evening, Errington accompanied them, in order to have the
satisfaction of escorting his beautiful betrothed as far as
her own door. They were all three very silent—the *bonde*
was pensive, Thelma shy, and Errington himself was too
happy for speech. Arriving at the farmhouse, they saw
Sigurd curled up under the porch, playing idly with the
trailing rose-branches, but, on hearing their footsteps, he

looked up, uttered a wild exclamation, and fled. Güldmar tapped his own forehead significantly.

"He grows worse and worse, the poor lad!" he said somewhat sorrowfully. "And yet there is a strange mingling of foresight and wit with his wild fancies. Wouldst thou believe it, Thelma, child," and here he turned to his daughter and encircled her waist with his arm—"he seemed to know how matters were with thee and Philip, when I was yet in the dark concerning them!"

This was the first allusion her father had made to her engagement, and her head drooped with a sort of sweet shame.

"Nay, now, why hide thy face?" went on the old man cheerily. "Didst thou think I would grudge my bird her summer-time? Not I! And little did I hope for thee, my darling, that thou wouldst find a shelter worthy of thee in this wild world!" He paused a moment, looking tenderly down upon her, as she nestled in mute affection against his breast,—then addressing himself to Errington, he went on—

"We have a story in our Norse religion, my lad, of two lovers who declared their passion to each other, on one stormy night in the depth of winter. They were together in a desolate hut on the mountains, and around them lay unbroken tracts of frozen snow. They were descended from the gods, and therefore the gods protected them—and it happened that after they had sworn their troth, the doors of the snow-bound hut flew suddenly open, and lo! the landscape had changed—the hills were gay with grass and flowers,—the sky was blue and brilliant, the birds sang, and everywhere was heard the ripple of waters let loose from their icy fetters, and gamboling down the rocks in the joyous sun. This was the work of the goddess Friga,— the first kiss exchanged by the lovers she watched over, banished Winter from the land, and Spring came instead. 'Tis a pretty story, and true all the world over—true for all men and women of all creeds! It must be an ice- bound heart indeed that will not warm to the touch of love —and mine, though aged, grows young again in the joy of my children." He put his daughter gently from him to- wards Philip, saying with more gravity, "Go to him, child! —go—with thy old father's blessing! And take with thee the three best virtues of a wife,—truth, humility, and obe- dience. Good night, my son!" and he wrung Errington's hand with fervor. "You'll take longer to say good night to Thelma," and he laughed, "so I'll go in and leave you to it!"

And with a good-natured nod, he entered the house whistling a tune as he went, that they might not think he imagined himself lonely or neglected,—and the two lovers paced slowly up and down the garden-path together, exchanging those first confidences which to outsiders seem so eminently foolish, but which to those immediately concerned are most wonderful, delightful, strange, and enchanting beyond all description. Where, from a practical point of view, is the sense of such questions as these— "When did you love me first?" "What did you feel when I said so-and-so?" "Have you dreamt of me often?" "Will you love me always, always, always?" and so on *ad infinitum*. "Ridiculous rubbish!" exclaims the would-be strong-minded, but secretly savage old maid,—and the selfishly matter-of-fact, but privately fidgety and lonely old bachelor. Ah! but there are those who could tell you that at one time or another of their lives this "ridiculous rubbish" seemed far more important than the decline and fall of empires,—more necessary to existence than light and air,—more fraught with hope, fear, suspense, comfort, despair, and anxiety than anything that could be invented or imagined! Philip and Thelma,—man and woman in the full flush of youth, health, beauty, and happiness,—had just entered their Paradise,—their fairy-garden,—and every little flower and leaf on the way had special, sweet interest for them. Love's indefinable glories,—Love's proud possibilities,—Love's long ecstasies,—these, like so many spirit-figures, seemed to smile and beckon them on, on, on, through golden seas of sunlight,—through flower-filled fields of drowsy entrancement,—through winding ways of rose-strewn and lily-scented leafage,—on, on, with eyes and hearts absorbed in one another,—unseeing any end to the dreamlike wonders that, like some heavenly picture-scroll, unrolled slowly and radiantly before them. And so they murmured those unwise, tender things which no wisdom in the world has ever surpassed, and when Philip at last said "Good night!" with more reluctance than Romeo, and pressed his parting kiss on his love's sweet, fresh mouth,— the riddle with which he had puzzled himself so often was resolved at last,—life *was* worth living, worth cherishing, worth ennobling. The reason of all things seemed clear to him,—Love, and Love only, supported, controlled, and grandly completed the universe! He accepted this answer to all perplexities,—his heart expanded with a sense of large content—his soul was satisfied.

Meanwhile, during his friend's absence from the yacht, Lorimer took it upon himself to break the news to Duprèz and Macfarlane. These latter young gentleman had had their suspicions already, but they were not quite prepared to hear them so soon confirmed. Lorimer told the matter in his own way.

" I say, you fellows!" he remarked carelessly, as he sat smoking in their company on deck, " you'd better look out! If you stare at Miss Güldmar too much, you'll have Phil down upon you!"

" Ha, ha!" exclaimed Duprèz slyly, " the dear Phil-eep is in love?"

" Something more than that," said Lorimer, looking absently at the cigarette he held between his fingers,—" he's an engaged man."

" Engaged!" cried Macfarlane excitedly. " Ma certes! He has the deevil's own luck! He's just secured for himself the grandest woman in the warld!"

" *Je le crois bien!*" said Duprèz gravely, nodding his head several times. " Phil-eep is a wise boy! He is the fortunate one! I am not for marriage at all—no! not for myself,—it is to tie one's hands, to become a prisoner,—and that would not suit me; but if I were inclined to captivity, I should like Mademoiselle Güldmar for my beautiful gaoler. And beautiful she is, *mon Dieu!* . . . beyond all comparison!"

Lorimer was silent, so was Macfarlane. After a pause Duprèz spoke again.

" And do you know, *cher* Lorimer, when our Phil-eep will marry?"

" I haven't the slightest idea," returned Lorimer. " I know he's engaged, that's all."

Suddenly Macfarlane broke into a chuckling laugh.

" I say, Lorimer," he said, with his deep-set, small grey eyes sparkling with mischief. " 'Twould be grand fun to see auld Dyceworthy's face when he hears o't. By the Lord! He'll fall to cursin' an' swearin' like ma pious aunt in Glasgie, or that auld witch that cursed Miss Thelma yestreen!"

"An eminently unpleasant old woman *she* was!" said Lorimer musingly. "I wonder what she meant by it!"

"She meant, *mon cher*," said Duprèz airily, "that she knew herself to be ugly and venerable, while Mademoiselle was youthful and ravishing,—it is a sufficient reason to excite profanity in the mind of a lady!"

"Here comes Errington!" said Macfarlane, pointing to the approaching boat that was coming swiftly back from the Güldmars' pier. "Lorimer, are we to congratulate him?"

"If you like!" returned Lorimer. "I dare say he won't object."

So that as soon as Sir Philip set foot on the yacht, his hands were cordially grasped, and his friends outvied each other in good wishes for his happiness. He thanked them simply and with a manly straightforwardness, entirely free from the usual affected embarrassment that some modern young men think it seemly to adopt under similar circumstances.

"The fact is," he said frankly, "I congratulate myself,— I'm more lucky than I deserve, I know!"

"What a sensation she will make in London, Phil!" said Lorimer suddenly. "I've just thought of it! Good Heavens! Lady Winsleigh will cry for sheer spite and vexation!"

Philip laughed. "I hope not," he said. "I should think it would need immense force to draw a tear from her ladyship's cold bright eyes."

"She used to like you awfully, Phil!" said Lorimer. "You were a great favorite of hers."

"All men are her favorites with the exception of one— her husband!" observed Errington gaily. "Come along, let's have some champagne to celebrate the day! We'll propose toasts and drink healths—we've got a fair excuse for jollity this evening."

They all descended into the saloon, and had a merry time of it, singing songs and telling good stories, Lorimer being the gayest of the party, and it was long past midnight when they retired to their cabins, without even looking at the wonders of, perhaps, the most gorgeous sky that had yet shone on their travels—a sky of complete rose-color, varying from the deepest shade up to the palest, in which the sun glowed with a subdued radiance like an enormous burning ruby.

Thelma saw it, standing under her house-porch, where her father had joined her,—Sigurd saw it,—he had come out from some thicket where he had been hiding, and he now sat, in a humble, crouching posture at Thelma's feet. All three were silent, reverently watching the spreading splendor of the heavens. Once Güldmar addressed his daughter in a soft tone.

"Thou are happy, my bird?"

She smiled—the expression of her face was almost divine in its rapture.

"Perfectly happy, my father!"

At the sound of her dulcet voice, Sigurd looked up. His large blue eyes were full of tears, he took her hand and held it in his meagre and wasted one.

"Mistress!" he said suddenly, "do you think I shall soon die?"

She turned her pitying eyes down upon him, startled by the vibrating melancholy of his tone.

"Thou wilt die, Sigurd," answered Güldmar gently, "when the gods please,—not one second sooner or later. Art thou eager to see Valhalla?"

Sigurd nodded dreamily. "They will understand me there!" he murmured. "And I shall grow straight and strong and brave! Mistress, if you meet me in Valhalla, you will love me!"

She stroked his wild fair locks. "I love you now, Sigurd," she said tenderly. "But perhaps we shall all love each other better in heaven."

"Yes, yes!" exclaimed Sigurd, patting her hand caressingly. "When we are all dead, dead! When our bodies crumble away and turn to flowers and birds and butterflies, —and our souls come out like white and red flames,—yes! . . . then we shall love each other and talk of such strange, strange things!" He paused and laughed wildly. Then his voice sank again into melancholy monotony—and he added: "Mistress, you are killing poor Sigurd!"

Thelma's face grew very earnest and anxious. "Are you vexed with me, dear?" she asked soothingly. "Tell me what it is that troubles you?"

Sigurd met her eyes with a look of speechless despair and shook his head.

"I cannot tell you!" he muttered. "All my thoughts have gone to drown themselves one by one in the cold sea! My heart was buried yesterday, and I saw it sealed down into its coffin. There is something of me left,—something that dances before me like a flame,—but it will not rest, it does not obey me. I call it, but it will not come! And I am getting tired, mistress—very, very tired!" His voice broke, and a low sob escaped him,—he hid his face in the folds of her dress. Güldmar looked at the poor fellow compassionately.

"The wits wander further and further away!" he said to his daughter in a low tone. " 'Tis a mind like a broken rainbow, split through by storm—'twill soon vanish. Be patient with him, child,—it cannot be for long!"

"No, not for long!" cried Sigurd, raising his head brightly. "That is true—not for long! Mistress, will you come to-morrow with me and gather flowers? You used to love to wander with your poor boy in the fields,—but you have forgotten,—and I cannot find any blossoms without you! They will not show themselves unless you come! Will you? dear, beautiful mistress! will you come?"

She smiled, pleased to see him a little more cheerful. "Yes, Sigurd," she said; "I will come. We will go together early to-morrow morning and gather all the flowers we can find. Will that make you happy?"

"Yes!" he said, softly kissing the hem of her dress. "It will make me happy—for the last time."

Then he rose in an attitude of attention, as though he had been called by some one at a distance,—and with a grave, preoccupied air he moved away, walking on tip-toe as though he feared to interrupt the sound of some soft invisible music. Güldmar sighed as he watched him disappear.

"May the gods make us thankful for a clear brain when we have it!" he said devoutly; and then turning to his daughter, he bade her good night, and laid his hands on her golden head in silent but fervent blessing. "Child," he said tremulously, "in the new joys that await thee, never forget how thy old father loves thee!"

Then, not trusting himself to say more, he strode into the house and betook himself to slumber. Thelma followed his example, and the old farmhouse was soon wrapped in the peace and stillness of the strange night—a night of glittering sunshine. Sigurd alone was wakeful,—he lay at the foot of one of the tallest pine-trees, and stared persistently at the radiant sky through the network of dark branches. Now and then he smiled as though he saw some beatific vision—sometimes he plucked fitfully at the soft long moss on which he had made his couch, and sometimes he broke into a low, crooning song. God alone knew the broken ideas, the dim fancies, the half-born desires, that glimmered like pale ghosts in the desert of his brain,—God alone, in the great Hereafter, could solve the problen of his sorrows and throw light on his soul's darkness.

It was past six in the morning when he arose, and smoothing back his tangled locks, went to Thelma's window and sat down beneath it, in mute expectancy. He had not long to wait,—at the expiration of ten or fifteen minutes, the little lattice was thrown wide open, and the girl's face, fresh as a rose, framed in a shower of amber locks, smiled down upon him.

"I am coming, Sigurd!" she cried softly and joyously. "How lovely the morning is! Stay for me there! I shall not be long."

And she disappeared, leaving her window open. Sigurd heard her singing little scraps of song to herself, as she moved about in the interior of her room. He listened, as though his soul were drawn out of him by her voice,—but presently the rich notes ceased, and there was a sudden silence. Sigurd knew or guessed the reason of that hush, —Thelma was at her prayers. Instinctively the poor forlorn lad folded his wasted hands—most piteously and most imploringly he raised his bewildered eyes to the blue and golden glory of the sky. His conception of God was indefinable ; his dreams of heaven, chaotic minglings of fairy-land with Valhalla,—but he somehow felt that wherever Thelma's holy aspirations turned, there the angels must be listening.

Presently she came out of the house, looking radiant as the morning itself,—her luxuriant hair was thrown back over her shoulders, and fell loosely about her in thick curls, simply confined by a knot of blue ribbon. She carried a large osier basket, capacious, and gracefully shaped.

"Now, Sigurd," she called sweetly, "I am ready! Where shall we go?"

Sigurd hastened to her side, happy and smiling.

"Across there," he said, pointing toward the direction of Bosekop. "There is a stream under the trees that laughs to itself all day—you know it, mistress? And the poppies are in the field as you go—and by the banks there are the

heart's-ease flowers—we cannot have too many of *them!*
Shall we go?"

"Wherever you like, dear," answered Thelma tenderly,
looking down from her stately height on the poor stunted
creature at her side, who held her dress as though he were
a child clinging to her as his sole means of guidance. "All
the land is pleasant to-day."

They left the farm and its boundaries. A few men were
at work on one of Güldmar's fields, and these looked up,—
half in awe, half in fear,—as Thelma and her fantastic
servitor passed along.

"'Tis a fine wench!" said one man, resting on his spade,
and following with his eyes the erect, graceful figure of his
employer's daughter.

"Maybe, maybe!" said another gruffly; "but a fine
wench is a snare of the devil! Do ye mind what Lovisa
Elsland told us?"

"Ay, ay," answered the first speaker, "Lovisa knows,—
Lovisa is the wisest woman we have in these parts—that's
true! The girl's a witch, for sure!"

And they resumed their work in gloomy silence. Not
one of them would have willingly labored on Olaf Güldmar's land, had not the wages he offered been above the
usual rate of hire,—and times were bad in Norway. But
otherwise, the superstitious fear of him was so great that
his fields might have gone untilled and his crops ungath-
ered,—however, as matters stood, none of them could deny
that he was a good paymaster, and just in his dealings with
those whom he employed.

Thelma and Sigurd took their way in silence across a
perfumed stretch of meadow-land,—the one naturally fertile spot in that somewhat barren district. Plenty of flowers blossomed at their feet, but they did not pause to gather
these, for Sigurd was anxious to get to the stream where
the purple pansies grew. They soon reached it—it was a
silvery clear ribbon of water that unrolled itself in bright
folds, through green, transparent tunnels of fern and waving grass—leaping now and then with a swift dash over a
smooth block of stone or jagged rock—but for the most
part gliding softly, with a happy, self-satisfied murmur, as
though it were some drowsy spirit dreaming joyous dreams.
Here nodded the grave, purple-leaved pansies,—legendary
consolers of the heart,—their little, quaint, expressive
physiognomies turned in every direction; up to the sky, as

though absorbing the sunlight,—down to the ground, with
an almost severe air of meditation, or curled sideways on
their stems in a sort of sly reflectiveness.

Sigurd was among them at once—they were his friends,
—his playmates, his favorites,—and he gathered them
quickly yet tenderly, murmuring as he did so, " Yes, you
must all die; but death does not hurt; no! life hurts, but
not death! See! as I pluck you, you all grow wings and
fly away—away to other meadows, and bloom again." He
paused, and a puzzled look came into his eyes. He turned
toward Thelma, who had seated herself on a little knoll
just above the stream, " Tell me, mistress," he said, " do the
flowers go to heaven? "

She smiled. " I think so, dear Sigurd," she said; " I
hope so! I am almost sure they do."

Sigurd nodded with an air of satisfaction.

" That is right," he observed. " It would never do to
leave them behind, you know! They would be missed, and
we should have to come down again and fetch them——"
A crackling among the branches of some trees startled him,
—he looked round, and uttered a peculiar cry like the cry
of a wild animal, and exclaimed, " Spies, spies! ha! ha!
secret, wicked faces that are afraid to show themselves!
Come out! Mistress, mistress! make them come out! "

Thelma rose, surprised as his gesticulations, and came
towards him; to her utter astonishment she found herself
confronted by old Lovisa Elsland, and the Reverend Mr.
Dyceworthy's servant, Ulrika. On both women's faces
there was a curious expression of mingled fear, triumph,
and malevolence. Lovisa was the first to break silence.

" At last! " she croaked, in a sort of slow, monotonous
tone. " At last, Thelma Güldmar, the Lord has delivered
you into my hands! "

Thelma drew Sigurd close to her, and slipped one arm
around him.

" Poor soul! " she said softly, with sweet pitying eyes
fixed fearlessly on the old hag's withered, evil visage.
" You must be tired, wandering about on the hills as you
do! If you are her friend," she added, addressing Ulrika,
" why do you not make her rest at home and keep warm?
She is so old and feeble! "

" Feeble! " shrieked Lovisa; " feeble! " And she seemed
choking with passion. " If I had my fingers at your
throat, you should then see if I am feeble! I——" Ulrika

13

pulled her by the arm, and whispered something which had the effect of calming her a little. " Well," she said, " you speak then! I can wait!"

Ulrika cleared her husky voice, and fixed her dull eyes on the girl's radiant countenance.

" You must go away," she said coldly and briefly. " You and your father, and this creature," and she pointed contemptuously to the staring Sigurd. " Do you understand? You must leave the Altenfjord. The people are tired of you—tired of bad harvests, ill-luck, sickness, and continued poverty. You are the cause of all our miseries,—and we have resolved you shall not stay among us. Go quickly,— take the blight and pestilence of your presence elsewhere! Go! or if you will not——"

" We shall burn, burn, burn, and utterly destroy!" interrupted Lovisa, with a sort of eldritch shriek. " The strong pine rafters of Olaf Güldmar's dwelling shall be kindled into flame to light the hills with crimson, far and near! Not a plank shall be spared!—not a vestige of his pride be left——"

" Stop!" said Thelma quietly. " What do you mean? You must both be very mad or very wicked! You want us to go away—you threaten to set fire to our home— why? We have done you no harm. Tell me, poor soul!" and she turned with queenly forbearance to Lovisa, " is it for Britta's sake that you would burn the house she lives in? That is not wise! You cursed me the other day,— and why? What have I done that you should hate me?"

The old woman regarded her with steadfast, cruel eyes.

" You are your mother's child!" she said. " I hated her—I hate you! You are a witch!—the village knows it —Mr. Dyceworthy knows it! Mr. Dyceworthy says we shall be justified in the Lord's sight for wreaking evil upon you! Evil, evil be on those of evil deeds!"

" Then shall the evil fall on Mr. Dyceworthy," said the girl calmly. " He is wicked in himself,—and doubly wicked to encourage *you* in wickedness. He is ignorant and false —why do you believe in such a man?"

" He is a saint—a saint!" cried Lovisa wildly. " And shall the daughter of Satan withstand his power?" And she clapped her hands in a sort of fierce ecstasy.

Thelma glanced at her pityingly and smiled. " A saint! Poor thing, how little you know him!" she said. " And it is a pity you should hate me, for I have done you no wrong. I would do good to all if I knew how,—tell me can I comfort you, or make your life more cheerful? It must be hard to be so old and all alone!"

"Your death would comfort me!" returned Lovisa grimly. "Why do you keep Britta from me?"

"I do not keep her," Thelma answered. "She stays with me because she is happy. Why do you grudge her, her happiness? And as for burning my father's house, surely you would not do so wicked and foolish a thing!— but still, you must do as you choose, for it is not possible that we shall leave the Altenfjord to please you."

Here Ulrika started forward angrily. "You defy us!" she cried. "You will not go?" And in her excitement she seized Thelma's arm roughly.

This action was too much for Sigurd; he considered it an attack on the person of his beloved mistress and he resented it at once in his own fashion. Throwing himself on Ulrika with sudden ferocity, he pushed and beat her back as though he were a wolf-hound struggling with refractory prey; and though the ancient Lovisa rushed to the rescue, and Thelma imploringly called upon her zealous champion to desist,—all remonstrances were unavailing, till Sigurd had reduced his enemy to the most abject and whimpering terror.

"A demon—a demon!" she sobbed and moaned, as the valiant dwarf at last released her from his clutches; and, tossing his long, fair locks over his misshapen shoulders, laughed loudly and triumphantly with delight at his victory. "Lovisa! Lovisa Elsland! this is your doing; you brought this upon me! I may die now, and you will not care! O Lord, Lord, have mercy——"

Suddenly she stopped; her eyes dilated,—her face grew grey with the sickening pallor of fear. Slowly she raised her hand and pointed to Sigurd—his fantastic dress had become disordered in the affray, and his jacket was torn open, —and on his bare chest a long red scar in the shape of a cross was distinctly visible. "That scar!" she muttered. "How did he get that scar?"

Lovisa stared at her in impatient derision. Thelma was too surprised to answer immediately, and Sigurd took it upon himself to furnish what he considered a crushing reply.

"Odin's mark!" he said, patting the scar with much elation. "No wonder you are afraid of it! Everybody

knows it—birds, flowers, trees, and stars! Even you—you
are afraid!"

And he laughed again, and snapped his fingers in her
face. The woman shuddered violently. Step by step she
drew near to the wondering Thelma, and spoke in low and
trembling accents, without a trace of her former anger.

"They say you are wicked," she said slowly, "and that
the devil has your soul ready, before you are dead! But
I am not afraid of you. No; I will forgive you, and pray
for you, if you will tell me, . . ." She paused, and then
continued, as with a strong effort. "Yes—tell me *who* is
this Sigurd?"

"Sigurd is a fou dling," answered Thelma simply. "He
was floating about in th Fjord in a basket, and my father
saved him. He was quite a baby. He had this scar on his
chest then. He has lived with us ever since."

Ulrika looked at her searchingly,—then bent her head,—
whether in gratitude or despair it was difficult to say.

"Lovisa Elsland," she said monotonously, "I am going
home. I cannot help you any longer! I am tired—ill."
Here she suddenly broke down, and, throwing up her arms
with a wild gesture, she cried, "O God, God! O God!"
and burst into a stormy passion of sobs and tears.

Thelma, touched by her utter misery, would have offered
consolation, but Lovisa repelled her with a fierce gesture.

"Go!" said the old woman harshly. "You have cast
your spells upon her—I am witness of your work! And shall
you escape just punishment? No; not while there is a God
in heaven, and I, Lovisa Elsland, live to perform His bidding! Go,—white devil that you are!—go and carry misfortune upon misfortune to your fine gentleman-lover!
Ah!" and she chuckled maliciously as the girl recoiled
from her, her proud face growing suddenly paler, "have I
touched you there? Lie in his breast, and it shall be as
though a serpent stung him,—kiss his lips, and your touch
shall be poison,—live in doubt, and die in misery! Go! and
may all evil follow you!"

She raised her staff and waved it majestically, as though
she drew a circle in the air,—Thelma smiled pityingly, but
deigned no answer to her wild ravings.

"Come, Sigurd!" she said simply, "let us return home.
It is growing late—father will wonder where we are."

"Yes, yes," agreed Sigurd, seizing the basket full of the
pansies he had plucked. "The sunshine is slipping away,

and we cannot live with shadows! These are not real women, mistress; they are dreams—black dreams,—I have often fought with dreams, and I know how to make them afraid! See how the one weeps because she knows me,— and the other is just going to fall into a grave. I can hear the clods thrown on her head—thump—thump! It does not take long to bury a dream! Come, mistress, let us follow the sunshine!"

And, taking the hand she extended towards him, he turned away, looking back once, however, to call out loudly—

"Good-bye, bad dreams!"

As they disappeared behind the trees, Lovisa turned angrily to the still-sobbing Ulrika.

"What is this folly?" she exclaimed, striking her staff fiercely into the ground. "Art mad or bewitched?"

Ulrika looked up,—her plain face swollen and stained with weeping.

"O Lord, have mercy upon me! O Lord, forgive me!" she moaned. "I did not know it—how *could* I know?"

Lovisa grew so impatient that she seized her by the shoulder and shook her violently.

"Know what?" she cried; "know what?"

"Sigurd is my son!" said Ulrika, with a sort of solemn resignation,—then, with a sudden gesture, she threw her hands above her head, crying, "My son, my son! The child I thought I had killed! The Lord be praised I did not murder him!"

Lovisa Elsland seemed stupefied with surprise. "Is this the truth?" she asked at last, slowly and incredulously.

"The truth, the truth!" cried Ulrika passionately. "It is always the truth that comes to light! He is my child, I tell you! . . . I gave him that scar!" She paused, shuddering, and continued in a lower tone, "I tried to kill him with a knife, but when the blood flowed, it sickened me, and I could not! He was an infant abortion—the evil fruit of an evil deed—and I threw him out to the waves,— as I told you, long ago. You have had good use of my confession, Lovisa Elsland; you have held me in your power by means of my secret, but now—"

The old woman interrupted her with a low laugh of contempt and malice.

"As the parents are, so are the children!" she said scorn-

fully. " Your lover must have been a fine man, Ulrika, if
the son is like his father ! "

Ulrika glared at her vengefully, then drew herself up with
an air of defiance.

" I care nothing for your taunts, Lovisa Elsland ! " she
said. " You can do me no harm ! All is over between us !
I will help in no mischief against the Güldmars. Whatever their faults, they saved—my child ! "

" Is that so great a blessing ? " asked Lovisa ironically.

" It makes your threats useless," answered Ulrika. " You
cannot call me *murderess* again ! "

" Coward and fool ! " shrieked Lovisa. " Was it *your* intent that the child should live ? Were you not glad to think
it dead ? And cannot I spread the story of your infamy
through all the villages where you are known ? Is not the
wretched boy himself a living witness of the attempt you
made to kill him ? Does not that scar speak against you ?
Would not Olaf Güldmar relate the story of the child's
rescue to any one that asked him ? Would you like all Bosekop to know of your intrigue with an escaped criminal, who
was afterwards caught and hung ! The virtuous Ulrika—
the zealous servant of the Gospel—the pious, praying
Ulrika ! " and the old woman trembled with rage and excitement. " Out of my power ? Never, never ! As long as
there is breath in my body I will hold you down ! *Not* a
murderess, you say——? "

" No," said Ulrika very calmly, with a keen look, " I am
not—but you *are !* "

CHAPTER XVI.

"Il n'y a personne qui ait eu autant á souffrir á votre sujet que
moi depuis ma naissance ! aussi je vous supplie á deux genoux et au
nom de Dieu, d'avoir pitié de moi ! "—*Old Breton Ballad.*

IN a few more days Thelma's engagement to Sir Philip
Bruce-Errington was the talk of the neighborhood. The
news spread gradually, having been, in the first place,
started by Britta, whose triumph in her mistress's happiness was charming to witness. It reached the astonished
and reluctant ears of the Reverend Mr. Dyceworthy, whose
rage was so great that it destroyed his appetite for twenty-
four hours. But the general impression in the neighborhood, where superstition maintained so strong a hold on the

primitive and prejudiced minds of the people, was that the
reckless young Englishman would rue the day on which he
wedded " the white witch of the Altenfjord."

Güldmar was regarded with more suspicion than ever, as
having used some secret and diabolical influence to promote
the match ; and the whole party were, as it seemed, tabooed,
and looked upon as given up to the most unholy practices.

Needless to say, the opinions of the villagers had no
effect whatever on the good spirits of those who were thus
unfavorably criticised, and it would have been difficult to
find a merrier group than that assembled one fine morning
in front of Güldmar's house, all equipped from top to toe
for some evidently unusually lengthy and arduous mountain
excursion. Each man carried a long, stout stick, portable
flask, knapsack, and rug—the latter two articles strapped
together and slung across the shoulder—and they all presented an eminently picturesque appearance, particularly
Sigurd, who stood at a little distance from the others, leaning on his tall staff and gazing at Thelma with an air of
peculiar pensiveness and abstraction.

She was at that moment busied in adjusting Errington's
knapsack more comfortably, her fair, laughing face turned
up to his, and her bright eyes alight with love and tender
solicitude.

" I've a good mind not to go at all," he whispered in her
ear. " I'll come back and stay with you all day."

" You foolish boy ! " she answered merrily. " You would
miss seeing the grand fall—all for what ? To sit with me
and watch me spinning, and you would grow so very sleepy !
Now, if I were a man, I would go with you."

" I'm very glad you're not a man ! " said Errington,
pressing the little hand that had just buckled his shoulder-
strap. " Though I wish you *were* going with us. But I
say, Thelma, darling, won't you be lonely ? "

She laughed gaily. " Lonely ? I ! Why, Britta is with
me—besides, I am never lonely *now*." She uttered the last
word softly, with a shy, upward glance. " I have so much
to think about——" She paused and drew her hand
away from her lover's close clasp. " Ah," she resumed,
with a mischievous smile, " you are a conceited boy ! You
want to be missed ! You wish me to say that I shall feel
most miserable all the time you are away ! If I do, I shall
not tell you ! "

" Thelma, child ? " called Olaf Güldmar, at this juncture,

"keep the gates bolted and doors barred while we are absent. Remember, thou and Britta must pass the night alone here,—we cannot be at home ti'. late in the evening of to-morrow. Let no one inside the garden, and deny thyself to all comers. Dost thou hear "

"Yes, father," she responded meekly.

"And let Britta keep good guard that her crazy hag of a grandam come not hither to disturb or fright thee with her croaking,—for thou hast not even Sigurd to protect thee."

"Not even Sigurd!" said that personage, with a meditative smile. "No, mistress; not even poor Sigurd!"

"One of us might remain behind," suggested Lorimer, with a side-look at his friend.

"Oh no, no!" exclaimed Thelma anxiously. "It would vex me so much! Britta and I have often been alone before. We are quite safe, are we not, father?"

"Safe enough!" said the old man, with a laugh. "I know of no one save Lovisa Elsland who has the courage to face thee, child! Still, pretty witch as thou art, 'twill not harm thee to put the iron bar across the house door, and to lock fast the outer gate when we have gone. This done, I have no fear of thy safety. Now," and he kissed his daughter heartily, "now lads, 'tis time we were on the march! Sigurd, my boy, lead on!"

"Wait!" cried Sigurd, springing to Thelma's side. "I must say good-bye!" And he caught the girl's hand and kissed it,—then plucking a rose, he left it between her fingers. "That will remind you of Sigurd, mistress! Think of him once to-day!—once again when the midnight glory shines. Good-bye, mistress! that is what the dead say, . . . Good-bye!"

And with a passionate gesture of farewell, he ran and placed himself at the head of the little group that waited for him, saying exultingly—

"Now follow me! Sigurd knows the way! Sigurd is the friend of all the wild waterfall! Up the hills,—across the leaping stream,—through the sparkling foam!" And he began chanting to himself a sort of wild mountain song.

Macfarlane looked at him dubiously. "Are ye sure?" he said to Güldmar. "Are ye sure that wee chap kens whaur he's gaun? He'll no lead us into a ditch an' leave us there, mistakin' it for the Fall?"

Güldmar laughed heartily. "Never fear! Sigurd's the

best guide you can have, in spite of his fancies. He knows
all the safest and surest paths; and Njedegorze is no easy
place to reach, I can tell you!"

"*Pardon!* How is it called?" asked Duprèz eagerly.

"Njedegorze."

The Frenchman shrugged his shoulders. "I give it
up!" he said smilingly. "Mademoiselle Güldmar, if anything happens to me at this cascade with the name unpro-
nounceable, you will again be my doctor, will you not?"

Thelma laughed as she shook hands with him. "Nothing
will happen," she rejoined; "unless, indeed, you catch cold
by sleeping in a hut all night. Father, you must see that
they do not catch cold!"

The *bonde* nodded, and motioned the party forward,
Sigurd leading the way,—Errington, however, lingered behind on pretense of having forgotten something, and, drawing his betrothed in his arms, kissed her fondly.

"Take care of yourself, darling!" he murmured,—and
then hurrying away he rejoined his friends, who had discreetly refrained from looking back, and therefore had not
seen the lovers embrace.

Sigurd, however, had seen it, and the sight apparently
gave fresh impetus to his movements, for he sprang up the
adjacent hill with so much velocity that those who followed
had some difficulty to keep up with him,—and it was not till
they were out of sight of the farmhouse that he resumed
anything like a reasonable pace.

As soon as they had disappeared, Thelma turned into the
house and seated herself at her spinning-wheel. Britta soon
entered the room, carrying the same graceful implement of
industry, and the two maidens sat together for some time
in a silence unbroken, save by the low melodious whirring
of the two wheels, and the mellow complaints of the strutting doves on the window-sill.

"Fröken Thelma!" said Britta at last, timidly.

"Yes, Britta?" And her mistress looked up inquiringly.

"Of what use is it for you to spin now?" queried the
little handmaid. "You will be a great lady, and great
ladies do not work at all!"

Thelma's wheel revolved more and more slowly, till at
last it stopped altogether.

"Do they not?" she said half inquiringly and musingly.
"I think you must be wrong, Britta. It is impossible that

there should be people who are always idle. I do not know
what great ladies are like."

"I do!" And Britta nodded her curly head sagaciously.
"There was a girl from Hammerfest who went to Christiania to seek service—she was handy at her needle, and a
fine spinner, and a great lady took her right away from
Norway to London. And the lady bought her spinning-
wheel for a curiosity she said,—and put it in the corner of
a large parlor, and used to show it to her friends, and they
would all laugh and say, ' How pretty!' And Jansena,—
that was the girl—never span again—she wore linen that
she got from the shops,—and it was always falling into
holes, and Jansena was always mending, mending, and it
was no good!"

Thelma laughed. "Then it is better to spin, after all,
Britta—is it not?"

Britta looked dubious. "I do not know," she answered;
"but I am sure great ladies do not spin. Because, as I
said to you, Fröken, this Jansena's mistress was a great
lady, and she never did anything,—no! nothing at all,—
but she put on wonderful dresses, and sat in her room, or
was driven about in a carriage. And that is what you will
do also, Fröken!"

"Oh no, Britta," said Thelma decisively. "I could not
be so idle. Is it not fortunate I have so much linen ready?
I have quite enough for marriage."

The little maid looked wistful. "Yes, dear Fröken,"
she murmured hesitatingly; "but I was thinking if it is
right for you to wear what you have spun. Because, you
see, Jansena's mistress had wonderful things all trimmed
with lace,—and they would all come back from the washing
torn and hanging in threads, and Jansena had to mend
those as well as her own clothes. You see, they do not
last at all—and they cost a large sum of money; but it is
proper for great ladies to wear them."

"I am not sure of that, Britta," said Thelma, still musingly. "But still, it may be—my bridal things may not
please Philip. If you know anything about it, you must
tell me what is right."

Britta was in a little perplexity. She had gathered
some idea from her friend Jansena concerning life in London,—she had even a misty notion of what was meant by a
"trousseau" with all its dainty, expensive, and often useless fripperies; but she did not know how to explain her-

self to her young mistress, whose simple, almost severe tastes would, she instinctively felt, recoil from anything like ostentation in dress, so she was discreetly silent.

"You know, Britta," continued Thelma gently, "I shall be Philip's wife, and I must not vex him in any little thing. But I do not quite understand. I have always dressed in the same way,—and he has never said that he thought me wrongly clothed."

And she looked down with quite a touching pathos at her straight, white woolen gown, and smoothed its folds doubtfully. The impulsive Britta sprang to her side and kissed her with girlish and unaffected enthusiasm.

"My dear, my dear! You are more lovely and sweet than anybody in the world!" she cried. "And I am sure Sir Philip thinks so too!"

A beautiful roseate flush suffused Thelma's cheeks, and she smiled.

"Yes, I know he does!" she replied softly. "And, after all, it does not matter what one wears."

Britta was meditating,—she looked lovingly at her mistress's rippling wealth of hair.

"Diamonds!" she murmured to herself in a sort of satisfied soliloquy. "Diamonds, like those you have on your finger, Fröken,—diamonds all scattered among your curls like dew-drops! And white satin, all shining, shining!—people would take you for an angel!"

Thelma laughed merrily. "Britta, Britta! You are talking such nonsense! Nobody dresses so grandly except queens in fairy-tales."

"Do they not?" and the wise Britta looked more profound than ever. "Well, we shall see, dear Fröken—we shall see!"

"*We?*" queried Thelma with surprised emphasis.

Her little maid blushed vividly, and looked down demurely, twisting and untwisting the string of her apron.

"Yes, Fröken," she said in a low tone. "I have asked Sir Philip to let me go with you when you leave Norway."

"Britta!" Thelma's astonishment was too great for more than this exclamation.

"Oh, my dear! don't be angry with me!" implored Britta, with sparkling eyes, rosy cheeks, and excited tongue all pleading eloquently together, "I should die here without you! I told the *bonde* so; I did, indeed! And then I went to Sir Philip—he is such a grand gentleman,—

so proud and yet so kind,—and I asked him to let me still be your servant. I said I knew all great ladies had a maid, and if I was not clever enough I could learn, and—and—" here Britta began to sob, " I said I did not want any wages —only to live in a little corner of the same house where you were,—to sew for you, and see you, and hear your voice sometimes——" Here the poor little maiden broke down altogether and hid her face in her apron crying bitterly.

The tears were in Thelma's eyes too, and she hastened to put her arm round Britta's waist, and tried to soothe her by every loving word she could think of.

" Hush, Britta dear ! you must not cry," she said tenderly. " What did Philip say ? "

" He said," jerked out Britta convulsively, " that I was a g-good little g-girl, and that he was g-glad I wanted to g-go ! " Here her two sparkling wet eyes peeped out of the apron inquiringly, and seeing nothing but the sweetest affection on Thelma's attentive face, she went on more steadily. " He p-pinched my cheek, and he laughed—and he said he would rather have me for your maid than anybody —there ! "

And this last exclamation was uttered with so much defiance that she dashed away the apron altogether, and stood erect in self-congratulatory glory, with a particularly red little nose and very trembling lips. Thelma smiled, and caressed the tumbled brown curls.

" I am very glad, Britta ! " she said earnestly. " Nothing could have pleased me more ! I must thank Philip. But it is of father I am thinking—what will father and Sigurd do ? "

" Oh, that is all settled, Fröken," said Britta, recovering herself rapidly from her outburst. " The *bonde* means to go for one of his long voyages in the *Valkyrie*—it is time she was used again, I'm sure,—and Sigurd will go with him. It will do them both good—and the tongues of Bosekop can waggle as much as they please, none of us will be here to mind them ! "

" And you will escape your grandmother ! " said Thelma amusedly, as she once more set her spinning-wheel in motion.

Britta laughed delightedly. " Yes ! she will not find her way to England without some trouble ! " she exclaimed. " Oh, how happy I shall be ! And you "—she looked pleadingly at her mistress—"you do not dislike me for your servant?"

"Dislike!" and Thelma gave her a glance of mingled reproach and tenderness. "You know how fond I am of you, Britta! It will be like having a little bit of my old home always with me."

Silently Britta kissed her hand, and then resumed her work. The monotonous murmur of the two wheels recommenced,—this time pleasantly accompanied by the rippling chatter of the two girls, who, after the fashion of girls all the world over, indulged in many speculations as to the new and strange life that lay before them.

Their ideas were of the most primitive character,—Britta had never been out of Norway, and Thelma's experiences, apart from her home life, extended merely to the narrow and restricted bounds of simple and severe convent discipline, where she had been taught that the pomps and vanities of the world were foolish and transient shows, and that nothing could please God more than purity and rectitude of soul. Her character was formed, and set upon a firm basis —firmer than she herself was conscious of. The nuns who had been entrusted with her education had fulfilled their task with more than their customary zeal—they were interested in the beautiful Norwegian child for the sake of her mother, who had also been their charge. One venerable nun in particular had bestowed a deep and lasting benefit on her, for, seeing her extraordinary beauty, and forestalling the dangers and temptations into which the possession of such exceptional charms might lead her, she adopted a wise preventive course, that cased her as it were in armor, proof against all the assailments of flattery. She told the girl quite plainly that she was beautiful,—but at the same time made her aware that beauty was common,—that she shared it alike with birds, flowers, trees, and all the wonderful objects of nature—moreover, that it was nothing to boast of, being so perishable.

"Suppose a rose foolish enough to boast of its pretty leaves," said the gentle *religieuse* on one occasion. "They all fall to the ground in a short time, and become decayed and yellow—it is only the fragrance, or the *soul* of the rose that lasts." Such precepts, that might have been wasted on a less sensitive and thoughtful nature, sank deeply into Thelma's mind—she accepted them not only in theory but in practice, and the result was that she accepted her beauty as she accepted her health,—as a mere natural occurrence—no more. She was taught that the three principal virtues of a woman were chastity, humility, and obedience,—these were the laws of God, fixed and immutable, which no one dared break without committing grievous and unpardonable sin. So she thought, and according to her thoughts she lived. What a strange world, then, lay before her in the contemplated change that was about to take place in the even tenor of her existence! A world of intrigue and folly —a world of infidelity and falsehood!—how would she meet it? It was a question she never asked herself—she thought London a sort of magnified Christiania, or at best, the Provençal town of Arles on a larger scale. She had heard her father speak of it, but only in a vague way, and she had been able to form no just idea even to herself of the enormous metropolis crowded to excess with its glad and sorrowful, busy and idle, rich and poor millions. England itself floated before her fancy as a green, fertile, embowered island where Shakespeare had lived—and it delighted her to know that her future home, Errington Manor, was situated in Warwickshire, Shakespeare's county. Of the society that awaited her she had no notion,—she was prepared to "keep house" for her husband in a very simple way—to spin his household linen, to spare him all trouble and expense, and to devote herself body and soul to his service. As may be well imagined, the pictures she drew of her future married life, as she sat and span with Britta on that peaceful afternoon, were widely different to the destined reality that every day approached her more nearly.

Meantime, while the two girls were at home and undisturbed in the quiet farm house, the mountaineering party, headed by Sigurd, were well on their way towards the great Fall of Njedegorze. They had made a toilsome ascent of the hills by the side of the Alten river—they had climbed over craggy boulders and slippery rocks, sometimes wading knee-deep in the stream, or pausing to rest and watch the salmon leap and turn glittering somersaults in the air close above the diamond-clear water,—and they had beguiled their fatigue with songs and laughter, and the telling of fantastic legends and stories in which Sigurd had shone at his best—indeed, this unhappy being was in a singularly clear and rational frame of mind, disposed, too, to be agreeable even towards Errington. Lorimer, who for reasons of his own, had kept a close watch on Sigurd ever since his friend's engagement to Thelma, was surprised and gratified at this change in his former behavior, and encouraged him in it, while Errington himself responded to the dwarf's proffered friendship, and walked beside him, chatting cheerfully, during the most part of the excursion to the Fall. It was a long and exceedingly difficult journey—and in some parts dangerous—but Sigurd proved himself worthy of the commendations bestowed on him by the *bonde*, and guided them by the easiest and most secure paths, till at last, about seven o'clock in the evening, they heard the rush and roar of the rapids below the Fall, and with half an hour's more exertion, came in sight of them, though not as yet of the Fall itself. Yet the rapids were grand enough to merit attention—and the whole party stopped to gaze on the whirling wonders of water that, hissing furiously, circled round and round giddily in wheels of white foam, and then, as though enraged, leaped high over obstructing stones and branches, and rushed onward and downward to the smoother length of the river.

The noise was deafening,—they could not hear each other speak unless by shouting at the top of their voices, and even then the sounds were rendered almost indistinct by the riotous uproar. Sigurd, however, who knew all the ins and outs of the place, sprang lightly on a jutting crag, and, putting both hands to his mouth, uttered a peculiar, shrill, and far-reaching cry. Clear above the turmoil of the restless waters, that cry was echoed back eight distinct times from the surrounding rocks and hills. Sigurd laughed triumphantly.

"You see!" he exclaimed, as he resumed his leadership of the party, "they all know me! They are obliged to answer me when I call—they dare not disobey!" And his blue eyes flashed with that sudden wild fire that generally foretold some access of his particular mania.

Errington saw this and said soothingly, "Of course not, Sigurd! No one would dream of disobeying you! See how we follow you to-day—we all do exactly what you tell us."

"We are sheep, Sigurd," added Lorimer lazily; "and you are the shepherd!"

Sigurd looked from one to the other half doubtingly, half cunningly. He smiled.

"Yes!" he said. "You will follow me, will you not? Up to the very top of the Fall?"

" By all means ! " answered Sir Philip gaily. " Any-where you choose to go ! "

Sigurd seemed satisfied, and lapsing into the calm, composed manner which had distinguished him all day, he led the way as before, and they resumed their march, this time in silence, for conversation was well-nigh impossible. The nearer they came to the yet invisible Fall, the more thunderous grew the din—it was as though they approached some vast battle-field, where opposing armies were in full action, with all the tumult of cannonade and musketry. The ascent grew steeper and more difficult—at times the high barriers of rocks seemed almost impassable,—often they were compelled to climb over confused heaps of huge stones, through which the eddying water pushed its way with speed and fury,—but Sigurd's precision was never at fault,—he leaped crag after crag swiftly and skillfully, always lighting on a sure foothold, and guiding the others to do the same. At last, at a sharp turn of one of these rocky eminences, they perceived an enormous cloud of white vapor rising up like smoke from the earth, and twisting itself as it rose, in swaying, serpentine folds, as though some giant spirit-hand were shaking it to and fro like a long flowing veil in the air. Sigurd paused and pointed forward.

" Njedegorze ! " he cried.

They all pressed on with some excitement. The ground vibrated beneath their feet with the shock of the falling torrent, and the clash and uproar of the disputing waters rolled in their ears like the grand, sustained bass of some huge cathedral organ. Almost blinded by the spray that dashed its disdainful drops in their faces, deafened by the majestic, loud, and ceaseless eloquence that poured its persuasive force into the splitting hearts of the rocks around them,—breathless with climbing, and well-nigh tread out, they struggled on, and broke into one unanimous shout of delight and triumph when they at last reached the small hut that had been erected for the convenience of travellers who might choose that way to journey to the Altenfjord,—and stood face to face with the magnificent cascade, one of the grandest in Norway. What a sublime spectacle it was ! —that tempest of water sweeping sheer down the towering rocks in one straight, broad, unbroken sheet of foam ! A myriad rainbows flashed in the torrent and vanished, to reappear again instantly with redoubled lustre,—while the glory of the evening sunlight glittering on one side of the fall made it gleam like a sparkling shower of molten gold.

"Njedegorze!" cried Sigurd again, giving a singularly musical pronunciation to the apparently uncouth name. "Come! still a little further,—to the top of the Fall!"

Olaf Güldmar, however, paid no attention to this invitation. He was already beginning to busy himself with preparations for passing the night comfortably in the hut before mentioned. Stout old Norseman as he was, there were limits to his endurance, and the arduous exertions of the long day had brought fatigue to him as well as to the rest of the party.

Macfarlane was particularly exhausted. His frequent pulls at the whiskey flask had been of little or no avail as a support to his aching limbs, and, now he had reached his destination, he threw himself full length on the turf in front of the hut and groaned most dismally.

Lorimer surveyed him amusedly, and stood beside him, the very picture of a cool young Briton whom nothing could possibly discompose.

"Done up—eh, Sandy?" he inquired.

"Done up!" growled Macfarlane. "D'ye think I'm a Norseman or a jumping Frenchy?" This with a look of positive indignation at the lively Duprèz, who, if tired, was probably too vain to admit it, for he was strutting about, giving vent to his genuine admiration of the scene before him with the utmost freshness and enthusiasm. "I'm just a plain Scotchman, an' no such a fule at climbin' either! Why, man, I've been up Goatfell in Arran, an' Ben Lomond an' Ben Nevis—there's a mountain for ye, if ye like! But a brae like this, wi' a' the stanes lyin' helter-skelter, an' crags that ye can barely hold on to—and a mad chap guidin' ye on at the speed o' a leapin' goat—I tell ye, I havena been used to't." Here he drew out his flask and took another extensive pull at it. Then he added suddenly, "Just look at Errington! He'll be in a fair way to break his neck if he follows yon wee crazy loon any further."

At these words Lorimer turned sharply round, and perceived his friend following Sigurd step by step up a narrow footing in the steep ascent of some rough, irregular crags that ran out and formed a narrow ledge, ending in a sharp point, jutting directly over the full fury of the waterfall. He watched the two climbing figures for an instant without any anxiety,—then he suddenly remembered that Philip

14

had promised to go with Sigurd " to the top of the Fall."
Acting on a rapid impulse which he did not stop to explain
to himself, Lorimer at once started off after them,—but the
ascent was difficult ; they were some distance ahead, and
though he shouted vociferously, the roar of the cascade rendered his voice inaudible. Gaining on them, however, by
slow degrees, he was startled when all at once they disappeared at the summit—and, breathless with his rapid
climb, he paused, bewildered. By-and-by he saw Sigurd
creeping cautiously out along the rocky shelf that overhung
the tumbling torrent—his gaze grew riveted with a sort of
deadly fascination on the spot.

"Good God!" he muttered under his breath. "Surely
Phil will not follow him *there !*"

He watched with strained eyes,—and a smothered cry
escaped him as Errington's tall figure, erect and bold, appeared on that narrow and dangerous platform! He never
knew how he clambered up the rest of the slippery ascent.
A double energy seemed given to his active limbs. He
never paused again for one second till he also stood on the
platform, without being heard or perceived by either Sigurd or Philip. Their backs were turned to him, and he
feared to move or speak, lest a sudden surprised movement
on their parts should have the fatal result of precipitating
one or both into the fall. He remained, therefore, behind
them, silent and motionless,—looking, as they looked, at
the terrific scene below. From that point, Njedegorze was
as a huge boiling caldron, from which arose twisted wreaths
and coiling lengths of white vapor, faintly colored with gold
and silvery blue. Dispersing in air, these mists took all
manner of fantastic forms,—ghostly arms seemed to wave
and beckon, ghostly hands to unite in prayer,—and fluttering creatures in gossamer draperies of green and crimson
appeared to rise and float, and retire and shrink, to noth-
ingness again in the rainbow drift and sweep of whirling
foam. Errington gazed unconcernedly down on the seething abyss. He pushed back his cap from his brow, and let
the fresh wind play among his dark, clustering curls. His
nerves were steady, and he surveyed the giddily twisting
wheels of shining water, without any corresponding giddiness in his own brain. He had that sincere delight in a
sublime natural spectacle, which is the heritage of all who
possess a poetic and artistic temperament ; and though he
stood on a frail ledge of rock, from which one false or un-

wary step might send him to certain destruction, he had not the slightest sense of possible danger in his position. Withdrawing his eyes from the Fall, he looked kindly down at Sigurd, who in turn was staring up at him with a wild fixity of regard.

"Well, old boy," he said cheerfully, " this is a fine sight! Have you had enough of it? Shall we go back?"

Sigurd drew imperceptibly nearer. Lorimer, from his point of vantage behind a huge bowlder, drew nearer also.

"Go back?" echoed Sigurd. "Why should we go back?"

"Why, indeed!" laughed Errington, lightly balancing himself on the trembling rocks beneath him. "Except that I should scarcely think this is the best place on which to pass the night! Not enough room, and too much noise! What say you?"

"Oh, brave, brave, fool!" cried the dwarf in sudden ex-citement. "Are you not *afraid?*"

The young baronet's keen eyes glanced him over with amused wonder.

"What of?" he demanded coolly. Still nearer came Sigurd—nearer also came the watchful, though almost in-visible Lorimer.

"Look down there!" continued Sigurd in shrill tones, pointing to the foaming gulf. "Look at the *Elf-danz*— see the beautiful spirits with the long pale green hair and glittering wings! See how they beckon, beckon, beckon! They want some one to join them—look how their white arms wave,—they throw back their golden veils and smile at us! They call to *you*—you with the strong figure and the proud eyes—why do you not go to them? They will kiss and caress you—they have sweet lips and snow-white bosoms,—they will love you and take care of you—they are as fair as Thelma!"

"Are they? I doubt it!" and Errington smiled dream-ily as he turned his head again towards the fleecy whirl of white water, and saw at once with an artist's quick eye what his sick-brained companion meant by the *Elf-danz*, in the fan-tastic twisting, gliding shapes tossed up in the vaporous mist of the Fall. "But I'll take your word, Sigurd, with-out making the elves' personal acquaintance! Come along —this place is bad for you—we'll dance with the green-haired nymphs another time."

And with a light laugh he was about to turn away, when

he was surprised by a sudden, strange convulsion of Sigurd's countenance—his blue eyes flashed with an almost phosphorescent lustre,—his pale skin flushed deeply red, and the veins in his forehead started into swelled and knotted prominence.

"Another time!" he screamed loudly; "no, no! Now—now! Die, robber of Thelma's love! Die—die—*die!*"

Repeating these words like quick gasps of fury, he twisted his meager arms tightly round Errington, and thrust him fiercely with all his might towards the edge of the Fall. For one second Philip strove against him—the next, he closed his eyes—Thelma's face smiled on his mind in that darkness as though in white farewell—the surging blood roared in his ears with more thunder than the terrific tumble of the torrent—"God!" he muttered, and *then*—then he stood safe on the upper part of the rocky platform with Lorimer's strong hand holding him in a vice-like grasp, and Lorimer's face, pale, but looking cheerfully into his. For a moment he was too bewildered to speak. His friend loosened him and laughed rather forcedly—a slight tremble of his lips was observable under his fair moustache.

"By Jove, Phil," he remarked in his usual nonchalant manner, "that was rather a narrow shave! Fortunate I happened to be there!"

Errington gazed about him confusedly. "Where's Sigurd?" he asked.

"Gone! Ran off like a 'leapin' goat,' as Sandy elegantly describes him. I thought at first he meant to jump over the Fall, in which case I should have been compelled to let him have his own way, as my hands were full. But he's taken a safe landward direction."

"Didn't he try to push me over?"

"Exactly! He was quite convinced that the mermaids wanted you. But I considered that Miss Thelma's wishes had a prior claim on my regard."

"Look here, old man," said Errington suddenly, "don't jest about it! You saved my life!"

"Well!" and Lorimer laughed. "Quite by accident, I assure you."

"*Not* by accident!" and Philip flushed up, looking very handsome and earnest. "I believe you followed us up here thinking something might happen. Now didn't you?"

"Suppose I did," began Lormier, but he was interrupted

by his friend, who seized his hand, and pressed it with a warm, close, affectionate fervor. Their eyes met—and Lorimer blushed as though he had performed some action meriting blame rather than gratitude. "That'll do, old fellow," he said almost nervously. "As we say in polite society when some one crushes our favorite corn under his heel—don't mention it! You see Sigurd *is* cracked,— there's not the slightest doubt about that,—and he's hardly accountable for his vagaries. Then I know something about him that perhaps you don't. He loves your Thelma!"

They were making the descent of the rocks together, and Errington stopped short in surprise.

"Loves Thelma! You mean as a brother——"

"Oh no, I don't! I mean that he loves her as brothers often love other people's sisters—his affection is by no means fraternal—if it were only *that*——"

"I see!" and Philip's eyes filled with a look of grave compassion. "Poor fellow! I understand his hatred of me now. Good Heavens! how he must suffer! I forgive him with all my heart. But—I say, Thelma has no idea of this!"

"Of course not. And you'd better not tell her. What's the good of making her unhappy?"

"But how did *you* learn it?" inquired Philip, with a look of some curiosity at his friend.

"Oh, I!" and Lormier laughed carelessly; "I was always an observing sort of fellow—fond of putting two and two together and making four of them, when I wasn't too exhausted and the weather wasn't too hot for the process. Sigurd's rather attached to me—indulges me with some specially private ravings now and then—I soon found out his secret, though I believe the poor little chap doesn't understand his own feelings himself."

"Well," said Errington thoughtfully, "under the circumstances you'd better not mention this affair of the Fall to Güldmar. It will only vex him. Sigurd won't try such a prank again."

"I'm not so sure of that," replied Lorimer; "but you know enough now to be on your guard with him." He paused and looked up with a misty softness in his frank blue eyes—then went on in a subdued tone—"When I saw you on the edge of that frightful chasm, Phil——" He broke off as if the recollection were too painful, and exclaimed suddenly—"Good God! if I had lost you!"

Errington clapped one hand on his shoulder.

"Well! What if you had?" he asked almost mirthfully, though there was a suspicious tremble in his ringing voice.

"I should have said with Horatio, 'I am more an antique Roman than a Dane,'—and gone after you," laughed Lorimer. "And who knows what a jolly banquet we might not have been enjoying in the next world by this time? If I believe in anything at all, I believe in a really agreeable heaven—nectar and ambrosia, and all that sort of thing, and Hebes to wait upon you."

As he spoke they reached the sheltering hut, where Güldmar, Duprèz, and Macfarlane were waiting rather impatiently for them.

"Where's Sigurd?" cried the *bonde.*

"Gone for a ramble on his own account," answered Errington readily. "You know his fancies!"

"I wish his fancies would leave him," grumbled Güldmar. "He promised to light a fire and spread the meal—and now, who knows whither he has wandered?"

"Never mind, sir," said Lorimer. "Engage me as a kitchen-boy. I can light a fire, and can also sit beside it when it is properly kindled. More I cannot promise. As the housemaids say when they object to assist the cook,—it would be *beneath* me."

"Cook!" cried Duprèz, catching at this word. "I can cook! Give me anything to broil. I will broil it! You have coffee—I will make it!" And in the twinkling of an eye he had divested himself of his coat, turned up his cuffs, and manufactured the cap of a *chef* out of a newspaper which he stuck jauntily on his head. "Behold me, *messieurs, à votre service!*"

His liveliness was infectious; they all set to work with a will, and in a few moments a crackling wood-fire blazed cheerily on the ground, and the gipsy preparations for the *al fresco* supper went on apace amid peals of laughter. Soon the fragrance of steaming coffee arose and mingled itself with the resinous odors of the surrounding pine-trees, —while Macfarlane distinguished himself by catching a fine salmon trout in a quiet nook of the rushing river, and this Duprèz cooked in a style that would have done honor to a *cordon bleu.* They made an excellent meal, and sang songs in turn and told stories,—Olaf Güldmar, in particular, related eerie legends of the *Dovre-fjelde,* and many a striking history of ancient origin, full of terror and superstition, —concerning witches, devils, and spirits both good and evil, who are still believed to have their abode on the Norwegian hills,—for, as the *bonde* remarked with a smile, " when civilization has driven these unearthly beings from every other refuge in the world, they will always be sure of a welcome in Norway."

It was eleven o'clock when they at last retired within the hut to rest for the night, and the errant Sigurd had not returned. The sun shone brilliantly, but there was no window to the small shed, and light and air came only through the door, which was left wide open. The tired travellers lay down on their spread-out rugs and blankets, and wishing each other a cheerful " good night," were soon fast asleep. Errington was rather restless, and lay awake for some little time, listening to the stormy discourse of the Fall; but at last his eyelids yielded to the heaviness that oppressed them, and he sank into a light slumber.

Meanwhile the imperial sun rode majestically downwards to the edge of the horizon,—and the sky blushed into the pale tint of a wild rose, that deepened softly and steadily with an ever-increasing fiery brillance as the minutes glided noiselessly on to the enchanted midnight hour. A wind began to rustle mysteriously among the pines—then gradually growing wrathful, strove to whistle a loud defiance to the roar of the tumbling waters. Through the little nooks and crannies of the roughly constructed cabin, where the travellers slept, it uttered small wild shrieks of warning or dismay—and, suddenly, as though touched by an invisible hand, Sir Philip awoke. A crimson glare streaming through the open door dazzled his drowsy eyes—was it a forest on fire? He started up in dreamy alarm,—then remembered where he was. Realizing that there must be an exceptionally fine sky to cast so ruddy a reflection on the ground, he threw on his cloak and went outside.

What a wondrous, almost unearthly scene greeted him! His first impulse was to shout aloud in sheer ecstasy—his next to stand silent in reverential awe. The great Fall was no longer a sweeping flow of white foam—it had changed to a sparkling shower of rubies, as though some great genie, tired of his treasures, were flinging them away by giant handfuls, in the most reckless haste and lavish abundance. From the bottom of the cascade a crimson vapor arose, like smoke from flame, and the whirling rapids, deeply red for the most part, darkened here and there into an olive-green flecked with gold, while the spray, tossed high over interrupting rocks and boulders, glittered as it fell like small fragments of broken opal. The sky was of one dense uniform rose-color from west to east,—soft and shimmering as a broad satin pavilion freshly unrolled,—the sun was invisible, hidden behind the adjacent mountains, but his rays touched some peaks in the distance, on which white wreaths of snow lay, bringing them into near and sparkling prominence.

The whole landscape was transformed—the tall trees, rustling and swaying in the now boisterous wind, took all flickering tints of color on their trunks and leaves,—the grey stones and pebbles turned to lumps of gold and heaps of diamonds, and on the other side of the rapids, a large tuft of heather in a cleft of the rocks glowed with extraordinary vividness and warmth, like a suddenly kindled fire. A troop of witches dancing wildly on the sward,—a ring of fairies,—kelpies tripping from crag to crag,—a sudden chorus of sweet-voiced water-nymphs—nothing unreal or fantastical would have surprised Errington at that moment. Indeed, he almost expected something of the kind —the scene was so eminently fitted for it.

"Positively, I must wake Lorimer," he thought to himself. "He oughtn't to miss such a gorgeous spectacle as this."

He moved a little more in position to view the Fall. What was that small dark object running swiftly yet steadily along on the highest summit of those jutting crags? He rubbed his eyes amazedly—was it—could it be *Sigurd?* He watched it for a moment,—then uttered a loud cry as he saw it pause on the very ledge of rock from which but a short while since, he himself had been so nearly precipitated. The figure was now distinctly visible, outlined in black against the flaming crimson of the sky,—it stood upright and waved its arms with a frantic gesture. There was no mistaking it—it *was* Sigurd!

Without another second's hesitation Errington rushed back to the hut and awoke, with clamorous alarm, the rest of the party. His brief explanation sufficed—they all hurried forth in startled excitement. Sigurd still occupied his hazardous position, and as they looked at him he seemed to dance wildly nearer the extreme edge of the rocky platform. Old Güldmar turned pale. "The gods preserve him!" he muttered in his beard—then turning he began resolutely to make the ascent of the rocks with long, rapid strides—the young men followed him eager and almost breathless, each and all bent upon saving Sigurd from the danger in which he stood, and trying by different ways to get more quickly near the unfortunate lad and call, or draw him back by force from his point of imminent deadly peril. They were more than half-way up, when a piercing cry rang clearly above the thunderous din of the fall—a cry that made them pause for a moment.

Sigurd had caught sight of the figures advancing to his rescue, and was waving them back with eloquent gesture of anger and defiance. His small misshapen body was alive with wrath,—it seemed as though he were some dwarf king ruling over the glittering crimson torrent, and grimly forbidding strangers to enter on the boundaries of his magic territory. They, however, pressed on with renewed haste, —and they had nearly reached the summit when another shrill cry echoed over the sunset-colored foam.

Once more they paused they were in full view of the distraught Sigurd, and he turned his head towards them, shaking back his long fair hair with his old favorite gesture and laughing in apparent glee. Then he suddenly raised his arms, and, clasping his hands together, poised himself as though he were some winged thing about to fly.

"Sigurd! Sigurd!" shouted Güldmar, his strong voice tremulous with anguish. "Come back! come back to Thelma!"

At the sound of that beloved name, the unhappy creature seemed to hesitate, and, profiting by that instant of irresolution, Errington and Lorimer rushed forward——Too late! Sigurd saw them coming, and glided with stealthy caution to the very brink of the torrent, where there was scarcely any foothold—there he looked back at his would-be rescuers with an air of mystery and cunning, and broke into a loud derisive laugh.

Then—still with clasped hands and smiling face—unheeding the shout of horror that broke from those who beheld him—he leaped, and fell! Down, down into the roaring abyss! For one half-second—one lightning flash—his twisted figure, like a slight black speck was seen against the wide roseate glory of the tumbling cascade—then it disappeared, engulfed and lost for ever! Gone,—with all his wild poet fancies and wandering dreams—gone, with his unspoken love and unguessed sorrows—gone where dark things shall be made light,—and where the broken or tangled chain of the soul's intelligence shall be mended and made perfect by the tender hands of the All-Wise and the All-Loving One, whose ways are too gloriously vast for our finite comprehension.

"Gone, mistress!" as he would have said to the innocent cause of his heart's anguish. "Gone where I shall grow straight and strong and brave! Mistress, if you meet me in Valhalla, you will love me!"

CHAPTER XVII.

"Do not, I pray you, think evilly of so holy a man! He has a sore combat against the flesh and the devil!"—*The Maid of Honor.*

THE horror-stricken spectators of the catastrophe stood for a minute inert and speechless,—stupefied by its suddenness and awful rapidity. Then with one accord they hurried down to the level shore of the torrent, moved by the unanimous idea that they might possibly succeed in rescuing Sigurd's frail corpse from the sharp teeth of the jagged rocks, that, piercing upwards through the foam of the roaring rapids, were certain to bruise, tear, and disfigure it beyond all recognition. But even this small satisfaction was denied them. There was no sign of a floating or struggling body anywhere visible. And while they kept an eager look-out, the light in the heavens slowly changed. From burning crimson it softened to a tender amethyst hue, as smooth and delicate as the glossy pale tint of the purple clematis,—and with it the rosy foam of the Fall graduated to varying tints of pink, from pink to tender green, and lastly, it became as a shower of amber wine. Güldmar spoke first in a voice broken by deep emotion.

"'Tis all over with him, poor lad!" he said, and tears glittered thickly in his keen old eyes. "And—though the gods, of a surety, know best—this is an end I looked not for! A mournful home-returning shall we have—for how to break the news to Thelma is more than I can tell!"

And he shook his head sorrowfully while returning the warm and sympathizing pressure of Errington's hand.

"You see," he went on, with a wistful look at the grave and compassionate face of his accepted son-in-law—"the boy was no boy of mine, 'tis true—and the winds had more than their share of his wits—yet—we knew him from a baby— and my wife loved him for his sad estate, which he was not to blame for. Thelma, too—he was her first playmate——"

The *bonde* could trust himself to say no more, but turned abruptly away, brushing one hand across his eyes, and was silent for many minutes. The young men, too, were silent,—Sigurd's determined suicide had chilled and sickened them. Slowly they returned to the hut to pass the remaining hours of the night—though sleep was, of course, after what they had witnessed, impossible. They remained awake, therefore, talking in low tones of the fatal event, and listening to the solemn *sough* of the wind through the pines, that sounded to Errington's ears like a monotonous forest dirge. He thought of the first time he had ever seen the unhappy creature whose wandering days had just ended,—of that scene in the mysterious shell cavern,—of the wild words he had then uttered—how strangely they came back to Philip's memory now!

"You have come as a thief in the golden midnight, and the thing you seek is the life of Sigurd! Yes—yes! it is true—the spirit cannot lie! You must kill, you must steal—see how the blood drips, drop by drop, from the heart of Sigurd! and the jewel you steal,—ah! what a jewel! You shall not find such another in Norway!" Was not the hidden meaning of these incoherent phrases rendered somewhat clear now? though how the poor lad's disordered imagination had been able thus promptly to conjure up with such correctness, an idea of Errington's future relations with Thelma, was a riddle impossible of explanation. He thought, too, with a sort of generous remorse, of that occasion when Sigurd had visited him on board the yacht to implore him to leave the Altenfjord. He realized everything,—the inchoate desires of the desolate being, who, though intensely capable of loving, felt himself in a dim, sad way, unworthy of love,—the struggling passions in him that clamored for utterance—the instinctive dread and jealousy of a rival, while knowing that he was both physically and mentally unfitted to compete with one,—all these things passed through Philip's mind, and filled him with a most profound pity for the hidden sufferings, the tortures and inexplicable emotions which had racked Sigurd's darkened soul. And, still busy with these reflections, he turned on his arm as he lay, and whispered softly to his friend who was close by him—

"I say, Lorimer,—I feel as if I had been to blame some-how in this affair! If I had never come on the scene, Sigurd would still have been happy in his own way."

Lorimer was silent. After a pause, Errington went on still in the same low tone.

"Poor little fellow! Do you know, I can't imagine any-thing more utterly distracting than having to see such a woman as Thelma day after day,—loving her all the time, and knowing such love to be absolutely hopeless! Why, it was enough to make him crazier than ever!"

Lorimer moved restlessly. "Yes, it must have been hard on him!" he answered at last, in a gentle, somewhat sad tone. "Perhaps it's as well he's out of it all. Life is infinitely perplexing to many of us. By this time he's no doubt wiser than you or I, Phil,—he could tell us the rea-son why love is such a blessing to some men, and such a curse to others!"

Errington made no answer, and they relapsed into si-lence—silence which was almost unbroken save by an oc-casional deep sigh from Olaf Güldmar and a smothered ex-clamation such as, "Poor lad, poor lad! Who would have thought it?"

With the early dawn they were all up and ready for the homeward journey,—though with very different feelings to those with which they had started on their expedition. The morning was dazzlingly bright and clear,—and the cat-aract of Njedegorze rolled down in glittering folds of creamy white and green, uttering its ceaseless psalm of praise to the Creator in a jubilant roar of musical thunder. They paused and looked at it for the last time before leaving,—it had assumed for them a new and solemn aspect—it was Sigurd's grave. The *bonde* raised his cap from his rough white hair,—instinctively the others followed his example.

"May the gods grant him good rest!" said the old man reverently. "In the wildest waters they say there is a calm underflow,—maybe the lad has found it and is glad to sleep." He paused and stretched his hands forth with an eloquent and touching gesture. "Peace be with him!"

Then, without more words, and as though disdaining his own emotion, he turned abruptly away, and began to de-scend the stony and precipitous hill, up which Sigurd had so skillfully guided them the day before. Macfarlane and Duprèz followed him close,—Macfarlane casting more than once a keen look over the rapids.

" 'Tis a pity we couldna find his body," he said in a low tone.

Duprèz shrugged his shoulders. Sigurd's death had shocked him considerably by its suddenness, but he was too much of a volatile Frenchman to be morbidly anxious about securing the corpse.

" I think not so at all," he said. " Of what use would it be? To grieve *mademoiselle?* to make her cry? That would be cruel,—I would not assist in it! A dead body is not a sight for ladies,—believe me, things are best as they are."

They went on, while Errington and Lorimer lingered yet a moment longer.

" A magnificent sepulchre! " said Lorimer, dreamily eyeing for the last time the sweeping flow of the glittering torrent. " Better than all the monuments ever erected! Upon my life, I would not mind having such a grave myself! Say what you like, Phil, there was something grand in Sigurd's choice of a death. We all of us have to get out of life somehow one day—that's certain—but few of us have the chance of making such a triumphant exit! "

Errington looked at him with a grave smile. " How you talk, George! " he said half-reproachfully. " One would think you envied the end of that unfortunate, half-witted fellow! You've no reason to be tired of your life, I'm sure, —all your bright days are before you."

" Are they? " And Lorimer's blue eyes looked slightly melancholy. " Well, I dare say they are! Let's hope so at all events. There need be something before me,—there isn't much behind except wasted opportunities. Come on, Phil! "

They resumed their walk, and soon rejoined the others. The journey back to the Altenfjord was continued all day with but one or two interruptions for rest and refreshment. It was decided that on reaching home, old Güldmar should proceed a little in advance, in order to see his daughter alone first, and break to her the news of the tragic event that had occurred,—so that when, after a long and toilsome journey, they caught sight, at about eight in the evening, of the familiar farmhouse through the branches of the trees that surrounded and sheltered it, they all came to a halt.

The young men seated themselves on a pleasant knoll under some tall pines, there to wait a quarter of an hour or

so, while the *bonde* went forward to prepare Thelma. On
second thoughts, the old man asked Errington to accompany him,—a request to which he very readily acceded,
and these two, leaving the others to follow at their leisure,
went on their way rapidly. They arrived at, and entered
the garden,—their footsteps made a crunching noise on the
pebbly path,—but no welcoming face looked forth from any
of the windows of the house. The entrance door stood
wide open,—there was not a living soul to be seen but the
kitten asleep in a corner of the porch, and the doves
drowsing on the roof in the sunshine. The deserted
air of the place was unmistakable, and Güldmar and Errington exchanged looks of wonder not unmixed with
alarm.

" Thelma! Thelma! " called the *bonde* anxiously. There
was no response. He entered the house and threw open the
kitchen door. There was no fire,—and not the slightest sign
of any of the usual preparations for supper.

" Britta! " shouted Güldmar. Still no answer. " By the
gods! " he exclaimed, turning to the astonished Philip,
" this is a strange thing! Where can the girls be? I
have never known both of them to be absent from the
house at the same time. Go down to the shore, my lad,
and see if Thelma's boat is missing, while I search the
garden."

Errington obeyed—hurrying off on his errand with a
heart beating fast from sudden fear and anxiety. For he
knew Thelma was was not likely to have gone out of her
own accord, at the very time she would have naturally expected her father and his friends back, and the absence of
Britta too, was, to say the least of it, extraordinary. He
reached the pier very speedily, and saw at a glance that the
boat was gone. He hastened back to report this to Güldmar, who was making the whole place resound with his
shouts of " Thelma! " and " Britta! " though he shouted
altogether in vain.

" Maybe," he said dubiously, on hearing of the missing
boat—" Maybe the child has gone on the Fjord—'tis often
her custom,—but, then, where is Britta? Besides, they
must have expected us—they would have prepared supper
—they would have been watching for our return. No,
no! there is something wrong about this—'tis altogether
unusual."

And he looked about him in a bewildered way, while Sir

Philip, noting his uneasiness, grew more and more uneasy himself.

"Let me go and search for them, sir," he said, eagerly. "They may be in the woods, or up towards the orchard."

Güldmar shook his head and drew his fuzzy white brows together in puzzled meditation—suddenly he started and struck his staff forcibly on the ground.

"I have it!" he exclaimed. "That old hag Lovisa is at the bottom of this!"

"By Jove!" cried Errington. "I believe you're right! What shall we do?"

At that moment, Lorimer, Duprèz, and Macfarlane came on the scene, thinking they had kept aloft long enough,—and the strange disappearance of the two girls was rapidly explained to them. They listened astonished and almost incredulous, but agreed with the *bonde* as to Lovisa's probable share in the matter.

"Look here!" said Lorimer excitedly. "I'm not in the least tired,—show me the way to Talvig, where that old screech-owl lives, and I'll go there straight as a gun! Shouldn't wonder if she has not forced away her grandchild, in which case Miss Thelma may have gone after her."

"I'll come with you!" said Errington. "Let's lose no time about it."

But Güldmar shook his head. "'Tis a long way, my lads,—and you do not know the road. No—'twill be better we should take the boat and pull over to Bosekop; there we can get a carriole to take two of us at least to Talvig——"

He stopped, interrupted by Macfarlane, who looked particularly shrewd.

"I should certainly advise ye to try Boskop first," he remarked cautiously. "Mr. Dyceworthy might be able to provide ye with valuable information."

"Dyceworthy!" roared the *bonde*, becomming inflammable at once. "He knows little of me or mine, thank the gods! and I would not by choice step within a mile of his dwelling. What makes you think of him, sir?"

Lorimer laid a hand soothingly on his arm.

"Now, my dear Mr. Güldmar, don't get excited! Mac is right. I dare say Dyceworthy knows as much in his way as the ancient Lovisa. At any rate, it isn't his fault if he

does not. Because you see——" Lorimer hesitated and
turned to Errington. "You tell him, Phil! you know all
about it."

"The fact is," said Errington, while Güldmar gazed from
one to the other in speechless amazement, "Thelma hasn't
told you because she knew how angry you'd be—but Dyceworthy asked her to marry him. Of course she refused
him, and I doubt if he's taken his rejection very resignedly."

The face of the old farmer as he heard these words was a
study. Wonder, contempt, pride, and indignation struggled
for the mastery on his rugged features.

"Asked—her—to—marry—him!" he repeated slowly.
"By the sword of Odin! Had I known it I would have
throttled him!" His eyes blazed and he clenched his hand.
"Throttled him, lads! I would! Give me the chance and
I'll do it now! I tell you, the mere look of such a man as
that is a desecration to my child,—liar and hypocrite as he
is! may the gods confound him!" He paused—then suddenly bracing himself up, added. "I'll away to Bosekop
at once—they've been afraid of me there for no reason—
I'll teach them to be afraid of me in earnest! Who'll come
with me?"

All eagerly expressed their desire to accompany him
with the exception of one,—Pierre Duprèz,—he had disappeared.

"Why, where has he gone?" demanded Lorimer in some
surprise.

"I canna tell," replied Macfarlane. "He just slipped
awa' while ye were haverin' about Dyceworthy—he'll maybe
join us at the shore."

To the shore they at once betook themselves, and were
soon busied in unmooring Güldmar's own rowing-boat, which,
as it had not been used for some time, was rather a tedious
business,—moreover they noted with concern that the tide
was dead against them.

Duprèz did not appear,—the truth is, that he had taken
into his head to start off for Talvig on foot without waiting
for the others. He was fond of an adventure and here was
one that suited him precisely—to rescue distressed damsels
from the grasp of persecutors. He was tired, but he managed to find the road,—and he trudged on determinedly,
humming a song of Béranger's as he walked to keep him
cheerful. But he had not gone much more than a mile,

when he discerned in the distance a carriole approaching him,—and approaching so swiftly that it appeared to swing from side to side of the road at imminent risk of upsetting altogether. There seemed to be one person in it—an excited person too, who lashed the stout little pony and urged it on to fresh exertions with gesticulations and cries. That plump buxom figure—that tumbled brown hair streaming wildly on the breeze,—that round rosy face—why! it was Britta! Britta, driving all alone, with the reckless daring of a Norwegian peasant girl accustomed to the swaying, jolting movement of the carriole as well as the rough roads and sharp turnings. Nearer she came and nearer—and Duprèz hailed her with a shout of welcome. She saw him, answered his call, and drove still faster,—soon she came up beside him, and without answering his amazed questions, she cried breathlessly—

"Jump in—jump in! We must go on as quickly as possible to Bosekop! Quick—quick! Oh my poor Fröken! The old villain! Wait till I get at him!"

"But, my *leet-le* child!" expostulated Pierre, climbing up into the queer vehicle—"What is all this? I am in astonishment—I understand not at all! How comes it that you are run away from home, and Mademoiselle also?"

Britta only waited till he was safely seated, and then lashed the pony with redoubled force. Away they clattered at a break-neck pace, the Frenchman having much ado to prevent himself from being jolted out again on the road.

"It is a wicked plot!" she then exclaimed, panting with excitement—"a wicked, wicked plot! This afternoon Mr. Dyceworthy's servant came and brought Sir Philip's card. It said that he had met with an accident and had been brought back to Bosekop, and that he wished the Fröken to come to him at once. Of course, the darling believed it all —and she grew so pale, so pale! And she went straight away in her boat all by herself! Oh my dear—my dear!"

Britta gasped for breath, and Duprèz soothingly placed an arm round her waist, an action which the little maiden seemed not to be aware of. She resumed her story—"Then the Fröken had not been gone so very long, and I was watching for her in the garden, when a woman passed by— a friend of my grandmother's. She called out—'Hey, Britta! Do you know they have got your mistress down at Talvig, and they'll burn her for a witch before they sleep!' 'She has gone to Bosekop,' I answered, 'so I know you tell

15

a lie.' 'It is no lie,' said the old woman, 'old Lovisa has her this time for sure.' And she laughed and went away. Well, I did not stop to think twice about it—I started off for Talvig at once—I ran nearly all the way. I found my grandmother alone—I asked her if she had seen the Fröken? She screamed and clapped her hands like a mad woman! she said that the Fröken was with Mr. Dyceworthy—Mr. Dyceworthy would know what to do with her!"

" *Sapristi!* " ejaculated Duprèz. " This is serious!"

Britta glanced anxiously at him, and went on. " Then she tried to shut the doors upon me and beat me—but I escaped. Outside I saw a man I knew with his carriole, and I borrowed it of him and came back as fast as I could —but oh! I am so afraid—my grandmother said such dreadful things!"

" The others have taken a boat to Bosekop," said Duprèz, to re-assure her. " They may be there by now."

Britta shook her head. " The tide is against them—no! we shall be there first. But," and she looked wistfully at Pierre, " my grandmother said Mr. Dyceworthy had sworn to ruin the Fröken. What did she mean, do you think?"

Duprèz did not answer,—he made a strange grimace and shrugged his shoulders. Then he seized the whip and lashed the pony.

" Faster, faster, *mon chere!* " he cried to that much-astonished, well-intentioned animal. " It is not a time to sleep, *ma foi!* " Then to Britta—" My little one, you shall see! We shall disturb the good clergyman at his peaceful supper—yes indeed! Be not afraid!"

And with such reassuring remarks he beguiled the rest of the way, which to both of them seemed unusually long, though it was not much past nine when they rattled into the little village called by courtesy a town, and came to a halt within a few paces of the minister's residence. Everything was very quiet—the inhabitants of the place retired to rest early—and the one principal street was absolutely deserted. Duprèz alighted.

" Stay you here, Britta," he said, lightly kissing the hand that held the pony's reins. " I will make an examination of the windows of the house. Yes—before knocking at the door! You wait with patience. I will let you know everything!"

And with a sense of pleasureable excitement in his mind, he stole softly along on tip-toe—entered the minister's garden, fragrant with roses and mignonette, and then, attracted by the sound of voices, went straight up to the parlor window. The blind was down and he could see nothing, but he heard Mr. Dyceworthy's bland persuasive tones, echoing out with a soft sonorousness, as though he were preaching to some refractory parishioner. He listened attentively.

" Oh strange, strange ! " said Mr. Dyceworthy. " Strange that you will not see how graciously the Lord hath delivered you into my hands ! Yea,—and no escape is possible ! For lo, you yourself, Fröken Thelma," Duprèz started, " you yourself came hither unto my dwelling, a woman all unprotected, to a man equally unprotected,—and who, though a humble minister of saving grace, is not proof against the offered surrender of your charms ! Make the best of it, my sweet girl !—make the best of it ! You can never undo what you have done to-night."

" Coward ! . . . coward ! " and Thelma's rich low voice caused Pierre to almost leap forward from the place where he stood concealed. " You,—*you* made me come here—*you* sent me that card—*you* dared to use the name of my betrothed husband, to gain your vile purpose ! *You* have kept me locked in this room all these hours—and do you think you will not be punished ? I will let the whole village know of your treachery and falsehood ! "

Mr. Dyceworthy laughed gently. " Dear me, dear me ! " he remarked sweetly. " How pretty we look in a passion, to be sure ! And we talk of our ' betrothed husband ' do we ? Tut-tut ! Put that dream out of your mind, my dear girl—Sir Philip Bruce-Errington will have nothing to do with you after your little escapade of to-night ! Your honor is touched !—yes, yes ! and honor is everything to such a man as he. As for the ' card ' you talk about, I never sent a card—not I ! " Mr. Dyceworthy made this assertion in a tone of injured honesty. " Why should I ! No—no ! You came here of your own accord,—that is certain and——" here he spoke more slowly and with a certain malicious glee, " I shall have no difficulty in proving it to be so, should the young man Errington ask me for an explanation ! Now you had better give me a kiss and make the peace ! There's not a soul in the place who will believe anything you say against me ; *you*, a reputed witch, and I, a minister of the Gospel. For your father I care nothing, a poor sinful pagan can never injure a servant of the Lord.

Come now, let me have that kiss! I have been very patient
—I am sure I deserve it!"

There was a sudden rushing movement in the room, and
a slight cry.

"If you touch me!" cried Thelma, "I will kill you! I
will! God will help me!"

Again Mr. Dyceworthy laughed sneeringly. "God will
help you!" he exclaimed as though in wonder. "As if God
ever helped a *Roman!* Fröken Thelma, be sensible. By
your strange visit to me to-night you have ruined your
already damaged character—I say you have ruined it,—and
if anything remains to be said against you, *I* can say it—
moreover, I *will!*"

A crash of breaking window-glass followed these words,
and before Mr. Dyceworthy could realize what had happened, he was pinioned against his own wall by an active,
wiry, excited individual, whose black eyes sparkled with
gratified rage, whose clenched fist was dealing him severe
thumps all over his fat body.

"Ha, ha! You will, will you!" cried Duprèz, literally
dancing up against him and squeezing him as though he
were a jelly. "You will tell lies in the service of *le Bon
Dieu?* No—not quite, not yet!" And still pinioning him
with one hand, he dragged at his collar with the other till
he succeeded, in spite of the minister's unwieldly efforts to
defend himself, in rolling him down upon the floor, where he
knelt upon him in triumph. "Voila! Je sais faire *la boxe,*
moi!" Then turning to Thelma, who stood an amazed
spectator of the scene, her flushed cheeks and tear-swollen
eyes testifying to the misery of the hours she had passed,
he said, "Run, Mademoiselle, run! The little Britta is
outside, she has a pony-car—she will drive you home. I
will stay here till Phil-eep comes. I shall enjoy myself! I
will begin—Phil-eep with finish! Then we will return to
you."

Thelma needed no more words, she rushed to the door,
threw it open, and vanished like a bird in air. Britta's joy
at seeing her was too great for more than an exclamation of
welcome,—and the carriole, with the two girls safely in it,
was soon on its rapid way back to the farm. Meanwhile,
Olaf Güldmar, with Errington and the others, had just
landed at Bosekop after a heavy pull across the Fjord, and
they made straight for Mr. Dyceworthy's house, the *bonde*
working himself up as he walked into a positive volcano of

wrath. Finding the street-door open as it had just been left by the escaped Thelma, they entered, and on the threshold of the parlor, stopped abruptly, in amazement at the sight that presented itself. Two figures were rolling about on the floor, apparently in a close embrace,—one large and cumbrous, the other small and slight. Sometimes they shook each other,—sometimes they lay still,—sometimes they recommenced rolling. Both were perfectly silent, save that the larger personage seemed to breathe somewhat heavily. Lorimer stepped into the room to secure a better view— then he broke into an irrepressible laugh.

" It's Duprèz," he cried, for the benefit of the others that stood at the door. " By Jove! How did he get here, I wonder ? "

Hearing his name, Duprèz looked up from that portion of My. Dyceworthy's form in which he had been burrowing, and smiled radiantly.

" Ah, *cher* Lorimer! Put your knee here, will you ? So! that is well—I will rest myself! " And he rose, smoothing his roughened hair with both hands, while Lorimer in obedience to his request, kept one knee artistically pressed on the recumbent figure of the minister. " Ah! and there is our Phil-eep, and Sandy, and Monsieur Güldmar! But I do not think," here he beamed all over, " there is much more to be done! He is one bruise, I assure you! He will not preach for many Sundays ;—it is bad to be so fat—he will be so exceedingly suffering ! "

Errington could not forbear smiling at Pierre's equanimity.

" But what has happened? " he asked. " Is Thelma here ? "

" She *was* here," answered Duprèz. " The religious had decoyed her here by means of some false writing,—supposed to be from you. He kept her locked up here the whole afternoon. When I came he was making love and frightening her,—I am pleased I was in time. But "—and he smiled again—" he is well beaten ! "

Sir Philip strode up to the fallen Dyceworthy, his face darkening with wrath.

" Let him go, Lorimer," he said sternly. Then, as the reverend gentleman slowly struggled to his feet, moaning with pain, he demanded, " What have you to say for yourself, sir ? Be thankful if I do not give you the horse-whipping you deserve, you scoundrel ! "

" Let me get at him ! " vociferated Güldmar at this juncture, struggling to free himself from the close grasp of the prudent Macfarlane. " I have longed for such a chance! Let me get at him ! "

But Lorimer assisted to restrain him from springing forward,—and the old man chafed and swore by his gods in vain.

Mr. Dyceworthy meanwhile meekly raised his eyes, and folded his hands with a sort of pious resignation.

" I have been set upon and cruelly abused," he said mournfully, " and there is no part of me without ache and soreness ! " He sighed deeply. " But I am punished rightly for yielding unto carnal temptation, put before me in the form of the maiden who came hither unto me with delusive entrancements——"

He stopped, shrinking back in alarm from the suddenly raised fist of the young baronet.

" You'd better be careful ! " remarked Philip coolly, with dangerously flashing eyes ; " there are four of us here, remember ! "

Mr. Dyceworthy coughed, and resumed an air of outraged dignity.

" Truly, I am aware of it ! " he said ; " and it surpriseth me not at all that the number of the ungodly outweigheth that of the righteous ! Alas ! ' why do the heathen rage so furiously together ? ' Why, indeed ! Except that ' in their hearts they imagine a vain thing ! ' I pardon you, Sir Philip, I freely pardon you ! And you also, sir," turning gravely to Duprèz, who received his forgiveness with a cheerful and delighted bow. " You can indeed injure—and you *have* injured this poor body of mine—but you cannot touch the *soul !* No, nor can you hinder that freedom of speech "—here his malignant smile was truly diabolical— " which is my glory, and which shall forever be uplifted against all manner of evil-doers, whether they be fair women and witches, or misguided pagans——"

Again he paused, rather astonished at Errington's scornful laugh.

" You low fellow ! " said the baronet. " From Yorkshire, are you ? Well, I happen to know a good many people in that part of the world—and I have some influence there, too. Now, understand me—I'll have you hounded out of the place ! You shall find it too hot to hold you—that I swear ! Remember ! I'm a man of my word ! And if you dare to mention the name of Miss Güldmar disrespectfully, I'll thrash you within an inch of your life ! "

Mr. Dyceworthy blinked feebly, and drew out his hand-kerchief.

" I trust, Sir Philip," he said mildly, " you will recon-sider your words! It would ill beseem you to strive to do me harm in the parish were my ministrations are welcome, as appealing to that portion of the people who follow the godly Luther. Oh yes,"—and he smiled cheerfully—" you will reconsider your words. In the meantime—I—I"—he stammered slightly—" I apologize! I meant naught but good to the maiden—but I have been misunder-stood, as is ever the case with the servants of the Lord. Let us say no more about it! I forgive!—let us all for-give! I will even extend my pardon to the pagan yon-der——"

But the " pagan " at that moment broke loose from the friendly grasp in which he had been hitherto held, and strode up to the minister, who recoiled like a beaten cur from the look of that fine old face flushed with just indig-nation, and those clear blue eyes fiery as the flash of steel.

" Pagan, you call me! " he cried. " I thank the gods for it—I am proud of the title! I would rather be the veriest savage that ever knelt in untutored worship to the great forces of Nature, than such a *thing* as you—a slinking, un-clean animal, crawling coward-like between earth and sky, and daring to call itself a *Christian!* Faugh! Were I the Christ, I should sicken at sight of you! "

Dyceworthy made no reply, but his little eyes glittered evilly.

Errington, not desiring any further prolongation of the scene, managed to draw the irate *bonde* away, saying in a low tone—

" We've had enough of this, sir! Let us get home to Thelma."

" I was about to suggest a move," added Lorimer. " We are only wasting time here."

" Ah! " exclaimed Duprèz radiantly—" and Monsieur Dyceworthy will be glad to be in bed! He will be very stiff to-morrow, I am sure! Here is a lady who will at-tend him."

This with a courteous salute to the wooden-faced Ulrika, who suddenly confronted them in the little passage. She seemed surprised to see them, and spoke in a monotonous dreamy tone, as though she walked in her sleep.

" The girl has gone? " she added slowly.

Duprèz nodded briskly. " She has gone! And let me tell you, madame, that if it had not been for you, she would not have com(here at all. You took that card to her?"

Ulrika frowned. "I was compelled," she said. "*She* made me take it. I promised." She turned her dull eyes slowly on Güldmar. "It was Lovisa's fault. Ask Lovisa about it." She paused, and moistened her dry lips with her tongue. "Where is your crazy lad?" she asked, almost anxiously. "Did he come with you?"

"He is dead!" answered Güldmar, with grave coldness.

"Dead!" And to their utter amazement, she threw up her arms and burst into a fit of wild laughter. "Dead! Thank God! Thank God! Dead! And through no fault of mine! The Lord be praised! He was only fit for death —never mind how he died—it is enough that he is dead— dead! I shall see him no more—he cannot curse me again! —the Lord be thankful for all His mercies!"

And her laughter ceased—she threw her apron over her head and broke into a passion of weeping.

"The woman must be crazy!" exclaimed the *bonde*, thoroughly mystified,—then placing his arm through Errington's, he said impatiently, "You're right, my lad! We've had enough of this. Let us shake the dust of this accursed place off our feet and get home. I'm tired out!"

They left the minister's dwelling and made straight for the shore, and were soon well on their journey back to the farm across the Fjord. This time the tide was with them— the evening was magnificent, and the coolness of the breeze, the fresh lapping of the water against the boat, and the brilliant tranquility of the landscape, soon calmed their over-excited feelings. Thelma was waiting for them under the porch as usual, looking a trifle paler than her wont, after all the worry and fright and suspense she had undergone,—but the caresses of her father and lover soon brought back the rosy warmth on her fair face, and restored the lustre to her eyes. Nothing was said about Sigurd's fate just then,—when she asked for her faithful servitor, she was told he had " gone wandering as usual," and it was not till Errington and his friends returned to their yacht that old Güldmar, left alone with his daughter, broke the sad news to her very gently. But the shock, so unexpected and terrible, was almost too much for her already overwrought nerves,—and such tears were shed for Sigurd as

Sigurd himself might have noted with gratitude. Sigurd—the loving, devoted Sigurd—gone for ever! Sigurd,—her playmate,—her servant,—her worshiper,—dead! Ah, how tenderly she mourned him!—how regretfully she thought of his wild words! "Mistress, you are killing poor Sigurd!" Wistfully she wondered if, in her absorbing love for Philip, she had neglected the poor crazed lad,—his face, in all its pale, piteous appeal, haunted her, and her grief for his loss was the greatest she had ever known since the day on which she had seen her mother sink into the last long sleep. Britta, too, wept and would not be comforted—she had been fond of Sigurd in her own impetuous little way,—and it was some time before either she or her mistress could calm themselves sufficiently to retire to rest. And long after Thelma was sleeping, with tears still wet on her cheeks, her father sat alone under his porch, lost in melancholy meditation. Now and then he ruffled his white hair impatiently with his hand,—his daughter's adventure in Mr. Dyceworthy's house had vexed his proud spirit. He knew well enough that the minister's apology meant nothing—that the whole village would be set talking against Thelma more, even than before,—that there was no possibility of preventing scandal so long as Dyceworthy was there to start it. He thought and thought and puzzled himself with probabilities—till at last, when he finally rose to enter his dwelling for the night, he muttered half-aloud. "If it must be, it must! And the sooner the better now, I think, for the child's sake."

The next morning Sir Philip arrived unusually early,—and remained shut up with the *bonde*, in private conversation for more than an hour. At the expiration of that time, Thelma was called, and taken into their confidence. The result of their mysterious discussion was not immediately evident,—though for the next few days, the farm-house lost its former tranquility and became a scene of bustle and excitement. Moreover, to the astonishment of the Bosekop folk, the sailing-brig known as the *Valkyrie*, belonging to Olaf Güldmar, which had been hauled up high and dry on the shore for many months, was suddenly seen afloat on the Fjord, and Valdemar Svensen, Errington's pilot, appeared to be busily engaged upon her decks, putting everything in ship-shape order. It was no use asking *him* any questions—he was not the man to gratify impertinent curiosity. By-and-by a rumor got about in the village—

Lovisa had gained her point in one particular,—the Güldmars were going away—going to leave the Altenfjord!

At first, the report was received with incredulity—but gained ground, as people began to notice that several packages were being taken in boats from the farm-house to both the *Eulalie* and the *Valkyrie.* These preparations excited a great deal of interest and inquisitiveness,—but no one dared ask for information as to what was about to happen. The Reverend Mr. Dyceworthy was confined to his bed "from a severe cold"—as he said, and therefore was unable to perform his favorite mission of spy;—so that when, one brilliant morning, Bosekop was startled by the steam-whistle of the *Eulalie* blowing furiously, and echoing far and wide across the surrounding rocky islands, several of the lounging inhabitants paused on the shore, or sauntered down to the rickety pier, to see what was the cause of the clamor. Even the long-suffering minister crawled out of bed and applied his fat, meek visage to his window, from whence he could command an almost uninterrupted view of the glittering water. Great was his amazement, and discomfiture to see the magnificent yacht moving majestically out of the Fjord, with Güldmar's brig in tow behind her, and the English flag fluttering gaily from her middle-mast, as she curtsied her farewell to the dark mountains, and glided swiftly over the little hissing waves. Had Mr. Dyceworthy been possessed of a field-glass, he might have been able to discern on her deck, the figure of a tall, fair girl, who, drawing her crimson hood over her rich hair, stood gazing with wistful, dreamy blue eyes, at the fast receding shores of the Altenfjord—eyes that smiled and yet were tearful.

"Are you sorry, Thelma?" asked Errington gently, as he passed one arm tenderly round her. "Sorry to trust your life to me?"

She laid her little hand in playful reproach against his lips.

"Sorry! you foolish boy! I am glad and grateful! But it is saying good-bye to one's old life, is it not? The dear old home!—and poor Sigurd!"

Her voice trembled, and bright tears fell.

"Sigurd is happy,"—said Errington gravely, taking the hand that caressed him, and reverently kissing it. "Believe me, love,—if he had lived some cruel misery might have befallen him—it is better as it is!"

Thelma did not answer for a minute or two—then she said suddenly—

" Philip, do you remember where I saw you first ? "

" Perfectly ! " he answered, looking fondly into the sweet upturned face. " Outside a wonderful cavern, which I afterwards explored."

She started and seemed surprised. " You went inside ? —you saw——? "

" Everything ! "—and Philip related his adventure of that morning, and his first interview with Sigurd. She listened attentively—then she whispered softly—

" My mother sleeps there, you know,—yesterday I went to take her some flowers for the last time. Father came with me—we asked her blessing. And I think she will give it, Philip—she must know how good you are and how happy I am."

He stroked her silky hair tenderly and was silent. The *Eulalie* had reached the outward bend of the Altenfjord, and the station of Bosekop was rapidly disappearing. Olaf Güldmar and the others came on deck to take their last look of it.

" I shall see the old place again, I doubt not, long before you do, Thelma, child," said the stout old *bonde*, viewing, with a keen, fond glance, the stretch of the vanishing scenery. " Though when once you are safe married at Christiania, Valdemar Svensen and I will have a fine toss on the seas in the *Valkyrie*,—and I shall grow young again in the storm and drift of the foam and the dark wild waves ! Yes—a wandering life suits me—and I am not sorry to have a taste of it once more. There's nothing like it—nothing like a broad ocean and a sweeping wind ! "

And he lifted his cap and drew himself erect, inhaling the air like an old warrior scenting battle. The others listened, amused at his enthusiasm,—and, meanwhile, the Altenfjord altogether disappeared, and the *Eulalie* was soon plunging in a rougher sea. They were bound for Christiania, where it was decided Thelma's marriage should at once take place —after which Sir Philip would leave his yacht at the disposal of his friends, for them to return in it to England. He himself intended to start directly for Germany with his bride, a trip in which Britta was to accompany them as Thelma's maid. Olaf Güldmar, as he had just stated, purposed making a voyage in the *Valkyrie*, as soon as he should get her properly manned and fitted, which he meant to do at Christiania.

Such were their plans,—and, meanwhile, they were all together on the *Eulalie*,—a happy and sociable party,—Errington having resigned his cabin to the use of his fair betrothed, and her little maid, whose delight at the novel change in her life, and her escape from the persecution of her grandmother, was extreme. Onward they sailed,—past the grand Lofoden Islands and all the magnificent scenery extending thence to Christiansund, while the inhabitants of Bosekop looked in vain for their return to the Altenfjord.

The short summer there was beginning to draw to a close,—some of the birds took their departure from the coast,—the dull routine of the place went on as usual, rendered even duller by the absence of the " witch " element of discord,—a circumstance that had kept the superstitious villagers, more or less on a lively tension of religious and resentful excitement—and by-and-by, the rightful minister of Bosekop came back to his duties and released the Reverend Charles Dyceworthy, who straightway returned to his loving flock in Yorkshire. It was difficult to ascertain whether the aged Lovisa was satisfied or wrathful, at the departure of the Güldmars with her granddaughter Britta in their company—she kept herself almost buried in her hut at Talvig, and saw no one but Ulrika, who seemed to grow more respectably staid than ever, and who, as a prominent member of the Lutheran congregation, distinguished herself greatly by her godly bearing and uncompromising gloom.

Little by little, the gossips ceased to talk about the disappearance of the " white witch " and her father—little by little they ceased to speculate as to whether the rich Englishman, Sir Philip Errington, really meant to marry her —a consummation of things which none of them seemed to think likely—the absence of their hated neighbors, was felt by them as a relief, while the rumored fate of the crazy Sigurd was of course looked upon as evidence of fresh crime on the part of the " pagan," who was accused of having, in some way or other, caused the unfortunate lad's death. And the old farm-house on the pine-covered knoll was shut up and silent,—its doors and windows safely barred against wind and rain,—and only the doves, left to forage for themselves, crooned upon its roof all day, or strutting on the deserted paths, ruffled their plumage in melancholy meditation, as though wondering at the absence of the fair ruling spirit of the place, whose smile had been brighter than the sunshine. The villagers avoided it as though it were haunted—the roses drooped and died untended,—and by degrees the old homestead grew to look like a quaint little picture of forgotten joys, with its deserted porch and fading flowers.

Meanwhile, a thrill of amazement, incredulity, disappointment, indignation, and horror, rushed like a violent electric shock through the upper circles of London society, arousing the deepest disgust in the breasts of match-making matrons, and seriously ruffling the pretty feathers of certain bird-like beauties who had just began to try their wings, and who " had expectations." The cause of the sensation was very simple. It was an announcement in the *Times*—under the head of " Marriages "—and ran as follows :—

" At the English Consulate, Christiania, Sir Philip Bruce-Errington, Bart., to Thelma, only daughter of Olaf Güldmar, *Bonde*, of the Altenfjord, Norway. No cards."

BOOK II

THE LAND OF MOCKERY

CHAPTER XXIV

BOOK II.

THE LAND OF MOCKERY.

CHAPTER XVIII.

"There's nothing serious in mortality:
     All is but toys."

MACBETH.

" I THINK," said Mrs. Rush-Marvelle deliberately, laying
down the *Morning Post* beside her breakfast-cup, " I think
his conduct is perfectly disgraceful ! "

Mr. Rush-Marvelle, a lean gentleman with a sallow,
clean-shaven face and an apologetic, almost frightened manner, looked up hastily.

" Of whom are you speaking, my dear ? " he inquired.

" Why, of that wretched young man Bruce-Errington !
He ought to be ashamed of himself ! "

And Mrs. Marvelle fixed her glasses more firmly on her
small nose, and regarded her husband almost reproachfully.
" Don't tell me, Montague, that you've forgotten that scandal about him ! He went off last year, in the middle of
the season, to Norway, in his yacht, with three of the very
fastest fellows he could pick out from his acquaintance—
regular reprobates, so I'm told—and after leading the
most awful life out there, making love to all the peasant
girls in the place, he married one of them,—a common
farmer's daughter. Don't you remember? We saw the
announcement of his marriage in the *Times*."

" Ah yes, yes ! " And Mr. Rush-Marvelle smiled a propitiatory smile, intended to soothe the evidently irritated
feelings of his better-half, of whom he stood always in
awe. " Of course, of course ! A very sad *mésalliance*.
Yes, yes ! Poor fellow ! And is there fresh news of him ? "

" Read *that*,"—and the lady handed the *Morning Post*
across the table, indicating by a dent of her polished fin-
ger-nail, the paragraph that had offended her sense of social
dignity. Mr. Marvelle read it with almost laborious care

—though it was remarkably short and easy of comprehension.

"Sir Philip and Lady Bruce-Errington have arrived at their house in Prince's Gate from Errington Manor."

"Well, my dear?" he inquired, with a furtive and anxious glance at his wife. "I suppose—er—it—er—it was to be expected?"

"No, it was *not* to be expected," said Mrs. Rush-Marvelle, rearing her head, and heaving her ample bosom to and fro in rather a tumultuous manner. "Of course it was to be expected that Bruce-Errington would behave like a fool —his father was a fool before him. But I say it was *not* to be expected that he would outrage society by bringing that common wife of his to London, and expecting *us* to receive her! The thing is perfectly scandalous! He has had the decency to keep away from town ever since his marriage—part of the time he has staid abroad, and since January he has been at his place in Warwickshire,—and this time—observe this!" and Mrs. Marvelle looked most impressive—"not a soul has been invited to the Manor— not a living soul! The house used to be full of people during the winter season—of course, now, he dare not ask anybody lest they should be shocked at his wife's ignorance. That's as clear as daylight! And now he has the impudence to actually bring her here,—into *society!* Good Heavens! He must be mad! He will be laughed at wherever he goes!"

Mr. Rush-Marvelle scratched his bony chin perplexedly.

"It makes it a little awkward for—for you," he remarked feelingly.

"Awkward! It is abominable!" And Mrs. Marvelle rose from her chair, and shook out the voluminous train of her silken breakfast-gown, an elaborate combination of crimson with grey chinchilla fur. "I shall have to call on the creature—just imagine it! It is most unfortunate for me that I happen to be one of Bruce-Errington's oldest friends—otherwise I might have passed him over in some way—as it is I can't. But fancy having to meet a great coarse peasant woman, who, I'm certain, will only be able to talk about fish and whale-oil! It is really *quite* dreadful!"

Mr. Rush-Marvelle permitted himself to smile faintly.

"Let us hope she will not turn out so badly," he said soothingly,—"but, you know, if she proves to be—er—a common person of,—-er—a very uneducated type—you can always let her drop gently—quite gently ! "

And he waved his skinny hand with an explanatory flourish.

But Mrs. Marvelle did not accept his suggestion in good part.

" You know nothing about it," she said somewhat testily. " Keep to your own business, Montague, such as it is. The law suits your particular form of brain—society does not. You would never be in society at all if it were not for me— now you know you wouldn't ! "

" My love," said Mr. Marvelle, with a look of meek admiration at his wife's majestic proportions. " I am aware of it ! I always do you justice. You are a remarkable woman ! "

Mrs. Marvelle smiled, somewhat mollified. " You see," she then condescended to explain—" the whole thing is so extremely disappointing to me. I wanted Marcia Van Clupp to go in for the Errington stakes,—it would have been such an excellent match,—money on both sides. And Marcia would have been just the girl to look after that place down in Warwickshire—the house is going to rack and ruin, in *my* opinion."

" Ah, yes ! " agreed her husband mildly. " Van Clupp is a fine girl—a *very* fine girl ! No end of ' go ' in her. And so Errington Manor needs a good deal of repairing, perhaps?" This query was put by Mr. Marvelle, with his head very much on one side, and his bilious eyes blinking drowsily.

" I don't know about repairs," replied Mrs. Marvelle. " It is a magnificent place, and certainly the grounds are ravishing. But one of the best rooms in the house, is the former Lady Errington's boudoir—it is full of old-fashioned dirty furniture, and Bruce-Errington won't have it touched, —he will insist on keeping it as his mother left it. Now that is ridiculous—perfectly morbid ! It's just the same thing with his father's library—he won't have that touched either—and the ceiling wants fresh paint, and the windows want new curtains—and all sorts of things ought to be done. Marcia would have managed all that splendidly—she'd have had everything new throughout—Americans are so quick, and there's no nonsensical antiquated sentiment about Marcia."

" She might even have had new pictures and done away

16

with the old ones," observed Mr. Marvelle, with a feeble
attempt at satire. His wife darted a keen look at him,
but smiled a little too. She was not without a sense of
humor.

"Nonsense, Montague! She knows the value of works
of art better than many a so-called connoisseur. I won't
have you make fun of her. Poor girl! She *did* speculate
on Bruce-Errington,—you know he was very attentive to
her, at that ball I gave just before he went off to Norway."

"He certainly seemed rather amused by her," said Mr.
Marvelle. "Did she take it to heart when she heard he was
married?"

"I should think not," replied Mrs. Marvelle loftily. "She
has too much sense. She merely said, 'All right! I must
stick to Masherville!'"

Mr. Marvelle nodded blandly. "Admirable,—admirable!"
he murmured, with a soft little laugh. "A *very* clever girl
—a very bright creature! And really there are worse
fellows than Masherville! The title is old."

"Yes, the title is all very well," retorted his wife—"but
there's no money—or at least very little."

"Marcia has sufficient to cover any deficit?" suggested
Mr. Marvelle, in a tone of meek inquiry.

"An American woman *never* has sufficient," declared
Mrs. Marvelle. "You know that as well as I do. And
poor dear Mrs. Van Clupp has so set her heart on a really
brilliant match for her girl—and I had positively promised
she should have Bruce-Errington. It is really too bad!"
And Mrs. Marvelle paced the room with a stately, sweeping
movement, pausing every now and then to glance at herself
approvingly in the mirror above the chimney-piece, while
her husband resumed his perusal of the *Times*. By-and-by
she said abruptly—

"Montague!"

Mr. Marvelle dropped his paper with an alarmed air.

"My dear!"

"I shall go to Clara Winsleigh this morning—and see
what she means to do in the matter. Poor Clara! She must
be disgusted at the whole affair!"

"She had rather a liking for Errington, hadn't she?" inquired Mr. Marvelle, folding up the *Times* in a neat parcel,
preparatory to taking it with him in order to read it in peace
on his way to the Law Courts.

"Liking? Well!" And Mrs. Marvelle, looking at her·

self once more in the glass, carefully arranged the ruffle of
Honiton lace about her massive throat,—"It was a little
more than liking—though, of course, her feelings were perfectly proper, and all that sort of thing,—at least, I suppose
they were! She had a great friendship for him,—one of
those emotional, perfectly spiritual and innocent attach-
ments, I believe, which are so rare in this wicked world."
Mrs. Marvelle sighed, then suddenly becoming practical
again, she continued. "Yes, I shall go there and stop to
luncheon, and talk this thing over. Then I'll drive on to
the Van Clupps, and bring Marcia home to dinner. I suppose you don't object?"

"Object!" Mr. Marvelle made a deprecatory gesture,
and raised his eyes in wonder. As if he dared object to
anything whatsoever that his wife desired!

She smiled graciously as he approached, and respectfully
kissed her smooth cool cheek, before taking his departure for
his daily work as a lawyer in the city, and when he was
gone, she betook herself to her own small boudoir, where
she busied herself for more than an hour in writing letters,
and answering invitations.

She was, in her own line, a person of importance. She
made it her business to know everything and everybody—
she was fond of meddling with other people's domestic concerns, and she had a finger in every family pie. She was,
moreover, a regular match-maker,—fond of taking young
ladies under her maternal wing, and "introducing" them to
the proper quarters, and when, as was often the case, a distinguished American of many dollars but no influence
offered her three or four hundred guineas for chaperoning
his daughter into English society and marrying her well,
Mrs. Rush-Marvelle pocketed the *douceur* quite gracefully,
and did her best for the girl. She was a good-looking
woman, tall, portly, and with an air of distinction about her,
though her features were by no means striking, and the
smallness of her nose was out of all proportion to the
majesty of her form—but she had a very charming smile,
and a pleasant, taking manner, and she was universally admired in that particular "set" wherein she moved. Girls
adored her, and wrote her gushing letters, full of the most
dulcet flatteries—married ladies on the verge of a scandal
came to her to help them out of their difficulties—old
dowagers, troubled with rheumatism or refractory daughters, poured their troubles into her sympathizing ears—in

short, her hands were full of other people's business to such an extent that she had scarcely any leisure to attend to her own. Mr. Rush-Marvelle,——but why describe this gentleman at all? He was a mere nonentity—known simply as the husband of Mrs. Rush-Marvelle. He knew he was nobody—and, unlike many men placed in a similar position, he was satisfied with his lot. He admired his wife intensely, and never failed to flatter her vanity to the utmost excess, so that, on the whole, they were excellent friends, and agreed much better than most married people.

It was about twelve o'clock in the day, when Mrs. Rush-Marvelle's neat little brougham and pair stopped at Lord Winsleigh's great house in Park Lane. A gorgeous flunkey threw open the door with a virtuously severe expression on his breakfast-flushed countenance,—an expression which relaxed into a smile of condescension on seeing who the visitor was.

"I suppose Lady Winsleigh is at home, Briggs?" inquired Mrs. Marvelle, with the air of one familiar with the ways of the household.

"Yes'm," replied Briggs slowly, taking in the "style" of Mrs Rush-Marvelle's bonnet, and mentally calculating its cost. "Her ladyship is in the boo-dwar."

"I'll go there," said Mrs. Marvelle, stepping into the hall, and beginning to walk across it, in her own important and self-assertive manner. "You needn't announce me."

Briggs closed the street-door, settled his powdered wig, and looked after her meditatively. Then he shut up one eye in a sufficiently laborious manner and grinned. After this he retired slowly to a small ante-room, where he found the *World* with its leaves uncut. Taking up his master's ivory paper-knife, he proceeded to remedy this slight inconvenience,—and, yawning heavily, he seated himself in a velvet arm-chair, and was soon absorbed in perusing the pages of the journal in question.

Meanwhile Mrs. Marvelle, in her way across the great hall to the "boo-dwar," had been interrupted and nearly knocked down by the playful embrace of a handsome boy, who sprang out upon her suddenly with a shout of laughter, —a boy of about twelve years old, with frank, bright blue eyes and clustering dark curls.

"Hullo, Mimsey!" cried this young gentleman—"here you are again! Do you want to see papa? Papa's in there!"—pointing to the door from which he had emerged

—"he's correcting my Latin exercise. Five good marks to-day, and I'm going to the circus this afternoon! Isn't it jolly?"

"Dear me, Ernest!" exclaimed Mrs. Marvelle half crossly, yet with an indulgent smile,—"I wish you would not be so boisterous! You've nearly knocked my bonnet off."

"No, I haven't," laughed Ernest; "it's as straight as— wait a bit!" And waving a lead pencil in the air, he drew an imaginary stroke with it. "The middle feather is bobbing up and down just on a line with your nose—it couldn't be better!"

"There, go along, you silly boy!" said Mrs. Marvelle, amused in spite of herself. "Get back to your lessons. There'll be no circus for you if you don't behave properly! I'm going to see your mother."

"Mamma's reading," announced Ernest. "Mudie's cart has just been and brought a lot of new novels. Mamma wants to finish them all before night. I say, are you going to stop to lunch?"

"Ernest, why are you making such a noise in the passage?" said a gentle, grave voice at this juncture. "I am waiting for you, you know. You haven't finished your work yet. Ah, Mrs. Marvelle! How do you do?"

And Lord Winsleigh came forward and shook hands. "You will find her ladyship in, I believe. She will be delighted to see you. This young scapegrace," here he caressed his son's clustering curls tenderly—"has not yet done with his lessons—the idea of the circus to-day seems to have turned his head."

"Papa, you promised you'd let me off Virgil this morning!" cried Ernest, slipping his arm coaxingly through his father's. Lord Winsleigh smiled. Mrs. Rush-Marvelle shook her head with a sort of mild reproachfulness.

"He really ought to go to school," she said, feigning severity. "You will find him too much for you, Winsleigh, in a little while."

"I think not," replied Lord Winsleigh, though an anxious look troubled for an instant the calm of his deep-set grey eyes. "We get on very well together, don't we, Ernest?" The boy glanced up fondly at his father's face and nodded emphatically. "At a public-school, you see, the boys are educated on hard and fast lines—all ground down to one pattern,—there's no chance of any originality possible. But don't let me detain you, Mrs. Marvelle—you have no doubt much to say to Lady Winsleigh. Come, Ernest! If I let you off Virgil, you must do the rest of your work thoroughly."

And with a courteous salute, the grave, kindly-faced nobleman re-entered his library, his young son clinging to his arm and pouring forth boyish confidences, which seemingly received instant attention and sympathy,—while Mrs. Rush-Marvelle looked after their retreating figures with something of doubt and wonder on her placid features. But whatever her thoughts, they were not made manifest just then. Arriving at a door draped richly with old-gold plush and satin, she knocked.

"Come in!" cried a voice that, though sweet in tone, was also somewhat petulant.

Mrs. Marvelle at once entered, and the occupant of the room sprang up in haste from her luxurious reading-chair, where she was having her long tresses brushed out by a prim-looking maid, and uttered an exclamation of delight.

"My dearest Mimsey!" she cried, "this is quite *too* sweet of you! You're just the very person I wanted to see!" And she drew an easy fauteuil to the sparkling fire,—for the weather was cold, with that particularly cruel coldness common to an English May,—and dismissed her attendant. "Now sit down, you dear old darling," she continued, "and let me have all the news!"

Throwing herself back on her lounge, she laughed, and tossed her waving hair loose over her shoulders, as the maid had left it,—then she arranged, with a coquettish touch here and there, the folds of her pale pink dressing-gown, showered with delicate Valenciennes. She was undeniably a lovely woman. Tall and elegantly formed, with an almost regal grace of manner, Clara, Lady Winsleigh, deserved to be considered, as she was, one of the reigning beauties of the day. Her full dark eyes were of a bewitching and dangerous softness,—her complexion was pale, but of such a creamy, transparent pallor as to be almost brilliant,—her mouth was small and exquisitely shaped. True,—her long eyelashes were not altogether innocent of "kohl,"—true, there was a faint odor about her as of rare perfumes and cosmetics,—true, there was something not altogether sin- cere or natural even in her ravishing smile and fascinating ways—but few, save cynics, could reasonably dispute her physical perfections, or question the right she had to tempt and arouse the passions of men, or to trample underfoot, with an air of insolent superiority, the feelings of women less fair and fortunate. Most of her sex envied her,—but Mrs. Rush-Marvelle, who was past the prime of life, and, who, moreover, gained her social successes through intelligence and tact alone, was far too sensible to grudge any woman her beauty. On the contrary, she was a frank admirer of handsome persons, and she surveyed Lady Winsleigh now through her glasses with a smile of bland approval.

" You are looking very well, Clara," she said. " Let me see—you went to Kissingen in the summer, didn't you ? "

" Of course I did," laughed her ladyship. " It was delicious ! I suppose you know Lennie came after me there ! Wasn't it ridiculous ! "

Mrs. Marvelle coughed dubiously. " Didn't Winsleigh put in an appearance at all ? " she asked.

Lady Clara's brow clouded. " Oh yes ! For a couple of weeks or so. Ernest came with him, of course, and they rambled about together all the time. The boy enjoyed it."

" I remember now," said Mrs. Marvelle. " But I've not seen anything of you since you came back, Clara, except once in the park and once at the theatre. You've been all the time at Winsleigh Court—by-the-by, was Sir Francis Lennox there too ? "

" Why, naturally ! " replied the beauty, with a cool smile. " He follows me everywhere like a dog ! Poor Lennie ! "

Again the elder lady coughed significantly.

Clara Winsleigh broke into a ringing peal of laughter, and rising from her lounge, knelt beside her visitor in a very pretty coaxing attitude.

" Come, Mimsey ! " she said, " you are not going to be ' proper ' at this time of day ! That would be a joke ! Darling, indulgent, good old Mimsey !—you don't mean to turn into a prim, prosy, cross Mrs. Grundy ! I won't believe it ! And you mustn't be severe on poor Lennie—he's such a docile, good boy, and really not bad-looking ! "

Mrs. Marvelle fidgeted a little on her chair. " I don't want to talk about *Lennie,* as you call him," she said, rather testily—" Only I think you'd better be careful how far you go with him. I came to consult you on something quite different. What are you going to do about the Bruce-Errington business ? You know it was in the *Post* to-day that they've arrived in town. The idea of Sir

Philip bringing his common wife into society!—It's too ridiculous!"

Lady Winsleigh sprang to her feet, and her eyes flashed disdainfully.

"What am I going to do?" she repeated, in accents of bitter contempt. "Why, receive them, of course! It will be the greatest punishment Bruce-Errington can have! I'll get all the best people here that I know—and he shall bring his peasant woman among them, and blush for her! It will be the greatest fun out! Fancy a Norwegian farmer's girl lumbering along with her great feet and red hands! . . . and, perhaps, not knowing whether to eat an ice with a spoon or with her fingers! I tell you Bruce-Errington will be ready to die for shame—and serve him right too!"

Mrs. Marvelle was rather startled at the harsh, derisive laughter with which her ladyship concluded her excited observations, but she merely observed mildly—

"Well, then, you will leave cards?"

"Certainly?"

"Very good—so shall I," and Mrs. Marvelle sighed resignedly. "What must be, must be! But it's really dreadful to think of it all—I would never have believed Philip Errington could have so disgraced himself!"

"He is no gentleman!" said Lady Winsleigh freezingly. "He has low tastes and low desires. He and his friend Lorimer are two *cads*, in my opinion!"

"Clara!" exclaimed Mrs. Marvelle warningly. "You were fond of him once!—now, don't deny it!"

"Why should I deny it?" and her ladyship's dark eyes blazed with concentrated fury. "I loved him! There! I would have done anything for him! He might have trodden me down under his feet! He knew it well enough—cold, cruel, heartless cynic as he was and is! Yes, I loved him!—but I *hate* him now!"

And she stamped her foot to give emphasis to her wild words. Mrs. Marvelle raised her hands and eyes in utter amazement.

"Clara, Clara! Pray, pray be careful! Suppose any one else heard you going on in this manner! Your reputation would suffer, I assure you! Really, you're horribly reckless! Just think of your husband——"

"My husband!" and a cold gleam of satire played round Lady Winsleigh's proud mouth. She paused and laughed a little. Then she resumed in her old careless way —" You must be getting very goody-goody, Mimsey, to talk to me about my husband! Why don't you read me a lecture on the duties of wives and the education of children? I am sure you know how profoundly it would interest me!"

She paced up and down the room slowly while Mrs Marvelle remained discreetly silent. Presently there came a tap at the door, and the gorgeous Briggs entered. He held himself like an automaton, and spoke as though repeating a lesson.

" His lordship's compliments, and will her la'ship lunch in the dining-room to-day?"

" No," said Lady Winsleigh curtly. " Luncheon for myself and Mrs. Marvelle can be sent up here."

Briggs still remained immovable. " His lordship wished to know if Master Hernest was to come to your la'ship before goin' out?"

" Certainly not!" and Lady Winsleigh's brows drew together in a frown. " The boy is a perfect nuisance!"

Briggs bowed and vanished. Mrs. Rush-Marvelle grew more and more restless. She was a good-hearted woman, and there was something in the nature of Clara Winsleigh that, in spite of her easy-going conscience, she could not altogether approve of.

" Do you never lunch with your husband, Clara?" she asked at last.

Lady Winsleigh looked surprised. " Very seldom. Only when there is company, and I am compelled to be present. A domestic meal would be too *ennuyant!* I wonder you can think of such a thing! And we generally dine out."

Mrs. Marvelle was silent again, and, when she did speak, it was on a less delicate matter.

" When is your great ' crush,' Clara?" she inquired. " You sent me a card, but I forget the date."

" On the twenty-fifth," replied Lady Winsleigh. " This is the fifteenth. I shall call on Lady Bruce-Errington "— here she smiled scornfully—" this afternoon—and to-morrow I shall send them their invitations. My only fear is whether they mayn't refuse to come. I would not miss the chance for the world! I want my house to be the first in which her peasant-ladyship distinguishes herself by her blunders!"

" I'm afraid it'll be quite a scandal!" sighed Mrs. Rush-

Marvelle. "Quite! Such a pity! Bruce-Errington was such a promising, handsome young man!"

At that moment Briggs appeared again with an elegantly set luncheon-tray, which he placed on the table with a flourish.

"Order the carriage at half-past three," commanded Lady Winsleigh. "And tell Mrs. Marvelle's coachman that he needn't wait,—I'll drive her home myself."

"But, my dear Clara," remonstrated Mrs. Marvelle, " I must call at the Van Clupps'——"

"I'll call there with you. I owe them a visit. Has Marcia caught young Masherville yet?"

"Well," hesitated Mrs. Marvelle, "he is rather slippery, you know—so undecided and wavering!"

Lady Winsleigh laughed. "Never mind that! Marcia's a match for him! Rather a taking girl—only *what* an accent! My nerves are on edge whenever I hear her speak."

"It's a pity she can't conquer that defect," agreed Mrs. Marvelle. "I know she has tried. But, after all, they're not the best sort of Americans——"

"The *best* sort! I should think not! But they're of the *richest* sort, and that's something, Mimsey! Besides, though everybody knows what Van Clupp's father was, they make a good pretense at being well-born,—they don't cram their low connections down your throat, as Bruce-Errington wants to do with his common wife. They ignore all their vulgar belongings delightfully! They've been cruelly 'cut' by Mrs. Rippington—she's American—but, then, she's perfect style. Do you remember that big 'at home' at the Van Clupp's when they had a band to play in the back-yard, and everybody was deafened by the noise? Wasn't it quite too ridiculous!"

Lady Winsleigh laughed over this reminiscence, and then betook herself to the consideration of lunch,—a tasty meal which both she and Mrs. Marvelle evidently enjoyed, flavored as it was with the high spice of scandal concerning their most immediate and mutual friends, who were, after much interesting discussion, one by one condemned as of "questionable" repute, and uncertain position. Then Lady Winsleigh summoned her maid, and was arrayed *cap-à-pie* in "carriage-toilette," while Mrs. Marvelle amused herself by searching the columns of *Truth* for some new tit-bit of immorality connected with the royalty or nobility of England. And at half-past three precisely, the two ladies drove off together in an elegant victoria drawn by a dashing pair of greys, with a respectably apoplectic coachman on the box, supported by the stately Briggs, in all the glory of the olive-green and gold liveries which distinguished the Winsleigh equipage. By her ladyship's desire, they were driven straight to Prince's Gate.

" We may as well leave our cards together," said Clara, with a malicious little smile, " though I hope to goodness the creature won't be at home."

Bruce-Errington's town-house was a very noble-looking mansion—refined and simple in outer adornment, with a broad entrance, deep portico, and lofty windows—windows which fortunately were not spoilt by gaudy hangings of silk or satin in " æsthetic " colors. The blinds were white —and, what could be seen of the curtains from the outside, suggested the richness of falling velvets, and gold-woven tapestries. The drawing-room balconies were full of brilliant flowers, shaded by quaint awnings of Oriental pattern, thus giving the place an air of pleasant occupation and tasteful elegance.

Lady Winsleigh's carriage drew up at the door, and Briggs descended.

" Inquire if Lady Bruce-Errington is at home," said his mistress. " And if not, leave these cards."

Briggs received the scented glossy bits of pasteboard in his yellow-gloved hand with due gravity, and rang the bell marked " Visitors " in his usual ponderous manner, with a force that sent it clanging loudly through the corridors of the stately mansion. The door was instantly opened by a respectable man with grey hair and a gentle, kindly face, who was dressed plainly in black, and who eyed the gorgeous Briggs with the faintest suspicion of a smile. He was Errington's butler, and had served the family for twenty-five years.

" Her ladyship is driving in the Park," he said in response to the condescending inquiries of Briggs. " She left the house about half an hour ago."

Briggs thereupon handed in the cards, and forthwith reported the result of his interview to Lady Winsleigh, who said with some excitement—

" Turn into the Park and drive up and down till I give further orders."

Briggs mutely touched his hat, mounted the box, and the

carriage rapidly bowled in the required direction, while
Lady Winsleigh remarked laughingly to Mrs. Marvelle—

"Philip is sure to be with his treasure! If we can catch
a glimpse of her, sitting, staring open-mouthed at everything, it will be amusing! We shall then know what to
expect."

Mrs. Marvelle said nothing, though she too was more or
less curious to see the "peasant" addition to the circle of
fashionable society,—and when they entered the Park, both
she and Lady Winsleigh kept a sharp look-out for the first
glimpse of the quiet grey and silver of the Bruce-Errington liveries. They watched, however, in vain—it was not
yet the hour for the crowding of the Row—and there was
not a sign of the particular equipage they were so desirous
to meet. Presently Lady Winsleigh's face flushed—she
laughed, and bade her coachman come to a halt.

"It is only Lennie," she said in answer to Mrs. Marvelle's
look of inquiry. "I *must* speak to him a moment!"

And she beckoned coquettishly to a slight, slim young
man with a dark moustache and rather handsome features,
who was idling along on the footpath, apparently absorbed
in a reverie, though it was not of so deep a character that
he failed to be aware of her ladyship's presence—in fact he
had seen her as soon as she appeared in the Park. He saw
everything apparently without looking—he had lazily
drooping eyes, but a swift under-glance which missed no
detail of whatever was going on. He approached now with
an excessively languid air, raising his hat slowly, as though
the action bored him.

"How do, Mrs. Marvelle!" he drawled lazily, addressing
himself first to the elder lady, who responded somewhat
curtly,—then leaning his arms on the carriage door, he fixed
Lady Winsleigh with a sleepy stare of admiration. "And
how is our Clara? Looking charming, as usual! By
Jove! Why weren't you here ten minutes ago? You
never saw such a sight in your life! Thought the whole
Row was going crazy, 'pon my soul!"

"Why, what happened?" asked Lady Winsleigh, smiling graciously upon him. "Anything extraordinary?"

"Well, I don't know what you'd call extraordinary;"
and Sir Francis Lennox yawned and examined the handle
of his cane attentively. "I suppose if Helen of Troy came
driving full pelt down the Row all of a sudden, there'd be
some slight sensation!"

"Dear me!" said Clara Winsleigh pettishly. "You talk in enigmas to-day. What on earth do you mean?"

Sir Francis condescended to smile. "Don't be waxy, Clara!" he urged—" I mean what I say—a new Helen appeared here to-day, and instead of 'tall Troy' being on fire, as Dante Rossetti puts it, the Row was in a burning condition of excitement—fellows on horseback galloped the whole length of the Park to take a last glimpse of her—her carriage dashed off to Richmond after taking only four turns. She is simply magnificent!"

"Who is she?" and in spite of herself, Lady Winsleigh's smile vanished and her lips quivered.

"Lady Bruce-Errington," answered Sir Francis readily. "The loveliest woman in the world, I should say! Phil was beside her—he looks in splendid condition—and that meek old secretary fellow sat opposite—Neville—isn't that his name? Anyhow they seemed as jolly as pipers,—as for that woman, she'll drive everybody out of their wits about her before half the season's over."

"But she's a mere peasant!" said Mrs. Marvelle loftily. "Entirely uneducated—a low, common creature!"

"Ah, indeed!" and Sir Francis again yawned extensively. "Well, I don't know anything about that! She was exquisitely dressed, and she held herself like a queen. As for her hair—I never saw such wonderful hair,—there's every shade of gold in it."

"Dyed!" said Lady Winsleigh, with a sarcastic little laugh. "She's been in Paris,—I dare say a good *coiffeur* has done it for her there artistically!"

This time Sir Francis's smile was a thoroughly amused one.

"Commend me to a woman for spite!" he said carelessly. "But I'll not presume to contradict you, Clara! You know best, I dare say! Ta-ta! I'll come for you to-night,—you know we're bound for the theatre together. By-bye, Mrs. Marvelle! You look younger than ever!"

And Sir Francis Lennox sauntered easily away, leaving the ladies to resume their journey through the Park. Lady Winsleigh looked vexed—Mrs. Marvelle bewildered.

"Do you think," inquired this latter, "she can really be so wonderfully lovely?"

"No, I don't!" answered Clara snappishly. "I dare say she's a plump creature with a high color—men like fat women with brick-tinted complexions—they think it's healthy. Helen of Troy indeed! Pooh! Lennie must be crazy."

The rest of their drive was very silent,—they were both absorbed in their own reflections. On arriving at the Van Clupps', they found no one at home—not even Marcia—so Lady Winsleigh drove her " dearest Mimsey " back to her own house in Kensington, and there left her with many expressions of tender endearment—then, returning home, proceeded to make an elaborate and brilliant toilette for the enchantment and edification of Sir Francis Lennox that evening. She dined alone, and was ready for her admirer when he called for her in his private hansom, and drove away with him to the theatre, where she was the cynosure of many eyes; meanwhile her husband, Lord Winsleigh, was pressing a good-night kiss on the heated forehead of an excited boy, who, plunging about in his little bed and laughing heartily, was evidently desirous of emulating the gambols of the clown who had delighted him that afternoon at Hengler's.

" Papa! could you stand on your head and shake hands with your foot? " demanded this young rogue, confronting his father with towzled curls and flushed cheeks.

Lord Winsleigh laughed. " Really, Ernest, I don't think I could ! " he answered good-naturedly. " Haven't you talked enough about the circus by this time? I thought you were ready for sleep, otherwise I should not have come up to say good-night."

Ernest studied the patient, kind features of his father for a moment, and then slipped penitently under the bed-clothes, settling his restless young head determinedly on the pillow.

" I'm all right now ! " he murmured, with a demure, dimpling smile. Then, with a tender upward twinkle of his merry blue eyes, he added, " Good-night, papa dear ! God bless you ! "

A sort of wistful pathos softened the grave lines of Lord Winsleigh's countenance as he bent once more over the little bed, and pressed his bearded lips lightly on the boy's fresh cheek, as cool and soft as a rose-leaf.

" God bless you, little man ! " he answered softly, and there was a slight quiver in his calm voice. Then he put out the light and left the room, closing the door after him with careful noiselessness. Descending the broad stairs slowly, his face changed from its late look of tenderness to one of stern and patient coldness, which was evidently its habitual expression. He addressed himself to Briggs, who was lounging aimlessly in the hall.

" Her ladyship is out ? "

" Yes, my lord! Gone to the theayter with Sir Francis Lennox."

Lord Winsleigh turned upon him sharply. " I did not ask you, Briggs, *where* she had gone, or *who* accompanied her. Have the goodness to answer my questions simply, without adding useless and unnecessary details."

Briggs's mouth opened a little in amazement at his master's peremptory tone, but he answered promptly—

" Very good, my lord ! "

Lord Winsleigh paused a moment, and seemed to consider. Then he said—

" See that her ladyship's supper is prepared in the dining-room. She will most probably return rather late. Should she inquire for me, say I am at the Carlton."

Again Briggs responded, " Very good, my lord ! " And, like an exemplary servant as he was, he lingered about the passage while Lord Winsleigh entered his library, and, after remaining there some ten minutes or so, came out again in hat and great coat. The officious Briggs handed him his cane, and inquired—

" 'Ansom, my lord ? "

" Thanks, no. I will walk."

It was a fine moonlight night, and Briggs stood for some minutes on the steps, airing his shapely calves and watching the tall, dignified figure of his master walking, with the upright, stately bearing which always distinguished him, in the direction of Pall Mall. Park Lane was full of crowding carriages with twinkling lights, all bound to the different sources of so-called " pleasure " by which the opening of the season is distinguished. Briggs surveyed the scene with lofty indifference, sniffed the cool breeze, and, finding it somewhat chilly, re-entered the house and descended to the servant's hall. Here all the domestics of the Winsleigh household were seated at a large table loaded with hot and savory viands,—a table presided over by a robust and perspiring lady, with a very red face and sturdy arms bare to the elbow.

" Lor', Mr. Briggs ! " cried this personage, rising respectfully as he approached, " 'ow late you are ! Wot 'ave you been a-doin' on ? 'Ere I've been a-keepin' your lamb-chops

and truffles 'ot all this time, and if they's dried up 'taint my
fault, nor that of the hoven, which is as good a hoven as
you can wish to bake in. . . ."

She paused breathless, and Briggs smiled blandly.

"Now, Flopsie!" he said in a tone of gentle severity.
"Excited again—as usual! It's bad for your 'elth—very
bad! *Hif* the chops is dried, your course is plain—cook
some more! Not that I am enny ways particular—but
chippy meat is bad for a delicate digestion. And you would
not make me hill, my Flopsie, would you?"

Whereupon he seated himself, and looked condescendingly round the table. He was too great a personage to be
familiar with such inferior creatures as housemaids, scullery-
girls, and menials of that class,—he was only on intimate
terms with the cook, Mrs. Flopper, or, as he called her,
"Flopsie,"—the coachman, and Lady Winsleigh's own
maid, Louise Rénaud, a prim, sallow-faced Frenchwoman,
who, by reason of her nationality, was called by all the inhabitants of the kitchen, "mamzelle," as being a name both
short, appropriate, and convenient.

On careful examination, the lamb-chops turned out satisfactorily—"chippiness" was an epithet that could not
justly be applied to them,—and Mr. Briggs began to eat
them leisurely, flavoring them with a glass or two of fine
port out of a decanter which he had taken the precaution to
bring down from the dining-room sideboard.

"I *ham* late," he then graciously explained—"not that I
was detained in enny way by the people upstairs. The gay
Clara went out early, but I was absorbed in the evenin'
papers—Winsleigh forgot to ask me for them. But he'll
see them at his club. He's gone there now on foot—poor
fellah!"

"I suppose *she's* with the same party?" grinned the fat
Flopsie, as she held a large piece of bacon dipped in vinegar
on her fork, preparatory to swallowing it with a gulp.

Briggs nodded gravely. "The same! Not a fine man
at all, you know—no leg to speak of, and therefore no
form. Legs—*good* legs—are beauty. Now, Winsleigh's
not bad in that particular,—and I dare say Clara can hold
her own,—but I wouldn't bet on little Francis."

Flopsie shrieked with laughter till she had a "stitch in
her side," and was compelled to restrain her mirth.

"Lor', Mr. Briggs!" she gasped, wiping the moisture
from her eyes, "you are a regular one, aren't you! Mussy

on us, you ought to put all wot you say in the papers—you'd make your fortin!"

"Maybe, maybe, Flospie," returned Briggs with due dignity. "I will not deny that there may be wot is called 'sparkle' in my natur. And 'sparkle' is wot is rekwired in polite literatoor. Look at 'Hedmund' and ''Enery!' Sparkle again,—read their magnificent productions, the *World* and *Truth,*—all sparkle, every line! It is the secret of success, Flospie—be a sparkler and you've got everything before you."

Louise Rénaud looked across at him half-defiantly. Her prim, cruel mouth hardened into a tight line.

"To spark-el?" she said—"that is what we call *étinceler* —*éclater.* Yes, I comprehend! Miladi is one spark-el! But one must be a very good jewel to spark-el always—yes —yes—not a sham!"

And she nodded a great many times, and ate her salad very fast. Briggs surveyed her with much complacency.

"You are a talented woman, Mamzelle," he said, "very talented! I admire your ways—I really do!"

Mamzelle smiled with a gratified air, and Briggs settled his wig, eyeing her anew with fresh interest.

"*Wot* a witness you would be in a divorce case!" he continued enthusiastically. "You'd be in your helement!"

"I should—I should indeed!" exclaimed Mamzelle, with sudden excitement,—then as suddenly growing calm, she made a rapid gesture with her hands—"But there will be no divorce. Milord Winsleigh is a fool!"

Briggs appeared doubtful about this, and meditated for a long time over his third glass of port with the profound gravity of a philosopher.

"No, Mamzelle," he said at last, when he rose from the table to return to his duties upstairs—"No! there I must differ from you. I am a close observer. Wotever Winsleigh's faults,—and I do not deny that they are many,—he is a gentleman—that I *must* admit—and with *hevery* respect for you, Mamzelle—I can assure you he's no fool!"

And with these words Briggs betook himself to the library to arrange the reading-lamp and put the room in order for his master's return, and as he did so, he paused to look at a fine photograph of Lady Winsleigh that stood on the oak escritoire, opposite her husband's arm-chair.

"No," he muttered to himself. "Wotever he thinks of some goings-on, he ain't blind nor deaf—that's certain

And I'd stake my character and purfessional reputation on
it—wotever he is, he's no fool!"

For once in his life, Briggs was right. He was generally
wrong in his estimat of both persons and things—but it so
happened on this particular occasion that he had formed a
perfectly correct judgment.

CHAPTER XIX.

> "Could you not drink her gaze like wine?
>   Yet in its splendor swoon
> Into the silence languidly,
>   As a tune into a tune?"
>
> DANTE ROSSETTI.

ON the morning of the twenty-fifth of May, Thelma, Lady
Bruce-Errington, sat at breakfast with her husband in their
sun-shiny morning-room, fragrant with flowers and melodious with the low piping of a tame thrush in a wild gilded
cage, who had the sweet habit of warbling his strophes to
himself very softly now and then, before venturing to give
them full-voiced utterance. A bright-eyed, feathered poet
he was, and an exceeding favorite with his fair mistress,
who occasionally leaned back in her low chair to look at
him and murmur an encouraging "Sweet, sweet!" which
caused the speckled plumage on his plump breast to ruffle
up with suppressed emotion and gratitude.

Philip was pretending to read the *Times*, but the huge,
self-important printed sheet had not the faintest interest
for him,—his eyes wandered over the top of its columns to
the golden gleam of his wife's hair, brightened just then
by the sunlight streaming through the window,—and finally he threw it down beside him with a laugh.

"There's no news," he declared. "There never *is* any
news!"

Thelma smiled, and her deep-blue eyes sparkled.

"No?" she half inquired—then taking her husband's
cup from his hand to re-fill it with coffee, she added, "but I
think you do not give yourself time to find the news,
Philip. You will never read the papers more than five
minutes."

"My dear girl," said Philip gaily, "I am more conscien-
tious than you are, at any rate, for you never read them at
all!"

" Ah, but you must remember," she returned gravely,
" that is because I do not understand them! I am not
clever. They seem to me to be all about such dull things
—unless there is some horrible murder or ruel'y or accident—and I would rather not hear of these. I do prefer
books always—because the books last, and news is never
certain—it may not even be true."

Her husband looked at her fondly ; his thoughts were evidently very far away from newspapers and their contents.

As she met his gaze, the rich color flushed her soft cheeks
and her eyes drooped shyly under their long lashes. Love,
with her, had not yet proved an illusion,—a bright toy to
be snatched hastily and played with for a brief while, and
then thrown aside as broken and worthless. It seemed to
her a most marvellous and splendid gift of God, increasing
each day in worth and beauty,—widening upon her soul
and dazzling her life in ever new and expanding circles of
glory. She felt as if she could never sufficiently understand it,—the passionate adoration Philip lavished upon
her, filled her with a sort of innocent wonder and gratitude,
while her own overpowering love and worship of him, sometimes startled her by its force into a sweet shame and hesitating fear. To her mind he was all that was great, strong,
noble, and beautiful—he was her master, her king,—and
she loved to pay him homage by her exquisite humility,
clinging tenderness, and complete, contented submission.
She was neither weak nor timid,—her character, moulded
on grand and simple lines of duty, saw the laws of Nature
in their true light, and accepted them without question.
It seemed to her quite clear that man was the superior,—
woman the inferior, creature—and she could not understand the possibility of any wife not rendering instant and
implicit obedience to her husband, even in trifles.

Since her wedding-day no dark cloud had crossed her
heaven of happiness, though she had been a little confused
and bewildered at first by the wealth and dainty luxury
with which Sir Philip had delighted to surround her. She
had been married quietly at Christiania, arrayed in one of
her own simple white gowns, with no ornament save a cluster of pale blush-roses, the gift of Lorimer. The ceremony
was witnessed by her father and Errington's friends,—and
when it was concluded they had all gone on their several
ways,—old Güldmar for a " toss " on the Bay of Biscay,—
the yacht *Eulalie*, with Lorimer, Macfarlane, and Duprèz

on board, back to England, where these gentlemen had separated to their respective homes,—while Errington, with
his beautiful bride, and Britta in demure and delighted attendance on her, went straight to Copenhagen. From
there they travelled to Hamburg, and through Germany to
the Schwarzwald, where they spent their honeymoon at a
quiet little hotel in the very heart of the deep-green Forest.

Days of delicious dreaming were these,—days of roaming
on the emerald green turf under the stately and odorous
pines, listening to the dash of the waterfalls, or watching
the crimson sunset burning redly through the darkness of
the branches,—and in the moonlit evenings sitting under
the trees to hear the entrancing music of a Hungarian
string-band, which played divine and voluptuous melodies
of the land,—" lieder " and " walzer " that swung the heart
away on a golden thread of sound to a paradise too sweet
to name! Days of high ecstacy, and painfully passionate
joy!—when " love, love!" palpitated in the air, and
struggled for utterance in the jubilant throats of birds, and
whispered wild suggestions in the rustling of the leaves!
There were times when Thelma,—lost and amazed and
overcome by the strength and sweetness of the nectar held
to her innocent lips by a smiling and flame-winged *Eros*,—
would wonder vaguely whether she lived indeed, or whether
she were not dreaming some gorgeous dream, too brilliant
to last? And even when her husband's arms most surely
embraced her, and her husband's kiss met hers in all the
rapture of victorious tenderness, she would often question
herself as to whether she were worthy of such perfect happiness, and she would pray in the depths of her pure heart
to be made more deserving of this great and wonderful gift
of love—this supreme joy, almost too vast for her comprehension.

On the other hand, Errington's passion for his wife was
equally absorbing—she had become the very moving-spring
of his existence. His eyes delighted in her beauty,—but
more than this, he revelled in and reverenced the crystal-
clear purity and exquisite refinement of her soul. Life assumed for him a new form,—studied by the light of
Thelma's straightforward simplicity and intelligence, it
was no longer, as he had once been inclined to think, a
mere empty routine,—it was a treasure of inestimable
value fraught with divine meanings. Gradually, the touch
of modern cynicism that had at one time threatened to

spoil his nature, dropped away from him like the husk
from an ear of corn,—the world arrayed itself in bright
and varying colors—there was good—nay, there was glory
—in everything.

With these ideas, and the healthy satisfaction they engendered, his heart grew light and joyous,—his eyes more
lustrous,—his step gay and elastic,—and his whole appearance was that of man at his best,—man, as God most
surely meant him to be—not a rebellious, feebly-repining,
sneering wretch, ready to scoff at the very sunlight,—but
a being both brave and intelligent, strong and equably balanced in temperament, and not only contented, but absolutely glad to be alive,—glad to feel the blood flowing
through the veins,—glad and grateful for the gifts of
breathing and sight.

As each day passed, the more close and perfect grew the
sympathies of husband and wife,—they were like two notes
of a perfect chord, sounding together in sweetest harmony.
Naturally, much of this easy and mutual blending of character and disposition arose from Thelma's own gracious
and graceful submissiveness,—submissiveness which, far
from humiliating her, actually placed her (though she
knew it not) on a throne of almost royal power, before
which Sir Philip was content to kneel—an ardent worshipper of her womanly sweetness. Always without question
or demur, she obeyed his wishes implicitly,—though, as
has been before mentioned, she was at first a little overpowered and startled by the evidences of his wealth, and
did not quite know what to do with all the luxuries and
gifts he heaped upon her. Britta's worldly prognostica-
tions had come true,—the simple gowns her mistress had
worn at the Altenfjord were soon discarded for more costly
apparel,—though Sir Philip had an affection for his wife's
Norwegian costumes, and in his heart thought they were
as pretty, if not prettier, than the most perfect triumphs
of a Parisian *modiste.*

But in the social world, Fashion, the capricious deity,
must be followed, if not wholly, yet in part; and so
Thelma's straight, plain garments were laid carefully by as
souvenirs of the old days, and were replaced by toilettes of
the most exquisite description,—some simple,—some costly,
—and it was difficult to say in which of them the lovely
wearer looked her best. She herself was indifferent in the
matter—she dressed to please Philip,—if he was satisfied,

she was happy—she sought nothing further. It was Britta
whose merry eyes sparkled with pride and admiration
when she saw her "Fröken" arrayed in gleaming silk or
sweeping velvets, with the shine of rare jewels in her rippling hair,—it was Britta who took care of all the dainty
trifles that gradually accumulated on Thelma's dressing-
table,—in fact, Britta had become a very important personage in her own opinion. Dressed neatly in black, with a
coquettish muslin apron and cap becomingly frilled, she
was a very taking little maid, with her demure rosy face
and rebellious curls, though very different to the usual
trained spy whose officious ministrations are deemed so
necessary by ladies of position, whose lofty station in life
precludes them from the luxury of brushing their own
hair. Britta's duties were slight—she invented most of
them—yet she was always busy sewing, dusting, packing,
or polishing. She was a very wide-awake little person, too,
—no hint was lost upon her,—and she held her own wherever she went with her bright eyes and sharp tongue.
Though secretly in an unbounded state of astonishment at
everything new she saw, she was too wise to allow this to
be noticed, and feigned the utmost coolness and indifference, even when they went from Germany to Paris, where
the brilliancy and luxury of the shops almost took away
her breath for sheer wonderment.

In Paris, Thelma's wardrobe was completed—a certain
Madame Rosine, famous for "artistic arrangements," was
called into requisition, and viewing with a professional eye
the superb figure and majestic carriage of her new customer, rose to the occasion in all her glory, and resolved
that Miladi Bruce-Errington's dresses should be the wonder
and envy of all who beheld them.

"For," said Madame, with a grand air, "it is to do me
justice. That form so magnificent is worth draping,—it
will support my work to the best advantage. And persons
without figures will hasten to me and entreat me for costumes, and will think that if I dress them I can make them
look as well as Miladi. And they will pay!"—Madame
shook her head with much shrewdness—"Mon Dieu! they
will pay!—and that they still look frightful will not be my
fault."

And undoubtedly Madame surpassed her usual skill in all
she did for Thelma,—she took such pains, and was so successful in all her designs, that "Miladi," who did not as a

rule show more than a very ordinary interest in her toilette, found it impossible not to admire the artistic taste, harmonious coloring, and exquisite fit of the few choice gowns supplied to her from the " Maison Rosine "—and only on one occasion had she any discussion with the celebrated *modiste*. This was when Madame herself, with much pride, brought home an evening dress of the very palest and tenderest sea-green silk, showered with pearls and embroidered in silver, a perfect *chef-d' œuvre* of the dressmaker's art. The skirt, with its billowy train and peeping folds of delicate lace, pleased Thelma,—but she could not understand the bodice, and she held that very small portion of the costume in her hand with an air of doubt and wonderment. At last she turned her grave blue eyes inquiringly on Madame.

" It is not finished ? " she asked. " Where is the upper part of it and the sleeves ? "

Madame Rosine gesticulated with her hands and smiled.

" Miladi, there is no more ! " she declared. " Miladi will perceive it is for the evening wear—it is *dècolletée*—it is to show to everybody Miladi's most beautiful white neck and arms. The effect will be ravishing ! "

Thelma's face grew suddenly grave—almost stern.

" You must be very wicked ! " she said severely, to the infinite amazement of the vivacious Rosine. " You think I would show myself to people half clothed ? How is it possible ! I would not so disgrace myself ! It would bring shame to my husband ! "

Madame was almost speechless with surprise. What strange lady was this who was so dazzlingly beautiful and graceful, and yet so ignorant of the world's ways ? She stared,—but was soon on the defensive.

" Miladi is in a little error ! " she said rapidly and with soft persuasiveness. " It is *la mode*. Miladi has perhaps lived in a country where the fashions are different. But if she will ask the most amiable Sieur Bruce-Errington, she will find that her dress is quite in keeping with *les convenances*."

A pained blush crimsoned Thelma's fair cheek. " I do not like to ask my husband such a thing," she said slowly, " but I must. For I could not wear this dress without shame. I cannot think he would wish me to appear in it as you have made it—but——" She paused, and taking up the objectionable bodice, she added gently—" You will kindly wait here, madame, and I will see what Sir Philip says."

And she retired, leaving the *modiste* in a state of much astonishment, approaching resentment. The idea was outrageous,—a woman with such divinely fair skin,—a woman with the bosom of a Venus, and arms of a shape to make sculptors rave,—and yet she actually wished to hide these beauties from the public gaze! It was ridiculous—utterly ridiculous,—and Madame sat fuming impatiently, and sniffing the air in wonder and scorn. Meanwhile Thelma, with flushing cheeks and lowered eyes, confided her difficulty to Philip, who surveyed the shocking little bodice she brought for his inspection with a gravely amused, but very tender, smile.

" There certainly doesn't seem much of it, does there, darling?" he said. " And so you don't like it?"

" No," she confessed frankly—" I think I should feel quite undressed in it. I often wear just a little opening at the throat—but this——! Still, Philip, I must not displease you—and I will always wear what you wish, even if it is uncomfortable to myself."

" Look here, my pet," and he encircled her waist fondly with his arm, " Rosine is quite right. The thing's perfectly fashionable,—and there isn't a woman in society who wouldn't be perfectly charmed with it. But your ideas are better than Rosine's and all society's put together. Obey your own womanly instinct, Thelma!"

" But what do *you* wish?" she asked earnestly. " You must tell me. It is to please you that I live."

He kissed her. " You want me to issue a command about the affair?" he said half laughingly.

She smiled up into his eyes. " Yes!—and I will obey!"

" Very well! Now listen!" and he held her by both hands, and looked with sudden gravity into her sweet face —" Thelma, my wife, thus sayeth your lord and master,— despise the vulgar indecencies of fashion, and you will gratify me more than words can say ;—keep your pure and beautiful self sacred from the profaning gaze of the multitude,—sacred to me and my love for you, and I shall be the proudest man living! Finally,"—and he smiled again— " give Rosine back this effort at a bodice, and tell her to make something more in keeping with the laws of health and modesty. And Thelma—one more kiss! You are a darling!"

She laughed softly and left him, returning at once to the irate dressmaker who waited for her.

" I am sorry," she said very sweetly, " to have called you wicked ! You see, I did not understand ! But though this style of dress is fashionable, I do not wish to wear it—so you will please make me another bodice, with a small open square at the throat, and elbow-sleeves,—and you will lose nothing at all—for I shall pay you for this one just the same. And you must quite pardon me for my mistake and hasty words ! "

Maladi's manner was so gracious and winning, that Madame Rosine found it impossible not to smile in a soothed and mollified way,—and though she deeply regretted that so beautiful a neck and arms were not to be exposed to public criticism, she resigned herself to the inevitable, and took away the offending bodice, replacing it in a couple of days by one much prettier and more becoming by reason of its perfect modesty.

On leaving Paris, Sir Philip had taken his wife straight home to his fine old Manor in Warwickshire. Thelma's delight in her new abode was unbounded—the stately oaks that surrounded it,—the rose-gardens, the conservatories,—the grand rooms, with their fine tapestries, oak furniture, and rare pictures,—the splendid library, the long, lofty drawing-rooms, furnished and decorated after the style of Louis Quinze,—all filled her with a tender pride and wistful admiration. This was Philip's home ! and she was here to make it bright and glad for him !—she could imagine no fairer fate. The old servants of the place welcomed their new mistress with marked respect and evident astonishment at her beauty, though, when they knew her better, they marvelled still more at her exceeding gentleness and courtesy. The housekeeper, a stately white-haired dame, who had served the former Lady Errington, declared she was " an angel "—while the butler swore profoundly that " he knew what a queen was like at last ! "

The whole household was pervaded with an affectionate eagerness to please her, though, perhaps, the one most dazzled by her entrancing smile and sweet consideration for his comfort was Edward Neville, Sir Philip's private secretary and librarian,—a meek, mild-featured man of some five and forty years old, whose stooping shoulders, grizzled hair, and weak eyes gave him an appearance of much greater age. Thelma was particularly kind to Neville, having heard his history from her husband. It was brief and sad. He had married a pretty young girl whom he had found earning a bare subsistence as a singer in provincial music-halls,— loving her, he had pitied her unprotected state, and had res- cued her from the life she led—but after six months of com- parative happiness, she had suddenly deserted him, leaving no clue as to where or why she had gone. His grief for her loss, weighed heavily upon his mind—he brooded incessantly upon it—and though his profession was that of a music- master and organist, he grew so abstracted and inattentive to the claims of the few pupils he had, that they fell away from him one by one—and, after a bit, he lost his post as organist to the village church as well. This smote him deeply, for he was passionately fond of music, and was, moreover, a fine player,—and it was at this stage of his mis- fortunes that he met by chance Bruce-Errington. Philip, just then, was almost broken-hearted—his father and mother had died suddenly within a week of one another,—and he, finding the blank desolation of his home unbearable, was anxious to travel abroad for a time, so soon as he could find some responsible person in whose hands to leave the charge of the Manor, with its invaluable books and pictures, during his absence.

Hearing Neville's history through a mutual friend, he decided, with his usual characteristic impulse, that here was the very man for him—a gentleman by birth, rumored to be an excellent scholar,—and he at once offered him the post he had in view,—that of private secretary at a salary of £200 per annum. The astonished Neville could not at first believe in his good fortune, and began to stammer forth his gratitude with trembling lips and moistening eyes,—but Errington cut him short by declaring the whole thing set- tled, and desiring him to enter on his duties at once. He was forthwith installed in his position,—a highly enviable one for a man of his dreamy and meditative turn of mind. To him, literature and music were precious as air and light, he handled the rare volumes on the Errington book-shelves with lingering tenderness, and often pored over some diffi- cult manuscript, or dusty folio till long past midnight, al- most forgetful of his griefs in the enchantment thus engen- dered. Nor did he lack his supreme comforter, music,— there was a fine organ at the lower end of the long library, and seated at his beloved instrument, he wiled away many an hour,—steeping his soul in the divine and solemn melodies of Palestrina and Pergolesi, till the cruel sorrow that had darkened his life seemed nothing but a bad dream, and the face of his wife as he had first known it, fair, trustful, and plaintive, floated before his eyes unchanged, and arousing in him the old foolish throbbing emotions of rapture and passion that had gladdened the bygone days.

He never lost the hope of meeting her again, and from time to time he renewed his search for her, though all uselessly—he studied the daily papers with an almost morbid anxiety lest he should see the notice of her death—and he would even await each post with a heart beating more rapidly than usual, in case there should be some letter from her, imploring forgiveness, explaining everything, and summoning him once more to her side. He found a true and keenly sympathizing friend in Sir Philip, to whom he became profoundly attached,—to satisfy his wishes, to forward his interests, to attend to his affairs with punctilious exactitude—all this gave Neville the supremest happiness. He felt some slight doubt and anxiety, when he first received the sudden announcement of his patron's marriage, —but all forebodings as to the character and disposition of the new Lady Bruce-Errington fled like mist before sunshine, when he saw Thelma's fair face and felt her friendly hand-clasp.

Every morning on her way to the breakfast-room, she would look in at the door of his little study, which adjoined the library, and he learned to watch for the first glimmer of her dress, and to listen for her bright "Good morning, Mr. Neville!" with a sensation of the keenest pleasure. It was a sort of benediction on the whole day. A proud man was he when she asked him to give her lessons on the organ,— and never did he forget the first time he heard her sing. He was playing an exquisite "Ave Maria," by Stradella, and she, standing by her husband's side was listening, when she suddenly exclaimed—

"Why, we used to sing that at Arles!"—and her rich, round voice pealed forth clear, solemn, and sweet, following with pure steadiness the sustained notes of the organ. Neville's heart thrilled,—he heard her with a sort of breathless wonder and rapture, and when she ceased, it seemed as though heaven had closed upon him.

"One cannot praise such a voice as that!" he said. "It would be a kind of sacrilege. It is divine!"

After this, many were the pleasant musical evenings they

all passed together in the grand old library, and,—as Mrs, Rush-Marvelle had so indignantly told her husband,—no visitors were invited to the Manor during that winter. Errington was perfectly happy—he wanted no one but his wife, and the idea of entertaining a party of guests who would most certainly interfere with his domestic enjoyment, seemed almost abhorrent to him. The county-people called,—but missed seeing Thelma, for during the daytime she was always out with her husband taking long walks and rambling excursions to the different places hallowed by Shakespeare's presence,—and when she, instructed by Sir Philip, called on the county-people, they also seemed to be never at home.

And so, as yet, she had made no acquaintances, and now that she had been married eight months and had come to London, the same old story repeated itself. People called on her in the afternoon just at the time when she went out driving,—when she returned their visits, she, in her turn, found them absent. She did not as yet understand the mystery of having " a day " on which to receive visitors in shoals—a day on which to drink unlimited tea, talk platitudes, and utterly bored and exhausted at the end thereof— in fact, she did not see the necessity of knowing many people,—her husband was all-sufficient for her,—to be in his society was all she cared for. She left her card at different houses because he told her to do so, but this social duty amused her immensely.

" It is like a game ! " she declared, laughing, " some one comes and leaves these little cards which explain who *they* are, on *me*,—then I go and leave *my* little cards and yours, explaining who *we* are on that some one—and we keep on doing this, yet we never see each other by any chance ! It is so droll ! "

Errington did not feel called upon to explain what was really the fact,—namely, that none of the ladies who had left cards on his wife had given her the option of their " at home " day on which to call,—he did not think it necessary to tell her what he knew very well, that his " set," both in county and town, had resolved to " snub " her in every petty fashion they could devise,—that he had already received several invitations which, as they did not include her, he had left unanswered,—and that the only house to which she had as yet been really asked in proper form was that of Lady Winsleigh. He was more amused than vexed

at the resolute stand made by the so-called " leaders " of
society against her, knowing as he did, most thoroughly,
how she must conquer them all in the end. She had been
seen nowhere as yet but in the Park, and Philip had good
reason to be contented with the excitement her presence had
created there,—but he was a little astonished at Lady
Winsleigh's being the first to extend a formal welcome to
his unknown bride. Her behavior seemed to him a little
suspicious,—for he certainly could not disguise from himself
that she had at one time been most violently and recklessly
in love with him. He recollected one or two most painful
scenes he had had with her, in which he had endeavored to
recall her to a sense of the duty she owed to her husband,
—and his face often flushed with vexation when he thought
of her wild and wicked abandonment of despair, her tears,
her passion, and distracted, dishonoring words. Yet she
was the very woman who now came forward in the very
front of society to receive his wife !—he could not quite
understand it. After all, he was a man,—and the sundry
artful tricks and wiles of fashionable ladies were, naturally,
beyond him. Thelma had never met Lady Winsleigh—not
even for a passing glance in the Park,—and when she received the invitation for the grand reception at Winsleigh
House, she accepted it, because her husband wished her so
to do, not that she herself anticipated any particular pleasure from it. When the day came round at last she
scarcely thought of it, till at the close of their pleasant
breakfast *tête-à-tête* described at the commencement of this
chapter, Philip suddenly said,—

" By-the-by, Thelma, I have sent to the bank for the Errington diamonds. They'll be here presently. I want you
to wear them to-night."

Thelma looked puzzled and inquiring.

" To-night ? What is it that we do ? I forget ! Oh ! now I
know—it is to go to Lady Winsleigh. What will it be like,
Philip ? "

" Well, there'll be heaps of people all cramming and
crowding up the stairs and down them again,—you'll
see all those women who have called on you, and you'll
be introduced to them,—I dare say there'll be some
bad music and an indigestible supper—and—and—that's
all ! "

She laughed and shook her head reproachfully.

" I cannot believe you, my naughty boy ! " she said, rising

from her seat, and kneeling beside him with arms round his neck, and soft eyes gazing lovingly into his. "You are nearly as bad as that very bad Mr. Lorimer, who will always see strange vexations in everything! I am quite sure Lady Winsleigh will not have crowds up and down her stairs,—that would be bad taste. And if she has music, it will be good—and she would not give her friends a supper to make them ill."

Philip did not answer. He was studying every delicate tint in his wife's dazzling complexion and seemed absorbed.

"Wear that one gown you got from Worth," he said abruptly. "I like it—it suits you."

"Of course I will wear it if you wish," she answered, laughing still. "But why? What does it matter? You want me to be something very splendid in dress to-night?"

Philip drew a deep breath. "I want you to eclipse every woman in the room!" he said with remarkable emphasis.

She grew rather pensive. "I do not think that would be pleasant," she said gravely. "Besides, it is impossible. And it would be wrong to wish me to make every one else dissatisfied with themselves. That is not like you, my Philip!"

He touched with tender fingers the great glistening coil of hair that was twisted up at the top of her graceful head.

"Ah, darling! You don't know what a world it is, and what very queer people there are in it! Never mind? . . . don't bother yourself about it. You'll have a good bird's-eye view of society to-night, and you shall tell me afterwards how you like it. I shall be curious to know what you think of Lady Winsleigh."

"She is beautiful, is she not?"

"Well, she is considered so by most of her acquaintances, and by herself," he returned with a smile.

"I do like to see very pretty faces," said Thelma warmly; "it is as if one looked at pictures. Since I have been in London I have seen so many of them—it is quite pleasant. Yet none of these lovely ladies seem to me as if they were really happy or strong in health."

"Half of them have got nervous diseases and all sorts of things wrong with them from over-much tea and tight lacing," replied Errington. and the few who *are* tolerably healthy are too bouncing by half, going in for hunting and such-like amusements till they grow blowsy and fat, and coarse as tom-boys or grooms. They can never hit the *juste milieu.* Well!" and he rose from the breakfast-table. "I'll go and see Neville and attend to business. We'll drive out this afternoon for some fresh air, and afterwards you must rest, my pet—for you'll find an 'at home' more tiring than climbing a mountain in Norway."

He kissed, and left her to her usual occupations, of which she had many, for she had taken great pains to learn all the details of the work in the Errington Establishment,—in fact, she went every morning to the little room where Mistress Parton, the housekeeper, received her with much respect and affection, and duly instructed her on every point of the domestic management and daily expenditure, so that she was thoroughly acquainted with everything that went on.

She had very orderly quiet ways of her own, and though thoughtful for the comfort and well-being of the lowest servant in her household she very firmly checked all extravagance and waste, yet in such a gentle, unobtrusive manner that her control was scarcely felt—though her husband at once recognized it in the gradually decreasing weekly expenses, while to all appearance, things were the same as ever. She had plenty of clear, good common sense,—she saw no reason why she should waste her husband's wealth simply because it was abundant,—so that under her mild sway, Sir Philip found himself getting richer without any trouble on his own part. His house assumed an air of lighter and more tasteful elegance,—flowers, always arranged by Thelma herself, adorned the rooms,— birds filled the great conservatory with their delicious warblings, and gradually that strange fairy sweet fabric known as " Home " rose smilingly around him. Formerly he had much disliked his stately town mansion—he had thought it dull and cold—almost gloomy,—but now he considered it charming, and wondered he had missed so many of its good points before.

And when the evening for Lady Winsleigh's "crush" came,—he looked regretfully round the lovely luxurious drawing-room with its bright fire, deep easy chairs, books, and grand piano, and wished he and his wife could remain at home in peace. He glanced at his watch—it was ten o'clock. There was no hurry—he had not the least intention of arriving at Winsleigh House too early. He knew what the effect of Thelma's entrance would be—and he smiled as he thought of it. He was waiting for her now,—he himself was ready in full evening dress—and remarkably handsome he looked. He walked up and down restlessly for a minute or so,—then taking up a volume of Keats, he threw himself into an easy chair and soon became absorbed. His eyes were still on the printed page, when a light touch on his shoulder startled him,—a soft, half-laughing voice inquired—

"Philip! Do I please you?"

He sprang up and faced her,—but for a moment could not speak. The perfection of her beauty had never ceased to arouse his wonder and passionate admiration,—but on this night, as she stood before him, arrayed in a simple, trailing robe of ivory-tinted velvet, with his family diamonds flashing in a tiara of light on her hair, glistening against the whiteness of her throat and rounded arms, she looked angelically lovely—so radiant, so royal, and withal so innocently happy, that, wistfully gazing at her, and thinking of the social clique into which she was about to make her entry, he wondered vaguely whether he was not wrong to take so pure and fair a creature among the false glitter and reckless hypocrisy of modern fashion and folly. And so he stood silent, till Thelma grew anxious.

"Ah, you are not satisfied!" she said plaintively. "I am not as you wish! There is something wrong."

He drew her closely into his arms, kissing her with an almost pathetic tenderness.

"Thelma, my love, my sweet one!" and his strong voice trembled. "You do not know—how should you? what I think of you! Satisfied? Pleased? Good Heavens— what little words those are to express my feelings! I can tell you how you look, for nothing can ever make *you* vain. You are beautiful! . . . you are the most beautiful woman I have ever seen, and you look your very best tonight. But you are more than beautiful—you are good and pure and true, while society is—— But why should I destroy your illusions? Only, my wife,—we have been all in all to each other,—and now I have a foolish feeling as if things were going to be different—as if we should not be so much together—and I wish—I wish to God I could keep you all to myself without anybody's interference!"

She looked at him in wonder, though she smiled.

"But you have changed, my boy, since the morning," she said. "Then you did wish me to be particular in dress,—and to wear your jewels, for this Lady Winsleigh. Now your eyes are sad, and you seem as if you would rather not go at all. Well, is it not easy to remain at home? I will take off these fine things, and we will sit together and read. Shall it be so?"

He laughed. "I believe you would do it if I asked you!" he said.

"But, of course! I am quite happy alone with you. I care nothing for this party,—what is it to me if you do not wish to go?"

He kissed her again. "Thelma, don't spoil me too much! If you let me have my own way to such an extent, who knows what an awful domestic tyrant I may become! No, dear—we must go to-night—there's no help for it. You see we've accepted the invitation, and it's no use being churlish. Besides, after all "—he gazed at her admiringly—" I want them to see my Norwegian rose! Come along! The carriage is waiting."

They passed out into the hall, where Britta was in attendance with a long cloak of pale-blue plush lined with white fur, in which she tenderly enveloped her beloved "Fröken," her rosy face beaming with affectionate adoration as she glanced from the fair diamond-crowned head down to the point of a small pearl-embroidered shoe that peeped beneath the edge of the rich, sheeny white robe, and saw that nothing was lacking to the most perfect toilette that ever woman wore.

"Good-night, Britta!" said Thelma kindly. "You must not sit up for me. You will be tired."

Britta smiled—it was evident she meant to outwatch the stars, if necessary, rather than allow her mistress to be unattended on her return. But she said nothing—she waited at the door while Philip assisted his wife into the carriage —and still stood musingly under the wide portico, after they had driven away.

"Hadn't you better come in, Miss Britta?" said the butler respectfully,—he had a great regard for her ladyship's little maid.

Britta, recalled to herself, started, turned, and re-entered the hall.

"There will be many fine folks there to-night, I suppose?" she asked.

18

The butler rubbed his nose perplexedly. " Fine folks?
At Winsleigh House? Well, as far as clothes go, I dare say
there will. But there'll be no one like her ladyship—no
one! " And he shook his grey head emphatically.

" Of course not! " said Britta, with a sort of triumphant
defiance. " We know that very well, Morris! There's no
one like her ladyship anywhere in the wide world! But I
tell you what—I think a great many people will be jealous
of her."

Morris smiled. " You may take your oath of that, Miss
Britta," he said with placid conviction. " Jealous! Jealous
isn't the word for it! Why," and he surveyed Britta's
youthful countenance with fatherly interest, " you're only a
child as it were, and you don't know the world much.
Now, I've been five and twenty years in this family, and I
knew Sir Philip's mother, the Lady Eulalie—he named his
yacht after her. Ah! she was a sweet creature—she came
from Austria, and she was as dark as her present ladyship
is fair. Wherever she went, I tell you, the women were
ready to cry for spite and envy of her good looks—and
they would say anything against her they could invent.
That's the way they go on sometimes in society, you
know."

" As bad as in Bosekop," murmured Britta, more to herself than to him, " only London is a larger place." Then
raising her voice again, she said, " Perhaps there will be
some people wicked enough to hate her ladyship, Morris? "

" I shouldn't wonder," said Morris philosophically. " I
shouldn't wonder at all! There's a deal of hate about one
way or another,—and if a lady is as beautiful as an angel,
and cuts out everybody wherever she goes, why you can't
expect the other ladies to be very fond of her. 'Tisn't in
human nature—at least not in feminine human nature.
Men don't care much about their looks, one way or the
other, unless they're young chaps—then one has a little patience with them and they come all right."

But Britta had become meditative again. She went slowly
up into her mistress's room and began arranging the few
trifles that had been left in disorder.

" Just fancy! "—she said to herself—" some one may hate
the Fröken even in London just as they hated her in Bosekop, because she is so unlike everybody else. I shall keep
my eyes open,—and I shall soon find out any wickedness
against her! My beautiful, dear darling! I believe the

world is a cruel place after all,—but *she* shan't be made unhappy in it, if I can help it!"

And with this emphatic declaration, she kissed a little
shoe of Thelma's that she was just putting by—and,
smoothing her curls, went down to her supper.

CHAPTER XX.

" Such people there are living and flourishing in the world,—Faithless, Hopeless, Charityless,—let us have at them, dear friends, with
might and main ! "—THACKERAY.

WHO can adequately describe the thrilling excitement attending an aristocratic " crush,"—an extensive, sweeping-
off-of-old-scores " at home,"—that scene of bewildering confusion which might be appropriately set forth to the minds
of the vulgar in the once-popular ditty, " Such a getting-
up-stairs I never did see ! " Who can paint in sufficiently
brilliant colors the mere *outside* of a house thus distinguished by this strange festivity, in which there is no actual pleasure,—this crowding of carriages—this shouting of
small boys and policemen?—who can, in words, delineate
the various phases of lofty indignation and offense on the
countenances of pompous coachmen, forced into contention
with vulgar but good-natured " cabbys "—for right of way ?
. . . who can sufficiently set forth the splendors of a
striped awning avenue, lined on both sides with a collection of tropical verdure, hired for the occasion at so much
per dozen pots, and illuminated with Chinese lanterns !
Talk of orange groves in Italy and the languid light of a
southern moon ! What are they compared to the marvels
of striped awning ? Mere trees—mere moonlight—(poor
products of Nature!) do not excite either wonder or envy
—but, strange to say, an awning avenue invariably does !
As soon as it is erected in all its bland suggestiveness,
no matter at what house, a small crowd of street-arabs
and nursemaids collect to stare at it,—and when tired of
staring, pass and repass under it with peculiar satisfaction ; the beggar, starving for a crust, lingers doubtfully
near it, and ventures to inquire of the influenza-smitten
crossing-sweeper whether it is a wedding or a party ? And
if Awning Avenue means matrimony, the beggar waits to
see the guests come out; if, on the contrary, it stands
for some evening festivity, he goes, resolving to return at

the appointed hour, and try if he cannot persuade one
" swell " at least to throw him a penny for his night's
supper. Yes—a great many people endure sharp twinges
of discontent at the sight of Awning Avenue,—people who
can't afford to give parties, and who wish they could,—
pretty, sweet girls who never go to a dance in their lives,
and long with all their innocent hearts for a glimpse,—
just *one* glimpse !—of what seems to them inexhaustible,
fairy-like delight,—lonely folks, who imagine in their simplicity that all who are privileged to pass between the
lines of hired tropical foliage aforementioned, must perforce
be the best and most united of friends—hungry men and
women who picture, with watering mouths, the supper-
table that lies *beyond* the awning, laden with good things,
of the very names of which they are hopelessly ignorant,
—while now and then a stern, dark-browed Thinker or two
may stalk by and metaphorically shake his fist at all the
waste, extravagance, useless luxury, humbug, and hypocrisy Awning Avenue usually symbolizes, and may mutter
in his beard, like an old-fashioned tragedian, " A time *will*
come ! " Yes, Sir Thinker !—it will most undoubtedly—
it *must*—but not through you—not through any mere human agency. Modern society contains within itself the
seed of its own destruction,—the most utter Nihilist that
ever swore deadly oath need but contain his soul in patience and allow the seed to ripen. For God's justice is
as a circle that slowly surrounds an evil and as slowly
closes on it with crushing and resistless force,—and feverish, fretting humanity, however nobly inspired, can do
nothing either to hasten or retard the round, perfect, absolute and Divine Law. So let the babes of the world
play on, and let us not frighten them with stories of earth-
quakes ; they are miserable enough as it is, believe it !
—their toys are so brittle, and snap in their feeble hands
so easily, that one is inclined to pity them ! And Awning Avenue, with its borrowed verdure and artificial light,
is frequently erected for the use of some of the most
wretched among the children of the earth,—children who
have trifled with and lost everything,—love, honor, hope,
and faith, and who are travelling rapidly to the grave
with no consolation save a few handfuls of base coin,
which they must, perforce, leave behind them at the last.

So it may be that the crippled crossing-sweeper outside
Winsleigh House is a very great deal happier than the

master of that stately mansion. He has a new broom,—and Master Ernest Winsleigh has given him two oranges, and a rather bulky stick of sugar candy. He is a *protègè* of Ernest's—that bright handsome boy considers it a "jolly shame"—to have only one leg,—and has said so with much emphasis,—and though the little sweeper himself has never regarded his affliction quite in that light, he is exceedingly grateful for the young gentleman's patronage and sympathy thus frankly expressed. And on this particular night of the grand reception he stands, leaning on his broom and munching his candy, a delighted spectator of the scene in Park Lane,—the splendid equipages, the prancing horses, the glittering liveries, the excited cabmen, the magnificent toilettes of the ladies, the solemn and resigned deportment of the gentlemen,—and he envies none of them— not he! Why should he? His oranges are in his pocket— untouched as yet—and it is doubtful whether the crowding guests at the Winsleigh supper-table shall find anything there to yield them such entire enjoyment as he will presently take in his humble yet refreshing desert. And he is pleased as a child at a pantomime—the Winsleigh "at home" is a show that amuses him,—and he makes sundry remarks on "'im" and "'er" in a meditative *sotto voce*. He peeps up Awning Avenue heedless of the severe eye of the policeman on guard,—he sweeps the edge of the crimson felt foot-cloth tenderly with his broom,—and if he has a desire ungratified, it is that he might take a peep just for a minute inside the front door, and see how "they're all a'goin' it!"

And how *are* they a'goin' it! Well, not very hilariously, if one may judge by the aspect of the gentlemen in the hall and on the stairs,—gentlemen of serious demeanor, who are leaning, as though exhausted, against the banisters, with a universal air of profound weariness and dissatisfaction. Some of these are young fledglings of manhood,—callow birds who, though by no means innocent,—are more or less inexperienced,—and who have fluttered hither to the snare of Lady Winsleigh's "at home," half expecting to be allowed to make love to their hostess, and so have something to boast of afterwards,—others are of the middle-aged complacent type, who, though infinitely bored, have condescended to "look in" for ten minutes or so, to see if there are any pretty women worth the honor of their criticism— others again (and these are the most unfortunate) are the

" nobodies "—or husbands, fathers, and brothers of " beauties," whom they have dutifully escorted to the scene of
triumph, in which they, unlucky wights! are certainly not
expected to share.   A little desultory conversation goes on
among these stair-loungers,—conversation mingled with
much dreary yawning,—a trained opera-singer is shaking
forth chromatic roulades and trills in the great drawing-room
above,—there is an incessant stream of people coming and
going,—there is the rustle of silk and satin,—perfume
shaken out of lace kerchiefs, and bouquets oppresses the
warm air,—the heat is excessive,—and there is a never-ending monotonous hum of voices, only broken at rare intervals by the " society laugh "—that unmeaning giggle on
the part of the women,—that strained " ha, ha, ha !." on the
part of the men, which is but the faint ghostly echo of the
farewell voice of true mirth.

Presently, out of the ladies' cloak-room come two fascinating figures—the one plump and matronly, with grey hair
and a capacious neck glittering with diamonds,—the other
a slim girl in pale pink, with dark eyes and a ravishing
complexion, for whom the lazy gentlemen on the stairs
make immediate and respectful room.

" How d'ye do, Mrs. Van Clupp?" says one of the
loungers.

" Glad to see you, Miss Marcia!" says another, a sandy-
haired young man, with a large gardenia in his button-
hole, and a glass in his eye.

At the sound of his voice Miss Marcia stops and regards
him with a surprised smile.   She is very pretty, is Marcia,
—bewitchingly pretty,—and she has an air of demure grace
and modesty about her that is perfectly charming.   Why!
oh, why does she not remain in that sylph-like attitude of
questioning silence?   But she speaks—and the charm is
broken.

" Waal now!   Dew tell!" she exclaims.   " I thought
yew were in Pa-ar—is!   Ma, would yew have concluded to
find Lord Algy here?   This is *too* lovely!   If I'd known
yew were coming I'd have stopped at home—yes, I would
—that's so!"

And she nods her little head, crowned with its glossy
braids of chestnut hair, in a very coquettish manner,
while her mother, persistently beaming a stereotyped company smile on all around her, begins to ascend the stairs,

beckoning her daughter to follow. Marcia does so, and Lord Algernon Masherville escorts her.

" You—you didn't mean that?" he stammers rather feebly—" You—you don't mind my being here, do you? I'm—I'm *awfully* glad to see you again, you know—and—er—all that sort of thing!"

Marcia darts a keen glance at him,—the glance of an observant, clear-headed magpie.

" Oh yes! I dare say!" she remarks with airy scorn. " S'pect *me* to believe *yew!* Waal! Did yew have a good time in Pa-ar—is?"

" Fairly so," answers Lord Masherville indifferently. " I only came back two days ago. Lady Winsleigh met me by chance at the theatre, and asked me to look in to-night for ' some fun ' she said. Have you any idea what she meant?"

" Of course!" says the fair New Yorker, 'with a little nasal laugh,—" don't *yew* know? We're all here to see the fisherwoman from the wilds of Norway,—the creature Sir Philip Errington married last year. I conclude she'll give us fits all round, don't yew?"

Lord Masherville, at this, appears to hesitate. His eyeglass troubles him, and he fidgets with its black string. He is not intellectual—he is the most vacillating, most meek and timid of mortals—but he is a gentleman in his own poor fashion, and has a sort of fluttering chivalry about him, which, though feeble, is better than none.

" I really cannot tell you, Miss Marcia," he replies almost nervously. " I hear—at the Club,—that—that Lady Bruce-Errington is a great beauty."

" Dew tell!" shrieks Marcia, with a burst of laughter. " Is she really though! But I guess her looks won't mend her grammar any way!"

He makes no reply, as by this time they have reached the crowded drawing-room, where Lady Winsleigh, radiant in ruby velvet and rose-brilliants, stands receiving her guests, with a cool smile and nod for mere acquaintances,— and a meaning flash of her dark eyes for her intimates, and a general air of haughty insolence and perfect self-satisfaction pervading her from head to foot. Close to her is her husband, grave, courtly, and kind to all comers, and fulfilling his duty as host to perfection,—still closer is Sir Francis Lennox, who in the pauses of the incoming tide of guests finds occasion to whisper trifling nothings in her tiny white ear, and even once ventures to arrange more tastefully a falling cluster of pale roses that rests lightly on the brief shoulder-strap (called by courtesy a sleeve) which keeps her ladyship's bodice in place.

Mrs. Rush-Marvelle is here too, in all her glory,—her good-humored countenance and small nose together beam with satisfaction,—her voluminous train of black satin showered with jet gets in everybody's way,—her ample bosom heaves like the billowy sea, somewhat above the boundary line of transparent lace that would fain restrain it—but in this particular she is prudence itself compared with her hostess, whose charms are exhibited with the un-blushing frankness of a ballet-girl,—and whose example is followed, it must be confessed, by most of the women in the room. Is Mr. Rush-Marvelle here? Oh yes—after some little trouble we discover him,—squeezed against the wall and barricaded by the grand piano,—in company · with a large album, over which he pores, feigning an almost morbid interest in the portraits of persons he has never seen, and never will see. Beside him is a melancholy short man with long hair and pimples, who surveys the increasing crowd in the room with an aspect that is almost tragic. Once or twice he eyes Mr. Marvelle dubiously as though he would speak—and, finally, he *does* speak, tapping that album-en-tranced gentleman on the arm with an energy that is some-what startling.

"It is to blay I am here!" he announces. "To blay ze biano! I am great artist!" He rolls his eyes wildly and with a sort of forced calmness proceeds to enumerate on his fingers—"Baris, Vienna, Rome, Berlin, St. Betersburg—all know me! All resbect me! See!" And he holds out his button-hole in which there is a miniature red ribbon. "From ze Emberor! Kaiser Wilhelm!" He exhibits a ring on his little finger. "From ze Tsar!" Another rapid movement and a pompous gold watch is thrust before the bewildered gaze of his listener. "From my bubils in Baris! I am bianist—I am here to blay!"

And raking his fingers through his long locks, he stares defiantly around him. Mr. Rush-Marvelle is a little fright-ened. This is an eccentric personage—he must be soothed. Evidently he must be soothed!

"Yes, yes, I quite understand!" he says, nodding per-suasively at the excited genius. "You are here to play. Exactly! Yes, yes! We shall all have the pleasure of hearing you presently. Delightful, I'm sure! You are the celebrated Herr—?"

"Machtenklinken," adds the pianist haughtily. "Ze celebrated Machtenklinken!"

"Yes—oh—er,—yes!" And Mr. Marvelle grapples desperately with this terrible name. "Oh—er—yes! I— er know you by reputation Herr—er—Machten——. Oh, er—yes! Pray excuse me for a moment!"

And thankfully catching the commanding eye of his wife, he scrambles hastily away from the piano and joins her. She is talking to the Van Clupps, and she wants him to take away Mr. Van Clupp, a white-headed, cunning-look-ing old man, for a little conversation, in order that she may be free to talk over certain naughty bits of scandal with Mrs. Van Clupp and Marcia.

To-night there is no place to sit down in all the grand extent of the Winsleigh drawing-rooms,—puffy old dowa-gers occupy the sofas, ottomans, and chairs, and the largest and most brilliant portion of the assemblage are standing, grinning into each other's faces with praiseworthy and polite pertinacity, and talking as rapidly as though their lives depended on how many words they could utter within the space of two minutes. Mrs. Rush-Marvelle, Mrs. Van Clupp and Marcia make their way slowly through the gab-bling, pushing, smirking crowd till they form a part of the little *coterie* immediately round Lady Winsleigh, to whom, at the first opportunity, Mrs. Marvelle whispers—

"Have they come?"

"The modern Paris and the new Helen?" laughs Lady Clara, with a shrug of her snowy shoulders. "No, not yet. Perhaps they won't turn up at all! Marcia dear, you look *quite* charming! Where is Lord Algy?"

"I guess he's not a thousand miles away!" returns Mar-cia, with a knowing twinkle of her dark eyes. "He'll hang round here presently! Why,—there's Mr. Lorimer worry-ing in at the doorway!"

"Worrying in" is scarcely the term to apply to the polite but determined manner in which George Lorimer coolly elbows a passage among the heaving bare shoulders, backs, fat arms, and long trains that seriously obstruct his passage, but after some trouble he succeeds in his efforts to reach his fair hostess, who receives him with rather a super-cilious uplifting of her delicate eyebrows.

"Dear me, Mr. Lorimer, you are quite a stranger!" she

observes somewhat satirically. "We thought you had
made up your mind to settle in Norway!"

"Did you really, though!" and Lorimer smiles languidly.
"I wonder at that,—for you knew I came back from that
region in the August of last year."

"And since then I suppose you have played the hermit?"
inquires her ladyship indifferently, unfurling her fan of os-
trich feathers and waving it slowly to and fro.

"By no means! I went off to Scotland with a friend,
Alec Macfarlane, and had some excellent shooting. Then,
as I never permit my venerable mamma to pass the winter
in London, I took her to Nice, from which delightful spot
we returned three weeks ago."

Lady Winsleigh laughs. "I did not ask you for a cate-
gorical explanation of your movements, Mr. Lorimer," she
says lightly—"I'm sure I hope you enjoyed yourself?"

He bows gravely. "Thanks! Yes,—strange to say, I
did manage to extract a little pleasure here and there out
of the universal dryness of things."

"Have you seen your friend, Sir Philip, since he came to
town?" asks Mrs. Rush-Marvelle in her stately way.

"Several times. I have dined with him and Lady Errington frequently. I understand they are to be here to-
night?"

Lady Winsleigh fans herself a little more rapidly, and
her full crimson lips tighten into a thin, malicious line.

"Well, I asked them, of course,—as a matter of form,"
she says carelessly,—"but I shall, on the whole, be rather
relieved if they don't come."

A curious, amused look comes over Lorimer's face.

"Indeed! May I ask why?"

"I should think the reason ought to be perfectly apparent to you"—and her ladyship's eyes flash angrily. "Sir
Philip is all very well—he is by birth a gentleman,—but
the person he has married is not a lady, and it is an exceedingly unpleasant duty for me to have to receive her."

A faint tinge of color flushes Lorimer's brow. "I
think," he says slowly, "I think you will find yourself mistaken, Lady Winsleigh. I believe——" Here he pauses,
and Mrs. Rush-Marvelle fixes him with a stony stare.

"Are we to understand that she is educated?" she inquires freezingly. "Positively well-educated?"

Lorimer laughs. "Not according to the standard of
modern fashionable requirements!" he replies.

Mrs. Marvelle sniffs the air portentously,—Lady Clara curls her lip. At that moment everybody makes respectful way for one of the most important guests of the evening— a broad-shouldered man of careless attire, rough hair, fine features, and keen, mischievous eyes—a man of whom many stand in wholesome awe,—Beaufort Lovelace, or as he is commonly called. "Beau" Lovelace, a brilliant novelist, critic, and pitiless satirist. For him society is a game,—a gay humming-top which he spins on the palm of his hand for his own private amusement. Once a scribbler in an attic, subsisting bravely on bread and cheese and hope, he now lords it more than half the year in a palace of fairy-like beauty on the Lago di Como,—and he is precisely the same person who was formerly disdained and flouted by fair ladies because his clothes were poor and shabby, yet for whom they now practise all the arts known to their sex, in fruitless endeavors to charm and conciliate him. For he laughs at them and their pretty ways,—and his laughter is merciless. His arrowy glance discovers the "poudre de riz" on their blooming cheeks,—the carmine on their lips, and the "kohl" on their eyelashes. He knows purchased hair from the natural growth—and he has a cruel eye for discerning the artificial contour of a "made-up" figure. And like a merry satyr dancing in a legendary forest, he capers and gambols in the vast fields of Humbug—all forms of it are attacked and ridiculed by his powerful and pungent pen,—he is a sort of English Heine, gathering in rich and daily harvests from the never-perishing incessantly-growing crop of fools. And as he,—in all the wickedness of daring and superior intellect,—approaches, Lady Wins-leigh draws herself up with the conscious air of a beauty who knows she is nearly perfect,—Mrs. Rush-Marvelle makes a faint endeavor to settle the lace more modestly over her rebellious bosom,—Marcia smiles coquettishly, and Mrs. Van Clupp brings her diamond pendant (value, a thousand guineas) more prominently forward,—for as she thinks, poor ignorant soul! "wealth always impresses these literary men more than anything!" In one swift glance Beau Lovelace observes all these different movements,—and the inner fountain of his mirth begins to bubble. "What fun those Van Clupps are!" he thinks. "The old woman's got a diamond plaster on her neck! Horrible taste! She's anxious to show how much she's worth, I suppose! Mrs. Marvelle wants a shawl, and Lady Clara a bodice. By

Jove! What sights the women do make of themselves!"

But his face betrays none of these reflections,—its expression is one of polite gravity, though a sudden sweetness smooths it as he shakes hands with Lord Winsleigh and Lorimer,—a sweetness that shows how remarkably handsome Beau can look if he chooses. He rests one hand on Lorimer's shoulder.

"Why, George, old boy, I thought you were playing the dutiful son at Nice? Don't tell me you've deserted the dear old lady! Where is she? You know I've got to finish that argument with her about her beloved Byron."

Lorimer laughs. "Go and finish it when you like, Beau," he answers. "My mother's all right. She's at home. You know she's always charmed to see you. She's delighted with that new book of yours."

"Is she? She finds pleasure in trifles then——"

"Oh no, Mr. Lovelace!" interrupts Lady Clara, with a winning glance. "You must not run yourself down! The book is exquisite! I got it at once from the library, and read every line of it!"

"I am exceedingly flattered!" says Lovelace, with a grave bow, though there is a little twinkling mockery in his glance. "When a lady so bewitching condescends to read what I have written, how can I express my emotion!"

"The press is unanimous in its praise of you," remarks Lord Winsleigh cordially. "You are quite the lion of the day!"

"Oh quite!" agrees Beau laughing. "And do I not roar 'as sweet as any nightingale'? But I say, where's the new beauty?"

"I really do not know to whom you allude, Mr. Lovelace," replies Lady Winsleigh coldly. Lorimer smiles and is silent. Beau looks from one to the other amusedly.

"Perhaps I've made a mistake," he says, "but the Duke of Roxwell is responsible. He told me that if I came here to-night I should see one of the loveliest women living,—Lady Bruce-Errington. He saw her in the park. I think *this* gentleman"—indicating Sir Francis Lennox, who bites his moustache vexedly—"said quite openly at the Club last night that she *was* the new beauty,—and that she would be here this evening."

Lady Winsleigh darts a side glance at her "Lennie" that is far from pleasant.

" Really it's perfectly absurd ! " she says, with a scornful
toss of her head. " We shall have housemaids and bar-
girls accepted as ' quite the rage ' next. I do not know
Sir Philip's wife in the least,—I hear she was a common
farmer's daughter. I certainly invited her to-night out of
charity and kindness in order that she might get a little
accustomed to society—for, of course, poor creature ! entirely ignorant and uneducated as she is, everything will
seem strange to her. But she has not come——"

" SIR PHILIP AND LADY BRUCE-ERRINGTON ! " announces
Briggs at this juncture.

There is a sudden hush—a movement of excitement,—
and the groups near the door fall apart staring, and struck
momentarily dumb with surprise, as a tall, radiant figure
in dazzling white, with diamonds flashing on a glittering
coil of gold hair, and wondrous sea-blue earnest eyes, passes
through their midst with that royal free step and composed
grace of bearing that might distinguish an Empress of
many nations.

" Good heavens ! What a magnificent woman ! " mutters
Beau Lovelace—" Venus realized ! "

Lady Winsleigh turns very pale,—she trembles and can
scarcely regain her usual composure as Sir Philip, with a
proud tenderness lighting up the depths of his hazel eyes,
leads this vision of youth and perfect loveliness up to her,
saying simply—

" Lady Winsleigh, allow me to introduce to you—my
wife ! Thelma, this is Lady Winsleigh."

There is a strange sensation in Lady Winsleigh's throat
as though a very tight string were suddenly drawn round
it to almost strangling point—and it is certain that she
feels as though she must scream, hit somebody with her
fan, and rush from the room in an undignified rage. But
she chokes back these purely feminine emotions—she smiles
and extends her jewelled hand.

" So good of you to come to-night ! " she says sweetly.
" I have been longing to see you, Lady Errington ! I dare
say you know your husband is quite an old acquaintance of
mine ! "

And a langourous glance, like fire seen through smoke,
leaps from beneath her silky eyelashes at Sir Philip—but
he sees it not—he is chatting and laughing gaily with Lorimer and Beau Lovelace.

" Indeed, yes ! " answers Thelma, in that soft low voice

of hers, which had such a thrilling richness within it—" and it is for that reason I am very glad to meet you. It is always pleasant for me to know my husband's friends."

Here she raises those marvellous, innocent eyes of hers and smiles;—why does Lady Winsleigh shrink from that frank and childlike openness of regard? Why does she, for one brief moment, hate herself?—why does she so suddenly feel herself to be vile and beneath contempt? God only knows!—but the first genuine blush that has tinged her ladyship's cheek for many a long day, suddenly spreads a hot and embarrassing tide of crimson over the polished pallor of her satiny skin, and she says hurriedly—

" I must find you some people to talk to. This is my dear friend, Mrs. Rush-Marvelle—I am sure you will like each other. Let me introduce Mrs. Van Clupp to you— Mrs. Van Clupp, and Miss Van Clupp! "

The ladies bow stiffly while Thelma responds to their prim salutation with easy grace.

" Sir Francis Lennox "—continues Lady Winsleigh, and there is something like a sneer in her smile, as that gentle. man makes a deep and courtly reverence, with an unmistakable look of admiration in his sleepy tiger-brown eyes, —then she turns to Lord Winsleigh and adds in a casual way, " My husband ! " Lord Winsleigh advances rather eagerly—there is a charm in the exquisite nobility of Thelma's face that touches his heart and appeals to the chivalrous and poetical part of his nature.

" Sir Philip and I have known each other for some years," he says, pressing her little fair hand cordially. " It is a great pleasure for me to see you to-night, Lady Errington,—I realize how very much my friend deserves to be congratulated on his marriage ! "

Thelma smiles. This little speech pleases her, but she does not accept the compliment implied to herself.

" You are very kind, Lord Winsleigh "—she answers; " I am glad indeed that you like Philip. I do think with you that he deserves every one's good wishes. It is my great desire to make him always happy."

A brief shadow crosses Lord Winsleigh's thoughtful brow, and he studies her sweet eyes attentively. Is she sincere? Does she mean what she says? Or is she, like others of her sex, merely playing a graceful part? A slight sigh escapes him,—absolute truth, innocent love, and stainless purity are written in such fair, clear lines on that perfect countenance that the mere idea of questioning her sincerity seems a sacrilege.

" Your desire is gratified, I am sure," he returns, and his voice is somewhat sad. " I never saw him looking so well He seems in excellent spirits."

" Oh, for that ! " and she laughs. " He is a very light-hearted boy ! But once he would tell me very dreadful things about the world—how it was not at all worth living in—but I do think he must have been lonely. For he is very pleased with everything now, and finds no fault at all ! "

" I can quite understand that ! " and Lord Winsleigh smiles, though that shadow of pain still rests on his brow.

Mrs. Rush-Marvelle and the Van Clupps are listening to the conversation with straining ears. What strange person is this ? She does not talk bad grammar, though her manner of expressing herself is somewhat quaint and foreign. But she is babyish—perfectly babyish ! The idea of any well-bred woman condescending to sing the praises of her own husband in public ! Absurd ! " Deserves every-one's good wishes ! "—pooh ! her " great desire is to make him always happy ! "—what utter rubbish !—and he is a " light-hearted boy ! " Good gracious !—what next ? Marcia Van Clupp is strongly inclined to giggle, and Mrs. Van Clupp is indignantly conscious that the Errington diamonds far surpass her own, both for size and lustre.

At that moment Sir Philip approaches his wife, with George Lorimer and Beau Lovelace. Thelma's smile at Lorimer is the greeting of an old friend—a sun-bright glance that makes his heart beat a little quicker than usual. He watches her as she turns to be introduced to Lovelace,—while Miss Van Clupp, thinking of the relent-less gift of satire with which that brilliant writer is endowed, looks out for " some fun "—for, as she confides in a low tone to Mrs. Marvelle—" she'll never know how to talk to that man ! "

" Thelma," says Sir Philip, " this is the celebrated author, Beaufort Lovelace,—you have often heard me speak of him."

She extends both her hands, and her eyes deepen and flash.

" Ah ! you are one of those great men whom we all love and admire ! " she says, with direct frankness,—and the cynical Beau, who has never yet received so sincere a com-

pliment, feels himself coloring like a school-girl. "I am so
very proud to meet you! I have read your wonderful
book, ' Azaziel,' and it made me glad and sorry together.
For why do you draw a noble example and yet say at the
same time that it is impossible to follow it? Because in
one breath you inspire us to be good, and yet you tell us
we shall never become so! That is not right,—is it?"

Beau meets her questioning glance with a grave smile.

"It is most likely entirely wrong from *your* point of
view, Lady Errington," he said. "Some day we will talk
over the matter. You shall show me the error of my ways.
Perhaps you will put life, and the troublesome business of
living, in quite a new light for me! You see, we novelists
have an unfortunate trick of looking at the worst or most
ludicrous side of everything—we can't help it! So many
apparently lofty and pathetic tragedies turn out, on close
examination, to be the meanest and most miserable of
farces,—it's no good making them out to be grand Greek
poems when they are only base doggerel rhymes. Besides, it's the fashion nowadays to be *chiffonniers* in literature—to pick up the rags of life and sort them in all their
uncomeliness before the morbid eyes of the public. What's
the use of spending thought and care on the manufacture
of a jewelled diadem, and offering it to the people on a velvet cushion, when they prefer an *olla-podrida* of cast-off
clothing, dried bones and candle-ends? In brief, what
would it avail to write as grandly as Shakespeare or Scott,
when society clamors for Zola and others of his school?"

There was a little group round them by this time,—men
generally collected wherever Beau Lovelace aired his opinions,—and a double attraction drew them together now in
the person of the lovely woman to whom he was holding
forth.

Marcia Van Clupp stared mightily—surely the Norwegian
peasant would not understand Beau's similes,—for they were
certainly incomprehensible to Marcia. As for his last remark—why! she had read all Zola's novels in the secrecy
of her own room, and had gloated over them;—no words
could describe her intense admiration of books that were so
indelicately realistic! "He is jealous of other writers, I
suppose," she thought; "these literary people hate each
other like poison."

Meanwhile Thelma's blue eyes looked puzzled. "I do
not know that name," she said. "Zola!—what is he? He

cannot be great. Shakespeare I know,—he is the glory of
the world, of course; I think him as noble as Homer.
Then for Walter Scott—I love all his beautiful stories—I
have read them many, many times, nearly as often as I
have read Homer and the Norse Sagas. And the world
must surely love such writings—or how should they last so
long?" She laughed and shook her bright head archly.
" *Chiffonnier! Point du tout! Monsieur, les divines pen-
seés que vous avez donné au monde ne sont pas des chif-
fons.*"

Beau smiled again, and offered her his arm. " Let me
find you a chair!" he said. " It will be rather a difficult
matter,—still I can but try. You will be fatigued if you
stand too long." And he moved through the swaying
crowd, with her little gloved hand resting lightly on his
coat-sleeve,—while Marcia Van Clupp and her mother exchanged looks of wonder and dismay. The " fisherwoman "
could speak French,—moreover, she could speak it with a
wonderfully soft and perfect accent,—the " person " had
studied Homer and Shakespeare, and was conversant with
the best literature,—and, bitterest sting of all, the " peasant "
could give every woman in the room a lesson in deportment,
grace, and perfect taste in dress. Every costume looked
tawdy beside her richly flowing velvet draperies—every low
bodice became indecent compared with the modesty of that
small square opening at Thelma's white throat—an opening just sufficient to display her collar of diamonds—and
every figure seemed either dumpy and awkward, too big or
too fat, or too lean and too lanky—when brought into contrast with her statuesque outlines.

The die was cast,—the authority of Beau Lovelace was
nearly suprem in fashionable and artistic circles, and from
the moment he was seen devoting his attention to the " new
beauty," excit d whispers began to flit from mouth to
mouth,—" She will be the rage this season! "—" We must
ask her to come to us! "—"*Do* ask Lady Winsleigh to introduce us! "—" She *must* come to *our* house! " and so on.
And Lady Winsleigh was neither blind nor deaf—she saw
and heard plainly enough that her reign was over, and in
her secret soul she was furious. The " common farmer's
daughter " was neither vulgar nor uneducated—and she
was surpassingly lovely—even Lady Winsleigh could not
deny so plain and absolute a fact. But her ladyship was a
woman of the world, and she perceived at once that Thelma

was not. Philip had married a creature with the bodily
loveliness of a goddess and the innocent soul of a child—
and it was just that child-like, pure soul looking serenely
out of Thelma's eyes that had brought the long-forgotten
blush of shame to Clara Winsleigh's cheek. But that feeling of self-contempt soon passed—she was no better and no
worse than other women of her set, she thought—after all,
what had she to be ashamed of? Nothing, except—except
—perhaps, her " little affair " with " Lennie." A new emotion now stirred her blood—one of malice and hatred,
mingled with a sense of outraged love and ungratified passion—for she still admired Philip to a foolish excess. Her
dark eyes flashed scornfully as she noted the attitude of Sir
Francis Lennox,—he was leaning against the marble man-
tel-piece, stroking his moustache with one hand, absorbed
in watching Thelma, who, seated in an easy chair which
Beau Lovelace had found for her, was talking and laughing
gaily with those immediately around her, a group which
increased in size every moment, and in which the men were
most predominant.

"Fool!" muttered Lady Winsleigh to herself, apostro-
phizing " Lennie " in this uncomplimentary manner.
" Fool! I wonder if he thinks I care! He may play hired
lacquey to all the women in London if he likes! He looks
a prig compared to Philip!"

And her gaze wandered,—Philip was standing by his
wife, engaged in an animated conversation with Lord
Winsleigh. They were all near the grand piano—and Lady
Clara, smoothing her vexed brow, swept her ruby velvets
gracefully up to that quarter of the room. Before she
could speak, the celebrated Herr Machtenklinken confronted her with some sternness.

" Your ladyshib vill do me ze kindness to remember," he
said, loftily, " zat I am here to blay! Zere has been no
obbortunity—ze biano could not make itself to be heard in
zis fery moch noise. It is bossible your ladyshib shall require not ze music zis efening? In zat case I shall take
my fery goot leave."

Lady Winsleigh raised her eyes with much supercilious-
ness.

" As you please," she said coolly. " If *you* are so indifferent to your advantages—then all I can say is, so am I!
You are, perhaps, known on the Continent, Herr Machten-

klinken,—but not here—and I think you ought to be more grateful for my influence."

So saying, she passed on, leaving the luckless pianist in a state of the greatest indignation.

" *Gott in Himmel!* " he gasped, in a sort of infuriated *sotto voce.* " Ze Emberor himself would not have speak to me so! I come here as a favor—her ladyshib do not offer me one *pfenning,*—ach! ze music is not for such beoble! I shall brefer to blay to bigs! Zere is no art in zis coun-try!——"

And he began to make his way out of the room, when he was overtaken by Beau Lovelace, who had followed him in haste.

"Where are you off to, Hermann?" he asked good-naturedly. " We want you to play. There is a lady here who heard you in Paris quite recently—she admires you immensely. Won't you come and be introduced to her?"

Herr Machtenklinken paused, and a smile softened his hitherto angry countenance.

" You are fery goot, Mr. Lofelace," he remarked—" and I would do moch for *you*—but her ladyshib understands me not—she has offend me—it is better I should take my leave."

" Oh, bother her ladyship! " said Beau lightly. " Come along, and give us something in your best style."

So saying, he led the half-reluctant artist back to the piano, where he was introduced to Thelma, who gave him so sweet a smile that he was fairly dazzled.

" It is you who play Schumann so beautifully," she said. " My husband and I heard you at one of Lamoureux's con-certs in Paris. I fear," and she looked wistfully at him, " that you would think it very rude and selfish of me if I asked you to play just one little piece? Because, of course, you are here to enjoy yourself, and talk to your friends, and it seems unkind to take you away from them! "

A strange moisture dimmed the poor German's eyes. This was the first time in England that the " celebrate " had been treated as a friend and a gentleman. Up to this moment, at all the " at homes " and " assemblies," he had not been considered as a guest at all,—he was an " artist," " a good pianist,"—" a man who had played before the Em-peror of Germany "—and he was expected to perform for nothing, and be grateful for the " influence " exercised on his behalf—influence which as yet had not put one single extra guinea in his pocket. Now, here was a great lady almost apologizing for asking him to play, lest it should take him away from his "friends"! His heart swelled with emotion and gratitude—the poor fellow had no " friends " in London, except Beau Lovelace, who was kind to him, but who had no power in the musical world,—and as Thelma's gentle voice addressed him, he could have knelt and kissed her little shoe for her sweet courtesy and kindness.

" Miladi," he said, with a profound reverence, " I will blay for you with bleasure,—it will be a joy for ze music to make itself beautiful for you! "

And with this fantastic attempt at a compliment, he seated himself at the instrument and struck a crashing chord to command silence.

The hum of conversation grew louder than ever—and to Thelma's surprise Lady Winsleigh seated herself by her and began to converse. Herr Machtenklinken struck another chord,—in vain! The deafening clamor of tongues continued, and Lady Winsleigh asked Thelma with much seeming interest if the scenery was very romantic in Norway?

The girl colored deeply, and after a little hesitation, said

" Excuse me,—I would rather not speak till the music is over. It is impossible for a great musician to think his thoughts out properly unless there is silence. Would it not be better to ask every one to leave off talking while this gentleman plays? "

Clara Winsleigh looked amused. " My dear, you don't know them," she said carelessly. " They would think me mad to propose such a thing! There are always a few who listen."

Once more the pianist poised his hands over the keys of the instrument,—Thelma looked a little troubled and grieved. Beau Lovelace saw it, and acting on a sudden impulse, turned towards the chattering crowds, and, holding up his hand, called, " Silence, please! "

There was an astonished hush. Beau laughed. " We want to hear some music," he said, with the utmost coolness. " Conversation can be continued afterwards." He then nodded cheerfully towards Herr Machtenklinken, who, inspired by this open encouragement, started off like a racehorse into one of the exquisite rambling preludes of Chopin. Gradually, as he played, his plain face took upon itself a noble, thoughtful, rapt expression,—his wild eyes softened,—his furrowed, frowning brow smoothed,—and, meeting the grave, rare blue eyes of Thelma, he smiled. His touch grew more and more delicate and tender—from the prelude he wandered into a nocturne of plaintive and exceeding melancholy, which h played with thrilling and exquisite pathos—anon, he glided into one of those dreamily joyous yet sorrowful mazurkas, that remind one of bright flowers growing in wild luxuriance over lonely and forsaken graves. The " celebratę " had reason to boast of himself—he was a perfect master of the instrument,—and as his fingers closed on the final chord, a hearty burst of applause rewarded his efforts, led by Lovelace and Lorimer. He responded by the usual bow,—but his real gratitude was all for Thelma. For her he had played his best—and he had seen tears in her lovely eyes. He felt as proud of her appreciation as of the ring he had received from the Tsar,—and bent low over the fair hand she extended to him.

" You must be very happy," she said, " to feel all those lovely sounds in your heart! I hope I shall see and hear you again some day,—I thank you so very much for the pleasure you have given me! "

Lady Winsleigh said nothing—and she listened to Thelma's words with a sort of contempt.

" Is the girl half-witted ? " she thought. " She must be, or she would not be so absurdly enthusiastic ! The man plays well,—but it is his profession to play well—it's no good praising these sort of people,—they are never grateful, and they always impose upon you." Aloud she asked Sir Philip—

" Does Lady Errington play ? "

" A little," he answered. " She sings."

At once there was a chorus of inanely polite voices round the piano, " Oh, *do* sing, Lady Errington ! Please, give us one song ! " and Sir Francis Lennox, sauntering up, fixed his languorous gaze on Thelma's face, murmuring, " You will not be so cruel as to refuse us such delight ? "

" But, of course not ! " answered the girl, greatly surprised at all these unnecessary entreaties. " I am always pleased to sing." And she drew off her long loose gloves and seated herself at the piano without the least affectation of reluctance. Then, glancing at her husband with a bright smile, she asked, "What song do you think will be best, Philip?"

"One of those old Norse mountain-songs," he answered.

She played a soft minor prelude—there was not a sound in the room now—everybody pressed towards the piano, staring with a curious fascination at her beautiful face and diamond-crowned hair. One moment—and her voice, in all its passionate, glorious fullness, rang out with a fresh vibrating tone that thrilled to the very heart—and the foolish crowd that gaped and listened was speechless, motionless, astonished, and bewildered.

A Norse mountain-song was it? How strange, and grand, and wild! George Lorimer stood apart—his eyes ached with restrained tears. He knew the melody well—and up before him rose the dear solemnity of the Altenguard hills, the glittering expanse of the Fjord, the dear old farmhouse behind its cluster of pines. Again he saw Thelma as he had seen her first—clad in her plain white gown, spinning in the dark embrasure of the rose-wreathed window—again the words of the self-destroyed Sigurd came back to his recollection, "Good things may come for others —but for you the heavens are empty!" He looked at her now,—Philip's wife—in all the splendor of her rich attire;— she was lovelier than ever, and her sweet nature was as yet unspoilt by all the wealth and luxury around her.

"Good God! what an *infeqno* she has come into!" he thought vaguely. "How will she stand these people when she gets to know them? The Van Clupps, the Rush-Marvelles, and others like them,—and as for Clara Winsleigh——" He turned to study her ladyship attentively. She was sitting quite close to the piano—her eyes were cast down, but the rubies on her bosom heaved quickly and restlessly, and she furled and unfurled her fan impatiently. "I shouldn't wonder," he went on meditating gravely, "if she doesn't try and make some mischief somehow. She looks it."

At that moment Thelma ceased singing, and the room rang with applause. Herr Machtenklinken was overcome with admiration.

"It is a voice of heaven!" he said in a rapture.

The fair singer was surrounded with people.

"I hope," said Mrs. Van Clupp, with her usual ill-bred eagerness to ingratiate herself with the titled and wealthy,

"I hope you will come and see me, Lady Errington? I am at home every Friday evening to my friends."

"Oh yes," said Thelma, simply. "But I am not your friend yet! When we do know each other better I will come. We shall meet each other many times first,—and then you will see if you like me to be your friend. Is it not so?"

A scarcely concealed smile reflected itself on the faces of all who heard this naïve, but indefinite acceptance of Mrs. Van Clupp's invitation, while Mrs. Van Clupp herself was somewhat mortified, and knew not what to answer. This Norwegian girl was evidently quite ignorant of the usages of polite society, or she would at once have recognized the fact that an " at home " had nothing whatsoever to do with the obligations of friendship—besides, as far as friendship was concerned, had not Mrs. Van Clupp tabooed several of her own blood-relations and former intimate acquaintances? . . . for the very sensible reason that while she had grown richer, they had grown poorer. But now Mrs. Rush-Marvelle sailed up in all her glory, with her good-natured smile and matronly air. She was a privileged person, and she put her arm round Thelma's waist.

"You must come to me, my dear," she said with real kindness—her motherly heart had warmed to the girl's beauty and innocence,—" I knew Philip when he was quite a boy. He will tell you what a dreadfully old woman I am! You must try to like me for his sake."

Thelma smiled radiantly. "I always wish to like Philip's friends," she said frankly. "I do hope I shall please you!"

A pang of remorse smote Mrs. Rush-Marvelle's heart as she remembered how loth she had been to meet Philip's " peasant " wife,—she hesitated,—then, yielding to her warm impulse, drew the girl closer and kissed her fair rose-tinted cheek.

"You please everybody, my child," she said honestly. ' Philip is a lucky man! Now I'll say good night, for it is getting late,—I'll write to you to-morrow and fix a day for you to come and lunch with me."

"But you must also come and see Philip," returned Thelma, pressing her hand.

"So I will—so I will!" and Mrs. Rush-Marvelle nodded beamingly, and made her way up to Lady Winsleigh, saying, "Bye-bye, Clara! Thanks for a most charming evening!"

Clara pouted. "Going already, Mimsey?" she queried, —then, in a lower tone, she said, "Well! what do you think of her?"

"A beautiful child—no more!" answered Mrs. Marvelle, —then, studying with some gravity the brilliant brunette face before her, she added in a whisper, "Leave her alone, Clara,—don't make her miserable! You know what I mean! It wouldn't take much to break her heart."

Clara laughed harshly and played with her fan.

"Dear me, Mimsey! . . . you are perfectly outrageous! Do you think I'm an ogress ready to eat her up? On the contrary, I mean to be a friend to her."

Mrs. Marvelle still looked grave.

"I'm glad to hear it," she said; "only some friends are worse than declared enemies."

Lady Winsleigh shrugged her shoulders.

"Go along, Mimsey,—go home to bed!" she exclaimed impatiently. "You are *intense!* I hate sentimental philosophy and copy-book platitudes!" She laughed again and folded her hands with an air of mock penitence, "There! I didn't mean to be rude! Good-night, dear old darling!"

"Good-night, Clara!" and Mrs. Marvelle, summoning her timid husband from some far corner, where he had remained in hiding, took her departure with much stateliness.

A great many people were going down to supper by this time, but Sir Philip was tired of the heat and glare and noise, and whispered as much to Thelma, who at once advanced to bid her hostess farewell.

"Won't you have some supper?" inquired her ladyship. "Don't go yet!"

But Thelma was determined not to detain her husband a moment longer than he wished—so Lady Winsleigh, seeing remonstrances were of no avail, bade them both an effusive good-night.

"We must see a great deal of each other!" she said, pressing Thelma's hands warmly in her own: "I hope we shall be quite dear friends!"

"Thank you!" said Thelma, "I do hope so too, if you wish it so much. Good-night, Lord Winsleigh!"

"Let me escort you to your carriage," said her noble host, at once offering her his arm.

"And allow me to follow," added Beau Lovelace, slipping his arm through Errington's, to whom he whispered, "How dare you, sir! How dare you be such a provokingly happy man in this miserable old world?" Errington laughed—and the little group had just reached the door of the drawing-room when Thelma suddenly turned with a look of inquiry in her eyes.

"Where is Mr. Lorimer?" she said. "I have forgotten to say good-night to him, Philip."

"Here I am, Lady Errington," and Lorimer sauntered forward with rather a forced smile,—a smile which altogether vanished, leaving his face strangely pale, as she stretched out her hand to him, and said laughingly—

"You bad Mr. Lorimer! Where were you? You know it would make me quite unhappy not to wish you good-night. Ah, you are a very naughty brother!"

"Come home with us, George," said Sir Philip eagerly. "Do, there's a good fellow!"

"I can't, Phil!" answered Lorimer, almost pathetically. "I can't to-night—indeed, I can't! Don't ask me!" And he wrung his friend's hand hard,—and then bravely met Thelma's bright glance.

"Forgive me!" he said to her. "I know I ought to have presented myself before—I'm a dreadfully lazy fellow, you know! Good-night!"

Thelma regarded him steadfastly.

"You look,—what is it you call yourself sometimes—*seedy?*" she observed. "Not well at all. Mind you come to us to morrow!"

He promised—and then accompanied them down to their carriage—he and Beau Lovelace assisting to cover Thelma with her fur cloak, and being the last to shake hands with Sir Philip as he sprang in beside his wife, and called to the coachman "Home!" The magic word seemed to effect the horses, for they started at a brisk trot, and within a couple of minutes the carriage was out of sight. It was a warm star-lit evening,—and as Lorimer and Lovelace re-entered Winsleigh House, Beau stole a side-glance at his silent companion.

"A plucky fellow!" he mused; "I should say he'd die game. Tortures won't wring his secret out of him." Aloud he said, "I say, haven't we had enough of this? Don't let us sup here—nothing but unsubstantial pastry and claret-cup—the latter abominable mixture would kill me. Come on to the Club, will you?"

Lorimer gladly assented—they got their over-coats from the officious Briggs, tipped him handsomely, and departed arm in arm. The last glimpse they caught of the Winsleigh festivities was Marcia Van Clupp sitting on the stairs, polishing off with much gusto the wing and half-breast of a capon,—while the mild Lord Masherville stood on the step just above her, consoling his appetite with a spoonful of tepid yellow jelly. He had not been able to secure any capon for himself—he had been frightened away by the warning cry of "Ladies first!" shouted forth by a fat gentleman, who was on guard at the head of the supper-table, and who had already secreted five plates of different edibles for his own consumption, in a neat corner behind the window-curtains. Meanwhile, Sir Philip Bruce-Errington, proud, happy, and triumphant, drew his wife into a close embrace as they drove home together, and said, "You were the queen of the evening, my Thelma! Have you enjoyed yourself?"

"Oh, I do not call that enjoyment!" she declared. "How is it possible to enjoy anything among so many strangers?"

"Well, what is it?" he asked laughingly.

She laughed also. "I do not know indeed what it is!" she said. "I have never been to anything like it before. It did seem to me as if all the people were on show for some reason or other. And the gentlemen did look very tired—there was nothing for them to do. Even you, my boy! You made several very big yawns! Did you know that?"

Philip laughed more than ever. "I didn't know it, my pet!" he answered; "but I'm not surprised. Big yawns are the invariable result of an 'at home.' Do you like Beau Lovelace?"

"Very much," she answered readily. "But, Philip, I should not like to have so many friends as Lady Winsleigh. I thought friends were rare?"

"So they are! She doesn't care for these people a bit. They are mere acquaintances."

"Whom does she care for then?" asked Thelma suddenly. "Of course I mean after her husband. Naturally she loves him best."

"Naturally," and Philip paused, adding, "she has her son—Ernest—he's a fine bright boy—he was not there tonight. You must see him some day. Then I think her favorite friend is Mrs. Rush-Marvelle."

" I do like that lady too," said Thelma. " She spoke very kindly to me and kissed me."

" Did she really ! " and Philip smiled. " I think she was more to be congratulated on taking the kiss than you in receiving it ! But she's not a bad old soul,—only a little too fond of money. But, Thelma, whom do *you* care for most ? You did tell me once, but I forget ! "

She turned her lovely face and star-like eyes upon him, and, meeting his laughing look, she smiled.

" How often must I tell you ! " she murmured softly. " I do think you will never tire of hearing ! You know that it is you for whom I care most, and that all the world would be empty to me without you ! Oh, my husband—my darling ! do not make me try to tell you how much I love you ! I cannot—my heart is too full ! "

The rest of their drive homeward was very quiet—there are times when silence is more eloquent than speech.

CHAPTER XXI.

" A small cloud, so slight as to be a mere speck on the fair blue sky, was all the warning we received."—PLINY.

AFTER that evening great changes came into Thelma's before peaceful life. She had conquered her enemies, or so it seemed,—society threw down all its barricades and rushed to meet her with open arms. Invitations crowded upon her, —often she grew tired and bewildered in the multiplicity of them all. London life wearied her,—she preferred the embowered seclusion of Errington Manor, the dear old house in green-wooded Warwickshire. But the " season " claimed her,—its frothy gaieties were deemed incomplete without her—no " at home " was considered quite " the " thing unless she was present. She became the centre of a large and ever-widening social circle,—painters, poets, novelists, wits, *savants*, and celebrities of high distinction crowded her rooms, striving to entertain her as well as themselves with that inane small talk and gossip too often practiced by the wisest among us,—and thus surrounded, she began to learn many puzzling and painful things of which in her old Norwegian life, she had been happily ignorant.

For instance, she had once imagined that all the men and women of culture who followed the higher professions must perforce be a sort of " Joyous Fraternity," superior to other mortals not so gifted,—and, under this erroneous impression, she was at first eager to know some of the so-called " great " people who had distinguished themselves in literature or the fine arts. She had fancied that they must of necessity be all refined, sympathetic, large-hearted, and noble-minded—alas! how grievously was she disappointed! She found, to her sorrow, that the tree of modern Art bore but few wholesome roses and many cankered buds—that the " Joyous Fraternity " were not joyous at all—but, on the contrary, inclined to dyspepsia and discontentment. She found that even poets, whom she had fondly deemed were the angel-guides among the children of this earth,—were most of them painfully conceited, selfish in aim and limited in thought,—moreover, that they were often so empty of all true inspiration, that they were actually able to hate and envy one another with a sort of womanish spite and temper, —that novelists, professing to be in sympathy with the heart of humanity, were no sooner brought into contact one with another, than they plainly showed by look, voice, and manner, the contempt they entertained for each other's work,—that men of science were never so happy as when trying to upset each other's theories ;—that men of religious combativeness were always on the alert to destroy each other's creeds,—and that, in short, there was a very general tendency to mean jealousies, miserable heart-burnings and utter weariness all round.

On one occasion, she, in the sweetest simplicity, invited two lady authoresses of note to meet at one of her " at homes," . . . she welcomed both the masculine-looking ladies with a radiant smile, and introduced them, saying gently,—" You will be so pleased to know each other! " But the stony stare, stiff nod, portentous sniff, and scornful smile with which these two eminent females exchanged cold greetings, were enough to daunt the most sympathetic hostess that ever lived—and when they at once retired to different corners of the room and sat apart with their backs turned to one another for the remainder of the evening, their attitude was so uncompromising that it was no wonder the gentle Thelma felt quite dismayed and wretched at the utter failure of the *rencontre.*

" They would *not* be sociable ! " she afterwards complained to Lady Winsleigh. " They *tried* to be as rude to each other as they could ! "

Lady Winsleigh laughed. " Of course ! " she said.

" What else *did* you expect! But if you want some fun, ask a young, pretty, and brilliant authoress (there are a few such) to meet an old, ugly and dowdy one (and there are many such), and watch the dowdy one's face! It will be a delicious study of expression, I assure you!"

But Thelma would not try this delicate experiment,—in fact, she began rather to avoid literary people, with the exception of Beau Lovelace. His was a genial, sympathetic nature, and, moreover, he had a winning charm of manner which few could resist. He was not a bookworm,—he was not, strictly speaking, a literary man,—and he was entirely indifferent to public praise or blame. He was, as he himself expressed it, " a servant and worshipper of literature," and there is a wide gulf of difference between one who serves literature for its own sake and one who uses it basely as a tool to serve himself.

But in all her new and varied experiences, perhaps Thelma was most completely bewildered by the women she met. Her simple Norse beliefs in the purity and gentleness of womanhood were startled and outraged,—she could not understand London ladies at all. Some of them seemed to have no idea beyond dress and show,—others looked upon their husbands, the lawful protectors of their name and fame, with easy indifference, as though they were mere bits of household furniture,—others, having nothing better to do, " went in " for spiritualism,—the low spiritualism that manifests itself in the turning of tables and moving of sideboards—not the higher spiritualism of an improved, perfected, and saint-like way of life—and these argued wildly on the theory of matter passing through matter, to the extent of declaring themselves able to send a letter or box through the wall without making a hole in it,—and this with such obstinate gravity as made Thelma fear for their reason. Then there were the women-atheists,—creatures who had voluntarily crushed all the sweetness of the sex within them—foolish human flowers without fragrance, that persistently turned away their faces from the sunlight and denied its existence, preferring to wither, profitless, on the dry stalk of their own theory;—there were the " platform-women," unnatural products of an unnatural age,—there were the great ladies of the aristocracy who turned with scorn from a case of real necessity, and yet spent hundreds of pounds on private theatricals wherein they might have the chance of displaying themselves in extravagant costumes,—and there were the " professional " beauties, who, if s ddenly deprived of elegant attire and face-cosmetics, turned out to be no beauties at all, but very ordinary, unin· telligent persons.

"What is the exact meaning of the term, ' professional beauty '?" Thelma had asked Beau Lovelace on one occa. sion. "I suppose it is some very poor beautiful woman who takes money for showing herself to the public, and having her portraits sold in the shops ? And who is it that pays her ? "

Lovelace broke into a laugh. " Upon my word, Lady Errington,—you have put the matter in a most original but indubitably correct light! Who pays the ' professional beauty,' you ask ? Well, in the case of Mrs. Smith-Gres- ham, whom you met the other day, it is a certain Duke who pays her to the tune of several thousands a year. When he gets tired of her, or she of him, she'll find somebody else—or perhaps she'll go on the stage and swell the list of bad amateurs. She'll get on somehow, as long as she can find a fool ready to settle her dressmaker's bill."

" I do not understand ! " said Thelma,—and her fair brows drew together in that pained grave look that was becoming rather frequent with her now.

And she began to ask fewer questions concerning the various strange phases of social life that puzzled her,—why, for instance, religious theorists made so little practical use of their theories,—why there were cloudy-eyed eccentrics who admired the faulty drawing of Watts, and the common- place sentence-writing of Walt Whitman,—why members of Parliament talked so much and did so little,—why new poets, however nobly inspired, were never accepted unless they had influential friends on the press,—why painters al- ways married their models or their cooks, and got heartily ashamed of them afterwards,—and why people all round said so many things they did not mean. And confused by the general insincerity, she clung,—poor child !—to Lady Winsleigh, who had the tact to seem what she was not,— and the cleverness to probe into Thelma's nature and find out how translucently clear and pure it was—a perfect well of sweet water, into which one drop of poison, or better still, several drops, gradually and insidiously instilled, might in time taint its flavor and darken its brightness. For if a woman have an innocent, unsuspecting soul as del- icate as the curled cup of a Nile lily, the more easily will it droop and wither in the heated grasp of a careless, cruel hand. And to this flower-crushing task Lady Winsleigh set herself,—partly for malice pretense against Errington, whose coldness to herself in past days had wounded her vanity, and partly for private jealousy of Thelma's beauty and attractiveness.

Within a short time she had completely won the girl's confidence and affection,—Sir Philip, forgetting his former suspicions of her, was touched and disarmed by the attachment and admiration she openly displayed towards his young wife,—she and Thelma were constantly seen together, and Mrs. Rush-Marvelle, far-sighted as she generally was, often sighed doubtfully and rubbed her nose in perplexity as she confessed she " couldn't quite understand Clara." But Mrs. Rush-Marvelle had her hands full of other matters,—she was aiding and abetting Marcia Van Clupp to set traps for that mild mouse Lord Masherville,—and she was too much absorbed in this difficult and delicate business to attend to anything else just then. Otherwise, it is possible she might have scented danger for Thelma's peace of mind, and being good-natured, might have warded it off before it approached too closely,—but, like policeman who are never within call when wanted, so friends are seldom at hand when their influence might be of real benefit.

The Van Clupps were people Thelma could not get on with at all—she tried to do so because Mrs. Rush-Marvelle had assured her they were " charming "—and she liked Mrs. Marvelle sufficiently well to be willing to please her. But, in truth, these rich and vulgar Yankees seemed to her mind less to be esteemed than the peasants of the Altenfjord, who in many instances possessed finer tact and breeding than old Van Clupp, the man of many dollars, whose father had been nothing but a low navvy, but of whom he spoke now with smirking pride as a real descendant of the Pilgrim Fathers. An odd thing it is, by the way, how fond some Americans are of tracing back their ancestry to these virtuous old gentlemen! The Van Clupps were of course not the best types of their country—they were of that class who, because they have money, measure everything by the money-standard, and hold even a noble poverty in utter contempt. Poor Van Clupp! It was sometimes pitiable to see him trying to be a gentleman—" going in " for " style " —to an excess that was ludicrous,—cramming his house with expensive furniture like an upholsterer's show-room,—

drinking his tea out of pure Sévres, with a lofty ignorance of its beauty and value,—dressing his wife and daughter like shilling fashion-plates, and having his portrait taken in precisely the same attitude as that assumed by the Duke of Wrigglesbury when his Grace sat to the same photographer! It was delicious to hear him bragging of his pilgrim ancestor,—while in the same breath he would blandly sneer at certain " poor gentry " who could trace back their lineage to Cœur de Lion! But because the Erringtons were rich as well as titled persons, Van Clupp and his belongings bent the servile knee before them, flattering Thelma with that ill-judged eagerness and zealous persistency which distinguish inborn vulgarity, and which, far from pleasing her, annoyed and embarrassed her because she could not respond sincerely to such attentions.

There were many others too, not dollar-crusted Americans, whose excessive adulation and ceaseless compliment vexed the sincere, frank spirit of the girl,—a spirit fresh and pure as the wind blowing over her own Norse mountains. One of these was Sir Francis Lennox, that fashionable young man of leisure,—and she had for him an instinctive, though quite unreasonable aversion. He was courtesy itself—he spared no pains to please her. Yet she felt as if his basilisk brown eyes were always upon her,—he seemed to be ever at hand, ready to watch over her in trifles, such as the passing of a cup of tea, the offering of her wrap,—the finding of a chair,—the holding of a fan,—he was always on the alert, like a remarkably well-trained upper servant. She could not, without rudeness, reject such unobtrusive, humble services,—and yet—they rendered her uncomfortable, though she did not quite know why. She ventured to mention her feeling concerning him to her friend Lady Winsleigh, who heard her timid remarks with a look on her face that was not quite pleasant.

" Poor Sir Francis! " her ladyship said with a slight, mocking laugh. " He's never happy unless he plays puppy-dog! Don't mind him, Thelma! He won't bite, I assure you,—he means no harm. It's only his little way of making himself agreeable! "

George Lorimer, during this particular " London season," fled the field of action, and went to Paris to stay with Pierre Duprèz. He felt that it was dangerous to confront the fair enemy too often, for he knew in his own honest heart that his passion for Thelma increased each time he saw her—so, he avoided her. She missed him very much from her circle of intimates, and often went to see his mother, Mrs. Lorimer, one of the sweetest old ladies in the world,—who had at once guessed her son's secret, but, like a prudent dame, kept it to herself. There were few young women as pretty and charming as old Mrs. Lorimer, with her snow-white parted hair and mild blue eyes, and voice as cheery as the note of a thrush in spring-time. After Lady Winsleigh, Thelma liked her best of all her new friends, and was fond of visiting her quiet little house in Kensington,—for it was very quiet, and seemed like a sheltered haven of rest from the great rush of frivolity and folly in which the fashionable world delighted.

And Thelma was often now in need of rest. As the season drew towards its close, she found herself strangely tired and dispirited. The life she was compelled to lead was all unsuited to her nature—it was artificial and constrained,—and she was often unhappy. Why? Why, indeed! She did her best,—but she made enemies everywhere. Again, why? Because she had a most pernicious,—most unpleasant habit of telling the truth. Like Socrates, she seemed to say—" If any man should appear to me not to possess virtue, but to pretend that he does, I shall reproach him." This she expressed silently in face, voice, and manner,—and, like Socrates, she might have added that she went about "perceiving, indeed, and grieving and alarmed that she was making herself odious." For she discovered, by degrees, that many people looked strangely upon her—that others seemed afraid of her—and she continually heard that she was considered " eccentric." So she became more reserved—even cold,—she was content to let others argue about trifles, and air their whims and follies without offering an opinion on any side.

And by-and-by the first shadow began to sweep over the fairness of her married life. It happened at a time when she and her husband were not quite so much together,—society and its various claims had naturally separated them a little, but now a question of political ambition separated them still more. Some well-intentioned friends had persuaded Sir Philip to stand for Parliament—and this idea no sooner entered his head, than he decided with impulsive ardor that he had been too long without a " career,"—and a " career " he must have in order to win distinction for his wife's sake. Therefore, summoning his secretary, Neville, to his aid, he plunged headlong into the seething, turgid waters of English politics, and shut himself up in his library day after day, studying blue-books, writing and answering letters, and drawing up addresses,—and with the general proneness of the masculine mind to attend to one thing only at a time, he grew so absorbed in his work that his love for Thelma, though all unchanged and deep as ever, fell slightly into the background of his thoughts. Not that he neglected her,—he simply concerned himself more with other things. So it happened that a certain indefinable sense of loss weighed upon her,—a vague, uncomprehended solitude began to encompass her,—a solitude even more keenly felt when she was surrounded by friends than when she was quite alone,—and as the sweet English June drew to its end, she grew languid and listless, and her blue eyes often filled with sudden tears. Her little watch-dog, Britta, began to notice this, and to wonder concerning the reason of her mistress's altered looks.

"It is this dreadful London," thought Britta. "So hot and stifling—there's no fresh air for her. And all this going about to balls and parties and shows—no wonder she is tired out!"

But it was something more than mere fatigue that made Thelma's eyes look sometimes so anxious, so gravely meditative and earnest. One day she seemed so much abstracted and lost in painful musings that Britta's loving heart ached, and she watched her for some moments without venturing to say a word. At last she spoke out bravely—

"Fröken!"—she paused,—Thelma seemed not to hear her. "Fröken!—has anything vexed or grieved you to-day?"

Thelma started nervously. "Vexed me—grieved me?" she repeated. "No, Britta—why do you ask?"

"You look very tired, dear Fröken," continued Britta gently. "You are not as bright as you were when we first came to London."

Thelma's lips quivered. "I—I am not well, Britta," she murmured, and suddenly her self-control gave way, and she broke into tears. In an instant Britta was kneeling by her, coaxing and caressing her, and calling her by every endearing name she could think of, while she wisely forbore from asking any more questions. Presently her sobs grew calmer,—she rested her fair head against Britta's shoulder and smiled faintly. At that moment a light tap was heard outside, and a voice called—

"Thelma! Are you there?"

Britta opened the door, and Sir Philip entered hurriedly and smiling—but stopped short to survey his wife in dismay.

"Why, my darling!" he exclaimed distressfully. "Have you been crying?"

Here the discreet Britta retired.

Thelma sprang to her husband and nestled in his arms.

"Philip, do not mind it," she murmured. "I felt a little sad—it is nothing! But tell me—you *do* love me? You will never tire of me? You have always loved me, I am sure?"

He raised her face gently with one hand, and looked at her in surprise.

"Thelma—what strange questions from *you!* Love you? Is not every beat of my heart for you? Are you not my life, my joy—my everything in this world?" And he pressed her passionately in his arms and kissed her.

"You have never loved any one else so much?" she whispered, half abashed.

"Never!" he answered readily. "What makes you ask such a thing?"

She was silent. He looked down at her flushing cheeks and tear-wet lashes attentively.

"You are fanciful to-day, my pet," he said at last. "You've been tiring yourself too much. You must rest. You'd better not go to the Brilliant Theatre to-night—it's only a burlesque, and is sure to be vulgar and noisy. We'll stop at home and spend a quiet evening together—shall we?"

She raised her eyes half wistfully and smiled. "I should like that very, very much, Philip!" she murmured; "but you know we did promise Clara to go with her to-night. And as we are so soon to leave London and return to Warwickshire, I should not like to disappoint her."

"You are very fond of Clara?" he asked suddenly.

"Very!" She paused and sighed slightly. "She is so kind and clever—much more clever than I can ever be—and she knows many things about the world which I do not. And she admires you so much, Philip!"

"Does she indeed?" Philip laughed and colored a little.

" Very good of her, I'm sure ! And so you'd really like to go to the Brilliant to-night ? "

" I think so," she said hesitatingly. " Clara says it will be very amusing. And you must remember how much I enjoyed ' Faust ' and ' Hamlet.' "

Errington smiled. " You'll find the Brilliant perform-ance very different to either," he said amusedly. " You don't know what a burlesque is like ! "

" Then I must be instructed," replied Thelma, smiling also, " I need to learn many things. I am very ignorant ! "

" Ignorant ! " and he swept aside with a caressing touch the clustering hair from her broad, noble brow. " My darling, you possess the greatest wisdom—the wisdom of innocence. I would not change it for all the learning of the sagest philosphers ! "

" You really mean that ? " she asked half timidly.

" I really mean that ! " he answered fondly. " Little sceptic ! As if I would ever say anything to you that I did *not* mean ! I shall be glad when we're out of London and back at the Manor—then I shall have you all to myself again—for a time, at least."

She raised her eyes full of sudden joy,—all traces of her former depression had disappeared.

" And *I* shall have *you !* " she said gladly. " And we shall not disappoint Lady Winsleigh to-night, Philip—I am not tired—and I shall be pleased to go to the theatre."

" All right ! " responded Philip cheerfully. " So let it be ! Only I don't believe you'll like the piece,—though it certainly won't make you cry. Yet I doubt if it will make you laugh, either. However, it will be a new experience for you."

And a new experience it decidedly was,—an experience, too, which brought some strange and perplexing results to Thelma of which she never dreamed.

She went to the Brilliant, accompanied by Lady Wins-leigh and her husband,—Neville, the secrĕtary, making the fourth in their box ; and during the first and second scene of the performance the stage effects were so pretty and the dancing so graceful that she nearly forgot the bewildered astonishment she had at first felt at the extreme scantiness of apparel worn by the ladies of the ballet. They repre-sented birds, bees, butterflies, and the other winged deni-zens of the forest-world,—and the *tout-ensemble* was so fairy-like and brilliant with swift movement, light, and color that the eye was too dazzled and confused to note objectionable details. But in the third scene, when a plump, athletic young woman leaped on the stage in the guise of a humming-bird, with a feather tunic so short that it was a mere waist-belt of extra width,—a flesh-colored bodice about three inches high, and a pair of blue wings attached to her fat shoulders, Thelma started and half rose from her seat in dismay, while a hot tide of color crimsoned her cheeks. She looked nervously at her husband.

" I do not think this is pleasant to see," she said in a low tone. " Would it not be best to go away ? I—I think I would rather be at home."

Lady Winsleigh heard and smiled,—a little mocking smile.

" Don't be silly, child ! " she said. " If you leave the theatre just now you'll have every one staring at you. That woman's an immense favorite—she is the success of the piece. She's got more diamonds than either you or I."

Thelma regarded her friend with a sort of grave wonder, —but said nothing in reply. If Lady Winsleigh liked the performance and wished to remain, why,—then politeness demanded that Thelma should not interfere with her pleasure by taking an abrupt leave. So she resumed her seat, but withdrew herself far behind the curtain of the box, in a corner where the stage was almost invisible to her eyes. Her husband bent over her and whispered—

" I'll take you home if you wish it, dear ! only say the word."

She shook her head.

" Clara enjoys it ! " she answered somewhat plaintively. " We must stay."

Philip was about to address Lady Winsleigh on the subject, when suddenly Neville touched him on the arm.

" Can I speak to you alone for a moment, Sir Philip ? " he said in a strange, hoarse whisper. " Outside the box— away from the ladies—a matter of importance ! "

He looked as if he were about to faint. He gasped rather than spoke these words; his face was white as death, and his eyes had a confused and bewildered stare.

" Certainly ! " answered Philip promptly, though not without an accent of surprise,—and, excusing their absence briefly to his wife and Lady Winsleigh, they left the box together. Meanwhile the well-fed " Humming-Bird " was capering extravagantly before the footlights, pointing

her toe in the delighted face of the stalls and singing in a
in a loud, coarse voice the following refined ditty—

"Oh my ducky, oh my darling, oh my duck, duck, duck!
  If you love me you must have a little pluck, pluck, pluck!
  Come and put your arms around me, kiss me once, twice, thrice,
  For kissing may be naughty, but, by Jingo! it is nice!
                    Once, twice, thrice!
                    Nice, nice, nice!
                    Bliss, bliss, bliss!
                    Kiss, kiss, kiss!
        Kissing may be naughty, but it's nice!"

There were several verses in this graceful poem, and each
one was hailed with enthusiastic applause. The "Humming-
Bird" was triumphant, and when her song was concluded
she executed a startling *pas-seul* full of quaint and astonishing surprises, reaching her superbest climax when she
backed off the stage on one portly leg,—kicking the other
in regular time to the orchestra. Lady Winsleigh laughed,
and leaning towards Thelma, who still sat in her retired
corner, said with a show of kindness—

"You dear little goose! You must get accustomed to
this kind of thing—it takes with the men immensely. Why,
even your wonderful Philip has gone down behind the
scenes with Neville—you may be sure of that!"

The startled, pitiful astonishment in the girl's face
might have touched a less callous heart than Lady Winsleigh's,—but her ladyship was prepared for it and only
smiled.

"Gone behind the scenes! To see that dreadful woman!"
exclaimed Thelma in a low pained tone. "Oh no, Clara!
He would not do such a thing. Impossible!"

"Well, my dear, then where is he? He has been gone
quite ten minutes. Look at the stalls—all the men are out
of them! I tell you Violet Vere draws everybody of the
male sex after her! At the end of all her 'scenes' she has
a regular reception—for men only—of course! Ladies not
admitted!" And Clara Winsleigh laughed. "Don't look
so shocked for heaven's sake, Thelma,—you don't want
your husband to be a regular nincompoop! He must have
his amusements as well as other people. I believe you want
him to be like a baby, tied to your apron-string! You'll
find that an awful mistake,—he'll get tired to death of you,
sweet little Griselda though you are!"

Thelma's face grew very pale, and her hand closed more
tightly on the fan she held.

" You have said that so very, very often lately, Clara ! "
she murmured. " You seem so sure that he will get tired
—that all men get tired. I do not think you know Philip
—he is not like any other person I have ever met. And
why should he go behind the scenes to such a person as
Violet Vere——"

At that moment the box-door opened with a sharp click,
and Errington entered alone. He looked disturbed and
anxious.

" Neville is not well," he said abruptly, addressing his
wife. " I've sent him home. He wouldn't have been able
to sit this thing out." And he glanced half angrily towards
the stage—the curtain had just gone up again and displayed the wondrous Violet Vere still in her " humming-
bird " character, swinging on the branch of a tree and
(after the example of all humming-birds) smoking a cigar
with brazen-faced tranquillity.

" I am sorry he is ill," said Thelma gently. " That is why
you were so long away ? "

" Was I long ? " returned Philip somewhat absently.
" I didn't know it. I went to ask a question behind the
scenes."

Lady Winsleigh coughed and glanced at Thelma, whose
eyes dropped instantly.

" I suppose you saw Violet Vere ? " asked Clara.

" Yes, I saw her," he replied briefly. He seemed irritable and vexed—moreover, decidedly impatient. Presently
he said—

" Lady Winsleigh, would you mind very much if we left
this place and went home? I'm rather anxious about Neville—he's had a shock. Thelma doesn't care a bit about
this piece, I know, and if you are not very much absorbed——"

Lady Winsleigh rose instantly, with her usual ready
grace.

" My dear Sir Philip ! " she said sweetly. " As if I would
not do anything to oblige you ! Let us go by all means !
These burlesques *are* extremely fatiguing ! "

He seemed relieved by her acquiescence—and smiled that
rare sweet smile of his, which had once played such havoc
with her ladyship's sensitive feelings. They left the theatre,
and were soon on their way home, though Thelma was
rather silent during the drive. They dropped Lady Winsleigh at her own door, and after they had bidden her a cor-

dial good night, and were going on again towards home,
Philip, turning towards his wife, and catching sight of her
face by the light of a street-lamp, was struck by her extreme
paleness and weary look.

" You are very tired, my darling, I fear ? " he inquired,
tenderly encircling her with one arm. " Lean your head
on my shoulder—so ! "

She obeyed, and her hand trembled a little as he took
and held it in his own warm, strong clasp.

" We shall soon be home ! " he added cheerily. " And I
think we must have no more theatre-going this season.
The heat and noise and glare are too much for you."

" Philip," said Thelma suddenly. " Did you really go behind the scenes to-night ? "

" Yes, I did," he answered readily. " I was obliged to
go on a matter of business—a very disagreeable and unpleasant matter too."

" And what was it ? " she asked timidly, yet hopefully.

" My pet, I can't tell you ! I wish I could ! It's a
secret I'm bound not to betray—a secret which involves
the name of another person who'd be wretched if I were to
mention it to you. There,—don't let us talk about it any
more ! "

" Very well, Philip," said Thelma resignedly,—but
though she smiled, a sudden presentiment of evil depressed
her. The figure of the vulgar, half-clothed, painted creature known as Violet Vere rose up mockingly before her
eyes,—and the half-scornful, half-jesting words of Lady
Winsleigh rang persistently in her ears.

On reaching home, Philip went straight to Neville's little
study and remained with him in earnest conversation for a
long time—while Thelma went to bed, and lay restless
among her pillows, puzzling her brain with strange forebodings and new and perplexing ideas, till fatigue overpowered her, and she fell asleep with a few tear-drops wet
on her lashes. And that night Philip wondered why his
sweet wife talked so plaintively in her sleep,—though he
smiled as he listened to the drift of those dove-like mur-
murings.

" No one knows how my boy loves me," sighed the
dreaming voice. " No one in all the world ! How should
he tire ? Love can never tire ! "

Meanwhile, Lady Winsleigh, in the seclusion of her own

boudoir, penned a brief note to Sir Francis Lennox as follows—

" DEAR OLD LENNIE,

" I saw you in the stalls at the theatre this evening, though you pretended not to see me. What a fickle creature you are! not that I mind in the very least. The virtuous Bruce-Errington left his saintly wife and me to talk little platitudes together, while he, decorously accompanied by his secretary, went down to pay court to Violet Vere. How stout she is getting! Why don't you men advise her to diet herself? I know you also went behind the scenes —of course, *you* are an *ami intime*—promising boy you are, to be sure! Come and lunch with me to-morrow, if you're not too lazy.

" Yours ever,
" CLARA."

She gave this missive to her maid, Louise Rénaud, to post,—that faithful attendant took it first to her own apartment where she ungummed the envelope neatly by the aid of hot water, and read every word of it. This was not an exceptional action of hers,—all the letters received and sent by her mistress were subjected to the same process,—even those that were sealed with wax she had a means of opening in such a manner that it was impossible to detect that they had been tampered with.

She was a very clever French maid was Louise,—one of the cleverest of her class. Fond of mischief, ever suspicious, always on the alert for evil, utterly unscrupulous and malicious, she was an altogether admirable attendant for a lady of rank and fashion, her skill as a *coiffeur* and needle-woman always obtaining for her the wages she so justly deserved. When will wealthy women reared in idleness and luxury learn the folly of keeping a trained spy attached to their persons ?—a spy whose pretended calling is merely to arrange dresses and fripperies (half of which she invariably steals), but whose real delight is to take note of all her mistress's incomings and outgoings, tempers and tears—to watch her looks, her smiles and frowns,—and to start scandalous gossip concerning her in the servants' hall, from whence it gradually spreads to the society newspapers —for do you think these estimable and popular journals are never indebted for their " reliable " information to the " honest " statements of discharged footman or valet ?

Briggs, for instance, had tried his hand at a paragraph or
two concerning the "Upper Ten," and with the aid of a
dictionary, had succeeded in expressing himself quite
smartly, though in ordinary conversation his h's were often
lacking or superfluous, and his grammar doubtful.
Whether he persuaded any editor to accept his literary efforts is quite another matter—a question to which the answer must remain for ever enveloped in mystery,—but if
he *did* appear in print (it is only an if!)he must have been
immensely gratified to consider that his statements were
received with gusto by at least half aristocratic London,
and implicitly believed as having emanated from the "best
authorities." And Louise Rénaud having posted her mistress's letter at last, went down to visit Briggs in his private pantry, and to ask him a question.

"Tell me," she said rapidly, with her tight, prim smile.
"You read the papers—you will know. What lady is that
of the theatres—Violet Vere?"

Briggs laid down the paper he was perusing and surveyed
her with a superior air.

"What, Vi?" he exclaimed with a lazy wink. "Vi, of
the Hopperer-Buff? You've 'erd of 'er surely, Mamzelle?
No? There's not a man (as is worth calling a man) about
town, as don't know *'er!* Dukes, Lords, an' Royal 'Igh-
nesses—she's the style for 'em! Mag-ni-ficent creetur! all
legs and arms! I won't deny but wot I 'ave an admiration
for 'er myself—I bought a 'arf-crown portrait of 'er quite
recently." And Briggs rose slowly and searched in a
mysterious drawer which he invariably kept locked.

"'Ere she is, as large as life, Mamzelle," he continued,
exhibiting a "promenade" photograph of the actress in
question. "There's a neck for you! There's form! Vi,
my dear, I saloot you!" and he pressed a sounding kiss on
the picture—"you're one in a million! Smokes and drinks
like a trooper, Mamzelle!" he added admiringly, as Louise
Rénaud studied the portrait attentively. "But with all 'er
advantages, you would not call 'er a lady. No—that term
would be out of the question. She is wot we men would
call an enchantin' female!" And Briggs kissed the tips of
his fingers and waved them in the air as he had seen certain
foreign gentlemen do when enthusiastic.

"I comprehend," said the French maid, nodding emphatically. "Then, if she is so, what makes that proud Seigneur
Bruce-Errington visit her?" Here she shook her finger at

Briggs. " And leave his beautiful lady wife, to go and see her?" Another shake. " And that *miserable* Sieur Lennox to go also? Tell me that!" She folded her arms, like Napoleon at St. Helena, and smiled again that smile which was nothing but a sneer. Briggs rubbed his nose contemplatively.

" Little Francis can go ennywheres," he said at last. " He's laid out a good deal of tin on Vi and others of 'er purfession. You cannot make enny-think of that young feller but a cad. I would not accept 'im for my pussonal attendant. No! But Sir Philip Bruce-Errington——" He paused, then continued, " Air you sure of your facts, Mamzelle?"

Mamzelle was so sure, that the bow on her cap threatened to come off with the determined wagging of her head.

" Well," resumed Briggs, " Sir Philip may, like hothers, consider it 'the thing' you know, to 'ang on as it were to Vi. But I '*ad* thought 'im superior to it. Ah! poor 'uman natur, as 'Uxley says!" and Briggs sighed. " Lady Errington is a sweet creetur, Mamzelle—a *very* sweet creetur! *Has* a rule I find the merest nod of my 'ed a sufficient saloot to a woman of the aristocracy—but for '*er*, Mamzelle, I never fail to show 'er up with a court bow!" And involuntarily Briggs bowed then and there in his most elegant manner. Mamzelle tightened her thin lips a little and waved her hand expressively.

" She is an angel of beauty!" she said, " and Miladi Winsleigh is jealous—ah, *Dieu!* jealous to death of her! She is innocent too—like a baby—and she worships her husband. That is an error! To worship a man is a great mistake—she will find it so. Men are not to be too much loved—no, no!"

Briggs smiled in superb self-consciousness. " Well, well! I will not deny, Mamzelle, that it spoils us," he said complacently. " It certainly spoils us! ' When lovely woman stoops to folly,'—the hold, hold story!"

" You will r-r-r-emember," said Mamzelle, suddenly stepping up very close to him and speaking with a strong accent, " what I have said to-night! Monsieur Briggs, you will r-remember! There will be mees-cheef! Yes—there will be mees-cheef to Sieur Bruce-Errington, and when there is,—I—I, Louise Rénaud—I know who ees at the bottom of eet!"

So saying, with a whirl of her black silk dress and a flash

of her white muslin apron, she disappeared. Briggs, left alone, sauntered to a looking-glass hanging on the wall and studied with some solicitude a pimple that had recently appeared on his clean-shaven face.

"Mischief!" he soliloquized. "I des-say! Whenever a lot of women gets together, there's sure to be mischief. Dear creeturs! They love it like the best Clicquot. Sprightly young pusson is Mamzelle. Knows who's at the bottom of 'eet,' does she? Well—she's not the only one as knows the same thing. As long as doors 'as cracks and key'oles, it ain't in the least difficult to find out wot goes on inside boo-dwars and drorin'-rooms. And 'ighly interestin' things one 'ears now and then—'ighly interestin'!"

And Briggs leered suavely at his own reflection, and then resumed the perusal of his paper. He was absorbed in the piquant, highly flavored details of a particularly disgraceful divorce case, and he was by no means likely to disturb himself from his refined enjoyment for any less important reason than the summons of Lord Winsleigh's bell, which rang so seldom that, when it did, he made it a point of honor to answer it immediately, for, as he said—

"His lordship knows wot is due to me, and I knows wot is due to 'im—therefore it 'appens we are able to ekally respect each other!"

CHAPTER XXII.

> "If thou wert honorable,
> Thou would'st have told this tale for virtue, not
> For such an end thou seek'st ; as base, as strange.
> Thou wrong'st a gentleman who is as far
> From thy report, as thou from honor."
>
> *Cymbeline.*

SUMMER in Shakespeare Land! Summer in the heart of England—summer in wooded Warwickshire,—a summer brilliant, warm, radiant with flowers, melodious with the songs of the heaven-aspiring larks, and the sweet, low trill of the forest-hidden nightingales. Wonderful and divine it is to hear the wild chorus of nightingales that sing beside Como in the hot languorous nights of an Italian July— wonderful to hear them maddening themselves with love and music, and almost splitting their slender throats with the bursting bubbles of burning song,—but there is something, perhaps, more dreamily enchanting still,—to hear them warbling less passionately but more plaintively, beneath the drooping leafage of those grand old trees, some of which may have stretched their branches in shadowy benediction over the sacred head of the grandest poet in the world. Why travel to Athens,—why wander among the Ionian Isles for love of the classic ground? Surely, though the clear-brained old Greeks were the founders of all noble literature, they have reached their fulminating point in the English Shakespeare,—and the Warwickshire lanes, decked simply with hawthorn and sweet-briar roses, through which Mary Arden walked leading her boy-angel by the hand, are sacred as any portion of that earth once trodden by the feet of Homer and Plato.

So, at least, Thelma thought, when, released from the bondage of London social life, she found herself once more at Errington Manor, then looking its loveliest, surrounded with a green girdle of oak and beech, and set off by the beauty of velvety lawns and terraces, and rose-gardens in full bloom. The depression from which she had suffered fell away from her completely—she grew light-hearted as a child, and flitted from room to room, singing to herself for pure gladness. Philip was with her all day now, save for a couple of hours in the forenoon which he devoted to letter-writing in connection with his Parliamentary aspirations,—and Philip was tender, adoring and passionate as lovers may be, but as husbands seldom are. They took long walks together through the woods,—they often rambled across the fragrant fields to Anne Hathaway's cottage, which was not very far away, and sitting down in some sequestered nook, Philip would pull from his pocket a volume of the immortal Plays, and read passages aloud in his fine mellow voice, while Thelma, making posies of the meadow flowers, listened entranced. Sometimes, when he was in a more business-like humor, he would bring out Cicero's Orations, and after pondering over them for a while would talk very grandly about the way in which he meant to speak in Parliament.

"They want dash and fire there," he said, "and these qualities must be united with good common sense. In addressing the House, you see, Thelma, one must rouse and interest the men—not bore them. You can't expect fellows to pass a Bill if you've made them long for their beds all the time you've been talking about it."

Thelma smiled and glanced over his shoulder at " Cicero's Orations."

" And do you wish to speak to them like Cicero, my boy?" she said gently. " But I do not think you will find that possible. Because when Cicero spoke it was in a different age and to very different people—people who were glad to learn how to be wise and brave. But if you were Cicero himself, do you think you would be able to impress the English Parliament?"

" Why not, dear?" asked Errington with some fervor. " I believe that men, taken as men, *pur et simple*, are the same in all ages, and are open to the same impressions. Why should not modern Englishmen be capable of receiving the same lofty ideas as the antique Romans, and acting upon them?"

" Ah, do not ask *me* why," said Thelma, with a plaintive little shake of her head—" for *I* cannot tell you! But remember how many members of Parliament we did meet in London—and where were their lofty ideas? Philip, had they any ideas at all, do you think? There was that very fat gentleman who is a brewer,—well, to hear him talk, would you not think all England was for the making of beer? And he does not care for the country unless it continues to consume his beer! It was to that very man I said something about *Hamlet*, and he told me he had no interest for such nonsense as Shakespeare and play-going— his time was taken up at the ' '*Ouse.*' You see, he is a member of Parliament—yet it is evident he neither knows the language nor the literature of his country! And there must be many like him, otherwise so ignorant a person would not hold such a position—and for such men, what would be the use of a Cicero?"

Philip leaned back against the trunk of the tree under which they were sitting, and laughed.

" You may be right, Thelma,—I dare say you are. There's certainly too much beer represented in the House— I admit that. But, after all, trade is the great moving-spring of national prosperity,—and it would hardly be fair to refuse seats to the very men who help to keep the country going."

" I do not see that," said Thelma gravely,—" if those men are ignorant, why should they have a share in so important a thing as Government? They may know all about beer, and wool, and iron,—but perhaps they can only judge what is good for themselves, not what is best for the whole country, with all its rich and poor. I do think that only the wisest scholars and most intelligent persons should be allowed to help in the ruling of a great nation."

" But the people choose their own rulers," remarked Errington reflectively.

" Ah, the poor people ! " sighed Thelma. " They know so very little,—and they are taught so badly ! I think they never do quite understand what they do want,—they are the same in all histories,—like little children, they get bewildered and frightened in any trouble, and the wisest heads are needed to think for them. It is, indeed, most cruel to make them puzzle out all difficulty for themselves ! "

" What a little sage you are, my pet ! " laughed Philip, taking her hand on which the marriage-ring and its accompanying diamond circlet, glistened brilliantly in the warm sunlight. " Do you mean to go in for politics ? "

She shook her head. "No, indeed ! That is not woman's work at all. The only way in which I think about such things, is that I feel the people cannot all be wise,—and that it seems a pity the wisest and greatest in the land should not be chosen to lead them rightly."

" And so under the circumstances, you think it's no use my trying to *pose* as a Cicero ? " asked her husband amusedly. She laughed—with a very tender cadence in her laughter.

" It would not be worth your while, my boy," she said. " You know I have often told you that I do not see any great distinction in being a member of Parliament at all. What will you do ? You will talk to the fat brewer perhaps, and he will contradict you—then other people will get up and talk and contradict each other,—and so it will go on for days and days—meanwhile the country remains exactly as it was, neither better nor worse,—and all the talking does no good ! It is better to be out of it,—here together, as we are to-day."

And she raised her dreamy blue eyes to the sheltering canopy of green leaves that overhung them—leaves thick-clustered and dewy, through which the dazzling sky peeped in radiant patches. Philip looked at her,—the rapt expression of her upward gaze,—the calm, untroubled sweetness of her fair face,—were such as might well have suited one of Raffaelle's divinest angels. His heart beat quickly —he drew closer to her, and put his arm round her.

"Your eyes are looking at the sky, Thelma," he whispered. "Do you know what that is? Heaven looking into heaven! And do you know which of the two heavens I prefer?" She smiled, and turning, met his ardent gaze with one of equal passion and tenderness.

"Ah, you *do* know!" he went on, softly kissing the side of her slim white throat. "I thought you couldn't possibly make a mistake!" He rested his head against her shoulder, and after a minute or two of lazy comfort, he resumed. "You are not ambitious, my Thelma! You don't seem to care whether your husband distinguishes himself in the ''Ouse,' as our friend the brewer calls it, or not. In fact, I don't believe you care for anything save—love! Am I not right, my wife?"

A wave of rosy color flushed her transparent skin, and her eyes filled with an earnest, almost pathetic languor.

"Surely of all things in the world," she said in a low tone,—"Love is best?"

To this he made prompt answer, though not in words—his lips conversed with hers, in that strange, sweet language which, though unwritten, is everywhere comprehensible,—and then they left their shady resting-place and sauntered homeward hand in hand through the warm fields fragrant with wild thyme and clover.

Many happy days passed thus with these lovers—for lovers they still were. Marriage had for once fulfilled its real and sacred meaning—it had set Love free from restraint, and had opened all the gateways of the only earthly paradise human hearts shall ever know,—the paradise of perfect union and absolute sympathy with the one thing beloved on this side eternity.

The golden hours fled by all too rapidly,—and towards the close of August there came an interruption to their felicity. Courtesy had compelled Bruce-Errington and his wife to invite a few friends down to visit them at the Manor before the glory of the summer-time was past,—and first among the guests came Lord and Lady Winsleigh and their bright boy, Ernest. Her ladyship's maid, Louise Rénaud, of course, accompanied her ladyship,—and Briggs was also to the fore in the capacity of Lord Winsleigh's personal attendant. After these, George Lorimer arrived—he had avoided the Erringtons all the season,—but he could not very well refuse the pressing invitation now given him without seeming churlish,—then came Beau Lovelace, for a few days only, as with the commencement of September he would be off as usual to his villa on the Lago di Como. Sir Francis Lennox, too, made his appearance frequently in a casual sort of way—he " ran down," to use his own expression, now and then, and made himself very agreeable, especially to men, by whom he was well liked for his invariable good-humor and extraordinary proficiency in all sports and games of skill. Another welcome visitor was Pierre Duprèz, lively and sparkling as ever,—he came from Paris to pass a fortnight with his " cher Phil-eep," and make merriment for the whole party. His old admiration for Britta had by no means decreased,—he was fond of waylaying that demure little maiden on her various household errands, and giving her small posies of jessamine and other sweet-scented blossoms to wear just above the left-hand corner of her apron-bib, close to the place where the heart is supposed to be. Olaf Güldmar had been invited to the Manor at this period,—Errington wrote many urgent letters, and so did Thelma, entreating him to come,—for nothing would have pleased Sir Philip more than to have introduced the fine old Odin worshipper among his fashionable friends, and to have heard him bluntly and forcibly holding his own among them, putting their faint and languid ways of life to shame by his manly, honest, and vigorous utterance. But Güldmar had only just returned to the Altenfjord after nearly a year's absence, and his hands were too full of work for him to accept his son-in-law's invitation.

" The farm lands have a waste and dreary look," he wrote, " though I let them to a man who should verily have known how to till the soil trodden by his fathers—and as for the farmhouse, 'twas like a hollow shell that has lain long on the shore and become brown and brittle—for thou knowest no human creature has entered there since we departed. However, Valdemar Svensen and I, for sake of company, have resolved to dwell together in it, and truly we have nearly settled down to the peaceful contemplation of our past days,—so Philip, and thou, my child Thelma, trouble not concerning me. I am hale and hearty, the gods be thanked,—and may live on in hope to see you both next spring or summer-tide. Your happiness keeps this old man young—so grudge me not the news of your delights wherein I am myself delighted."

One familiar figure was missing from the Manor household,—that of Edward Neville. Since the night at the

21

Brilliant, when he had left the theatre so suddenly, and
gone home on the plea of illness, he had never been quite
the same man. He looked years older—he was strangely
nervous and timid—and he shrank away from Thelma as
though he were some guilty or tainted creature. Surprised
at this, she spoke to her husband about it,—but he, hurriedly, and with some embarrassment, advised her to " let
him alone "—his " nerves were shaken "—his " health was
feeble "—and that it would be kind on her part to refrain
from noticing him or asking him questions. So she refrained—but Neville's behavior puzzled her all the same.
When they left town, he implored, almost piteously, to be
allowed to remain behind,—he could attend to Sir Philip's
business so much better in London, he declared, and he had
his way. Errington, usually fond of Neville's society, made
no attempt whatever to persuade him against his will,—so
he stayed in the half-shut-up house in Prince's Gate through
all the summer heat, poring over parliamentary documents
and pamphlets,—and Philip came up from the country once
a fortnight to visit him, and transact any business that
might require his personal attention.

On one of the last and hottest days in August, a grand
garden-party was given at the Manor. All the county people were invited, and they came eagerly, though, before
Thelma's social successes in London, they had been reluctant to meet her. Now, they put on their best clothes, and
precipitated themselves into the Manor grounds like a flock
of sheep seeking land on which to graze,—all wearing their
sweetest propitiatory smirk—all gushing forth their admiration of " that *darling* Lady Errington "—all behaving
themselves in the exceptionally funny manner that county
people affect,—people who are considered somebodies in the
small villages their big houses dominate,—but who, when
brought to reside in London, become less than the minnows
in a vast ocean. These good folks were not only anxious to
see Lady Errington—they wanted to *say* they had seen her,
—and that she had spoken to *them*, so that they might, in
talking to their neighbors, mention it in quite an easy,
casual way, such as—" Oh, I was at Errington Manor the
other day, and Lady Errington said to me——." Or—" Sir
Philip is *such* a charming man ! I was talking to his lovely
wife, and he asked me——" etc., etc. Or—" You've no idea
what large strawberries they grow at the Manor ! Lady
Errington showed me some that were just ripening—mag-

nificent!" And so on. For in truth this *is* "a mad world, my masters,"—and there is no accounting for the inexpressibly small follies and mean toadyisms of the people in it.

Moreover, all the London guests who were visiting Thelma came in for a share of the county magnates' servile admiration. They found the Winsleighs "*so* distingué"—Master Ernest instantly became "that *dear* boy!"—Beau Lovelace was "so dreadfully clever, you know!"—and Pierre Duprèz "quite *too* delightful!"

The grounds looked very brilliant—pink-and-white marquees were dotted here and there on the smooth velvet lawns—bright flags waved from different quarters of the gardens, signals of tennis, archery, and dancing,—and the voluptuous waltz-music of a fine Hungarian band rose up and swayed in the air with the downward floating songs of the birds and the dash of fountains in full play. Girls in pretty light summer costumes made picturesque groups under the stately oaks and beeches,—gay laughter echoed from the leafy shrubberies, and stray couples were seen sauntering meditatively through the rose-gardens, treading on the fallen scented petals, and apparently too much absorbed in each other to notice anything that was going on around them. Most of these were lovers, of course—intending lovers, if not declared ones,—in fact, Eros was very busy that day among the roses, and shot forth a great many arrows, aptly aimed, out of his exhaustless quiver.

Two persons there were, however,—man and woman,—who, walking in that same rose-avenue, did not seem, from their manner, to have much to do with the fair Greek god,—they were Lady Winsleigh and Sir Francis Lennox. Her ladyship looked exceedingly beautiful in her clinging dress of Madras lace, with a bunch of scarlet poppies at her breast, and a wreath of the same vivid flowers in her picturesque Leghorn hat. She held a scarlet-lined parasol over her head, and from under the protecting shadow of this silken pavilion, her dark, lustrous eyes flashed disdainfully as she regarded her companion. He was biting an end of his brown moustache, and looked annoyed, yet lazily amused too.

"Upon my life, Clara," he observed, "you are really awfully down on a fellow, you know! One would think you never cared twopence about me!"

"Too high a figure!" retorted Lady Winsleigh, with a hard little laugh. "I never cared a brass farthing!"

He stopped short in his walk and stared at her.

"By Jove! you *are* cool!" he ejaculated. "Then what did you mean all the time?"

"What did *you* mean?" she asked defiantly.

He was silent. After a slight, uncomfortable pause, he shrugged his shoulders and smiled.

"Don't let us have a scene!" he observed in a bantering tone. "Anything but that!"

"Scene!" she exclaimed indignantly. "Pray when have you had to complain of me on that score?"

"Well, don't let me have to complain now," he said coolly.

She surveyed him in silent scorn for a moment, and her full, crimson lips curled contemptuously.

"What a brute you are!" she muttered suddenly between her set pearly teeth.

"Thanks, awfully!" he answered, taking out a cigarette and lighting it leisurely. "You are really charmingly candid, Clara! Almost as frank as Lady Errington, only less polite!"

"I shall not learn politeness from *you*, at any rate," she said,—then altering her tone to one of studied indifference, she continued coldly, "What do you want of me? We've done with each other, as you know. I believe you wish to become gentleman-lacquey to Bruce-Errington's wife, and that you find it difficult to obtain the situation. Shall I give you a character?"

He flushed darkly, and his eyes glittered with an evil lustre.

"Gently, Clara! Draw it mild!" he said languidly. "Don't irritate me, or I *may* turn crusty! You know, if I chose, I could open Bruce-Errington's eyes rather more widely than you'd like with respect to the *devoted affection* you entertain for his beautiful wife." She winced a little at this observation—he saw it and laughed,—then resumed: "At present I'm really in the best of humors. The reason I wanted to speak to you alone for a minute or two was, that I'd something to say which might possibly please you. But perhaps you'd rather not hear it?"

She was silent. So was he. He watched her closely for a little—noting with complacency the indignant heaving of her breast and the flush on her cheeks,—signs of the strong repression she was putting upon her rising temper.

"Come, Clara, you may as well be amiable," he said.

" I'm sure you'll be glad to know that the virtuous Philip is not immaculate after all. Won't it comfort you to think that he's nothing but a mortal man like the rest of us ? . . . and that with a little patience your charms will most probably prevail with him as easily as they once did with me ? Isn't that worth hearing ? "

' I don't understand you," she replied curtly.

" Then you are very dense, my dear girl," he remarked smilingly. " Pardon me for saying so! But I'll put it plainly and in as few words as possible. The moral Bruce-Errington, like a great many other ' moral ' men I know, has gone in for Violet Vere,—and I dare say you understand what *that* means. In the simplest language, it means that he's tired of his domestic bliss and wants a change."

Lady Winsleigh stopped in her slow pacing along the gravel-walk, and raised her eyes steadily to her companion's face.

" Are you sure of this ? " she asked.

" Positive ! " replied Sir Francis, flicking the light ash off his cigarette delicately with his little finger. " When you wrote me that note about the Vere, I confess I had my suspicions. Since then they've been confirmed. I know for a fact that Errington has had several private interviews with Vi, and has also written her a good many letters. Some of the fellows in the green-room tease her about her new conquest, and she grins and admits it. Oh, the whole thing's plain enough ! Only last week, when he went up to town to see his man Neville on business he called on Vi at her own apartments in Arundel Street, Strand. She told me so herself—we're rather intimate, you know,—though of course she refused to mention the object of his visit. Honor among thieves ! " and he smiled half mockingly.

Lady Winsleigh seemed absorbed, and walked on like one in a dream. Just then, a bend in the avenue brought them in full view of the broad terrace in front of the Manor, where Thelma's graceful figure, in a close-fitting robe of white silk crêpe, was outlined clearly against the dazzling blue of the sky. Several people were grouped near her,— she seemed to be in animated conversation with some of them, and her face was radiant with smiles. Lady Winsleigh looked at her,—then said suddenly in a low voice—

" It will break her heart ! "

Sir Francis assumed an air of polite surprise. " Pardon ! Whose heart ? "

She pointed slightly to the white figure on the terrace.
" Hers ! Surely you must know that ? "

He smiled. " Well—isn't that precisely what you desire,
Clara ? Though, for my part, I don't believe in the brittle-
ness of hearts—they seem to me to be made of exceptionally tough material. However, if the fair Thelma's heart
cracks ever so widely, I think I can undertake to mend it ! "

Clara shrugged her shoulders. " You ! " she exclaimed
contemptuously.

He stroked his moustache with feline care and nicety.
" Yes—I ! If not, I've studied women all my life for
nothing ! "

She broke into a low peal of mocking laughter—turned,
and was about to leave him, when he detained her by a
slight touch on her arm.

" Stop a bit ! " he said in an impressive *sotto-voce.* " A
bargain's a bargain all the world over. If I undertake to
keep you cognizant of Bruce-Errington's little goings-on in
London,—information which, I dare say, you can turn to
good account,—you must do something for me. I ask very
little. Speak of me to Lady Errington—make her think
well of me,—flatter me as much as you used to do when we
fancied ourselves terrifically in love with each other—(a
good joke, wasn't it !)—and, above all, make her *trust* me !
Do you understand ? "

" As Red Riding-Hood trusted the Wolf and was eaten
up for her innocence," observed Lady Winsleigh. " Very
well ! I'll do my best. As I said before, you want a character. I'm sure I hope you'll obtain the situation you so
much desire ! I can state that you made yourself fairly
useful in your last place, and that you left because your
wages were not high enough ! "

And with another sarcastic laugh, she moved forward
towards the terrace where Thelma stood. Sir Francis followed at some little distance with no very pleasant expression on his features. A stealthy step approaching him
from behind made him start nervously—it was Louise
Rénaud, who, carrying a silver tray on which soda-water
bottles and glasses made an agreeable clinking, tripped demurely past him without raising her eyes. She came directly out of the rose-garden,—and, as she overtook her
mistress on the lawn, that lady seemed surprised, and
asked—

" Where have you been, Louise ? "

" Miladi was willing that I should assist in the attendance to-day," replied Louise discreetly. " I have waited upon Milord Winsleigh, and other gentlemen in the summer-house at the end of the rose-garden."

And with one furtive glance of her black, bead-like eyes at Lady Winsleigh's face, she made a respectful sort of half-curtsy and went her way.

Later on in the afternoon, when it was nearing sunset, and all other amusements had given way to the delight of dancing on the springy green turf to the swinging music of the band,—Briggs, released for a time from the duties of assisting the waiters at the splendid refreshment-table (duties which were pleasantly lightened by the drinking of a bottle of champagne which he was careful to reserve for his own consumption), sauntered leisurely through the winding alleys and fragrant shrubberies which led to the most unromantic portion of the Manor grounds,—namely, the vegetable-garden. Here none of the butterflies of fashion found their way,—the suggestions offered by growing cabbages, turnips, beans, and plump, yellow-skinned marrows were too prosaic for society bantams who require refined surroundings in which to crow their assertive platitudes. Yet it was a peaceful nook—and there were household odors of mint and thyme and sweet marjoram, which were pleasant to the soul of Briggs, and reminded him of roast goose on Christmas Day, with all its attendant succulent delicacies. He paced the path slowly,—the light of the sinking sun blazing gloriously on his plush breeches, silver cordons and tassels,—for he was in full-dress livery in honor of the fête, and looked exceedingly imposing. Now and then he glanced down at his calves with mild approval, —his silk stockings fitted them well, and they had a very neat and shapely appearance.

" I *'ave* developed," he murmured to himself. " There ain't a doubt about it ! One week of country air, and I'm a different man ;—the effecks of overwork 'ave disappeared. Flopsie won't know these legs of mine when I get back,— they've improved surprisingly." He stopped to survey a bed of carrots. " Plenty of Cressy there," he mused. " Cressy's a noble soup, and Flopsie makes it well,—a man might do wuss than marry Flopsie. She's a widder, and a *leetle* old—just a leetle old for me—but——" Here he sniffed delicately at a sprig of thyme he had gathered, and smiled consciously. Presently he perceived a small, plump,

pretty figure approaching him, no other than Britta, looking particularly charming in a very smart cap, adorned
with pink-ribbon bows, and a very elaborately frilled muslin
apron. Briggs at once assumed his most elegant and conquering air, straightened himself to his full height and
kissed his hand to her with much condescension. She
laughed as she came up to him, and the dimples in her
round cheeks appeared in full force.

"Well, Mr. Briggs," she said, "are you enjoying yourself?"

Briggs smiled down upon her benevolently. "I am!"
he responded graciously. "I find the hair refreshing. And
you, Miss Britta?"

"Oh, I'm very comfortable, thank you!" responded
Britta demurely, edging a little away from his arm, which
showed an unmistakable tendency to encircle her waist,—
then glancing at a basket she held full of grapes, just cut
from the hot house, she continued, "These are for the supper-table. I must be quick, and take them to Mrs. Parton."

"Must you?" and Briggs asked this question with quite
an unnecessary amount of tenderness, then resuming his
dignity, he observed, "Mrs. Parton is a very worthy woman
—an excellent 'ousekeeper. But she'll no doubt excuse you
for lingering a little, Miss Britta—especially in *my* company."

Britta laughed again, showing her pretty little white teeth
to the best advantage. "Do you think she will?" she said
merrily. "Then I'll stop a minute, and if she scolds me
I'll put the blame on you!"

Briggs played with his silver tassels and, leaning gracefully against a plum-tree, surveyed her with a critical eye.

"I was not able," he observed, "to see much of you in
town. Our people were always a' visitin' each other, and
yet our meetings were, as the poet says, 'few and far
between.'"

Britta nodded indifferently, and perceiving a particularly
ripe gooseberry on one of the bushes close to her, gathered
it quickly and popped it between her rosy lips. Seeing
another equally ripe, she offered it to Briggs, who accepted
it and ate it slowly, though he had a misgiving that by so
doing he was seriously compromising his dignity. He resumed his conversation.

"Since I've been down 'ere, I've 'ad more opportunity to
observe you. I 'ope you will allow me to say I think very

'ighly of you." He waved his hand with the elegance of a Sir Charles Grandison. "Very 'ighly indeed! Your youth is most becoming to you! If you only 'ad a little more *chick*, there'd be nothing left to desire!"

"A little more—*what*?" asked Britta, opening her blue eyes very wide in puzzled amusement.

"*Chick!*" replied Briggs, with persistent persuasiveness. "*Chick*, Miss Britta, is a French word much used by the aristocracy. Coming from Norway, an 'avin' perhaps a very limited experience, you mayn't 'ave 'erd it—but eddicated people 'ere find it very convenient and expressive. *Chick* means style,—*the* thing, *the* go, *the* fashion. For example, everythink your lady wears is *chick!*"

"Really!" said Britta, with a wandering and innocent air. "How funny! It doesn't sound like French, at all, Mr. Briggs,—it's more like English."

"Perhaps the Paris accent isn't familiar to you yet," remarked Briggs majestically. "Your stay in the gay metropolis was probably short. Now, I 'ave been there many times —ah, Paris, Paris!" he paused in a sort of ecstacy, then, with a side leer, continued—"You'd 'ardly believe 'ow wicked I am in Paris, Miss Britta! I am, indeed! It is something in the hair of the Bollyvards, I suppose! And the caffy life excites my nerves."

"Then you shouldn't go there," said Britta gravely, though her eyes twinkled with repressed fun. "It can't be good for you. And, oh! I'm so sorry, Mr. Briggs, to think that *you* are ever wicked!" And she laughed.

"It's not for long," explained Briggs, with a comically satisfied, yet penitent, look. "It is only a sort of breaking out,—a fit of 'igh spirits. Hall men are so at times! It's *chick* to run a little wild in Paris. But, Miss Britta, if *you* were with me I should never run wild!" Here his arm made another attempt to get round her waist—and again she skillfully, and with some show of anger, avoided it.

"Ah, you're very 'ard upon me," he then observed. "Very, very, 'ard! But I won't complain, my—my dear gal—one day you'll know me better!" He stopped and looked at her very intently. "Miss Britta," he said abruptly, "you've a great affection for your lady, 'aven't you?"

Instantly Britta's face flushed, and she was all attention.

"Yes, indeed!" she answered quickly. "Why do you ask, Mr. Briggs?"

Briggs rubbed his nose perplexedly. "It is not easy to explain," he said. "To run down my own employers wouldn't be in my line. But I've an idea that Clara—by which name I allude to my Lord Winsleigh's lady,—is up to mischief. She 'ates *your* lady, Miss Britta—'ates 'er like poison!"

"Hates her!" cried Britta in astonishment. "Oh, you must be mistaken, Mr. Briggs! She is as fond of her as she can be—almost like a sister to her!"

"Clara's a fine actress," murmured Briggs, more to himself than to his companion. "She'd beat Violet Vere on 'er own ground." Raising his voice a little, he turned gallantly to Britta and relieved her of the basket she held.

"Hallow me!" he said. "We'll walk to the 'ouse together. On the way I'll explain—and you'll judge for yourself. The words of the immortal bard, whose county we are in, occur to me as *aprerpo*,—' There are more things in 'evin and 'erth, 'Oratio,—than even the most devoted domestic can sometimes be aweer of.'"

And gently sauntering by Britta's side, Briggs began to converse in low and confidential tones,—she listened with strained and eager attention,—and she was soon receiving information that startled her and set her on the alert.

Talk of private detectives and secret service! Do private detectives ev·r discover so much as the servants of a man's own household?—servants who are aware of the smallest trifles,—who know the name and position of every visitor that comes and goes,—who easily learn to recognize the handwriting on every letter that arrives—who laugh and talk in their kitchens over things that their credulous masters and mistresses imagine are unknown to all the world save themselves,—who will judge the morals of a Duke, and tear the reputation of a Duchess to shreds, for the least, the most trifling error of conduct! If you can stand well with your servants, you can stand well with the whole world—if not—carry yourself as haughtily as you may—your pride will not last long, depend upon it!

Meanwhile, as Briggs and Britta strolled in the side paths of the shrubbery, the gay guests of the Manor were dancing on the lawn. Thelma did not dance,—she reclined in a low basket-chair, fanning herself. George Lorimer lay stretched in lazy length at her feet, and near her stood her husband, together with Beau Lovelace and Lord Winsleigh. At a little distance, under the shadow of a noble beech, sat

Mrs. Rush-Marvelle and Mrs. Van Clupp in earnest conversation. It was to Mrs. Marvelle that the Van Clupps
owed their invitation for this one day down to Errington
Manor,—for Thelma herself was not partial to them. But
she did not like to refuse Mrs. Marvelle's earnest entreaty
that they should be asked,—and that good-natured, scheming lady having gained her point, straightway said to Marcia Van Clupp somewhat severely—

"Now, Marcia, this is your last chance. If you don't
hook Masherville at the Carringten fête, you'll lose him!
You mark my words!"

Marcia had dutifully promised to do her best, and she
was not having what she herself called "a good hard time
of it." Lord Algy was in one of his most provokingly vacillating moods—moreover, he had a headache, and felt bilious. Therefore he would not dance—he would not play
tennis—he did not understand archery—he was disinclined
to sit in romantic shrubberies or summer-houses, as he had
a nervous dread of spiders—so he rambled aimlessly about
the grounds with his hands in his pockets, and perforce
Marcia was compelled to ramble too. Once she tried what
effect an opposite flirtation would have on his mind, so she
coquetted desperately with a young country squire, whose
breed of pigs was considered the finest in England—but
Masherville did not seem to mind it in the least. Nay, he
looked rather relieved than otherwise, and Marcia, seeing
this, grew more resolute than ever.

"I guess I'll pay him out for this!" she thought as
she watched him feebly drinking soda-water for his headache. "He's a man that wants ruling, and ruled he shall
be!"

And Mrs. Rush-Marvelle and Mrs. Van Clupp observed
her manœuvres with maternal interest, while the cunning-
faced, white-headed Van Clupp conversed condescendingly
with Mr. Rush-Marvelle, as being a nonentity of a man
whom he could safely patronize.

As the glory of the sunset paled, and the delicate, warm
hues of the summer twilight softened the landscape, the
merriment of the brilliant assembly seemed to increase. As
soon as it was dark, the grounds were to be illuminated by
electricity, and dancing was to be continued indoors—the
fine old picture-gallery being the place chosen for the purpose. Nothing that could add to the utmost entertainment
of the guests had been forgotten, and Thelma, the fair mis-

tress of these pleasant revels, noting with quiet eyes the evident enjoyment of all present, felt very happy and tranquil. She had exerted herself a good deal, and was now a little tired. Her eyes had a dreamy, far-off look, and she found her thoughts wandering, now and then, away to the Altenfjord—she almost fancied she could hear the sigh of the pines and the dash of the waves mingling in unison as they used to do when she sat at the old farm-house window and span, little dreaming then how her life would change—how all those familiar things would be swept away as though they had never been. She roused herself from this momentary reverie, and glancing down at the recumbent gentleman at her feet, touched his shoulder lightly with the edge of her fan.

" Why do you not dance, you very lazy Mr. Lorimer ? " she asked, with a smile.

He turned up his fair, half-boyish face to hers and laughed.

" Dance ! I ! Good gracious ! Such an exertion would kill me, Lady Errington—don't you know that ? I am of a Sultan-like disposition—I shouldn't mind having slaves to dance for me if they did it well—but I should look on from the throne whereon I sat cross-legged,—and smoke my pipe in peace."

" Always the same ! " she said lightly. " Are you never serious ? "

His eyes darkened suddenly. " Sometimes. Awfully so ! And in that condition I become a burden to myself and my friends."

" Never be serious ! " interposed Beau Lovelace, " it really isn't worth while ! Cultivate the humor of a Socrates, and reduce everything by means of close argument to its smallest standpoint, and the world, life, and time are no more than a pinch of snuff for some great Titantic god to please his giant nose withal ! "

" Your fame isn't worth much then, Beau, if we're to go by that line of argument," remarked Errington, with a laugh.

" Fame ! By Jove ! You don't suppose I'm such an arrant donkey as to set any store by fame ! " cried Lovelace, a broad smile lighting up his face and eyes. " Why, because a few people read my books and are amused thereby, —and because the Press pats me graciously on the back, and says metaphorically, ' Well done, little 'un ! ' or words to that effect, am I to go crowing about the world as if I were the only literary chanticleer? My dear friend, have you read 'Esdras'? You will find there that a certain king of Persia wrote to one 'Rathumus, a story-writer.' No doubt he was famous in his day, but,—to travesty *Hamlet,* 'where be his stories now?' Learn, from the deep oblivion into which poor Rathumus's literary efforts have fallen, the utter mockery and uselessness of so-called *fame!*"

"But there must be a certain pleasure in it while you're alive to enjoy it," said Lord Winsleigh. "Surely you derive some little satisfaction from your celebrity, Mr. Lovelace?"

Beau broke into a laugh, mellow, musical, and hearty.

"A satisfaction shared with murderers, thieves, divorced women, dynamiters, and other notorious people in general," he said. "They're all talked about—so am I. They all get written about—so do I. My biography is always being carefully compiled by newspaper authorities, to the delight of the reading public. Only the other day I learned for the first time that my father was a greengrocer, who went in for selling coals by the half-hundred and thereby made his fortune—my mother was an unsuccessful oyster-woman who failed ignominiously at Margate—moreover, I've a great many brothers and sisters of tender age whom I absolutely refuse to assist. I've got a wife somewhere, whom my literary success causes me to despise—and I have deserted children. I'm charmed with the accuracy of the newspapers—and I wouldn't contradict them for the world, —I find my biographies so original! They are the result of that celebrity which Winsleigh thinks enjoyable."

"But assertions of that kind are libels," said Errington. "You could prosecute."

"Too much trouble!" declared Beau. "Besides, five journals have disclosed the name of the town where I was born, and as they all contradict each other, and none of them are right, any contradiction on *my* part would be superfluous!"

They laughed,—and at that moment Lady Winsleigh joined them.

"Are you not catching cold, Thelma?" she inquired sweetly. "Sir Philip, you ought to make her put on something warm,—I find the air growing chilly."

At that moment the ever-ready Sir Francis Lennox approached with a light woolen wrap he had found in the hall.

" Permit me ! " he said gently, at the same time adroitly throwing it over Thelma's shoulders.

She colored a little,—she did not care for his attention, but she could not very well ignore it without seeming to be discourteous. So she murmured, " Thank you ! " and, rising from her chair, addressed Lady Winsleigh.

" If you feel cold, Clara, you will like some tea," she said. " Shall we go indoors, where it is ready ? "

Lady Winsleigh assented with some eagerness,—and the two beautiful women—the one dark, the other fair—walked side by side across the lawn into the house, their arms round each other's waists as they went.

" Two queens—and yet not rivals ? " half queried Lovelace, as he watched them disappearing.

" Their thrones are secure ! " returned Sir Philip gaily.

The others were silent. Lord Winsleigh's thoughts, whatever they were, deepened the lines of gravity on his face ; and George Lorimer, as he got up from his couch on the grass, caught a fleeting expression in the brown eyes of Sir Francis Lennox that struck him with a sense of unpleasantness. But he quickly dismissed the impression from his mind, and went to have a quiet smoke in the shrubbery.

CHAPTER XXIII.

" La rose du jardin, comme tu sais, dure peu, et la saison des roses est bien vite écoulée ! "—SAADI.

THELMA took her friend Lady Winsleigh to her own boudoir, a room which had been the particular pride of Sir Philip's mother. The walls were decorated with panels of blue silk in which were woven flowers of gold and silver thread,—and the furniture, bought from an old palace in Milan, was of elaborately carved wood inlaid with ivory and silver. Here a *tête-à-tête* tea was served for the two ladies, both of whom were somewhat fatigued by the pleasures of the day. Lady Winsleigh declared she must have some rest, or she would be quite unequal to the gaieties of the approaching evening, and Thelma herself was not sorry to escape for a little from her duties as hostess,—so the two remained together for some time in earnest conversation.

and Lady Winsleigh then and there confided to Thelma what she had heard reported concerning Sir Philip's intimate acquaintance with the burlesque actress, Violet Vere. And they were both so long absent that, after a while, Errington began to miss his wife, and, growing impatient, went in search of her. He entered the boudoir, and, to his surprise, found Lady Winsleigh there quite alone.

"Where is Thelma?" he demanded.

"She seems not very well—a slight headache or something of that sort—and has gone to lie down," replied Lady Winsleigh, with a faint trace of embarrassment in her manner. "I think the heat has been too much for her."

"I'll go and see after her,"—and he turned promptly to leave the room.

"Sir Philip!" called Lady Winsleigh. He paused and looked back.

"Stay one moment," continued her ladyship softly. "I have been for a long time so very anxious to say something to you in private. Please let me speak now. You—you know "—here she cast down her lustrous eyes—" before you went to Norway I—I was very foolish,——"

"Pray do not recall it," he said with kindly gravity. "*I* have forgotten it."

"That is so good of you!" and a flush of color warmed her delicate cheeks. "For if you have forgotten, you have also forgiven?"

"Entirely!" answered Errington,—and touched by her plaintive, self-reproachful manner and trembling voice, he went up to her and took her hands in his own. "Don't think of the past, Clara! Perhaps I also was to blame a little—I'm quite willing to think I was. Flirtation's a dangerous amusement at best." He paused as he saw two bright tears on her long, silky lashes, and in his heart felt a sort of remorse that he had ever permitted himself to think badly of her. "We are the best of friends now, Clara," he continued cheerfully, "and I hope we may always remain so. You can't imagine how glad I am that you love my Thelma!"

"Who would not love her!" sighed Lady Winsleigh gently, as Sir Philip released her hands from his warm clasp,—then raising her tearful eyes to his she added wistfully, "You must take great care of her, Philip—she is so sensitive,—I always fancy an unkind word would kill her."

"She'll never hear one from me!" he returned, with so

tender and earnest a look on his face, that Lady Winsleigh's heart ached for jealousy. " I must really go and see how she is. She's been exerting herself too much to-day. Excuse me ! " and with a courteous smile and bow he left the room with a hurried and eager step.

Alone, Lady Winsleigh smiled bitterly. " Men are all alike ! " she said half aloud. " Who would think he was such a hypocrite ? Fancy his dividing his affection between two such contrasts as Thelma and Violet Vere ! However, there's no accounting for tastes. As for man's fidelity, I wouldn't give a straw for it—and for his morality——! " She finished the sentence with a scornful laugh, and left the boudoir to return to the rest of the company.

Errington, meanwhile, knocked softly at the door of his wife's bedroom—and receiving no answer, turned the handle noiselessly and went in. Thelma lay on the bed, dressed as she was, her cheek resting on her hand, and her face partially hidden. Her husband approached on tiptoe, and lightly kissed her forehead. She did not stir,—she appeared to sleep profoundly.

" Poor girl ! " he thought, " she's tired out, and no wonder, with all the bustle and racket of these people ! A good thing if she can rest a little before the evening closes in."

And he stole quietly out of the room, and meeting Britta on the stairs told her on no account to let her mistress be disturbed till it was time for the illumination of the grounds. Britta promised,—Britta's eyes were red—one would almost have fancied she had been crying. But Thelma was not asleep—she had felt her husband's kiss,— her heart had beat as quickly as the wing of a caged wild bird at his warm touch,—and now he had gone she turned and pressed her lips ,passionately on the pillow where his hand had leaned. Then she rose languidly from the bed, and, walking slowly to the door, locked it against all comers. Presently she began to pace the room up and down,—up and down,—her face was very white and weary, and every now and then a shuddering sigh broke from her lips.

" Can I believe it ? Oh no !—I cannot—I will not ! " she murmured. " There must be some mistake—Clara has heard wrongly." She sighed again. " Yet—if it is so,— he is not to blame—it is I—I who have failed to please him. Where—how have I failed ? "

A pained, puzzled look filled her grave blue eyes, and she stopped in her walk to and fro.

"It cannot be true!" she said half aloud,—"it is altogether unlike him. Though Clara says—and she has known him so long!—Clara says he loved *her* once—long before he saw me—my poor Philip!—he must have suffered by that love!—perhaps that is why he thought life so wearisome when he first came to the Altenfjord—ah! the Altenfjord!"

A choking sob rose in her throat—but she repressed it. "I must try not to weary him," she continued softly—"I must have done so in some way, or he would not be tired. But as for what I have heard,—it is not for me to ask him questions. I would not have him think that I mistrust him. No—there is some fault in me—something he does not like, or he would never go to——" She broke off and stretched out her hands with a sort of wild appeal. "Oh, Philip! my darling!" she exclaimed in a sobbing whisper. "I always knew I was not worthy of you—but I thought, —I hoped my love would make amends for all my shortcomings!"

Tears rushed into her eyes, and she turned to a little arched recess, shaded by velvet curtains—her oratory— where stood an exquisite white marble statuette of the Virgin and Child. There she knelt for some minutes, her face hidden in her hands, and when she rose she was quite calm, though very pale. She freshened her face with cold water, rearranged her disordered hair,—and then went downstairs, thereby running into the arms of her husband who was coming up again to look, as he said, at his "Sleeping Beauty."

"And here she is!" he exclaimed joyously. "Have you rested enough, my pet?"

"Indeed, yes!" she answered gently. "I am ashamed to be so lazy. Have you wanted me, Philip?"

"I always want you," he declared. "I am never happy without you."

She smiled and sighed. "You say that to please me," she said half wistfully.

"I say it because it is true!" he asserted proudly, putting his arm round her waist and escorting her in this manner down the great staircase. "And you know it, you sweet witch! You're just in time to see the lighting up of the grounds. There'll be a good view from the picture-gallery

22

—lots of the people have gone in there—you'd better come too, for it's chilly outside."

She followed him obediently, and her reappearance among her guests was hailed with enthusiasm,—Lady Winsleigh being particular effusive, almost too much so.

"Your headache has quite gone, dearest, hasn't it?" she inquired sweetly.

Thelma eyed her gravely. "I did not suffer from the headache, Clara," she said. "I was a little tired, but I am quite rested now."

Lady Winsleigh bit her lips rather vexedly, but said no more, and at that moment exclamations of delight broke from all assembled at the brilliant scene that suddenly flashed upon their eyes. Electricity, that radiant sprite whose magic wand has lately been bent to the service of man, had in less than a minute played such dazzling pranks in the gardens that they resembled the fabled treasure-houses discovered by Aladdin. Every tree glittered with sparkling clusters of red, blue, and green light—every flower-bed was bordered with lines and circles of harmless flame, and the fountains tossed up tall columns of amber, rose, and amethyst spray against the soft blue darkness of the sky, in which a lustrous golden moon had just risen. The brilliancy of the illuminations showed up several dark figures strolling in couples about the grounds—romantic persons evidently, who were not to be persuaded to come indoors, even for the music of the band, which just then burst forth invitingly through the open windows of the picture-gallery.

Two of these pensive wanderers were Marcia Van Clupp and Lord Algernon Masherville,—and Lord Algy was in a curiously sentimental frame of mind, and weak withal, " comme une petite queue d' agneau affligè." He had taken a good deal of soda and brandy for his bilious headache, and, physically, he was much better,—but mentally he was not quite his ordinary self. By this it must not be understood that he was at all unsteadied by the potency of his medicinal tipple—he was simply in a bland humor—that peculiar sort of humor which finds strange and mystic beauty in everything, and contemplates the meanest trifles with emotions of large benevolence. He was conversational too, and inclined to quote poetry—this sort of susceptibleness often affects gentlemen after they have had an excellent dinner flavored with the finest Burgundy. Lord

Algy was as mild, as tame, and as flabby as a sleeping jelly-fish,—and in this inoffensive, almost tender mood of his, Marcia pounced upor him. She looked ravishingly pretty in the moonlight, with a white wrap thrown carelessly round her head and shoulders, and her bold, bird-like eyes sparkling with excitement (for who that knows the pleasure of sports, is not excited when the fox is nearly run to earth?), and she stood with him beside one of the smaller illuminated fountains, raising her small white hand every now and then to catch some of the rainbow drops, and then with a laugh she would shake them off her little pearly nails into the air again. Poor Masherville could not help gazing at her with a lack-lustre admiration in his pale eyes,—and Marcia, calculating every move in her own shrewd mind, saw it. She turned her head away with a petulant yet coquettish movement.

"My patience!" she exclaimed; "yew *kin* stare! Yew'll know me again when yew see me,—say?"

"I should know you anywhere," declared Masherville, nervously fumbling with the string of his eye-glass. "It's impossible to forget *your* face, Miss Marcia!"

She was silent,—and kept that face turned from him so long that the gentle little lord was surprised. He approached her more closely and took her hand—the hand that had played with the drops in the fountain. It was such an astonishingly small hand—so very fragile-looking and tiny, that he was almost for putting up his eye-glass to survey it, as if it were a separate object in a museum. But the faintest pressure of the delicate fingers he held startled him, and sent the most curious thrill through his body—and when he spoke he was in such a flutter that he scarcely knew what he was saying.

"Miss—Miss Marcia!" he stammered, "have—have I said—anything to—to offend you?"

Very slowly, and with seeming reluctance, she turned her head towards him, and—oh, thou mischievous Puck, that sometimes takest upon thee the semblance of Eros, what skill is thine! . . . there were tears in her eyes—real tears—bright, large tears that welled up and fell through her long lashes in the most beautiful, touching, and becoming manner! "And," thought Marcia to herself, "if I don't fetch him now, I never will!" Lord Algy was quite frightened—his poor brain grew more and more bewildered.

"Why—Miss Marcia! I say! Look here!" he mumbled in his extremity, squeezing her little hand tighter and tighter. "What—what *have* I done! Good gracious! You—you really mustn't cry, you know—I say—look here! Marcia! I wouldn't vex you for the world!"

"Yew bet yew wouldn't!" said Marcia, with slow and nasal plaintiveness. "I like that! That's the way yew English talk. But yew kin hang round a girl a whole season and make all her folks think badly of her—and—and —break her heart—yes—that's so!" Here she dried her eyes with a filmy lace handkerchief. "But don't *yew* mind me! I kin bear it. I kin worry through!" And she drew herself up with dignified resignation—while Lord Algy stared wildly at her, his feeble mind in a whirl. Presently she smiled most seductively, and looked up with her dark, tear-wet eyes to the moon.

"I guess it's a good night for lovers!" she said, sinking her ordinary tone to an almost sweet cadence. "But we're not of that sort, are we?"

The die was cast! She looked so charming—so irresistible, that Masherville lost all hold over his wits. Scarcely knowing what he did, he put his arm round her waist. Oh, what a warm, yielding waist! He drew her close to his breast, at the risk of breaking his most valuable eyeglass,—and felt his poor weak soul in a quiver of excitement at this novel and delicious sensation.

"We are—we are of that sort!" he declared courageously. "Why should you doubt it, Marcia?"

"I believe *yew* if *yew* say so," responded Marcia. "But I guess yew're only fooling me!"

"Fooling you!" Lord Algy was so surprised that he released her quite suddenly from his embrace—so suddenly that she was a little frightened. Was she to lose him, after all?

"Marcia," he continued mildly, yet with a certain manliness that did not ill become him. "I—I hope I am too much of—of a gentleman to—to '*fool*' any woman, least of all you, after I have, as you say, compromised you in society by my—my attentions. I—I have very little to offer you—but such as it is, is yours. In—in short, Marcia, I— I will try to make you happy if you can—can care for me enough to—to—marry me!"

Eureka! The game was won! A vision of Masherville Park, Yorkshire, that "well-timbered and highly desirable residence," as the auctioneers would describe it, flitted before Marcia's eyes,—and, filled with triumph, she went straight into her lordly wooer's arms, and kissed him with thorough transatlantic frankness. She was really grateful to him. Ever since she had come to England, she had plotted and schemed to become " my lady " with all the vigor of a purely republican soul,—and now at last, after hard fighting, she had won the prize for which her soul had yearned. She would in future belong to the English aristocracy—that aristocracy which her relatives in New York pretended to despise, yet openly flattered,—and with her arms round the trapped Masherville's neck, she foresaw the delight she would have in being toadied by them as far as toadyism could be made to go.

She is by no means presented to the reader as a favorable type of her nation—for, of course, every one knows there are plenty of sweet, unselfish, guileless American girls, who are absolutely incapable of such unblushing marriage-scheming as hers,—but what else could be expected from Marcia? Her grandfather, the navvy, had but recently become endowed with Pilgrim-Father Ancestry,—and her maternal uncle was a boastful pork-dealer in Cincinnati. It was her bounden duty to ennoble the family somehow,—surely, if any one had a right to be ambitious, she was that one! And wild proud dreams of her future passed through her brain, little Lord Algy quivered meekly under her kiss, and returned it with all the enthusiasm of which he was capable. One or two faint misgivings troubled him as to whether he had not been just a little too hasty in making a serious *bona fide* offer of marriage to the young lady by whose Pilgrim progenitors he was not deceived. He knew well enough what her antecedents were, and a faint shudder crossed him as he thought of the pork-dealing uncle, who would, by marriage, become *his* uncle also. He had long been proud of the fact that the house of Masherville had never, through the course of centuries, been associated, even in the remotest manner with trade—and now !——

" Yet, after all," he mused, " the Marquis of Londonderry openly advertises himself as a coal-merchant, and the brothers-in-law of the Princess Louise are in the wine trade and stock-broking business,—and all the old knightly blood of England is mingling itself by choice with that of the lowest commoners—what's the use of my remaining aloof, and refusing to go with the spirit of the age? Besides, Marcia loves me, and it's pleasant to be loved !"

Poor Lord Algy. He certainly thought there could be no question about Marcia's affection for him. He little dreamed that it was to his title and position she had become so deeply attached,—he could not guess that after he had married her there would be no more Lord Masherville worth mentioning—that that individual, once independent, would be entirely swallowed up and lost in the dashing personality of Lady Masherville, who would rule her husband as with a rod of iron.

He was happily ignorant of his future, and he walked in the gardens for some time with his arm round Marcia's waist, in a very placid and romantic frame of mind. By-and-by he escorted her into the house, where the dancing was in full swing—and she, with a sweet smile, bidding him wait for her in the refreshment-room, sought for and found her mother, who as usual, was seated in a quiet corner with Mrs. Rush-Marvelle, talking scandal.

" Well? " exclaimed these two ladies, simultaneously and breathlessly.

Marcia's eyes twinkled. " Guess he came in as gently as a lamb ! " she said.

They understood her. Mrs. Rush-Marvelle rose from her chair in her usual stately and expensive manner.

" I congratulate you, my dear ! " kissing Marcia affectionately on both cheeks. " Bruce Errington would have been a better match,—but, under the circumstances, Masherville is really about the best thing you could do. You'll find him quite easy to manage ! " This with an air as though she were recommending a quiet pony.

" That's so ! " said Marcia carelessly, " I guess we'll pull together somehow. Mar-ma," to her mother—" yew kin turn on the news to all the folks yew meet—the more talk the better ! I'm not partial to secrets ! " And with a laugh, she turned away.

Then Mrs. Van Clupp laid her plump, diamond-ringed hand on that of her dear friend, Mrs. Marvelle.

" You have managed the whole thing beautifully," she said, with a grateful heave of her ample bosom. " Such a clever creature as you are ! " She dropped her voice to a mysterious whisper. " You shall have that cheque to-morrow, my love ! "

Mrs. Rush-Marvelle pressed her fingers cordially.

" Don't hurry yourself about it ! "—she returned in the same confidential tone. " I dare say you'll want me to arrange the wedding and the 'crush' afterwards. **I can wait till then.**"

"No, no! that's a separate affair," declared **Mrs. Van Clupp.** "I must insist on your taking the promised **two** hundred. You've been really so *very* energetic!"

"Well, I *have* worked rather hard," said Mrs. Marvelle, with modest self-consciousness. "You see nowadays it's so difficult to secure suitable husbands for the girls who ought to have them. Men *are* such slippery creatures!"

She sighed—and Mrs. Van Clupp echoed the sigh,— and then these two ladies,—the nature of whose intimacy may now be understood by the discriminating reader,— went together to search out those of their friends and acquaintances who were among the guests that night, and to announce to them (in the strictest confidence, of course!) the delightful news of "dear Marcia's engagement." Thelma heard of it, and went at once to proffer her congratulations to Marcia in person.

"I hope you will be very, very happy!" she said simply, yet with such grave earnestness in her look and voice that the "Yankee gel" was touched to a certain softness and seriousness not at all usual with her, and became so winning and gentle to Lord Algy that he felt in the seventh heaven of delight with his new position as affianced lover to so charming a creature.

Meanwhile George Lorimer and Pierre Duprèz were chatting together in the library. It was very quiet there, —the goodly rows of books, the busts of poets and philosophers,—the large, placid features of the Pallas Athene crowning an antique pedestal,—the golden pipes of the organ gleaming through the shadows,—all these gave a solemn, almost sacred aspect to the room. The noise of the dancing and festivity in the distant picture-gallery did not penetrate here, and Lorimer sate at the organ, drawing out a few plaintive strains from its keys as he talked.

"It's your fancy, Pierre," he said slowly. "Thelma may be a little tired to-day, perhaps—but I know she's perfectly happy."

"I think not so," returned Duprèz. "She has not the brightness—the angel look— *les yeux d' enfant,*—that we beheld in her at that far Norwegian Fjord. Britta **is** anxious for her."

Lorimer looked up, and smiled a little.

"Britta? It's always Britta with you, *mon cher!* One would think——" he paused and laughed.

"Think what you please!" exclaimed Duprèz, with a defiant snap of his fingers. "I would not give that little person for all the *grandes dames* here to-day! She is charming—and she is *true!—Ma foi!* to be true to any one is a virtue in this age! I tell you, my good boy, there is something sorrowful—heavy—on *la belle* Thelma's mind—and Britta, who sees her always, feels it—but she cannot speak. One thing I will tell you—it is a pity she is so fond of Miladi Winsleigh."

"Why?" asked Lorimer, with some eagerness.

"Because——" he stopped abruptly as a white figure suddenly appeared at the doorway, and a musical voice addressed them—

"Why, what are you both doing here, away from everybody?" and Thelma smiled as she approached. "You are hermits, or you are lazy! People are going in to supper. Will you not come also?"

"*Ma foi!*" exclaimed Duprèz; "I had forgotten! I have promised your most charming mother, *cher* Lorimer, to take her in to this same supper. I must fly upon the wings of chivalry!"

And with a laugh, he hurried off, leaving Thelma and Lorimer alone together. She sank rather wearily into a chair near the organ, and looked at him.

"Play me something!" she said softly.

A strange thrill quivered through him as he met her eyes —the sweet, deep, earnest eyes of the woman he loved. For it was no use attempting to disguise it from himself —he loved her passionately, wildly, hopelessly; as he had loved her from the first.

Obedient to her wish, his fingers wandered over the organ-keys in a strain of solemn, weird, yet tender melancholy—the grand, rich notes pealed forth sobbingly—and she listened, her hands clasped idly in her lap. Presently he changed the theme to one of more heart-appealing passion—and a strange wild minor air, like the rushing of the wind across the mountains, began to make itself heard through the subdued rippling murmur of his improvised accompaniment. To his surprise and fear, she started up, pressing her hands against her ears.

"Not that—not that song, my friend!" she cried, almost

imploringly. "Oh, it will break my heart! Oh, the Altenfjord!" And she gave way to a passion of weeping.

"Thelma! Thelma!" and poor Lorimer, rising from the organ, stood gazing at her in piteous dismay,—every nerve in his body wrung to anguish by the sound of her sobbing. A mad longing seized him to catch her in his arms,—to gather her and her sorrows, whatever they were, to his heart!—and he had much ado to restrain himself.

"Thelma," he presently said, in a gentle voice that trembled just a little, "Thelma, what is troubling you? You call me your brother—give me a brother's right to your confidence." He bent over her and took her hand. "I—I can't bear to see you cry like this! Tell me—what's the matter? Let me fetch Philip."

She looked up with wild wet eyes and quivering lips.

"Oh no—no!" she murmured, in a tone of entreaty and alarm. "Do not,—Philip must not know—I do wish him always to see me bright and cheerful—and—it is nothing! It is that I heard something which grieved me——"

"What was it?" asked Lorimer, remembering Duprèz's recent remarks.

"Oh, I would not tell you!" she said eagerly, drying her eyes and endeavoring to smile, "because I am sure it was a mistake, and all wrong—and I was foolish to fancy that such a thing could be, even for a moment. But when one does not know the world, it seems cruel——"

"Thelma, what do you mean?" and George surveyed her in some perplexity. "If any one's been bothering or vexing you, just you tell Phil all about it. Don't have any secrets from him,—he'll soon put everything straight, whatever it is."

She shook her head slightly. "Ah, you do not understand!" she said pathetically, "how should you? Because you have not given your life away to any one, and it is all different with you. But when you do love—if you are at all like me,—you will be so anxious to always seem worthy of love—and you will hide all your griefs away from your beloved,—so that your constant presence shall not seem tiresome. And I would not for all the world trouble Philip with my silly fancies—because then he might grow more weary still——"

"*Weary!*" interrupted Lorimer, in an accent of emphatic surprise. "Why, you don't suppose Phil's tired of you,

Thelma? That *is* nonsense indeed! He worships you! Who's been putting such notions into your head?"

She rose from her chair quite calm and very pale, and laid her two trembling hands in his.

"Ah, you also will mistake me," she said, with touching sweetness, "like so many others who think me strange in my speech and manner. I am sorry I am not like other women,—but I cannot help it. What I do wish you to under-stand is that I never suppose anything against my Philip —he is the noblest and best of men! And you must promise not to tell him that I was so foolish as to cry just now because you played that old song I sang to you both so often in Norway—it was because I felt a little sad—but it was only a fancy,—and I would not have him troubled with such things. Will you promise?"

"But what has made you sad?" persisted Lorimer, still puzzled.

"Nothing—nothing indeed," she answered, with almost feverish earnestness. "You yourself are sometimes sad, and can you tell why?"

Lorimer certainly could have told why,—but he remained silent, and gently kissed the little hands he held.

"Then I mustn't tell Philip of your sadness?" he asked softly, at last. "But will you tell him yourself, Thelma? Depend upon it, it's much better to have no secrets from him. The least grief of yours would affect him more than the downfall of a kingdom. You know how dearly he loves you!"

"Yes—I know!" she answered, and her eyes brightened slowly. "And that is why I wish him always to see me happy!" She paused, and then added in a lower tone, "I would rather die, my friend, than vex him for one hour!"

George still held her hands and looked wistfully in her face. He was about to speak again, when a cold, courteous voice interrupted them.

"Lady Errington, may I have the honor of taking you in to supper?"

It was Sir Francis Lennox. He had entered quite noise-lessly—his footsteps making no sound on the thick velvet-pile carpet, and he stood quite close to Lorimer, who dropped Thelma's hands hastily and darted a suspicious glance at the intruder. But Sir Francis was the very pic-ture of unconcerned and bland politeness, and offered Thelma his arm with the graceful ease of an accomplished courtier. She was, perforce, compelled to accept it—and she was slightly confused, though she could not have told why.

"Sir Philip has been looking everywhere for you," continued Sir Francis amicably. "And for you also," he added, turning slightly to Lorimer. "I trust I've not abruptly broken off a pleasant *tête-à-tête*?"

Lorimer colored hotly. "Not at all," he said rather brusquely. "I've been strumming on the organ, and Lady Errington has been good enough to listen to me."

"You do not *strum*," said Thelma, with gentle reproach. "You play very beautifully."

"Ah! a charming accomplishment!" observed Sir Francis, with his under-glance and covert smile, as they all three wended their way out of the library. "I regret I have never had time to devote myself to acquiring some knowledge of the arts. In music I am a positive ignoramus! I can hold my own best in the field."

"Yes, you're a great adept at hunting, Lennox," remarked Lorimer suddenly, with something sarcastic in his tone. "I suppose the quarry never escapes you?"

"Seldom!" returned Sir Francis coolly. "Indeed, I think I may say, never!"

And with that, he passed into the supper-room, elbowing a way for Thelma, till he succeeded in placing her near the head of the table, where she was soon busily occupied in entertaining her guests and listening to their chatter; and Lorimer, looking at her once or twice, saw, to his great relief, that all traces of her former agitation had disappeared, leaving her face fair and radiant as a spring morning.

CHAPTER XXIV.

"A generous fierceness dwells with innocence,
And conscious virtue is allowed some pride."

DRYDEN.

THE melancholy days of autumn came on apace, and by-and-by the Manor was deserted. The Bruce-Errington establishment removed again to town, where business, connected with his intending membership for Parliament, occupied Sir Philip from morning till night. The old insidious feeling of depression returned and hovered over Thelma's mind like a black bird of ill omen, and though she did her best to shake it off she could not succeed. People began to notice her deepening seriousness and the wistful melancholy of her blue eyes, and made their remarks thereon when they saw her at Marcia Van Clupp's wedding, an event which came off brilliantly at the commencement of November, and which was almost entirely presided over by Mrs. Rush-Marvelle. That far-seeing matron had indeed urged on the wedding by every delicate expedient possible.

"Long engagements are a great mistake," she told Marcia,—then, in a warning undertone she added, "Men are capricious nowadays,—they're all so much in demand, —better take Masherville while he's in the humor."

Marcia accepted this hint and took him,—and Mrs. Rush-Marvelle heaved a sigh of relief when she saw the twain safely married, and off to the Continent on their honeymoon-trip,—Marcia all sparkling and triumphant,—Lord Algy tremulous and feebly ecstatic.

"Thank Heaven *that's* over!" she said to her polite and servile husband. "I never had such a troublesome business in my life! That girl's been nearly two seasons on my hands, and I think five hundred guineas not a bit too much for all I've done."

"Not a bit—not a bit!" agreed Mr. Marvelle warmly. "Have they—have they——" here he put on a most benevolent side-look—"quite settled with you, my dear?"

"Every penny," replied Mrs. Marvelle calmly. "Old Van Clupp paid me the last hundred this morning. And poor Mrs. Van Clupp is so *very* grateful!" She sighed placidly, and appeared to meditate. Then she smiled sweetly and, approaching Mr. Marvelle, patted his shoulder caressingly. "I think we'll do the Italian lakes, dear— what do you say?"

"Charming—charming!" declared, not her lord and master, but her slave and vassal. "Nothing could be more delightful!"

And to the Italian lakes accordingly they went. A great many people were out of town,—all who had leisure and money enough to liberate themselves from the approaching evils of an English winter, had departed or were departing,—Beau Lovelace had gone to Como,—George Lorimer had returned with Duprèz to Paris, and Thelma had very few visitors except Lady Winsleigh, who was more often with her now than ever. In fact, her ladyship was more like one of the Errington household than any-

thing else,—she came so frequently and stayed so long.
She seemed sincerely attached to Thelma,—and Thelma
herself, too single-hearted· and simple to imagine that such
affection could be feigned, gave her in return, what Lady
Winsleigh had never succeeded in winning from any
woman,—a pure, trusting, and utterly unsuspecting love,
such as she would have lavished on a twin-born sister.
But there was one person who was not deceived by Lady
Winsleigh's charm of manner, and grace of speech. This
was Britta. Her keen eyes flashed a sort of unuttered defiance into her ladyship's beautiful, dark languishing ones
—she distrusted her, and viewed the intimacy between her
and the "Fröken" with entire disfavor. Once she ventured to express something of her feeling on the matter to
Thelma—but Thelma had looked so gently wondering and
reproachful that Britta had not courage to go on.

"I am so sorry, Britta," said her mistress, "that you do
not like Lady Winsleigh—because I am very fond of her.
You must try to like her for my sake."

But Britta pursed her lips and shook her head obstinately. However, she said no more at the time, and
decided within herself to wait and watch the course of
events. And in the meantime she became very intimate
with Lady Winsleigh's maid, Louise Rénaud, and Briggs,
and learned from these two domestic authorities many
things which greatly tormented and puzzled her little
brain,—things over which she pondered deeply without arriving at any satisfactory conclusion.

On her return to town, Thelma had been inexpressibly
shocked at the changed appearance of her husband's secretary, Edward Neville. At first she scarcely knew him, he
had altered so greatly. Always inclined to stoop, his
shoulders were now bent as by the added weight of twenty
years—his hair, once only grizzled, was now quite grey—
his face was deeply sunken and pale, and his eyes by contrast looked large and wild, as though some haunting
thought were driving him to madness. He shrank so nervously from her gaze, that she began to fancy he must have
taken some dislike to her,—and though she delicately refrained from pressing questions upon him personally, she
spoke to her husband about him, with real solicitude. "Is
Mr. Neville working too hard?" she asked one day. "He
looks very ill."

Her remark seemed to embarrass Philip,—he colored and seemed confused.

"Does he? Oh, I suppose he sleeps badly. Yes, I remember, he told me so. You see, the loss of his wife has always preyed on his mind—he never loses hope of—of—that is—he is always trying to—you know!—to get her back again."

"But do you think he will ever find her?" asked Thelma. "I thought you said it was a hopeless case?"

"Well—I think so, certainly—but, you see, it's no good dashing his hopes—one never knows—she *might* turn up any day—it's a sort of chance!"

"I wish I could help him to search for her," she said compassionately. "His eyes do look so full of sorrow," she paused and added musingly, "almost like Sigurd's eyes sometimes."

"Oh, he's not losing his wits," said Philip hastily, "he's quite patient, and—and all that sort of thing. Don't bother about him, Thelma, he's all right!"

And he fumbled hastily with some papers, and began to talk of something else. His embarrassed manner caused her to wonder a little at the time as to the reason of it,—but she had many other things to think about, and she soon forgot a conversation that might have proved a small guiding-link in the chain of events that were soon about to follow quickly one upon another, shaking her life to its very foundation. Lady Winsleigh found it almost impossible to get her on the subject of the burlesque actress, Violet Vere, and Sir Philip's supposed admiration for that notorious stage-siren.

"I do not believe it," she said firmly, "and you—you must not believe it either, Clara. For wherever you heard it, it is wrong. We should dishonor Philip by such a thought—you are his friend, and I am his wife—we are not the ones to believe anything against him, even if it could be proved—and there are no proofs."

"My dear," responded her ladyship easily. "You can get proofs for yourself if you like. For instance, ask Sir Philip how often he has seen Miss Vere lately,—and hear what he says."

Thelma colored deeply. "I would not question my husband on such a subject," she said proudly.

"Oh well! if you are so fastidious!" And Lady Winsleigh shrugged her shoulders.

" I am not fastidious," returned Thelma, " only I do wish to be worthy of his love,—and I should not be so if I doubted him. No, Clara, I will trust him to the end."

Clara Winsleigh drew nearer to her, and took her hand.

" Even if he were unfaithful to you ? " she asked in a low, impressive tone.

" Unfaithful ! " Thelma uttered the word with a little cry. " Clara, dear Clara, you must not say such a word ! Unfaithful ! That means that my husband would love some one more than me !—ah ! that is impossible ! "

" Suppose it were possible ? " persisted Lady Winsleigh, with a cruel light in her dark eyes. " Such things have been ! "

Thelma stood motionless, a deeply mournful expression on her fair, pale face. She seemed to think for a moment, then she spoke.

" I would never believe it ! " she said solemnly. " Never, unless I heard it from his own lips, or saw it in his own writing, that he was weary of me, and wanted me no more."

" And then ? "

" Then "—she drew a quick breath—" I should know what to do. But, Clara, you must understand me well, even if this were so, I should never blame him—no—not once ! "

" Not blame him ? " cried Lady Winsleigh impatiently. " Not blame him for infidelity ? "

A deep blush swept over her face at the hated word " infidelity," but she answered steadily—

" No. Because, you see, it would be my fault, not his. When you hold a flower in your hand for a long time, till all its fragrance has gone, and you drop it because it no longer smells sweetly—you are not to blame—it is natural you should wish to have something fresh and fragrant,—it is the flower's fault because it could not keep its scent long enough to please you. Now, if Philip were to love me no longer, I should be like that flower, and how would *he* be to blame ? He would be good as ever, but I—I should have ceased to seem pleasant to him—that is all ! "

She put this strange view of the case quite calmly, as if it were the only solution to the question. Lady Winsleigh heard her, half in contemptuous amusement, half in dismay. " What can I do with such a woman as this," she thought. " And fancy Lennie imagining for a moment that *he* could have any power over her ' " Aloud, she said—

" Thelma, you're the oddest creature going—a regular heathen child from Norway! You've set up your husband as an idol, and you're always on your knees before him. It's awfully sweet of you, but it's quite absurd, all the same. Angelic wives always get the worst of it, and so you'll see! Haven't you heard that?"

" Yes, I have heard it,' she answered, smiling a little. " But only since I came to London. In Norway, it is taught to women that to be patient and obedient is best for every one. It is not so here. But I am not an angelic wife, Clara, and so the ' worst of it ' will not apply to me. Indeed, I do not know of any ' worst ' that I would not bear for Philip's sake."

Lady Winsleigh studied the lovely face, eloquent with love and truth, for some moments in silence ;—a kind of compunction pricked her conscience. Why destroy all that beautiful faith? Why wound that grandly trusting nature? The feeling was but momentary.

" Philip *does* run after the Vere," she said to herself— " it's true, there's no mistake about it, and she ought to know of it. But she won't believe without proofs—what proofs can I get, I wonder?" And her scheming brain set to work to solve this problem.

In justice to her, it must be admitted, she had a good deal of seeming truth on her side. Sir Philip's name *had* somehow got connected with that of the leading actress at the Brilliant, and more people than Lady Winsleigh began to make jocose whispering comments on his stage " *amour*," —comments behind his back, which he was totally unaware of. Nobody knew quite how the rumor had first been started. Sir Francis Lennox seemed to know a good deal about it, and he was an " intimate " of the " Vere " magic circle of attraction. And though they talked, no one ventured to say anything to Sir Philip himself ;—the only two among his friends who would have spoken out honestly were Beau Lovelace and Lorimer, and these were absent.

One evening, contrary to his usual custom, Sir Philip went out after the late dinner. Before leaving, he kissed his wife tenderly, and told her on no account to sit up for him—he and Neville were going to attend to a little matter of business which might detain them longer than they could calculate. After they had gone, Thelma resigned herself to a lonely evening, and, stirring the fire in the drawing-room to a cheerful blaze, she sat down beside it.

First, she amused herself by reading over some letters recently received from her father,—and then, yielding to a sudden fancy, she drew her spinning-wheel from the corner where it always stood, and set it in motion. She had little time for spinning now, but she never quite gave it up, and as the low, familiar whirring sound hummed pleasantly on her ears, she smiled, thinking how quaint and almost incongruous her simple implement of industry looked among all the luxurious furniture, and costly nick-nacks by which she was surrounded.

"I ought to have one of my old gowns on," she half murmured, glancing down at the pale-blue silk robe she wore, "I am too fine to spin!"

And she almost laughed as the wheel flew round swiftly under her graceful manipulations. Listening to its whirr, whirr, whirr, she scarcely heard a sudden knock at the street-door, and was quite startled when the servant, Morris, announced—

"Sir Francis Lennox!"

Surprised, she rose from her seat at the spinning-wheel with a slight air of hauteur. Sir Francis, who had never in his life seen a lady of title and fashion in London engaged in the primitive occupation of spinning, was entirely delighted with the picture before him,—the tall, lovely woman with her gold hair and shimmering blue draperies, standing with such stateliness beside the simple wooden wheel, the antique emblem of household industry. Instinctively he thought of Marguerite;—but Marguerite as a crowned queen, superior to all temptations of either man or fiend.

"Sir Philip is out," she said, as she suffered him to take her hand.

"So I was aware!" returned Lennox easily. "I saw him a little while ago at the door of the Brilliant Theatre."

She turned very pale,—then controlling the rapid beating of her heart by a strong effort, she forced a careless smile, and said bravely—

"Did you? I am very glad—for he will have some amusement there, perhaps, and that will do him good. He has been working so hard!"

She paused. He said nothing, and she went on more cheerfully still—

"Is it not a very dismal, wet evening! Yes!—and you must be cold. Will you have some tea?"

23

"Tha-anks!" drawled Sir Francis, staring at her admir-ingly. "If it's not too much trouble——"

"Oh no!" said Thelma. "Why should it be?" And she rang the bell and gave the order. Sir Francis sank lazily back in an easy chair, and stroked his moustache slowly. He knew that his random hit about the theatre had struck home,—but she allowed the arrow to pierce and possibly wound her heart without showing any outward sign of dis-composure. "A plucky woman!" he considered, and won-dered how he should make his next move. She, meanwhile, smiled at him frankly, and gave a light twirl to her spin-ning-wheel.

"You see!" she said, "I was amusing myself this evening by imagining that I was once more at home in Norway."

"Pray don't let me interrupt the amusement," he re-sponded, with a sleepy look of satisfaction shooting from beneath his eyelids. "Go on spinning, Lady Errington! . . . I've never seen any one spin before."

At that moment Morris appeared with the tea, and handed it to Sir Francis,—Thelma took none, and as the servant retired, she quietly resumed her occupation. There was a short silence, only broken by the hum of the wheel. Sir Francis sipped his tea with a meditative air, and studied the fair woman before him as critically as he would have studied a picture.

"I hope I'm not in your way?" he asked suddenly. She looked up surprised.

"Oh no—only I am sorry Philip is not here to talk to you. It would be so much pleasanter."

"Would it?" he murmured rather rather dubiously and smiling. "Well—I shall be quite contented if *you* will talk to me, Lady Errington!"

"Ah, but I am not at all clever in conversation," re-sponded Thelma quite seriously. "I am sure you, as well as many others, must have noticed that. I never do seem to say exactly the right thing to please everybody. Is it not very unfortunate?"

He laughed a little. "I have yet to learn in what way you do *not* please everybody," he said, dropping his voice to a low, caressing cadence. "Who, that sees you, does not admire—and—and love you?"

She met his languorous gaze without embarrassment,—

while the childlike openness of her regard confused and slightly shamed him.

"Admire me? Oh yes!" she said somewhat plaintively. "It is that of which I am so weary! Because God has made one pleasant in form and face,—to be stared at and whispered about, and have all one's dresses copied!—all that is so small and common and mean, and does vex me so much!"

"It is the penalty you pay for being beautiful," said Sir Francis slowly, wondering within himself at the extraordinary incongruity of a feminine creature who was actually tired of admiration.

She made no reply—the wheel went round faster than before. Presently Lennox set aside his emptied cup, and drawing his chair a little closer to hers, asked—

"When does Errington return?"

"I cannot tell you," she answered. "He said that he might be late. Mr. Neville is with him."

There was another silence. "Lady Errington," said Sir Francis abruptly—"pray excuse me—I speak as a friend, and in your interests,—how long is this to last?"

The wheel stopped. She raised her eyes,—they were grave and steady.

"I do not understand you," she returned quietly. "What is it that you mean?"

He hesitated—then went on, with lowered eyelids and a half-smile.

"I mean—what all our set's talking about—Errington's queer fancy for that actress at the Brilliant."

Thelma still gazed at him fixedly. "It is a mistake," she said resolutely, "altogether a mistake. And as you are his friend, Sir Francis, you will please contradict this report—which is wrong, and may do Philip harm. It has no truth in it at all——"

"No truth!" exclaimed Lennox. "It's true as Gospel! Lady Errington, I'm sorry for it—but your husband is deceiving you most shamefully!"

"How dare you say such a thing!" she cried, springing upright and facing him,—then she stopped and grew very pale—but she kept her eyes upon him. How bright they were! What a chilling pride glittered in their sea-blue depths!

"You are in error," she said coldly. "If it is wrong to visit this theatre you speak of, why are *you* so often seen

there—and why is not some harm said of *you?* It is not
your place to speak against my husband. It is shameful and
treacherous! You do forget yourself most wickedly!"

And she moved to leave the room. But Sir Francis interposed.

"Lady Errington," he said very gently, "don't be hard
upon me—pray forgive me! Of course I've no business
to speak—but how can I help it? When I hear every one
at the clubs discussing you, and pitying you, it's impossible to listen quite unmoved! I'm the least among your
friends, I know,—but I can't bear this sort of thing to go
on,—the whole affair will be dished up in the society papers
next!"

And he paced the room half impatiently,—a very well-
feigned expression of friendly concern and sympathy on
his features. Thelma stood motionless, a little bewildered
—her head throbbed achingly, and there was a sick sensation of numbness creeping about her.

"I tell you it is all wrong!" she repeated with an effort.
"I do not understand why these people at the clubs should
talk of me, or pity me. I do not need any pity! My husband is all goodness and truth,"—she stopped and gathered
courage as she went on. "Yes! he is better, braver, nobler
than all other men in the world, it seems to me! He gives
me all the joy of my life—each day and night I thank God
for the blessing of his love!"

She paused again. Sir Francis turned and looked at her
steadily. A sudden thought seemed to strike her, for she
advanced eagerly, a sweet color flushing the pallor of her
skin.

"You can do so much for me if you will!" she said, laying her hand on his arm. "You can tell all these people
who talk so foolishly that they are wrong,—tell them how
happy I am! And that my Philip has never deceived me
in any matter, great or small!"

"Never?" he asked with a slight sneer. "You are sure?"

"Sure!" she answered bravely. "He would keep nothing from me that it was necessary or good for me to know.
And I—oh! I might pass all my life in striving to please
him, and yet I should never, never be worthy of all his tenderness and goodness! And that he goes many times to a
theatre without me—what is it? A mere nothing—a trifle
to laugh at! It is not needful to tell me of such a small
circumstance!"

As she spoke she smiled—her form seemed to dilate with a sort of inner confidence and rapture.

Sir Francis stared at her half shamed,—half savage. The beautiful, appealing face, bright with simple trust, roused him to no sort of manly respect or forbearance,—the very touch of the blossom-white hand she had laid so innocently on his arm, stung his passion as with a lash—as he had said, he was fond of hunting—he had chased the unconscious deer all through the summer, and now that it had turned to bay with such pitiful mildness and sweet pleading, why not draw the knife across its slim throat without mercy?

"Really, Lady Errington!" he said at last sarcastically, "your wifely enthusiasm and confidence are indeed charming! But, unfortunately, the proofs are all against you. Truth is truth, however much you may wish to blind your eyes to its manifestations. I sincerely wish Sir Philip were present to hear your eloquent praises of him, instead of being where he most undoubtedly is,—in the arms of Violet Vere!"

As he said these words she started away from him and put her hands to her ears as though to shut out some discordant sound—her eyes glowed feverishly. A cold shiver shook her from head to foot.

"That is false—false!" she muttered in a low, choked voice. "How can you—how dare you?"

She ceased, and with a swaying, bewildered movement, as though she were blind, she fell senseless at his feet.

In one second he was kneeling beside her. He raised her head on his arm,—he gazed eagerly on her fair, still features. A dark contraction of his brows showed that his thoughts were not altogether righteous ones. Suddenly he laid her down again gently, and, springing to the door, locked it. Returning, he once more lifted her in a half-reclining position, and encircling her with his arms, drew her close to his breast and kissed her. He was in no hurry for her to recover—she looked very beautiful—she was helpless—she was in his power. The silvery ting-ling of the clock on the mantel-piece striking eleven startled him a little—he listened painfully—he thought he heard some one trying the handle of the door he had locked. Again—again he kissed those pale, unconscious lips! Presently, a slight shiver ran through her frame—she sighed, and a little moan escaped her. Gradually, as warmth and sensation returned

to her, she felt the pressure of his embrace, and murmured—

"Philip! Darling,—you have come back earlier,—I
thought——"

Here she opened her eyes and met those of Sir Francis,
who was eagerly bending over her. She uttered an exclamation of alarm, and strove to rise. He held her still more
closely.

"Thelma—dear, dearest Thelma! Let me comfort you,
—let me tell you how much I love you!"

And before she could divine his intent, he pressed his lips
passionately on her pale cheek. With a cry she tore herself violently from his arms and sprang to her feet, trembling
in every limb.

"What—what is this?" she exclaimed wrathfully. "Are
you mad?"

And still weak and confused from her recent attack of
faintness, she pushed back her hair from her brows and regarded him with a sort of puzzled horror.

He flushed deeply, and set his lips hard.

"I dare say I am," he answered, with a bitter laugh;
"in fact, I know I am! You see, I've betrayed my miserable secret. Will you forgive me, Lady Errington—
Thelma?" He drew nearer to her, and his eyes darkened
with restrained passion. "Matchless beauty!—adorable
woman, as you are!—will you not pardon my crime, if
crime it be—the crime of loving you? For I do love you!
—Heaven only knows how utterly and desperately!"

She stood mute, white, almost rigid, with that strange
look of horror frozen, as it were, upon her features. Em-
boldened by her silence, he approached and caught her
hand,—she wrenched it from his grasp and motioned him
from her with a gesture of such royal contempt that he
quailed before her. All suddenly the flood-gates of her
speech were loosened,—the rising tide of burning indignation that in its very force had held her dumb and motionless, now broke forth unrestrainedly.

"O God!" she cried impetuously, a magnificent glory of
disdain flashing in her jewel-like eyes, "what *thing* is this
that calls itself a man?—this thief of honor,—this pretended friend? What have I done, sir, that you should
put such deep disgrace as your so-called *love* upon me?—
what have I *seemed*, that you thus dare to outrage me by
the pollution of your touch? I,—the wife of the noblest

gentleman in the lan⌐! Ah!" and she drew a long breath
—"and it is you who speak against my husband—*you!*
She smiled scornfully,—then with more calmness continued
—" You will leave my house, sir, at once! . . . and
never presume to enter it again!"

And she stepped towards the bell. He looked at her with
an evil leer.

" Stop a moment!" he said coolly. " Just one moment
before you ring. Pray consider! The servant cannot possibly enter, as the door is locked."

" You *dared* to lock the door!" she exclaimed, a sudden
fear chilling her heart as she remembered similar manœuvres on the part of the Reverend Mr. Dyceworthy—
then another thought crossed her mind, and she began to
retreat towards a large painted panel of " Venus " disport-
ing among cupids and dolphins in the sea. Sir Francis
sprang to her side, and caught her arm in an iron grip—his
face was aflame with baffled spite and vindictiveness.

" Yes, I *dared!*" he muttered with triumphant malice.
" And I dared do more than that! You lay unconscious in
my arms,—you beautiful, bewitching Thelma, and I kissed
you—ay! fifty times! You can never undo those kisses!
You can never forget that *my* lips, as well as your husband's, have rested on yours—I have had that much joy
that shall never be taken away from me! And if I choose,
even now,"—and he gripped her more closely—" yes, even
now I will kiss you, in spite of you!—who is to prevent
me? I will force you to love me, Thelma——"

Driven to bay, she struck him with all her force in the
face, across the eyes.

" Traitor!—liar!—coward!" she gasped breathlessly
" Let me go!"

Smarting with the pain of the blow, he unconsciously
loosened his grasp—she rushed to the " Venus " panel, and
to his utter discomfiture and amazement he saw it open and
close behind her. She disappeared suddenly and noiselessly as if by magic. With a fierce exclamation, he threw
his whole weight against that secret sliding door—it resisted all his efforts. He searched for the spring by which
it must have opened,—the whole panel was perfectly smooth
and apparently solid, and the painted " Venus " reclining
on her dolphin's back seemed as though she smiled mockingly at his rage and disappointment.

While he was examining it, he heard the sudden, sharp,

and continuous ringing of an electric bell somewhere in the house, and with a guilty flush on his face he sprang to the drawing-room door and unlocked it. He was just in time, for scarcely had he turned the key, when Morris made his appearance. That venerable servitor looked round the room in evident surprise.

" Did her ladyship ring ? " he inquired, his eyes roving everywhere in search of his mistress. Sir Francis collected his wits, and forced himself to seem composed.

" No," he said coolly. " *I* rang." He adopted this false-hood as a means of exit. " Call a hansom, will you ? "

And he sauntered easily into the hall, and got on his hat and great-coat. Morris was rather bewildered,—but, obedient to the command, blew the summoning cab-whistle, which was promptly answered. Sir Francis tossed him half a crown, and entered the vehicle, which clattered away with him in the direction of Cromwell Road. Stopping at a par-ticular house in a side street leading from thence, he bade the cabman wait,—and, ascending the steps, busied himself for some moments in scribbling something rapidly in pencil on a leaf of his note-book by the light of the hanging-lamp in the doorway. He then gave a loud knock, and inquired of the servant who answered it—

" Is Mr. Snawley-Grubbs in ? "

" Yes, sir,"—the reply came rather hesitatingly—" but he's having a party to-night."

And, in fact, the scraping of violins and the shuffle of dancing feet were distinctly audible overhead.

" Oh, well, just mention my name—Sir Francis Lennox. Say I will not detain him more than five minutes."

He entered, and was ushered into a small ante-room while the maid went to deliver her message. He caught sight of his own reflection in a round mirror over the man-tel-piece, and his face darkened as he saw a dull red ridge across his forehead—the mark of Thelma's well-directed blow,—the sign-manual of her scorn. A few minutes passed, and then there came in to him a large man in an ex-pensive dress-suit,—a man with a puffy, red, Silenus-like countenance—no other than Mr. Snawley-Grubbs, who hailed him with effusive cordiality.

" My dear, Sir Francis ! " he said in a rich, thick, uncom-fortable voice. " This is an unexpected pleasure ! Won't you come upstairs ? My girls are having a little informal dance—just among themselves and their own young friends

—quite simple,—in fact an unpretentious little affair!" And he rubbed his fat hands, on which twinkled two or three large diamond rings. "But we shall be charmed if you will join us!"

"Thanks, not this evening," returned Sir Francis. "It's rather too late. I should not have intruded upon you at this hour—but I thought you might possibly like this paragraph for the *Snake*."

And he held out with a careless air the paper on which he had scribbled but a few minutes previously. Mr. Snawley-Grubbs smiled,—and fixed a pair of elegant gold-rimmed eye-glasses on his inflamed crimson nose.

"I must tell you, though," he observed, before reading, "that it is too late for this week, at any rate. We've gone to press already."

"Never mind!" returned Sir Francis indifferently. "Next week will do as well."

And he furtively watched Mr. Snawley-Grubbs while he perused the pencilled scrawl. That gentleman, however, as Editor and Proprietor of the *Snake*—a new, but highly successful weekly " society " journal, was far too dignified and self-important to allow his countenance to betray his feelings. He merely remarked, as he folded up the little slip very carefully.

"Very smart! very smart, indeed! Authentic, of course?"

Sir Francis drew himself up haughtily. "You doubt my word?"

"Oh dear, no!" declared Mr. Snawley-Grubbs hastily, venturing to lay a soothing hand on Sir Francis's shoulder. "Your position, and all that sort of thing—— Naturally you *must* be able to secure correct information. You can't help it! I assure you the *Snake* is infinitely obliged to you for a great many well-written and socially exciting paragraphs. Only, you see, I myself should never have thought that so extreme a follower of the exploded old doctrine of *noblesse oblige*, as Sir Philip Bruce-Errington, would have started on such a new line of action at all. But, of course, we are all mortal!" And he shook his round, thick head with leering sagacity. "Well!" he continued after a pause. "This shall go in without fail next week, I promise you."

"You can send me a hundred copies of the issue," said

Sir Francis, taking up his hat to go. " I suppose you're not afraid of an action for libel ? "

Mr. Snawley-Grubbs laughed—nay, he roared,—the idea seemed so exquisitely suited to his sense of humor.

"Afraid? My dear fellow, there's nothing I should like better! It would establish the *Snake*, and make my fortune! I would even go to prison with pleasure. Prison, for a first-class misdemeanant, as I should most probably be termed, is perfectly endurable." He laughed again, and escorted Sir Francis to the street-door, where he shook hands heartily. " You are sure you won't come upstairs and join us? No? Ah, I see you have a cab waiting. Good-night, good-night ! "

And the Snawley-Grubbs door being closed upon him, Sir Francis re-entered his cab, and was driven straight to his bachelor lodgings in Piccadilly. He was in a better humor with himself now,—though he was still angrily conscious of a smart throbbing across the eyes, where Thelma's ringed hand had struck him. He found a brief note from Lady Winsleigh awaiting him. It ran as follows :—

" You're playing a losing game this time,—she will believe nothing without proofs—and even then it will be difficult. You had better drop the pursuit, I fancy. For once a woman's reputation will escape you ! "

He smiled bitterly as he read these last words.

" Not while a society paper exists ! " he said to himself. "As long as there are editors willing to accept the word of a responsible man of position, for any report, the chastest Diana that ever lived shall not escape calumny ! She wants proofs, does she? She shall have them—by Jove ! she shall ! "

And instead of going to bed, he went off to a bijou villa in St. John's Wood,—an elegantly appointed little place, which he rented and maintained,—and where the popular personage known as Violet Vere, basked in the very lap of luxury.

Meanwhile, Thelma paced up and down her own boudoir, into which she had escaped through the sliding panel which had baffled her admirer. Her whole frame trembled as she thought of the indignity to which she had been subjected during her brief unconsciousness,—her face burned with bitter shame,—she felt as if she were somehow poisonously infected by those hateful kisses of Lennox.—all her womanly and wifely instincts were outraged. Her first impulse was to tell he husband everything the instant he returned. It was she who had rung the bell which had startled Sir Francis, and she was surprised that her summons was not answered. She rang again, and Britta appeared.

" I wanted Morris," said Thelma quickly.

" He thought it was the drawing-room bell," responded Britta meekly, for her " Fröken " looked very angry. " I saw him in the hall just now, letting out Sir Francis Lennox."

" Has he gone? " demanded Thelma eagerly.

Britta's wonder increased. " Yes, Fröken !"

Thelma caught her arm. " Tell Morris never, never to let him inside the house again—*never !* " and her blue eyes flashed wrathfully. " He is a wicked man, Britta ! You do not know how wicked he is !"

" Oh yes, I do !" and Britta regarded her mistress very steadfastly. " I know quite well ! But, then, I must not speak ! If I dared, I could tell you some strange things, dear Fröken—but you will not hear me. You know you do not wish me to talk about your grand new friends, Fröken, but——" she paused timidly.

" Oh, Britta, dear ! " said Thelma affectionately taking her hand. " You know they are not so much my friends as the friends of Sir Philip,—and for this reason I must never listen to anything against them. Do you not see? Of course their ways seem strange to us—but, then, life in London is so different to life in Norway,—and we cannot all at once understand——" she broke off, sighing a little. Then she resumed—" Now you will give Morris my message, Britta—and then come to me in my bedroom—I am tired, and Philip said I was not to wait up for him."

Britta departed, and Thelma went rather slowly up-stairs. It was now nearly midnight, and she felt languid and weary. Her reflections began to take a new turn. Suppose she told her husband all that had occurred, he would most certainly go to Sir Francis and punish him in some way— there might then be a quarrel in which Philip might suffer —and all sorts of evil consequences would perhaps result from her want of reticence. If, on the other hand, she said nothing, and simply refused to receive Lennox, would not her husband think such conduct on her part strange ? She puzzled over these questions till her head ached—and finally resolved to keep her own counsel for the present,—after what had happened, Sir Francis would most probably not in-

trude himself again into her presence. "I will ask Mrs.
Lorimer what is best to do," she thought. "She is old and
wise, and she will know."

That night, as she laid her head on her pillow, and Britta
threw the warm *eidredon* over her, she shivered a little and
asked—

"Is it not very cold, Britta?"

"Very!" responded her little maid. "And it is beginning to snow."

Thelma looked wistful. "It is all snow and darkness
now at the Altenfjord," she said.

Britta smiled. "Yes, indeed, Fröken! We are better
off here than there."

"Perhaps!" replied Thelma a little musingly, and then
she settled herself as though to sleep.

Britta kissed her hand, and retired noiselessly. When
she had gone, Thelma opened her eyes and lay broad awake
looking at the flicker of rosy light flung on the ceiling from
the little suspended lamp in her oratory. All snow and
darkness at the Altenfjord! How strange the picture
seemed! She thought of her mother's sepulchre,—how
cold and dreary it must be,—she could see in fancy the
long pendent icicles fringing the entrance to the sea-king's
tomb,—the spot where she and Philip had first met,—she
could almost hear the slow, sullen plash of the black Fjord
against the shore. Her maiden life in Norway—her school-
days at Arles,—these were now like dreams,—dreams that
had passed away long, long ago. The whole tenor of her
existence had changed,—she was a wife,—she was soon to
be a mother,—and with this near future of new and sacred
joy before her, why did she to-night so persistently look
backward to the past?

As she lay quiet, watching the glimmering light upon the
wall, it seemed as though her room were suddenly filled with
shadowy forms,—she saw her mother's sweet, sad, suffering
face,—then her father's sturdy figure and fine, frank features,—then came the flitting shape of the hapless Sigurd,
whose plaintive voice she almost imagined she could hear,
—and feeling that she was growing foolishly nervous, she
closed her eyes, and tried to sleep. In vain,—her mind began to work on a far more unpleasing train of thought.
Why did not Philip return? Where was he? As though
some mocking devil had answered her, the words, "In the
arms of Violet Vere!" as uttered by Sir Francis Lennox,

recurred to her. Overcome by her restlessness, she started up,—she determined to get out of bed, and put on her dressing-gown and read,—when her quick ears caught the sound of steps coming up the stair-case. She recognized her husband's firm tread, and understood that he was followed by Neville, whose sleeping-apartment was on the floor above. She listened attentively—they were talking together in low tones on the landing outside her door.

" I think it would be much better to make a clean breast of it," said Sir Philip. " She will have to know some day."

" Your wife? For God's sake, don't tell her! " Neville's voice replied. " Such a disgraceful——" Here his words sank to a whisper, and Thelma could not distinguish them. Another minute, and her husband entered with soft precaution, fearing to awake her—she stretched out her arms to welcome him, and he hastened to her with an exclamation of tenderness and pleasure.

." My darling! Not asleep yet ? "

She smiled,—but there was something very piteous in her smile, had the dim light enabled him to perceive it.

"No, not yet, Philip! And yet I think I have been dreaming of—the Altenfjord."

" Ah! it must be cold there now," he answered lightly. " It's cold enough here, in all conscience. To-night there is a bitter east wind, and snow is falling."

She heard this account of the weather with almost morbid interest. Her thoughts instantly betook themselves again to Norway, and dwelt there. To the last,—before her aching eyes closed in the slumber she so sorely needed,—she seemed to be carried away in fancy to a weird stretch of gloom-enveloped landscape where she stood entirely alone, vaguely wondering at the dreary scene. " How strange it seems! " she murmured almost aloud. " All snow and darkness at the Altenfjord! "

CHAPTER XXV.

" Le temps où nous nous sommes aimés n'a guère duré, jeune fille ; il a passé comme un coup de vent! "

Old Breton Ballad.

THE next morning dawned, cold and dismal. A dense yellow fog hung over the metropolis like a pall—the street-

lamps were lighted, but their flare scarcely illumined the
thoroughfares, and the chill of the snow-burdened air pene-
trated into the warmest rooms, and made itself felt even by
the side of the brightest fires. Sir Philip woke with an
uncomfortable sense of headache and depression, and grumbled,—as surely every Englishman has a right to grumble,
at the uncompromising wretchedness of his country's winter
climate. His humor was not improved when a telegram
arrived before breakfast, summoning him in haste to a dull
town in one of the Midland counties, on pressing business
connected with his candidature for Parliament.

"What a bore!" he exclaimed, showing the missive to
his wife. "I *must* go,—and I shan't be able to get back to-
night. You'll be all alone, Thelma. I wish you'd go to the
Winsleighs!"

"Why?" said Thelma quietly. "I shall much prefer to
be here. I do not mind, Philip. I am accustomed to be
alone."

Something in her tone struck him as particularly sad,
and he looked at her intently.

"Now, my darling," he said suddenly, "if this Parliamentary bother is making you feel worried or vexed in any
way, I'll throw it all up—by Jove, I will!" And he drew
her into his warm embrace. "After all," he added, with a
laugh, "what does it matter! The country can get on without me!"

Thelma smiled a little.

"You must not talk so foolishly, Philip," she said tenderly. "It is wrong to begin a thing of importance, and
not go through with it. And I am not worried or vexed at
all. What would people say of me if I, your wife, were, for
my own selfish comfort and pleasure of having you always
with me, to prevent you from taking a good place among
the men of your nation? Indeed, I should deserve much
blame! And so, though it is a gloomy day for you, poor
boy,—you must go to this place where you are wanted, and
I shall think of you all the time you are gone, and shall be
so happy to welcome you home to-morrow!"

And she kissed and clung to him for a moment in silence.
All that day Philip was haunted by the remembrance of
the lingering tenderness of her farewell embrace. By ten
o'clock he was gone, taking Neville with him; and after her
household duties were over, Thelma prepared herself to go
and lunch with old Mrs. Lorimer, and see what she would

advise concerning the affair of Sir Francis Lennox. But, at the same time, she resolved that nothing should make her speak of the reports that were afloat about her husband and Violet Vere.

" I know it is all false," she said to herself over and over again. " And the people here are as silly as the peasants in Bosekop, ready to believe any untruth so long as it gives them something to talk about. But they may chatter as they please—I shall not say one word, not even to Philip—for it would seem as if I mistrusted him."

Thus she put away all the morbid fancies that threatened to oppress her, and became almost cheerful.

And while she made her simple plans for pleasantly passing the long, dull day of her husband's enforced absence, her friend, Lady Winsleigh, was making arrangements of a very different nature. Her ladyship had received a telegram from Sir Francis Lennox that morning. The pink missive had apparently put her in an excellent humor, though, after reading it, she crumpled it up and threw it in the waste-paper basket, from which receptacle, Louise Rénaud, her astute attendant, half an hour later extracted it, secreting it in her own pocket for private perusal at leisure. She ordered her brougham, saying she was going out on business,—and before departing, she took from her dressing-case certain bank-notes and crammed them hastily into her purse—a purse which, in all good faith, she handed to her maid to put in her sealskin muff-bag. Of course, Louise managed to make herself aware of its contents,—but when her ladyship at last entered her carriage her unexpected order, " To the Brilliant Theatre, Strand," was sufficient to startle Briggs, and cause him to exchange surprise signals with " Mamzelle," who merely smiled a prim, incomprehensible smile.

" *Where* did your la'ship say ? " asked Briggs dubiously.

" Are you getting deaf, Briggs ? " responded his mistress pleasantly. " To the Brilliant Theatre ! " She raised her voice, and spoke with distinct emphasis. There was no mistaking her. Briggs touched his hat,—in the same instant he winked at Lousie, and then the carriage rolled away.

At night, the Brilliant Theatre is a pretty little place,—comfortable, cosy, bright, and deserving of its name;—in broad day, it is none of these things. A squalid dreariness seems to have settled upon it—it has a peculiar atmosphere of its own—an atmosphere dark, heavy, and strangely flavored with odors of escaping gas and crushed orange-peel. Behind the scenes, these odors mingle with a chronic, all-pervading smell of beer—beer, which the stranger's sensitive nose detects directly, in spite of the choking clouds of dust which arise from the boards at the smallest movement of any part of the painted scenery. The Brilliant had gone through much ill-fortune—its proprietors never realized any financial profit till they secured Violet Vere. With her came prosperity. Her utter absence of all reserve—the frankness with which she threw modesty to the winds,—the vigor with which she danced a regular " break-down,"—roaring a comic song of the lowest type, by way of accompaniment,—the energetic manner in which, metaphorically speaking, she kicked at the public with her shapely legs,—all this overflow of genius on her part drew crowds to the Brilliant nightly, and the grateful and happy managers paid her a handsome salary, humored all her caprices, and stinted and snubbed for her sake, all the rest of the company. She was immensely popular—the " golden youth " of London raved about her dyed hair, painted eyes, and carmined lips—even her voice, as coarse as that of a dustman, was applauded to the echo, and her dancing excited the wildest enthusism. Dukes sent her presents of diamond ornaments—gifts of value which they would have possibly refused to their own wives and daughters,—Royal Highnesses thought it no shame to be seen lounging near her stage dressing-room door,—in short, she was in the zenith of her career, and, being thoroughly unprincipled, audaciously insolent, and wholly without a conscience,—she enjoyed herself immensely.

At the very time when Lady Winsleigh's carriage was nearing the Strand, the grand morning rehearsal of a new burlesque was " on " at the Brilliant—and Violet's harsh tones, raised to a sort of rough masculine roar, were heard all over the theatre, as she issued commands or made complaints according to her changeful humors. She sat in an elevated position above the stage on a jutting beam of wood painted to resemble the gnarled branch of a tree,—swinging her legs to and fro and clinking the heels of her shoes together in time to the mild scraping of a violin, the player whereof was " trying over " the first few bars of the new " jig " in which she was ere long to distinguish herself. She was a handsome woman, with a fine, fair skin, and large, full, dark eyes—she had a wide mouth, which, nearly always on the grin, displayed to the full her strong white teeth,—her figure was inclined to excessive *embonpoint*, but this rather endeared her to her admirers than otherwise,— many of these gentlemen being prone to describe her fleshly charms by the epithet " Prime!" as though she were a fatting pig or other animal getting ready for killing.

" Tommy! Tommy!" she screeched presently. " Are you going to sleep? Do you expect me to dance to a dirge, you lazy devil!"

Tommy, the player of the violin, paused in his efforts, and looked up drearily. He was an old man, with a lean, long body and pinched features—his lips had a curious way, too, of trembling when he spoke, as if he were ready to cry.

" I can't help it," he said slowly. " I don't know it yet. I must practice it a bit at home. My sight's not so good as it used to be————"

> " Such a pair of optics, love, you've never, never seen—
> One my mother blacked last night, the tother it is green!"

sang Violet, to the infinite delight of all the unwashed-looking supernumeraries and ballet-girls, who were scattered about the stage, talking and laughing.

" Shut up, Tommy!" she continued. " You're always talking about your eyesight. I warn you, if you say too much about it you'll lose your place. We don't want blind fiddlers in the Brilliant. Put down you catgut screamer, and fetch me a pint. Ask for the Vere's own tipple— they'll twig!"

Tommy obeyed, and shuffled off on his errand. As he departed,—a little man with a very red face, wearing a stove-pipe hat very much on one sid, bounced on the stage as if some one had thrown him there like a ball.

" Now, ladies, ladies!" he shouted warningly. "Attention! Once again, please! The last figure once again!" The straggling groups scrambled hastily into something like order, and the little man continued—" One, two, three! Advance—retreat—left, right! Very well, indeed! Arms up a little more, Miss Jenkins—so! toes well pointed—curtsy—retire! One, two, three! swift slide to the left wing—forward! Round—take hands—all smile, please!" This general smile was apparently not quite satisfactory, for he repeated persuasively—" All smile, please!

So! Round again—more quickly—now break the circle in centre—enter Miss Vere——" he paused, growing still redder in the face, and demanded, " Where is Miss Vere ? "

He was standing just beneath the painted bough of the sham tree, and in one second his hat was dexterously kicked off, and two heels met with a click round his neck.

" Here I am, pickaninny ! " retorted Miss Vere holding him fast in this novel embrace, amid the laughter of the supers. " You're getting as blind as Tommy ! Steady, steady now, donkey !—steady—woa ! " And in a thrice she stood upright, one foot planted firmly on each of his shoulders.

" No weight, am I, darling ? " she went on jeeringly, and with an inimitably derisive air she put up an eye-glass and surveyed the top of his head. " You want a wig, my dear —you do, indeed ! Come with me to-morrow, and I'll buy you one to suit your complexion. Your wife won't know you ! "

And with a vigorous jump she sprang down from her position, managing to give him a smart hit on the nose as she did so—and leaping to the centre of the stage, she posed herself to commence her dance—when Tommy came creeping back in his slow and dismal fashion, bearing something in a pewter pot.

" That's the ticket ! " she cried as she perceived him. " I'm as dry as a whole desert ! Give it here ! " And she snatched the mug from the feeble hand of her messenger and began drinking eagerly.

The little red-faced man interposed. " Now, Miss Vi," he said, " is that brandy ? "

" Rather so ! " returned the Vere, with a knowing wink, " and a good many things besides. It's a mixture. The 'Vere's Own !' Ha, ha ! Might be the name of a regiment ! "

And she burried her mouth and nose again in the tankard.

" Look here," said the little man again. " Why not wait till after the dance ? It's bad for you before."

" Oh, is it, indeed ! " screamed Violet, raising her face, which became suddenly and violently flushed. " O good Lord ! Are you a temperance preacher ? Teach your granny ! Bad for me ? Say another word, and I'll box your ears for you ! You braying jackass !—you snivelling idiot ! Who makes the Brilliant draw ? You or I ? Tell me that, you staring old———"

Here Tommy, who had for some minutes been vainly endeavoring to attract her attention, raised his weak voice to
a feeble shout.

"I say, Miss Vere! I've been trying to tell you, but
you won't listen! There's a lady waiting to see you!"

"A what?" she asked.

"A lady!" continued Tommy, in loud tones. "A lady
of *title!* Wants to see you in private! Won't detain you
long!"

Violet Vere raised her pewter mug once more, and
drained off its contents.

"Lord, ain't I honored!" she said, smacking her lips with
a grin. "A lady of title to see me! Let her wait! Now
then!" and snapping her fingers, she began her dance, and
went through it to the end, with her usual vigor and frankness. When she had finished, she turned to the red-faced
man who had watched her evolutions with much delight in
spite of the abuse she had heaped upon him, and said with
an affected, smirking drawl—

"Show the lady of title into my dressing-room! I shall
be ready for her in ten minutes. Be sure to mention that I
am very shy,—and unaccustomed to company!"

And, giggling gently like an awkward school-girl, she
held down her head with feigned bashfulness, and stepped
mincingly across the stage with such a ludicrous air of
prim propriety, that all her associates burst out laughing,
and applauded her vociferously. She turned and curtsied
to them demurely—then suddenly raising one leg in a hor-
izontal position, she twirled it rapidly in their faces,—then
she gave a little shocked cough behind her hand, grinned,
and vanished.

When, in the stipulated ten minutes, she was ready to
receive her unknown visitor, she was quite transformed.
She had arrayed herself in a trailing gown of rich black
velvet, fastened at the side with jet clasps—a cluster of natural, innocent, white violets nestled in the fall of Spanish
lace at her throat—her face was pale with pearl-powder,—
and she had eaten a couple of scented bon-bons to drown
the smell of her recent brandy-tipple. She reclined gracefully in an easy chair, pretending to read, and she rose with
an admirably acted air of startled surprise, as one of the
errand boys belonging to the Brilliant tapped at her door,
and in answer to her "Come in!" announced, "Lady Winsleigh!"

A faint, sweet, questioning smile played on the Vere's wide mouth.

"I am not aware that I have the honor of——" she began, modulating her voice to the requirements of fashionable society, and wondering within herself "what the d——l" this woman in the silk and sable-fur costume wanted.

Lady Winsleigh in the meantime stared at her with cold, critical eyes.

"She is positively rather handsome," she thought. "I can quite imagine a certain class of men losing their heads about her." Aloud she said—

"I must apologize for this intrusion, Miss Vere! I dare say you have never heard my name—I am not fortunate enough to be famous,—as *you* are." This with a killing satire in her smile. "May I sit down? Thanks! I have called upon you in the hope that you may perhaps be able to give me a little information in a private matter—a matter concerning the happiness of a very dear friend of mine." She paused—Violet Vere sat silent. After a minute or two, her ladyship continued in a somewhat embarrassed manner—

"I believe you know a gentleman with whom I am also acquainted—Sir Philip Bruce-Errington."

Miss Vere raised her eyes with charming languor and a slow smile.

"Oh yes!"

"He visits you, doesn't he?"

"Frequently!"

"I'm afraid you'll think me rude and inquisitive," continued Lady Winsleigh, with a coaxing air, "but—but may I ask——"

"Anything in the world," interrupted Violet coolly. "Ask away! But I'm not bound to answer."

Lady Winsleigh reddened with indignation. "What an insulting creature!" she thought. But, after all, she had put herself in her present position, and she could not very well complain if she met with a rebuff. She made another effort.

"Sir Francis Lennox told me——" she began.

The Vere interrupted her with a cheerful laugh.

"Oh, you come from him, do you? Now, why didn't you tell me that at first? It's all right! You're a great friend of Lennie's, aren't you?"

Lady Winsleigh sat erect and haughty, a deadly chill of disgust and fear at her heart. This creature called her quondam lover, " Lennie "—even as she herself had done,—and she, the proud, vain woman of society and fashion shuddered at the idea that there should be even this similarity between herself and the " thing " called Violet Vere. She replied stiffly—

" I have known him a long time."

" He's a nice fellow," went on Miss Vere easily—" a *leetle* stingy sometimes, but never mind that! You want to know about Sir Philip Errington, and I'll tell you. He's chosen to mix himself up with some affairs of mine——"

" What affairs ? " asked Lady Winsleigh rather eagerly.

" They don't concern you," returned Miss Vere calmly, " and we needn't talk about them! But they concern Sir Philip,—or he thinks they do, and insists on seeing me about them, and holding long conversations, which bore me excessively ! "

She yawned slightly, smothering her yawn in a dainty lace handkerchief, and then went on—

" He's a moral young man, don't you know—and I never could endure moral men! I can't get on with them at all ! "

" Then you don't like him ? " questioned Lady Winsleigh in rather a disappointed tone.

" No, I don't ! " said the Vere candidly. " He's not my sort. But, Lord bless you ! I know how he's getting talked about because he comes here—and serve him right too ! He shouldn't meddle with my business." She paused suddenly and drew a letter from her pocket,—laughed and tossed it across the table.

" You can read that, if you like," she said indifferently. " He wrote it, and sent it round to me last night."

Lady Winsleigh's eyes glistened eagerly,—she recognized Errington's bold, clear hand at once,—and as she read, an expression of triumph played on her features. She looked up presently and said—

" Have you any further use for this letter, Miss Vere? Or—will you allow me to keep it ? "

The Vere seemed slightly suspicious of this proposal, but looked amused too.

" Why, what do you want it for ? " she inquired bluntly. " To tease him about me ? "

Lady Winsleigh forced a smile. " Well—perhaps ! " she

admitted, then with an air of gentleness and simplicity she
continued, " I think, Miss Vere, with you, that it is very
wrong of Sir Philip,—very absurd of him, in fact—to interfere with your affairs, whatever they may be,—and as it
is very likely annoying to you——"

" It *is*," interrupted Violet decidedly.

" Then, with the help of this letter—which, really—
really—excuse me for saying it!—quite compromises him,"
and her ladyship looked amiably concerned about it, " I
might perhaps persuade him not to—to—intrude upon you
—you understand? But if you object to part with the letter, never mind! If I did not fear to offend you, I should
ask you to exchange it for—for something more—well! let
us say, something more substantial——"

" Don't beat about the bush!" said Violet, with a sudden
oblivion of her company manners. " You mean money?"

Lady Winsleigh smiled. " As you put it so frankly, Miss
Vere——" she began.

" Of course! I'm always frank," returned the Vere,
with a loud laugh. " Besides, what's the good of pretending? Money's the only thing worth having—it pays your
butcher, baker, and dressmaker—and how are you to get
along if you *can't* pay them, I'd like to know! Lord! if
all the letters I've got from fools were paying stock instead
of waste-paper, I'd shut up shop, and leave the Brilliant to
look out for itself!"

Lady Winsleigh felt she had gained her object, and she
could now afford to be gracious.

" That would be a great loss to the world," she remarked
sweetly. " An immense loss! London could scarcely get
on without Violet Vere!" Here she opened her purse and
took out some bank-notes, which she folded and slipped inside an envelope. " Then I may have the letter?" she continued.

" You may and welcome!" returned Violet.

Lady Winsleigh instantly held out the envelope, which she
as instantly clutched. " Especially if you'll tell Sir Philip
Errington to mind his own business!" She paused, and a
dark flush mounted to her brow—one of those sudden
flushes that purpled rather than crimsoned her face. " Yes,"
she repeated, " as he's a friend of yours, just tell him I said
he was to mind his own business! Lord! what does he
want to come here and preach at me for! I don't want his
sermons! Moral!" here she laughed rather hoarsely, " I'm

as moral as any one on the stage! Who says I'm not! Take 'em all round—there's not a soul behind the footlights more open and above-board than I am!"

And her eyes flashed defiantly.

"She's been drinking?" thought Lady Winsleigh disgustedly. In fact, the "Vere's Own" tipple had begun to take its usual effect, which was to make the Vere herself both blatant and boisterous.

"I'm sure," said her ladyship with frigid politeness, "that you are everything that is quite charming, Miss Vere! I have a great respect for the—the oraments of the English stage. Society has quite thrown down its former barriers, you know!—the members of your profession are received in the very best circles——"

"I ain't!" said Violet, with ungrammatical candor. "Your Irvings and your Terrys, your Mary Andersons and your Langtrys,—they're good enough for your fine drawing-rooms, and get more invitations out than they can accept. And none of them have got half my talent, I tell you! Lord bless my soul! if they're respectable enough for you,—so am I!"

And she struck her hand emphatically on the table. Lady Winsleigh looked at her with a slight smile.

"I must really say good-bye!" she said, rising and gathering her furs about her. "I could talk with you all the morning, Miss Vere, but I have so many engagements! Besides I mustn't detain *you!* I'm so much obliged to you for your kind reception of me!"

"Don't mention it!" and Violet glanced her over with a kind of sullen sarcasm. "I'm bound to please Lennie when I can, you know!"

Again Lady Winsleigh shivered a little, but forced herself to shake hands with the notorious stage-Jezebel.

"I shall come and see you in the new piece," she said graciously. "I always take a box on first nights? And your dancing is so exquisite! The very poetry of motion! So pleased to have met you! Good-bye!"

And with a few more vague compliments and remarks about the weather, Lady Winsleigh took her departure. Left alone, the actress threw herself back in her chair and laughed.

"That woman's up to some mischief," she exclaimed *sotto voce*, "and so is Lennie! I wonder what's their little game? *I* don't care, as long as they'll keep the high-and-

mighty Errington in his place. I'm tired of him! Why
does he meddle with *my* affairs?" Her brows knitted into
a frown. "As if he or anybody else could persuade me to
go back to——," she paused, and bit her lips angrily.
Then she opened the envelope Lady Winsleigh had left with
her, and pulled out the bank-notes inside. "Let me see—
five, ten, fifteen, twenty! Not bad pay, on the whole! It'll
just cover the bill for my plush mantle. Hullo! Who's
there?"

Some one knocked at her door.

"Come in!" she cried.

The feeble Tommy presented himself. His weak mouth
trembled more than ever, and he was apparently conscious
of this, for he passed his hand nervously across it two or
three times.

"Well, what's up?" inquired the "star" of the Brilliant,
fingering her bank-notes as she spoke.

"Miss Vere," stammered Tommy, "I venture to ask you
a favor,—could you kindly, very kindly lend me ten
shillings till to-morrow night? I am so pressed just now—
and my wife is ill in bed—and——" he stopped, and his
eyes sought her face hopefully, yet timidly.

"You shouldn't have a wife, Tommy!" averred Violet
with blunt frankness. "Wives are expensive articles.
Besides, I never lend. I never give—except to public
charities where one's name gets mentioned in the papers.
I'm obliged to do that, you know, by way of advertisement.
Ten shillings! Why, I can't afford ten pence! My bills
would frighten you, Tommy! There go along, and don't
cry, for goodness sake! Let your fiddle cry for you!"

"Oh, Miss Vere," once more pleaded Tommy, "if you
knew how my wife suffers——"

The actress rose and stamped her foot impatiently.

"Bother your wife!" she cried angrily, "and you too!
Look out! or I tell the manager we've got a beggar at the
Brilliant. Don't stare at me like that! Go to the d—l
with you!"

Tommy slunk off abashed and trembling, and the Vere
began to sing, or rather croak, a low comic song, while she
threw over her shoulders a rich mantle glittering with embroidered trimmings, and poised a coquettish Paris model
hat on her thick uptwisted coils of hair. Thus attired, she
passed out of her dressing-room, locking the door behind
her, and after a brief conversation with the jocose acting

manager, whom she met on her way out, she left the theatre, and took a cab to the Criterion, where the young Duke of Moorlands, her latest conquest, had invited her to a sumptuous luncheon with himself and friends, all men of fashion, who were running through what money they had as fast as they could go.

Lady Winsleigh, on her way home, was tormented by sundry uncomfortable thoughts and sharp pricks of conscience. Her interview with Violet Vere had instinctively convinced her that Sir Philip was innocent of the intrigue imputed to him, and yet,—the letter she had now in her possession seemed to prove him guilty. And though she felt herself to be playing a vile part, she could not resist the temptation of trying what the effect would be of this compromising document on Thelma's trusting mind. It was undoubtedly a very incriminating epistle—any lawyer would have said as much, while blandly pocketing his fee for saying it. It was written off in evident haste, and ran as follows :—

" Let me see you once more on the subject you know of. Why will you not accept the honorable position offered to you ? There shall be no stint of money—all the promises I have made I am quite ready to fulfill—you shall lose nothing by being gentle. Surely you cannot continue to seem so destitute of all womanly feeling and pity ? I will not believe that you would so deliberately condemn to death a man who has loved, and who loves you still so faithfully, and who, without you, is utterly weary of life and brokenhearted ! Think once more—and let my words carry more weight with you !

" BRUCE-ERRINGTON."

This was all, but more than enough !

" I wonder what he means," thought Lady Winsleigh. " It looks as if he were in love with the Vere and she refused to reciprocate. It *must* be that. And yet that doesn't accord with what the creature herself said about his ' preaching at her.' He wouldn't do that if he were in love."

She studied every word of the letter again and again, and finally folded it up carefully and placed it in her pocketbook.

" Innocent or guilty, Thelma must see it," she decided.

" I wonder how she'll take it! If she wants a proof—it's one she'll scarcely deny. Some women would fret themselves to death over it—but I shouldn't wonder if she sat down under it quite calmly without a word of complaint." She frowned a little. " Why must *she* always be superior to others of her sex! How I detest that still solemn smile of hers and those big baby-blue eyes! I think if Philip had married any other woman than she—a woman more like the rest of us who'd have gone with her time,—I could have forgiven him more easily. But to pick up a Norwegian peasant and set her up as a sort of moral finger-post to society—and then to go and compromise himself with Violet Vere—that's a kind of thing I *can't* stand! I'd rather be anything in the world than a humbug!"

. Many people desire to be something they are not, and her ladyship quite unconsciously echoed this rather general sentiment. She was, without knowing it, such an adept in society humbug, that she even humbugged herself. She betrayed herself as she betrayed others, and told little soothing lies to her own conscience as she told them to her friends. There are plenty of women like her,—women of pleasant courtesy and fashion, to whom truth is mere coarseness,—and with whom polite lying passes for perfect breeding. She was not aware, as she was driven along Park Lane to her own residence, that she carried with her on the box of her brougham a private detective in the person of Briggs. Perched stiffly on his seat, with arms tightly folded, this respectable retainer was quite absorbed in meditation, so much so that he exchanged not a word with his friend, the coachman, beside him. He had his own notions of propriety,—he considered that his mistress had no business whatever to call on an actress of Violet Vere's repute, —and he resolved that whether he were reproved for over-officiousness or not, nothing should prevent him from casually mentioning to Lord Winsleigh the object of her ladyship's drive that morning.

" For," mused Briggs gravely, " a lady 'as responsibilities, and 'owever she forgets 'erself, appearances 'as to be kep' up."

With the afternoon, the fog which had hung over the city all day, deepened and darkened. Thelma had lunched with Mrs. Lorimer, and had enjoyed much pleasant chat with that kindly, cheerful old lady. She had confided to her, part of the story of Sir Francis Lennox's conduct, carefully avoiding every mention of the circumstance which had given rise to it,—namely, the discussion about Violet Vere. She merely explained that she had suddenly fainted, in which condition Sir Francis had taken advantage of her helplessness to insult her.

Mrs. Lorimer was highly indignant. "Tell your husband all about it, my dear!" she advised. "He's big enough, and strong enough, to give that little snob a good trouncing! My patience! I wish George were in London—he'd lend a hand and welcome!"

And the old lady nodded her head violently over the sock she was knitting,—the making of socks for her beloved son was her principal occupation and amusement.

"But I hear," said Thelma, "that it is against the law to strike any one, no matter how you have been insulted. If so,—then Philip would be punished for attacking Sir Francis, and that would not be fair."

"You didn't think of that, child, when you struck Lennox yourself," returned Mrs. Lorimer, laughing. "And I guarantee you gave him a good hard blow,—and serve him right! Never mind what comes of it, my dearie—just tell your husband as soon as ever he comes home, and let him take the matter into his own hands. He's a fine man—he'll know how to defend the pretty wife he loves so well!" And she smiled, while her shining knitting-needles clicked faster than ever.

Thelma's face saddened a little. "I think I am not worthy of his love," she said sorrowfully.

Mrs. Lorimer looked at her with some inquisitiveness.

"What makes you say that, my dear?"

"Because I feel it so much," she replied. "Dear Mrs. Lorimer, you cannot, perhaps, understand—but when he married me, it seemed as if the old story of the king and the beggar-maid were being repeated over again. I sought nothing but his love—his love was, and is my life! These riches—these jewels and beautiful things he surrounds me with—I do not care for them at all, except for the reason that he wishes me to have them. I scarcely understand their value, for I have been poor all my life, and yet I have wanted nothing. I do not think wealth is needful to make one happy. But love—ah! I could not live without it— and now—now——" She paused, and her eyes filled with sudden tears.

"Now what?" asked Mrs. Lorimer gently.

" Now," continued the girl in a low voice, " my heart is always afraid! Yes! I am afraid of losing my husband's love. Ah, do not laugh at me, dear Mrs. Lorimer! You know people who are much together sometimes get tired,— tired of seeing the same face always,—the same form——"

" Are *you* tired, dearie?" asked the old lady meaningly.

" I? Tired of Philip? I am only happy when he is with me!" And her eyes deepened with passionate tender- ness. " I would wish to live and die beside him, and I should not care if I never saw another human face than his!'

" Well, and don't you think he has the same feelings for you?"

" Men are different, I think," returned Thelma musingly " Now, love is everything to me—but it may not be every- thing to Philip. I do believe that love is only part of a man's life, while it is *all* a woman's. Clara told me once that most husbands wearied of their wives, though they would not always confess it——"

" Clara Winsleigh's modern social doctrines are false, my dear!" interrupted Mrs. Lorimer quickly. " She isn't sat- isfied with her own marriage, and she thinks everybody must be as discontented as herself. Now, my husband and I lived always together for five and twenty years,—and we were lovers to the last day, when my darling died with his hand in mine—and—and—if it hadn'ὸ been for my boy,—I should have died too!"

And two bright tears fell glittering on the old lady's knit- ting.

Thelma took her hand and kissed it fondly. " I can un- derstand that," she said softly; " but still,—still I do be. lieve it is difficult to keep love when you have won it! It is, perhaps, easy to win—but I am sure it is hard to keep!"

Mrs. Lorimer looked at her earnestly.

" My dear child, don't let that frivolous Winsleigh woman put nonsense into your pretty head. You are too sensible to take such a morbid view of things,—and you mustn't allow your wholesome fresh nature to be contam- inated by the petulant, wrong-headed notions that cloud the brains of idle, fashionable, useless women. Believe me, good men don't tire of their wives—and Sir Philip is a good man. Good wives never weary their husbands—and you are a good wife—and you will be a good, sweet mother. Think of that new delight so soon coming for you,—and leave all the modern, crazy, one-sided notions of human life to the French and Russian novelists. Tut-tut!" continued the old lady tenderly. "A nice little ladyship you are,— worrying yourself about nothing! Send Philip to me when he comes home—I'll scold him for leaving his bird to mope in her London cage!"

"I do not mope," declared Thelma. "And you must not scold him, please! Poor boy! He is working so very hard, and has so much to attend to. He wants to distinguish himself for—for my sake!"

"That looks very much as if he were tired of you!" laughed Mrs. Lorimer. "Though I dare say you'd like him to stay at home and make love to you all day! Silly girl! You want the world to be a sort of Arcadia, with you as Phyllis, and Sir Philip as Corydon! My dear, we're living in the nineteenth century, and the days of fond shepherds and languishing shepherdesses are past!"

Thelma laughed too, and felt soon ashamed of her depression. The figure of Violet Vere now and then danced before her like a mocking will-o'-the-wisp—but her pride forbade her to mention this,—the actual source of all her vague troubles.

She left Mrs. Lorimer's house, which was near Holland Park, about four o'clock, and as she was passing Church Street, Kensington, she bade her coachman drive up to the Carmelite Church there, familiarly known as the "Carms." She entered the sacred edifice, where the service of Benediction was in progress; and, kneeling down, she listened to the exquisite strains of the solemn music that pealed through those dim and shadowy aisles, and a sense of the most perfect peace settled soothingly on her soul. Clasping her gentle hands, she prayed with innocent and heartfelt earnestness—not for herself,—never for herself,—but always, always for that dear, most dear one, for whom every beat of her true heart was a fresh vow of undying and devoted affection.

"Dear God!" she whispered, "if I love him too much, forgive me! Thou who art all Love, wilt pardon me this excess of love! Bless my darling always, and teach me how to be more worthy of Thy goodness and his tenderness!"

And when she left the church, she was happier and more light-hearted than she had been for many a long day. She drove home, heedless of the fog and cold, dismal aspect of the weather, and resolved to go and visit Lady Winsleigh in the evening, so that when Philip came back on the morrow, she might be able to tell him that she had amused herself, and had not been lonely.

But when she arrived at her own door, Morris, who opened it, informed her that Lady Winsleigh was waiting in the drawing-room to see her, and had been waiting some time. Thelma hastened thither immediately, and held out her hands joyously to her friend.

"I am so sorry you have had to wait, Clara!" she began. "Why did you not send word and say you were coming? Philip is away and will not be back to-night, and I have been lunching with Mrs. Lorimer, and—why, what makes you look so grave?"

Lady Winsleigh regarded her fixedly. How radiantly lovely the young wife looked!—her cheeks had never been more delicately rosy, or her eyes more brilliant. The dark fur cloak she wore with its rich sable trimmings, and the little black velvet *toque* that rested on her fair curls, set off the beauty of her clear skin to perfection, and her rival, who stood gazing at her with such close scrutiny, envied her more than ever as she was once again reluctantly forced to admit to herself the matchless loveliness of the innocent creature whose happiness she now sought to destroy.

"Do I look grave, Thelma?" she said with a slight smile. "Well, perhaps I've a reason for my gravity. And so your husband is away?"

"Yes. He went quite early this morning,—a telegram summoned him and he was obliged to go." Here she drew up a chair to the fire, and began to loosen her wraps. "Sit down, Clara! I will ring for tea."

"No, don't ring," said Lady Winsleigh. "Not yet! I want to talk to you privately." She sank languidly on a velvet lounge and looked Thelma straight in the eyes.

"Dear Thelma," she continued in a sweetly tremulous, compassionate voice. "Can you bear to hear something very painful and shocking, something that I'm afraid will grieve you very much?"

The color fled from the girl's fair face—her eyes grew startled.

"What do you mean, Clara? Is it anything about— about Philip?"

Lady Winsleigh bent her head in assent, but remained silent.

"If," continued Thelma, with a little return of the rosy hue to her cheeks. "If it is something else about that—

that person at the theatre, Clara, I would rather not hear it! I think I have been wrong in listening to any such stories—it is so seldom that gossip of any kind is true. It is not a wife's duty to receive scandals about her husband. And suppose he does see Miss Vere, how do I know that it may not be on business for some friend of his?—because I do know that on that night when he went behind the scenes at the Brilliant, he said it was on business. Mr. Lovelace used often to go and see Miss Mary Anderson, all to persuade her to take a play written by a friend of his—and Philip, who is always kind-hearted, may perhaps be doing something of the same sort. I feel I have been wicked to have even a small doubt of my husband's love,—so, Clara, do not let us talk any more on a subject which only displeases me."

"You must choose your own way of life, of course," said Lady Winsleigh coldly. "But you draw rather foolish comparisons, Thelma. There is a wide difference between Mary Anderson and Violet Vere. Besides, Mr. Lovelace is a bachelor,—he can do as he likes and go where he likes without exciting comment. However, whether you are angry with me or not, I feel I should not be your true friend if I did not show you—*this*. You know your husband's writing!"

And she drew out the fatal letter, and continued, watching her victim as she spoke, "This was sent by Sir Philip to Violet Vere last night,—she gave it to me herself this morning."

Thelma's hand trembled as she took the paper.

"Why should I read it?" she faltered mechanically.

Lady Winsleigh raised her eyebrows and frowned impatiently.

"Why—why? Because it is your duty to do so! Have you no pride? Will you allow your husband to write such a letter as that to another woman,—and *such* a woman too! without one word of remonstrance? You owe it to yourself—to your own sense of honor—to resent and resist such treatment on his part! Surely the deepest love cannot pardon deliberate injury and insult."

"My love can pardon anything," answered the girl in a low voice, and then slowly, very slowly, she opened the folded sheet—slowly she read every word it contained,— words that stamped themselves one by one on her bewildered brain and sent it reeling into darkness and vacancy.

She felt sick and cold—she stared fixedly at her husband's familiar handwriting. "A man who has loved and who loves you still, and who without you is utterly weary and broken-hearted!"

Thus he wrote of himself to—to Violet Vere! It seemed incredible—yet it was true! She heard a rushing sound in her ears—the room swung round dizzily before her eyes—yet she sate, still, calm and cold, holding the letter and speaking no word.

Lady Winsleigh watched her, irritated at her passionless demeanor.

"Well!" she exclaimed at last. "Have you nothing to say?"

Thelma looked up, her eyes burning with an intense feverish light.

"Nothing!" she replied.

"*Nothing?*" repeated her ladyship with emphatic astonishment.

"Nothing against Philip," continued the girl steadily. "For the blame is not his, but mine! That he is weary and broken-hearted must be my fault—though I cannot yet understand what I have done. But it must be something, because if I were all that he wished he would not have grown so tired." She paused and her pale lips quivered. "I am sorry," she went on with dreamy pathos, "sorrier for him than for myself, because now I see I am in the way of his happiness." A quiver of agony passed over her face, —she fixed her large bright eyes on Lady Winsleigh, who instinctively shrank from the solemn speechless despair of that penetrating gaze.

"Who gave you this letter, Clara?" she asked calmly.

"I told you before,—Miss Vere herself."

"Why did she give it to you?" continued Thelma in a dull, sad voice.

Lady Winsleigh hesitated and stammered a little. "Well, because—because I asked her if the stories about Sir Philip were true. And she begged me to ask him not to visit her so often." Then, with an additional thought of malice, she said softly. "She doesn't wish to wrong you, Thelma,—of course, she's not a very good woman, but I think she feels sorry for you!"

The girl uttered a smothered cry of anguish, as though she had been stabbed to the heart. She!—to be actually *pitied* by Violet Vere, because she had been unable to keep her husband's love! This idea tortured her very soul,—but she was silent.

"I thought you were my friend, Clara?" she said suddenly, with a strange wistfulness.

"So I am, Thelma," murmured Lady Winsleigh, a guilty flush coloring her cheeks.

"You have made me very miserable," went on Thelma gravely, and with pathetic simplicity, "and I am sorry indeed that we ever met. I was so happy till I knew you!—and yet I was very fond of you! I am sure you mean everything for the best, but I cannot think it is so. And it is all so dark and desolate now—why have you taken such pains to make me sad? Why have you so often tried to make me doubt my husband's love?—why have you come to-day so quickly to tell me I have lost it? But for you, I might never have known this sorrow,—I might have died soon, in happy ignorance, believing in my darling's truth as I believe in God!"

Her voice broke, and a hard sob choked her utterance. For once Lady Winsleigh's conscience smote her—for once she felt ashamed, and dared not offer consolation to the innocent soul she had so wantonly stricken. For a minute or two there was silence—broken only by the monotonous ticking of the clock and the crackling of the fire.

Presently Thelma spoke again. "I will ask you to go away now and leave me, Clara," she said simply. "When the heart is sorrowful, it is best to be alone. Good-bye!" And she gently held out her hand.

"Poor Thelma!" said Lady Winsleigh, taking it with an affectation of tenderness. "What will you do?"

Thelma did not answer; she sat mute and rigid.

"You are thinking unkindly of me just now," continued Clara softly; "but I felt it was my duty to tell you the worst at once. It's no good living in a delusion! I'm very, very sorry for you, Thelma!"

Thelma remained perfectly silent. Lady Winsleigh moved towards the door, and as she opened it looked back at her. The girl might have been a lifeless figure for any movement that could be perceived about her. Her face was white as marble—her eyes were fixed on the sparkling fire—her very hands looked stiff and pallid as wax, as they lay clasped in her lap—the letter—the cruel letter,—had fallen at her feet. She seemed as one in a trance of misery—and so Lady Winsleigh left her.

25

CHAPTER XXVI.

"O my lord, O Love,
I have laid my life at thy feet;
Have thy will thereof
For what shall please thee is sweet!"

SWINBURNE.

SHE roused herself at last. Unclasping her hands, she pushed back her hair from her brows and sighed heavily. Shivering as with intense cold, she rose from the chair she had so long occupied, and stood upright, mechanically gathering around her the long fur mantle that she had not as yet taken off. Catching sight of the letter where it lay, a gleaming speck of white on the rich dark hues of the carpet, she picked it up and read it through again calmly and comprehensively,—then folded it up carefully as though it were something of inestimable value. Her thoughts were a little confused,—she could only realize clearly two distinct things,—first, that Philip was unhappy,—secondly, that she was in the way of his happiness. She did not pause to consider how this change in him had been effected,—moreover, she never imagined that the letter he had written could refer to any one but himself. Hers was a nature that accepted facts as they appeared—she never sought for ulterior motives or disguised meanings. True, she could not understand her husband's admiration for Violet Vere, "But then"—she thought—"many other men admire her too. And so it is certain there must be something about her that wins love,—something I cannot see!"

And presently she put aside all other considerations, and only pondered on one thing,—how should she remove herself from the path of her husband's pleasure? For she had no doubt but that she was an obstacle to his enjoyment. He had made promises to Violet Vere which he was "ready to fulfill,"—he offered her "an honorable position,"—he desired her "not to condemn him to death,"—he besought her to let his words "carry more weight with her."

"It is because I am here," thought Thelma wearily. "She would listen to him if I were gone!" She had the strangest notions of wifely duty—odd minglings of the stern Norse customs with the gentler teachings of Christianity,—yet in both cases the lines of woman's life were clearly defined in one word—obedience. Most women, receiving an apparent proof of a husband's infidelity, would have made what is termed a "scene,"—would have confronted him with rage and tears, and personal abuse,— but Thelma was too gentle for this,—too gentle to resist what seemed to be Philip's wish and will, and far too proud to stay where it appeared evident she was not wanted. Moreover she could not bear the idea of speaking to him on such a subject as his connection with Violet Vere,—the hot color flushed her cheeks with a sort of shame as she thought of it.

Of course, she was weak—of course, she was foolish,— we will grant th t she was anything the reader chooses to call her. It is much better for a woman nowadays to be defiant rather than yielding,—aggressive, not submissive,— violent, not meek. We all know that! To abuse a husband well all round, is the modern method of managing him! But poor, foolish, loving, sensitive Thelma had nothing of the magnificent strength of mind possessed by most wives of to-day,—she could only realize that Philip —her Philip—was "utterly weary and broken-hearted "— for the sake of another woman—and that other woman actually pitied *her!* She pitied herself too, a little vaguely —her brows ached and thro bed violently—there was a choking sensation in her throat, but she could not weep. Tears would have relieved her tired brain, but no tears fell. She strove to decide on some immediate plan of action,—Philip would be home to-morrow,—she recoiled at the thought of meeting him, knowing what she knew. Glancing dreamily at her own figure, reflected by the lamplight in the long mirror opposite, she recognized that she was fully attired in outdoor costume—all save her hat, which she had taken off after her first greeting of Lady Winsleigh, and which was still on the table at her side. She looked at the clock,—it was five minutes to seven. Eight o'clock was her dinner-hour, and thinking of this, she suddenly rang the bell. Morris immediately answered it.

"I shall not dine at home," she said in her usual gentle voice; "I am going to see some friend this evening. I may not be back till—till late."

" Very well, my lady," and Morris retired without seeing anything remarkable in his mistress's announcement. Thelma drew a long breath of relief as he disappeared, and, steadying her nerves by a strong effort, passed into her own boudoir,—the little sanctum specially endeared to her by Philip's frequent presence there. How cosy and comfortable a home-nest it looked !—a small fire glowed warmly in the grate, and Britta, whose duty it was to keep this particular room in order, had lit the lamp,—a rosy globe supported by a laughing cupid,—and had drawn the velvet curtains close at the window to keep out the fog and chilly air —there were fragrant flowers on the table,—Thelma's own favorite lounge was drawn up to the fender in readiness for her,—opposite to it stood the deep, old-fashioned easy chair in which Philip always sat. She looked round upon all these familiar things with a dreary sense of strangeness and desolation, and the curves of her sweet mouth trembled a little and drooped piteously. But her resolve was taken, and she did not hesitate or weep. She sat down to her desk and wrote a few brief lines to her father—this letter she addressed and stamped ready for posting.

Then for a while she remained apparently lost in painful musings, playing with the pen she held, and uncertain what to do. Presently she drew a sheet of note-paper toward her, and began, " My darling boy." As these words appeared under her hand on the white page, her forced calm nearly gave way,—a low cry of intense agony escaped from her lips, and, dropping the pen, she rose and paced the room restlessly, one hand pressed against her heart as though that action could still its rapid beatings. Once more she essayed the hard task she had set herself to fulfill—the task of bidding farewell to the husband in whom her life was centred. Piteous, passionate words came quickly from her overcharged and almost breaking heart—words, tender, touching,—full of love, and absolutely free from all reproach. Little did she guess as she wrote that parting letter, what desperate misery it would cause to the receiver !—

When she had finished it, she felt quieted—even more composed than before. She folded and sealed it—then put it out of sight and rang for Britta. That little maiden soon appeared, and seemed surprised to see her mistress still in walking costume.

" Have you only just come in, Fröken ? " she ventured to inquire.

" No, I came home some time ago," returned Thelma gently. " But I was talking to Lady Winsleigh in the drawing-room,—and as I am going out again this evening I shall not require to change my dress. I want you to post this letter for me, Britta."

And she held out the one addressed to her father, Olaf Güldmar. Britta took it, but her mind still revolved the question of her mistress's attire.

" If you are going to spend the evening with friends," she suggested, " would it not be better to change ? "

" I have on a velvet gown," said Thelma, with a rather wearied patience. " It is quite dressy enough for where I am going." She paused abruptly, and Britta looked at her inquiringly.

" Are you tired, Fröken Thelma ? " she asked. " You are so pale ! "

" I have a slight headache," Thelma answered. " It is nothing,—it will soon pass. I wish you to post that letter at once, Britta."

" Very well, Fröken." Britta still hesitated. " Will you be out all the evening ? " was her next query.

" Yes."

" Then perhaps you will not mind if I go and see Louise, and take supper with her ? She has asked me, and Mr. Briggs "—here Britta laughed—" is coming to see if I can go. He will escort me, he says ! " And she laughed again.

Thelma forced herself to smile. " You can go, by all means, Britta ! But I thought you did not like Lady Winsleigh's French maid ? "

" I don't like her much," Britta admitted—" still, she means to be kind and agreeable, I think. And "—here she eyed Thelma with a mysterious and important air—" I want to ask her a question about something very particular."

" Then, go and stay as long as you like, dear," said Thelma, a sudden impulse off affection causing her to caress softly her little maid's ruffled brown curls, " I shall not be back till—till quite late. And when you return from the post, I shall be gone—so—good-bye ! "

" Good-bye ! " exclaimed Britta wonderingly. " Why, where are you going ? One would think you were starting on a long journey. You speak so strangely, Fröken ! "

" Do I ? " and Thelma smiled kindly. " It is because my

head aches, I suppose. But it is not strange to say good.
bye, Britta ! "

Britta caught her hand. " Where are you going ? " she
persisted.

" To see some friends," responded Thelma quietly. " Now
do not ask any more questions, Britta, but go and post my
letter. I want father to get it as soon as possible, and you
will lose the post if you are not very quick."

Thus reminded, Britta hastened off, determining to run
all the way, in order to get back before her mistress left the
house. Thelma, however, was too quick for her. As soon
as Britta had gone, she took the letter she had written to
Philip, and slipped it within the pages of a small volume
of poems he had lately been reading. " It was a new book,
entitled " Gladys the Singer," and its leading *metif* was
the old, never-exhausted subject of a woman's too faithful
love, betrayal, and despair. As she opened it, her eyes fell
by chance on a few lines of hopeless yet musical melancholy, which, like a sad song heard suddenly, made her
throat swell with rising yet restrained tears. They ran
thus :—

> "Oh ! I can drown, or, like a broken lyre,
> Be thrown to earth, or cast upon a fire,—
> I can be made to feel the pangs of death,
> And yet be constant to the quest of breath,—
> Our poor pale trick of living through the lies
> We name Existence when that 'something' dies
> Which we call Honor. Many and many a way
> Can I be struck or fretted night or day
> In some new fashion,—or condemn'd the while
> To take for food the semblance of a smile,—
> The left-off rapture of a slain caress,—"

Ah !—she caught her breath sobbingly, " The left-off rapture of a slain caress ! " Yes,—that would be her portion
now if—if she stayed to receive it. But she would not
stay ! She turned over the volume abstractedly, scarcely
conscious of the action,—and suddenly, as if the poet-
writer of it had been present to probe her soul and make
her inmost thoughts public, she read :—

> " Because I am unlov'd of thee to-day,
> And undesired as sea-weeds in the sea ! "

Yes !—that was the " because " of everything that swayed
her sorrowful spirit,—" because " she was " unlov'd and
undesired."

She hesitated no longer, but shut the book with her farewell letter inside it, and put it back in its former place on the little table beside Philip's arm-chair. Then she considered how she should distinguish it by some mark that should attract her husband's attention toward it,—and loosening from her neck a thin gold chain on which was suspended a small diamond cross with the names " Philip " and " Thelma " engraved at the back, she twisted it round the little book, and left it so that the sparkle of the jewels should be seen distinctly on the cover. Now was there anything more to be done ? She divested herself of all her valuable ornaments, keeping only her wedding-ring and its companion circlet of brilliants,—she emptied her purse of all money save that which was absolutely necessary for her journey—then she put on her hat, and began to fasten her long cloak slowly, for her fingers were icy cold and trembled very strangely. Stay,—there was her husband's portrait, —she might take that, she thought, with a sort of touching timidity. It was a miniature on ivory—and had been painted expressly for her,—she placed it inside her dress, against her bosom.

" He has been too good to me," she murmured ; " and I have been too happy,—happier than I deserved to be. Excess of happiness must always end in sorrow."

She looked dreamily at Philip's empty chair—in fancy she could see his familiar figure seated there, and she sighed as she thought of the face she loved so well,—the passion of his eyes,—the tenderness of his smile. Softly she kissed the place where his head had rested,—then turned resolutely away.

She was giving up everything, she thought, to another woman,—but then—that other woman, however incredible it seemed, was the one Philip loved best,—his own written words were a proof of this. There was no choice therefore, —his pleasure was her first consideration,—everything must yield to that, so she imagined,—her own life was nothing, in her estimation, compared to his desire. Such devotion as hers was of course absurd—it amounted to weak self-immolation, and would certainly be accounted as supremely foolish by most women who have husbands, and who, when they swear to " obey," mean to break the vow at every convenient opportunity—but Thelma could not alter her strange nature, and, with her, obedience meant the extreme letter of the law of utter submission.

Leaving the room she had so lately called her own, she passed into the entrance-hall. Morris was not there, and she did not summon him,—she opened the street-door for herself, and shutting it quietly behind her, she stood alone in the cold street, where the fog had now grown so dense that the lamp-posts were scarcely visible. She walked on for a few paces rather bewildered and chilled by the piercing bitterness of the air,—then, rallying her forces, she hailed a passing cab, and told the man to take her to Charing Cross Station. She was not familiar with London—and Charing Cross was the only great railway terminus she could just then think of.

Arrived there, the glare of the electric light, the jostling passengers rushing to and from the trains, the shouts and wrangling of porters and cabmen, confused her not a little, —and the bold looks of admiration bestowed on her freely by the male loungers sauntering near the doors of the restaurant and hotel, made her shrink and tremble for shame. She had never travelled entirely alone before—and she began to be frightened at the pandemonium of sights and noises that surged around her. Yet she never once thought of returning,—she never dreamed of going to any of her London friends, lest on hearing of her trouble they might reproach Philip—and this Thelma would not have endured. For the same reason, she had said nothing to Britta.

In her then condition, it seemed to her that only one course lay open for her to follow,—and that was to go quietly home,—home to the Altenfjord. No one would be to blame for her departure but herself, she thought,—and Philip would be free. Thus she reasoned,—if, indeed, she reasoned at all. But there was such a frozen stillness in her soul—her senses were so numbed with pain, that as yet she scarcely realized either what had happened or what she herself was doing. She was as one walking in sleep—the awakening, bitter as death, was still to come.

Presently a great rush of people began to stream towards her from one of the platforms, and trucks of luggage, heralded by shouts of, " Out of the way, there ! " and " By'r leave ! " came trundling rapidly along—the tidal train from the Continent had just arrived.

Dismayed at the increasing confusion and uproar, Thelma addressed herself to an official with a gold band round his hat.

"Can you tell me," she asked timidly, "where I shall take a ticket for Hull ?'

The man glanced at the fair, anxious face, and smiled good-humoredly.

"You've come to the wrong station, miss," he said. "You want the Midland line."

"The Midland?" Thelma felt more bewildered than ever.

"Yes,—the *Midland*," he repeated rather testily. "It's a good way from here—you'd better take a cab."

She moved away,—but started and drew herself back into a shadowed corner, coloring deeply as the sound of a rich, mellifluous voice, which she instantly recognized, smote suddenly on her ears.

"And as I before remarked, my good fellow," the voice was saying, "I am not a disciple of the semi-obscure. If a man has a thought which is worth declaring, let him declare it with a free and noble utterance—don't let him wrap it up in multifarious parcels of dreary verbosity! There's too much of that kind of thing going on nowadays—in England, at least. There's a kind of imitation of art which isn't art at all,—a morbid, bilious, bad imitation. You only get close to the real goddess in Italy. I wish I could persuade you to come and pass the winter with me there?"

It was Beau Lovelace who spoke, and he was talking to George Lorimer. The two had met in Paris,—Lovelace was on his way to London, where a matter of business summoned him for a few days, and Lorimer, somewhat tired of the French capital, decided to return with him. And here they were,—just arrived at Charing Cross,—and they walked across the station arm in arm, little imagining who watched them from behind the shelter of one of the waiting-room doors, with a yearning sorrow in her grave blue eyes. They stopped almost opposite to her to light their cigars,— she saw Lorimer's face quite distinctly, and heard his answer to Lovelace.

"Well, I'll see what I can do about it, Beau! You know my mother always likes to get away from London in winter—but whether we ought to inflict ourselves upon you,—you being a literary man too——"

"Nonsense, you won't interfere in the least with the flow of inky inspiration," laughed Beau. "And as for your mother, I'm in love with her, as you are aware! I admire her almost as much as I do Lady Bruce-Errington—and that's saying a great deal! By-the-by, if Phil can get through his share of this country's business, he might do worse than bring his beautiful Thelma to the Lake of Como for a while. I'll ask him!"

And having lit their Havannas successfully, they walked on and soon disappeared. For one instant Thelma felt strongly inclined to run after them, like a little forlorn child that had lost its way,—and, unburdening herself of all her miseries to the sympathetic George, entreat, with tears, to be taken back to that husband who did not want her any more. But she soon overcame this emotion,—and calling to mind the instructions of the official personage whose advice she had sought, she hurried out of the huge, brilliantly lit station, and taking a hansom, was driven, as she requested, to the Midland. Here the rather gloomy aspect of the place oppressed her as much as the garish bustle of Charing Cross had bewildered her,—but she was somewhat relieved when she learned that a train for Hull would start in ten minutes. Hurrying to the ticket-office she found there before her a kindly faced woman with a baby in her arms, who was just taking a third-class ticket to Hull, and as she felt lonely and timid, Thelma at once decided to travel third-class also, and if possible in the same compartment with this cheerful matron, who, as soon as she had secured her ticket, walked away to the train, hushing her infant in her arms as she went. Thelma followed her at a little distance—and as soon as she saw her enter a third-class carriage, she hastened her steps and entered also, quite thankful to have secured some companionship for the long cold journey. The woman glanced at her a little curiously—it was strange to see so lovely and young a creature travelling all alone at night,—and she asked kindly——

"Be you goin' fur, miss?"

Thelma smiled—it was pleasant to be spoken to, she thought.

"Yes," she answered. "All the way to Hull."

"'Tis a cold night for a journey," continued her companion.

"Yes, indeed," answered Thelma. "It must be cold for your little baby."

And unconsciously her voice softened and her eyes grew sad as she looked across at the sleeping infant.

" Oh, he's as warm as toast!" laughed the mother cheerily. "He gets the best of everything, he do. It's yourself that's looking cold, my dear in spite of your warm cloak. Will ye have this shawl?"

And she offered Thelma a homely gray woollen wrap with much kindly earnestness of manner.

" I am quite warm, thank you," said Thelma gently, accepting the shawl, however, to please her fellow-traveller. " It is a headache I have which makes me look pale. And I am very, very tired!"

Her voice trembled a little,—she sighed and closed her eyes. She felt strangely weak and giddy,—she seemed to be slipping away from herself and from all the comprehension of life,—she wondered vaguely who and what she was. Had her marriage with Philip been all a dream?—perhaps she had never left the Altenfjord after all! Perhaps she would wake up presently and see the old farm-house quite unchanged, with the doves flying about the roof, and Sigurd wandering under the pines as was his custom. Ah, dear Sigurd! Poor Sigurd! he had loved her, she thought— nay, he loved her still,—he could not be dead! Oh, yes,— she must have been dreaming,—she felt certain she was lying on her own little white bed at home, asleep ;—she would by-and-by open her eyes and get up and look through her little latticed window, and see the sun sparkling on the water, and the *Eulalie* at the anchor in the Fjord—and her father would ask Sir Philip and his friends to spend the afternoon at the farm-house—and Philip would come and stroll with her through the garden and down to the shore, and would talk to her in that low, caressing voice of his,— and though she loved him dearly, she must never, never let him know of it, because she was not worthy! . . . She woke from these musings with a violent start and a sick shiver running through all her frame,—and looking wildly about her, saw that she was reclining on some one's shoulder,—some one was dabbing a wet hankerchief on her forehead—her hat was off and her cloak was loosened.

" There, my dear, you're better now!" said a kindly voice in her ear. "Lor! I thought you was dead—that I did! 'Twas a bad faint indeed. And with the train jolting along like this too! It was lucky I had a flask of cold water with me. Raise your head a little—that's it! Poor thing,—you're as white as a sheet! You're not fit to travel, my dear—you're not indeed."

Thelma raised herself slowly, and with a sudden impulse kissed the good woman's honest, rosy face, to her intense astonishment and pleasure.

" You are very kind to me ! " she said tremulously. " I am so sorry to have troubled you. I do feel ill—but it will soon pass."

And she smoothed her ruffled hair, and sitting up erect, endeavored to smile. Her companion eyed her pale face compassionately, and taking up her sleeping baby from the shawl on which she had laid it while ministering to Thelma's needs, began to rock it slowly to and fro. Thelma, meanwhile, became sensible of the rapid movement of the train.

" We have left London ? " she asked with an air of surprise.

" Nearly half an hour ago, my dear." Then, after a pause, during which she had watched Thelma very closely, she said—

" I think you're married, aren't you, dearie ? "

" Yes." Thelma answered, a slight tinge of color warming her fair pale cheeks.

" Your husband, maybe, will meet you at Hull ? "

" No,—he is in London," said Thelma simply. " I am going to see my father."

This answer satisfied her humble friend, who, noticing her extreme fatigue and the effort it cost her to speak, forbore to ask any more questions, but good-naturedly recommended her to try and sleep. She slept soundly herself for the greater part of the journey ; but Thelma was now feverishly wide awake, and her eyeballs ached and burned as though there were fire behind them.

Gradually her nerves began to be wound up to an extreme tension of excitement—she forgot all her troubles in listening with painful intentness to the rush and roar of the train through the darkness. The lights of passing stations and signal-posts gleamed like scattered and flying stars—there was the frequent shriek of the engine-whistle, —the serpent-hiss of escaping steam. She peered through the window—all was blackness ; there seemed to be no earth, no sky,—only a sable chaos, through which the train flew like a flame-mouthed demon. Always that rush and roar ! She began to feel as if she could stand it no longer. She must escape from that continuous, confusing sound—it maddened her brain. Nothing was easier ; she would open the carriage-door and get out! Surely she could manage to jump off the step, even though the train was in motion!

Danger! She smiled at that idea,—there was no danger; and, if there was, it did not much matter. Nothing mattered now,—now that she had lost her husband's love. She glanced at the woman opposite, who slept profoundly—the baby had slipped a little from its mother's arms, and lay with its tiny face turned towards Thelma. It was a pretty creature, with soft cheeks and a sweet little mouth,—she looked at it with a vague, wild smile. Again, again that rush and roar surged like a storm in her ears and distracted her mind! She rose suddenly and seized the handle of the carriage door. Another instant, and she would have sprung to certain death,—when suddenly the sleeping baby woke, and, opening its mild blue eyes, gazed at her.

She met its glance as one fascinated,—almost unconsciously her fingers dropped from the door-handle,—the little baby still looked at her in dreamlike, meditative fashion, —its mother slept profoundly. She bent lower and lower over the child. With a beating heart she ventured to touch the small, pink hand that lay outside its wrappings like a softly curved rose-leaf. With a sort of elf-like confidence and contentment the feeble, wee fingers closed and curled round hers,—and held her fast! Weak as a silken thread, yet stronger in its persuasive force than a grasp of iron, that soft, light pressure controlled and restrained her, . . . very gradually the mists of her mind cleared,—the rattling, thunderous dash of the train grew less dreadful, less monotonous, less painful to her sense of hearing,—her bosom heaved convulsively, and all suddenly her eyes filled with tears—merciful tears, which at first welled up slowly, and were hot as fire, but which soon began to fall faster and faster in large, bright drops down her pale cheeks. Seeing that its mother still slept, she took the baby gently into her own fair arms,—and rocked it to and fro with many a sobbing murmur of tenderness;—the little thing smiled drowsily and soon fell asleep again, all unconscious that its timely look and innocent touch had saved poor Thelma's life and reason.

She, meanwhile, wept on softly, till her tired brain and heart were somewhat relieved of their heavy burden,—the entanglement of her thoughts became unravelled,—and, though keenly aware of the blank desolation of her life, she was able to raise herself in spirit to the Giver of all Love and Consolation, and to pray humbly for that patience and resignation which now alone could serve her needs. And she communed with herself and God in silence, as the train rushed on northwards. Her fellow-traveller woke up as they were nearing their destination, and, seeing her holding the baby, was profuse in her thanks for this kindness. And when they at last reached Hull, about half an hour after midnight, the good woman was exceedingly anxious to know if she could be of any service,—but Thelma gently, yet firmly, refused all her offers of assistance.

They parted in the most friendly manner,—Thelma kissing the child, through whose unconscious means, as she now owned to herself, she had escaped a terrible death,—and then she went directly to a quiet hotel she knew of, which was kept by a native of Christiania, a man who had formerly been acquainted with her father. At first, when this worthy individual saw a lady arrive, alone, young, richly dressed, and without luggage, he was inclined to be suspicious,—but as soon as she addressed him in Norwegian, and told him who she was, he greeted her with the utmost deference and humility.

" The daughter of Jarl Güldmar," he said, continuing to speak in his own tongue, " honors my house by entering it ! "

Thelma smiled a little. " The days of the great Jarls are past, Friedhof," she replied somewhat sadly, " and my father is content to be what he is,—a simple *bonde.*"

Friedhof shook his head quite obstinately. " A Jarl is always a Jarl," he declared. " Nothing can alter a man's birth and nature. And the last time I saw Valdemar Svensen,—he who lives with your father now,—he was careful always to speak of the *Jarl*, and seldom or never did he mention him in any other fashion. And now, noble Fröken, in what manner can I serve you ? "

Thelma told him briefly that she was going to see her father on business, and that she was desirous of starting for Norway the next day as early as possible.

Friedhof held up his hands in amazement. " Ah ! most surely you forget," he exclaimed, using the picturesque expressions of his native speech, " that this is the sleeping time of the sun ! Even at the Hardanger Fjord it is dark and silent,—the falling streams freeze with cold on their way ; and if it is so at the Hardanger, what will it be at the Alten? And there is no passenger ship going to Christiania or Bergen for a fortnight!"

Thelma clasped her hands in dismay. "But I *must* go!" she cried impatiently; "I must, indeed, good Friedhof! I cannot stay here! Surely, surely there is some vessel that would take me,—some fishing boat,—what does it matter how I travel, so long as I get away?"

The landlord looked at her rather wonderingly. "Nay, if it is indeed so urgent, noble Fröken," he replied, "do not trouble, for there is a means of making the journey. But for *you*, and in such bitter weather, it seems a cruelty to speak of it. A steam cargo-boat leaves here for Hammerfest and the North Cape to-morrow—it will pass the Altenfjord. No doubt you could go with that, if you so choose, —but there will be no warmth or comfort, and there are heavy storms on the North Sea. I know the captain; and 'tis true he takes his wife with him, so there would be a woman on board,—yet——"

Thelma interrupted him. She pressed two sovereigns into his hand.

"Say no more, Friedhof," she said eagerly. "You will take me to see this captain—you will tell him I must go with him. My father will thank you for this kindness to me, even better than I can."

"It does not seem to me a kindness at all," returned Friedhof with frank bluntness. "I would be loth to sail the seas myself in such weather. And I thought you were so grandly married, Fröken Güldmar,—though I forget your wedded name,—how comes it that your husband is not with you?"

"He is very busy in London," answered Thelma. "He knows where I am going. Do not be at all anxious, Friedhof,—I shall make the journey very well and I am not afraid of storm or wild seas."

Friedhof still looked dubious, but finally yielded to her entreaties and agreed to arrange her passage for her in the morning.

She stayed at his hotel that night, and with the very early dawn accompanied him on board the ship he had mentioned. It was a small, awkwardly built craft, with an ugly crooked black funnel out of which the steam was hissing and spitting with quite an unnecessary degree of violence—the decks were wet and dirty, and the whole vessel was pervaded with a sickening smell of whale-oil. The captain, a gruff red-faced fellow, looked rather surlily at his unexpected passenger—but was soon mollified by her gentle manner, and the readiness with which she paid the money he demanded for taking her.

"You won't be very warm," he said, eyeing her from head to foot—"but I can lend you a rug to sleep in."

Thelma smiled and thanked him. He called to his wife, a thin, overworked-looking creature, who put up her head from a window in the cabin, at his summons.

"Here's a lady going with us," he announced. "Look after her, will you?" The woman nodded. Then, once more addressing himself to Thelma, he said, "We shall have nasty weather and a wicked sea!"

"I do not mind!" she answered quietly, and turning to Friedhof who had come to see her off, she shook hands with him warmly and thanked him for the trouble he had taken in her behalf. The good landlord bade her farewell somewhat reluctantly,—he had a presentiment that there was something wrong with the beautiful, golden-haired daughter of the *Jarl*—and that perhaps he ought to have prevented her making this uncomfortable and possibly perilous voyage. But it was too late now,—and at a little before seven o'clock, the vessel,—which rejoiced in the name of the *Black Polly*,—left the harbor, and steamed fussily down the Humber in the teeth of a sudden storm of sleet and snow.

Her departure had no interest for any one save Friedhof, who stood watching her till she was no more than a speck on the turbid water. He kept his post, regardless of the piercing cold of the gusty, early morning air, till she had entirely disappeared, and then returned to his own house and his daily business in a rather depressed frame of mind. He was haunted by the pale face and serious eyes of Thelma—she looked very ill, he thought. He began to reproach himself,—why had he been such a fool as to let her go?—why had he not detained her?—or at any rate, persuaded her to rest a few days in Hull? He looked at the threatening sky and the falling flakes of snow with a shiver.

"What weather!" he muttered, "and there must be a darkness as of death at the Altenfjord!"

Meanwhile the *Black Polly*—unhandsome as she was in appearance, struggled gallantly with and overcame an army of furious waves that rose to greet her as she rounded

Spurn Head, and long ere Thelma closed her weary eyes in an effort to sleep, was plunging, shivering, and fighting her slow way through shattering mountainous billows and a tempest of sleet, snow, and tossing foam across the wild North Sea.

CHAPTER XXVII.

" What of her glass without her ?   The blank grey
There, where the pool is blind of the moon's face—
Her dress without her ?   The tossed empty space
Of cloud-rack whence the moon has passed away ! "
DANTE G. ROSSETTI.

" Good God ! " cried Errington impatiently. " What's the matter ? Speak out ! "

He had just arrived home. He had barely set foot within his own door, and full of lover-like ardor and eager-ness was about to hasten to his wife's room,—when his old servant Morris stood in his way trembling and pale-faced, —looking helplessly from him to Neville,—who was as much astonished as Sir Philip, at the man's woe-begone appearance.

" Something has happened," he stammered faintly at last. " Her ladyship—— "

Philip started—his heart beat quickly and then seemed to grow still with a horrible sensation of fear.

" What of her ? " he demanded in low hoarse tones. " Is she ill ? "

Morris threw up his hands with a gesture of despair.

" Sir Philip, my dear master ! " cried the poor old man. " I do not know whether she is ill or well—I cannot guess ! My lady went out last night at a little before eight o'clock, —and—and she has never come home at all ! We cannot tell what has become of her ! She has gone ! "

And tears of distress and anxiety filled his eyes. Philip stood mute. He could not understand it. All color fled from his face—he seemed as though he had received a sud-den blow on the head which had stunned him.

" Gone ! " he said mechanically. " Thelma—my wife gone ! Why should she go ? "

And he stared fixedly at Neville, who laid one hand soothingly on his arm.

" Perhaps she is with friends," he suggested. " She may be at Lady Winsleigh's or Mrs. Lorimer's."

26

"No, no!" interrupted Morris. "Britta, who stayed up all night for her, has since been to every house that my lady visits and no one has seen or heard of her!"

"Where is Britta?" demanded Philip suddenly.

"She has gone again to Lady Winsleigh's," answered Morris, "she says it is there that mischief has been done,—I don't know what she means!"

Philip shook off his secretary's sympathetic touch, and strode through the rooms to Thelma's boudoir. He put aside the velvet curtains of the portiére with a noiseless hand—somehow he felt as if, in spite of all he had just heard, she *must* be there as usual to welcome him with that serene sweet smile which was the sunshine of his life. The empty desolate air of the room smote him with a sense of bitter pain,—only the plaintive warble of her pet thrush, who was singing to himself most mournfully in his gilded cage, broke the heavy silence. He looked about him vacantly. All sorts of dark forebodings crowded on his mind, —she must have met with some accident, he thought with a shudder,—for that she would depart from him in this sudden way of her own accord for no reason whatsoever seemed to him incredible—impossible.

"What have I done that she should leave me?" he asked half aloud and wonderingly. Everything that had seemed to him of worth a few hours ago became valueless in this moment of time. What cared he now for the business of Parliament—for distinction or honors among men? Nothing—less than nothing! Without her, the world was empty —its ambitions, its pride, its good, its evil, seemed but the dreariest and most foolish trifles!

"Not even a message?" he thought. "No hint of where she meant to go—no word of explanation for me? Surely I must be dreaming—my Thelma would never have deserted me!"

A sort of sob rose in his throat, and he pressed his hand strongly over his eyes to keep down the womanish drops that threatened to overflow them. After a minute or two, he went to her desk and opened it, thinking that there perhaps she might have left a note of farewell. There was nothing—nothing save a little heap of money and jewels. These Thelma had herself placed, before her sorrowful, silent departure, in the corner where he now found them.

More puzzled than ever, he glanced searchingly round the room—and his eyes were at once attracted by the sparkle of the diamond cross that lay uppermost on the cover of "Gladys the Singer," the book of poems which was in its usual place on his own reading table. In another second he seized it—he unwound the slight gold chain—he opened the little volume tremblingly. Yes!—there was a letter within its pages addressed to himself,—now, now he should know all! He tore it open with feverish haste—two folded sheets of paper fell out,—one was his own epistle to Violet Vere, and this, to his consternation, he perceived first. Full of a sudden misgiving he laid it aside, and began to read Thelma's parting words.

"My darling boy," she wrote—

"A friend of yours and mine brought me the enclosed letter and though, perhaps, it was wrong of me to read it, I hope you will forgive me for having done so. I do not quite understand it, and I cannot bear to think about it—but it seems that you are tired of your poor Thelma! I do not blame you, dearest, for I am sure that in some way or other the fault is mine, and it does grieve me so much to think you are unhappy! I know that I am very ignorant of many things, and that I am not suited to this London life —and I fear I shall never understand its ways. But one thing I can do, and that is to let you be free, my Philip— quite free! And so I am going back to the Altenfjord, where I will stay till you want me again, if you ever do. My heart is yours and I shall always love you till I die,— and though it seems to me just now better that we should part, to give you greater ease and pleasure, still you must always remember that I have no reproaches to make to you. I am only sorry to think my love has wearied you,— for you have been all goodness and tenderness to me. And so that people shall not talk about me or you, you will simply say to them that I have gone to see my father, and they will think nothing strange in that. Be kind to Britta, —I have told her nothing, as it would only make her miserable. Do not be angry that I go away—I cannot bear to stay here, knowing all. And so, good-bye, my love, my dearest one!—if you were to love many women more than me, I still should love you best—I still would gladly die to serve you. Remember this always,—that, however long we may be parted, and though all the world should come between us, I am, and ever shall be your faithful wife,

" THELMA."

The ejaculation that broke from Errington's lips as he finished reading this letter was more powerful than reverent. Stinging tears darted to his eyes—he pressed his lips passionately on the fair writing.

" My darling—my darling ! " he murmured. " What a miserable misunderstanding ! "

Then without another moment's delay he rushed into Neville's study and cried abruptly—

" Look here ! It's all your fault."

" *My* fault ! " gasped the amazed secretary.

" Yes—your fault ! " shouted Errington almost beside himself with grief and rage. " Your fault, and that of your accursed *wife*, Violet Vere ! "

And he dashed the letter, the cause of all the mischief, furiously down on the table. Neville shrank and shivered, —his grey head drooped, he stretched out his hands appealingly.

" For God's sake, Sir Philip, tell me what I've done ? " he exclaimed piteously.

Errington strode up and down the room in a perfect fever of impatience.

" By Heaven, it's enough to drive me mad ! " he burst forth.

" Your wife !—your wife !—confound her ! When you first discovered her in that shameless actress, didn't I want to tell Thelma all about it—that very night ?—and didn't you beg me not to do so ? Your silly scruples stood in the way of everything ! I was a fool to listen to you—a fool to meddle in your affairs—and—and I wish to God I'd never seen or heard of you ! "

Neville turned very white, but remained speechless.

" Read that letter ! " went on Philip impetuously. " You've seen it before ! It's the last one I wrote to your wife imploring her to see you and speak with you. Here it comes, the devil knows how, into Thelma's hands. She's quite in the dark about *your* secret, and fancies I wrote it on my own behalf ! It looks like it too—looks exactly as if I were pleading for myself and breaking my heart over that detestible stage-fiend—by Jove ! it's too horrible ! " And he gave a gesture of loathing and contempt.

Neville heard him in utter bewilderment. " Not possible ! " he muttered. " Not possible—it can't be ! "

" Can't be ? It *is !* " shouted Philip. " And if you'd let me tell Thelma everything from the first, all this wouldn't have happened. And you ask me what you've done! *Done!* You've parted me from the sweetest, dearest girl in the world!"

And throwing himself into a chair, he covered his face with his hand and a great uncontrollable sob broke from his lips.

Neville was in despair. Of course, it was his fault—he saw it all clearly. He painfully recalled all that had happened since that night at the Brilliant Theatre when with a sickening horror he had discovered Violet Vere to be no other than Violet Neville,—his own little violet! . . . as he had once called her—his wife that he had lost and mourned as though she were some pure dead woman lying sweetly at rest in a quiet grave. He remembered Thelma's shuddering repugnance at the sight of her,—a repugnance which he himself had shared—and which made him shrink with fastidious aversion, from the idea of confiding to any one but Sir Philip, the miserable secret of his connection with her. Sir Philip had humored him in this fancy, little imagining that any mischief would come of it—and the reward of his kindly sympathy was this,—his name was compromised, his home desolate, and his wife enstranged from him!

In the first pangs of the remorse and sorrow that filled his heart, Neville could gladly have gone out and drowned himself. Presently he began to think,—was there not some one else beside himself who might possibly be to blame for all this misery? For instance, who could have brought or sent that letter to Lady Errington? In her high station, she, so lofty, so pure, so far above the rest of her sex, would have been the last person to make any inquiries about such a woman as Violet Vere. How had it all happened? He looked imploringly for some minutes at the dejected figure in the chair without daring to offer a word of consolation. Presently he ventured a remark——

"Sir Philip!" he stammered. "It will soon be all right, —her ladyship will come back immediately. I myself will explain—it's—it's only a misunderstanding . . ."

Errington moved in his chair impatiently, but said nothing. Only a misunderstanding! How many there are who can trace back broken friendships and severed loves to that one thing—"only a misunderstanding!" The tenderest relations are often the most delicate and subtle, and "trifles light as air" may scatter and utterly destroy the sensitive gossamer threads extending between one heart and another, as easily as a child's passing foot destroys the spider's web woven on the dewy grass in the early mornings of spring.

Presently Sir Philip started up—his lashes were wet and his face was flushed.

"It's no good sitting here," he said, rapidly buttoning on his overcoat. "I must go after her. Let all the business go to the devil! Write and say I won't stand for Middleborough—I resign in favor of the Liberal candidate. I'm off to Norway to-night."

"To Norway!" cried Neville. "Has she gone *there*? At this season——"

He broke off, for at that moment Britta entered, looking the picture of misery. Her face was pale and drawn—her eyelids red and swollen, and when she saw Sir Philip, she gave him a glance of the most despairing reproach and indignation. He sprang up to her.

"Any news?" he demanded.

Britta shook her head mournfully, the tears beginning to roll again down her cheeks.

"Oh, if I'd only thought!" she sobbed, "if I'd only known what the dear Fröken meant to do when she said good-bye to me last night, I could have prevented her going— I could—I would have told her all I know—and she would have stayed to see you! Oh, Sir Philip, if you had only been here, that wicked, wicked Lady Winsleigh *couldn't* have driven her away!"

At this name such a fury filled Philip's heart that he could barely control himself. He breathed quickly and heavily.

"What of her?" he demanded in a low, suffocated voice. "What has Lady Winsleigh to do with it, Britta?"

"Everything!" cried Britta, though, as she glanced at his set, stern face and paling lips, she began to feel a little frightened. "She has always hated the Fröken, and been jealous of her—always! Her own maid, Louise, will tell you so—Lord Winsleigh's man, Briggs, will tell you so! They've listened at the doors, and they know all about it!" Britta made this statement with the most childlike candor. "And they've heard all sorts of wicked things—Lady Winsleigh was always talking to Sir Francis Lennox about the Fröken,—and now they've made her believe you do not care for her any more—they've been trying to make her believe everything bad of you for ever so many months

———" she paused, terrified at Sir Philip's increasing pallor.

"Go on, Britta," he said quietly, though his voice sounded strange to himself. Britta gathered up all her remaining stock of courage.

"Oh dear, oh dear!" she continued desperately, "I *don't* understand London people at all, and I never shall understand them. Everybody seems to want to be wicked! Briggs says that Lady Winsleigh was fond of *you*, Sir Philip,—then, that she was fond of Sir Francis Lennox,— and yet she has a husband of her own all the time! It is so very strange!" And the little maiden's perplexity appeared to border on distraction. "They would think such a woman quite mad in Norway! But what is worse than anything is that you—you, Sir Philip,—oh! I *won't* believe it," and she stamped her foot passionately, "I *can't* believe it! . . . . and yet everybody says that you go to see a dreadful, painted dancing woman at the theatre, and that you like her better than the Fröken,—it *isn't* true, is it?" Here she peered anxiously at her master—but he was absolutely silent. Neville made as though he would speak, but a gesture from Sir Philip's hand restrained him. Britta went on rather dispiritedly, "Anyhow, Briggs has just told me that only yesterday Lady Winsleigh went all by herself to see this actress, and that she got some letter there which she brought to the Fröken——" she recoiled suddenly with a little scream. "Oh, Sir Philip!—where are you going?"

Errington's hand came down on her shoulder, as he twisted her lightly out of his path and strode to the door.

"Sir Philip—Sir Philip!" cried Neville anxiously, hastening after him. "Think for a moment; don't do anything rash!" Philip wrung his hand convulsively. "Rash! My good fellow, it's a *woman* who has slandered me—what *can* I do? Her sex protects her!" He gave a short, furious laugh. "But— by God!—were she a man I'd shoot her dead!"

And with these words, and his eyes blazing with wrath, he left the room. Neville and Britta confronted each other in vague alarm.

"Where will he go?" half whispered Britta.

"To Winsleigh House, I suppose," answered Neville in the same low tone.

Just then the hall door shut with a loud bang, that echoed through the silent house.

"He's gone!" and as Neville said this he sighed and looked dubiously at his companion. "How do you know all this about Lady Winsleigh, Britta? It may not be true—it's only servants' gossip."

"Only servants' gossip!" exclaimed Britta. "And is that nothing? Why, in these grand houses like Lord Winsleigh's, the servants know everything! Briggs makes it his business to listen at the doors—he says it's a part of his duty. And Louise opens all her mistress's letters—she says she owes it to her own respectability to know what sort of a lady it is she serves. And she's going to leave, because she says her ladyship *isn't* respectable! There! what do you think of that! And Sir Philip will find out a great deal more than even *I* have told him—but oh! I *can't* understand about that actress!" And she shook her head despairingly.

"Britta," said Neville suddenly, "That actress is my wife!"

Britta started,—and her round eyes opened wide.

"Your wife, Mr. Neville?" she exclaimed.

Neville took off his spectacles and polished them nervously "Yes, Britta—my wife!"

She looked at him in amazed silence. Neville went on rubbing his glasses, and continued in rather dreamy, tremulous accents—

"Yes—I lost her years ago—I thought she was dead. But I found her—on the stage of the Brilliant Theatre. I—I never expected—*that!* I would rather she had died!" He paused and went on softly, "When I married her, Britta, she was such a dear little girl,—so bright and pretty!—and I—I fancied she was fond of me! Yes, I did, —of course, I was foolish—I've always been foolish, I think. And when—when I saw her on that stage I felt as if some one had struck me a hard blow—it seems as if I'd been stunned ever since. And though she knows I'm in London, she won't see me, Britta,—she won't let me speak to her even for a moment! It's very hard! Sir Philip has tried his best to persuade her to see me—he has talked to her and written to her about me; and that's not all,—he has even tried to make her come back to me—but it's all no use—and—and that's how all the mischief has arisen—do you see?"

Britta gazed at him still, with sympathy written on every line of her face,—but a great load had been lifted from her mind by his words—she began to understand everything.

"I'm so sorry for you, Mr. Neville!" she said. "But why didn't you tell all this to the Fröken?"

"I *couldn't!*" murmured Neville desperately. "She was there that night at the Brilliant,—and if you had seen how she looked when she saw—my wife—appeared on the stage! So pained, so sorry, so ashamed! and she wanted to leave the theatre at once. Of course, I ought to have told her,—I wish I had—but—somehow, I never could." He paused again. "It's all my stupidity, of course, Sir Philip is quite blameless—he has been the kindest, the best of friends to me——" his voice trembled more and more, and he could not go on. There was a silence of some minutes, during which Britta appeared absorbed in meditation, and Neville furtively wiped his eyes.

Presently he spoke again more cheerfully. "It'll soon be all right again, Britta!" and he nodded encouragingly. "Sir Philip says her ladyship has gone home to Norway, and he means to follow her to-night."

Britta nodded gravely, but heaved a deep sigh.

"And I posted her letter to her father!" she half murmured. "Oh, if I had only thought or guessed why it was written!"

"Isn't it rather a bad time of the year for Norway?" pursued Neville. "Why, there must be snow and darkness——"

"Snow and darkness at the Altenfjord!" suddenly cried Britta, catching at his words. "That's exactly what she said to me the other evening! Oh dear! I never thought of it—I never remembered it was the dark season!" She clasped her hands in dismay. "There is no sun at the Altenfjord now—it is like night—and the cold is bitter. And she is not strong—not strong enough to travel—and there's the North Sea to cross—oh, Mr. Neville," and she broke out sobbing afresh. "The journey will kill her,—I know it will! my poor, poor darling! I must go after her—I'll go with Sir Philip—I *won't* be left behind!"

"Hush, hush, Britta!" said Neville kindly, patting her shoulder. "Don't cry—don't cry!"

But he was very near crying himself, poor man, so shaken was he by the events of the morning. And he could not help admitting to himself the possibility that so long and trying a journey for Thelma in her present condition of health meant little else than serious illness—perhaps death. The only comfort he could suggest to the disconsolate Britta was, that at that time of year it was very probable there would be no steamer running to Christiansund or Bergen, and in that case Thelma would be unable to leave England, and would, therefore, be overtaken by Sir Philip at Hull.

Meanwhile, Sir Philip himself, in a white heat of restrained anger, arrived at Winsleigh House, and asked to see Lord Winsleigh immediately. Briggs, who opened the door to him, was a little startled at his haggard face and blazing eyes, even though he knew, through Britta, all about the sorrow that had befallen him. Briggs was not surprised at Lady Errington's departure,—that portion of his " duty " which consisted in listening at doors, had greatly enlightened him on many points,—all, save one—the reported connection between Sir Philip and Violet Vere. This seemed to be really true according to all appearances.

" Which it puzzles me," soliloquized the owner of the shapely calves. " It do, indeed. Yet I feels very much for Sir Philip,—I said to Flopsie this morning—' Flopsie, I feels for 'im ! ' Yes,—I used them very words. Only, of course, he shouldn't 'ave gone with Vi. She's a fine woman certainly—but skittish—d—d skittish ! I've allus made it a rule myself to avoid 'er on principle. Lor ! if I'd kep' company with 'er and the likes of 'er I shouldn't be the man I am ! " And he smiled complacently.

Lord Winsleigh, who was in his library as usual, occupied with his duties as tutor to his son Ernest, rose to receive Sir Philip with an air of more than his usual gravity.

" I was about to write to you, Errington," he began, and then stopped short, touched by the utter misery expressed in Philip's face. He addressed Ernest with a sort of nervous haste.

" Run away, my boy, to your own room. I'll send for you again presently."

Ernest obeyed. " Now," said Lord Winsleigh, as soon as the lad disappeared, " tell me everything, Errington. Is it true that your wife has left you ? "

" Left me ! " and Philip's eyes flashed with passionate anger. " No Winsleigh !—she's been driven away from me by the vilest and most heartless cruelty. She's been made to believe a scandalous and abominable lie against me—and she's gone! I—I—by Jove! I hardly like to say it to your face—but——"

" I understand!" a curious flicker of a smile shadowed rather than brightened Lord Winsleigh's stern features. " Pray speak quite plainly! Lady Winsleigh is to blame? I am not at all surprised!"

Errington gave him a rapid glance of wonder. He had always fancied Winsleigh to be a studious, rather dull sort of man, absorbed in books and the education of his son,—a man, more than half blind to everything that went on around him—and, moreover, one who deliberately shut his eyes to the frivolous coquetry of his wife,—and though he liked him fairly well, there had been a sort of vague contempt mingled with his liking. Now a new light was suddenly thrown on his character—there was something in his look, his manner, his very tone of voice,—which proved to Errington that there was a deep and forcible side to his nature of which his closest friends had never dreamed—and he was somewhat taken aback by the discovery. Seeing that he still hesitated, Winsleigh laid a hand encouragingly on his shoulder and said—

" I repeat—I'm not at all surprised! Nothing that Lady Winsleigh might do would cause me the slightest astonishment. She has long ceased to be my wife, except in name, —that she still bears that name and holds the position she has in the world is simply—for my son's sake! I do not wish,"—his voice quivered slightly—" I do not wish the boy to despise his mother. It's always a bad beginning for a young man's life. I want to avoid it for Ernest, if possible,—regardless of any personal sacrifice." He paused a moment—then resumed. " Now, speak out, Errington, and plainly,—for if mischief has been done and I can repair it in any way, you may be sure I will."

Thus persuaded, Sir Philip briefly related the whole story of the misunderstanding that had arisen concerning Neville's wife, Violet Vere.—and concluded by saying—

" It is, of course, only through Britta that I've just heard about Lady Winsleigh's having anything to do with it. Her information may not be correct—I hope it isn't,— but——"

Lord Winsleigh interrupted him. " Come with me," he said composedly. " We'll resolve this difficulty at once."

He led the way out of the library across the hall. Errington followed him in silence. He knocked at the door

of his wife's room,—in response to her " Come in ! " they
both entered. She was alone, reclining on a sofa, reading,
—she started up with a pettish exclamation at sight of her
husband, but observing who it was that came with him, she
stood mute, the color rushing to her cheeks with surprise
and something of fear. Yet she endeavored to smile, and
returned with her usual grace their somewhat formal salutations.

" Clara," then said Lord Winsleigh gravely, " I have to
ask you a question on behalf of Sir Philip Errington here,
—a question to which it is necessary for you to give the
plain answer. Did you or did you not procure this letter
from Violet Vere, of the Brilliant Theatre—and did you or
did you not, give it yourself yesterday into the hands of
Lady Bruce-Errington ? " And he laid the letter in question, which Philip had handed to him, down upon the table
before her.

She looked at it—then at him—then from him to Sir
Philip, who uttered no word—and lightly shrugged her
shoulders.

" I don't know what you are talking about," she said,
carelessly.

Sir Philip turned upon her indignantly.

" Lady Winsleigh, you *do* know——"

She interrupted him with a stately gesture.

" Excuse me, Sir Philip ! I am not accustomed to be
spoken to in this extraordinary manner. You forget yourself—my husband, I think, also forgets himself ! I know
nothing whatever about Violet Vere—I am not fond of the
society of actresses. Of course, I've heard about your admiration for her—that is common town-talk,—though my
informant on this point was Sir Francis Lennox."

" Sir Francis Lennox ! " cried Philip furiously. " Thank
God ! there's a man to deal with ! By Heaven, I'll choke
him with his own lie ! "

Lady Winsleigh raised her eyebrows in well-bred surprise.

" Dear me ! It is a lie, then ? Now, I should have
thought from all accounts that it was so very likely to be
true ! "

Philip turned white with passion. Her sarcastic smile,—
her mocking glance,—irritated him almost beyond endurance.

" Permit me to ask you, Clara," continued Lord Winsleigh calmly, " if you,—as you say, know nothing about

Violet Vere, why did you go to the Brilliant Theatre yesterday morning ? "

She flashed an angry glance at him.

" Why ? To secure a box for the new performance. Is there anything wonderful in that ? "

Her husband remained unmoved. " May I see the voucher for this box ? " he inquired.

" I've sent it to some friends," replied her ladyship haughtily. " Since when have you decided to become an inquisitor, my lord ? "

" Lady Winsleigh," said Philip suddenly and eagerly, " will you swear to me that you have said or done nothing to make my Thelma leave me ? "

" Oh, she *has* left you, has she ? " and Lady Clara smiled maliciously. " I thought she would ! Why don't you ask your dear friend, George Lorimer, about her ? He is madly in love with her, as everybody knows,—she is probably the same with him ! "

" Clara, Clara ! " exclaimed Lord Winsleigh in accents of deep reproach. " Shame on you ! Shame ! "

Her ladyship laughed amusedly. " Please don't be tragic ! " she said ; " it's too ridiculous ! Sir Philip has only himself to blame. Of course, Thelma knows about his frequent visits to the Brilliant Theatre. I told her all that Sir Francis said. Why should she be kept in the dark ? I dare say she doesn't mind—she's very fond of Mr. Lorimer ! "

Errington felt as though he must choke with fury. He forgot the presence of Lord Winsleigh—he forgot everything but his just indignation.

" My God ! " he cried passionately. " You *dare* to speak so !—*you !* "

" Yes I ! " she returned coolly, measuring him with a glance. " I dare ! What have you to say against *me ?* " She drew herself up imperiously.

Then turning to her husband, she said, " Have the goodness to take your excited friend away, my lord ! I am going out—I have a great many engagements this morning—and I really cannot stop to discuss this absurd affair any longer ! It isn't my fault that Sir Philip's excessive admiration for Miss Vere has become the subject of gossip—*I* don't blame him for it ! He seems extremely ill-tempered about it ; after all, ' *ce n'est que la verité qui blesse !* ' "

And she smiled maliciously.

CHAPTER XXVIII.

"For my mother's sake,
For thine and hers, O Love! I pity take
On all poor women. Jesu's will be done,
Honor for all, and infamy for none,
This side the borders of the burning lake."
ERIC MACKAY'S *Love-Letters of a Violinist.*

LORD WINSLEIGH did not move. Sir Philip fixed his eyes upon her in silence. Some occult fascination forced her to meet his glance, and the utter scorn of it stung her proud heart to its centre. Not that she felt much compunction—her whole soul was up in arms against him, and had been so from the very day she was first told of his unexpected marriage. His evident contempt now irritated her—she was angrier with him than ever, and yet—she had a sort of strange triumph in the petty vengeance she had designed—she had destroyed his happiness for a time, at least. If she could but shake his belief in his wife! she thought, vindictively. To that end she had thrown out her evil hint respecting Thelma's affection for George Lorimer, but the shaft had been aimed uselessly. Errington knew too well the stainless purity of Thelma to wrong her by the smallest doubt, and he would have staked his life on the loyalty of his friend. Presently he controlled his anger sufficiently to be able to speak, and still eyeing her with that straight, keen look of immeasurable disdain, he said in cold, deliberate accents—

"Your ladyship is in error,—the actress in question is the wife of my secretary, Mr. Neville. For years they have been estranged—my visits to her were entirely on Neville's behalf—my letters to her were all on the same subject. Sir Francis Lennox must have known the truth all along,— Violet Vere has been his mistress for the past five years!"

He uttered the concluding words with intense bitterness. A strange, bewildered horror passed over Lady Winsleigh's face.

"I don't believe it," she said rather faintly.

"Believe it or not, it is true!" he replied curtly. "Ask the manager of the Brilliant, if you doubt me. Winsleigh, it's no use my stopping here any longer. As her ladyship refuses to give any explanation——"

"Wait a moment, Errington," interposed Lord Winsleigh in his coldest and most methodical manner, "Her ladyship refuses—but *I* do not refuse! Her ladyship will not speak —she allows her husband to speak for her. Therefore," and he smiled at his astonished wife somewhat sardonically, "I may tell you at once, that her ladyship admits to having purchased from Violet Vere for the sum of £20, the letter which she afterwards took with her own hands to your wife." Lady Winsleigh uttered an angry exclamation.

"Don't interrupt me, Clara, if you please," he said, with an icy smile. "We have so many sympathies in common that I'm sure I shall be able to explain your unspoken meanings quite clearly." He went on, addressing himself to Errington, who stood utterly amazed.

"Her ladyship desires me to assure you that her only excuse for her action in this matter is, that she fully believed the reports her friend, Sir Francis Lennox, gave her concerning your supposed intimacy with the actress in question,—and that, believing it, she made use of it as much as possible for the purpose of destroying your wife's peace of mind and confidence in you. Her object was most purely feminine—love of mischief, and the gratification of private spite! There's nothing like frankness!" and Lord Winsleigh's face was a positive study as he spoke. "You see,"—he made a slight gesture towards his wife, who stood speechless, and so pale that her very lips were colorless— "her ladyship is not in a position to deny what I have said. Excuse her silence!"

And again he smiled—that smile as glitteringly chilled as a gleam of light on the edge of a sword. Lady Winsleigh raised her head, and her eyes met his with a dark expression of the uttermost anger. "Spy!" she hissed between her teeth,—then without further word or gesture, she swept haughtily away into her dressing-room, which adjoined the boudoir, and closed the door of communication, thus leaving the two men alone together.

Errington felt himself to be in a most painful and awkward position. If there was anything he more than disliked, it was a *scene*—particularly of a domestic nature. And he had just had a glimpse into Lord and Lady Winsleigh's married life, which, to him, was decidedly unpleasant. He could not understand how Lord Winsleigh had become cognizant of all he had so frankly stated—and then, why had he not told him everything at first, without waiting to declare it in his wife's presence? Unless, indeed, he wished to shame her? There was evidently something in the man's disposition and character that he, Philip, could not as yet comprehend,—something that certainly puzzled him, and filled him with vague uneasiness.

"Winsleigh, I'm awfully sorry this has happened," he began hurriedly, holding out his hand.

Lord Winsleigh grasped it cordially. "My dear fellow, so am I! Heartily sorry! I have to be sorry for a good many things rather often. But I'm specially grieved to think that your beautiful and innocent young wife is the victim in this case. Unfortunately I was told nothing till this morning, otherwise I might possibly have prevented all your unhappiness. But I trust it won't be of long duration. Here's this letter," he returned it as he spoke, "which in more than one way has cost so large a price. Possibly her ladyship may now regret her ill-gotten purchase."

"Pardon me," said Errington curiously, "but how did you know——"

"The information was pressed upon me very much," replied Lord Winsleigh evasively, "and from such a source that up to the last moment I almost refused to believe it." He paused, and then went on with a forced smile, "Suppose we don't talk any more about it, Errington? The subject's rather painful to me. Only allow me to ask your pardon for my wife's share in the mischief!"

Something in his manner of speaking affected Sir Philip.

"Upon my soul, Winsleigh," he exclaimed with sudden fervor, "I fancy you're a man greatly wronged!"

Lord Winsleigh smiled slightly. "You only *fancy*?" he said quietly. "Well,—my good friend, we all have our troubles—I dare say mine are no greater than those of many better men." He stopped short, then asked abruptly, "I suppose you'll see Lennox?"

Errington set his teeth hard. "I shall,—at once!" he replied. "And I shall probably thrash him within an inch of his life!"

"That's right! I shan't be sorry!" and Lord Winsleigh's hand clenched almost unconsciously. "I hope you understand, Errington, that if it hadn't been for my son, I should have shot that fellow long ago. I dare say you wonder,—and some others too,—why I haven't done it. But Ernest—poor little chap! . . . . he would have heard of it,—and the reason of it,—his young life is involved in mine—why should I bequeath him a dishonored mother's name? There—for heaven's sake, don't let me make a fool of myself!" and he fiercely dashed his hand across his eyes. "A duel or a divorce—or a horsewhipping—they all come to pretty much the same thing—all involve public scandal for the name of the woman who may be unhappily concerned—and scandal clings, like the stain on Lady Macbeth's hand. In your case you can act—*your* wife is above a shadow of suspicion—but I—oh, my God! how much women have to answer for in the miseries of this world!"

Errington said nothing. Pity and respect for the man before him held him silent. Here was one of the martyrs of modern social life—a man who evidently knew himself to be dishonored by his wife,—and who yet, for the sake of his son, submitted to be daily broken on the wheel of private torture rather than let the boy grow up to despise and slight his mother. Whether he were judged as wise or weak in his behavior there was surely something noble about him—something unselfish and heroic that deserved recognition. Presently Lord Winsleigh continued in calmer tones—

"I've been talking too much about myself, Errington, I fear—forgive it! Sometimes I've thought you misunderstood me——"

"I never shall again!" declared Philip earnestly.

Lord Winsleigh met his look of sympathy with one of gratitude.

"Thanks!" he said briefly,—and with this they shook hands again heartily, and parted. Lord Winsleigh saw his visitor to the door—and then at once returned to his wife's apartments. She was still absent from the boudoir—he therefore entered her dressing-room without ceremony.

There he found her,—alone, kneeling on the floor, her head buried in an arm-chair,—and her whole frame shaken with convulsive sobs. He looked down upon her with a strange wistful pain in his eyes,—pain mingled with compassion.

"Clara!" he said gently. She started and sprang up—confronting him with flushed cheeks and wet eyes.

"*You* here?" she exclaimed angrily. "I wonder you

dare to——" she broke off, confused by his keen, direct glance.

"It *is* a matter for wonder," he said quietly. "It's the strangest thing in the world that I—your husband—should venture to intrude myself into your presence! Nothing could be more out of the common. But I have something to say to you—something which must be said sooner or later—and I may as well speak now."

He paused,—she was silent, looking at him in a sort of sudden fear.

"Sit down," he continued in the same even tones. "You must have a little patience with me—I'll endeavor to be as brief as possible."

Mechanically she obeyed him and sank into a low fauteuil. She began playing with the trinkets on her silver chatelaine, and endeavored to feign the most absolute unconcern, but her heart beat quickly—she could not imagine what was coming next—her husband's manner and tone were quite new to her.

"You accused me just now," he went on, "of being a spy. I have never condescended to act such a part toward you, Clara. When I first married you I trusted you with my life, my honor, and my name, and though you have betrayed all three"—she moved restlessly as his calm gaze remained fixed on her—"I repeat,—though you have betrayed all three,—I have deliberately shut my eyes to the ruin of my hopes, in a loyal endeavor to shield you from the world's calumny. Regarding the unhappiness you have caused the Erringtons,—your own maid Louise Rénaud (who has given you notice of her intention to leave you) told me all she knew of your share in what I may call positive cruelty, towards a happy and innocent woman who has never injured you, and whose friend you declared yourself to be——"

"You believe the lies of a servant?" suddenly cried Lady Winsleigh wrathfully.

"Have not *you* believed the lies of Sir Francis Lennox, who is less honest than a servant?" asked her husband, his grave voice deepening with a thrill of passion. "And haven't you reported them everywhere as truths? But as regards your maid—I doubted her story altogether. She assured me she knew what money you took out with you yesterday, and what you returned with—and as the only place you visited in the morning was the Brilliant Theatre,

—after having received a telegram from Lennox, which she saw,—it was easy for her to put two and two together, especially as she noticed you reading the letter you had purchased—moreover "—he paused—" she has heard certain conversations between you and Sir Francis, notably one that took place at the garden-party in the summer at Errington Manor. Spy? you say? your detective has been paid by you,—fed and kept about your own person,—to minister to your vanity and to flatter your pride—that she has turned informer against you is not surprising. Be thankful that her information has fallen into no more malignant hands than mine!"

Again he paused—she was still silent—but her lips trembled nervously.

"And yet I was loth to believe everything"—he resumed half sadly—" till Errington came and showed me that letter and told me the whole story of his misery. Even then I thought I would give you one more chance—that's why I brought him to you and asked you the question before him. One look at your face told me you were guilty, though you denied it. I should have been better pleased had you confessed it! But why talk about it any longer?—the mischief is done—I trust it is not irreparable. I certainly consider that before troubling that poor girl's happiness,—you should have taken the precaution to inquire a little further into the truth of the reports you heard from Sir Francis Lennox,—he is not a reliable authority on any question whatsoever. You may have thought him so——" he stopped short and regarded her with sorrowful sternness—" I say, Clara, you may have thought him so, once—but *now?* Are you proud to have shared his affections with—Violet Vere?"

She uttered a sharp cry and covered her face with her hands,—an action which appeared to smite her husband to the heart,—for his voice trembled with deep feeling when he next spoke.

"Ah, best hide it, Clara!" he said passionately. "Hide that fair face I loved so well—hide those eyes in which I dreamed of finding my life's sunshine! Clara, Clara! What can I say to you, fallen rose of womanhood? How can I——" he suddenly bent over her as though to caress her, then drew back with a quick agonized sigh. "You thought me blind, Clara! . . . ." he went on in low tones, "blind to my own dishonor—blind to your faithlessness ;—

I tell you if you had taken my heart between your hands and wrung the blood out of it drop by drop, I could not have suffered more than I have done! Why have I been silent so long?—no matter why,—but *now*, now Clara,—this life of ours must end!"

She shuddered away from him.

"End it then!" she muttered in a choked voice. "You can do as you like,—you can divorce me."

"Yes," said Lord Winsleigh musingly. "I can divorce you! There will be no defense possible,—as you know. If witnesses are needed, they are to be had in the persons of our own domestics. The co-respondent in the case will not refute the charge against him,—and I, the plaintiff, *must* win my just cause. Do you realize it all, Clara? You, the well-known leader of a large social circle—you, the proud beauty and envied lady of rank and fashion,—you will be made a subject for the coarse jests of lawyers, —the very judge on the bench will probably play off his stale witticism at your expense,—your dearest friends will tear your name to shreds,—the newspapers will reek of your doings,—and honest housemaids reading of your fall from your high estate, will thank God that their souls and bodies are more chaste than yours! And last,—not least, —think when old age creeps on, and your beauty withers, —think of your son grown to manhood,—the sole heir to my name,—think of him as having but one thing to blush for—the memory of his dishonored mother!"

"Cruel—cruel!" she cried, endeavoring to check her sobs, and withdrawing her hands from her face. "Why do you say such things to me? Why did you marry me?"

He caught her hands and held them in a fast grip.

"Why? Because I loved you, Clara—loved you with all the tenderness of a strong man's heart! When I first saw you, you seemed to me the very incarnation of maiden purity and loveliness! The days of our courtship—the first few months of our marriage—what they were to you, I know not,—to me they were supreme happiness. When our boy was born, my adoration, my reverence for you increased—you were so sacred in my eyes, that I could have knelt and asked a benediction from these little hands"—here he gently loosened them from his clasp. "Then came the change—*what* changed you, I cannot imagine—it has always seemed to me unnatural, monstrous, incredible! There was no falling away in *my* affection, that I can swear! My curse upon the man who turned your heart from mine! So rightful and deep a curse is it that I feel it must some day strike home."

He paused and seemed to reflect. " Who is there more vile, more traitorous than he? " he went on. " Has he not tried to influence Errington's wife against her husband? For what base purpose? But Clara,—he is powerless against *her* purity and innocence ;—what, in the name of God, gave him power over *you* ? "

She drooped her head, and the hot blood rushed to her face.

" You've said enough!" she murmured sullenly. " If you have decided on a divorce, pray carry out your intention with the least possible delay. I cannot talk any more! I—I am tired! "

" Clara," said her husband solemnly, with a strange light in his eyes, " I would rather kill you than divorce you! "

There was something so terribly earnest in his tone that her heart beat fast with fear.

" Kill me ?—kill me? " she gasped, with white lips.

" Yes ! " he repeated, " kill you,—as a Frenchman or an Italian would,—and take the consequences. Yes—though an Englishman, I would rather do this than drag your frail poor womanhood through the mire of public scandal! I have, perhaps, a strange nature, but such as I am, I am. There are too many of our high-born families already, flaunting their immorality and low licentiousness in the face of the mocking, grinning populace,—I for one could never make up my mind to fling the honor of my son's mother to them, as though it were a bone for dogs to fight over. No —I have another proposition to make to you——"

He stopped short. She stared at him wonderingly. He resumed in methodical, unmoved, business-like tones.

" I propose, Clara, simply,—to leave you ! I'll take the boy and absent myself from this country, so as to give you perfect freedom and save you all trouble. There'll be no possibility of scandal, for I will keep you cognizant of my movements,—and should you require my presence at any time for the sake of appearances,—or—to shield you from calumny,—you may rely on my returning to you at once,— without delay. Ernèst will gain many advantages by travel,—his education is quite a sufficient motive for my departure, my interest in his young life being well known to all our circle. Moreover, with me—under my surveillance—he need never know anything against—against you. I have always taught him to honor and obey you in his heart."

Lord Winsleigh paused a moment—then went on, somewhat musingly;—"When he was quite little, he used to wonder why you didn't love him,—it was hard for me to hear him say that, sometimes. But I always told him that you did love him—but that you had so many visits to make, and so many friends to entertain, that you had no time to play with him. I don't think he quite understood,—but still—I did my best!"

He was silent. She had hidden her face again in her hands, and he heard a sound of smothered sobbing.

"I think," he continued calmly, "that he has a great reverence for you in his young heart—a feeling which partakes, perhaps, more of fear than love—still it is better than—disdain—or—or disrespect. I shall always teach him to esteem you highly,—but I think, as matters stand—if I relieve you of all your responsibilities to husband and son—you—Clara!—pray don't distress yourself—there's no occasion for this—Clara——"

For on a sudden impulse she had flung herself at his feet in an irrepressible storm of passionate weeping.

"Kill me, Harry!" she sobbed wildly, clinging to him. "Kill me! don't speak to me like this!—don't leave me! Oh, my God! don't, don't despise me so utterly! Hate me—curse me—strike me—do anything, but don't leave me as if I were some low thing, unfit for your touch,—I know I am, but oh, Harry! . . ." She clung to him more closely. "If you leave me I will not live,—I cannot! Have you no pity? Why would you throw me back alone —all, all alone, to die of your contempt and my shame!"

And she bowed her head in an agony of tears.

He looked down upon her a moment in silence.

"Your shame!" he murmured. "My wife——"

Then he raised her in his arms and drew her with a strange hesitation of touch, to his breast, as though she were some sick or wounded child, and watched her as she lay there weeping, her face hidden, her whole frame trembling in his embrace.

"Poor soul!" he whispered, more to himself than to her. "Poor frail woman! Hush, hush, Clara! The past is past! I'll make you no more reproaches. I—I *can't* hurt you, because I once so loved you—but now—now,—what *is* there left for me to do, but to leave you? You'll be happier so—you'll have perfect liberty—you needn't even think of me—unless, perhaps, as one dead and buried long ago ——"

She raised herself in his arms and looked at him piteously.

"Won't you give me a chance?" she sobbed. "Not one? If I had but known you better—if I had understood oh, I've been vile, wicked, deceitful—but I'm not happy Harry—I've never been happy since I wronged you! Won't you give me one little hope that I may win your love again,—no, not your love, but your pity? Oh, Harry have I lost all—all——"

Her voice broke—she could say no more.

He stroked her hair gently. "You speak on impulse just now, Clara," he said gravely yet tenderly. "You can't know your own strength or weakness. God forbid that *I* should judge you harshly! As you wish it, I will not leave you yet. I'll wait. Whether we part or remain together, shall be decided by your own actions, your own looks, your own words. You understand, Clara? You know my feelings. I'm content for the present to place my fate in your hands." He smiled rather sadly. "But for love, Clara—I fear nothing can be done to warm to life this poor perished love of ours. We can, perhaps, take hands and watch its corpse patiently together and say how sorry we are it is dead—such penitence comes always too late!"

He sighed, and put her gently away from him.

She turned up her flushed, tear-stained face to his.

"Will you kiss me, Harry?" she asked tremblingly. He met her eyes, and an exclamation that was almost a groan broke from his lips. A shudder passed through his frame.

"I can't, Clara! I can't—God forgive me!—Not yet!" And with that he bowed his head and left her.

She listened to the echo of his firm footsteps dying away, and creeping guiltily to a side-door she opened it, and watched yearningly his retreating figure till it had disappeared.

"Why did I never love him till now?" she murmured sobbingly. "Now, when he despises me—when he will not even kiss me?——" She leaned against the half-open door in an attitude of utter dejection, not caring to move, listening intently with a vague hope of hearing her husband's returning tread. A lighter step than his, however, came suddenly along from the other side of the passage and startled her a little—it was Ernest, looking the picture of boyish health and beauty. He was just going out for his usual ride—he lifted his cap with a pretty courtesy as he saw her, and said—

"Good-morning, mother!"

She looked at him with new interest,—how handsome the lad was!—how fresh his face!—how joyously clear those bright blue eyes of his! He, on his part, was moved by a novel sensation too—his mother,—his proud, beautiful, careless mother had been crying—he saw that at a glance, and his young heart beat faster when she laid her white hand, sparkling all over with rings, on his arm and drew him closer to her.

"Are you going to the Park?" she asked gently.

"Yes." Then recollecting his training in politeness and obedience he added instantly—"Unless you want me."

She smiled faintly. "I never do want you—do I, Ernest?" she asked half sadly. "I never want my boy at all." Her voice quivered,—and Ernest grew more and more astonished.

"If you do, I'll stay," he said stoutly, filled with a chivalrous desire to console his so suddenly tender mother of his, whatever her griefs might be. Her eyes filled again, but she tried to laugh.

"No dear—not now,—run along and enjoy yourself. Come to me when you return. I shall be at home all day. And,—stop Ernest—won't you kiss me?"

The boy opened his eyes wide in respectful wonderment, and his cheeks flushed with surprise and pleasure.

"Why, mother—of course!" And his fresh, sweet lips closed on hers with frank and unaffected heartiness. She held him fast for a moment and looked at him earnestly.

"Tell your father you kissed me—will you?" she said. "Don't forget!"

And with that she waved her hand to him, and retreated again into her own apartment. The boy went on his way somewhat puzzled and bewildered—did his mother love him, after all? If so, he thought—how glad he was!—how very glad! and what a pity he had not known it before!

CHAPTER XXIX.

"I heed not custom, creed, nor law;
 I care for nothing that ever I saw—
 I terribly laugh with an oath and sneer,
 When I think that the hour of Death draws near!"
                                                    W. WINTER.

ERRINGTON'S first idea, on leaving Winsleigh House, was to seek an interview with Sir Francis Lennox, and demand an explanation. He could not understand the man's motive for such detestable treachery and falsehood. His anger rose to a white heat as he thought of it, and he determined to " have it out " with him whatever the consequences might be. " No apology will serve his turn," he muttered. " The scoundrel! He has lied deliberately—and, by Jove, he shall pay for it ! "

And he started off rapidly in the direction of Piccadilly, but on the way he suddenly remembered that he had no weapon with him, not even a cane wherewith to carry out his intention of thrashing Sir Francis, and calling to mind a certain heavy horsewhip, that hung over the mantel-piece in his own room, he hailed a hansom, and was driven back to his house in order to provide himself with that imple-ment of castigation before proceeding further. On arriving at the door, to his surprise he found Lorimer who was just about to ring the bell.

" Why, I thought you were in Paris ? " he exclaimed.

" I came back last night," George began, when Morris opened the door, and Errington, taking his friend by the arm hurried him into the house. In five minutes he had unburdened himself of all his troubles—and had explained the misunderstanding about Violet Vere and Thelma's con-sequent flight. Lorimer listened with a look of genuine pain and distress on his honest face.

" Phil, you *have* been a fool ! " he said candidly. " A positive fool, if you'll pardon me for saying so. You ought to have told Thelma everything at first,—she's the very last woman in the world who ought to be kept in the dark about anything. Neville's feelings ? Bother Neville's feelings ! Depend upon it the poor girl has heard all manner of stories. She's been miserable for some time—Duprèz noticed it." And he related in a few words the little scene that had taken place at Errington Manor on the night of the garden-party, when his playing on the organ had moved her to such unwonted emotion.

Philip heard him in moody silence,—how had it happened, he wondered, that others,—comparative strangers, —had observed that Thelma looked unhappy, while he, her husband, had been blind to it? He could not make this out,—and yet it is a thing that very commonly happens. Our nearest and dearest are often those who are most in the dark respecting our private and personal sufferings, —we do not wish to trouble them,—and they prefer to think that everything is right with us, even though the rest of the world can plainly perceive that everything is wrong. To the last moment they will refuse to see death in our faces, though the veriest stranger meeting us casually, clearly beholds the shadow of the dark Angel's hand.

"*Apropos* of Lennox," went on Lorimer, sympathetically watching his friend, "I came on purpose to speak to you about him. I've got some news for you. He's a regular sneak and scoundrel. You can thrash him to your heart's content for he has grossly insulted your wife."

"*Insulted* her?" cried Errington furiously. "How,— what——"

"Give me time to speak!" And George laid a restraining hand on his arm. "Thelma visited my mother yesterday and told her that on the night before, when you had gone out, Lennox took advantage of your absence to come here and make love to her,—and she actually had to struggle with him, and even to strike him, in order to release herself from his advances. My mother advised her to tell you about it—and she evidently then had no intention of flight, for she said she would inform you of everything as soon as you returned from the country. And if Lady Winsleigh hadn't interfered, it's very probable that ——I say, where are you going?" This as Philip made a bound for the door.

"To get my horsewhip!" he answered.

"All right—I approve!" cried Lorimer. "But wait one instant, and see how clear the plot becomes. Thelma's beauty had maddened Lennox,—to gain her good opinion, as he thinks, he throws his mistress, Violet Vere, on *your* shoulders—(your ingenuous visits to the Brilliant Theatre

gave him a capital pretext for this) and as for Lady Winsleigh's share in the mischief, it's nothing but mere feminine
spite against you for marrying at all, and hatred of the
woman whose life is such a contrast to her own, and who
absorbs all your affection. Lennox has used her as his tool
and the Vere also, I've no doubt. The thing's as clear as
crystal. It's a sort of general misunderstanding all
round—one of those eminently unpleasant trifles that
very frequently upset the peace and comfort of the most
quiet and inoffensive persons. But the fault lies with *you*,
dear old boy!"

"With *me!*" exclaimed Philip.

"Certainly! Thelma's soul is as open as daylight—you
shouldn't have had any secret from her, however trifling.
She's not a woman ' on guard,'—she can't take life as the
most of us do, in military fashion, with ears pricked for
the approach of a spy, and prepared to expect betrayal
from her most familiar friends. She accepts things as they
appear, without any suspicion of mean ulterior designs.
It's a pity, of course!—it's a pity she can't be worldly-wise,
and scheme and plot and plan and lie like the rest of us!
However, *your* course is plain—first interview Lennox and
then follow Thelma. She can't have left Hull yet,—there
are scarcely any boats running to Norway at this season.
You'll overtake her I'm certain."

"By Jove, Lorimer!" said Errington suddenly. "Clara
Winsleigh sticks at nothing—do you know she actually had
the impudence to suggest that *you*,—you, of all people,—
were in love with Thelma!"

Lorimer flushed up, but laughed lightly. "How awfully
sweet of her! Much obliged to her, I'm sure! And how
did you take it Phil?"

"Take it? I didn't take it at all," responded Philip
warmly. "Of course, I knew it was only her spite—she'd
say anything in one of her tempers."

Lorimer looked at him with a sudden tenderness in his
blue eyes. Then he laughed again, a little forcedly, and
said—

"Be off, old man, and get that whip of yours! We'll
run Lennox to earth. Hullo! here's Britta!"

The little maid entered hurriedly at that moment,—she
came to ask with quivering lips, whether she might accompany Sir Philip in his intended journey to Norway.

"For if you do not find the Fröken at Hull, you will

want to reach the Altenfjord," said Britta, folding her hands resolutely in front of her apron, " and you will not get on without me. You do not know what the country is like in the depth of winter when the sun is asleep. You must have the reindeer to help you—and no Englishman knows how to drive reindeer. And—and—" here Britta's eyes filled—" you have not thought, perhaps, that the journey may make the Fröken very ill—and that when we find her—she may be dying——" and Britta's strength gave way in a big sob that broke from the depths of her honest, affectionate heart.

" Don't—*don't* talk like that, Britta!" cried Philip passionately. " I can't bear it! Of course, you shall go with me! I wouldn't leave you behind for the world! Get everything ready——" and in a fever of heat and impatience he began rumaging among some books on a side-shelf, till he found the time-tables he sought. " Yes,—here we are, —there's a train leaving for Hull at five—we'll take that. Tell Morris to pack my portmanteau, and you bring it along with you to the Midland railway-station this afternoon. Do you understand?"

Britta nodded emphatically, and hurried off at once to busy herself with these preparations, while Philip, all excitement, dashed off to give a few parting injunctions to Neville, and to get his horsewhip.

Lorimer, left alone for a few minutes, seated himself in an easy chair and began absently turning over the newspapers on the table. But his thoughts were far away, and presently he covered his eyes with one hand as though the light hurt them. When he removed it, his lashes were wet. " What a fool I am!" he muttered impatiently. " Oh Thelma, Thelma! my darling!—how I wish I could follow and find you and console you!—you poor, tender, resigned soul, going away like this because you thought you were not wanted—not wanted!—my God!—if you only knew how one man at least has wanted and yearned for you ever since he saw your sweet face!—Why can't I tear you out of my heart—why can't I love some one else? Ah Phil!— good, generous, kind old Phil!—he little guesses," he rose and paced the room up and down restlessly. " The fact is I oughtn't to be here at all—I ought to leave England altogether for a long time—till—till I get over it. The question is, *shall* I ever get over it? Sigurd was a wise boy—he found a short way out of all his troubles,—suppose

I imitate his example? No,—for a man in his senses that would be rather cowardly—though it might be pleasant!" He stopped in his walk with a pondering expression on his face. "At any rate, I won't stop here to see her come back—I couldn't trust myself,—I should say something foolish—I know I should! I'll take my mother to Italy— she wants to go; and we'll stay with Lovelace. It'll be a change—and I'll have a good stand-up fight with myself, and see if I can't come off the conqueror somehow! It's all very well to kill an opponent in battle but the question is, can a man kill his inner, grumbling, discontented, selfish Self? If he can't, what's the good of him?"

As he was about to consider this point reflectively, Errington entered, equipped for travelling, and whip in hand. His imagination had been at work during the past few minutes, exaggerating all the horrors and difficulties of Thelma's journey to the Altenfjord, till he was in a perfect fever of irritable excitement.

"Come on Lorimer!" he cried. "There's no time to lose! Britta knows what to do—she'll meet me at the station. I can't breathe in this wretched house a moment longer—let's be off!"

Plunging out into the hall, he bade Morris summon a hansom,—and with a few last instructions to that faithful servitor, and an encouraging kind word and shake of the hand to Neville, who with a face of remorseful misery, stood at the door to watch his departure,—he was gone. The hansom containing him and Lorimer rattled rapidly towards the abode of Sir Francis Lennox, but on entering Piccadilly, the vehicle was compelled to go so slowly on account of the traffic, that Errington, who every moment grew more and more impatient, could not stand it.

"By Jove! this is like a walking funeral!" he muttered. "I say Lorimer, let's get out! We can do the rest on foot."

They stopped the cabman and paid him his fare—then hurried along rapidly, Errington every now and then giving a fiercer clench to the formidable horsewhip which was twisted together with his ordinary walking-stick in such a manner as not to attract special attention.

"Coward and liar!" he muttered, as he thought of the man he was about to punish. "He shall pay for his dastardly falsehood—by Jove he shall! It'll be a precious long time before he shows himself in society any more!"

Then he addressed Lorimer. "You may depend upon it

he'll shout 'police! police!' and make for the door," he
observed. "You keep your back against it, Lorimer! I
don't care how many fines I've got to pay as long as I can
thrash him soundly!"

"All right!" Lorimer answered, and they quickened
their pace. As they neared the chambers which Sir
Francis Lennox rented over a fashionable jeweller's shop,
they became aware of a small procession coming straight
towards them from the opposite direction. *Something* was
being carried between four men who appeared to move with
extreme care and gentleness,—this something was surrounded by a crowd of boys and men whose faces were full
of morbid and frightened interest—the whole *cortége* was
headed by a couple of solemn policemen. "You spoke of a
walking funeral just now," said Lorimer suddenly. "This
looks uncommonly like one."

Errington made no reply—he had only one idea in his
mind,—the determination to chastise and thoroughly disgrace Sir Francis. "I'll hound him out of the clubs!" he
thought indignantly. "His own set shall know what a
liar he is—and if I can help it he shall never hold up his
head again!"

Entirely occupied as he was with these reflections, he
paid no heed to anything that was going on in the street,
and he scarcely heard Lorimer's last observation. So that
he was utterly surprised and taken aback, when he, with
Lorimer, was compelled to come to a halt before the very
door of the jeweller, Lennox's landlord, while the two
policemen cleared a passage through the crowd, saying in
low tones, "Stand aside, gentlemen, please!—stand aside,"
thus making gradual way for four bearers, who, as was now
plainly to be seen, carried a common wooden stretcher
covered with a cloth, under which lay what seemed, from
its outline, to be a human figure.

"What's the matter here?" asked Lorimer, with a curious cold thrill running through him as he put the simple
question.

One of the policemen answered readily enough.

"An accident, sir. Gentleman badly hurt. Down at
Charing Cross Station—tried to jump into a train when it
had started,—foot caught,—was thrown under the wheels
and dragged along some distance—doctor says he can't live,
sir."

"Who is he,—what's his name?"

" Lennox, sir—leastways, that's the name on his card—and this is the address. Sir Francis Lennox, I believe it is."

Errington uttered a sharp exclamation of horror,—at that moment the jeweller came out of the recesses of his shop with uplifted hands and bewildered countenance.

" An accident? Good Heavens!—Sir Francis! Up-stairs!—take him up-stairs!" Here he addressed the bearers. " You should have gone round to the private entrance—he mustn't be seen in the shop—frightening away all my customers—here, pass through!—pass through, as quick as you can!"

And they did pass through,—carrying their crushed burden tenderly along by the shining glass cases and polished counters, where glimmered and flashed jewels of every size and lustre for the adorning of the children of this world,—slowly and carefully, step by step, they reached the upper floor,—and there, in a luxurious apartment furnished with almost feminine elegance, they lifted the inanimate form from the stretcher and laid it down, still shrouded, on a velvet sofa, removing the last number of *Truth*, and two of Zola's novels, to make room for the heavy, unconscious head.

Errington and Lorimer stood at the doorway, completely overcome by the suddenness of the event—they had followed the bearers up-stairs almost mechanically,—exchanging no word or glance by the way,—and now they watched in almost breathless suspense while a surgeon who was present, gently turned back the cover that hid the injured man's features and exposed them to full view. Was *that* Sir Francis? that blood-smeared, mangled creature?—*that* the lascivious dandy,—the disciple of no-creed and self-worship? Errington shuddered and averted his gaze from that hideous face,—so horribly contorted,—yet otherwise deathlike in its rigid stillness. There was a grave hush. The surgeon still bent over him—touching here, probing there, with tenderness and skill,—but finally he drew back with a hopeless shake of his head.

" Nothing can be done," he whispered. " Absolutely nothing!"

At that moment Sir Francis stirred,—he groaned and opened his eyes;—what terrible eyes they were, filled with that look of intense anguish, and something worse than anguish,—fear—frantic fear—coward fear—fear that was almost more overpowering than his bodily suffering.

He stared wildly at the little group assembled—strange faces, so far as he could make them out, that regarded him with evident compassion,—what—what was all this—what did it mean? Death? No, no! he thought madly, while his brain reeled with the idea—death? What *was* death? —darkness, annihilation, blackness—all that was horrible— unimaginable! God! he would *not* die! God!—who *was* God? No matter—he would live;—he would struggle against this heaviness,—this coldness—this pillar of ice in which he was being slowly frozen—frozen—frozen!—inch by inch! He made a furious effort to move, and uttered a scream of agony, stabbed through and through by torturing pain.

"Keep still!" said the surgeon pityingly.

Sir Francis heard him not. He wrestled with his bodily anguish till the perspiration stood in large drops on his forehead. He raised himself, gasping for breath, and glared about him like a trapped beast of prey.

"Give me brandy!" he muttered chokingly. "Quick— quick! Are you going to let me die like a dog?—damn you all!"

The effort to move,—to speak,—exhausted his sinking strength—his throat rattled,—he clenched his fists and made as though he would spring off his couch—when a fearful contortion convulsed his whole body,—his eyes rolled up and became fixed—he fell heavily back,—*dead!*

Quietly the surgeon covered again what was now nothing,—nothing but a mutilated corpse.

"It's all over!" he announce briefly.

Errington heard these words in sickened silence. All over! Was it possible? So soon? All over!—and he had come too late to punish the would-be ravisher of his wife's honor,—too late! He still held the whip in his hand with which he had meant to chastise that—that distorted, mangled lump of clay yonder, . . . pah! he could not bear to think of it, and he turned away, faint and dizzy. He felt,—rather than saw the staircase,—down which he dreamily went, followed by Lorimer.

The two policemen were in the hall scribbling the cut-and-dry particulars of the accident in their note-books, which having done, they marched off, attended by a wandering, bilious-looking penny-a-liner who was anxious to

write a successful account of the " Shocking Fatality," as it
was called in the next day's newspapers. Then the
bearers departed cheerfully, carrying with them the empty
stretcher. Then the jeweller, who seemed quite unmoved
respecting the sudden death of his lodger, chatted amicably
with the surgeon about the reputation and various *de*-
merits of the deceased,—and Errington and Lorimer, as
they passed through the shop, heard him speaking of a
person hitherto unheard of, namely, Lady Francis Lennox,
who had been deserted by her husband for the past six
years, and who was living uncomplainingly the life of an
art-student in Germany with her married sister, maintain-
ing, by the work of her own hands, her one little child, a
boy of five.

" He never allowed her a farthing," said the conversational jeweller. " And she never asked him for one. Mr.
Wiggins, his lawyer—firm of Wiggins & Whizzer, Furni-
val's Inn,—told me all about his affairs. Oh yes—he was
a regular " masher "—tip-top! Not worth much, I should
say. He must have spent over a thousand a year in keeping up that little place at St. John's Wood for Violet
Vere. He owes me five hundred. However, Mr. Wiggins
will see everything fair, I've no doubt. I've just wired to
him, announcing the death. I don't suppose any one will
regret him—except, perhaps, the woman at St. John's
Wood. But I believe she's playing for a bigger stake just
now." And, stimulated by this thought, he drew out from
a handsome morocco case a superb pendant of emeralds
and diamonds—a work of art, that glittered as he displayed
it, like a star on a frosty night.

" Pretty thing, isn't it?" he said proudly. " Eight
hundred pounds, and cheap, too! It was ordered for Miss
Vere, two months ago, by the Duke of Moorlands. I see
he sold his collection of pictures the other day. Luckily
they fetched a tidy sum, so I'm pretty sure of the money
for this. He'll sell everything he's got to please her.
Queer? Oh, not at all! She's the rage just now,—I can't
see anything in her myself,—but I'm not a duke, you see
—I'm obliged to be respectable! "

He laughed as he returned the pendant to its nest of
padded amber satin, and Errington,—sick at heart to hear
such frivolous converse going on while that crushed and
lifeless form lay in the very room above,—unwatched, un-
cared-for,—put his arm through Lorimer's and left the shop,
28

Once in the open street, with the keen, cold air blowing against their faces, they looked at each other blankly. Piccadilly was crowded; the hurrying people passed and repassed,—there were the shouts of omnibus conductors and newsboys—the laughter of young men coming out of the St. James's Hall Restaurant; all was as usual,—as, indeed, why should it not? What matters the death of one man in a million? unless, indeed, it be a man whose life, like a torch, uplifted in darkness, has enlightened and cheered the world,—but the death of a mere fashionable " swell " whose chief talent has been a trick of lying gracefully—who cares for such a one? Society is instinctively relieved to hear that his place is empty, and shall know him more. But Errington could not immediately forget the scene he had witnessed. He was overcome by sensations of horror,—even of pity,—and he walked by his friend's side for some time in silence.

" I wish I could get rid of this thing! " he said suddenly, looking down at the horsewhip in his hand.

Lorimer made no answer. He understood his feeling, and realized the situation as sufficiently grim. To be armed with a weapon meant for the chastisement of a man whom Death had so suddenly claimed was, to say the least of it, unpleasant. Yet the horsewhip could scarcely be thrown away in Piccadilly—such an action might attract notice and comment. Presently Philip spoke again.

" He was actually married all the time! "

" So it seems; " and Lorimer's face expressed something very like contempt. " By Jove, Phil! he must have been an awful scoundrel! "

" Don't let's say any more about him—he's dead! " and Philip quickened his steps. " And what a horrible death! "

" Horrible enough, indeed! "

Again they were both silent. Mechanically they turned down towards Pall Mall.

" George," said Errington, with a strange awe in his tones, " it seems to me to-day as if there were death in the air. I don't believe in presentiments, but yet—yet I cannot help thinking—what if I should find my Thelma— *dead?* "

Lorimer turned very pale—a cold shiver ran through him, but he endeavored to smile.

" For God's sake, old fellow, don't think of anything so terrible! Look here, you're hipped—no wonder! and

you've got a long journey before you. Come and have
lunch. It's just two o'clock. Afterwards we'll go to the
Garrick and have a chat with Beau Lovelace—he's a first-
rate fellow for looking on the bright side of everything.
Then I'll see you off this afternoon at the Midland—what
do you say ? "

Errington assented to this arrangement, and tried to
shake off the depression that had settled upon him, though
dark forebodings passed one after the other like clouds
across his mind. He seemed to see the Altenguard hills
stretching drearily, white with frozen snow, around the
black Fjord; he pictured Thelma, broken-hearted, fancying
herself deserted, returning through the cold and darkness
to the lonely farm-house behind the now withered pines.
Then he began to think of the shell-cave where that other
Thelma lay hidden in her last deep sleep,—the wailing
words of Sigurd came freshly back to his ears, when the
poor crazed lad had likened Thelma's thoughts to his
favorite flowers, the pansies—" One by one you will gather
and play with her thoughts as though they were these
blossoms ; your burning hand will mar their color—they
will wither and furl up and die,—and you—what will you
care ? Nothing ! No man ever cares for a flower that is
withered,—not even though his own hand slew it ! "

Had he been to blame ? he mused, with a sorrowful
weight at his heart. Unintentionally, had he,—yes, he
would put it plainly,—had he neglected her, just a little ?
Had he not, with all his true and passionate love for her,
taken her beauty, her devotion, her obedience too much for
granted—too much as his right ? And in these latter
months, when her health had made her weaker and more in
need of his tenderness, had he not, in a sudden desire for
political fame and worldly honor, left her too much alone, a
prey to solitude and the often morbid musings which solitude engenders ?

He began to blame himself heartily for the misunderstanding that had arisen out of his share in Neville's unhappy secret. Neville had been weak and timid,—he had
shrunk nervously from avowing that the notorious Violet
Vere was actually the woman he had so faithfully loved
and mourned,—but he, Philip, ought not to have humored
him in these fastidious scruples—he ought to have confided
everything to Thelma. He remembered now that he had
once or twice been uneasy lest rumors of his frequent visits

to Miss Vere might possibly reach his wife's ears,—but, then, as his purpose was absolutely disinterested and harmless, he did not dwell on this idea, but dismissed it, and held his peace for Neville's sake, contenting himself with the thought that, " If Thelma *did* hear anything, she would never believe a word against me."

He could not quite see where his fault had been,—though a fault there was somewhere, as he uneasily felt—and he would no doubt have started indignantly had a small elf whispered in his ear the word " *Conceit.*" Yet that was the name of his failing—that and no other. How many men, otherwise noble-hearted, are seriously, though often unconsciously, burdened with this large parcel of blown-out Nothing! Sir Philip did not appear to be conceited—he would have repelled the accusation with astonishment,— not knowing that in his very denial of the fault, the fault existed. He had never been truly humbled but twice in his life,—once as he knelt to receive his mother's dying benediction,—and again when he first loved Thelma, and was uncertain whether his love could be returned by so fair and pure a creature. With these two exceptions, all his experience had tended to give him an excellent opinion of himself,—and that he should possess one of the best and loveliest wives in the world, seemed to him quite in keeping with the usual course of things. The feeling that it was a sheer impossibility for her to ever believe a word against him, rose out of this inward self-satisfaction—this one flaw in his otherwise bright, honest, and lovable character—a flaw of which he himself was not aware. Now, when for the third time his fairy castle of perfect peace and pleasure seemed shaken to its foundations,—when he again realized the uncertainty of life or death, he felt bewildered and wretched. His chiefest pride was centred in Thelma, and she—was gone! Again he reverted to the miserable idea that, like a melancholy refrain, haunted him—" What if I should find her *dead!* "

Absorbed in painful reflections, he was a very silent companion for Lorimer during the luncheon which they took at a quiet little restaurant well known to the *habitués* of Pall Mall and Regent Street. Lorimer himself had his own reasons for being equally depressed and anxious,—for did he not love Thelma as much as even her husband could?— nay, perhaps more, knowing his love was hopeless. Not always does possession of the adored object strengthen the adoration,—the rapturous dreams of an ideal passion have often been known to surpass reality a thousandfold. So the two friends exchanged but few words,—though they tried to converse cheerfully on indifferent subjects, and failed in the attempt. They had nearly finished their light repast, when a familiar voice saluted them.

" It *is* Errington,—I thocht I couldna be mistaken! How are ye both ? "

Sandy Macfarlane stood before them, unaltered, save that his scanty beard had grown somewhat longer. They had seen nothing of him since their trip to Norway, and they greeted him now with unaffected heartiness, glad of the distraction his appearance afforded them.

" Where do you hail from, Mac? " asked Lorimer, as he made the new-comer sit down at their table. " We haven't heard of you for an age."

" It *is* a goodish bit of time," assented Macfarlane, " but better late than never. I came up to London a week ago from Glasgie,—and my heed has been in a whirl ever since. Eh, mon! but it's an awfu' place !—maybe I'll get used to't after a wee whilie."

" Are you going to settle here, then? " inquired Errington, " I thought you intended to be a minister somewhere in Scotland? "

Macfarlane smiled, and his eyes twinkled.

" I hae altered ma opee-nions a bit," he said. " Ye see, ma aunt in Glasgie's deed——"

" I understand," laughed Lorimer. " You've come in for the old lady's money ? "

" Puir body! " and Sandy shook his head gravely. " A few hours before she died she tore up her will in a screamin' fury o' Christian charity and forethought,—meanin' to mak anither in favor o' leavin' a' her warld's trash to the Fund for Distributin' Bible Knowledge among the Heathen —but she never had time to fulfill her intention. She went off like a lamb,—and there being no will, her money fell to me, as the nearest survivin' relative—eh ! the puir thing ! —if her dees-imbodied spirit is anywhere aboot, she must be in a sair plight to think I've got it, after a' her curses ! "

" How much ? " asked Lorimer amused.

" Oh, just a fair seventy thousand or so," answered Macfarlane carelessly.

" Well done, Mac! " said Errington, with a smile, endeavoring to appear interested. " You're quite rich, then? I congratulate you!"

" Riches are a snare," observed Macfarlane, sententiously, " a snare and a decoy to both soul and body!" He laughed and rubbed his hands,—then added with some eagerness, " I say, how is Lady Errington?"

" She's very well," answered Sir Philip hurriedly, exchanging a quick look with Lorimer, which the latter at once understood. " She's away on a visit just now. I'm going to join her this afternoon."

" I'm sorry she's away," said Sandy, and he looked very disappointed; " but I'll see her when she comes back. Will she be long absent?"

" No, not long—a few days only "—and as Errington said this an involuntary sigh escaped him.

A few days only!—God grant it! But what—what if he should find her *dead*?

Macfarlane noticed the sadness of his expression, but prudently forbore to make any remark upon it. He contented himself with saying—

" Weel, ye've got a wife worth having—as I dare say ye know. I shall be glad to pay my respects to her as soon as she returns. I've got your address, Errington—will ye take mine?"

And he handed him a small card on which was written in pencil the number of a house in one of the lowest streets in the East-end of London. Philip glanced at it with some surprise.

" Is *this* where you live?" he asked with emphatic amazement.

" Yes. It's just the cleanest tenement I could find in that neighborhood. And the woman that keeps it is fairly respectable."

" But with your money," remonstrated Lorimer, who also looked at the card, " I rather wonder at your choice of abode. Why, my dear fellow, do you *know* what sort of a place it is?"

A steadfast, earnest, *thinking* look came into Macfarlane's deep-set, grey eyes.

" Yes, I do know, pairfectly," he said in answer to the question. " It's a place where there's misery, starvation, and crime of all sorts,—and there I am in the very midst of it—just where I want to be. Ye see, I was meant to be a meenister—one of those douce, cannie, comfortable bodies that drone in the pulpit about predestination and original sin, and so forth a—sort of palaver that does no good to ony resonable creature—an' if I had followed out this profession, I make nae doot that, with my aunt's seventy thousand, I should be a vera comfortable, respectable, selfish type of a man, who was decently embarked in an apparently important but really useless career——"

" Useless ? " interrupted Lorimer archly. " I say, Mac, take care! A minister of the Lord, *useless!* "

" I'm thinkin' there are unco few meen-isters o' the Lord in this warld," said Macfarlane musingly. " Maist o' them meen-ister to themselves, an' care na a wheen mair for Christ than Buddha. I tell ye, I was an altered man after we'd been to Norway—the auld pagan set me thinkin' mony an' mony a time—for, ma certes! he's better worthy respect than mony a so-called Christian. And as for his daughter—the twa great blue eyes o' that lassie made me fair ashamed o' mysel'. Why? Because I felt that as a meen-ister o' the Established Kirk, I was bound to be a sort o' heep-ocrite,—ony thinkin', reasonable man wi' a conscience canna be otherwise wi' they folk,—and ye ken, Errington, there's something in your wife's look that maks a body hesitate before tellin' a lee. Weel—what wi' her face an' the auld *bonde's* talk, I reflectit that I couldna be a meen-ister as meen-isters go,—an' that I must e'en follow oot the Testament's teachings according to ma own way o' thinkin'. First, I fancied I'd rough it abroad as a meesionary—then I remembered the savages at hame, an' decided to attend to them before onything else. Then my aunt's siller came in handy—in short, I'm just gaun to live on as wee a handfu' o' the filthy lucre as I can, an' lay oot the rest on the heathens o' London. An' it's as well to do't while I'm alive to see to't mysel'—for I've often observed that if ye leave your warld's gear to the poor when ye're deed, just for the gude reason that ye canna tak it to the grave wi' ye,—it'll melt in a wonderfu' way through the hands o' the ' secretaries ' an' ' distributors ' o' the fund, till there's naething left for those ye meant to benefit. Ye maunna think I'm gaun to do ony preachin' business down at East-end,—there's too much o' that an' tract-givin' already. The puir soul whose wee hoosie I've rented hadna tasted bit nor sup for three days—till I came an' startled her into a greetin' fit by takin' her rooms an' payin' her in advance—eh! mon, ye'd have thought I was a saint frae heaven if ye'd heard her blessin' me,—an' a gude curate had called on her just before and had given her a tract to dine on. Ye see, I maun mak mysel' a *friend* to the folk first, before I can do them gude—I maun get to the heart o' their troubles—an' troubles are plentiful in that quarter,— I maun live among them, an' be ane o' them. I wad mind ye that Christ Himsel' gave sympathy to begin with,—he did the preachin' afterwards."

"What a good fellow you are, Mac!" said Errington, suddenly seeing his raw Scotch friend with the perverse accent, in quite a new and heroic light.

Macfarlane actually blushed. "Nonsense, not a bit o't!" he declared quite nervously. "It's just pure selfishness, after a'—for I'm simply enjoyin' mysel' the hale day long. Last nicht, I found a wee cripple o' a laddie sittin' by himsel' in the gutter, munchin a potato skin. I just took him, —he starin' an' blinkin' like an owl at me,—and carried him into my room. There I gave him a plate o' barley broth, an' finished him up wi' a hunk o' gingerbread. Ma certes! Ye should ha' seen the rascal laugh. 'Twas better than lookin' at a play from a ten-guinea box on the grand tier!"

"By Jove, Sandy, you're a brick!" cried Lorimer, laughing to hide a very different emotion—"I had no idea you were that sort of chap."

"Nor had I," said Macfarlane quite simply—"I never fashed mysel' wi' thinkin' o' ither folks troubles at a'—I never even took into conseederation the meanin' o' the Testament teachings till—I saw your leddy wife, Errington." He paused a moment, then added gravely—"Yes— and I've aften fancied she maun be a real live angel,—an' I've sought always to turn my hand to something useful and worth the doin',—ever since I met her."

"I'll tell her so," said poor Philip, his heart aching for his lost love as he spoke, though he smiled. "It will give her pleasure to hear it."

Macfarlane blushed again like any awkward schoolboy.

"Oh, I dinna ken aboot that!" he said hurriedly. "She's just a grand woman anyway." Then, bethinking himself of another subject, he asked, "Have you heard o' the Reverend Mr. Dyceworthy lately?"

Errington and Lorimer replied in the negative.

Macfarlane laughed—his eyes twinkled. "It's evident ye never read police reports," he said—"Talk o' meen-isters,—he's a pretty specimen! He's been hunted out o' his place in Yorkshire for carryin' on love-affairs wi' the women o' his congregation. One day he locked himsel' in the vestry wi' the new-married wife o' one o' his preencipal supporters—an' he had a grand time of it—till the husband came an' dragged him oot an' thrashed him soundly. Then he left the neighborhood—an' just th' ither day—he turned up in Glasgie."

Macfarlane paused and laughed again.

"Well?" said Lorimer, with some interest—"Did you meet him there?"

"That did I—but no to speak to him—he was far too weel lookit after to need my services," and Macfarlane rubbed his great hands together with an irrepressible chuckle. "There was a crowd o' hootin' laddies round him, an' he was callin' on the heavens to bear witness to his purity. His hat was off—an' he had a black eye—an' a' his coat was covered wi' mud, an' a policeman was embracin' him vera affectionately by th' arm. He was in charge for drunken, disorderly, an' indecent conduct—an' the magistrate cam' down pretty hard on him. The case proved to be exceptionally outrageous—so he's sentenced to a month's imprisonment an' hard labor. Hard labor! Eh, mon! but that's fine! Fancy him at work—at real work for the first time in a' his days! Gude Lord! I can see him at it!"

"So he's come to that!" and Errington shrugged his shoulders with weary contempt. "I thought he would. His career as a minister is ended, that's one comfort!"

"Don't be too sure o' that!" said Sandy cautiously. "There's always America, ye ken. He can mak' a holy martyr o' himsel' there! He may gain as muckle a reputation as Henry Ward Beecher—ye cann ever tell what may happen—'tis a queer warld!"

"Queer, indeed!" assented Lorimer as they all rose and left the restaurant together. "If our present existence is the result of a fortuitous conglomeration of atoms,—I think the atoms ought to have been more careful what they were about, that's all I can say!"

They reached the open street, where Macfarlane shook hands and went his way, promising to call on Errington as soon as Thelma should be again at home.

"He's turned out quite a fine fellow," said Lorimer, when he had gone. "I should never have thought he had so much in him. He has become a philanthropist."

" I fancy he's better than an ordinary philanthropist," replied Philip. " Philanthropists often talk a great deal and do nothing."

" Like members of Parliament," suggested Lorimer, with a smile.

" Exactly so. By-the-by—I've resigned my candidateship."

" Resigned ? Why ? "

" Oh, I'm sick of the thing ! One has to be such a humbug to secure one's votes. I had a wretched time yesterday,—speechifying and trying to rouse up clodhoppers to the interests of their country,—and all the time my darling at home was alone, and breaking her heart about me ! By Jove ! if I'd only known ! When I came back this morning to all this misery—I told Neville to send in my resignation. I repeated the same thing to him the last thing before I left the house."

" But you might have waited a day or two," said Lorimer wonderingly. " You're such a fellow of impulse, Phil——"

" Well, I can't help it. I'm tired of politics. I began with a will, fancying that every member of the house had his country's interests at heart,—not a bit of it ! They're all for themselves—most of them, at any rate—they're not even sincere in their efforts to do good to the population. And it's all very well to stick up for the aristocracy ; but why, in Heaven's name, can't some of the wealthiest among them do as much as our old Mac is doing, for the outcast and miserable poor ? I see some real usefulness and good in *his* work, and I'll help him in it with a will—when—when Thelma comes back."

Thus talking, the two friends reached the Garrick Club, where they found Beau Lovelace in the reading-room, turning over some new books with the curious smiling air of one who believes there can be nothing original under the sun, and that all literature is mere repetition. He greeted them cheerfully.

" Come out of here," he said. " Come into a place where we can talk. There's an old fellow over there who's ready to murder any member who even whispers. We won't excite his angry passions. You know we're all literature-mongers here,—we've each got our own little particular stall where we sort our goods—our mouldy oranges, sour apples, and indigestible nuts,—and we polish them up to look tempting to the public. It's a great business, and we can't bear to be looked at while we're turning our apples with the best side outwards, and boiling our oranges to make them swell and seem big! We like to do our humbug in silence and alone."

He led the way into the smoking-room—and there heard with much surprise and a great deal of concern the story of Thelma's flight.

"Ingenuous boy!" he said kindly, clapping Philip on the shoulder. "How could you be such a fool as to think that repeated visits to Violet Vere, no matter on what business, would not bring the dogs of scandal yelping about your heels! I wonder you didn't see how you were compromising yourself!"

"He never told *me* a word about it," interposed Lorimer, "or else I should have given him a bit of my mind on the subject."

"Of course!" agreed Lovelace. "And—excuse me—why the devil didn't you let your secretary manage his domestic squabbles by himself?"

"He's very much broken down," said Errington. "A hopeless, frail, disappointed man. I thought I could serve him——"

"I see!" and Beau's eyes were bent on him with a very friendly look. "You're a first-rate fellow, Errington,—but you shouldn't fly off so readily on the rapid wings of impulse. Now I suppose you want to shoot Lennox—that can't be done—not in England at any rate."

"It can't be done at all, anywhere," said Lorimer gravely. "He's dead."

Beau Lovelace started back in amazement. "Dead! You don't say so! Why, he was dining last night at the Criterion—I saw him there."

Briefly they related the sudden accident that had occurred, and described its fatal result.

"He died horribly!" said Philip in a low voice. "I haven't got over it yet. That evil, tortured face of his haunts me."

Lovelace was only slightly shocked. He had known Lennox's life too well, and had depised it too thoroughly, to feel much regret now it was thus abruptly ended.

"Rather an unpleasant exit for such a fellow," he remarked. "Not æsthetic at all. And so you were going to castigate him?"

"Look!" and Philip showed him the horsewhip; "I've

been carrying this thing about all day,—I wish I could drop it in the streets; but if I did, some one would be sure to pick it up and return it to me."

"If it were a purse containing bank-notes you could drop it with the positive certainty of never seeing it again," laughed Beau. "Here, hand it over!" and he possessed himself of it. "I'll keep it till you come back. You leave for Norway to-night, then?"

"Yes. If I can. But it's the winter season—and there'll be all manner of difficulties. I'm afraid it's no easy matter to reach the Altenfjord at this time of year."

"Why not use your yacht, and be independent of obstacles?" suggested Lovelace.

"She's under repairs, worse luck!" sighed Philip despondingly. "She won't be in sailing condition for another month. No—I must take my chance—that's all. It's possible I may overtake Thelma at Hull—that's my great hope."

"Well, don't be down in the mouth about it, my boy!" said Beau sympathetically. "It'll all come right, depend upon it! Your wife's a sweet, gentle, noble creature,—and when once she knows all about the miserable mistake that has arisen, I don't know which will be greatest, her happiness or her penitence, for having misunderstood the position. Now let's have some coffee."

He ordered this refreshment from a passing waiter, and as he did so, a gentleman, with hands clasped behind his back, and a suave smile on his countenance, bowed to him with marked and peculiar courtesy as he sauntered on his way through the room. Beau returned the salute with equal politeness.

"That's Whipper," he explained with a smile, when the gentleman was out of earshot. "The best and most generous of men! He's a critic—all critics are large-minded and and generous, we know,—but he happens to be remarkably so. He did me the kindest turn I ever had in my life. When my first book came out, he fell upon it tooth and claw, mangled it, tore it to ribbons, metaphorically speaking, —and waved the fragments mockingly in the eyes of the public. From that day my name was made—my writings sold off with delightful rapidity, and words can never tell how I blessed, and how I still bless, Whipper! He always pitches into me—that's what's so good of him! We're awfully polite to each other, as you observe—and what is so perfectly charming is that he's quite unconscious how much he's helped me along! He's really a first-rate fellow. But I haven't yet attained the summit of my ambition,"— and here Lovelace broke off with a sparkle of fun in his clear steel-grey eyes.

" Why, what else do you want? "asked Lorimer laughing.

" I want," returned Beau solemnly, " I want to be jeered at by *Punch!* I want *Punch* to make mouths at me, and give me the benefit of his inimitable squeak and gibber. No author's fame is quite secure till dear old *Punch* has abused him. Abuse is the thing nowadays, you know. Heaven forbid that I should be praised by *Punch.* That would be frightfully unfortunate!"

Here the coffee arrived, and Lovelace dispensed it to his friends, talking gaily the while in an effort to distract Errington from his gloomy thoughts.

"I've just been informed on respectable authority, that Walt Whitman is the new Socrates," he said laughingly. " I felt rather stunned at the moment but I've got over it now. Oh, this deliciously mad London! what a gigantic Colney Hatch it is for the crazed folk of the world to air their follies in! That any reasonable Englishmen with such names as Shakespeare, Byron, Keats, and Shelley, to keep the glory of their country warm, should for one moment consider Walt Whitman a *poet!* Ye gods! Where are your thunderbolts!"

" He's an American, isn't he? " asked Errington.

" He is, my dear boy! An American whom the sensible portion of America rejects. We, therefore,—out of opposition,—take him up. His chief recommendation is that he writes blatantly concerning commonplaces,—regardless of music or rhythm. Here's a bit of him concerning the taming of oxen. He says the tamer lives in a

" ' Placid pastoral region.
There they bring him the three-year-olds and the four-year-olds to break them,—
Some are such beautiful animals, so lofty looking,—some are buff-colored, some mottled, one has a white line running along his back, some are brindled,
Some have wide flaring horns (a good sign!) look you! the bright hides
See the two with stars on their foreheads—see the round bodies and broad backs
How straight and square they stand on their legs——' "

" Stop, stop!" cried Lorimer, putting his hands to his

ears. " This is a practical joke, Beau! No one would call that jargon poetry!"

" Oh! wouldn't they though!" exclaimed Lovelace. " Let some critic of reputation once start the idea, and you'll have the good London folk who won't bother to read him for themselves, declaring him as fine as Shakespeare. The dear English muttons! fine Southdowns! fleecy baa-lambs! once let the Press-bell tinkle loudly enough across the fields of literature, and they'll follow, bleating sweetly in any direction! The sharpest heads in our big metropolis are those who know this, and who act accordingly."

" Then why don't *you* act accordingly?" asked Errington, with a faint smile.

" Oh, I? I can't! I never asked a favor from the Press in my life—but its little bell has tinkled for me all the same, and a few of the muttons follow, but not all. Are you off?" this, as they rose to take their leave. " Well, Errington, old fellow," and he shook hands warmly, " a pleasant journey to you, and a happy return home! My best regards to your wife. Lorimer, have you settled whether you'll go with me to Italy? I start the day after to-morrow."

Lorimer hesitated—then said, " All right! My mother's delighted at the idea,—yes, Beau! we'll come. Only I hope we shan't bore you."

" Bore me! you know me better than that," and he accompanied them out of the smoking-room into the hall, while Errington, a little surprised at this sudden arrangement, observed—

" Why, George—I thought you'd be here when we came back from Norway—to—to welcome Thelma, you know!"

George laughed. " My dear boy, I shan't be wanted! Just let me know how everything goes on. You—you see I'm in duty bound to take my mother out of London in winter."

" Just so!" agreed Lovelace, who had watched him narrowly while he spoke. " Don't grudge the old lady her southern sunshine, Errington! Lorimer wants brushing up a bit too—he looks seedy. Then I shall consider it settled—the day after to-morrow, we meet at Charing Cross— morning tidal express, of course,—never go by night service across the Channel if you can help it."

Again they shook hands and parted.

" Best thing that young fellow can do!" thought Love-face as he returned to the Club reading-room. " The sooner he gets out of this, into new scenes the better,—he's breaking his heart over the beautiful Thelma. By Jove! the boy's eyes looked like those of a shot animal whenever her name was mentioned. He's rather badly hit ! "

He sat down and began to meditate. " What can I do for him, I wonder ? " he thought. " Nothing, I suppose. A love of that sort can't be remedied. It's a pity—a great pity! And I don't know any woman likely to make a counter-impression on him. He'd never put up with an Italian beauty "—he paused in his reflections, and the color flushed his broad, handsome brow, as the dazzling vision of a sweet, piquant face with liquid dark eyes and rippling masses of rich brown hair came flitting before him—" unless he saw Angela," he murmured to himself softly,—" and he will not see her,—besides, Angela loves *me !* "

And after this, his meditations seemed to be particularly pleasant, to judge from the expression of his features. Beau was by no means ignorant of the tender passion—he had his own little romance, as beautiful and bright as a summer-day—but he had resolved that London, with its love of gossip, its scandal, and society papers,—London, that on account of his popularity as a writer, watched his movements and chronicled his doings in the most authoritative and incorrect manner,—London should have no chance of penetrating into the secret of his private life. And so far he had succeeded—and was likely still to succeed.

Meanwhile, as he still sat in blissful reverie, pretending to read a newspaper, though his thoughts were far away from it, Errington and Lorimer arrived at the Midland Station. Britta was already there with the luggage,—she was excited· and pleased—her spirits had risen at the prospect of seeing her mistress soon again,—possibly, she thought gladly, they might find her at Hull,—they might not have to go to Norway at all. The train came up to the platform —the tickets were taken,—and Sir Philip, with Britta, entered a first-class compartment, while Lorimer stood outside leaning with folded arms on the carriage-window, talking cheerfully.

" You'll find her all right, Phil, I'm positive ! " he said. " I think it's very probable she has been compelled to remain at Hull,—and even at the worst, Britta can guide you all over Norway, if necessary. Nothing will daunt *her.*"

And he nodded kindly to the little maid who had regained her rosy color and the sparkle of her eyes in the eagerness she felt to rejoin her beloved "Fröken." The engine-whistle gave a warning shriek—Philip leaned out and pressed his friend's hand warmly.

"Good-bye, old fellow! I'll write to you in Italy."

"All right—mind you do! And I say—give my love to Thelma!"

Philip smiled and promised. The train began to move,—slowly at first, then more quickly, till with clattering uproar and puffing clouds of white steam, it rushed forth from the station, winding through the arches like a black snake, till it had twisted itself rapidly out of sight. Lorimer, left alone, looked after it wistfully, with a heavy weight of un-uttered love and sorrow at his heart, and as he at last turned away, those haunting words that he had heard un-der the pines at the Altenfjord recurred again and again to his memory—the words uttered by the distraught Sigurd—and how true they were, he thought! how desperately, cruelly true!

"Good things may come for others—but for *you*, the heavens are empty!"

CHAPTER XXX.

"Honor is an old-world thing, but it smells sweet to those in whose hand it is strong."—OUIDA.

DISAPPOINTMENT upon disappointment awaited Errington at Hull. Unfortunately, neither he nor Britta knew of the existence of the good Norwegian innkeeper, Friedhof, who had assisted Thelma in her flight—and all their persistent and anxious inquiries elicited no news of her. Moreover, there was no boat of any kind leaving immediately for Nor-way—not even a whaler or fishing-smack. In a week's time,—possibly later,—there would be a steamer starting for Christiansund, and for this, Errington, though almost mad with impatience, was forced to wait. And in the mean-time, he roamed about the streets of Hull, looking eagerly at every fair-haired woman who passed him, and always hoping that Thelma herself would suddenly meet him face to face, and put her hands in his. He wrote to Neville and told him to send on any letters that might arrive for him, and by every post he waited anxiously for one from Thelma, but none came. To relieve his mind a little, he scribbled a long letter to her, explaining everything, telling her how ardently he loved and worshipped her—how he was on his way to join her at the Altenjford,—and ending by the most passionate vows of unchanging love and fidelity. He was somewhat soothed when he had done this—though he did not realize the fact that in all probability he himself might arrive before the letter. The slow, miserable days went on —the week was completed—the steamer for Christiansund started at last,—and, after a terribly stormy passage, he and the faithful Britta were landed there.

On arrival, he learned that a vessel bound for the North Cape had left on the previous day—there would not be another for a fortnight. Cursing his ill-luck, he resolved to reach the Altenfjord by land, and began to make arrangements accordingly. Those who knew the country well endeavored to dissuade him from this desperate project—the further north, the greater danger, they told him,—moreover, the weather was, even for Norway, exceptionally trying. Snow lay heavily over all the country he would have to traverse—the only means of conveyance was by carriole or *pulkha*—the latter a sort of sledge used by the Laplanders, made in the form of a boat, and generally drawn by reindeer. The capabilities of the carriole would be exhausted as soon as the snow-covered regions were reached—and to manage a *pulkha* successfully, required special skill of no ordinary kind. But the courageous little Britta made short work of all these difficulties—she could drive a *pulkha*,— she knew how to manage reindeer,—she entertained not the slightest doubt of being able to overcome all the obstacles on the way. At the same time, she frankly told Sir Philip that the journey would be a long one, perhaps occupying several days—that they would have to rest at different farms or *stations* on the road, and put up with hard fare— that the cold would be intense,—that often they would find it difficult to get relays of the required reindeer,—and that it might perhaps be wiser to wait for the next boat going to the North Cape.

But Errington would hear of no more delays—each hour that passed filled him with fresh anxieties—and once in Norway he could not rest. The idea that Thelma might be ill—dying—or dead—gained on him with redoubled force,—and his fears easily communicating themselves to Britta, who was to the full as impatient as he, the two

29

made up their minds, and providing every necessary for the journey they could think of, they started for the far sunless North, through a white, frozen land, which grew whiter and more silent the further they went,—even as the brooding sky above them grew darker and darker. The aurora borealis flashed its brilliant shafts of color against the sable breast of heaven,—the tall pines, stripped bare, every branch thick with snow and dropping icicles, stood,—pale ghosts of the forest,—shedding frozen tears—the moon, more like steel than silver, shone frostily cold, her light seeming to deepen rather than soften the dreariness of the land—and on—on—on—they went, Britta enveloped to the chin in furs, steadily driving the strange elfin-looking steeds with their horned heads casting long distorted shadows on the white ground,—and Philip beside her, urging her on with feverish impatience, while he listened to the smooth trot of the reindeer,—the tinkle of the bells on their harness, and the hiss of the sledge across the sparkling snow.

Meanwhile, as he thus pursued his long and difficult journey, rumor was very busy with his name in London. Everybody—that is, everybody worth consideration in the circle of the " Upper Ten "—was talking about him,— shrugging their shoulders, lifting their eyebrows and smiling knowingly, whenever he was mentioned. He became more known in one day than if he had served his country's interests in Parliament for years.

On the very morning after he had left the metropolis *en route* for Norway, that admirably conducted society journal, the *Snake*, appeared,—and of course, had its usual amount of eager purchasers, anxious to see the latest bit of aristocratic scandal. Often these good folks were severely disappointed—the *Snake* was sometimes so frightfully dull, that it had actually nothing to say against anybody— then, naturally, it was not worth buying. But this time it was really interesting—it knocked down—or tried to knock down—at one blow, a formerly spotless reputation—and " really—really ! " said the Upper Ten, " it was dreadful, but of course it was to be expected ! Those quiet, seemingly virtuous persons are always the worst when you come to know them, yet who would have thought it ! " And society read the assailing paragraph, and rolled it in its rank mouth, like a bon-bon, enjoying its flavor. It ran as follows :—

" We hear on excellent authority that the Norwegian

'beauty,' Lady Bruce-Errington, wife of Sir Philip Bruce-
Errington, is about to sue for a divorce on the ground of infidelity. The offending *dama* in the question is an admired
actress, well-known to the frequenters of the Brilliant
Theatre. But there are always two sides to these affairs,
and it is rumored that the fair Norwegian (who before her
marriage, we understand, was a great adept in the art of
milking reindeer on the shores of her native Fjord) has
private reasons of her own for desiring the divorce, not altogether in keeping with her stated reasons or her apparent
reserve. We are, however, always on the side of the fair
sex, and, as the faithless husband has made no secret of
his new *liaison*, we do not hesitate to at once pronounce in
the lady's favor. The case is likely to prove interesting
to believers in wedded happiness, combined with the strictest moral and religious sentiments."

Quite by accident this piece of would-be " smartness "
was seen by Beau Lovelace. He had a wholesome contempt for the *Snake*—and all its class,—he would never
have looked at it, or known of the paragraph, had not a
friend of his at the Garrick pointed it out to him with half
a smile and half a sneer.

" It's a damned lie ! " said Beau briefly.

" That remains to be proved ! " answered his friend, and
went away laughing.

Beau read it over and over again, his blood firing with
honest indignation. Thelma ! Thelma—that pure white
lily of womanhood,—was she to have her stainless life
blurred by the trail of such a thing as the *Snake ?*—and was
Errington's honor to be attainted in his absence, and he
condemned without a word uttered in his defence ?

" Detestable blackguard ! " muttered Lovelace, reverting
in his mind to the editor of the journal in question.
" What's his name I wonder ? " He searched and found it
at the top of a column—" Sole Editor and Proprietor,
C. Snawley-Grubbs, to whom all checks and post-office
orders should be made payable. The Editor cannot be responsible for the return of rejected MSS."

Beau noted the name, and wrote the address of the office
in his pocket-book, smiling curiously to himself the while.

" I'm almost glad Errington's out of the way, he said
half aloud. " He shan't see this thing if I can help it,
though I dare say some particularly affectionate friend will
send it to him, carefully marked. At any rate, he needn't

know it just yet—and as for Lorimer—shall I tell him? No, I won't. I'll have the game all to myself—and—by Jove! how I *shall* enjoy it!"

An hour later he stood in the office of the *Snake*, courteously inquiring for Mr. Snawley-Grubbs. Apparently he had come on horseback, for he held a riding-whip in his hand,—the very whip Errington had left with him the previous day. The inky, dirty, towzle-headed boy who presided in solitary grandeur over the *Snake's* dingy premises, stared at him inquiringly,—visitors of his distinguished appearance and manner being rather uncommon. Those who usually had business with the great Grubbs were of a different type altogether,—some of them discarded valets or footmen, who came to gain half a crown or five shillings by offering information as to the doings of their late masters and mistresses,—shabby "supers" from the theatres, who had secured the last bit of scandal concerning some celebrated stage or professional "beauty"—sporting men and turf gamblers of the lowest class,—unsuccessful dramatists and small verse writers—these, with now and then a few "ladies"—ladies of the bar-room, ballet, and demimonde, were the sort of persons who daily sought private converse with Grubbs—and Beau Lovelace, with his massive head, fine muscular figure, keen eyes, and self-assertive mien, was quite a novel specimen of manhood for the wondering observation of the office-boy, who scrambled off his high chair with haste and something of respect as he said—

"What name, sir, please?"

"Beaufort Lovelace," said the gentleman, with a bland smile. "Here is my card. Ask Mr. Grubbs whether he can see me for a few minutes. If he is engaged—editors generally *are* engaged—tell him I'll wait."

The boy went off in a greater hurry than ever. The name of Lovelace was quite familiar to him—he knew him, not as a distinguished novelist, but as "'im who makes such a precious lot of money." And he was breathless with excitement when he reached the small editorial chamber at the top of a dark, narrow flight of stairs, wherein sat the autocratic Snawley, smiling suavely over a heap of letters and disordered MSS. He glanced at the card which his ink-smeared attendant presented him.

"Ah, indeed!" he said condescendingly. "Lovelace—Lovelace? Oh yes—I suppose it must be the novelist of that name—yes!—show him up."

Shown up he was accordingly. He entered the room with a firm tread, and closed the door behind him!

"How do you do, my dear sir!" exclaimed Grubbs warmly. "You are well known to me by reputation! I am charmed—delighted to make the personal acquaintance of one who is—yes—let me say, who is a brother in litera-ture! Sit down, I beg of you!"

And he waved his hand towards a chair, thereby display-ing the great rings that glittered on his podgy fingers.

Beau, however, did not seat himself—he only smiled very coldly and contemptuously.

"We can discuss the fraternal nature of our relationship afterwards," he said satirically. "Business first. Pray, sir,—here he drew from his pocket the last number of the *Snake*—" are you the writer of this paragraph?"

He pointed to it, as he flattened the journal and laid it in front of the editor on the desk. Mr. Snawley-Grubbs glanced at it and smiled unconcernedly.

"No I am not. But I happen to know it is perfectly correct. I received the information on the highest—the very highest and most credible authority."

"Indeed!" and Beau's lip curled haughtily, while his hand clenched the riding-whip more firmly. "Then allow me to tell you, sir, that it is utterly false in every particular —moreover—that it is a gross libel,—published with delib-erate intent to injure those whom it presumes to mention, —and that, whoever wrote it,—you, sir, you alone are re-sponsible for a most mischievous, scandalous, and damnable lie!"

Mr. Grubbs was in no wise disconcerted. Honest indig-nation honestly expressed, always amused him—he was amused now.

"You're unduly excited, Mr. Lovelace," he said with a little laugh. "Permit me to remark that your language is rather extraordinary—quite *too* strong under the circum-stances! However, you're a privileged person—genius is always a little mad, or shall we say,—eccentric?— I sup-pose you are a friend of Sir Philip Errington, and you naturally feel hurt—yes—yes, I quite understand! But the scourge of the press—the wholesome, purifying scourge, cannot be withheld out of consideration for private or per-sonal feelings. No—no! There's a higher duty—the duty we owe to the public!"

"I tell you again," repeated Lovelace firmly—" the whole thing is a lie. *Will* you apologize?"

Mr. Grubbs threw himself back in his chair and laughed aloud.

"Apologize? My dear sir, you must be dreaming! Apologize? Certainly not! I cannot retract the statements I have made—and I firmly believe them to be true. And though there is a saying, 'the greater the truth the greater the libel,' I'm ready, sir, and, always have been ready, to sacrifice myself to the cause of truth. Truth, truth for ever! Tell the truth and shame the devil! You are at liberty to inform Sir Philip Errington from me, that as it is my object—a laudable and praiseworthy one, too, I think—to show up the awful immorality now reigning in our upper classes, I do not regret in the least the insertion of the paragraph in question. If it only makes him ashamed of his vices, I shall have done a good deed, and served the interests of society at large. At the same time, if he wishes to bring an action for libel——"

"You dog!" exclaimed Lovelace fiercely, approaching him with such a sudden rapid stride that the astonished editor sprang up and barricaded himself behind his own chair. "You hope for that, do you? An action for libel! nothing would please you better! To bring your scandalous printed trash into notoriety,—to hear your name shouted by dirty hawkers and newsboys—to be sentenced as a first-class misdemenent; ah, no such luck for you! I know the tricks of your vile trade! There are other ways of dealing with a vulgar bully and coward!"

And before the startled Grubbs could realize his position, Lovelace closed with him, bent him under, and struck the horsewhip smartly cross his back and shoulders. He uttered a yell of pain and fury, and strove vigorously to defend himself, but, owing to his obesity, his muscles were weak and flabby, and he was powerless against the activity and strength of his opponent. Lash after lash descended regularly and mercilessly—his cries, which gradually became like the roarings of a bull of Bashan, were unheard, as the office-boy below, profiting by a few idle moments, had run across the street to buy some chestnuts at a stall he particularly patronized. Beau thrashed on with increasing enjoyment—Grubbs resisted him less and less, till finally he slipped feebly down on the floor and grovelled there, gasping and groaning. Beau gave him one or **two** more artistic cuts, and stood above him, with the serene, triumphant smile of a successful athlete. Suddenly a loud peal of laughter echoed from the doorway,—a woman stood there, richly dressed in silk and fur, with diamonds sparkling in her ears and diamonds clasping the long boa at her throat. It was Violet Vere.

"Why, Snawley!" she cried with cheerful familiarity. "How are you? All broken, and no one to pick up the pieces! Serve you right! Got it at last, eh? Don't get up! You look so comfortable!"

"Bodily assault," gasped Grubbs. "I'll summons—call the police—call," his voice died away in inarticulate gurglings, and raising himself, he sat up on the floor in a sufficiently abject and ludicrous posture, wiping the tears of pain from his eyes. Beau looked at the female intruder and recognized her at once. He saluted her with cold courtesy, and turned again to Grubbs.

"*Will* you apologize?"

"No—I—I *won't!*"

Beau made another threatening movement—Miss Vere interposed.

"Stop a bit," she said, regarding him with her insolent eyes, in which lurked, however, an approving smile. "I don't know who you are, but you seem a fighting man! Don't go at him again till I've had a word. I say, Grubbs! you've been hitting at me in your trashy paper."

Grubbs still sat on the floor groaning.

"You must eat those words," went on the Vere calmly. "Eat 'em up with sauce for dinner. The 'admired actress well known at the Brilliant,' has nothing to do with the Bruce-Errington man,—not she! He's a duffer, a regular stiff one—no go about him anyhow. And what the deuce do you mean by calling me an offending *dama.* Keep your oaths to yourself, will you?"

Beau Lovelace was amused. Grubbs turned his watering eye from one to the other in wretched perplexity. He made an effort to stand up and succeeded.

"I'll have you arrested, sir?" he exclaimed shaking his fists at Beau, and quivering with passion, "on a charge of bodily assault—shameful bodily assault, sir!"

"All right!" returned Beau coolly. "If I were fined a hundred pounds for it, I should think it cheap for the luxury of thrashing such a hound!"

Grubbs quaked at the determined attitude and threatening eye of his assailant, and turned for relief to Miss Vere, whose smile, however, was not sympathetic.

"You'd better cave in!" she remarked airily. "You've got the worst of it, you know!"

She had long been on confidential terms with the *Snake* proprietor, and she spoke to him now with the candor of an old friend.

"Dear me, what do you expect of me!" he almost whimpered. "I'm not to blame! The paragraph was inserted without my knowledge by my sub-editor—he's away just now, and—there! why?" he cried with sudden defiance, "why don't you ask Sir Francis Lennox about it? He wrote the whole thing."

"Well, he's dead," said Miss Vere with the utmost coolness. "So it wouldn't be much use asking *him*. *He* can't answer,—you'll have to answer for him."

"I don't believe it!" exclaimed Mr. Grubbs. "He can't be dead!"

"Oh, yes, he can, and he *is*," retorted Violet. "And a good job too! He was knocked over by a train at Charing Cross. You'll see it in to-day's paper, if you take the trouble to look. And mind you contradict all that stuff about me in your next number—do you hear? I'm going to America with a Duke next month, and I can't afford to have my reputation injured. And I won't be called a '*dama*' for any penny-a-liner living." She paused, and again broke out laughing, "Poor old Snawley! You do look so sore! Ta-ta!" And she moved towards the door. Lovelace, always courteous, opened it for her. She raised her hard, bright eyes, and smiled.

"Thanks! Hope I shall see you again some day!"

"You are very good!" responded Beau gravely.

Either his tone, which was one chill indifference, or something in his look, irritated her suddenly—for a rush of hot color crimsoned her face, and she bit her lips vexedly as she descended the office-stairs.

"He's one of your high-and-mighty sort," she thought disdainfully, as she entered her cosy brougham and was driven away. "Quite too awfully moral!" She pulled a large, elaborately cut glass scent-bottle out of the pocket of her cloak, and, unscrewing the gold top, applied it, not to her nose but her mouth. It contained neat Cognac—and she drank a goodly gulp of it with evident relish, swallowing a scented bon-bon immediately afterwards to take away the suspicious odor. " Yes—quite too awfully moral ! " she repeated with a grin. " Not in my line at all ! Lord ! It's lucky there are not many such fellows about, or what would become of *me ?* A precious poor business I should make of it ! "

Meanwhile, Lovelace, left alone again with Mr. Grubbs, reiterated his demand for an apology. Grubbs made a rush for the door, as soon as Miss Vere had gone, with the full intention of summoning the police, but Beau coolly placed his back against it with resolute firmness, and flourished his whip defiantly.

" Come, sir, none of this nonsense ! " he said sternly. " I don't mean to leave this spot till I have satisfaction. If Sir Francis Lennox wrote that scandalous paragraph the greater rascal he,—and the more shame to you for inserting it. You, who make it your business to know all the dirty alleys and dark corners of life, must have known *his* character pretty thoroughly. There's not the slightest excuse for you. Will you apologize ?—and retract every word of that paragraph, in your next issue ? "

Grubbs, breathless with rage and fear, glared at him, but made no answer.

" If you refuse to comply," went on Beau deliberately, balancing the horsewhip lightly on his hand, " I'll just tell you what the consequences will be. I've thrashed you once—and I'll thrash you again. I have only to give the cue to several worthy fellows of my acquaintance, who don't care how much they pay for their fun, and each of them in turn will thrash you. As for an action for libel, don't expect it—but I swear there shan't be a safe corner in London for you. If, however, you publish next week a full retraction of your printed lie—why, then I—shall be only too happy to forget that such an individual as yourself burdens this planet. There are the two alternatives— choose !

Grubbs hesitated, but coward fear made him quail with the prospect of unlimited thrashings.

" Very well," he said sullenly. " Write what you want put in—I'll attend to it—I don't mind obliging Miss Vere. But all the same, I'll have *you* arrested ! "

Beau laughed. " Do so by all means ! " he said gaily. " I'll leave my address with you ! " He wrote rapidly a few lines on a piece of paper to the following effect—

We have to entirely contradict a statement we made

last week respecting a supposed forthcoming divorce case, in which Sir Philip Bruce-Errington was seriously impli-cated. There was no truth whatever in the statement, and we herewith apologize most humbly and heartily for having inadvertently given credence to a rumor which is now proved to be utterly false and without the slightest shadow of a foundation."

He handed this to Grubbs.

"Insert that word for word, at the head of your para-graphs," he said, "and you'll hear no more of me, unless you give me fresh provocation. And I advise you to think twice before you have me arrested—for I'll defend my own case, and—ruin you! I'm rather a dangerous customer to have much to do with! However, you've got my card—you know where to find me if you want me. Only you'd better send after me to-night if you do—to-morrow I may be absent."

He smiled, and drew on his gloves leisurely, eyeing mean-while the discomfited editor, who was furtively rubbing his shoulder where the lash had stung it somewhat severely.

"I'm exceedingly glad I've hurt you, Mr. Grubbs," he said blandly. "And the next time you want to call me your brother in literature, pray reflect on the manner in which my fraternal affection displayed itself! *Good* morn-ing!"

And he took his departure with a quiet step and serene manner, leaving Snawley-Grubbs to his own meditations, which were far from agreeable. He was not ignorant of the influence Beau Lovelace possessed, both on the press and in society—he was a general favorite,—a man whose opinions were quoted, and whose authority was accepted everywhere. If he appeared to answer a charge of assault against Grubbs, and defended his own case, he certainly would have the best of it. He might—he would have to pay a fine, but what did he care for that? He would hold up the *Snake* and its proprietor to the utmost ridicule and opprobrium—his brilliant satire and humor would carry all before it—and he, Snawley-Grubbs, would be still more utterly routed and humiliated. Weighing all these con-siderations carefully in his mind, the shrinking editor de-cided to sit down under his horsewhipping in silence and resignation.

It was not a very lofty mode of action—still, it was the

safest. Of course Violet Vere would spread the story all through *her* particular " set,"—it made him furious to think of this—yet there was no help for it. He would play the martyr, he thought—the martyr to the cause of truth,—the injured innocent entrapped by false information—he might possibly gain new supporters and sympathizers in this way if he played his cards carefully. He turned to the daily paper, and saw there chronicled the death of Sir Francis Lennox. It *was* true, then. Well! he was not at all affected by it—he merely committed the dead man in the briefest and strongest language to the very lowest of those low and sulphurous regions over which Satan is supposed to have full sway. Not a soul regretted Sir Francis —not even the Vere, whom he had kept and surrounded with every luxury for five years. Only one person, a fair, weary faced woman away in Germany shed a few tears over the lawyer's black-boardered letter that announced his death to her—and this was the deserted wife,—who had once loved him. Lady Winsleigh had heard the news,—she shuddered and turned very pale when her husband gently and almost pityingly told her of the sudden and unprepared end that had overtaken her quondam admirer—but she said nothing. She was presiding at the breakfast-table for the first time in many years—she looked somewhat sad and listless, yet lovelier so than in all the usual pride and assertive arrogance of her beauty. Lord Winsleigh read aloud the brief account of the accident in the paper—she listened dreamily, —still mute. He watched her with yearning eyes.

" An awful death for such a man, Clara ! " he said at last in a low tone.

She dared not look up—she was trembling nervously. How dreadful it was, she thought, to be thankful that a man was dead !—to feel a relief at his being no longer in this world ! Presently her husband spoke again more reservedly.

" No doubt you are greatly shocked and grieved," he said. " I should not have told you so suddenly—pardon me ! "

" I am not grieved," she murmured unsteadily. " It sounds horrible to say so—but I—I am afraid I am *glad !* "

" Clara ! "

She rose and came tremblingly towards him. She knelt at his feet, though he strove to prevent her,—she raised her large, dark eyes, full of dull agony, to his.

"I've been a wicked woman, Harry," she said, with a strange, imploring thrill of passion in her voice. "I am down—down in the dust before you! Look at me—don't forgive me—I won't ask that—you *can't* forgive me,—but *pity* me!"

He took her hands and laid them round his neck,—he drew her gently, soothingly,—closer, closer, till he pressed her to his heart.

"Down in the dust are you?" he whispered brokenly. "My poor wife! God forbid that I should keep you there!"

BOOK III.

THE LAND OF THE LONG SHADOW.

CHAPTER XXXI.

"They have the night, who had, like us, the day—
We, whom day binds, shall have the night as they—
We, from the fetters of the light unbound,
Healed of our wound of living, shall sleep sound!"
                                                    SWINBURNE.

NIGHT on the Altenfjord,—the long, long, changeless night of winter. The sharp snow-covered crests of the mountains rose in white appeal against the darkness of the sky,—the wild north wind tore through the leafless branches of the pine-forests, bringing with it driving pellets of stinging hail. Joyless and songless, the whole landscape lay as though frozen into sculptured stone. The Sun slept,—and the Fjord, black with brooding shadows, seemed silently to ask—where? Where was the great king of Light?—the glorious god of the golden hair and ruddy countenance?—the glittering warrior with the flaming shield and spear invincible? Where had he found his rest? By what strange enchantment had he fallen into so deep and long a drowsiness. The wind that had rioted across the mountains, rooting up great trees in its shrieking career northwards, grew hushed as it approached the Altenfjord—there a weird stillness reigned, broken only by the sullen and monotonous plash of the invisible waves upon the scarcely visible shore.

A few tiny, twinkling lights showed the irregular outline of Bosekop, and now and then one or two fishing-boats with sable sails and small colored lamps at mast and prow would flit across the inky water like dark messengers from another world bound on some mournful errand. Human figures, more shadowy than real, were to be seen occasionally moving on the pier, and to the left of the little town, as the eye

(461)

grew accustomed to the moveless gloom, a group of persons, like ghosts in a dream, could be dimly perceived, working busily at the mending of nets.

Suddenly a strange, unearthly glow flashed over the sombre scene,—a rosy radiance deepening to brilliant streaks of fire. The dark heavens were torn asunder, and through them streamed flaring pennons of light,—waving, trembling, dancing, luminous ribbons of red, blue, green, and a delicious amber, like the flowing of golden wine,—wider, higher, more dazzlingly lustrous, the wondrous glory shone aloft, rising upward from the horizon—thrusting long spears of lambent flame among the murky retreating clouds, till in one magnificent coruscation of resplendent beams a blazing arch of gold leaped from east to west, spanning the visible breath of the Fjord, and casting towards the white peaks above, vivid sparkles and reflections of jewel-like brightness and color. Here was surely the Rainbow Bridge of Odin—the glittering pathway leading to Valhalla! Long filmy threads of emerald and azure trailed downwards from it, like ropes of fairy flowers, binding it to the earth—above it hung a fleece-like nebulous whiteness,—a canopy through which palpitated sudden flashes of amethyst. Then, as though the arch were a bent bow for the hand of some heavenly hunter, crimson beams darted across it in swift succession, like arrows shot at the dark target of the world. Round and round swept the varying circles of color —now advancing—now retreating—now turning the sullen waters beneath into a quivering mass of steely green—now beating against the snow-covered hills till they seemed pinnacles of heaped-up pearls and diamonds. The whole landscape was transformed,—and the shadowy cluster of men and women on the shore paused in their toil, and turned their pale faces towards the rippling splendor,—the heavy fishing-nets drooping from their hands like dark webs woven by giant spiders.

"'Tis the first time we have seen the Arch of Death this year," said one in awed accents.

"Ay, ay!" returned another, with a sigh. "And some one is bound to cross it, whether he will or no. 'Tis a sure sign!"

"Sure!" they all agreed, in hushed voices as faint and far-off as the breaking of the tide against the rocks on the opposite coast.

As they spoke, the fairy-like bridge in the sky parted

asunder and vanished! The brilliant aurora borealis faded
by swift degrees—a few moments, and the land was again
enveloped in gloom.

It might have been midnight—yet by the clock it was but
four in the afternoon. Dreary indeed was the Altenfjord,
—yet the neighboring village of Talvag was even drearier.
There, desolation reigned supreme—it was a frozen region
of bitter, shelterless cold, where the poverty-stricken inhabitants, smitten by the physical torpor and mental stupefac-
tion engendered by the long, dark season, scarcely stirred
out of their miserable homes, save to gather extra fuel.
This is a time in Norway, when beyond the Arctic Circle,
the old gods yet have sway—when in spite of their persistent, sometimes fanatical, adherence to the strictest forms of
Christianity, the people almost unconsciously revert to the
superstitions of their ancestors. Gathering round the blazing pine-logs, they recount to one another in low voices the
ancient legends of dead and gone heroes,—and listening to
the yell of the storm-wind round their huts, they still fancy
they hear the wild war-cries of the Valkyries rushing past
at full gallop on their coal-black steeds, with their long hair
floating behind them.

On this particular afternoon the appearance of the
" Death-Arch," as they called that special form of the
aurora, had impressed the Talvig folk greatly. Some of
them were at the doors, and, regardless of the piercing
cold, occupied themselves in staring languidly at a reindeer
sledge which stood outside one of the more distant huts,
evidently waiting for some person within. The hoofs of
the animals made no impression on the hardened snow—
now and again they gently shook the tinkling bells on their
harness, but otherwise were very patient. The sledge was
in charge of a youthful Laplander—a hideous, stunted specimen of humanity, who appeared to be literally sewed up
from head to foot in skins.

This *cortége* was evidently an object of curiosity,—the
on-lookers eyed it askance, and with a sort of fear. For
did it not belong to the terrible *bonde*, Olaf Güldmar?—
and would not the Laplander,—a useful boy, well known in
Talvig,—come to some fatal harm by watching, even for a
few minutes, the property of an acknowledged pagan? Who
could tell? The very reindeer might be possessed by evil
spirits,—they were certainly much sleeker and finer than the
ordinary run of such animals. There was something un-

canny in the very look of them! Thus the stuperfied, unreasoning Talvig folk muttered, one to another, leaning drowsily out of their half-open doors.

" 'Tis a strange thing," said one man, " that woman as strong in the fear of the Lord as Lovisa Elsland should call for one of the wicked to visit her on her death-bed."

" Strange enough!" answered his neighbor, blinking over his pipe, and knocking down some of the icicles pendent from his roof. " But maybe it is to curse him with the undying curse of the godly."

" She's done that all her life," said the first speaker.

" That's true! She's been a faithful servant of the Gospel. All's right with her in the next world—she'll die easily."

" Was it for her the Death-Arch shone?" asked an old woman, suddenly thrusting her head, wrapped in a red woollen hood, out of a low doorway, through which the light of a fire sparkled from the background, sending vivid flashes across the snow.

The man who had spoken last shook his head solemnly.

" The Death-Arch never shone for a Christian yet," he said gravely. " No! There's something else in the wind. We can't see it—but it will come—it must come! That sign never fails."

And presently, tired of watching the waiting sledge and the passive Laplander, he retreated within his house, shutting his door against the darkness and the bitter wind. His neighbors followed his example,—and, save for two or three red glimmers of light here and there, the little village looked as though it had been deserted long ago—a picture of frost-bound silence and solitude.

Meanwhile, in Lovisa Elsland's close and comfortless dwelling, stood Olaf Güldmar. His strong, stately figure, wrapped in furs, seemed almost to fill the little place—he had thrown aside the thick scarf of *wadmel* in which he had been wrapped to the eyes while driving in the teeth of the wind,—and he now lifted his fur cap, thus displaying his silvery hair, ruddy features, and open, massive brow. At that moment a woman who was busying herself in putting fresh pine-logs on the smouldering fire, turned and regarded him intently.

" Lord, Lord!" she muttered—" 'tis a man of men,—he rejoiceth in his strength, even as the lion,—and of what avail shall the curse of the wicked avail against the soul that is firmly established ! "

Güldmar heard her not—he was looking towards a low pallet bed, on which lay, extended at full length, an apparently insensible form.

" Has she been long thus ? " he asked, in a low voice.

" Since last night," replied the woman—no other than Mr. Dyceworthy's former servant, Ulrika. " She wakened suddenly, and bade me send for you. To-day she has not spoken."

The *bonde* sighed somewhat impatiently. He approached the now blazing pine-logs, and as he drew off his thick fur driving-gloves, and warmed his hands at the cheerful blaze, Ulrika again fixed her dull eyes upon him with something of wonder and reluctant admiration. Presently she trimmed an oil-lamp, and set it, burning dimly, on the table. Then she went to the bed and bent over it,—after a pause of several minutes, she turned and made a beckoning sign with her finger. Güldmar advanced a little,—when a sudden eldritch shriek startled him back, almost curdling the blood in his veins. Out of the deep obscurity, like some gaunt spectre rising from the tomb, started a face, wrinkled, cadaverous, and distorted by suffering,—a face in which the fierce, fevered eyes glittered with a strange and dreadful brilliancy—the face of Lovisa Elsland, stern, forbidding, and already dark with the shadows of approaching death. She stared vacantly at Güldmar, whose picturesque head was illumined by the ruddy glow of the fire—and feebly shaded her eyes as though she saw something that hurt them. Ulrika raised her on her tumbled pillow, and saying, in cold, unmoved tones—" Speak now, for the time is short," she once more beckoned the *bonde* imperatively.

He approached slowly.

" Lovisia Elsland," he began in distinct tones, addressing himself to that ghastly countenance still partly shaded by one hand. " I am here—Olaf Gülmar. Dost thou know me ? "

At the sound of his voice, a strange spasm contorted the withered features of the dying woman. She bent her head as though to listen to some far-off echo, and held up her skinny finger as though enjoining silence.

" Know thee ! " she babbled whisperingly. " How should I not know the brown-haired Olaf ! Olaf of the merry eye—Olaf, the pride of the Norse maiden ? " She

30

lifted herself in a more erect attitude, and stretching out her lean arms, went on as though chanting a monotonous recitative. " Olaf, the wanderer over wild seas,—he comes and goes in his ship that sails like a white bird on the sparkling waters—long and silent are the days of his absence—mournful are the Fjelds and Fjords without the smile of Olaf—Olaf the King ! "

She paused, and Güldmar regarded her in pitying wonder. Her face changed to a new expression—one of wrath and fear.

" Stay, stay ! " she cried in penetrating accents. " Who comes from the South with Olaf? The clouds drive fast before the wind—clouds rest on the edge of the dark Fjord—sails red as blood flash against the sky—who comes with Olaf? Fair hair ripples against his breast like streaming sunbeams ; eyes blue as the glitter of the northern lights, are looking upon him—lips crimson and heavy with kisses for Olaf—ah ! " She broke off with a cry, and beat the air with her hands as though to keep some threatening thing away from her. " Back, back ! Dead bride of Olaf, torment me no more—back, I say ! See,"—and she pointed into the darkness before her—" The pale, pale face—the long glittering hair twisted like a snake of gold,—she glides along the path across the mountains,—the child follows !—the child ! Why not kill the child as well—why not ? "

She stopped suddenly with a wild laugh. The *bonde* had listened to her ravings with something of horror, his ruddy cheeks growing paler.

" By the gods, this is strange ! " he muttered. " She seems to speak of my wife,—yet what can she know of her ? "

For some moments there was silence. Lovisa seemed to have exhausted her strength. Presently, however, she put aside her straggling white hairs from her forehead, and demanded fiercely—

" Where is my grandchild ? Where is Britta ? "

Neither Güldmar nor Ulrika made any reply. But Britta's name recalled the old woman to herself, and when she spoke again it was quite collectedly, and in her usual harsh voice. She seemed to forget all that she had just uttered, for she turned her eyes upon the *bonde*, as though she had but then perceived him.

" So you are come, Olaf Güldmar ! " she said. " It is well,—for the hand of Death is upon me."

" It is well, indeed, if I can be of service, Lovisa Elsland," responded Güldmar, " though I am but a sorry consoler, holding, as I do, that death is the chief blessing, and in no way to be regretted at any time. Moreover, when the body grows too weak to support the soul, 'tis as well to escape from it with what speed we may."

" Escape—escape ? Where ? " asked Lovisa. " From the worm that dieth not ? From the devouring flame that is never quenched ? From the torturing thirst and heat and darkness of hell, who shall escape ? "

" Nay, if that is all the comfort thy creed can give thee," said the *bonde*, with a half-smile, " 'tis but a poor staff to lean on ! "

Lovisa looked at him mockingly. " And is thine so strong a prop to thy pride ? " she asked disdainfully. " Has Odin so endowed thee that thou shouldst boast of him ? Listen to me, Olaf Güldmar—I have but little strength remaining, and I must speak briefly. Thy wife——"

" What of her ? " said the *bonde* hastily. " Thou knewest her not."

" I knew her," said Lovisa steadily, " as the lightning knows the tree it withers—as the sea knows the frail boat it wrecks for sport on a windy day. Thou haughty Olaf ! I knew her well even as the broken heart knows its destroyer ! "

Güldmar looked perplexedly at Ulrika. " Surely she raves again ? " he said. Ulrika was silent.

" Rave ? Tell him I do not rave ! " cried Lovisa rising in her bed to utter her words with more strength and emphasis. " May be I have raved, but that is past ! The Lord, who will judge and condemn my soul, bear witness that I speak the truth ! Olaf Güldmar, rememberest thou the days when we were young ? "

" 'Tis long ago, Lovisa ! " replied the *bonde* with brief gentleness.

" Long ago ? It seems but yesterday ! But yesterday I saw the world all radiant with hope and joy and love—love that to you was a mere pastime—but with *me*——" She shuddered and seemed to lose herself in a maze of dreary recollections. " Love ! " she presently muttered—" ' love is strong as death,—jealousy is cruel as the grave—the coals thereof are coals of fire which hath a most vehement flame ! '

Even so! You, Olaf Güldmar, have forgotten what I remember,—that once in that yesterday of youth, you called
me fair,—once your lips branded mine ! Could I forget that
kiss ? Think you a Norse woman, bred in a shadow of the
constant mountains, forgets the first thrill of passion waked
in her soul ? Light women of those lands where the sun
ever shines on fresh follies, may count their loves by the
score,—but with us of the North, *one* love suffices to fill a
lifetime. And was not my life filled ? Filled to overflowing
with bitterness and misery ! For I loved you, proud Olaf !
—I loved you——" The *bonde* uttered an exclamation of
incredulous astonishment. Lovisa fixed her eyes on him
with a dark scorn. " Yes, I loved you,—scoffer and unbe-
liever as you were and are !—accursed of God and man ! I
loved you in spite of all that was said against you—nay, I
would have forsaken my creed for yours, and condemned
my soul to the everlasting burning for your sake ! I loved
you as *she*—that pale, fair, witch-like thing you wedded,
could never love——" Her voice died away in a sort of
despairing wail, and she paused.

" By my soul ! " said the *bonde*, astounded, and stroking
his white beard in some embarrassment. " I never knew
of this ! It is true that in the hot days of youth, mischief
is often done unwittingly. But why trouble yourself with
these memories, Lovisa ? If it be any comfort,—believe me,
I am sorry harm ever came to you through my thoughtless
jesting——"

" It matters not ! " and Lovisa regarded him with a
strange and awful smile. " I have had my revenge ! " She
stopped abruptly,—then went on—" 'Twas a fair bride you
chose, Olaf Güldmar—child of an alien from these shores,—
Thelma, with the treacherous laughter and light of the
South in her eyes and smile ! And I, who had known love,
made friends with hate——" She checked herself, and
looked full at the *bonde* with a fiendish joy sparkling in her
eyes. " She whom you wedded—she whom you loved so
well,—how soon she died ! "

There was something so suggestive and dreadful in the
expression of her face as she said this, that the stout heart
of the old *bonde*, pulsated more quickly with a sudden
vague distrust and dread. She gave him no time to speak,
but laying one yellow, claw-like hand on his arm, and raising her voice to a sort of yell, exclaimed triumphantly—

" Yes, yes ! how soon she died ! Bravely, bravely done !

And no one ever guessed the truth—no one ever knew I *killed* her!"

Güldmar uttered a sharp cry, and shook himself free from her touch. In the same instant his hand flew to the hilt of the hunting-knife in his girdle.

"*Killed* her! By the gods——"

Ulrika sprang before him. "Shame!" she cried sternly, "She is dying!"

"Too slowly for me!" exclaimed the *bonde* furiously.

"Peace—peace!" implored Ulrika. "Let her speak!"

"Strike, Olaf Güldmar!" said Lovisa, in a deep voice, harsh, but all untremulous—"Strike, pagan, with whom the law of blood is supreme—strike to the very center of my heart—I do not fear you! I killed her, I say—and therein I, the servant of the Lord, was justified! Think you that the Most High hath not commanded His elect to utterly destroy and trample underfoot their enemies?—and is not vengeance mine as well as thine, accursed slave of Odin?"

A spasm of pain here interrupted her—she struggled violently for breath—and Ulrika supported her. Güldmar stood motionless, white with restrained fury, his eyes blazing. Recovering by slow degrees, Lovisa once more spoke —her voice was weaker, and sounded a long way off.

"Yea, the Lord hath been on my side!" she said, and the hideous blasphemy rattled in her throat as it was uttered. "Listen—and hear how He delivered mine enemy into my hands. I watched her always—I followed her many and many a time, though she never saw me. I knew her favorite path across the mountains,—it led past a rocky chasm. On the edge of that chasm there was a broad, flat stone, and there she would sit often, reading, or watching the fishing-boats on the Fjord, and listening to the prattle of her child. I used to dream of that stone, and wonder if I could loosen it! It was strongly imbedded in the earth— but each day I went to it—each day I moved it! Little by little I worked—till a mere touch would have set it hurling downwards,—yet it looked as firm as ever." Güldmar uttered a fierce ejaculation of anguish—he put one hand to his throat as though he were stifling. Lovisa, watching him, smiled vindictively, and continued—

"When I had done all I could do, I lay in wait for her, hoping and praying—my hour came at last! It was a bright sunny morning—a little bird had been twittering above the very place—as it flew away, *she* approached—a book was in her hand,—her child followed her at some little distance off. Fortune favored me—a cluster of pansies had opened their blossoms a few inches below the stone,—she saw them,—and, light as a bird, sprang on it and reached forward to gather them—ah!"—and the wretched woman clapped her hands and broke into malignant laughter—"I can hear her quick shriek now—the crash of the stones and the crackle of branches as she fell down,—down to her death! Presently the child came running,—it was too young to understand—it sat down patiently waiting for its mother. How I longed to kill it! but it sang to itself like the bird that had flown away, and I could not! But *she* was gone—*she* was silent for ever—the Lord be praised for all His mercies! Was she smiling, Olaf Güldmar, when you found her—*dead?*"

A strange solemnity shadowed the *bonde's* features. He turned his eyes upon her steadily.

"Blessing and honor be to the gods of my fathers!" he said—"I found her—*living!*"

The change that came over Lovisa's face at these words was inexpressibly awful—she grew livid and her lips twitched convulsively.

"Living—living!" she gasped.

"Living!" repeated Güldmar sternly. "Vile hag! Your purpose was frustrated! Your crime destroyed her beauty and shortened her days—but she lived—lived for ten sweet, bitter years, hidden away from all eyes save mine,—mine that never grew tired of looking in her patient, heavenly face! Ten years I held her as one holds a jewel—and, when she died, her death was but a falling asleep in these fond arms——"

Lovisa raised herself with a sharp cry, and wrung her hands together—

"Ten years—ten years!" she moaned. "I thought her dead—and she lived on,—beloved and loving all the while. Oh God, God, why hast thou made a mockery of Thy servant!" She rocked herself to and fro—then looked up with an evil smile. "Nay, but she *suffered!* That was best. It is worse to suffer than to die. Thank God, she *suffered!*"

"Ay, she suffered!" said Güldmar fiercely, scarce able to restrain himself from seizing upon the miserable old woman and shaking the sinking life out of her—"And had

I but guessed who caused her sufferings, by the sword of Odin, I would have——"

Ulrika laid her hand on his suddenly upraised arm.

"Listen!" she whispered. A low wailing, like the cry of a distressed child, swept round and round the house, followed by a gust of wind and a clattering shower of hail-stones. A strange blue light leaped up from the sparkling log fire, and cast an unearthly glow through the room. A deep stillness ensued.

Then—steady and clear and resonant—a single sound echoed through the air, like a long note played on an exceedingly sweet silver trumpet. It began softly—swelled to a *crescendo*—then died delicately away. Güldmar raised his head—his face was full of rapt and expectant gravity,—his action, too, was somewhat singular, for he drew the knife from his girdle and kissed the hilt solemnly, returning it immediately to its sheath. At the same moment Lovisa uttered a loud cry, and flinging the coverings from her, strove to rise from her bed. Ulrika held her firmly,—she struggled feebly yet determinedly, gazing the while with straining, eager, glassy eyes into the gloom of the opposite corner.

"Darkness—darkness!" she muttered hoarsely,—"and the white faces of dead things! There—there they lie! —all still, at the foot of the black chasm—their mouths move without sound—what—what are they saying? I cannot hear—ask them to speak louder—louder! Ah!" and she uttered a terrified scream that made the rafters ring. "They move!—they stretch out their hands—cold, cold hands!—they are drawing me down to them—down—down—to that darkness! Hold me—hold me! don't let me go to them—Lord, Lord be merciful to me—let me live —live——" Suddenly she drew back in deadly horror, gesticulating with her tremulous lean hands as though it shut away the sight of some loathsome thing unveiled to her view. "Who is it"—she asked in an awful, shuddering whisper—" who is it that says there is no hell? *I see it!*" Still retreating backwards, backwards—the clammy dew of death darkening her affrighted countenance,—she turned her glazing eyes for the last time on Güldmar. Her lips twitched into a smile of dreadful mockery.

"May—thy gods—reward thee—Olaf Güldmar—even— as mine—are—rewarding—*me!*"

And with these words, her head dropped heavily on her

breast. Ulrika laid her back on her pillow, a corpse. The stern, cruel smile froze slowly on her dead features—gradually she became, as it were, a sort of ancient cenotaph, carved to resemble old age combined with unrepenting evil—the straggling white hair that rested on her wrinkled forehead looking merely like snow fallen on sculptured stone.

"Good Lord, have mercy on her soul!" murmured Ulrika piously, as she closed the upward staring eyes, and crossed the withered hands.

"Good devil, claim thine own!" said Güldmar, with proudly lifted arm and quivering, disdainful lips. "Thou foolish woman! Thinkest thou thy Lord makes place for murderers in His heaven? If so, 'tis well I am not bound there! Only the just can tread the pathway to Valhalla,—'tis a better creed!"

Ulrika looked at his superb, erect figure and lofty head, and a strangely anxious expression flitted across her dull countenance.

"Nay, *bonde*, we do not believe that the Lord accepteth murderers, without they repent themselves of their back-slidings,—but if with penitence they turn to Him even at the eleventh hour, haply they may be numbered among the elect."

Güldmar's eyes flashed. "I know not thy creed, woman, nor care to learn it! But, all the same, thou art deceived in thy vain imaginings. The Eternal Justice cannot err—call that justice Christ or Odin as thou wilt. I tell you, the soul of the innocent bird that perishes in the drifting snow is near and dear to its Creator—but the tainted soul that had yonder vile body for its tenement, was but a flame of the evil one, and accursed from the beginning,—it must return to him from whom it came. A heaven for such as she? Nay—rather the lowest circle of the furthest and fiercest everlasting fires—and thither do I commend her! Farewell!"

Rapidly muffling himself up in his wraps, he strode out of the house. He sprang into his sledge, throwing a generous gratuity to the small Laplander who had taken charge of it, and who now ventured to inquire—

"Has the good Lovisa left us?"

Güldmar burst into a hard laugh. "*Good!* By my soul! The folks of Talvig take up murderers for saints and criminals for guides! 'Tis a wild world! Yes—she

has gone—where all such blessed ones go—to—heaven!"
He shook his clenched fist in the air—then hastily gathering up the reins, prepared to start.

The Lapp, after the manner of his race, was easily frightened, and cowered back, terrified at the *bonde's* menacing gesture and fierce tone,—but quickly bethinking himself of the liberal fee he clutched in his palm, he volunteered a warning to this kingly old man with the streaming white hair and beard, and his keen eyes that were already fixed on the dark sweep of the rough, uneven road winding towards the Altenfjord.

" There is a storm coming, Jarl Güldmar!" he stammered.

Güldmar turned his head. " Why call me *Jarl?*" he demanded half angrily. " 'Tis a name I wear not."

He touched the reindeer lightly with his long whip—the sensitive beast started and sprang forward.

Once more the Lapp exclaimed, with increased excitement and uncouth gestures—

" Storm is coming!—wide—dark, deep! See how the sky stoops with the hidden snow!"

He pointed to the north, and there, low on the horizon, was a lurid red gleam like a smouldering fire, while just above it a greenish blackness of cloud hung heavy and motionless. Towards the central part of the heaven two or three stars shone with frosty brightness, and through a few fleecy ribbons of greyish mist limmered the uncertain promise of a faint moon.

Güldmar smiled slightly. " Storm coming?" he answered almost gaily. " That is well! Storm and I are old friends, my lad! Good night!"

Once more he touched his horned steeds, and with a jingle-jangle of musical bells and a scudding, slippery hissing across the hard snow, the sledge sped off with fairy-like rapidity, and in a few moments its one little guiding lantern disappeared in the darkness like a suddenly extinguished candle.

The Lapp stood pondering and gazing after it, with the *bonde's* money in his palm, till the cold began to penetrate even his thick skin-clothing and his fat little body, well anointed with whale-oil though it was,—and becoming speedily conscious of this, he scampered with extraordinary agility, considering the dimensions of his snow-shoes, into the hut where he had his dwelling, relating to all who choose to hear, the news of old Lovisa Elsland's death, and the account of his brief interview with the dreaded but generous pagan.

Ulrika, watching by the corpse of her aged friend, was soon joined by others bent on sharing her vigil, and the house was presently filled with woman's religious wailings and prayers for the departed. To all the curious inquiries that were made concerning the cause of Lovisa's desire to see the *bonde* before she died, Ulrika vouchsafed no reply, —and the villagers, who stood somewhat in awe of her as a woman of singular godliness and discreet reputation, soon refrained from asking any more questions. An ambitious young Lutheran preacher came, and, addressing himself to all assembled, loudly extolled the superhuman virtues of the dead " Mother of the village," as Lovisa had been called,—amid the hysterical weeping and moaning of the mourners, he begged them to look upon her " venerated face " and observe " the smile of God's own peace engraven there,"—and amid all his eloquence, and the shrieking excitement of his fanatical hearers, Ulrika alone was silent.

She sat stern and absorbed, with set lips and lowered eyelids at the head of the bed whereon the corpse was now laid out, grimly rigid,—with bound-up jaws, and clasped fingers like stiff, dried bones. Her thoughts dwelt gloomily and intently on Güldmar's words—" The Eternal Justice cannot err." Eternal Justice ! What sentence would Eternal Justice pass upon the crime of murder ?—or attempt to murder ? " I am guilty," the unhappy woman reflected, with a strong shudder chilling her veins, " guilty even as Lovisa ! I tried to kill my child—I thought, I hoped it was dead ! It was not my meaning that it should live. And this Eternal Justice, may be, will judge the intention more than the crime. O Lord, Lord ! save my soul ! Teach me how to escape from the condemning fires of Thine anger ! " Thus she prayed and wrestled with her accusing self in secret—despair and fear raging in her heart, though not a flicker of her inward agitation betrayed itself outwardly on her stolid, expressionless features.

Meanwhile the wind rose to a tearing, thunderous gale, and the night, already so dark, darkened yet more visibly. Olaf Güldmar, driving swiftly homewards, caught the first furious gust of the storm that came rushing onward from the North Cape, and as it swooped sideways against his light sledge, he was nearly hurled from his seat by the sudden violence of the shock. He settled himself more firmly, encouraging with a cheery word the startled reindeer, who stopped short,—stretching out their necks and sniffing the air, their hairy sides heaving with the strain of trotting against the blast, and the smoke of their breath steaming upwards in the frosty air like white vapor. The way lay now through a narrow defile bordered with tall pines,—and as the terrified animals, recovering, shook the tinkling bells on their harness, and once more resumed their journey, the road was comparatively sheltered, and the wind seemed to sink as suddenly as it rose. There was a hush—an almost ominous silence.

The sledge glided more slowly between the even lines of upright giant trees, crowned with icicles and draped in snow,—the *bonde* involuntarily loosened the reins of his elfin steeds, and again returned to those painful and solemn musings, from which the stinging blow of the tempest had for a moment roused him. The proud heart of the old man ached bitterly. What! All these years had passed, and he, the descendant of a hundred Vikings, had been cheated of justice! He had seen his wife,—the treasured darling of his days, suffering,—dying, inch by inch, year by year, with all her radiant beauty withered,—and he had never known her destroyer! Her fall from the edge of the chasm had been deemed by them both an accident, and yet—this wretched Lovisa Elsland—mad with misplaced, disappointed passion, jealousy, and revenge,—had lived on to the extreme of life, triumphant and unsuspected.

" I swear the gods have played me false in this! " he muttered, lifting his eyes in a sort of fierce appeal to the motionless pinetops stiff with frost. The mystery of the old hag's hatred of his daughter was now made clear—she resembled her mother too closely to escape Lovisa's malice. He remembered the curse she had called down upon the innocent girl,—how it was she who had untiringly spread abroad the report among the superstitious people of the place, that Thelma was a witch whose presence was a blight upon the land,—how she had decoyed her into the power of Mr. Dyceworthy—all was plain—and, notwithstanding her deliberate wickedness, she had lived her life without punishment! This was what made Güldmar's blood burn, and pulses thrill. He could not understand why the Higher Powers had permitted this error of justice, and, like many of his daring ancestors, he was ready to

fling defiance in the very face of Odin, and demand—
" Why,—O thou drowsy god, nodding over thy wine-cups,
—why didst thou do this thing ? "

Utter fearlessness,—bodily and spiritual,—fearlessness of
past, present, or future, life or death,—was Güldmar's
creed. The true Norse warrior spirit was in him—had he
been told, on heavenly authority, that the lowest range of
the ' Nastrond " or Scandinavian Hell, awaited him, he
would have accepted his fate with unflinching firmness
The indestructibility of the soul, and the certainty that it
must outlive even centuries of torture, and triumph gloriously in the end, was the core of the faith he professed.
As he glanced upwards, the frozen tree-tops, till then rigidly
erect, swayed slightly from side to side with a crackling
sound—but he paid no heed to this slight warning of a
fresh attack from the combative storm that was gathering
together and renewing its scattered forces. He began to
think of his daughter, and the grave lines on his face relaxed and softened.

" 'Tis all fair sailing for the child," he mused. " For that I
should be grateful! The world has been made a soft nest
for my bird,—I should not complain,—my own time is
short." His former anger calmed a little—the brooding
irritation of his mind became gradually soothed.

" Rose of my heart ! " he whispered, tenderly apostrophiz-
ing the memory of his wife,—that lost jewel of love, whose
fair body lay enshrined in the king's tomb by the Fjord.
" Wrongfully done to death as thou wert, and brief time as
we had for loving ;—in spite of thy differing creed, I feel
that I shall meet thee soon ! Yes—in the world beyond
the stars, they will bring thee to me in Valhalla,—whereso-
ever thou art, thou wilt not refuse to come ! The gods
themselves cannot unfasten the ties of love between us ! "

As he half thought, half uttered, these words, the reindeer again stopped abruptly, rearing their antlered heads
and panting heavily. Hark ! what was that ? A clear,
far-reaching note of music seemingly wakened from the
waters of the Fjord and rising upwards, upwards, with bell-
like distinctness ! Güldmar leaned from his motionless
sledge and listened in awe—it was the same sound he had
before heard as he stood by Lovisa Elsland's death-bed—
and was in truth nothing but a strong current of wind
blowing through the arched and honeycombed rocks by the
sea, towards the higher land,—creating the same effect as

though one should breathe forcibly through a pipe-like instrument of dried and hollow reeds,—and being rendered
more resonant by the intense cold, it bore a striking similarity to the full blast of a war-trumpet. For the worshipper of Odin, it had a significant and supernatural meaning,
—and he repeated his former action—that of drawing the
knife from his girdle and kissing the hilt. " If Death is
near me," he said in a loud voice, " I bid it welcome! The
gods know that I am ready!"

He waited as though expecting some answer—but there
was a brief, absolute silence. Then, with a wild shriek and
riotous uproar, the circling tempest,—before uncertain and
vacillating in its wrath,—pounced, eagle-like, downward
and grasped the mountains in its talons,—the strong pines
rocked backwards and forwards as though bent by Herculean hands, crashing their frosted branches madly together:
—the massive clouds in the sky opened and let fall their
burden of snow. Down came the large fleecy flakes, twisting dizzily round and round in a white waltz to the whirl
of the wind—faster—faster—heavier and thicker, till there
seemed no clear space in the air. Güldmar urged on the
reindeer, more anxious for their safety than his own—the
poor beasts were fatigued, and the blinding snow confused
them, but they struggled on patiently, encouraged by their
master's voice and the consciousness that they were nearing
home. The storm increased in fury—and a fierce gust of
frozen sleet struck the sledge like a strong hammer-stroke
as it advanced through the rapidly deepening snow-drifts—
its guiding lantern was extinguished. Güldmar did not
stop to relight it—he knew he was approaching his farm,
and he trusted to the instinct and sagacity of his steeds.

There was indeed but a short distance to go,—the
narrow wooded defile opened out on two roads, one leading
direct to Bosekop—the other, steep and tortuous, winding
down to the shore of the Fjord—this latter passed the
bonde's gate. Once out of the shadow of the pines, the way
would be more distinctly seen,—the very reindeer seemed
to be conscious of this, for they trotted more steadily,
shaking their bells in even and rhythmical measure. As
they neared the end of the long dark vista, a sudden bright-
blue glare quivered and sprang wave-like across the snow
—a fantastic storm-aurora that flashed and played among
the feathery falling flakes of white till they looked like
knots and closters of sparkling jewels. The extreme point

of the close defile was reached at last, and here the land
scape opened up wide, rocky and desolate—a weird picture,
—with the heavy clouds above repeatedly stabbed through
and through by the needle-pointed beams of the aurora
borealis,—and the blank whiteness of the ground below.
Just as the heads of the reindeer were turned into the
homeward road, half of the aurora suddenly faded, leaving the other half still beating out its azure brilliance
against the horizon. At the same instant, with abrupt
swiftness, a dark shadow,—so dark as to seem almost
palpable,—descended and fell directly in front of the advancing sledge—a sort of mist that appeared to block the
way.

Güldmar leaned forward and gazed with eager, straining
eyes into that drooping gloom—a shadow?—a mere vapor,
with the Northern Lights glimmering through its murky
folds? Ah no—no! For him it was something very different,—a heavenly phantasm, beautiful and grand, with
solemn meaning! He saw a Maiden, majestically tall, of
earnest visage and imperial mien,—her long black hair
streamed loose upon the wind—in one hand she held a shining shield—in the other a lifted spear! On her white
brow rested a glittering helmet,—her bosom heaved
beneath a corslet of pale gold—she fixed her divine, dark
eyes full upon his face and smiled! With a cry of wonder
and ecstacy the old man fell back in his sledge,—the reins
dropped from his hands,—" The Valkyrie! the Valkyrie! "
he exclaimed.

A mere breathing space, and the shadow vanished,—the
aurora came out again in unbroken splendor—and the
reindeer, feeling no restraint upon them, and terrified by
something in the air, or the ceaseless glitter, of the lights
in the sky, started off precipitately at full gallop. The
long reins trailed loosely over their backs, lashing their
sides as they ran—Güldmar, recovering from his momentary awe and bewilderment, strove to seize them, but in
vain. He called, he shouted,—the frightened animals were
utterly beyond control, and dashed madly down the steep
road, swinging the sledge from side to side, and entangling
themselves more and more with the loose reins, till, irritated
beyond endurance, confused and blinded by the flash of the
aurora and the dizzy whirl of the swiftly falling snow,
they made straight for a steep bank,—and before the *bonde*
had time to realize the situation and jump from the sledge

—crash! down they went with a discordant jangle of bells, their hoofs splitting a thin, sharp shelf of ice as they leaped forward,—dragging the light vehicle after them, and twisting it over and over till it was a mere wreck,—and throwing out its occupant head foremost against a jagged stone.

Then more scared than ever, they strove to clamber out of the gully into which they had recklessly sprung, but, foiled in these attempts, they kicked, plunged, and reared, —trampling heedlessly over the human form lying helpless among the shattered fragments of the sledge,—till tired out at last, they stood motionless, panting with terror. Their antlered heads cast fantastic patterns on the snow in the varying rose and azure radiance that rippled from the waving ribbons of the aurora,—and close to them, his slowly trickling life-blood staining the white ground,—his hair and beard glittering in the light like frosted silver,— his eyes fast closed as though he slept,—lay Olaf Güldmar unconscious—dying. The spear of the Valkyrie had fallen!

CHAPTER XXXII.

"Bury me not when I am dead—
Lay me not down in a dusty bed;
I could not bear the life down there,
With the wet worms crawling about my hair!"

ERIC MACKAY.

LONG hours passed, and the next day dawned, if the dim twilight that glimmered faintly across the Altenfjord could be called a dawn. The snow-fall had ceased,—the wind had sunk—there was a frost-bound, monotonous calm. The picturesque dwelling of the *bonde* was white in every part, and fringed with long icicles,—icicles drooped from its sheltering porch and gabled windows—the deserted dove-cote on the roof was a miniature ice-palace, curiously festooned with thin threads and crested pinnacles of frozen snow. Within the house there was silence,—the silence of approaching desolation. In the room where Thelma used to sit and spin, a blazing fire of pine sparkled on the walls, casting ruddy outward flashes through the frost-covered lattice-windows,—and here, towards the obscure noon, Olaf Güldmar awoke from his long trance of insensibility. He found himself at home, stretched on his own bed, and looked about him vacantly. In the earnest and watchful countenance that bent above his pillow, he slowly recognized his friend, companion, and servant, Valdemar Svensen, and though returning consciousness brought with it throbs of agonizing pain, he strove to smile, and feebly stretched out his hand. Valdemar grasped it—kissed it—and in spite of his efforts to restrain his emotion, a sigh, that was almost a groan, escaped him. The *bonde* smiled again,—then lay quiet for a few moments as though endeavoring to collect his thought. Presently he spoke—his voice was faint yet distinct.

"What has happened, Valdemar?" he asked. "How is it that the strength has departed from me?"

Svensen dropped on his knees by the bedside. "An accident, my Lord Olaf," he began falteringly.

Güldmar's eyes suddenly lightened. "Ah, I remember!" he said. "The rush down the valley—I remember all!" He paused, then added gently, "And so the end has come, Valdemar!"

Svensen uttered a passionate exclamation of distress.

"Let not my lord say so!" he murmured appealingly, with the air of a subject entreating favor from a king. "Or, if it must be, let me also travel with thee wherever thou goest!"

Olaf Güldmar's gaze rested on him with a musing tenderness.

"'Tis a far journey," he said simply. "And thou art not summoned." He raised his arm to test its force—for one second it was uplifted,—then it fell powerless at his side. "I am conquered!" he went on with a cheerful air. "The fight is over, Valdemar! Surely I have had a long battle, and the time for rest and reward is welcome." He was silent for a little, then continued, "Tell me—how—where didst thou find me? It seems I had a dream, strange, and glorious—then came a rushing sound of wheels and clanging bells,—and after that, a long deep silence."

Speaking in low tones, Valdemar briefly related the events of the past night. How he had heard the reindeer's gallop down the road, and the quick jangling of the bells on their harness, and had concluded that the *bonde* was returning home at extraordinary speed—,how these sounds had suddenly and unaccountably ceased,—how, after waiting for some time, and hearing nothing more, he had become greatly alarmed, and, taking a pine-torch, had gone

out to see what had occurred,—how he had found the reindeer standing by the broken sledge in the gully, and how,
after some search, he had finally discovered his master, lying half-covered by the snow, and grievously injured. How
he had lifted him and carried him into the house, ...

"By my soul!" interrupted the *bonde* cheerfully, "thou
must have found me no light weight, Valdemar! See
what a good thing it is to be a man—with iron muscles,
and strong limbs, and hardy nerve! By the Hammer of
Thor! the glorious gift of strong manhood is never half appreciated! As for me—I am a man no longer!"

He sighed a little, and, passing his sinewy hand across
his brow, lay back exhausted. He was racked by bodily
torture, but,—unflinching old hero as he was,—gave no
sign of the agonizing pain he suffered. Valdemar Svensen
had risen from his knees, and now stood gazing at him with
yearning, miserable eyes, his brown, weather-beaten visage
heavily marked with lines of grief and despair. He knew
that he was utterly powerless—that nothing could save the
noble life that was ebbing slowly away before him. His
long and varied experience as a sailor, pilot, and traveller
in many countries had given him some useful knowledge of
medicine and surgery, and if anything was possible to be
done, he could do it. But in this case no medical skill
would have been availing—the old man's ribs were crushed
in and his spine injured,—his death was a question of but a
few hours at the utmost, if so long.

"Olaf the King!" muttered the *bonde* presently.
"True! They make no mistakes yonder,—they know each
warrior by name and rank—'tis only in this world we are
subject to error. This world! By the gods! . . . 'tis but
a puff of thistle-down—or a light mist floating from the
sunset to the sea!"

He made a vigorous attempt to raise himself from his
pillow—though the excruciating anguish caused by his
movement, made him wince a little and grow paler.

"Wine, Valdemar! Fill the horn cup to the brim and
bring it to me—I must have strength to speak—before I
depart—on the last great journey."

Obediently and in haste, Svensen filled the cup he asked
for with old Lacrima Christi, of which there was always a
supply in this far Northern abode, and gave it to him,
watching him with a sort of superstitious reverence as he
drained off its contents and returned it empty.

"Ah! That warms this freezing blood of mine," he said, the lustre flashing back into his eyes. " 'Twill find fresh force to flow a brief while longer. Valdemar—I have little time to spend with thee—I feel death *here*,"—and he slightly touched his chest—" cold—cold and heavy. 'Tis nothing—a passing, chilly touch that sweeps away the world! But the warmth of a new, strong life awaits me—a life of never-ending triumph! The doors of Valhalla stand wide open—I heard the trumpet-call last night—I saw the dark-haired Valkyrie! All is well—and my soul is full of rejoicing. Valdemar—there is but one thing now thou hast to do for me,—the one great service thou hast sworn to render. *Fulfill thine oath!* "

Valdemar's brown cheek blanched,—his lips quivered,—he flung up his hands in wild appeal. The picturesque flow of his native speech gained new fervor and eloquence as he spoke.

"Not yet—not yet, my lord!" he cried passionately. "Wait but a little—there is time. Think for one moment —think! Would it not be well for my lord to sleep the last sleep by the side of his beloved Thelma—the star of the dark mountains—the moonbeam of the night of his life? Would not peace enwrap him there as with a soft garment, and would not his rest be lulled by the placid murmur of the sea? For the days of old time and storm and victory are past—and the dead slumber as stones in the silent pathways—why would my lord depart in haste as though he were wrathful, from the land he has loved? —from the vassal who implores his pardon for pleading against a deed he dares not do! "

" Dares not—dares not! " cried the *bonde*, springing up half-erect from his couch, in spite of pain, and looking like some enraged old lion with his tossed, streaming hair and glittering eyes. " Serf as thou art and coward! Thinkest thou an oath such as thine is but a thread of hair, to be snapped at thy pleasure? Wilt thou brave the wrath of the gods and the teeth of the Wolf of Nastrond? As surely as the seven stars shine on the white brow of Thor, evil shall be upon thee if thou refusest to perform the vow thou hast sworn! And shall a slave have strength to resist the dying curse of a King? "

The pride, the supreme authority,—the magnified strength of command that flushed the old man's features, were extraordinary and almost terrible in their impressive grandeur. If he indeed believed himself by blood a king and a descendant of kings,—he could not have shown a more forcible display of personal sovereignty. The effect of his manner on Valdemar was instantaneous,—the superstitious fears of that bronzed sea-wanderer were easily aroused. His head drooped—he stretched out his hands imploringly.

" Let not my lord curse his servant," he faltered. " It was but a tremor of the heart that caused my tongue to speak foolishly. I am ready—I have sworn—the oath shall be kept to its utmost end ! "

Olaf Güldmar's threatening countenance relaxed, and he fell back on his pillows.

" It is well ! " he said feebly and somewhat indistinctly. " Thy want of will maddened me—I spoke and lived in times that are no more—days of battle—and—glory—that are gone—from men—for ever. More wine, Valdemar !—I must keep a grip on this slippery life—and yet—I wander—wander into the—night——"

His voice ceased, and he sank into a swoon—a swoon that was like death. His breathing was scarcely perceptible, and Svensen, alarmed at his appearance, forced some drops of wine between his set lips, and chafed his cold hands with anxious solicitude. Slowly and very gradually he recovered consciousness and intelligence, and presently asked for a pencil and paper to write a few farewell words to his daughter. In the grief and bewilderment of the time, Valdemar entirely forgot to tell him that a letter from Thelma had arrived for him on the previous afternoon while he was away at Talvig,—and was even now on the shelf above the chimney, awaiting perusal. Güldmar, ignorant of this, began to write slowly and with firmness, disregarding his rapidly sinking strength. Scarcely had he begun the letter, however, than he looked up meaningly at Svensen, who stood waiting beside him.

" The time grows very short," he said imperatively. " Prepare everything quickly—go! Fear not—I shall live to see thee return—and to bless thee for thy faithful service."

As he uttered these words he smiled ;—and with one wistful, yearning look at him, Valdemar obediently and instantly departed. He left the house, carrying with him a huge pile of dry brushwood, and with the air of a man strung up to prompt action, rapidly descended the sloping path, thick with hardened snow, that led downwards to the Fjord. On reaching the shore, he looked anxiously about him. There was nothing in sight but the distant, twinkling lights of Bosekop—the Fjord itself was like a black pool, —so still that even the faintest murmur of its rippling against the *bonde's* own private pier could be heard,—the tide was full up.

Out of the reach of the encroaching waters, high and dry on the beach, was Güldmar's brig, the *Valkyrie*, transformed by the fingers of the frost into a white ship, fantastically draped with threads of frozen snow and pendent icicles. She was placed on a descending plank, to which she was attached by a chain and rope pulley,—so that at any time of the weather or tide she could be moved glidingly downwards into deep water—and this was what Valdemar occupied himself in doing. It was a hard task. The chains were stiff with the frost,—but, after some patient and arduous striving, they yielded to his efforts, and, with slow clank and much creaking complaint, the vessel slid reluctantly down and plunged forward, afloat at last. Holding her ropes, Valdemar sprang to the extreme edge of the pier and fastened her there, and then getting on board, he untied and began to hoist the sails. This was a matter of the greatest difficulty, but it was gradually and successfully accomplished; and a strange sight the *Valkyrie* then presented, resting nearly motionless on the black Fjord,—her stretched and frosted canvas looking like sheeted pearl fringed with silver,—her masts white with encrusted snow, and topped with pointed icicles. Leaving her for a moment, Valdemar quickly returned, carrying the pile of dry brushwood he had brought,—he descended with this into the hold of the ship, and returned without it. Glancing once more nervously about him, he jumped from the deck to the pier—thence to the shore—and as he did so a long dark wave rolled up and broke at his feet. The capricious wind had suddenly arisen,—and a moaning whisper coming from the adjacent hills gave warning of another storm.

Valdemar hurriedly retraced his steps back to the house, —his work with the *Valkyrie* had occupied him more than an hour—the *bonde*, his friend and master, might have died during his absence! There was a cold sickness at his heart —his feet seemed heavy as lead, and scarcely able to carry him along quickly enough—to his credulous and visionary mind, the hovering shadow of death seemed everywhere,—in every crackling twig he brushed against,—in every sough of the wakening gale that rustled among the bare pines. To his intense relief he found Güldmar lying calmly back among his pillows,—his eyes well open and clear, and an expression of perfect peace upon his features. He smiled as he saw his servant enter.

" All is in readiness ? " he asked.

Valdemar bent his head in silent assent.

The *bonde's* face lightened with extraordinary rapture.

" I thank thee, old friend ! " he said in low but glad accents. " Thou knowest I could not be at peace in any other grave. I have suffered in thine absence,—the sufferings of the body that, being yet strong in spite of age, is reluctant to take leave of life. But it is past ! I am as one numbed with everlasting frost,—and now I feel no pain. And my mind is like a bird that poises for a while over past and present, ere soaring into the far future. There are things I must yet say to thee, Valdemar,—give me thy close hearing, for my voice is weak."

Svensen drew closer, and stood in the humble attitude of one who waits a command from some supreme chief.

" This letter," went on the old man, giving him a folded paper, " is to the child of my heart, my Thelma. Send it to her—when—I am gone. It will not grieve her, I hope —for, as far as I could find words, I have expressed therein nothing but joy—the joy of a prisoner set free. Tell her, that with all the strength of my perishing body and escaping soul, I blessed her ! . . . her and the husband in whose arms she rests in safety." He raised his trembling hands solemnly—" The gods of my fathers and their attendant spirits have her young life in their glorious keeping !—the joy of love and purity and peace be on her innocent head for ever ! "

He paused,—the wind wailed mournfully round the house and shook the lattice with a sort of stealthy clatter, like a forlorn wanderer striving to creep in to warmth and shelter.

" Here, Valdemar," continued the *bonde* presently, in fainter accents, at the same time handing him another paper. " Here are some scrawled lines—they are plainly set forth and signed—which make thee master of this poor place and all that it contains."

A low, choked sob broke from Valdemar's broad breast— he covered his face with his hands.

"Of what avail?" he murmured brokenly. "When my lord departs, I am alone and friendless!"

The *bonde* regarded him with kindly pity.

"Tears from the stout heart?" he inquired with a sort of grave wonder. "Weep for life, Valdemar—not for death! Alone and friendless? Not while the gods are in heaven! Cheei thee—thou art strong and in vigorous pride of manhood—why should not bright days come for thee——" He broke off with a gasp—a sudden access of pain convulsed him and rendered his breathing difficult. By sheer force of will he mastered the cruel agony, though great drops of sweat stood on his brow when he at last found voice to continue—

"I thought all suffering was past," he said with a heroic smile. "This foolish flesh and blood of mine dies hard! But, as I was saying to thee, Valdemar—the farm is thine, and all it holds—save some few trifles I have set down to be given to my child. There is little worth in what I leave thee—the soil is hard and ungrateful—the harvest uncertain, and the cattle few. Even the reindeer—didst thou say they were injured by their fall last night?—I—I forget, ..."

"No harm has come to them," said Svensen hastily, seeing that the very effort of thinking was becoming too much for the old man. "They are safe and unhurt. Trouble not about these things!"

A strange, unearthly radiance transfigured Güldmar's visage.

"Trouble is departing swiftly from me," he murmured.

"Trouble and I shall know each other no more!" His voice died away inarticulately, and he was silent a little space. Suddenly, and with a rush of vigor that seemed superhuman, he raised himself nearly erect, and pointed outwards with a commanding gesture.

"Bear me hence!" he cried in ringing tones. "Hence to the mountains and the sea!"

With a sort of mechanical, swift obedience, Valdemar threw open the door—the wind rushed coldly into the house, bringing with it large feathery flakes of snow. A hand sledge stood outside the porch,—it was always there during the winter, being much used for visiting the outlying grounds of the farm,—and to this, Valdemar prepared to carry the *bonde* in his herculean arms. But, on being lifted from his couch, the old man, filled with strange, almost delirious force, declared himself able to stand,—and, though suffering deadly anguish at every step, did in truth manage to reach and enter the sledge, strongly supported by Valdemar. There, however, he fainted— and his faithful servant, covering his insensible form with furs, thought he was dead. But there was now no time for hesitation,—dead or living, Olaf Güldmar's will was law to his vassal,—an oath had been made and must be kept. To propel the sledge down to the Fjord was an easy matter—how the rest of his duty was accomplished he never knew.

He was conscious of staggering blindly onward, weighted with a heavy, helpless burden,—he felt the slippery pier beneath his feet—the driving snow and the icy wind on his face,—but he was as one in a dream, realizing nothing plainly, till with a wild start, he seemed to awake—and lo! he stood on the glassy deck of the *Valkyrie* with the body of his " King " stretched senseless before him! Had he brought him there? He could not remember what he had done during the past few mad minutes,—the earth and sky whirled dizzily around him,—he could grasp nothing tangible in thought or memory. But there, most certainly, Olaf Güldmar lay,—his pallid face upturned, his hair and beard as white as the snow that clung to the masts of his vessel—his hand clenched on the fur garment that enwrapped him as with a robe of royalty.

Dropping on his knees beside him, Valdemar felt his heart—it still throbbed fitfully and feebly. Watching the intense calm of the grand, rugged face, this stern, weather-worn sailor—this man of superstitious and heathen imaginations—gave way to womanish tears—tears that were the outcome of sincere and passionate grief. His love was of an exceptional type,—something like that of a faithful dog that refuses to leave the grave of its master,—he could contemplate death for himself with absolute indifference,—but not for the *bonde*, whose sturdy strength and splendid physique had seemed to defy all danger.

As he knelt and wept unrestrainedly, a soft change, a delicate transparency, swept over the dark bosom of the sky. Pale pink streaks glittered on the dusky horizon— darts of light began to climb upward into the clouds, and to plunge downward into the water,—the radiance spread, and gradually formed into a broad band of deep crimson, which burned with a fixed and intense glow—topaz-like rays flickered and streamed about it, as though uncertain what fantastic shape they should take to best display their brilliancy. This tremulous hesitation of varying color did not last long; the whole jewel-like mass swept together, expanding and contracting with extraordinary swiftness for a few seconds—then, suddenly and clearly defined in the sky, a Kingly Crown blazed forth—a Crown of perfect shape, its five points distinctly and separately outlined and flashing as with a million rubies and diamonds. The red lustre warmly tinged the pale features of the dying man, and startled Valdemar, who sprang to his feet and gazed at that mystic aureola with a cry of wonder. At the same moment Olaf Güldmar stirred, and began to speak drowsily without opening his eyes.

"Dawn on the sea!" he murmured. "The white waves gleam and sparkle beneath the prow, and the ship makes swift way through the water! It is dawn in my heart—the dawn of love for thee and me, my Thelma—fear not! The rose of passion is a hardy flower that can bloom in the north as well as in the south, believe me! Thelma—Thelma!"

He suddenly opened his eyes, and realizing his surroundings, raised himself half-erect.

"Set sail!" he cried, pointing with a majestic motion of his arm to the diadem glittering in the sky. "Why do we linger? The wind favors us, and the tide sweeps forward —forward! See how the lights beckon from the harbor!" He bent his brows and looked almost angrily at Svensen. "Do what thou hast to do!" and his tones were sharp and imperious. "I must press on!"

An expression of terror, pain, and pity passed over the sailor's countenance—for one instant he hesitated—the next, he descended into the hold of the vessel. He was absent for a very little space,—but when he returned his eyes were wild as though he had been engaged in some dark and criminal deed. Olaf Güldmar was still gazing at the brilliancy in the heavens, which seemed to increase in size and lustre as the wind rose higher. Svensen took his hand —it was icy cold, and damp with the dew of death.

"Let me go with thee!" he implored, in broken accent. "I fear nothing! Why should I not venture also on the last voyage?"

Güldmar made a faint but decided sign of rejection.

"The Viking sails alone to the grave of his fathers!" he said, with a serene and proud smile. "Alone—alone! Neither wife, nor child, nor vassal may have place with him in his ship—even so have the gods willed it. Farewell, Valdemar! Loosen the ropes and let me go!—thou servest me ill—hasten—hasten—I am weary of waiting——"

His head fell back,—that mysterious shadow which darkens the face of the dying a moment before dissolution, was on him now.

Just then a strange, suffocating odor began to permeate the air—little wreaths of pale smoke made their slow way through the boards of the deck—and a fierce gust of wind, blowing seawards from the mountains, swayed the *Valkyrie* uneasily to and fro. Slowly, and with evident reluctance, Sevensen commenced the work of detaching her from the pier,—feeling instinctively all the while that his master's dying eyes were fixed upon him. When but one slender rope remained to be cast off, he knelt by the old man's side and whispered tremblingly that all was done. At the same moment a small, stealthy tongue of red flame curled upwards through the deck from the hold,—and Güldmar, observing this, smiled.

"I see thou hast redeemed thine oath," he said, gratefully pressing Svensen's hand. "'Tis the last act of thine allegiance,—may the gods reward thy faithfulness! Peace be with thee!—we shall meet hereafter. Already the light shines from the Rainbow Bridge,—there,—there are the golden peaks of the hills and the stretch of the wide sea! Go, Valdemar!—delay no longer, for my soul is impatient —it burns, it struggles to be free! Go!—and—farewell!"

Stricken to the heart, and full of anguish,—yet serf-like in his submission and resignation to the inevitable,—Svensen kissed his master's hand for the last time. Then, with a sort of fierce sobbing groan, wrung from the very depths of his despairing grief, he turned resolutely away, and sprang off the vessel. Standing at the extreme edge of the pier, he let slip the last rope that bound her,—her sails filled and bulged outward,—her cordage creaked, she shuddered on the water—lurched a little—then paused.

In that brief moment a loud triumphant cry rang through the air. Olaf Güldmar leaped upright on the deck as though lifted by some invisible hand, and confronted his terrified servants, who gazed at him in fascinated amazement

and awe. His white hair gleamed like spun silver—his face
was transfigured, and wore a strange, rapt look of pale yet
splendid majesty—the dark furs that clung about him
trailed in regal folds to his feet.

"Hark!" he cried, and his voice vibrated with deep and
mellow clearness. "Hark to the thunder of the galloping
hoofs!—see—see the glitter of the shield and spear! She
comes—ah! Thelma! Thelma!" He raised his arms as
though in ecstacy. "Glory!—joy!—Victory!"

And, like a noble tree struck down by lightning, he fell
—dead!

Even as he fell, the *Valkyrie* plunged forward, driven
forcibly by a swooping gust of wind, and scudded out to the
Fjord like a wild bird flying before a tempest,—and, while
she thus fled, a sheet of flame burst through her sides and
blazed upwards, mingling a lurid, smoky glow with the clear
crimson radiance of the still brilliant and crown-like aurora.
Following the current, she made swift way across the dark
water in the direction of the island of Seiland, and presently
became a wondrous Ship of Fire! Fire flashed from her
masts—fire folded up her spars and sails in a devouring
embrace,—fire, that leaped and played and sent forth a million showering sparks hissingly into the waves beneath.

With beating heart and straining eyes, Valdemar Svensen crouched on the pier-head, watching, in mute agony, the
burning vessel. He had fulfilled his oath!—that strange
vow that had so sternly bound him,—a vow that was the
outcome of his peculiar traditions and pagan creed.

Long ago, in the days of his youth,—full of enthusiasm
for the worship of Odin and the past splendors of the race
of the great Norse warriors,—he had chosen to recognize in
Olaf Güldmar a true descendant of kings, who was by blood
and birth, though not in power, himself a king,—and tracing his legendary history back to old and half-forgotten
sources, he had proved, satisfactorily, to his own mind, that
he, Svensen, must lawfully, and according to old feudal
system, be this king's serf or vassal. And, growing more
and more convinced of this in his dreamy and imaginative
mind,—he had sworn a sort of mystic friendship and allegiance, which Güldmar had accepted, imposing on him, however, only one absolute command. This was that he should
be given the "crimson shroud" and sea-tomb of his war-
like ancestors,—for the idea that his body might be touched
by strange hands, shut in a close coffin, and laid in the

earth to moulder away to wormy corruption,—had been the one fantastic dread of the sturdy old pagan's life. And he had taken advantage of Svensen's devotion and obedience to impress on him the paramount importance of his solitary behest.

"Let no hypocritical prayers be chanted over my dumb corpse," he had said. "My blood would ooze from me at every pore were I touched by the fingers of a Lutheran! Save this goodly body that has served me so well from the inferior dust,—let the bright fire wither it, and the glad sea drown it,—and my soul, beholding its end afar off, shall rejoice and be satisfied. Swear by the wrath and thunder of the gods!—swear by the unflinching Hammer of Thor,— swear by the gates of Valhalla, and in the name of Odin! —and having sworn, the curse of all these be upon thee if thou fail to keep thy vow!"

And Valdemar had sworn. Now that the oath was kept—now that his promised obedience had been carried out to the extremest letter, he was as one stupefied. Shivering, yet regardless of the snow that began to fall thickly, he kept his post, staring, staring in drear fascination across the Fjord, where the *Valkyrie* drifted, now a mass of flame blown fiercely by the wind, and gleaming red through the flaky snow-storm.

The aurora borealis faded by gradual degrees, and the blazing ship was more than ever distinctly visible. She was seen from the shore of Bosekop, by a group of the inhabitants, who, rubbing their dull eyes, could not decide whether what they beheld was fire, or a new phase of the capricious, ever-changing Northern Lights,—the rapidly descending snow rendering their vision bewildered and uncertain. Any way, they thought very little about it,— they had had excitement of another kind in the arrival of Ulrika from Talvig, bringing accounts of the godly Lovisa Elsland's death.

Moreover, and English steam cargo-boat, bound for the North Cape, had, just an hour previously, touched at their harbor, to land a passenger,—a mysterious woman closely veiled, who immediately on arrival had hired a sledge, and had bidden the driver to take her to the house of Olaf Güldmar, an eight miles' journey through the drifted snow. All this was intensely interesting to the good, stupid, gossiping fisher-folks of Bosekop,—so much so, indeed, that they scarcely paid any heed to the spectacle of the fiery ship

swaying suggestively on the heaving water, and drifting
rapidly away—away towards the frosted peaks of Seiland.

Further and further she receded,—the flames around her
waving like banners in a battle—further and further still—
till Valdemar Svensen, from his station on the pier, began
to lose sight of her blazing timbers,—and, starting from his
reverie, he ran rapidly from the shore, up through the garden paths to the farm-house, in order to gain the summit,
and from that point of vantage, watch the last glimmering
spark of the Viking's burial. As he reached the house, he
stopped short and uttered a wild exclamation. There,—
under the porch hung with sparkling icicles,—stood
Thelma! . . . Thelma,—her face pale and weary, yet
smiling faintly,—Thelma with the glint of her wondrous
gold hair escaping from under her hat, and glittering on the
folds of her dark fur mantle.

"I have come home, Valdemar!" said the sweet, rich,
penetrating voice. "Where is my father?"

As a man distraught, or in some dreadful dream, Valdemar approached her—the strangeness of his look and
manner filled her with sudden fear,—he caught her hand and
pointed to the dark Fjord—to the spot where gleamed a
lurid waving wreath of flames.

"Fröken Thelma—he is *there!*" he gasped in choked,
hoarse tones. "*There*—where the gods have called him!"

With a faint shriek of terror, Thelma's blue eyes turned
toward the shadowy water,—as she looked, a long up-twist-
ing snake of fire appeared to leap from the perishing
Valkyrie,—a snake that twined its glittering coils rapidly
round and round on the wind, and as rapidly sank—down
—down—to one glimmering spark which glowed redly like
a floating lamp for a brief space,—and was then quenched
for ever! The ship had vanished! Thelma needed no explanation,—she knew her father's creed—she understood
all. Breaking loose from Valdemar's grasp, she rushed a
few steps forward with arms outstretched on the bitter,
snowy air.

"Father! father!" she cried aloud and sobbingly.
"Wait for me!—it is I Thelma!—I am coming—Father!"

The white world around her grew black—and, shuddering
like a shot bird, she fell senseless.

Instantly Valdemar raised her from the ground, and
holding her tenderly and reverently in his strong arms,
carried her, as though she were a child, into the house. . . .

The clouds darkened—the snow-storm thickened—the mountain-peaks, stern giants, frowned through their sleety veils at the arctic desolation of the land below them,—and over the charred and sunken corpse of the departed servant of Odin, sounded the solemn *De Profundis* of the sea.

CHAPTER XXXIII.

"The body is the storm ;
The soul the star beyond it, in the deep
Of Nature's calm. And, yonder, on the steep,
The Sun of Faith, quiescent, round, and warm ! "

LATE on that same night, the pious Ulrika was engaged in prayer. Prayer with her was a sort of fanatical wrestling of the body as well as of the soul,—she was never contented unless by means of groans and contortions she could manage to work up by degrees into a condition of hysteria resembling a mild epileptic attack, in which state alone she considered herself worthy to approach the Deity. On this occasion she had some difficulty to attain the desired result —her soul, as she herself expressed it, was " dry "—and her thoughts wandered,—though she pinched her neck and arms with the hard resoluteness of a sworn flagellant, and groaned, " Lord, have mercy on me a sinner ! " with indefatigable earnestness. She was considerably startled in the midst of these energetic devotions by a sudden jangling of sledge-bells, and a loud knocking—a knocking which threatened to break down the door of the small and humble house she inhabited. Hastily donning the coarse gown and bodice she had recently taken off in order to administer chastisement to her own flesh more thoroughly, she unfastened her bolts and bars, and, lifting the latch, was confronted by Valdemar Svensen, who, nearly breathless with swift driving through the snow-storm, cried out in quick gasps—

" Come with me—come ! She is dying ! "

" God help the man ! " exclaimed Ulrika startled. " *Who* is dying ? "

" She—the Fröken Thelma—Lady Errington—she is all alone up there," and he pointed distractedly in the direction from whence he had come. " I can get no one in Bosekop, —the women are cowards all,—all afraid to go near her," and he wrung his hands in passionate distress.

Ulrika pulled a thick shawl from the nail where it hung and wrapped it round her.

"I am ready," she said, and without more delay, stepped into the waiting sledge, while Valdemar, with an exclamation of gratitude and relief, took his place beside her. "But how is it?" she asked, as the reindeer started off at full speed, "how is it that the *bonde's* daughter is again at the Altenfjord?"

"I know not!" answered Svenson despairingly. "I would have given my life not to have told her of her father's death."

"Death!" cried Ulrika. "Olaf Güldmar *dead!* Impossible! Only last night I saw him in the pride of his strength,—and thought I never had beheld so goodly a man. Lord, Lord! That he should be *dead!*"

In a few words Svensen related all that had happened, with the exception of the fire-burial in the Fjord.

But Ulrika immediately asked, "Is his body still in the house?"

Svensen looked at her darkly. "Hast thou never heard, Ulrika," he said solemnly, "that the bodies of men who follow Olaf Güldmar's creed, disappear as soon as the life departs from them? It is a mystery—strange and terrible! But this is true—my master's sailing-ship has gone, and his body with it—and I know not where!"

Ulrika surveyed him steadily with a slow, incredulous smile. After a pause, she said—

"Fidelity in a servant is good, Valdemar Svensen! I know you well—I also know that a pagan shrinks from Christian burial. Enough said—I will ask no more—but if Olaf Güldmar's ship has gone, and he with it,—I warn you, the village will wonder."

"I cannot help it," said Svensen with cold brevity. "I have spoken truth—he has gone! I saw him die—and then vanish. Believe it or not as you will, I care not!"

And he drove on in silence. Ulrika was silent too.

She had known Valdemar Svenson for many years—he was a man universally liked and respected at all the harbors and different fishing-stations of Norway, and his life was an open book to everybody, with the exception of one page, which was turned down and sealed,—this was the question of his religious belief. No one knew what form of faith he followed,—it was only when he went to live with the *bonde*, after Thelma's marriage,—that the nature of his creed was dimly suspected. But Ulrika had no dislike for him on this account,—her opinions had changed very much during the past few months. As devout a Lutheran as ever, she began to entertain a little more of the true spirit of Christianity—that spirit of gentle and patient tolerance which, full of forbearance towards all humanity, is willing to admit the possibility of a little good in everything, even in the blind tenents of a heathen creed. Part of this alteration in her was due to the gratitude she secretly felt towards the Güldmar family, for having saved from destruction,—albeit unconscious of his parentage,—Sigurd, the child she had attempted to murder. The hideous malevolence of Lovisa Elsland's nature had shown her that there *may* be bad Lutherans,—the invariable tenderness displayed by the Güldmars for her unrecognized, helpless and distraught son,—had proved to her that there *may* be good heathens. Hearing thus suddenly of the *bonde's* death, she was strangely affected—she could almost have wept. She felt perfectly convinced that Svensen had made away with his master's body by some mysterious rite connected with pagan belief,—she knew that Güldmar himself, according to rumor, had buried his own wife in some unknown spot, with strange and weird ceremonials, but she was inclined to be tolerant,—and glancing at Svensen's grave, pained face from time 'o time as she sat beside him in the sledge, she resolved to ask him no more questions on the subject, but to accept and support, if necessary, the theory he had so emphatically set forth,—namely, the mystical evanishment of the corpse by some supernatural agency.

As they neared their ˉstination, she began to think of Thelma, the beautiful, proud girl whom she remembered best as standing on a little green-tufted hillock with a cluster of pansies in her hand, and Sigurd—Sigurd clinging fondly to her white skirts, with a wealth of passionate devotion in his upturned, melancholy, blue eyes. Ulrika had seen her but once since then,—and that was on the occasion when, at the threat of Lovisa Elsland, and the command of the Reverend Mr. Dyceworthy, she had given her Sir Philip Errington's card, with the false message written on it that had decoyed her for a time into the wily minister's power. She felt a thrill of shame as she remembered the part she had played in that cruel trick,—and reverting once more to the memory of Sigurd, whose tragic end at the Fall of Njedegorze she had learned through Valdemar, she resolved to make amends now that she had the chance, and to do her best for Thelma in her suffering and trouble.

" For who knows," mused Ulrika, " Whether it is not the Lord's hand that is extended towards me,—and that in the ministering to the wants of her whom I wronged, and whom my son so greatly loved, I may not thereby cancel the past sin, and work out my own redemption ! "

And her dull eyes brightened with hope, and her heart warmed,—she began to feel almost humane and sympathetic,—and was so eager to commence her office of nurse and consoler to Thelma that she jumped out of the sledge almost before it had stopped at the farm gate. Disregarding Valdemar's assistance, she clambered sturdily over the drifted heaps of slippery snow that blocked the deserted pathways, and made for the house,—Valdemar following her as soon as he had safely fastened up the sledge, which was not his own, he having in emergency borrowed it from a neighbor. As they approached, a sound came floating to meet them—a sound which made them pause and look at each other in surprise and anxiety. Some one was singing, —a voice full and clear, though with a strange, uncertain quiver in it, rippled out in wild strains of minor melody on the snow-laden air. For one moment Ulrika listened doubtedly, and then without more delay ran hastily forward and entered the house. Thelma was there,—sitting at the lattice window which she had thrown wide open to the icy blast,—she had taken off her cloak and hat, and her hair, unbound, fell about her in a great, glittering tangle of gold, —her hands were busy manipulating an imaginary spinning-wheel—her eyes were brilliant as jewels, but full of pain, terror, and pathos. She smiled a piteous smile as she became hazily conscious that there were others in the room —but she went on with her song—a mournful, Norwegian ditty,—till a sudden break in her voice caused her to put her hand to her throat and look up perplexedly.

" That song pleases you ? " she asked softly, " I am very glad ! Has Sigurd come home ? He wanders so much, poor boy ! Father, dear, you must tell him how wrong it is not to love Philip. Every one loves Philip—and I—I love him too, but he must never know that." She paused and sighed. " That is my secret,—the only one I have ! " And she drooped her fair head forlornly.

Moved by intense pity, such as she had never felt in all

her life before, Ulrika went up and tried to draw her gently
from the window.

"Poor thing, poor thing!" she said kindly. "Come
away with me, and lie down! You mustn't sit here,—let
me shut the lattice,—it's quite late at night, and too cold
for you, my dear."

"Too cold?" and Thelma eyed her wonderingly. "Why,
it is summer-time, and the sun never sets! The roses are
all about the walls—I gave one to Philip yesterday—a
little pale rose with a crimson heart. He wore it, and
seemed glad!"

She passed her hand across her forehead with a troubled
air, and watched Ulrika, who quietly closed the window
against the darkness and desolation of the night. "Are
you a friend?" she asked presently in anxious tones. "I
know so many that say they are my friends—but I am
afraid of them all—and I have left them. Do you know
why?" and she laid her hand on Ulrika's rough arm. "Because they tell me my Philip does not love me any more.
They are very cruel to say so, and I think it cannot be
true. I want to tell my father what they say—because he
will know—and if it is true, then I wish to die,—I could
not live! Will you take me to my father?"

The plaintive, pleading gentleness of her voice and look
brought more tears into Ulrika's eyes than had ever been
forced there by her devotional exercises,—and the miserable Valdemar, already broken-hearted by his master's
death, turned away and sobbingly cursed his gods for this
new and undeserved affliction. As the Italian peasantry
fall to abusing their saints in time of trouble, even so will
the few remaining believers in Norse legendary lore, upbraid their fierce divinities with the most reckless hardihood when things go wrong. There were times when Valdemar Svensen secretly quailed at the mere thought of the
wrath of Odin,—there were others when he was ready to
pluck the great god by the beard and beat him with the
flat of his own drawn Sword. This was his humor at the
present moment, as he averted his gaze from the pitiful
sight of his "King's" fair daughter all desolate and woe-
begone, her lovely face pale with anguish,—her sweet wits
wandering, and her whole demeanor that of one who is lost
in some dark forest, and is weary unto death. She studied
Ulrika's rough visage attentively, and presently noticed
the tears on her cheeks.

"You are crying!" she said in a tone of grave surprise. "Why? It is foolish to cry even when the heart aches. I have found that,—no one in the world ever pities you! But perhaps you do not know the world,—ah! it is very hard and cold;—all the people hide their feelings, and pretend to be what they are not. It is difficult to live so,— and I am tired!"

She rose from her chair, and stood up unsteadily, stretching out her little cold white hands to Ulrika, who folded them in her own strong coarse palms. "Yes—I am very tired!" she went on dreamily. "There seems to be nothing that is true—all is false and unreal—I cannot understand! But you seem kind,"—here her swaying figure tottered, and Ulrika drew her more closely to herself—"I think I know you—you came with me in the train, did you not? Yes—and the little baby smiled and slept in my arms nearly all the way." A violent shuddering seized her, and a quiver of agony passed over her face.

"Forgive me," she murmured, "I feel ill—very ill—and cold—but do not mind—I think—I am—dying!" She could scarcely articulate these last words—she sank forward, fainting, on Ulrika's breast, and that devout disciple of Luther, forgetting all her former dread of the "white witch of the Altenfjord"—only remembered that she held in her arms a helpless woman with all the sorrows and pangs of womanhood thick upon her,—and in this act of warm heart-expansion and timely tenderness, it may be that she cleansed her soiled soul in the sight of the God she worshipped, and won a look of pardon from the ever-watchful eyes of Christ.

As far as mundane matters were concerned, she showed herself a woman of prompt energy and decision. Laying Thelma gently down upon the very couch her dead father had so lately occupied, she sent the distracted Valdemar out to gather fresh pine-logs for the fire, and then busied herself in bringing down Thelma's own little bed from the upper floor, airing it with methodical care, and making it as warm and cosy as a bird's-nest. While she was engaged in these preparations, Thelma regained her consciousness, and began to toss and tumble and talk deliriously; but with it all she retained the innate gentleness and patience, and submitted to be undressed, though she began to sob pleadingly when Ulrika would have removed her husband's miniature from where it lay pressed against her bosom,—and taking it in her own hand she kissed and held it fast. One by one, the dainty articles of delicate apparel she wore were loosened and laid aside, Ulrika wondering at the embroidered linen and costly lace, the like of which was never seen in that part of Norway,—but wondering still more at the dazzling skin she thus unveiled, a skin as exquisitely soft and pure as the satiny cup of a Nile lily.

Poor Thelma sat resignedly watching her own attire taken from her, and allowing herself to be wrapped in a comfortable loose garment of white *wadmel*, as warm as eider-down, which Ulrika had found in a cupboard upstairs, and which, indeed, had once belonged to Thelma, she and Britta having made it together. She examined its texture now with some faint interest—then she asked plaintively—

"Are you going to bury me? You must put me to sleep with my mother—her name was Thelma, too. I think it is an unlucky name."

"Why, my dear?" asked Ulrika kindly, as she swept the rich tumbled hair from the girl's eyes, and began to braid it in one long loose plait, in order to give her greater ease.

Thelma sighed. "There is an old song that says——" She broke off. "Shall I sing it to you?" she asked with a wild look.

"No, no," said Ulrika. "Not now. By-and-by!" And she nodded her head encouragingly. "By-and-by! There'll be plenty of time for singing presently," and she laid her in bed, tucking her up warmly as though she were a very little child, and feeling strongly inclined to kiss her.

"Ah, but I should like to tell you, even if I must not sing—" and Thelma gazed up anxiously from her pillow—"only my head is so heavy, and full of strange noises—I do not know whether I can remember it."

"Don't try to remember it," and Ulrika stroked the soft cheek, with a curious yearning sensation of love tugging at her tough heartstrings. "Try to sleep—that will be better for you!" And she took from the fire a warm, nourishing drink she had prepared, and gave it to her. She was surprised at the eagerness with which the poor girl seized it.

"Lord help us, I believe she is light-headed for want of food!" she thought.

Such indeed was the fact,—Thelma had been several days on her journey from Hull, and during that time had eaten so little that her strength had entirely given way. The

provisions on board the *Black Polly* were extremely limited, and consisted of nothing but dried fish, hard bread,
and weak tea, without milk or sugar,—and in her condition
of health, her system had rebelled against this daily un-
tempting bill of fare. Ulrika's simple but sustaining
beverage seemed more than delicious to her palate,—she
drained it to the last drop, and, as she returned the cup, a
faint color came back to her cheeks and lips.

"Thank you," she said feebly. "You are very good to
me! And now I do quite know what I wished to say. It
was long ago—there was a queen, named Thelma, and some
one—a great warrior, loved her and found her fair. But
presently he grew tired of her face—and raised an army
against her, and took her throne by force, and crowned himself king of all her land. And the song says that Queen
Thelma wandered on the mountains all alone till she died—
it was a sad song—but I forget—the end."

And her voice trailed off into broken murmurs, her eyes
closed, and she slept. Ulrika watched her musingly and
tenderly—wondering what secret trouble weighed on the
girl's mind. When Valdemar Svensen presently looked in,
she made him a warning sign—and, hushing his footsteps,
he went away again. She followed him out into the kitchen,
where he had deposited his load of pine-wood, and began to
talk to him in low tones. He listened,—the expression
of grief and fear deepened on his countenance as he heard.

"Will she die?" he asked anxiously.

"Let us hope not," returned Ulrika. "But there is no
doubt she is very ill, and will be worse. What has brought
her here, I wonder? Do you know?"

Valdemar shook his head.

"Where is her husband?" went on Ulrika. "He ought
to be here. How could he have let her make such a
journey at such a time! Why did he not come with her?
There must be something wrong!"

Svensen looked, as he felt, completely perplexed and
despairing. He could think of no reason for Thelma's unexpected appearance at the Altenfjord—he had forgotten
all about the letter that had come from her to her father,—
the letter which was still in the house, unopened.

"Well, well! It is very strange!" Ulrika sighed resignedly. "But it is the Lord's will—and we must do our
best for her, that's all." And she began to enumerate a list
of things she wanted from Bosekop for her patient's sus-

tenance and comfort. " You must fetch all these," she said, " as soon as the day is fairly advanced." She glanced at the clock—it was just four in the morning. " And at the same time, you had better call at the doctor's house."

" He's away," interrupted Valdemar. " Gone to Christiania."

" Very well," said Ulrika composedly. " Then we must do without him. Doctors are never much use, any way,—maybe the Lord will help me instead."

And she returned to Thelma, who still slept, though her face was now feverishly flushed and her breathing hurried and irregular.

The hours of the new day,—day, though seeming night, passed on and it was verging towards ten o'clock when she woke, raving deliriously. Her father, Sigurd, Philip, the events of her life in London, the fatigues of her journey, were all jumbled fantastically together in her brain—she talked and sang incessantly, and, like some wild bird suddenly caged, refused to be quieted. Ulrika was all alone with her,—Valdemar having gone to execute his commissions in Bosekop,—and she had enough to do to make her remain in bed. For she became suddenly possessed by a strong desire to go sailing on the Fjord—and occasionally it took all Ulrika's strength to hold and keep her from springing to the window, whose white frosted panes seemed to have some fatal attraction for her wandering eyes.

She spoke of things strange and new to her attendant's ears—frequently she pronounced the names of Violet Vere and Lady Winsleigh with an accent of horror,—then she would talk of George Lorimer and Pierre Duprèz,—and she would call for Britta often, sometimes endearingly—sometimes impatiently.

The picture of her home in Warwickshire seemed to haunt her,—she spoke of its great green trees, its roses, its smooth sloping lawns—then she would begin to smile and sing again in such a weak, pitiful fashion that Ulrika,—her stern nature utterly melted at the sight of such innocent helpless distraction and sorrow,—could do nothing but fold the suffering creature in her arms, and rock her to and fro soothingly on her breast, the tears running down her cheeks the while.

And after long hours of bewilderment and anguish, Errington's child, a boy, was born—dead. With a regretful heart, Ulrika laid out the tiny corpse,—the withered blossom of a promised new delight, a minature form so fair and perfect that it seemed sheer cruelty on the part of nature to deny it breath and motion. Thelma's mind still wandered—she was hardly conscious of anything—and Ulrika was almost glad that this was so. Her anxiety was very great—she could not disguise from herself that Thelma's life was in danger,—and both she and Valdemar wrote to Sir Philip Errington, preparing him for the worst, and urging him to come at once,—little aware that the very night the lifeless child was born, was the same on which he had started from Hull for Christiansund, after his enforced waiting for the required steamer. There was nothing more to be done now, thought Ulrika piously, but to trust in the Lord and hope for the best. And Valdemar Svensen made with his own hands a tiny coffin for the body of the little dead boy who was to have brought such pride and satisfaction to his parents, and one day rowed it across the Fjord to that secret cave where Thelma's mother lay enshrined in stone. There he left it, feeling sure he had done well.

Ulrika asked him no questions—she was entirely absorbed in the duties that devolved upon her, and with an ungrudging devotion strange to see in her, watched and tended Thelma incessantly, scarcely allowing herself a minute's space for rest or food. The idea that her present ministration was to save her soul in the sight of the Lord, had grown upon her, and was now rooted firmly in her mind—she never gave way to fatigue or inattention,—every moan, every restless movement of the suffering girl, obtained her instant and tender solicitude, and when she prayed now, it was not for herself but for Thelma.

"Spare her, good Lord!" she would implore in the hyperbolical language she had drawn from her study of the Scriptures—"As the lily among thorns, so is she among the daughters! Cut her not off root and branch from the land of the living, for her countenance is comely, and as a bunch of myrrh which hath a powerful sweetness, even so must she surely be to the heart of her husband! Stretch forth Thy right hand, O Lord, and scatter healing, for the gates of death shall not prevail against Thy power!"

Day after day she poured out petitions such as these, and with the dogged persistency of a soldier serving Cromwell, believed that they would be granted,—though day after day Thelma seemed to grow weaker and weaker. She was still light-headed—her face grew thin and shadowy,—her hands were almost transparent in their whiteness and delicacy, and her voice was so faint as to be nearly inaudible. Sometimes Ulrika got frightened at her appearance, and heartily wished for medical assistance but this was not to be had. Therefore she was compelled to rely on the efficacy of one simple remedy,—a herbal drink to allay fever,—the virtues of which she had been taught in her youth,—this, and the healing mercies of mother Nature together with the reserved strength of her own constitution, were the threads on which Thelma's life hung.

Time passed on—and yet there was no news from Sir Philip. One night, sitting beside her exhausted patient, Ulrika fancied she saw a change on the wan face—a softer, more peaceful look than had been there for many days. Half in fear, half in hope, she watched,—Thelma seemed to sleep,—but presently her large blue eyes opened with a calm yet wondering expression in their clear depths. She turned slightly on her pillows, and smiled faintly.

" Have I been ill ? " she asked.

" Yes, my dear," returned Ulrika softly, overjoyed, yet afraid at the girl's returning intelligence. " Very ill. But you feel better now, don't you ? "

Thelma sighed, and raising her little wasted hand, examined it curiously. Her wedding and betrothal rings were so loose on her finger that they would have fallen off had they been held downwards. She seemed surprised at this, but made no remark. For some time she remained quiet, —steadfastly gazing at Ulrika, and evidently trying to make out who she was. Presently she spoke again.

" I remember everything now," she said, slowly. " I am at home, at the Altenfjord—and I know how I came—and also *why* I came." Here her lips quivered. " And I shall see my father no more, for he has gone—and I am all —all alone in the world ! " She paused—then added, " Do you think I am dying ? If so, I am very glad ! "

" Hush my dear ! " said Ulrika. " You mustn't talk in that way. Your husband is coming presently——" she broke off suddenly, startled at the look of utter despair in Thelma's eyes.

" You are wrong," she replied wearily. " He will not come—he cannot ! He does not want me any more ! "

And two large tears rolled slowly down her pale cheeks. Ulrika wondered, but forebore to pursue the subject further, fearing to excite or distress her,—and contented herself for the present with attending to her patient's bodily needs. She went to the fire, and began to pour out some nourishing soup, which she always had there in readiness,—and while she was thus engaged, Thelma's brain cleared more and more,—till with touching directness, and a new hope flushing her face, she asked softly and beseechingly for her child. " I forgot! " she said simply and sweetly. " Of course I am not alone any more. Do give me my baby —I am much better—nearly well—and I should like to kiss it."

Ulrika stood mute, taken aback by this demand. She dared not tell her the truth—she feared its effect on the sensitive mind that had so lately regained its balance. But while she hesitated, Thelma instinctively guessed all she strove to hide.

" It is dead! " she cried. " Dead!—and I never knew! "

And, burying her golden head in her pillows, she broke into a passion of convulsive sobbing. Ulrika grew positively desperate at the sound,—what *was* she to do? Everything seemed to go against her—she was inclined to cry herself. She embraced the broken-hearted girl, and tried to soothe her, but in vain. The long delirium and subsequent weakness,—combined with the secret trouble on her mind,—had deprived poor Thelma of all resisting power, and she wept on and on in Ulrika's arms till nature was exhausted, and she could weep no longer. Then she lay motionless, with closed eyes, utterly drained in body and spirit, scarcely breathing, and, save for a shivering moan that now and then escaped her, she seemed almost insensible. Ulrika watched her with darkening, meditative brows, —she listened to the rush of the storm-wind without,—it was past eleven o'clock at night. She began to count on her fingers—it was the sixteenth day since the birth of the child,—sixteen days exactly since she had written to Sir Philip Errington, informing him of his wife's danger—and the danger was not yet past. Thinking over all that had happened, and the apparent hopelessness of the case, she suddenly took a strange idea into her head. Retiring to a distant corner, she dropped on her knees.

" O Lord, God Almighty! " she said in a fierce whisper, " Behold, I have been Thy servant until now! I have wrestled with Thee in prayer till I am past all patience! If Thou wilt not hear my petition, why callest Thou Thyself good? Is it good to crush the already fallen? Is it good to have no mercy on the sorrowful? Wilt Thou condemn the innocent without reason? If so, thou art not the Holy One I imagined! Send forth Thy power *now*—now, while there is time! Rescue her that is lying under the shadow of death—for how has she offended Thee that she should die? Delay no longer, or how shall I put my trust in Thee? Send help speedily from Thine everlasting habitations—or, behold! I do forsake Thee—and my soul shall seek else-where for Eternal Justice!"

As she finished this extraordinary, half-threatening, and entirely blasphemous petition, the boisterous gale roared wildly round the house joining in chorus with the stormy dash of waves upon the coast—a chorus that seemed to Ulrika's ears like the sound of fiendish and derisive laughter.

She stood listening,—a trifle scared—yet with a sort of fanatical defiance written on her face, and she waited in sul-len patience evidently expecting an immediate answer to her outrageous prayer. She felt somewhat like a demagogue of the people, who boldly menaces an all-powerful sovereign, even while in dread of instant execution. There was a sharp patter of sleet on the window,—she glanced nervously at Thelma, who, perfectly still on her couch, looked more like a white, recumbent statue than a living woman. The wind shook the doors, and whistled shrilly through the crevices,—then, as though tired of its own wrath, surged away in hoarse murmurs over the tops of the creaking pines towards the Fjord, and there was a short, impressive silence.

Ulrika still waited—almost holding her breath in expec-tation of some divine manifestation. The brief stillness grew unbearable . . . . Hush! What was that! Jingle—jangle—jingle—jangle!—Bells! Sledge bells tinkling musically and merrily—and approaching swiftly, nearer—nearer! Now the sharp trotting roofs on the hard snow—then a sudden slackening of speed—the little metallic chimes rang slower and yet more slowly, till with a decisive and melodious clash they stopped!

Ulrika's heart beat thickly—her face flushed—she ad-vanced to Thelma's bedside, hoping, fearing,—she knew not what. There was a tread of firm, yet hurried, footsteps without—a murmur of subdued voices—a half-suppressed exclamation of surprise and relief from Valdemar,—and

then the door of the room was hastily thrown open, and a
man's tall figure, draped in what seemed to be a garment
of frozen snowflakes, stood on the threshold. The noise
startled Thelma—she opened her beautiful, tired, blue eyes.
Ah! what a divine rapture,—what a dazzling wonder and
joy flashed into them, giving them back their old lustre of
sunlight sparkling on azure sea! She sprang up in her
bed and stretched out her arms.

"Philip!" she cried sobbingly. "Philip! oh my darling! Try—try to love me again! . . . just a little!—before I die!"

As she spoke she was clasped to his breast,—folded to his
heart in that strong, jealous, passionate embrace with
which we who love, would fain shield our nearest and dearest from even the shadow of evil—his lips closed on hers,—
and in the sacred stillness that followed, Ulrika slipped
from the room, leaving husband and wife alone together.

CHAPTER XXXIV.

"I have led her home, my love, my only friend;
    There is none like her, none!
And never yet so warmly ran my blood,
    And sweetly on and on,
Calming itself to the long-wished-for end,
    Full to the banks, close on the promised good."
                                        TENNYSON.

BRITTA was in the kitchen, dragging off her snow-wet
cloak and fur mufflers, and crying heartily all the while.
The stalwart Svenson stood looking at her in perplexity,
now and then uttering a word of vague sympathy and consolation, to which she paid not the slightest heed. The poor
girl was tired out, and half-numb with the piercing cold,—
the excitement which had kept her up for days and days,
had yielded to the nervous exhaustion, which was its
natural result,—and she kept on weeping without exactly
knowing why she wept. Throughout the long and fatiguing
journey she had maintained unflinching energy and perse-
verence,—undaunted by storm, sleet, and darkness, she had
driven steadily over long miles of trackless snow—her instinct had guided her by the shortest and quickest routes—
she seemed to know every station and village on the way,—
she always managed to obtain relays of reindeer just when

they were needed,—in short, Errington would hardly have been able to reach the Altenfjord without her.

He had never realized to its full extent her strong, indomitable, devoted character, till he saw her hour after hour seated beside him in the *pulkha*, her hands tightly gripping the reins of the horned animals, whose ways she understood and perfectly controlled,—her bright, bird-like eyes fixed with watchful eagerness on the bewildering white landscape that opened out incessantly before her. Her common sense was never at fault—she forgot nothing—and with gentle but respectful firmness she would insist on Sir Philip's taking proper intervals of rest and refreshment at the different farms they passed on their road, though he, eager to press on, chafed and fretted at every little delay. They were welcomed all along their route with true Norse hospitality, though the good country-folk who entertained them could not refrain from astonishment at the idea of their having undertaken such a journey at such a season, and appeared to doubt the possibility of their reaching their destination at all. And now that they had reached it in safety, Britta's strength gave way. Valdemar Svensen had hastily blurted out the news of the *bonde's* death even while she and Sir Philip were alighting from their sledge— and in the same breath had told them of Thelma's dangerous illness. What wonder, then, that Britta sobbed hysterically, and refused to be comforted,—what wonder that she turned upon Ulrika as that personage approached, in a burst of unreasonable anger.

"Oh dear, oh dear!" she cried, "to think that the Fröken should be so ill—almost dying! and have nobody but *you* to attend to her!"

This, with a vindictive toss of the brown curls. Ulrika winced at her words—she was hurt, but she answered gently—

"I have done my best," she said with a sort of grave pathos, "I have been with her night and day—had she been a daughter of my own blood, I know not how I could have served her with more tenderness. And, surely, it has been a sore and anxious time with me also—for I, too, have learned to love her!"

Her set mouth quivered,—and Britta, seeing her emotion, was ashamed of her first hasty speech. She made an act of contrition at once by putting her arms round Ulrika's neck and kissing her—a proceeding which so much astonished that devout servant of Luther, that her dull eyes filled with tears.

"Forgive me!" said the impetuous little maiden. "I was very rude and very unkind! But if you love the Fröken, you will understand how I feel—how I wish I could have helped to take care of her. And oh! the *bonde!*"—here she gave way to a fresh burst of tears— "the dear, good, kind, brave *bonde!* That he should be dead!—oh! it is too cruel—too dreadful—I can hardly believe it!"

Ulrika patted her consolingly on the shoulder, but said nothing—and Valdemar sighed. Britta sought for her handkerchief, and dried her eyes—but, after a minute, began to cry again as recklessly as ever.

"And now"—she gasped—"if the Fröken—dies—I will die too. I will—you see if I don't! I w-w-won't live— without her!"

And such a big sob broke from her heaving bosom that it threatened to burst her trimly laced little bodice.

"She will not die," said Ulrika decisively. "I have had my fears—but the crisis is passed. Do not fret, Britta— there is no longer any danger. Her husband's love will lift the trouble from her heart—and strength will return more speedily than it left her."

And turning a little aside on the pretence of throwing more wood on the fire, she muttered inaudibly, "O Lord, verily thou hast done well to grant my just demand! Even for this will I remain Thy servant for ever!" After this parenthesis, she resumed the conversation,—Valdemar Svensen sitting silently apart,—and related all that had happened since Thelma's arrival at the Altenfjord. She also gave an account of Lovisa Elsland's death,—though Britta was not much affected by the loss of her grandmother.

"Dreadful old thing!" she said with a shudder. "I'm glad I wasn't with her! I remember how she cursed the Fröken,—perhaps her curse has brought all the trouble— if so, it's a good thing she's dead, for now everything will come right again. I used to fancy she had some crime to confess,—did she say anything wicked when she was dying?"

Ulrika avoided a direct reply to this question. What was the good of horrifying the girl by telling her that her deceased relative was to all intents and purposes a murderess?

She resolved to let the secret of old Lovisa's life remain
buried with her. Therefore she simply answered—

" Her mind wandered greatly,—it was difficult to hear
her last words. But it should satisfy you, Britta, to know
that she passed away in the fear of the Lord."

Britta gave a little half-dubious, half-scornful smile. She
had not the slightest belief in the sincerity of her late
grandmother's religious principles.

" I don't understand people who are so much *afraid* of
the Lord," she said. " They must have done something
wrong. If you always do your best, and try to be good,
you needn't fear anything. At least, that's my opinion."

" There is the everlasting burning," began Ulrika
solemnly.

" Oh, nonsense ! " exclaimed Britta quite impatiently. " I
don't believe it ! "

Ulrika started back in wonder and dismay. " You don't
believe it ! " she said in awed accents. " Are you also a
heathen ? "

" I don't know what you mean by a heathen," replied
Britta almost gaily. " But I can't believe that God, who
is so good, is going to everlastingly burn anybody. He
couldn't, you know ! It would hurt Him so much to see
poor creatures writhing about in flames for ever—*we* would
not be able to bear it, and I'm quite sure it would make
Him miserable even in heaven. Because He is all Love—
He says so,—He couldn't be cruel ! "

This frank statement of Britta's views presented such a
new form of doctrine to Ulrika's heavy mind that she was
almost appalled by it. God *couldn't* burn anybody for
ever—He was too good ! What a daring idea ! And yet
so consoling—so wonderful in the infinite prospect of hope
it offered, that she smiled,—even while she trembled to contemplate it. Poor soul ! She talked of heathens—being
herself the worst type of heathen—namely, a Christian
heathen. This sounds incongruous—yet it may be taken for
granted that those who profess to follow Christianity, and
yet make of God, a being malicious, revengeful, and of more
evil attributes than they possess themselves,—are as barbarous, as unenlightened, as hopelessly sunken in slavish
ignorance as the lowest savage who adores his idols of mud
and stone. Britta was quite unconscious of having said
anything out of the common—she was addressing herself to
Svensen.

"Where is the *bonde* buried, Valdemar?" she asked in a low tone.

He looked at her with a strange, mysterious smile.

"Buried? Do you suppose his body could mix itself with common earth? No!—he sailed away, Britta—away —yonder!"

And he pointed out through the window to the Fjord now invisible in the deep darkness.

Britta stared at him with roundly opened, frightened eyes—her face paled.

"Sailed away? You must be dreaming! Sailed away! How could he—if he was dead?"

Valdemar grew suddenly excited. "I tell you, he sailed away!" he repeated in a low, hoarse whisper. "Where is his ship, the *Valkyrie?* Try if you can find it anywhere— on sea or land! It has gone, and he has gone with it—like a king and warrior—to glory, joy, and victory! Glory—joy —victory!—those were his last words!"

Britta retreated, and caught Ulrika by the arm. "Is he mad?" she asked fearfully.

Valdemar heard her, and rose from his chair, a pained smile on his face.

"I am not mad, Britta," he said gently. "Do not be afraid! If grief for my master could have turned my brain, I had been mad ere this,—but I have all my wits about me, and I have told you the truth." He paused—then added, in a more ordinary tone, "You will need fresh logs of pine —I will go and bring them in."

And he went out. Britta gazed after him in speechless wonder.

"What does he mean?" she asked.

"What he says," returned Ulrika composedly. "You, like others, must have known that Olaf Güldmar's creed was a strange one—his burial has been strange—that is all!"

And she skillfully turned the conversation, and began to talk of Thelma, her sorrows and sufferings. Britta was most impatient to see her beloved "Fröken," and quite grudged Sir Philip the long time he remained alone with his wife.

"He *might* call me, if only for a moment," Britta thought plaintively. "I do so want to look at her dear face again! But men are all alike—as long as they've got what *they* want, they never think of anybody else. Dear me! I wonder how long I shall have to wait!" So she fumed and fretted, and sat by the kitchen-fire, drinking hot tea and talking to Ulrika—all the while straining her ears for the least sound or movement from the adjoining room. But none came—there was the most perfect silence. At last she could endure it no longer—and, regardless of Ulrika's remonstrances, she stole on tip-toe to the closed door that barred her from the sight of her heart's idol, and turning the handle softly, opened it and looked in. Sir Philip saw her, and made a little warning sign, though he smiled.

He was sitting by the bedside, and in his arms, nestled against his shoulder, Thelma rested. She was fast asleep. The lines of pain had disappeared from her sweet face—a smile was on her lips—her breath came and went with peaceful regularity,—and the delicate hue of a pale rose flushed her cheeks. Britta stood gazing on this fair sight till her affectionate little heart overflowed, and the ready tears dropped like diamonds from her curly lashes.

" Oh, my dear—my dear ! " she whispered in a sort of rapture when there was a gentle movement,—and two star-like eyes opened like blue flowers outspreading to the sun.

" Is that you, Britta?" asked a tender, wondering voice—and with a smothered cry of ecstacy, Britta sprang to seize the outstretched hand of her beloved Fröken, and cover it with kisses. And while Thelma laughed with pleasure to see her, and stroked her hair. Sir Philip described their long drive through the snow, and so warmly praised Britta's patience, endurance, and constant cheerfulness, that his voice trembled with its own earnestness, while Britta grew rosily red in her deep shyness and embarrassment, vehemently protesting that she had done nothing,—nothing at all to deserve so much commendation. Then, after much glad converse, Ulrika was called, and Sir Philip seizing her hand, shook it with such force and fervor that she was quite overcome.

" I don't know how to thank you ! " he said, his eyes sparkling with gratitude. " It's impossible to repay such goodness as yours ! My wife tells me how tender and patient and devoted you have been—that even when she knew nothing else, she was aware of your kindness. God bless you for it ! You have saved her life——"

" Ah, yes, indeed ! " interrupted Thelma gently. " And life has grown so glad for me again ! I do owe you so much."

" You owe me nothing," said Ulrika in those harsh, mo-

notonous tones which she had of late learned to modulate.
" Nothing. The debt is all on my side." She stopped ab-
ruptly—a dull red color flushed her face—her eyes dwelt on
Thelma with a musing tenderness.

Sir Philip looked at her in some surprise.

" Yes," she went on. " The debt is all on my side. Hear
me out, Sir Philip—and you too,—you ' rose of the northern forest,' as Sigurd used to call you ! You have not forgotten Sigurd ? "

" Forgotten him ? " said Thelma softly. " Never ! . . . I
loved him too well ! "

Ulrika's head dropped. " He was my son ! " she said.

There was a silence of complete astonishment. Ulrika
paused—then, as no one uttered a word, she looked up
boldly, and spoke with a sort of desperate determination.

" You see you have nothing to thank me for," she went
on, addressing herself to Sir Philip, while Thelma, leaning
back on her pillows, and holding Britta's hand, regarded
her with a new and amazed interest. " Perhaps, if you had
known what sort of a woman I am, you might not have
liked me to come near—*her*." And she motioned towards
Thelma. " When I was young—long ago—I loved——"
she laughed bitterly. " It seems a strange thing to say,
does it not ? Let it pass—the story of my love, my sin and
shame, need not be told here ! But Sigurd was my child—
born in an evil hour—and I—I strove to kill him at his
birth."

Thelma uttered a faint cry of horror. Ulrika turned an
imploring gaze upon her.

" Don't hate me ! " she said, her voice trembling. " Don't,
for God's sake, hate me ! You don't know what I have
suffered ! I was mad, I think, at the time—I flung the
child in the Fjord to drown ;—your father, Olaf Güldmar,
rescued him. I never knew that till long after ;—for years
the crime I had committed weighed upon my soul,—I prayed
and strove with the Lord for pardon, but always, always
felt that for me there was no forgiveness. Lovisa Elsland
used to call me " murderess ; " she was right—I *was* one,
or so I thought—till—till that day I met you, Fröken
Thelma, on the hills with Sigurd,—and the lad fought with
me." She shuddered,—and her eyes looked wild. " I
recognized him—no matter how ! . . . he bore my mark
upon him—he was my son—*mine !*—the deformed, crazy

creature who yet had wit enough to love *you*—you, whom then I hated—but now——"

She stopped and advanced a little closer to Thelma's bed-side.

"Now, there is nothing I would not do for you, my dear!" she said very gently. "But you will not need me any more. You understand what you have done for me,—you and your father? You have saved me by saving Sigurd,—saved *me* from being weighed down to hell with the crime of murder! And you made the boy happy while he lived. All the rest of my days spent in your service could not pay back the worth of that good deed. And most heartily do I thank the Lord that he has mercifully permitted me to tend and comfort you in the hour of trouble—and, moreover, that He has given me strength to speak and confess my sin and unworthiness before you ere I depart. For now the trouble is past, I must remove my shadow from your joy. God bless you!—and—try to think as kindly as you can of me for—for Sigurd's sake!"

Stooping, she kissed Thelma's hand,—and, before any one had time to speak a word, she left the room abruptly.

When, in a few minutes, Britta went to look after her, she was gone. She had departed to her own house in Bosekop, where she obstinately remained. Nothing would induce her to present herself again before Sir Philip or Thelma, and it was not till many days after they had left the Altenfjord that she was once more seen about the village. And then she was a changed being. No longer harsh or forbidding in manner, she became humble and gentle,—she ministered to the sick, and consoled the afflicted—but she was especially famous for her love of children. All the little ones of the place knew her, and were attracted by her,—and the time came when Ulrika, white-haired, and of peaceful countenance, could be seen knitting at her door in the long summer afternoons surrounded by a whole army of laughing, chattering, dimpled youngsters, who would play at hide-and-seek behind her chair, and clamber up to kiss her wrinkled cheeks, putting their chubby arms round her neck with that guileless confidence children show only to those whom they feel can appreciate such flattering attentions. Some of her acquaintance were wont to say that she was no longer the " godly " Ulrika—but however this might be, it is certain she had drifted a little nearer to the Author of all godliness, which,

—after all,—is the most we dare to strive for in all our differing creeds.

It was not long before Thelma began to recover. The day after her husband arrived, and Ulrika departed, she rose from her bed with Britta's assistance, and sat by the blazing fire, wrapped in her white gown and looking very fragile, though very lovely. Philip had been talking to her for some time, and now he sat at her feet, holding her hand in his, and watching her face, on which there was an expression of the most plaintive and serious penitence.

" I have been very wicked ! " she said, with such a quaint horror of herself that her husband laughed. " Now I look back upon it all, I think I have behaved so very badly ! because I ought never to have doubted you, my boy—no— not for all the Lady Winsleighs in the world. And poor Mr. Neville ! he must be so unhappy ! But it was that letter—that letter in your own writing, Philip ! "

" Of course ! " he answered soothingly. " No wonder you thought me a dreadful fellow ! But you won't do so again, will you, Thelma ? You will believe that you are the crown and centre of my life—the joy of all the world to me ? "

" Yes, I will ! " she said softly and proudly. " Though it is always the same, I never do think myself worthy ! But I must try to grow very conceited, and assure myself that I am very valuable ! so that then I shall understand everything better, and be wiser."

Philip laughed. " Talking of letters," he said suddenly, " here's one I wrote to you from Hull—it only got here to-day. Where it has been delayed is a mystery. You needn't read it—you know everything in it already. Then there's a letter on the shelf up there addressed in your writing—it seems never to have been opened."

He reached it down, and gave it to her. As she took it, her face grew very sad.

" It is the one I wrote to my father before I left London," she said. And her eyes filled with tears. " It came too late ! "

" Thelma," said Sir Philip then, very gently and gravely, " would you like—can you bear—to read your father's last words to you ? He wrote to you on his death-bed, and gave the letter to Valdemar——"

" Oh, let me see it ! " she murmured half-sobbingly. " Father,—dear father ! I knew he would not leave me without a word ! "

Sir Philip reverently opened the folded paper which Svensen had committed to his care that morning, and together they read the *bonde's* farewell. It ran as follows :—

"THELMA, MY BELOVED,

"The summons I have waited for has come at last, and the doors of Valhalla are set open to receive my soul. Wonder not that I depart with joy! Old as I am, I long for youth—the everlasting youth of which the strength and savor fails not. I have lived long enough to know the sameness of this world—though there is much therein to please the heart and eye of a man—but with that roving restlessness that was born within me, I desire to sail new seas and gaze on new lands, where a perpetual light shines that knows no fading. Grieve not for me—thou wilt remember that, unlike a Christian, I see in death the chiefest glory of life—and thou must not regret that I am eager to drain this cup of world-oblivion offered by the gods. I leave thee,—not sorrowfully,—for thou art in shelter and safety—the strong protection of thy husband's love defends thee and the safeguard of thine own innocence. My blessing upon him and thee! Serve him, Thelma mine, with full devotion and obedience—even as I have taught thee,—thus drawing from thy womanlife its best measure of sweetness,—keep the bright shield of thy truth untarnished—and live so that at the hour of thine own death-ecstasy thou mayest depart as easily as a song-bird soaring to the sun! I pass hence in happiness—if thou dost shed a tear thou wrongest my memory,—there is naught to weep for. Valdemar will give me the crimson shroud and ocean grave of my ancestors—but question him not concerning this fiery pomp of my last voyage—he is but a serf, and his soul is shaken to its very depths by sorrow. Let him be—he will have his reward hereafter. And now farewell, child of my heart—darling of mine age— clear mirror in which my later life has brightened to content! All partings are brief—we shall meet again—thou and I and Philip—and all who have loved or who love each other,—the journey heavenwards may be made by different roads, but the end—the glory—the immortality is the same! Peace be upon thee and on thy children and on thy children's children!

"Thy father,
"OLAF GÜLDMAR."

In spite of the brave old pagan's declaration that tears would wrong his memory, they dropped bright and fast from his daughter's eyes as she kissed again and again the words his dying hand had pencilled,—while Errington knew not which feeling gained the greater mastery over him,—grief for a good man's loss, or admiration for the strong, heroic spirit in which that good man had welcomed Death with rejoicing. He could not help comparing the *bonde's* departure from this life with that of Sir Francis Lennox, the man of false fashion, who had let slip his withered soul with an oath into the land of Nowhere. Presently Thelma grew calmer, and began to speak in hushed, soft tones—

"Poor Valdemar!" she said meditatively. "His heart must ache very much, Philip!"

Philip looked up inquiringly.

"You see, my father speaks of the 'crimson shroud,'" she went on. "That means that he was buried like many of the ancient Norwegian sea kings;—he was taken from his bed while dying and placed on board his own ship to breathe his last; then the ship was set on fire and sent out to sea. I always knew he wished it so. Valdemar must have done it all—for I,—I saw the last glimpse of the flames on the Fjord the night I came home! Oh, Philip!" and her beautiful eyes rested tenderly upon him, "it was all so dreadful—so desolate! I wanted—I prayed to die also! The world was so empty—it seemed as if there was nothing left!"

Philip, still sitting at her feet, encircled her with both arms, and drew her down to him.

"My Thelma!" he whispered, "there *is* nothing left—nothing at all worth living for,—save Love!"

"Ah! but that," she answered softly, "is everything!"

*   *   *   *   *   *

Is it so, indeed? Is Love alone worth living for—worth dying for? Is it the only satisfying good we can grasp at among the shifting shadows of our brief existence? In its various phases and different workings, is it, after all, the brightest radiance known in the struggling darkness of our lives?

Sigurd had thought so,—he had died to prove it. Philip thought so,—when once more at home in England with his recovered "treasure of the golden midnight" he saw her, like a rose refreshed by rain, raise her bright head in re-

newed strength and beauty, with the old joyous lustre
dancing in her eyes, and the smile of a perfect happiness
like summer sunshine on her fair face. Lord Winsleigh
thought so;—he was spending the winter in Rome with his
wife and son,—and there among the shadows of the Cæsars,
his long, social martyrdom ended, and he regained what he
had once believed lost for ever—his wife's affection. Clara,
gentle, wistful, with the softening shadow of a great sorrow
and a great repentance in her once too-brilliant eyes, was a
very different Clara to the dashing " beauty " who had fig-
ured so conspicuously in London society. She clung to
her husband with an almost timid eagerness as though she
dreaded losing him—and when he was not with her, she
seemed to rely entirely on her son, whom she watched with
a fond, almost melancholy pride, and who responded to her
tenderness though proffered so late, with the full-hearted
frankness of his impulsive, ardent nature. She wrote to
Thelma asking her pardon, and in return received such a
sweet, forgiving, generous letter as caused her to weep for
an hour or more. But she felt she could never again meet
the clear regard of those beautiful, earnest, truthful eyes—
never again could she stand in Thelma's presence, or call
her friend—that was all over. Still Love remained,—a
Love, chastened and sad, with dropping wings and a somewhat doubting smile,—yet it was Love—

> " Love, that keeps all the choir of lives in chime—
> Love, that is blood within the veins of time."

And Love, no matter how abused and maltreated, is a
very patient god, and even while suffering from undeserved
wounds, still works on, doing magical things. So that
poor Edward Neville, the forsaken husband of Violet Vere,
when he heard that that popular actress had died suddenly
in America from a fit of delirium tremens brought on by
excessive drinking, was able, by some gentle method known
only to Love and himself, to forget all her frailties—to ob-
literate from his memory the fact that he ever saw her on
the boards of the Brilliant Theatre,—and to think of her
henceforth only as the wife he had once adored, and who,
he decided in vague, dreamy fashion, must have died
young. Love also laid a firm hand on the vivacious Pierre
Duprèz—he who had long scoffed at the *jeu d' amour*,
played it at last in grave earnest,—and one bright season
he introduced his bride into Parisian society,—a charming

little woman, with very sparkling eyes and white teeth, who spoke French perfectly, though not with the "haccent" recommended by Briggs. It was difficult to recognize Britta in the *petite élégante* who laughed and danced and chattered her way through some of the best *salons* in Paris, captivating everybody as she went,—but there she was, all the same, holding her own as usual. Her husband was extremely proud of her—he was fond of pointing her out to people as something excessively precious and unique—and saying—"See her! That is my wife! From Norway! Yes—from the very utmost north of Norway! I love my country—certainly!—but I will tell you this much—if I had been obliged to choose a wife among French women— *ma foi!* I should never have married!"

And what of George Lorimer?—the idle, somewhat careless man of "modern" type, in whose heart, notwithstanding the supposed deterioration of the age, all the best and bravest codes of old-world chivalry were written? Had Love no fair thing to offer *him?* Was he destined to live out his life in the silent heroism of faithful, unuttered, unrequited, unselfish devotion? Were the heavens, as Sigurd had said, always to be empty? Apparently not,—for when he was verging towards middle age, a young lady besieged him with her affections, and boldly offered to be his wife any day he chose to name. She was a small person, not quite five years old, with great blue eyes and a glittering tangle of golden curls. She made her proposal one summer afternoon on the lawn at Errington Manor, in the presence of Beau Lovelace, on whose knee sat her little brother Olaf, a fine boy a year younger than herself. She had placed her dimpled arms round Lorimer's neck,—and when she so confidingly suggested marriage to her "Zordie," as she call him, she was rubbing her rosy, velvety cheek against his moustache with much sweet consideration and tenderness. Lovelace, hearing her, laughed aloud, whereat the little lady was extremely offended.

"I don't tare!" she said, with pretty defiance. "I do love oo, Zordie, and I will marry oo!"

George held her fondly to his breast as though she were some precious fragile flower of which not a petal must be injured.

"All right!" he answered gaily, though his voice trembled somewhat, "I accept! You shall be my little wife, Thelma. Consider it settled!"

Apparently she did so consider it, for from that day whenever she was asked her name, she announced herself proudly as " Zordie's 'ittle wife, Thelma "—to the great amusement of her father, Sir Philip, and that other Thelma, on whom the glory of motherhood had fallen like a new charm, investing both face and form with superior beauty and an almost divine serenity. But " Zordie's wife " took her *sobriquet* very seriously,—so much so, indeed, that by-and-by " Zordie " began to take it rather seriously himself —and to wonder whether, after all, marriages, unequal in point of age, might not occasionally turn out well. He condemned himself severely for the romanticism of thinking such thoughts, even while he indulged in them, and called himself " an old fool," though he was in the actual prime of manhood, and an exceedingly handsome fellow withal.

But when the younger Thelma came back at the age of sixteen from her convent school at Arles,—the same school where her mother had been before her,—she looked so like her mother, so very like, that his heart began to ache with the old, wistful, passionate longing he fancied he had stilled for ever. He struggled against this feeling for a while, till at last it became too strong for him,—and then, though he told himself it was absurd,—that a man past forty had no right to expect to win a girl's first love, he grew so reckless that he determined to risk his fate with her. One day, therefore, he spoke out, scarcely knowing what he said, and only conscious that his pulses were beating with abnormal rapidity. She listened to his tremulous, rather hesitating proposal with exceeding gravity, and appeared more surprised than displeased. Raising her glorious blue eyes— eyes in which her mother's noble, fearless look was faithfully reflected, she said simply, just in her mother's own quaint way—

" I do not know why you talk about this at all. I thought it was all settled long ago ! "

" Settled ! " faltered Lorimer astonished,—he was generally self-possessed, but this fair young lady's perfect equanimity far surpassed his at that moment—" Settled ! My darling ! my child—I am so much older than you are——"

" I don't like *boys !* " she declared, with stately disdain. " I was your wife when I was little—and I thought it was to be the same thing now I am big ! I told mother so, and she was quite pleased. But of course, if you don't want me——"

She was not allowed to finish her sentence, for Lorimer, with a sudden rush of joy that almost overpowered him, caught her in his arms and pressed the first lover's kiss on her pure, innocently smiling lips.

"Want you !" he murmured passionately, with a strange, sweet mingling of the past and present in his words. "I have always wanted—Thelma !"

THE END.

A. L. Burt's Catalogue of Books for Young People by Popular Writers, 52-58 Duane Street, New York ✌ ✌ ✌

BOOKS FOR GIRLS.

Alice's Adventures in Wonderland. By LEWIS CARROLL.

12mo, cloth, 42 illustrations, price 75 cents.

"From first to last, almost without exception, this story is delightfully droll, humorous and illustrated in harmony with the story."—New York Express.

Through the Looking Glass, and What Alice Found

There. By LEWIS CARROLL. 12mo, cloth, 50 illustrations, price 75 cents.

"A delight alike to the young people and their elders, extremely funny both in text and illustrations."—Boston Express.

Little Lucy's Wonderful Globe. By CHARLOTTE M.

YONGE. 12mo, cloth, illustrated, price 75 cents.

"This story is unique among tales intended for children, alike for pleasant instruction, quaintness of humor, gentle pathos, and the subtlety with which lessons moral and otherwise are conveyed to children, and perhaps to their seniors as well."—The Spectator.

Joan's Adventures at the North Pole and Elsewhere.

BY ALICE CORKRAN. 12mo, cloth, illustrated, price 75 cents.

"Wonderful as the adventures of Joan are, it must be admitted that they are very naturally worked out and very plausibly presented. Altogether this is an excellent story for girls."—Saturday Review.

Count Up the Sunny Days: A Story for Girls and Boys.

By C. A. JONES. 12mo, cloth, illustrated, price 75 cents.

"An unusually good children's story."—Glasgow Herald.

The Dove in the Eagle's Nest. By CHARLOTTE M.

YONGE. 12mo, cloth, illustrated, price $1.00.

"Among all the modern writers we believe Miss Yonge first, not in genius, but in this, that she employs her great abilities for a high and noble purpose. We know of few modern writers whose works may be so safely commended as hers."—Cleveland Times.

Jan of the Windmill. A Story of the Plains. By MRS.

J. H. EWING. 12mo, cloth, illustrated, price $1.00.

"Never has Mrs. Ewing published a more charming volume, and that is saying a very great deal. From the first to the last the book overflows with the strange knowledge of child-nature which so rarely survives childhood; and moreover, with inexhaustible quiet humor, which is never anything but innocent and well-bred, never priggish, and never clumsy."—Academy.

A Sweet Girl Graduate. By L. T. MEADE. 12mo, cloth,

illustrated, price $1.00.

"One of this popular author's best. The characters are well imagined and drawn. The story moves with plenty of spirit and the interest does not flag until the end too quickly comes."—Providence Journal.

For sale by all booksellers, or sent postpaid on receipt of price by the publisher, A. L. BURT, 52-58 Duane Street, New York.

BOOKS FOR GIRLS.

Six to Sixteen: A Story for Girls. By JULIANA
HORATIA EWING. 12mo, cloth, illustrated, price $1.00.

"There is no doubt as to the good quality and attractiveness of 'Six to Sixteen.' The book is one which would enrich any girl's book shelf."— St. James' Gazette.

The Palace Beautiful: A Story for Girls. By L. T.
MEADE. 12mo, cloth, illustrated, price $1.00.

"A bright and interesting story. The many admirers of Mrs. L. T. Meade in this country will be delighted with the 'Palace Beautiful' for more reasons than one. It is a charming book for girls."—New York Recorder.

A World of Girls: The Story of a School. By L. T.
MEADE. 12mo, cloth, illustrated, price $1.00.

"One of those wholesome stories which it does one good to read. It will afford pure delight to numerous readers. This book should be on every girl's book shelf."—Boston Home Journal.

The Lady of the Forest: A Story for Girls. By L. T.
MEADE. 12mo, cloth, illustrated, price $1.00.

"This story is written in the author's well-known, fresh and easy style. All girls fond of reading will be charmed by this well-written story. It is told with the author's customary grace and spirit."—Boston Times.

At the Back of the North Wind. By GEORGE MAC-
DONALD. 12mo, cloth, illustrated, price $1.00.

"A very pretty story, with much of the freshness and vigor of Mr. Macdonald's earlier work. . . . It is a sweet, earnest, and wholesome fairy story, and the quaint native humor is delightful. A most delightful volume for young readers."—Philadelphia Times.

The Water Babies: A Fairy Tale for a Land Baby.
By CHARLES KINGSLEY. 12mo, cloth, illustrated, price $1.00.

"The strength of his work, as well as its peculiar charms, consist in his description of the experiences of a youth with life under water in the luxuriant wealth of which he revels with all the ardor of a poetical nature."—New York Tribune.

Our Bessie. By ROSA N. CAREY. 12mo, cloth, illus-
strated, price $1.00.

"One of the most entertaining stories of the season, full of vigorous action, and strong in character-painting. Elder girls will be charmed with it, and adults may read its pages with profit."—The Teachers' Aid.

Wild Kitty. A Story of Middleton School. By L. T.
MEADE. 12mo, cloth, illustrated, price $1.00.

"Kitty is a true heroine—warm-hearted, self-sacrificing, and, as all good women nowadays are, largely touched with the enthusiasm of humanity. One of the most attractive gift books of the season."—The Academy.

A Young Mutineer. A Story for Girls. By L. T.
MEADE. 12mo, cloth, illustrated, price $1.00.

"One of Mrs. Meade's charming books for girls, narrated in that simple and picturesque style which marks the authoress as one of the first among writers for young people."—The Spectator.

For sale by all booksellers, or sent postpaid on receipt of price by the publisher, A. L. BURT, 52-58 Duane Street, New York.

BOOKS FOR GIRLS.

Sue and I. By MRS. O'REILLY. 12mo, cloth, illustrated, price 75 cents.

"A thoroughly delightful book, full of sound wisdom as well as fun."—Athenæum.

The Princess and the Goblin. A Fairy Story. By

GEORGE MACDONALD. 12mo, cloth, illustrated, price 75 cents.

"If a child once begins this book, it will get so deeply interested in it that when bedtime comes it will altogether forget the moral, and will weary its parents with importunities for just a few minutes more to see how everything ends."—Saturday Review.

Pythia's Pupils: A Story of a School. By EVA

HARTNER. 12mo, cloth, illustrated, price $1.00.

"This story of the doings of several bright school girls is sure to interest girl readers. Among many good stories for girls this is undoubtedly one of the very best."—Teachers' Aid.

A Story of a Short Life. By JULIANA HORATIA EWING.

12mo, cloth, illustrated, price $1.00.

"The book is one we can heartily recommend, for it is not only bright and interesting, but also pure and healthy in tone and teaching."—Courier.

The Sleepy King. A Fairy Tale. By AUBREY HOP-

WOOD AND SEYMOUR HICKS. 12mo, cloth, illustrated, price 75 cents.

"Wonderful as the adventures of Bluebell are, it must be admitted that they are very naturally worked out and very plausibly presented. Altogether this is an excellent story for girls."—Saturday Review.

Two Little Waifs. By MRS. MOLESWORTH. 12mo,

cloth, illustrated, price 75 cents.

"Mrs. Molesworth's delightful story of 'Two Little Waifs' will charm all the small people who find it in their stockings. It relates the adventures of two lovable English children lost in Paris, and is just wonderful enough to pleasantly wring the youthful heart."—New York Tribune.

Adventures in Toyland. By EDITH KING HALL. 12mo,

cloth, illustrated, price 75 cents.

"The author is such a bright, cheery writer, that her stories are always acceptable to all who are not confirmed cynics, and her record of the adventures is as entertaining and enjoyable as we might expect."—Boston Courier.

Adventures in Wallypug Land. By G. E. FARROW.

12mo, cloth, illustrated, price 75 cents.

"These adventures are simply inimitable, and will delight boys and girls of mature age, as well as their juniors. No happier combination of author and artist than this volume presents could be found to furnish healthy amusement to the young folks. The book is an artistic one in every sense."—Toronto Mail.

Fussbudget's Folks. A Story for Young Girls. By

ANNA F. BURNHAM. 12mo, cloth, illustrated, price $1.00.

"Mrs. Burnham has a rare gift for composing stories for children. With a light, yet forcible touch, she paints sweet and artless, yet natural and strong, characters."—Congregationalist.

For sale by all booksellers, or sent postpaid on receipt of price by the publisher, A. L. BURT, 52-58 Duane Street, New York.

BOOKS FOR GIRLS.

Mixed Pickles. A Story for Girls. By Mrs. E. M.

FIELD. 12mo, cloth, illustrated, price 75 cents.

"It is, in its way, a little classic, of which the real beauty and pathos can hardly be appreciated by young people. It is not too much to say of the story that it is perfect of its kind."—Good Literature.

Miss Mouse and Her Boys. A Story for Girls. By

MRS. MOLESWORTH. 12mo, cloth, illustrated, price 75 cents.

"Mrs. Molesworth's books are cheery, wholesome, and particularly well adapted to refined life. It is safe to add that she is the best English prose writer for children. A new volume from Mrs. Molesworth is always a treat."—The Beacon.

Gilly Flower. A Story for Girls. By the author of

"Miss Toosey's Mission." 12mo, cloth, illustrated, price $1.00.

"Jill is a little guardian angel to three lively brothers who tease and play with her. . . . Her unconscious goodness brings right thoughts and resolves to several persons who come into contact with her. There is no goodiness in this tale, but its influence is of the best kind."—Literary World.

The Chaplet of Pearls; or, The White and Black Ribau-

mont. By CHARLOTTE M. YONGE. 12mo, cloth, illustrated, price $1.00.

"Full of spirit and life, so well sustained throughout that grown-up readers may enjoy it as much as children. It is one of the best books of the season."—Guardian.

Naughty Miss Bunny: Her Tricks and Troubles. By

CLARA MULHOLLAND. 12mo, cloth, illustrated, price 75 cents.

"The naughty child is positively delightful. Papas should not omit the book from their list of juvenile presents."—Land and Water.

Meg's Friend. By ALICE CORKRAN. 12mo, cloth,

illustrated, price $1.00.

"One of Miss Corkran's charming books for girls, narrated in that simple and picturesque style which marks the authoress as one of the first among writers for young people."—The Spectator.

Averil. By ROSA N. CAREY. 12mo, cloth, illustrated,

price $1.00.

"A charming story for young folks. Averil is a delightful creature—piquant, tender, and true—and her varying fortunes are perfectly real-istic."—World.

Aunt Diana. By ROSA N. CAREY. 12mo, cloth, illus-

trated, price $1.00.

"An excellent story, the interest being sustained from first to last. This is, both in its intention and the way the story is told, one of the best books of its kind which has come before us this year."—Saturday Review.

Little Sunshine's Holiday: A Picture from Life. By

MISS MULOCK. 12mo, cloth, illustrated, price 75 cents.

"This is a pretty narrative of child life, describing the simple doings and sayings of a very charming and rather precocious child. This is a delightful book for young people."—Gazette.

For sale by all booksellers, or sent postpaid on receipt of price by the publisher, A. L. BURT, 52-58 Duane Street, New York.

BOOKS FOR GIRLS.

Esther's Charge. A Story for Girls. By ELLEN EVERETT
GREEN. 12mo, cloth, illustrated, price $1.00.

" . . . This is a story showing in a charming way how one little girl's jealousy and bad temper were conquered; one of the best, most suggestive and improving of the Christmas juveniles."—New York Tribune.

Fairy Land of Science. By ARABELLA B. BUCKLEY.
12mo, cloth, illustrated, price $1.00.

"We can highly recommend it; not only for the valuable information it gives on the special subjects to which it is dedicated, but also as a book teaching natural sciences in an interesting way. A fascinating little volume, which will make friends in every household in which there are children."—Daily News.

Merle's Crusade. By ROSA N. CAREY. 12mo, cloth,
illustrated, price $1.00.

"Among the books for young people we have seen nothing more unique than this book. Like all of this author's stories it will please young readers by the very attractive and charming style in which it is written."—Journal.

Birdie: A Tale of Child Life. By H. L. CHILDE-
PEMBERTON. 12mo, cloth, illustrated, price 75 cents.

"The story is quaint and simple, but there is a freshness about it that makes one hear again the ringing laugh and the cheery shout of children at play which charmed his earlier years."—New York Express.

The Days of Bruce: A Story from Scottish History.
By GRACE AGUILAR. 12mo, cloth, illustrated, price $1.00.

"There is a delightful freshness, sincerity and vivacity about all of Grace Aguilar's stories which cannot fail to win the interest and admiration of every lover of good reading."—Boston Beacon.

Three Bright Girls: A Story of Chance and Mischance.
By ANNIE E. ARMSTRONG. 12mo, cloth, illustrated, price $1.00.

"The charm of the story lies in the cheery helpfulness of spirit developed in the girls by their changed circumstances; while the author finds a pleasant ending to all their happy makeshifts. The story is charmingly told, and the book can be warmly recommended as a present for girls."—Standard.

Giannetta: A Girl's Story of Herself. By ROSA MUL-
HOLLAND. 12mo, cloth, illustrated, price $1.00.

"Extremely well told and full of interest. Giannetta is a true heroine—warm-hearted, self-sacrificing, and, as all good women nowadays are, largely touched with enthusiasm of humanity. The illustrations are unusually good. One of the most attractive gift books of the season."—The Academy.

Margery Merton's Girlhood. By ALICE CORKRAN.
12mo, cloth, illustrated, price $1.00.

"The experiences of an orphan girl who in infancy is left by her father to the care of an elderly aunt residing near Paris. The accounts of the various persons who have an after influence on the story are singularly vivid. There is a subtle attraction about the book which will make it a great favorite with thoughtful girls."—Saturday Review.

For sale by all booksellers, or sent postpaid on receipt of price by the publisher, A. L. BURT, 52-58 Duane Street, New York.

BOOKS FOR GIRLS.

Under False Colors: A Story from Two Girls' Lives.

By SARAH DOUDNEY. 12mo, cloth, illustrated, price $1.00.

"Sarah Doudney has no superior as a writer of high-toned stories—pure in style, original in conception, and with skillfully wrought out plots; but we have seen nothing equal in dramatic energy to this book."—Christian Leader.

Down the Snow Stairs; or, From Good-night to Good-

morning. By ALICE CORKRAN. 12mo, cloth, illustrated, price 75 cents.

"Among all the Christmas volumes which the year has brought to our table this one stands out facile princeps—a gem of the first water, bearing upon every one of its pages the signet mark of genius. . . . All is told with such simplicity and perfect naturalness that the dream appears to be a solid reality. It is indeed a Little Pilgrim's Progress."—Christian Leader.

The Tapestry Room: A Child's Romance. By MRS.

MOLESWORTH. 12mo, cloth, illustrated, price 75 cents.

"Mrs. Molesworth is a charming painter of the nature and ways of children; and she has done good service in giving us this charming juvenile which will delight the young people."—Athenæum, London.

Little Miss Peggy: Only a Nursery Story. By MRS.

MOLESWORTH. 12mo, cloth, illustrated, price 75 cents.

Mrs. Molesworth's children are finished studies. A joyous earnest spirit pervades her work, and her sympathy is unbounded. She loves them with her whole heart, while she lays bare their little minds, and expresses their foibles, their faults, their virtues, their inward struggles, their conception of duty, and their instinctive knowledge of the right and wrong of things. She knows their characters, she understands their wants, and she desires to help them.

Polly: A New Fashioned Girl. By L. T. MEADE.

12mo, cloth, illustrated, price $1.00.

Few authors have achieved a popularity equal to Mrs. Meade as a writer of stories for young girls. Her characters are living beings of flesh and blood, not lay figures of conventional type. Into the trials and crosses, and everyday experiences, the reader enters at once with zest and hearty sympathy. While Mrs. Meade always writes with a high moral purpose, her lessons of life, purity and nobility of character are rather inculcated by example than intruded as sermons.

One of a Covey. By the author of "Miss Toosey's

Mission." 12mo, cloth, illustrated, price 75 cents.

"Full of spirit and life, so well sustained throughout that grown-up readers may enjoy it as much as children. This 'Covey' consists of the twelve children of a hard-pressed Dr. Partridge out of which is chosen a little girl to be adopted by a spoiled, fine lady. We have rarely read a story for boys and girls with greater pleasure. One of the chief characters would not have disgraced Dickens' pen."—Literary World.

The Little Princess of Tower Hill. By L. T. MEADE.

12mo, cloth, illustrated, price 75 cents.

"This is one of the prettiest books for children published, as pretty as a pond-lily, and quite as fragrant. Nothing could be imagined more attractive to young people than such a combination of fresh pages and fair pictures; and while children will rejoice over it—which is much better than crying for it—it is a book that can be read with pleasure even by older boys and girls."—Boston Advertiser.

For sale by all booksellers, or sent postpaid on receipt of price by the publisher, A. L. BURT, 52-58 Duane Street, New York.

BOOKS FOR GIRLS.

Rosy. By MRS. MOLESWORTH. 12mo, cloth, illustrated, price 75 cents.

"Mrs. Molesworth, considering the quality and quantity of her labors, is the best story-teller for children England has yet known."

"This is a very pretty story. The writer knows children, and their ways well. The illustrations are exceedingly well drawn."—Spectator.

Esther: A Book for Girls. By ROSA N. CAREY. 12mo, cloth, illustrated, price $1.00.

"She inspires her readers simply by bringing them in contact with the characters, who are in themselves inspiring. Her simple stories are woven in order to give her an opportunity to describe her characters by their own conduct in seasons of trial."—Chicago Times.

Sweet Content. By MRS. MOLESWORTH. 12mo, cloth, illustrated, price 75 cents.

"It seems to me not at all easier to draw a lifelike child than to draw a lifelike man or woman: Shakespeare and Webster were the only two men of their age who could do it with perfect delicacy and success. Our own age is more fortunate, on this single score at least, having a larger and far nobler proportion of female writers; among whom, since the death of George Eliot, there is none left whose touch is so exquisite and masterly, whose love is so thoroughly according to knowledge, whose bright and sweet invention is so fruitful, so truthful, or so delightful as Mrs. Molesworth's."—A. C. Swinbourne.

Honor Bright; or, The Four-Leaved Shamrock. By the author of "Miss Toosey's Mission." 12mo, cloth, illustrated, price $1.00.

"It requires a special talent to describe the sayings and doings of children, and the author of 'Honor Bright,' 'One of a Covey,' possesses that talent in no small degree. A cheery, sensible, and healthy tale."—The Times.

The Cuckoo Clock. By MRS. MOLESWORTH. 12mo, cloth, illustrated, price 75 cents.

"A beautiful little story. It will be read with delight by every child into whose hands it is placed. . . . The author deserves all the praise that has been, is, and will be bestowed on 'The Cuckoo Clock.' Children's stories are plentiful, but one like this is not to be met with every day."—Pall Mall Gazette.

The Adventures of a Brownie. As Told to my Child. By MISS MULOCK. 12mo, cloth, illustrated, price 75 cents.

"The author of this delightful little book leaves it in doubt all through whether there actually is such a creature in existence as a Brownie, but she makes us hope that there might be."—Chicago Standard.

Only a Girl: A Tale of Brittany. From the French by C. A. JONES. 12mo, cloth, illustrated, price $1.00.

"We can thoroughly recommend this brightly written and homely narrative."—Saturday Review.

Little Rosebud; or, Things Will Take a Turn. By BEATRICE HARRADEN. 12mo, cloth, illustrated, price 75 cents.

"A most delightful little book. . . . Miss Harraden is so bright, so healthy, and so natural withal that the book ought, as a matter of duty, to be added to every girl's library in the land."—Boston Transcript.

For sale by all booksellers, or sent postpaid on receipt of price by the publisher, A. L. BURT, 52-58 Duane Street, New York.

BOOKS FOR GIRLS.

Girl Neighbors; or, The Old Fashion and the New. By

SARAH TYTLER. 12mo, cloth, illustrated, price $1.00.

"One of the most effective and quietly humorous of Miss Tytler's stories. 'Girl Neighbors' is a pleasant comedy, not so much of errors as of prejudices got rid of, very healthy, very agreeable, and very well written."—Spectator.

The Little Lame Prince and His Traveling Cloak. By

MISS MULOCK. 12mo, cloth, illustrated, price 75 cents.

"No sweeter—that is the proper word—Christmas story for the little folks could easily be found, and it is as delightful for older readers as well. There is a moral to it which the reader can find out for himself, if he chooses to think."—Cleveland Herald.

Little Miss Joy. By EMMA MARSHALL. 12mo, cloth,

illustrated, price 75 cents.

"A very pleasant and instructive story, told by a very charming writer in such an attractive way as to win favor among its young readers. The illustrations add to the beauty of the book."—Utica Herald.

The House that Grew. A Girl's Story. By MRS. MOLES-

WORTH. 12mo, cloth, illustrated, price 75 cents.

"This is a very pretty story of English life. Mrs. Molesworth is one of the most popular and charming of English story-writers for children. Her child characters are true to life, always natural and attractive, and her stories are wholesome and interesting."—Indianapolis Journal.

The House of Surprises. By L. T. MEADE. 12mo,

cloth, illustrated, price 75 cents.

"A charming tale of charming children, who are naughty enough to be interesting, and natural enough to be lovable; and very prettily their story is told. The quaintest yet most natural stories of child life. Simply delightful."—Vanity Fair.

The Jolly Ten: and their Year of Stories. By AGNES

CARR SAGE. 12mo, cloth, illustrated, price 75 cents.

The story of a band of cousins who were accustomed to meet at the "Pinery," with "Aunt Roxy." At her fireside they play merry games, have suppers flavored with innocent fun, and listen to stories—each with its lesson calculated to make the ten not less jolly, but quickly responsive to the calls of duty and to the needs of others.

Little Miss Dorothy. The Wonderful Adventures of

Two Little People. By MARTHA JAMES. 12mo, cloth, illustrated, price 75c.

"This is a charming little juvenile story from the pen of Mrs. James, detailing the various adventures of a couple of young children. Their many adventures are told in a charming manner, and the book will please young girls and boys."—Montreal Star.

Pen's Venture. A Story for Girls. By ELVIRTON

WRIGHT. 12mo, cloth, illustrated, price 75 cents.

Something Pen saw in the condition of the cash girls in a certain store gave her a thought; the thought became a plan; the plan became a venture—Pen's venture. It is amusing, touching, and instructive to read about it.

For sale by all booksellers, or sent postpaid on receipt of price by the publisher. A. L. BURT, 52-58 Duane Street, New York.